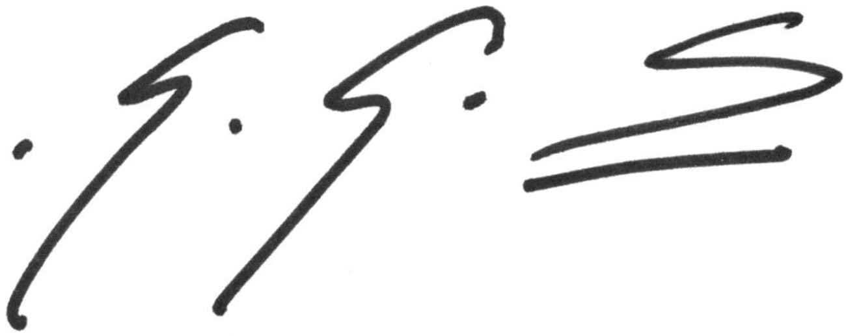

MIS(H)ADRA

IASMIN OMAR ATA

GALLERY 13

NEW YORK   LONDON   TORONTO   SYDNEY   NEW DELHI

Gallery 13
An Imprint of Simon & Schuster, Inc.
1230 Avenue of the Americas
New York, NY 10020

This book is a work of fiction. Any references to historical events, real people, or real places are used fictitiously. Other names, characters, places, and events are products of the author's imagination, and any resemblance to actual events or places or persons, living or dead, is entirely coincidental.

First Gallery 13 hardcover edition October 2017

GALLERY 13 and colophon are registered trademarks of Simon & Schuster, Inc.

For information about special discounts for bulk purchases, please contact Simon & Schuster Special Sales at 1-866-506-1949 or business@simonandschuster.com.

The Simon & Schuster Speakers Bureau can bring authors to your live event. For more information or to book an event, contact the Simon & Schuster Speakers Bureau at 1-866-248-3049 or visit our website at www.simonspeakers.com.

Manufactured in the United States of America

10 9 8 7 6 5 4 3 2 1

Library of Congress Cataloging-in-Publication Data is available.

ISBN 978-1-5011-6210-7
ISBN 978-1-5011-6214-5 (ebook)

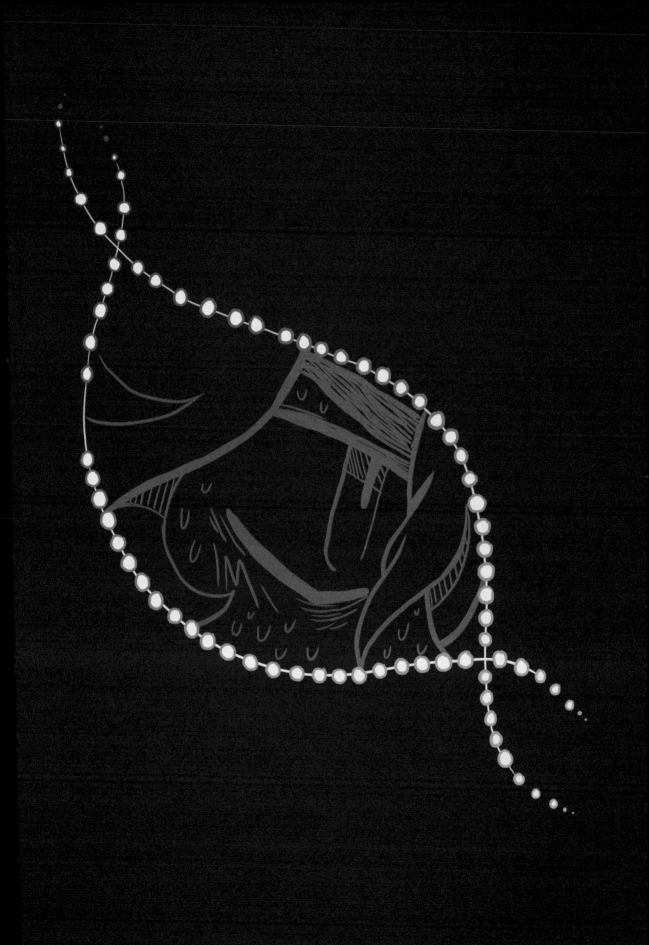

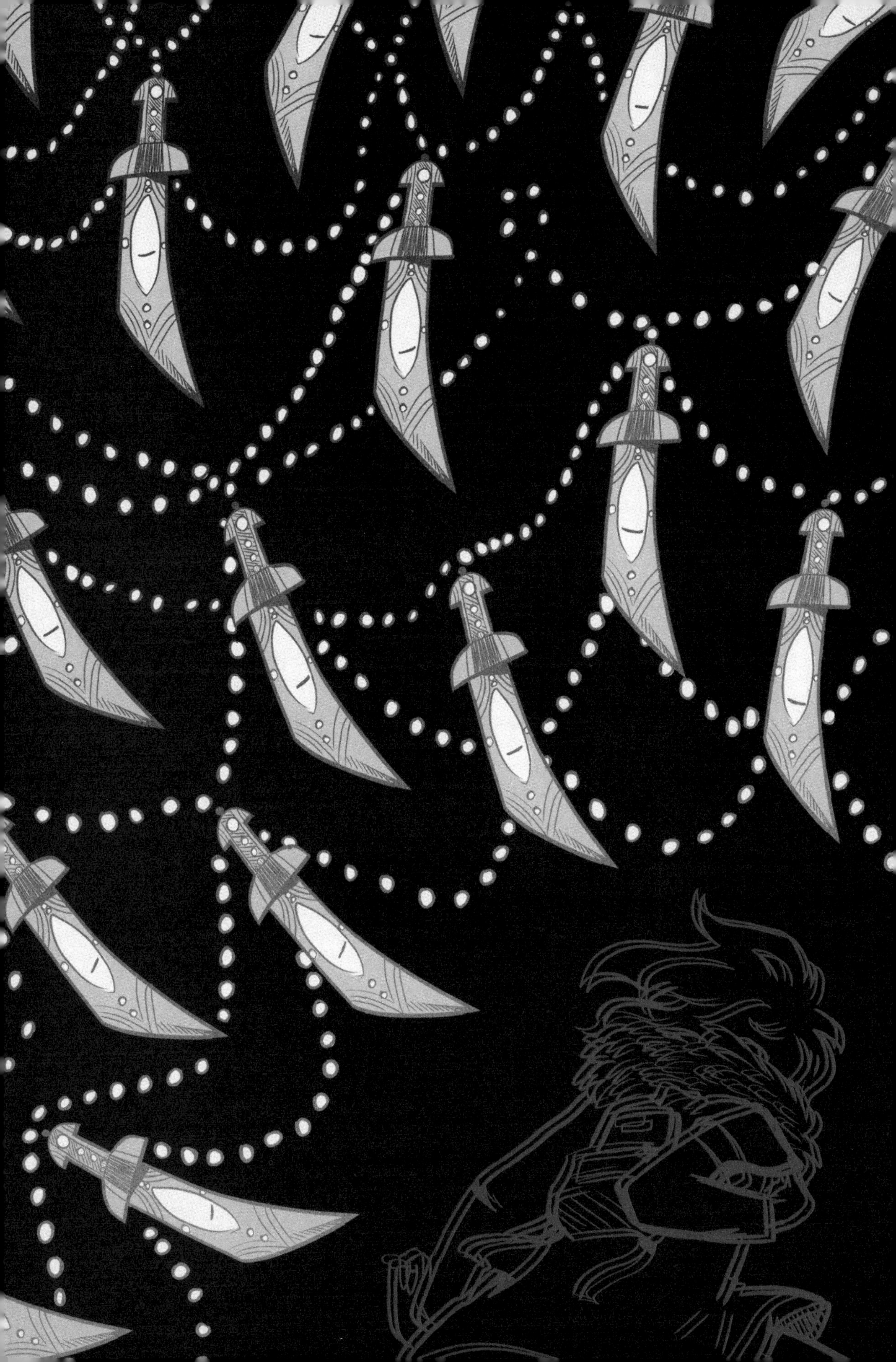

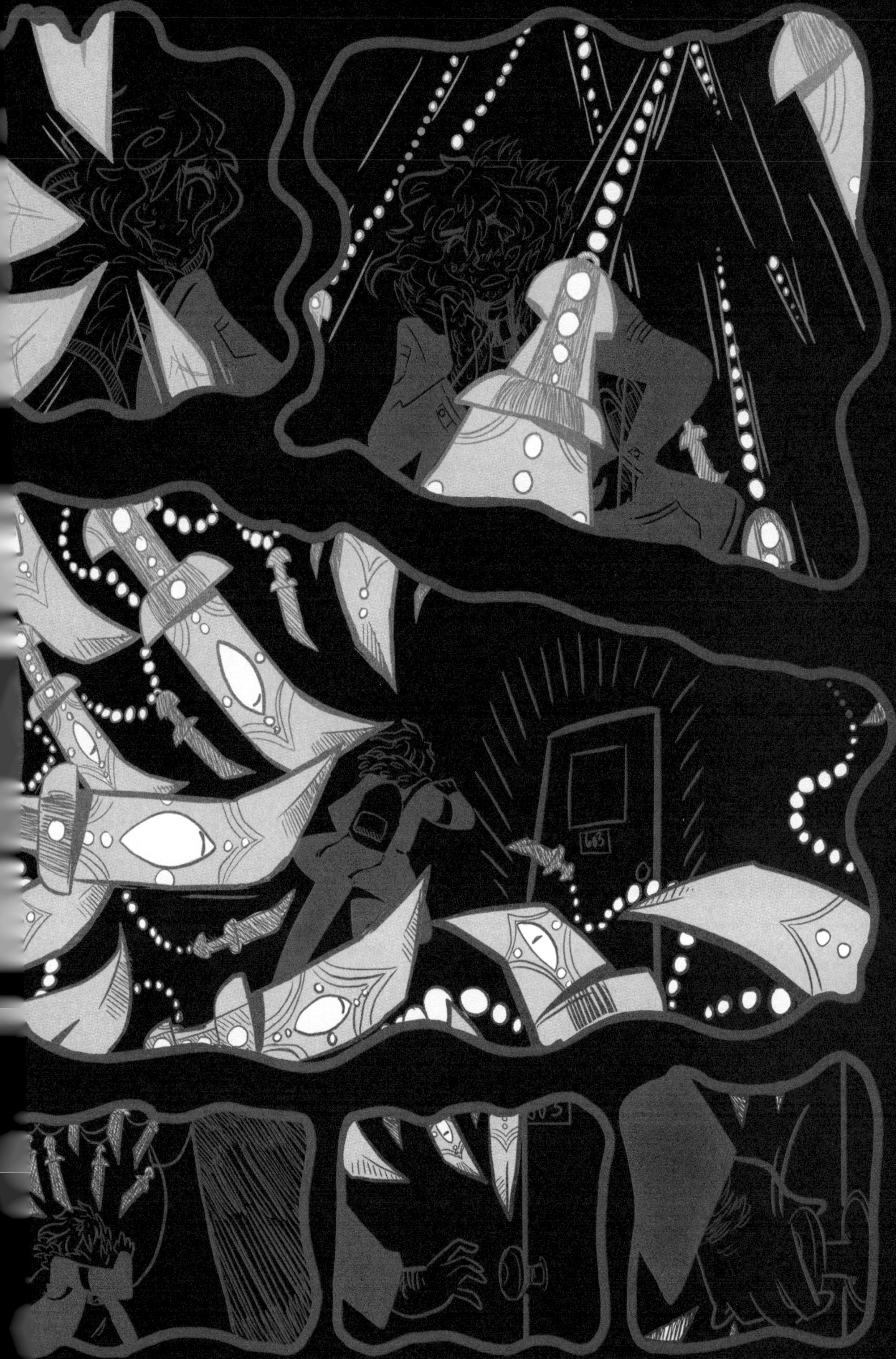

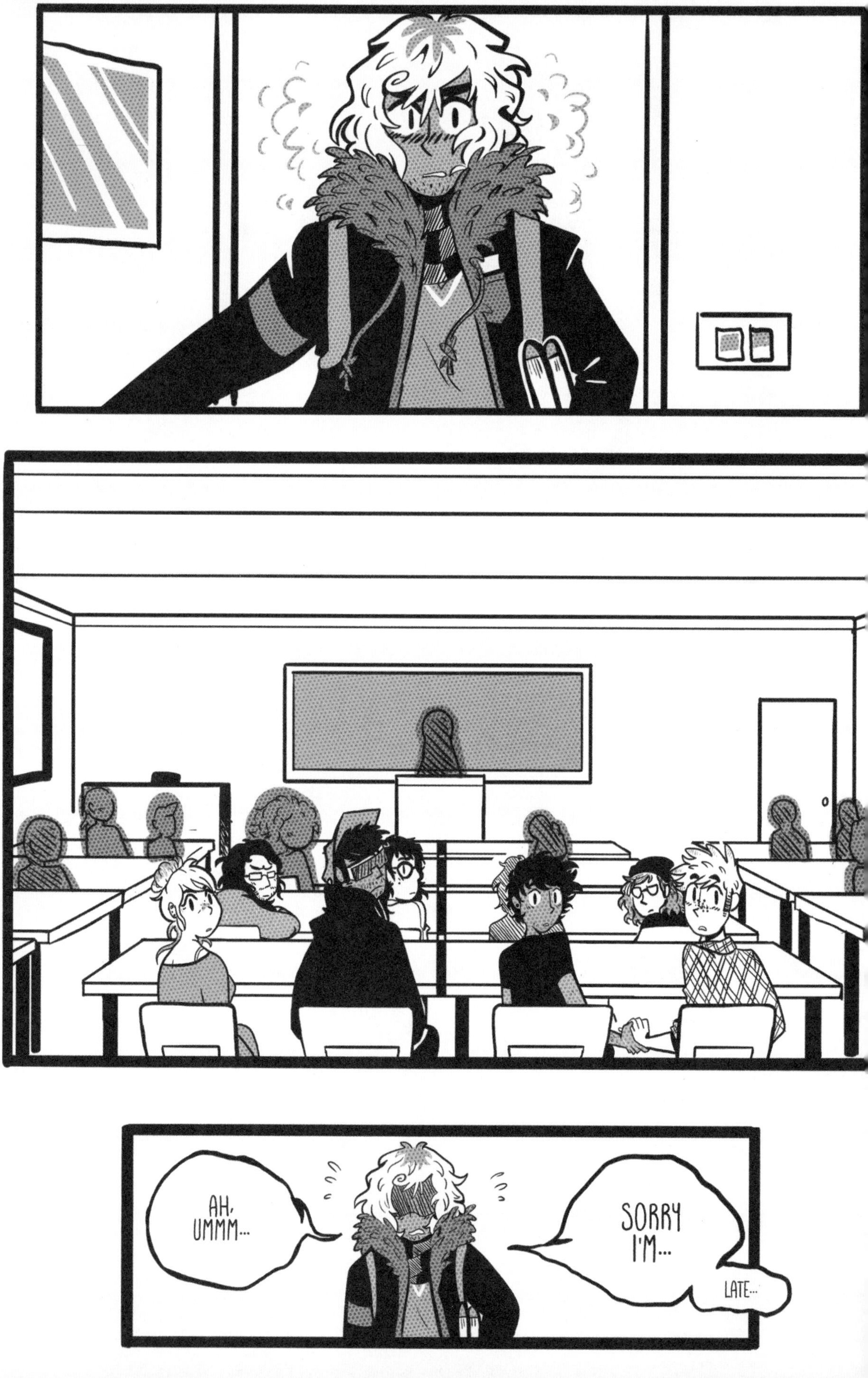
AH, UMMM...
SORRY I'M...
LATE...

LATE AGAIN, HUH?

WHOA.

AT LEAST HE ACTUALLY SHOWED UP.

UM, SO, ANYWAY... LIKE I WAS SAYING, MIDTERMS ARE COMING UP...

HE'S NEVER HERE.

AND HE NEVER HAS WORK TO SHOW.

DIDN'T YOU HEAR?

YOU ALL HAVE THE STUDY GUIDE ALREADY SO IF YOU STUDY TO THAT YOU'LL BE BUT JUST SO YOU... ERE WILL BE MULTIPLE CHOICE... ESTIONS.

THEY SAY HE HAS A DRUG PROBLEM OR SOMETHING AND ALMOST FAILED OUT.

NO WAY!

THERE WILL BE A DECENT AMOUNT OF QUESTIONS ABOUT THE CHAPTER ON GENDER POLITICS IN THE COUNTRIES OF THE... SO MAKE SURE YOU DO... SKI... ONE.

YEAH, HE MIGHT BE THE ONLY ONE IN OUR CLASS TO NOT WALK AT GRADUATION.

MAKES SENSE. I MEAN, LOOK AT HIM.

HE ALWAYS LOOKS LIKE HE'S ON SOMETHING.

EEK

HE HEARD US!

WHATEVER, IT'S PROBABLY ALL TRUE ANYWAY.

UGH

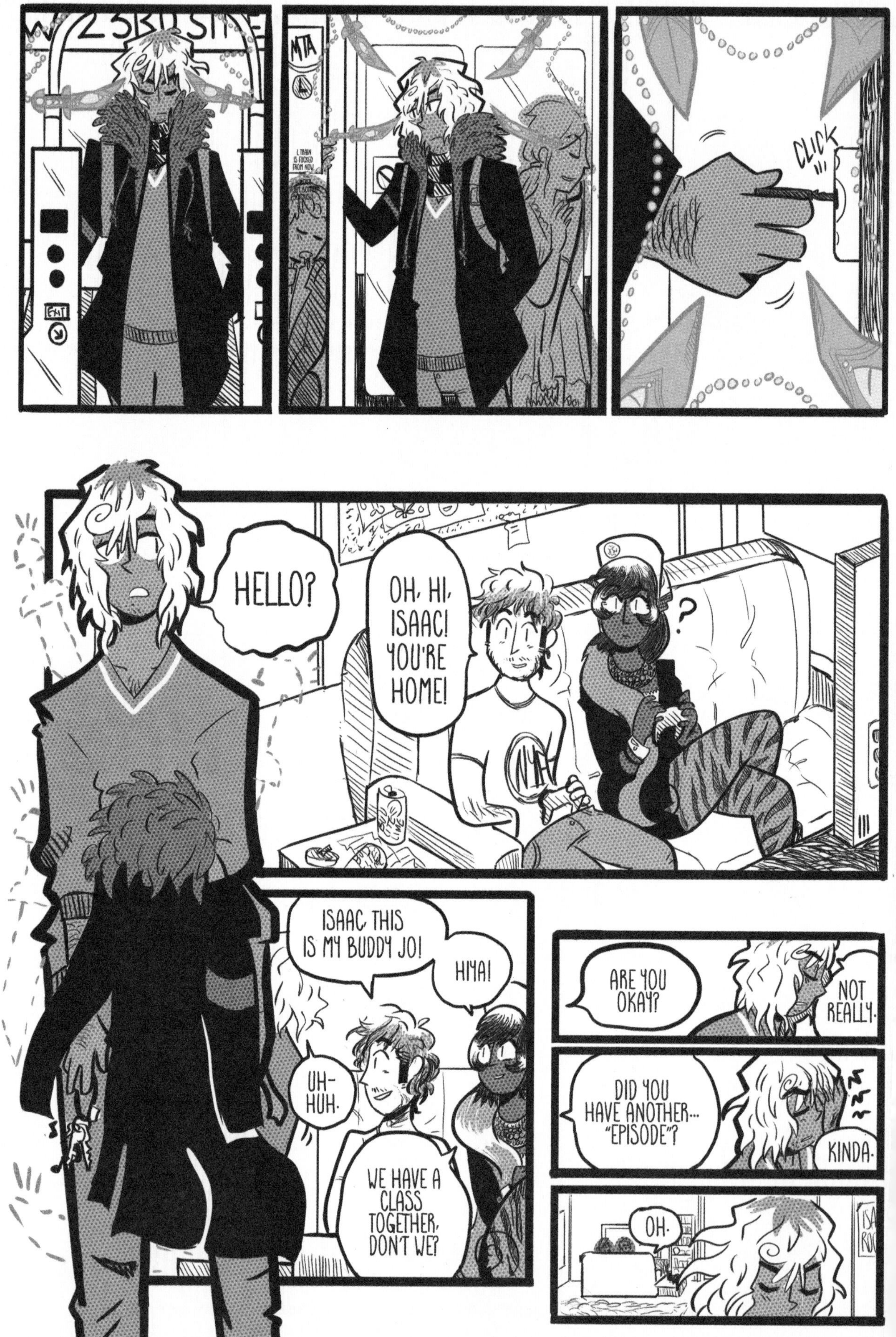
MTA
L TRAIN IS FUCKED FROM NOW
CLICK
HELLO?
OH, HI, ISAAC! YOU'RE HOME!
?
ISAAC, THIS IS MY BUDDY JO!
HIYA!
UH-HUH.
WE HAVE A CLASS TOGETHER, DON'T WE?
ARE YOU OKAY?
NOT REALLY.
DID YOU HAVE ANOTHER... "EPISODE"?
KINDA.
OH.

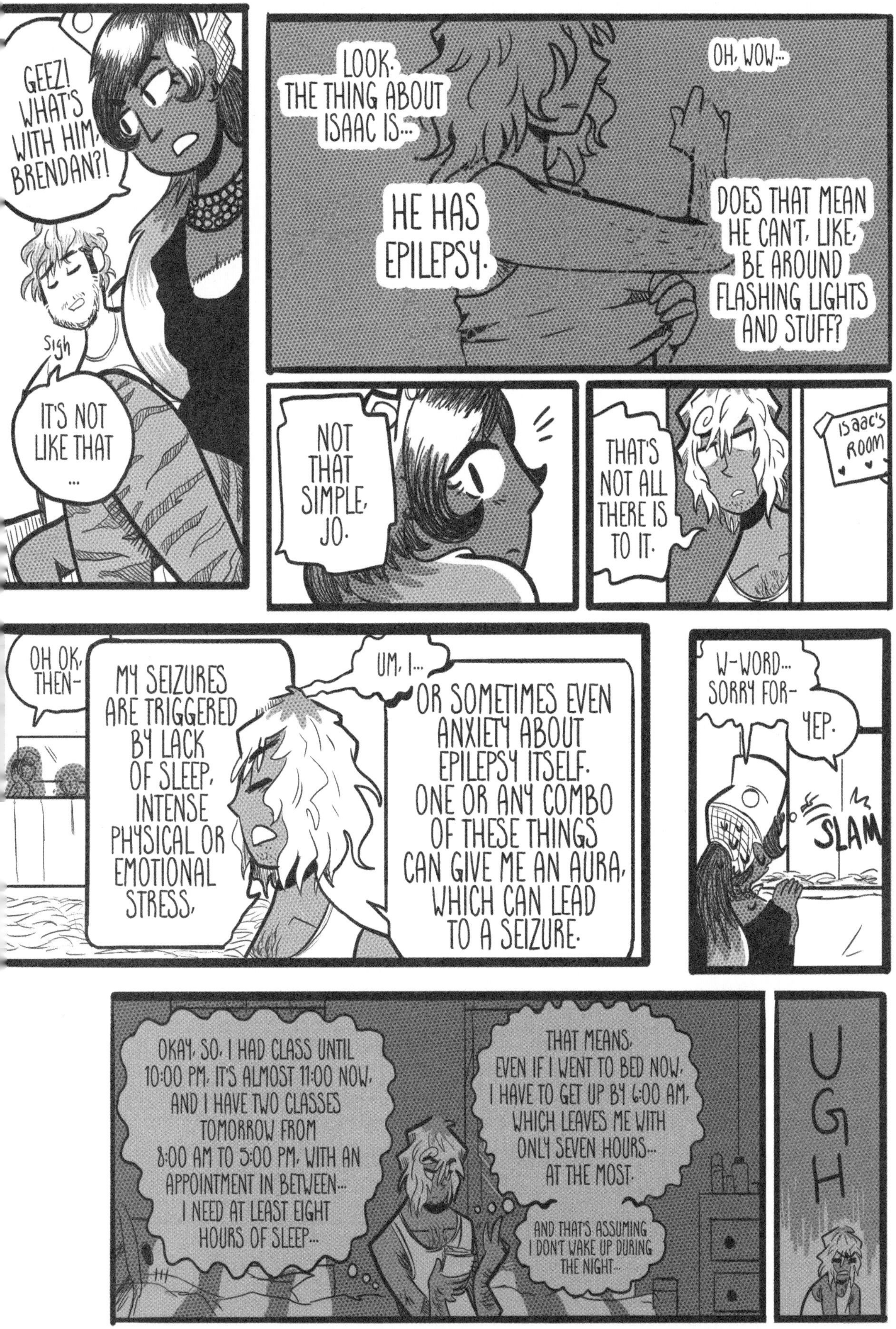
GEEZ! WHAT'S WITH HIM, BRENDAN?!
Sigh
IT'S NOT LIKE THAT ...
LOOK. THE THING ABOUT ISAAC IS...
HE HAS EPILEPSY.
OH, WOW...
DOES THAT MEAN HE CAN'T, LIKE, BE AROUND FLASHING LIGHTS AND STUFF?
NOT THAT SIMPLE, JO.
THAT'S NOT ALL THERE IS TO IT.
ISAAC'S ROOM
OH OK, THEN-
MY SEIZURES ARE TRIGGERED BY LACK OF SLEEP, INTENSE PHYSICAL OR EMOTIONAL STRESS,
UM, I...
OR SOMETIMES EVEN ANXIETY ABOUT EPILEPSY ITSELF. ONE OR ANY COMBO OF THESE THINGS CAN GIVE ME AN AURA, WHICH CAN LEAD TO A SEIZURE.
W-WORD... SORRY FOR-
YEP.
SLAM
OKAY, SO, I HAD CLASS UNTIL 10:00 PM, IT'S ALMOST 11:00 NOW, AND I HAVE TWO CLASSES TOMORROW FROM 8:00 AM TO 5:00 PM, WITH AN APPOINTMENT IN BETWEEN... I NEED AT LEAST EIGHT HOURS OF SLEEP...
THAT MEANS, EVEN IF I WENT TO BED NOW, I HAVE TO GET UP BY 6:00 AM, WHICH LEAVES ME WITH ONLY SEVEN HOURS... AT THE MOST.
AND THAT'S ASSUMING I DON'T WAKE UP DURING THE NIGHT...
UGH

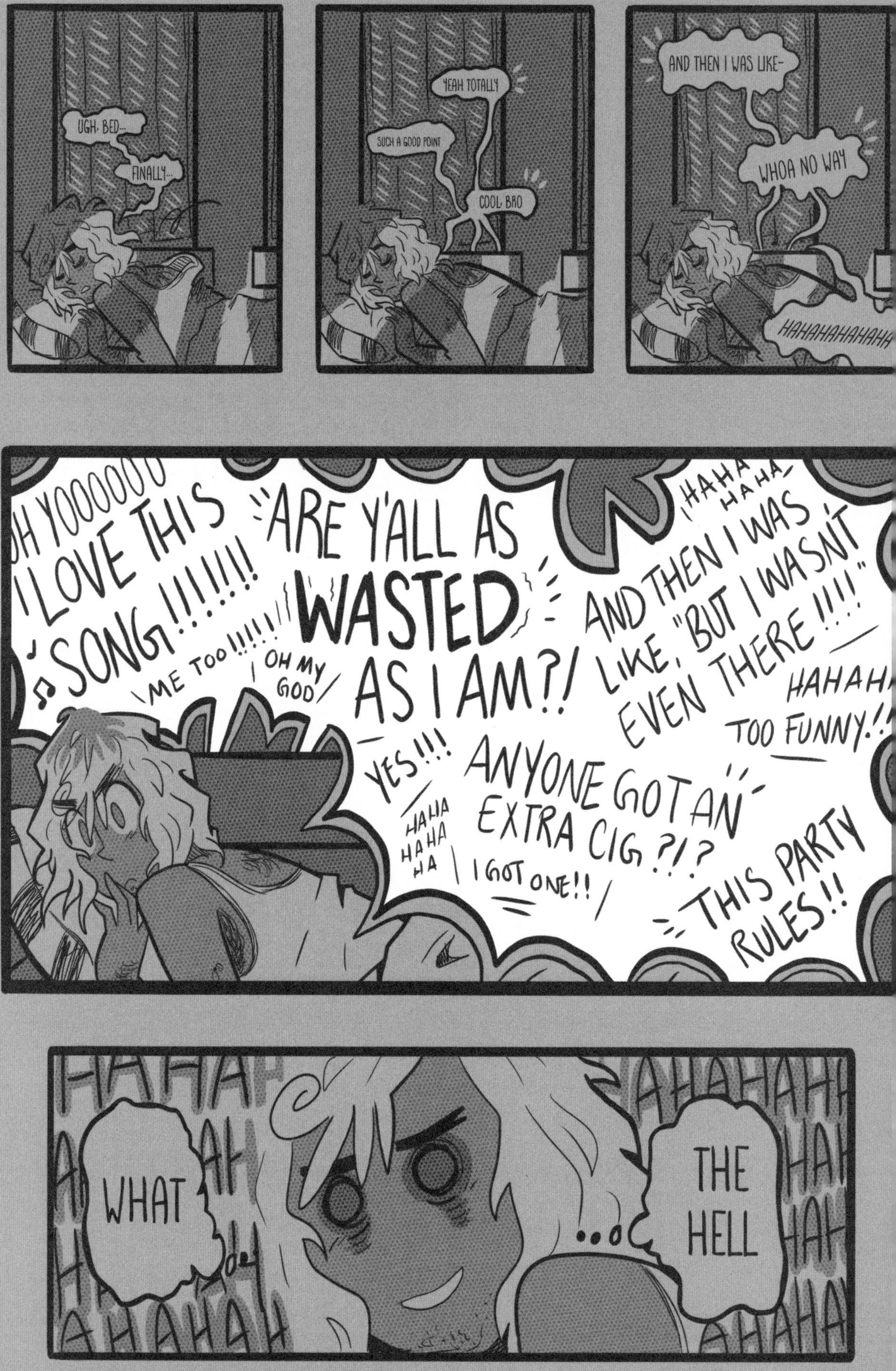

UGH, BED...
FINALLY...
SUCH A GOOD POINT
YEAH TOTALLY
COOL, BRO
AND THEN I WAS LIKE-
WHOA NO WAY
HAHAHAHAHAHH
OH YOOOOOO I LOVE THIS SONG!!!!!!!
ME TOO!!!!!
OH MY GOD
ARE Y'ALL AS WASTED AS I AM?!
HAHA HAHA
AND THEN I WAS LIKE, "BUT I WASN'T EVEN THERE!!!!"
HAHAH
TOO FUNNY!
YES!!!
HAHA HAHA HAHA HA
ANYONE GOT AN EXTRA CIG?!?
I GOT ONE!!
THIS PARTY RULES!!
HAHAH
AHAHAH
WHAT
THE HELL

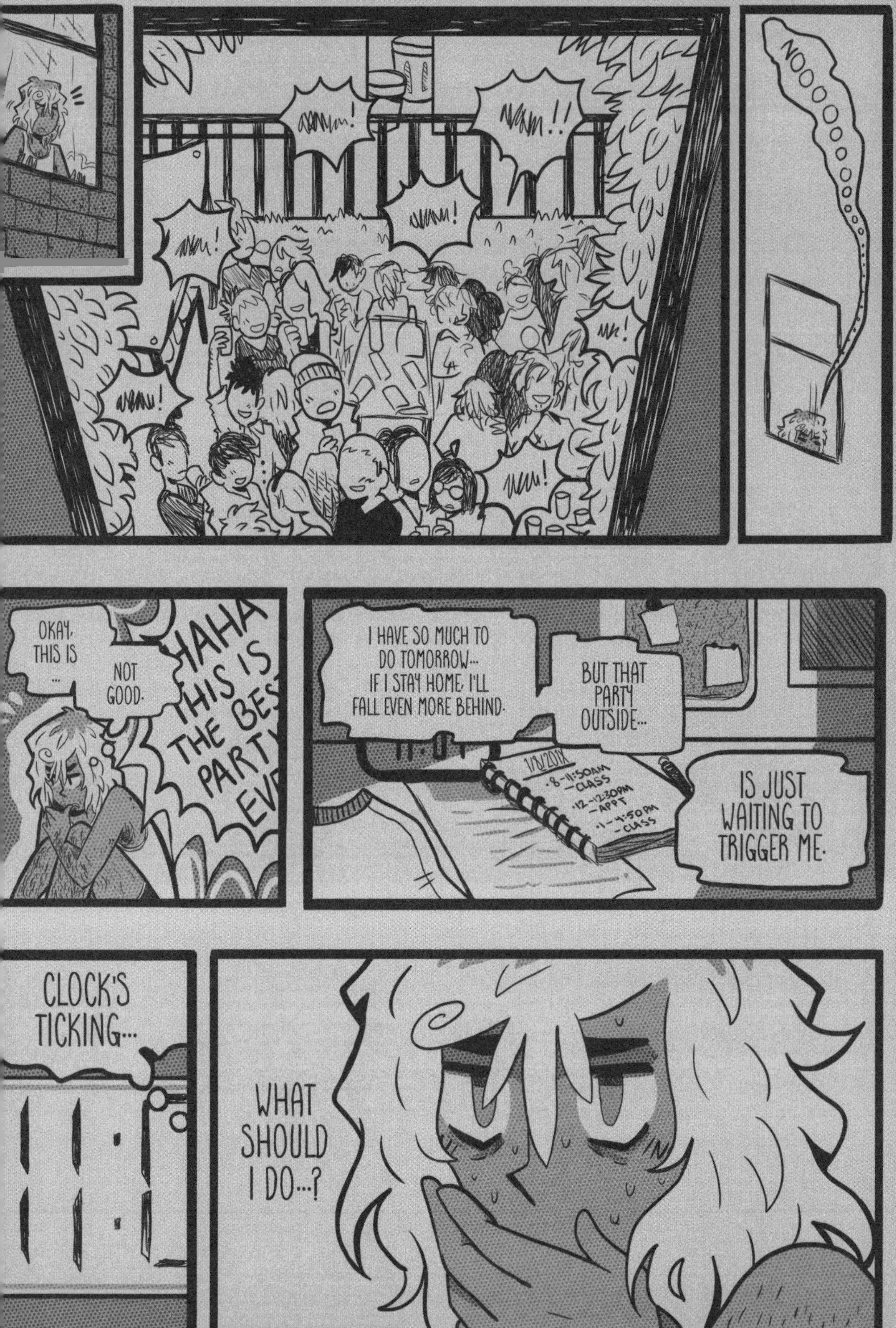
NOOOOOOOO
OKAY, THIS IS ...
NOT GOOD.
HAHA THIS IS THE BES PART EV
I HAVE SO MUCH TO DO TOMORROW... IF I STAY HOME, I'LL FALL EVEN MORE BEHIND.
BUT THAT PARTY OUTSIDE...
1/8/201X
•8-11:50AM -CLASS
•12-12:30PM -APPT
•1-4:50PM -CLASS
IS JUST WAITING TO TRIGGER ME.
CLOCK'S TICKING...
WHAT SHOULD I DO...?

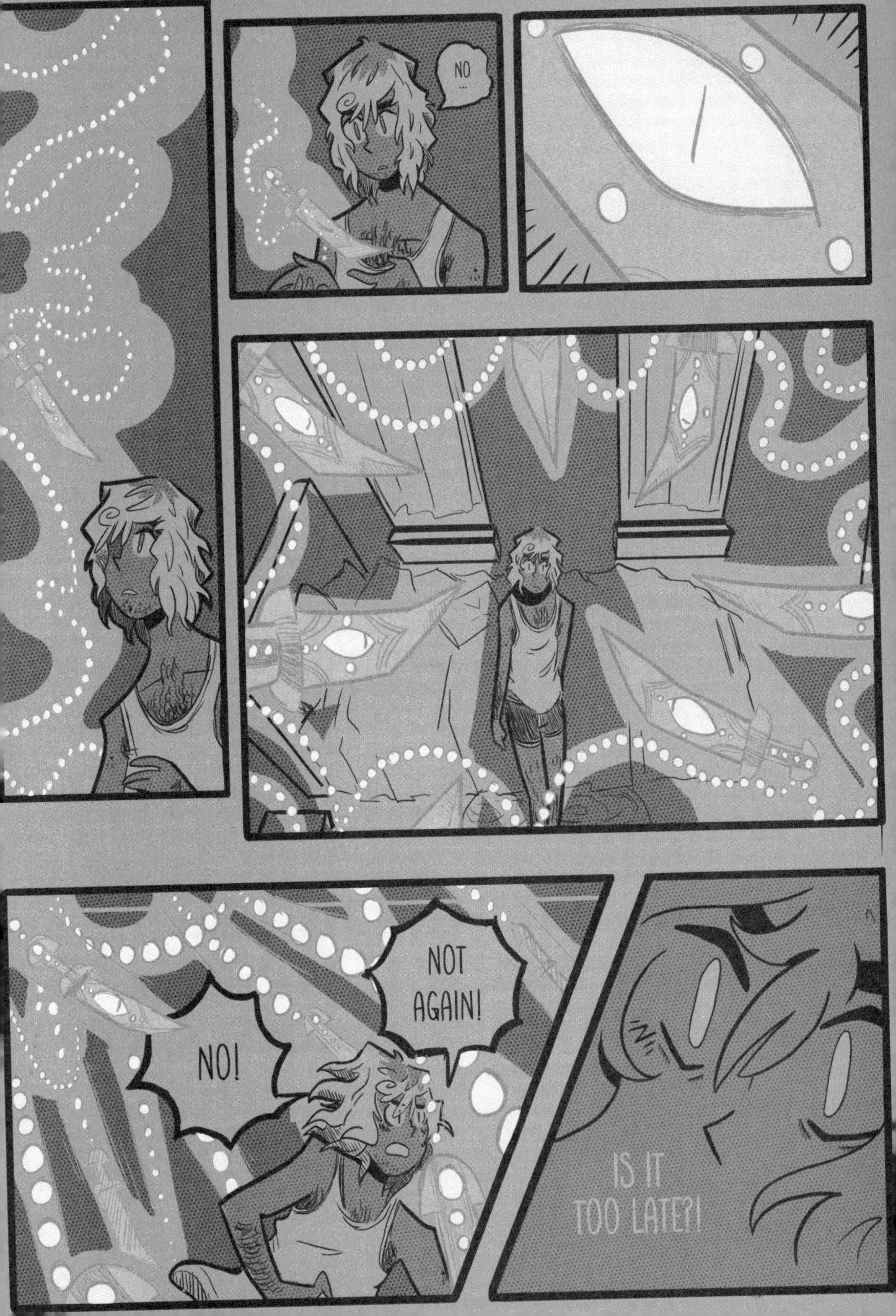
NO...
NO!
NOT AGAIN!
IS IT TOO LATE?!

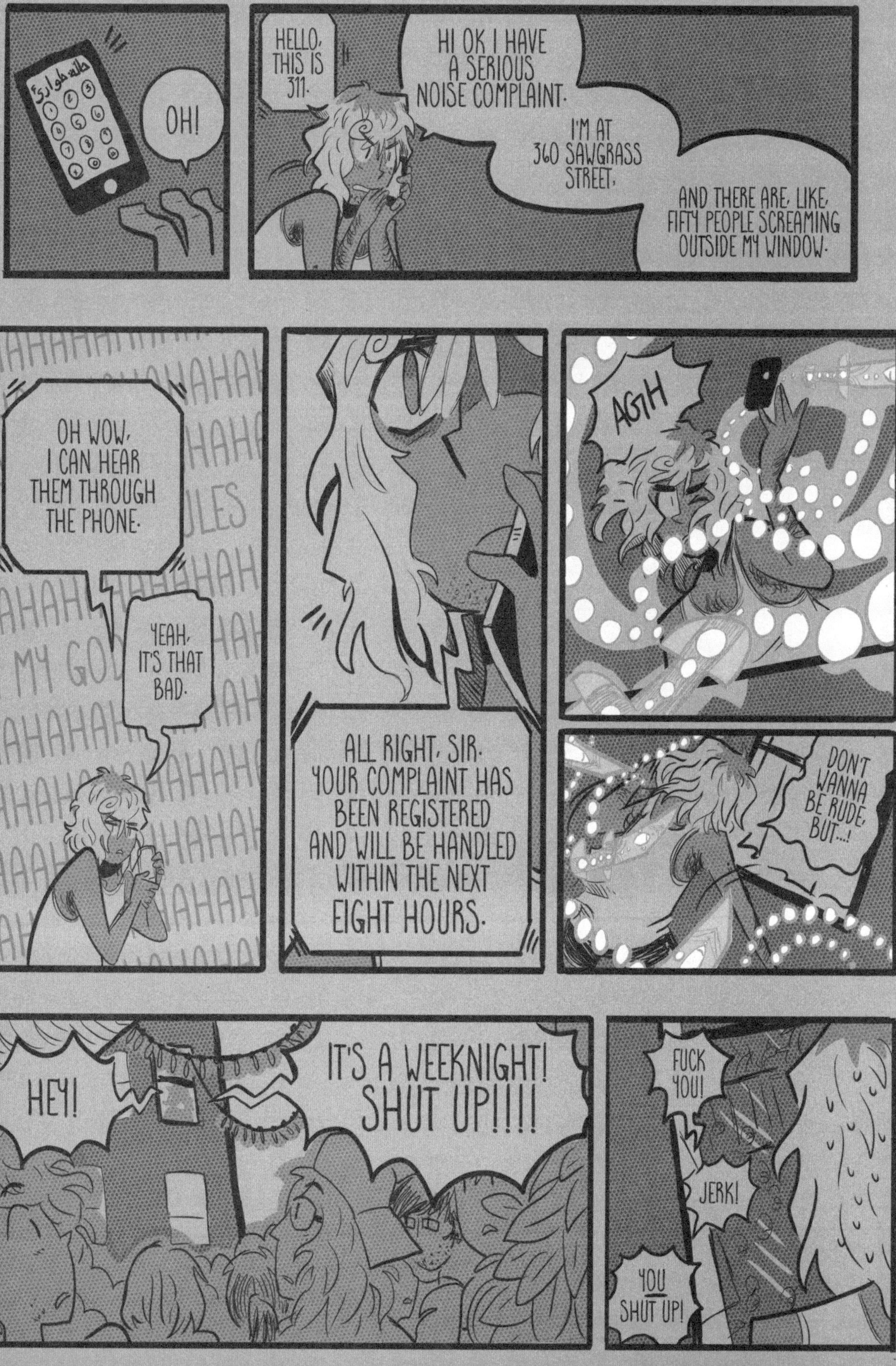

حالة طوارئ
OH!
HELLO, THIS IS 311.
HI OK I HAVE A SERIOUS NOISE COMPLAINT.
I'M AT 360 SAWGRASS STREET,
AND THERE ARE, LIKE, FIFTY PEOPLE SCREAMING OUTSIDE MY WINDOW.
OH WOW, I CAN HEAR THEM THROUGH THE PHONE.
YEAH, IT'S THAT BAD.
ALL RIGHT, SIR. YOUR COMPLAINT HAS BEEN REGISTERED AND WILL BE HANDLED WITHIN THE NEXT EIGHT HOURS.
AGH
DON'T WANNA BE RUDE, BUT...!
HEY!
IT'S A WEEKNIGHT! SHUT UP!!!!
FUCK YOU!
JERK!
YOU SHUT UP!

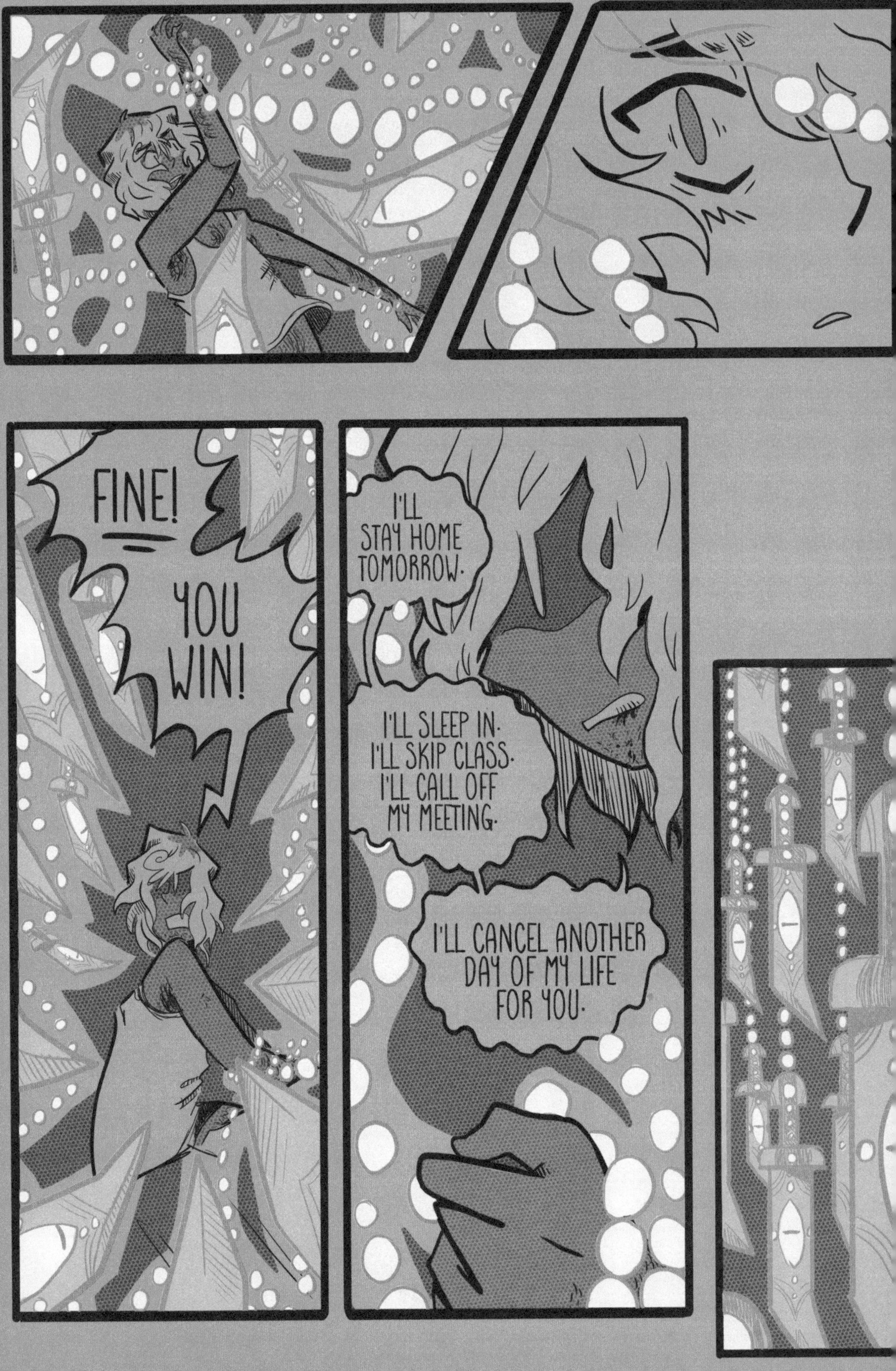
FINE!
YOU WIN!
I'LL STAY HOME TOMORROW.
I'LL SLEEP IN. I'LL SKIP CLASS. I'LL CALL OFF MY MEETING.
I'LL CANCEL ANOTHER DAY OF MY LIFE FOR YOU.

ARE YOU

HAPPY NOW?!

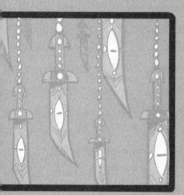

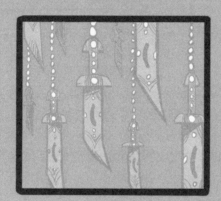

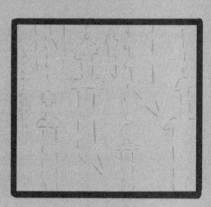

AHAHHHH

THIS RULES!

YEAH!

LET'S DO MORE SHOTS!

CHEERS!

TO OUR HEALTH!

IT'S GOOD TO BE ALIVE!

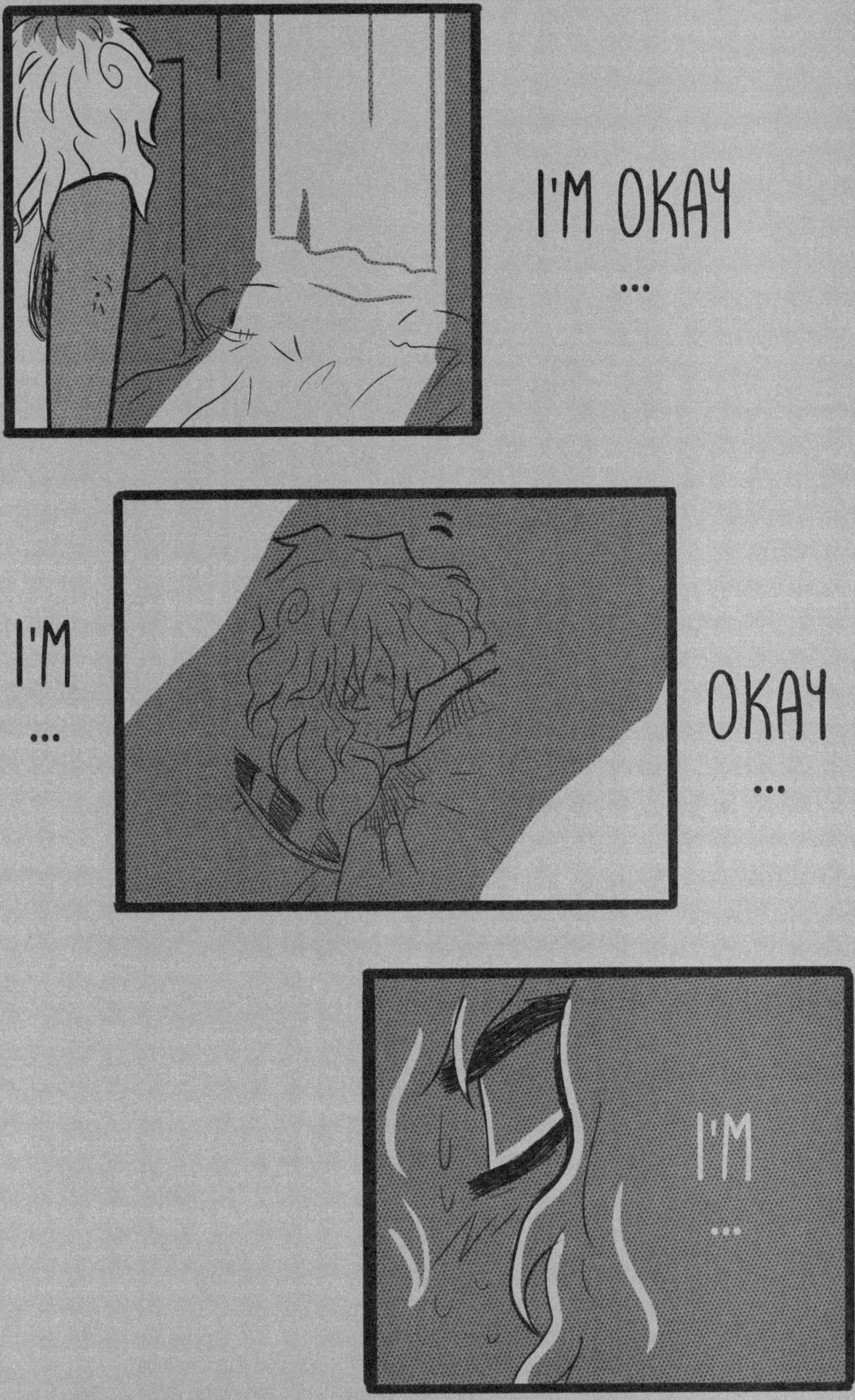
I'M OKAY
...
I'M
...
OKAY
...
I'M
...

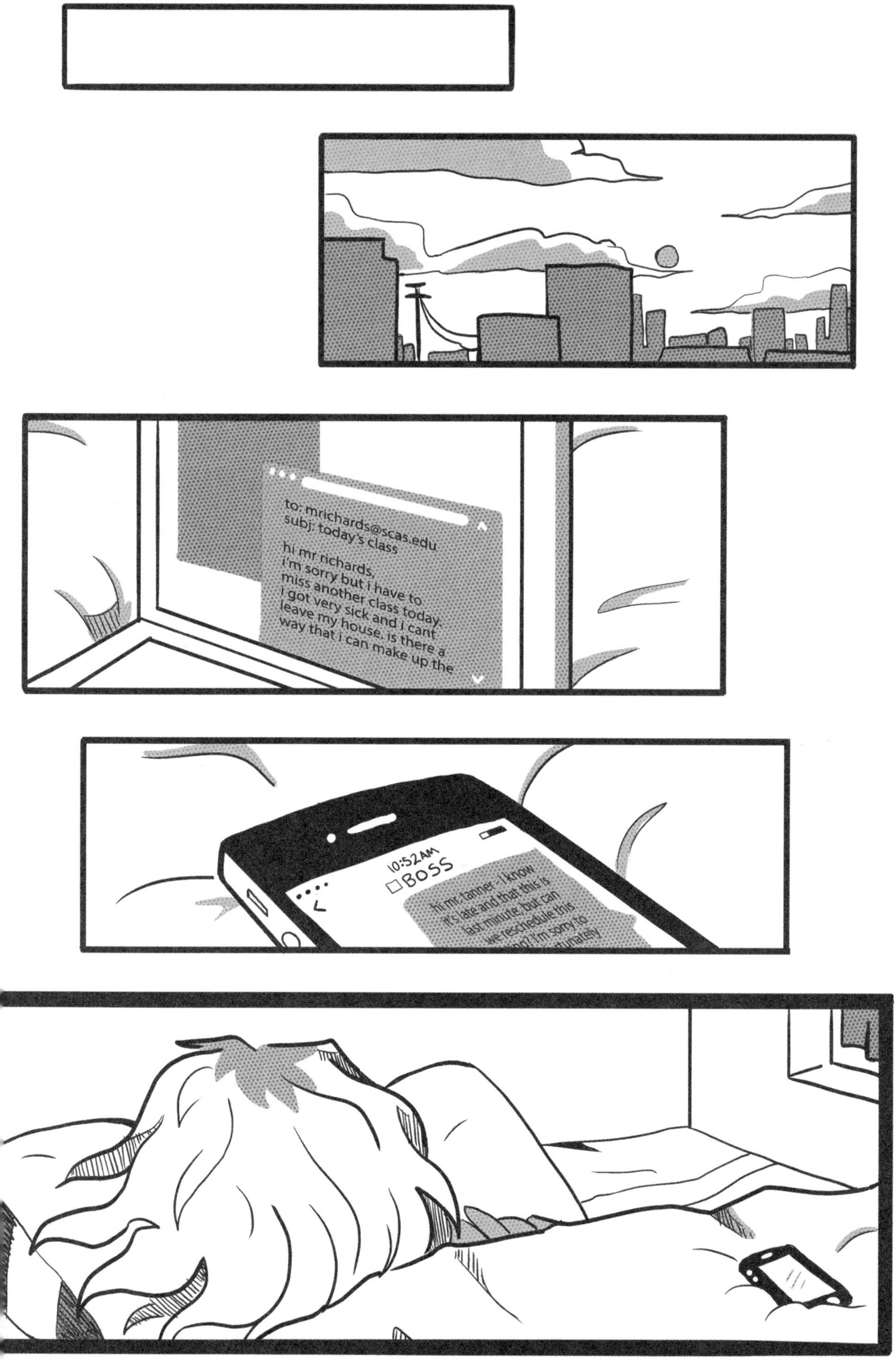
to: mrichards@scas.edu
subj: today's class
hi mr richards,
i'm sorry but i have to
miss another class today.
i got very sick and i cant
leave my house. is there a
way that i can make up the
10:52AM
BOSS
hi mr. tanner - I know
it's late and that this is
last minute, but can
we reschedule this

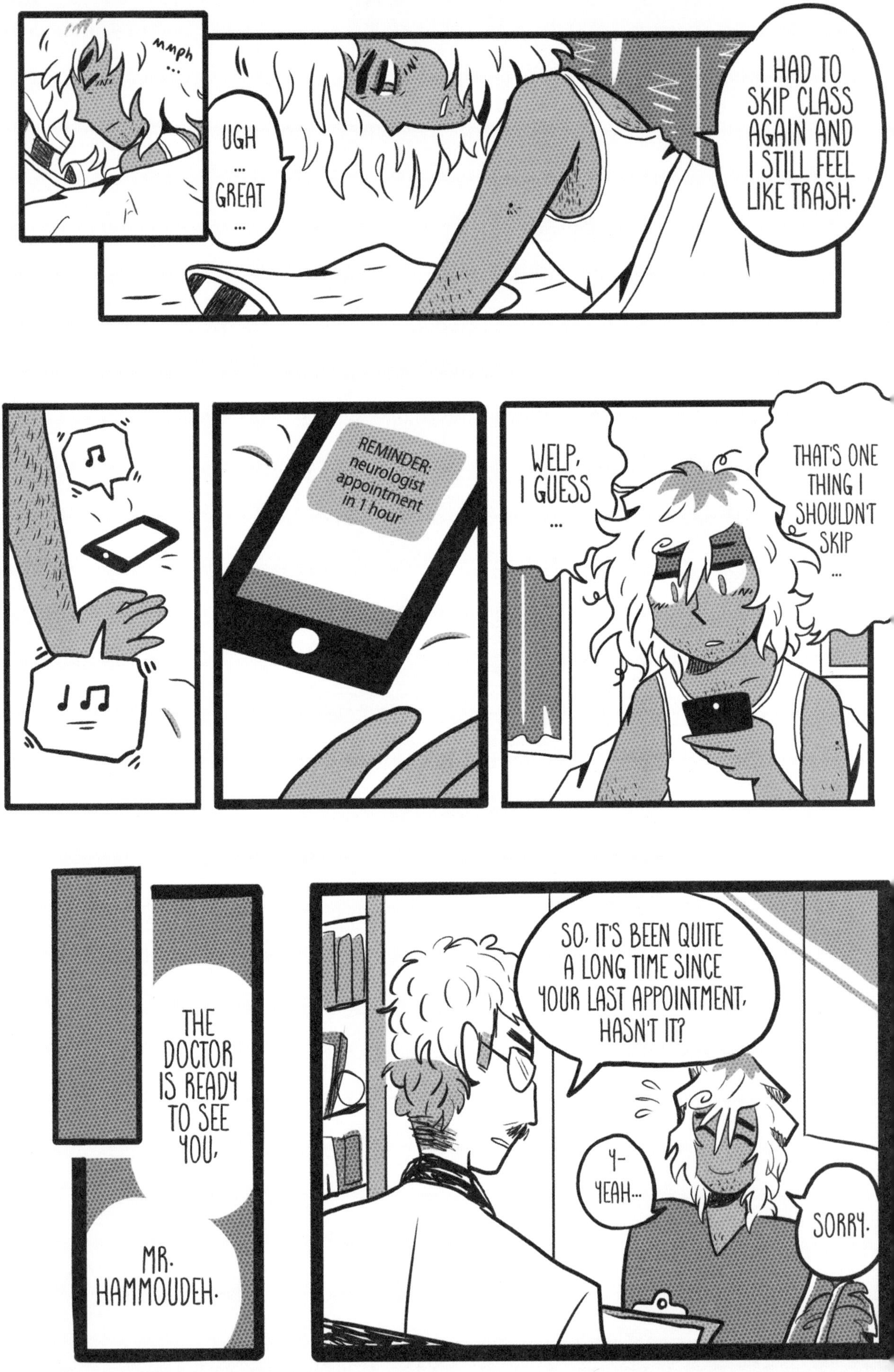

MMPH...
UGH ... GREAT ...
I HAD TO SKIP CLASS AGAIN AND I STILL FEEL LIKE TRASH.
REMINDER: neurologist appointment in 1 hour
WELP, I GUESS ...
THAT'S ONE THING I SHOULDN'T SKIP ...
THE DOCTOR IS READY TO SEE YOU,
MR. HAMMOUDEH.
SO, IT'S BEEN QUITE A LONG TIME SINCE YOUR LAST APPOINTMENT, HASN'T IT?
Y-YEAH...
SORRY.

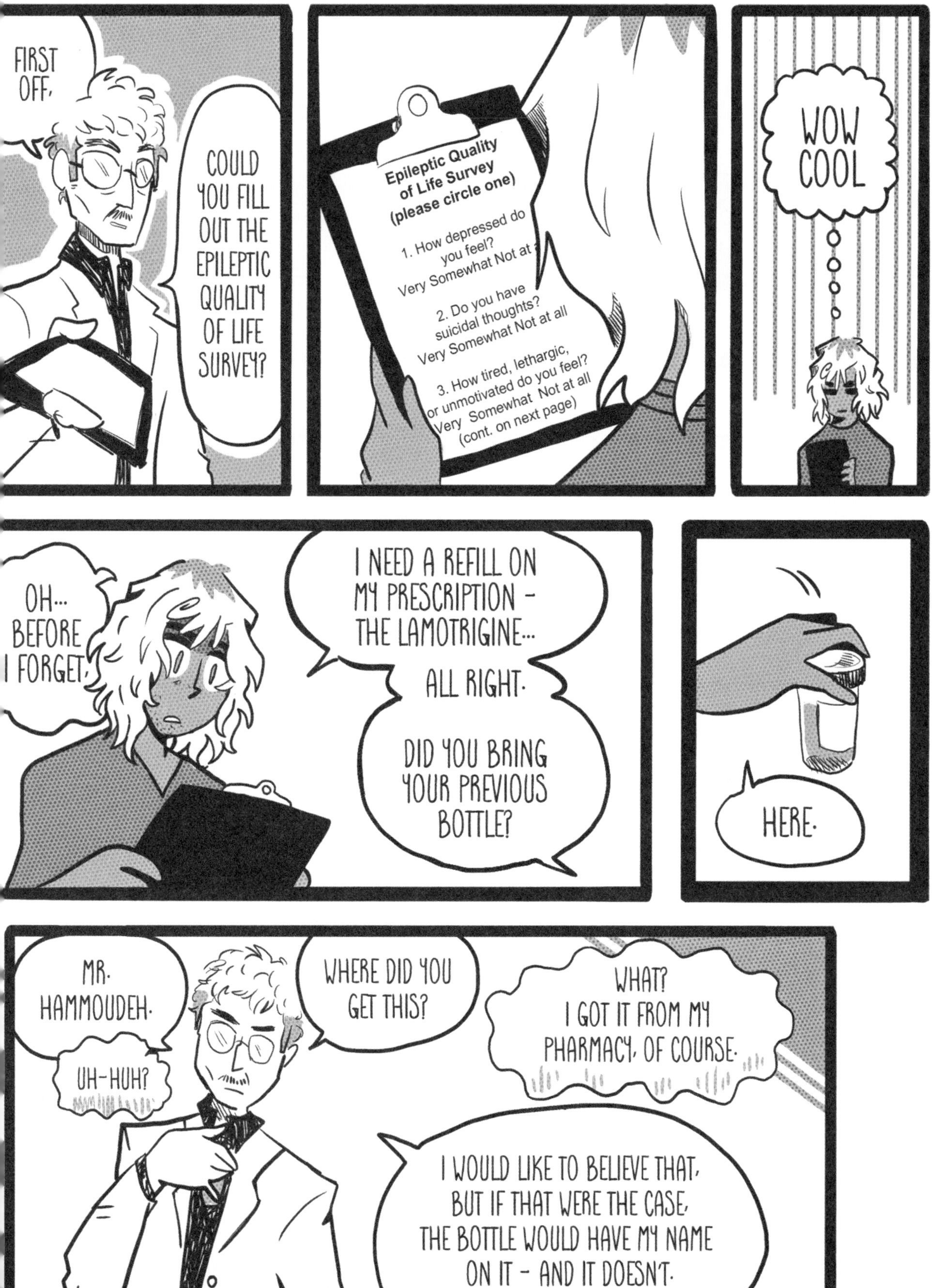
FIRST OFF,
COULD YOU FILL OUT THE EPILEPTIC QUALITY OF LIFE SURVEY?
Epileptic Quality of Life Survey (please circle one)
1. How depressed do you feel? Very Somewhat Not at
2. Do you have suicidal thoughts? Very Somewhat Not at all
3. How tired, lethargic, or unmotivated do you feel? Very Somewhat Not at all
(cont. on next page)
WOW COOL
OH... BEFORE I FORGET,
I NEED A REFILL ON MY PRESCRIPTION - THE LAMOTRIGINE...
ALL RIGHT.
DID YOU BRING YOUR PREVIOUS BOTTLE?
HERE.
MR. HAMMOUDEH.
UH-HUH?
WHERE DID YOU GET THIS?
WHAT? I GOT IT FROM MY PHARMACY, OF COURSE.
I WOULD LIKE TO BELIEVE THAT, BUT IF THAT WERE THE CASE, THE BOTTLE WOULD HAVE MY NAME ON IT - AND IT DOESN'T.

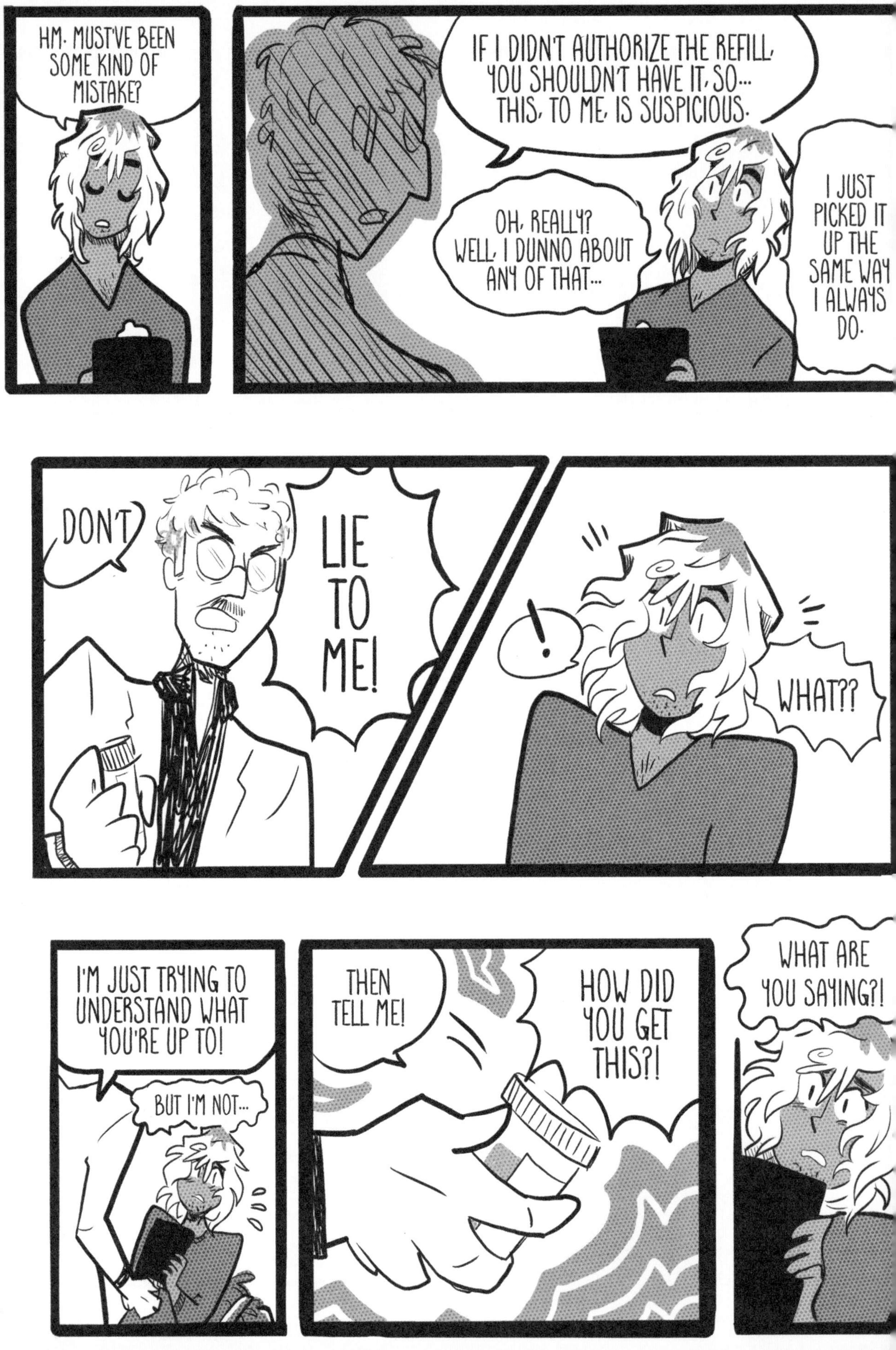
HM. MUST'VE BEEN SOME KIND OF MISTAKE?
IF I DIDN'T AUTHORIZE THE REFILL, YOU SHOULDN'T HAVE IT, SO... THIS, TO ME, IS SUSPICIOUS.
OH, REALLY? WELL, I DUNNO ABOUT ANY OF THAT...
I JUST PICKED IT UP THE SAME WAY I ALWAYS DO.
DON'T
LIE TO ME!
!
WHAT??
I'M JUST TRYING TO UNDERSTAND WHAT YOU'RE UP TO!
BUT I'M NOT...
THEN TELL ME!
HOW DID YOU GET THIS?!
WHAT ARE YOU SAYING?!

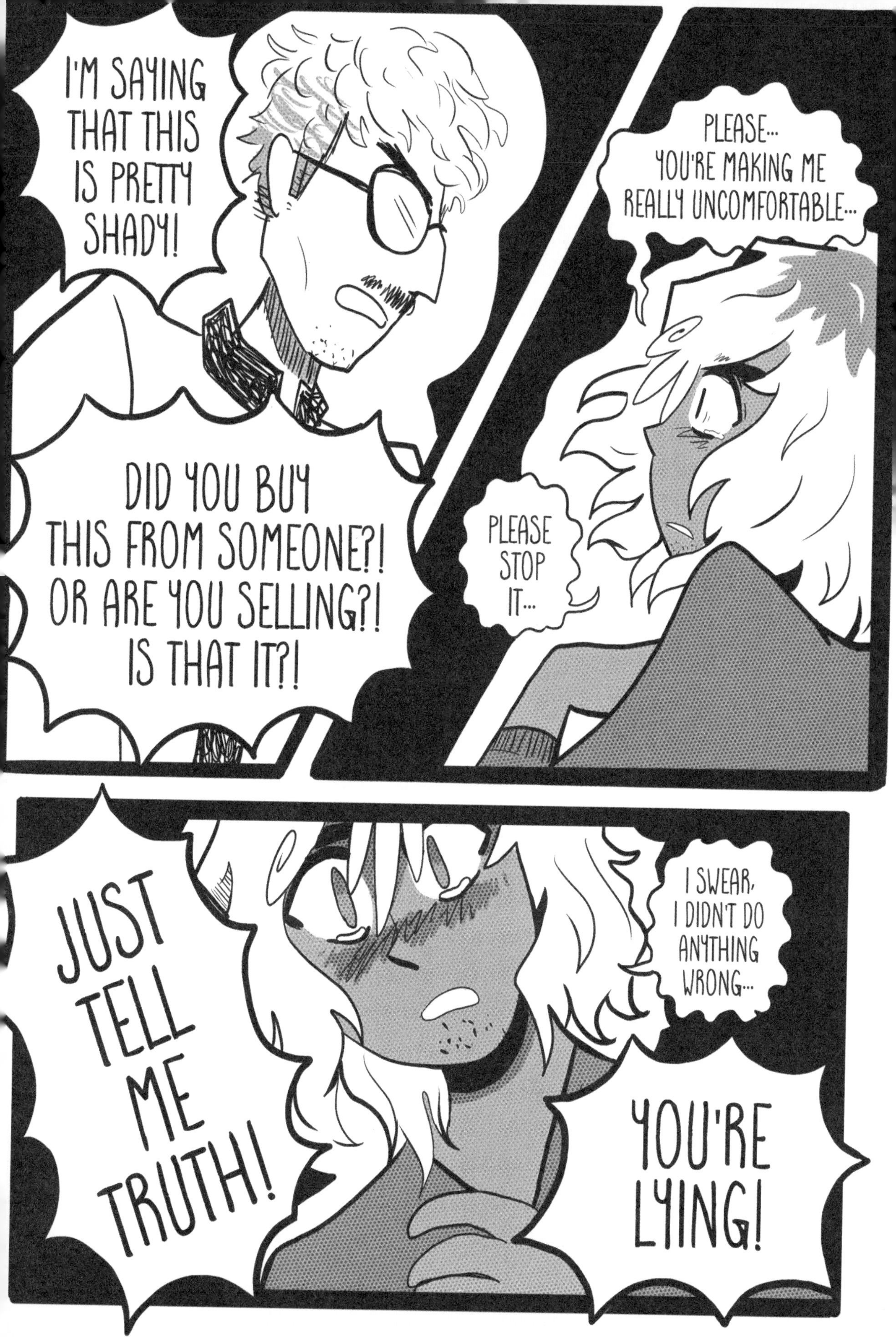
I'M SAYING THAT THIS IS PRETTY SHADY!
DID YOU BUY THIS FROM SOMEONE?! OR ARE YOU SELLING?! IS THAT IT?!
PLEASE... YOU'RE MAKING ME REALLY UNCOMFORTABLE...
PLEASE STOP IT...
JUST TELL ME TRUTH!
I SWEAR, I DIDN'T DO ANYTHING WRONG...
YOU'RE LYING!

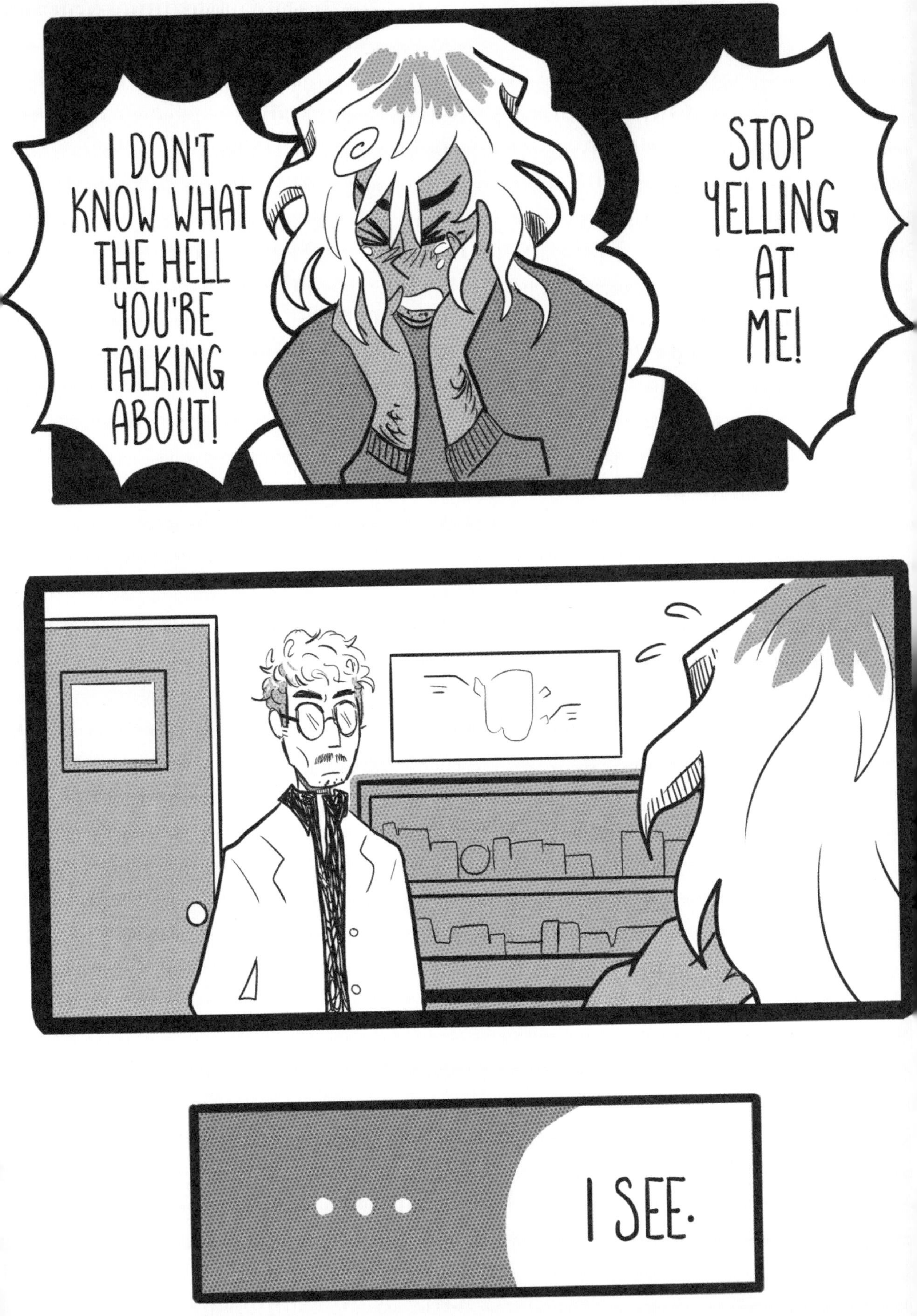
I DON'T KNOW WHAT THE HELL YOU'RE TALKING ABOUT!
STOP YELLING AT ME!
...
I SEE.

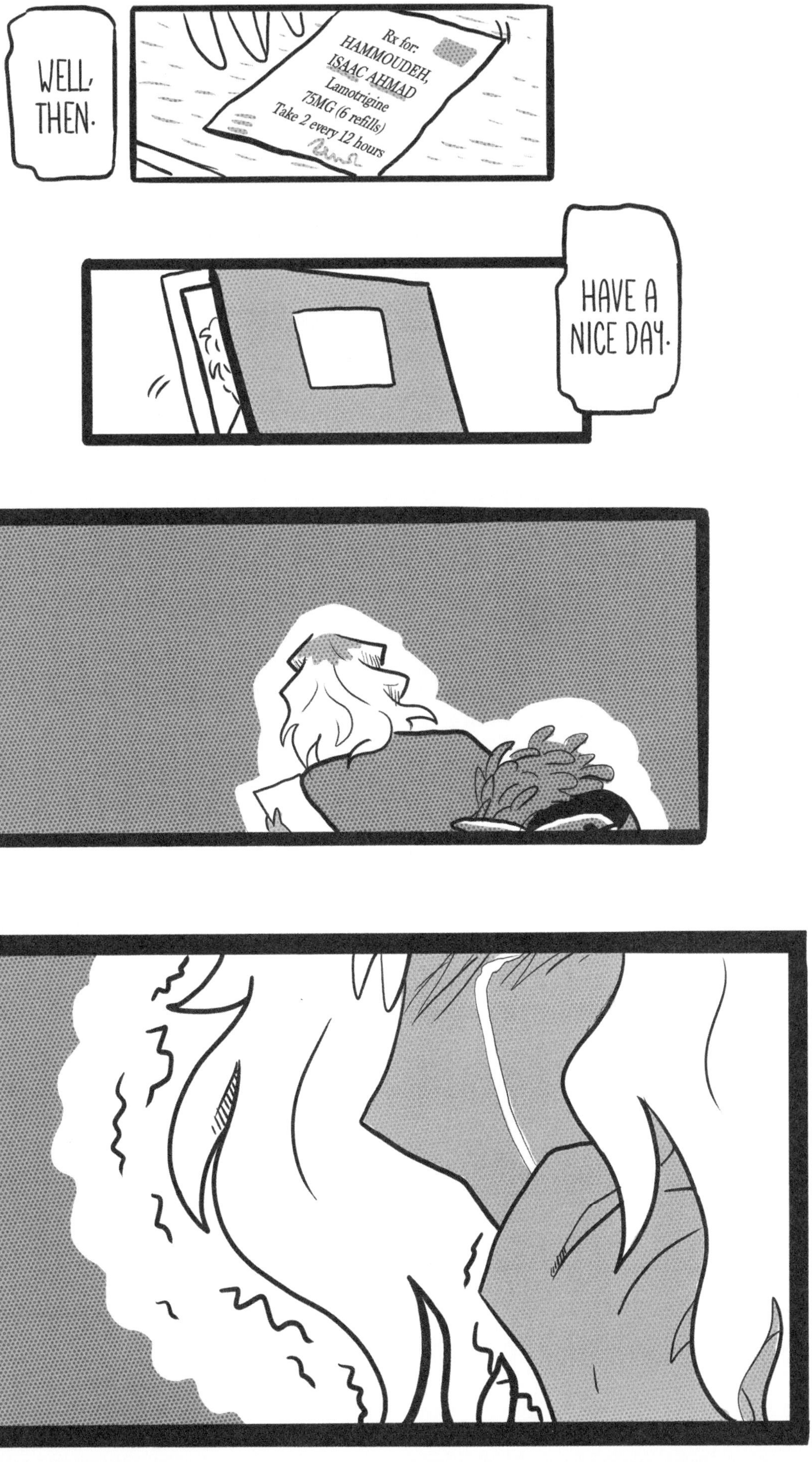
WELL, THEN.
Rx for:
HAMMOUDEH,
ISAAC AHMAD
Lamotrigine
75MG (6 refills)
Take 2 every 12 hours
HAVE A NICE DAY.

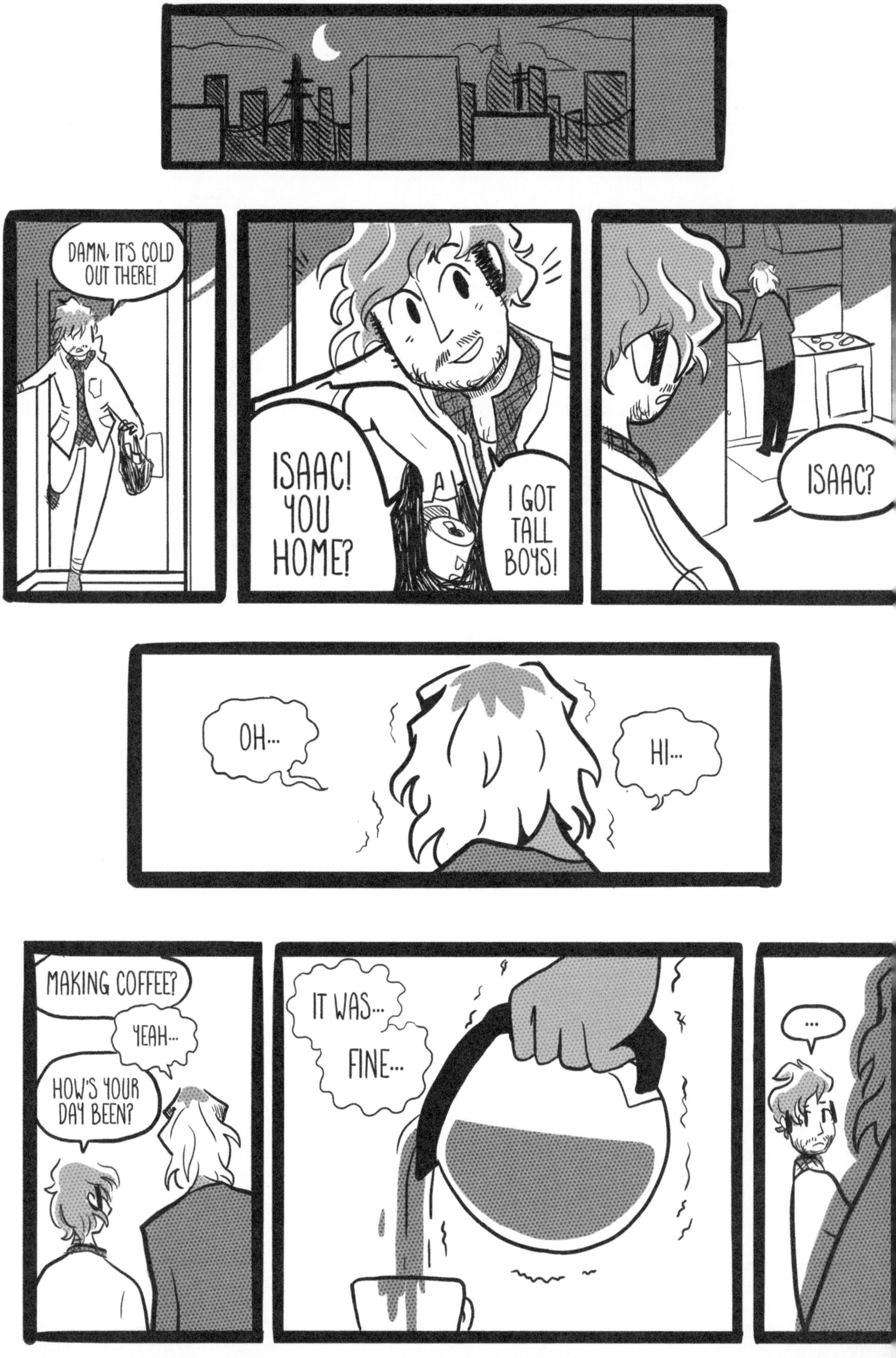
DAMN, IT'S COLD OUT THERE!
ISAAC! YOU HOME?
I GOT TALL BOYS!
ISAAC?
OH...
HI...
MAKING COFFEE?
YEAH...
HOW'S YOUR DAY BEEN?
IT WAS...
FINE...
...

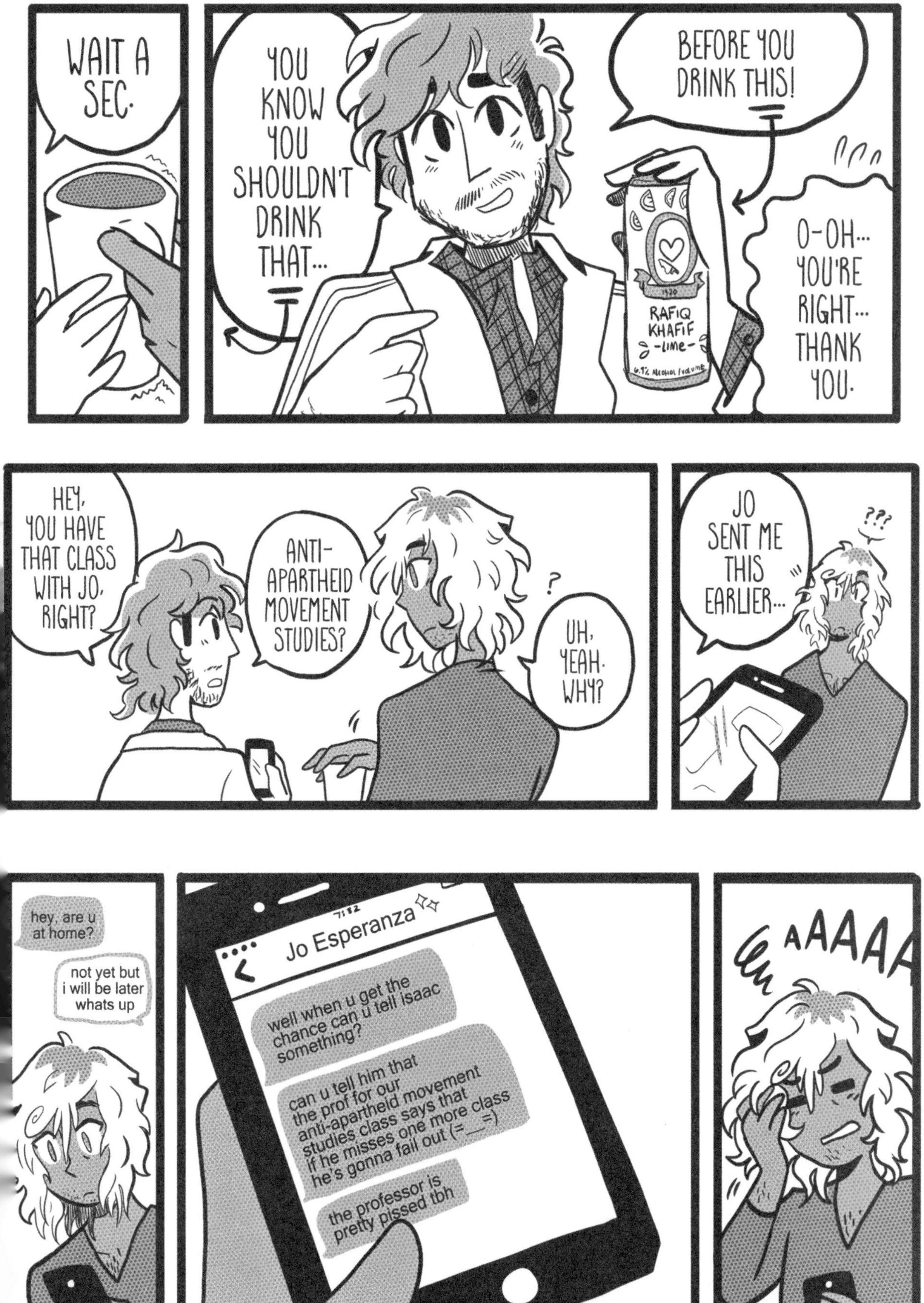
WAIT A SEC.
YOU KNOW YOU SHOULDN'T DRINK THAT...
BEFORE YOU DRINK THIS!
RAFIQ KHAFIF -lime-
O-OH... YOU'RE RIGHT... THANK YOU.
HEY, YOU HAVE THAT CLASS WITH JO, RIGHT?
ANTI-APARTHEID MOVEMENT STUDIES?
?
UH, YEAH. WHY?
JO SENT ME THIS EARLIER...
???
hey, are u at home?
not yet but i will be later whats up
Jo Esperanza
well when u get the chance can u tell isaac something?
can u tell him that the prof for our anti-apartheid movement studies class says that if he misses one more class he's gonna fail out (=__=)
the professor is pretty pissed tbh
AAAAA

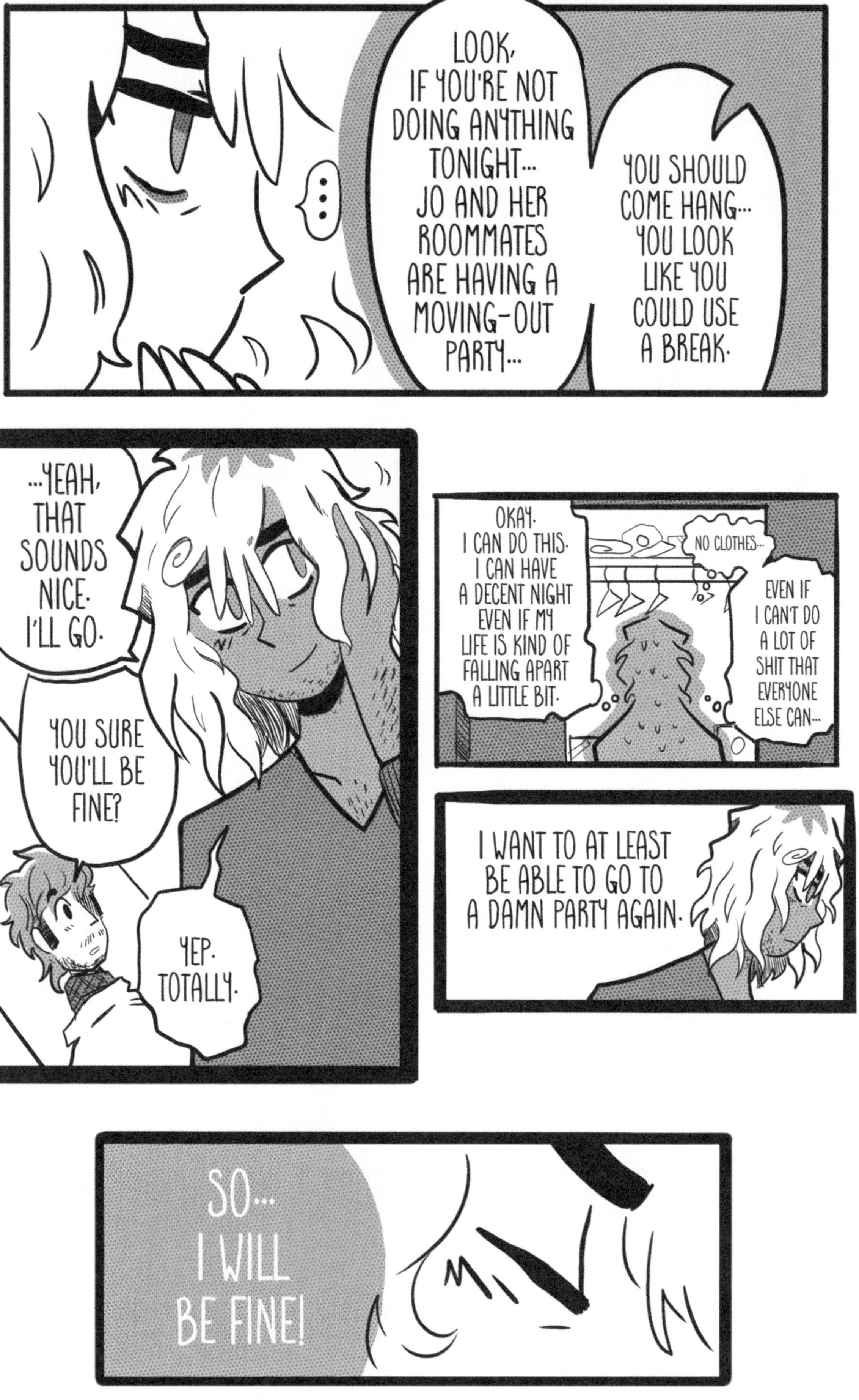
...
LOOK, IF YOU'RE NOT DOING ANYTHING TONIGHT... JO AND HER ROOMMATES ARE HAVING A MOVING-OUT PARTY...
YOU SHOULD COME HANG... YOU LOOK LIKE YOU COULD USE A BREAK.
...YEAH, THAT SOUNDS NICE. I'LL GO.
YOU SURE YOU'LL BE FINE?
YEP. TOTALLY.
OKAY. I CAN DO THIS. I CAN HAVE A DECENT NIGHT EVEN IF MY LIFE IS KIND OF FALLING APART A LITTLE BIT.
NO CLOTHES...
EVEN IF I CAN'T DO A LOT OF SHIT THAT EVERYONE ELSE CAN...
I WANT TO AT LEAST BE ABLE TO GO TO A DAMN PARTY AGAIN.
SO... I WILL BE FINE!

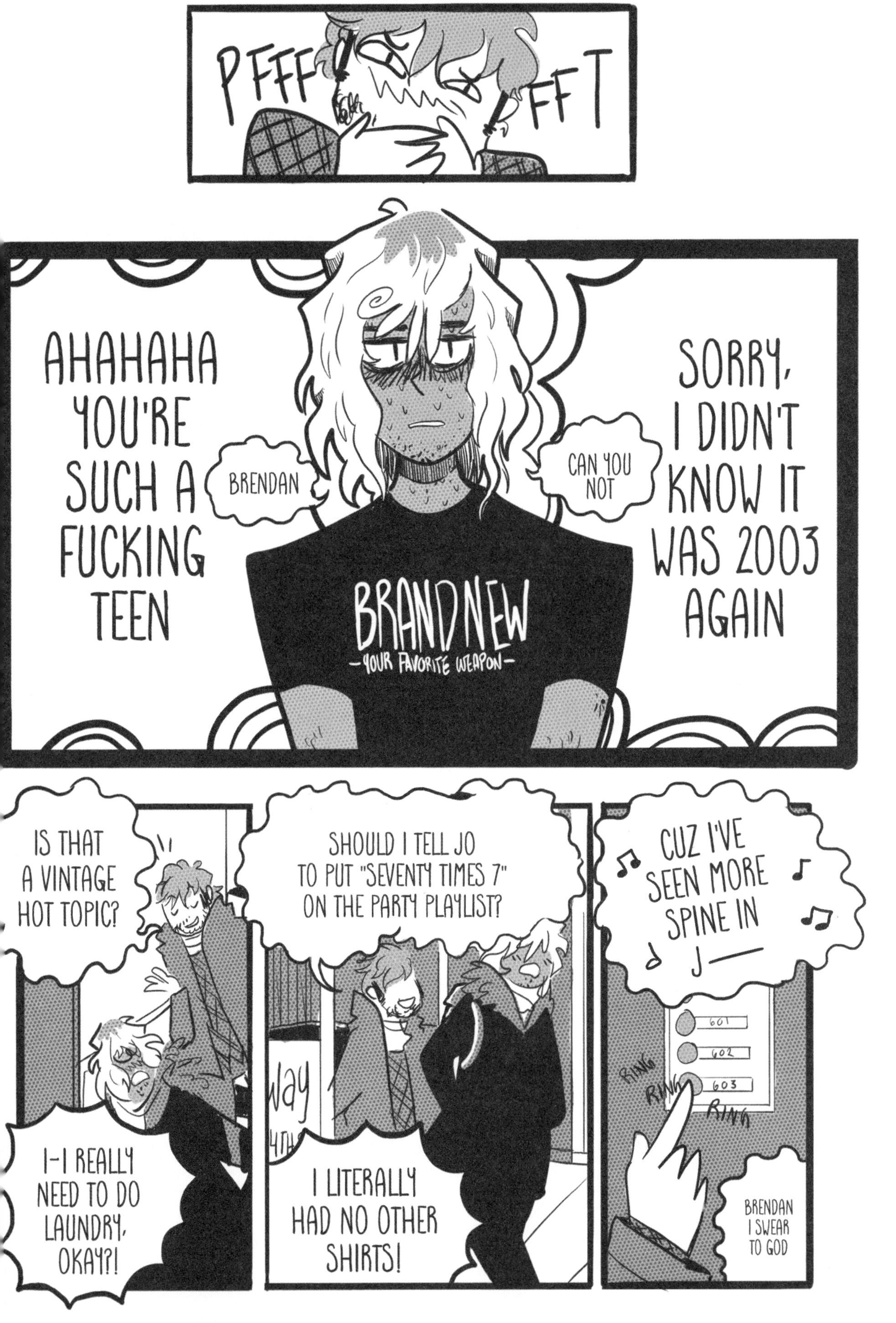
PFFF
FFT
AHAHAHA YOU'RE SUCH A FUCKING TEEN
BRENDAN
BRANDNEW
-YOUR FAVORITE WEAPON-
CAN YOU NOT
SORRY, I DIDN'T KNOW IT WAS 2003 AGAIN
IS THAT A VINTAGE HOT TOPIC?
I-I REALLY NEED TO DO LAUNDRY, OKAY?!
SHOULD I TELL JO TO PUT "SEVENTY TIMES 7" ON THE PARTY PLAYLIST?
I LITERALLY HAD NO OTHER SHIRTS!
CUZ I'VE SEEN MORE SPINE IN
601
602
603
RING
RING
RING
BRENDAN I SWEAR TO GOD

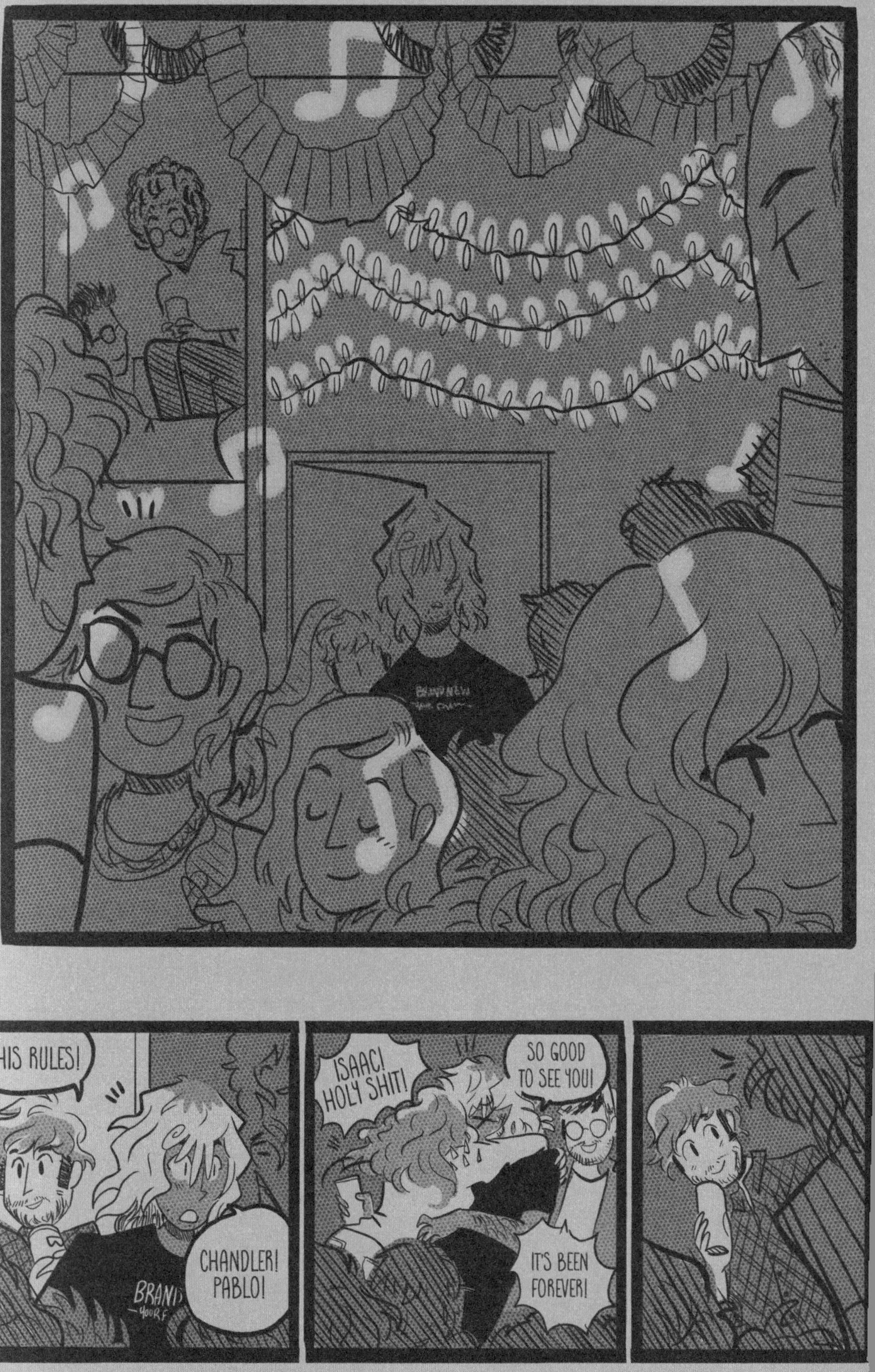
THIS RULES!
CHANDLER! PABLO!
ISAAC! HOLY SHIT!
SO GOOD TO SEE YOU!
IT'S BEEN FOREVER!

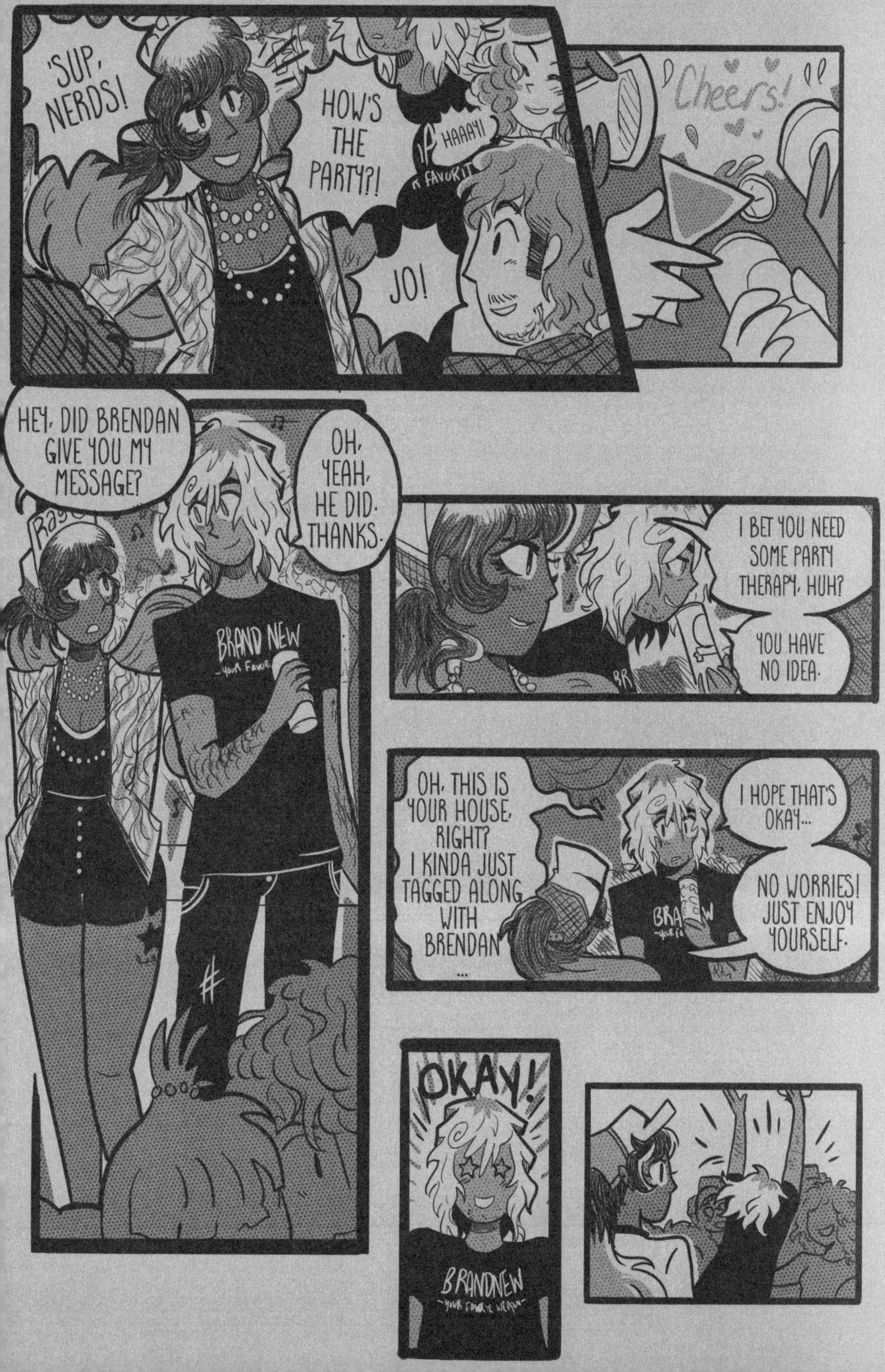
'SUP, NERDS!
HOW'S THE PARTY?!
HAAAY!
JO!
Cheers!
HEY, DID BRENDAN GIVE YOU MY MESSAGE?
OH, YEAH, HE DID. THANKS.
BRAND NEW
I BET YOU NEED SOME PARTY THERAPY, HUH?
YOU HAVE NO IDEA.
OH, THIS IS YOUR HOUSE, RIGHT? I KINDA JUST TAGGED ALONG WITH BRENDAN ...
I HOPE THAT'S OKAY...
NO WORRIES! JUST ENJOY YOURSELF.
OKAY!
BRANDNEW

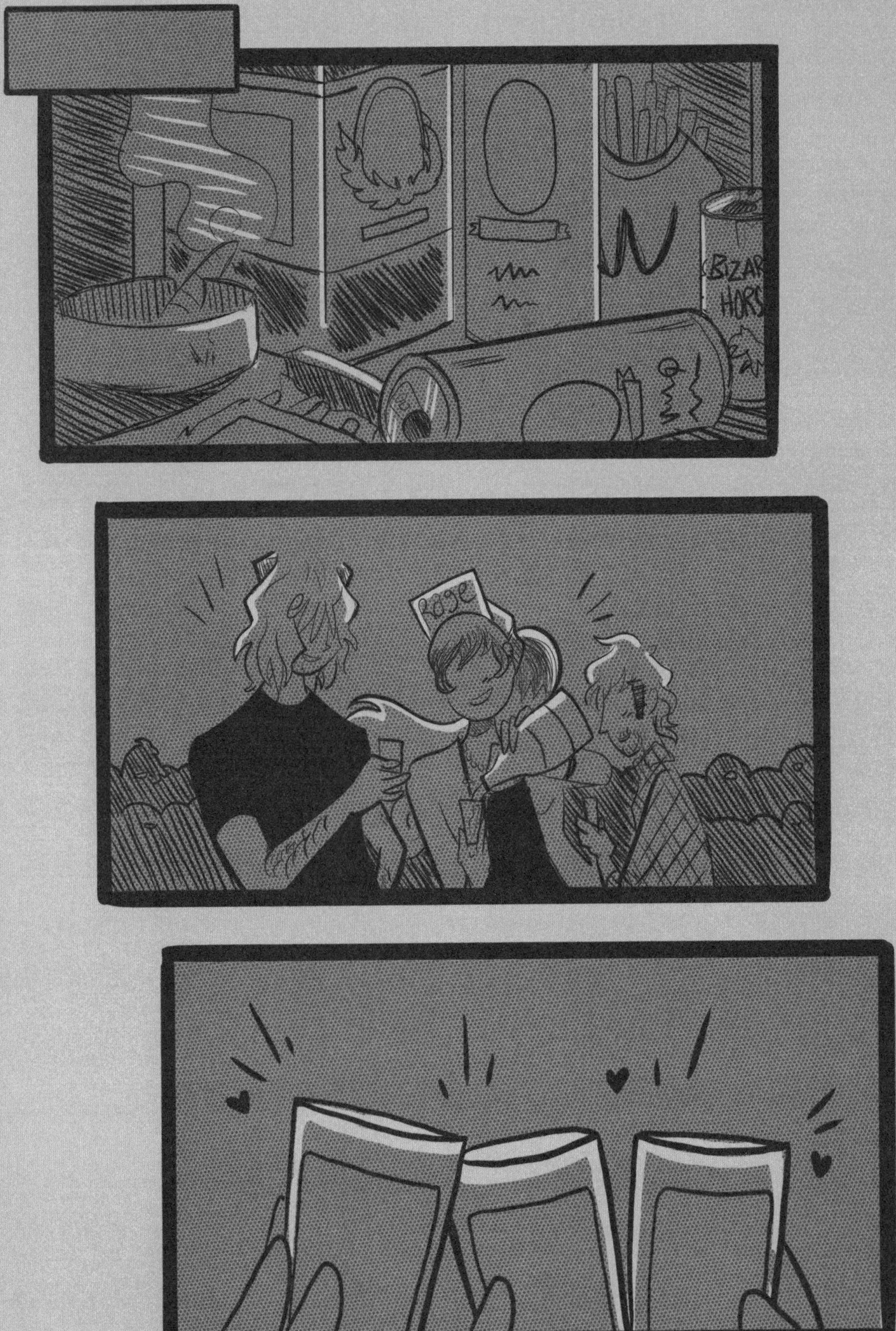
BIZAR
HORS
Rage

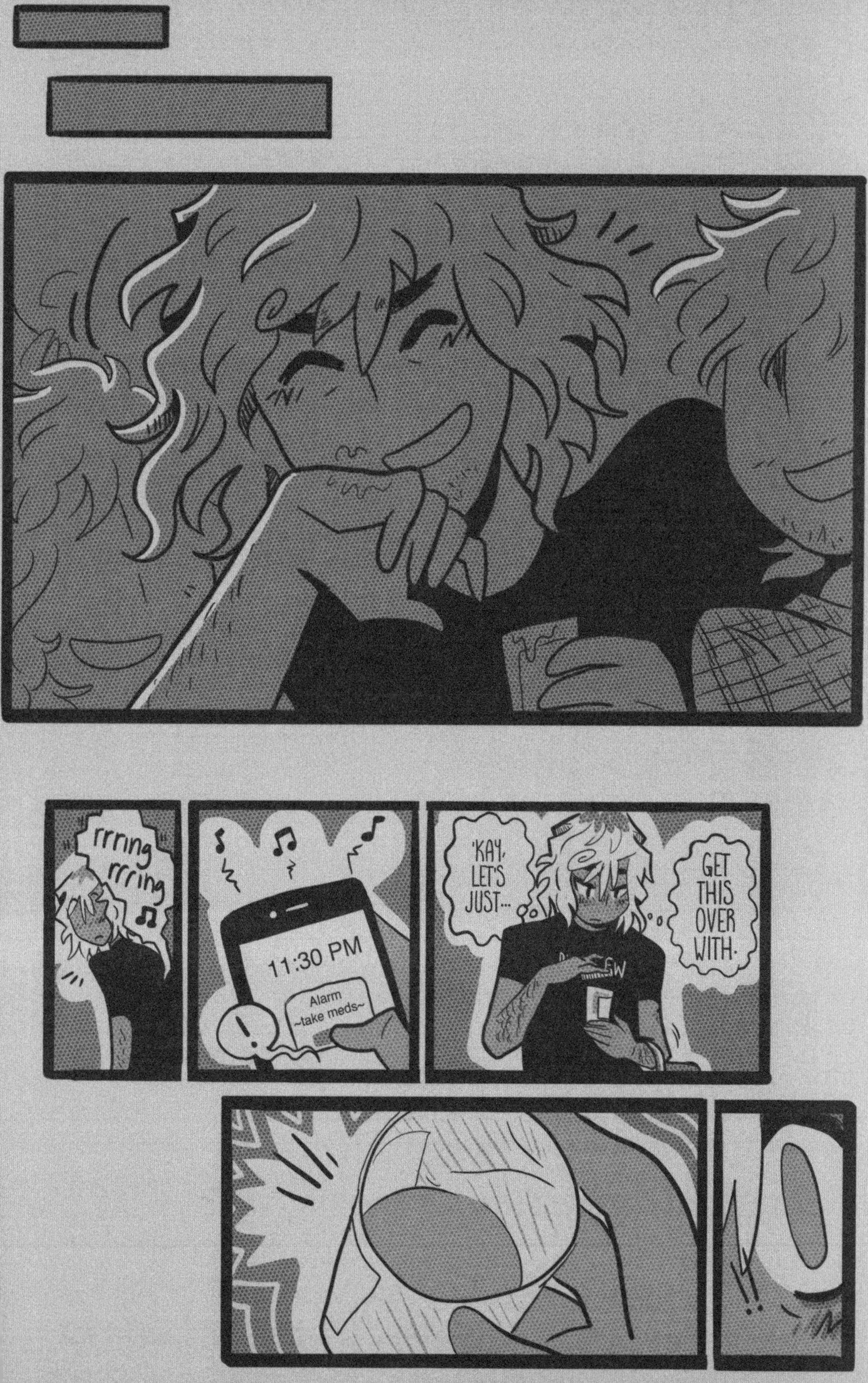
rrring rrring
11:30 PM
Alarm
~take meds~
'KAY, LET'S JUST...
GET THIS OVER WITH.

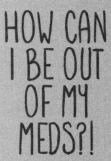

HOW CAN I BE OUT OF MY MEDS?!

NO, WAIT... MY APPOINTMENT EARLIER... BECAUSE OF WHAT HAPPENED...

I FORGOT TO GET MY REFILL ...

ISAAC?

OH, UMM ...

GOTTA GO TO THE BATH- ROOM...

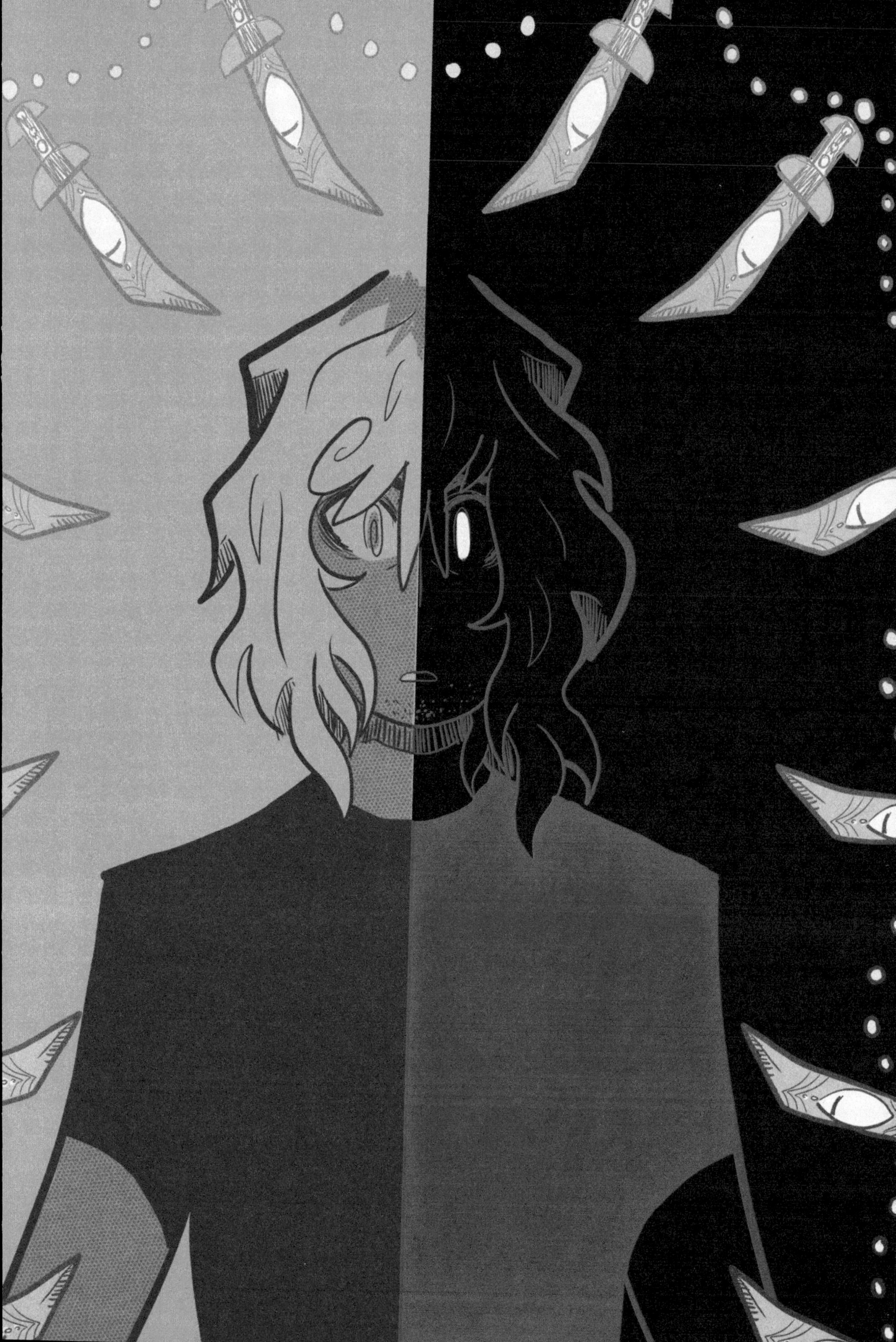

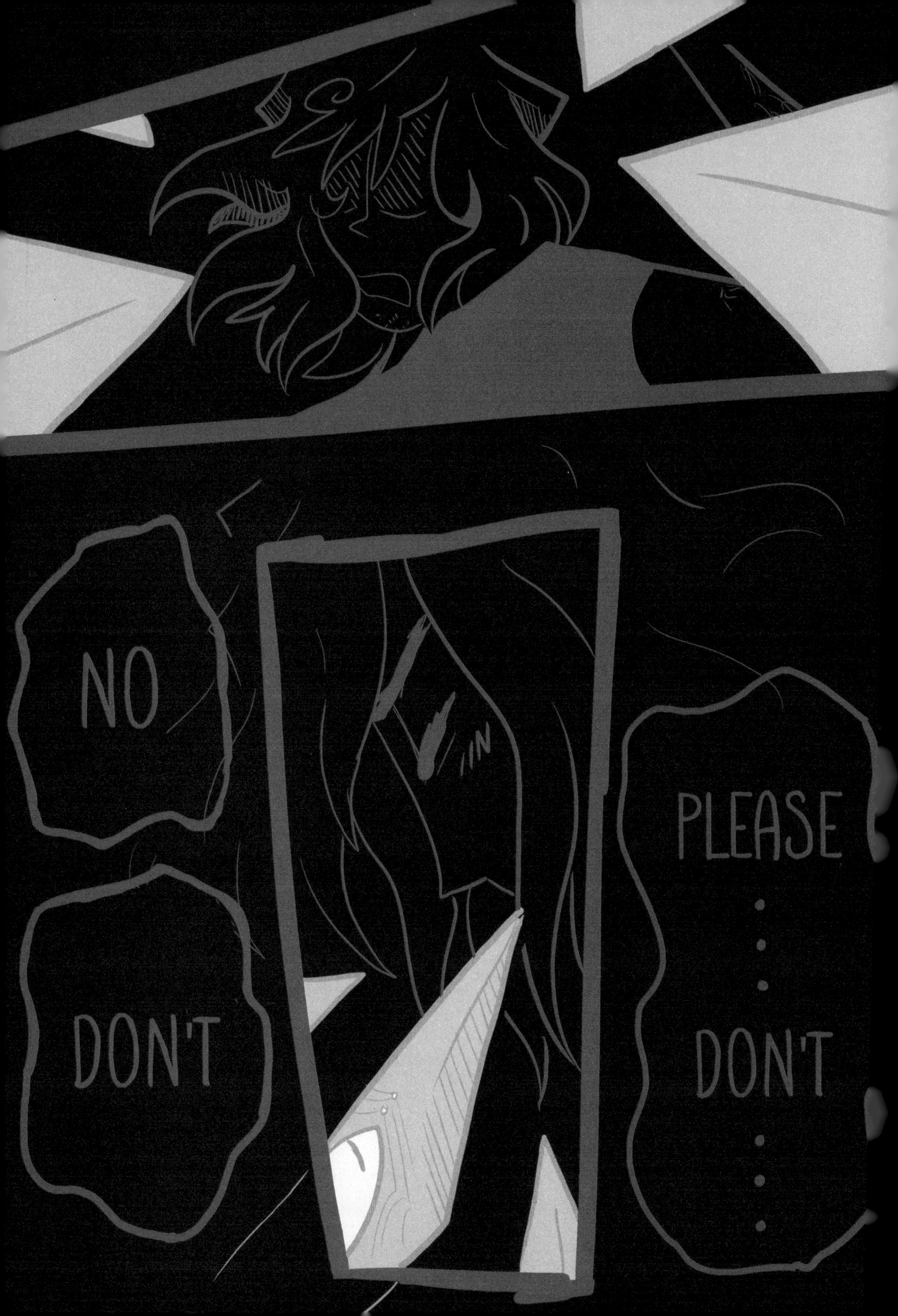
NO
DON'T
PLEASE . . . DON'T . . .

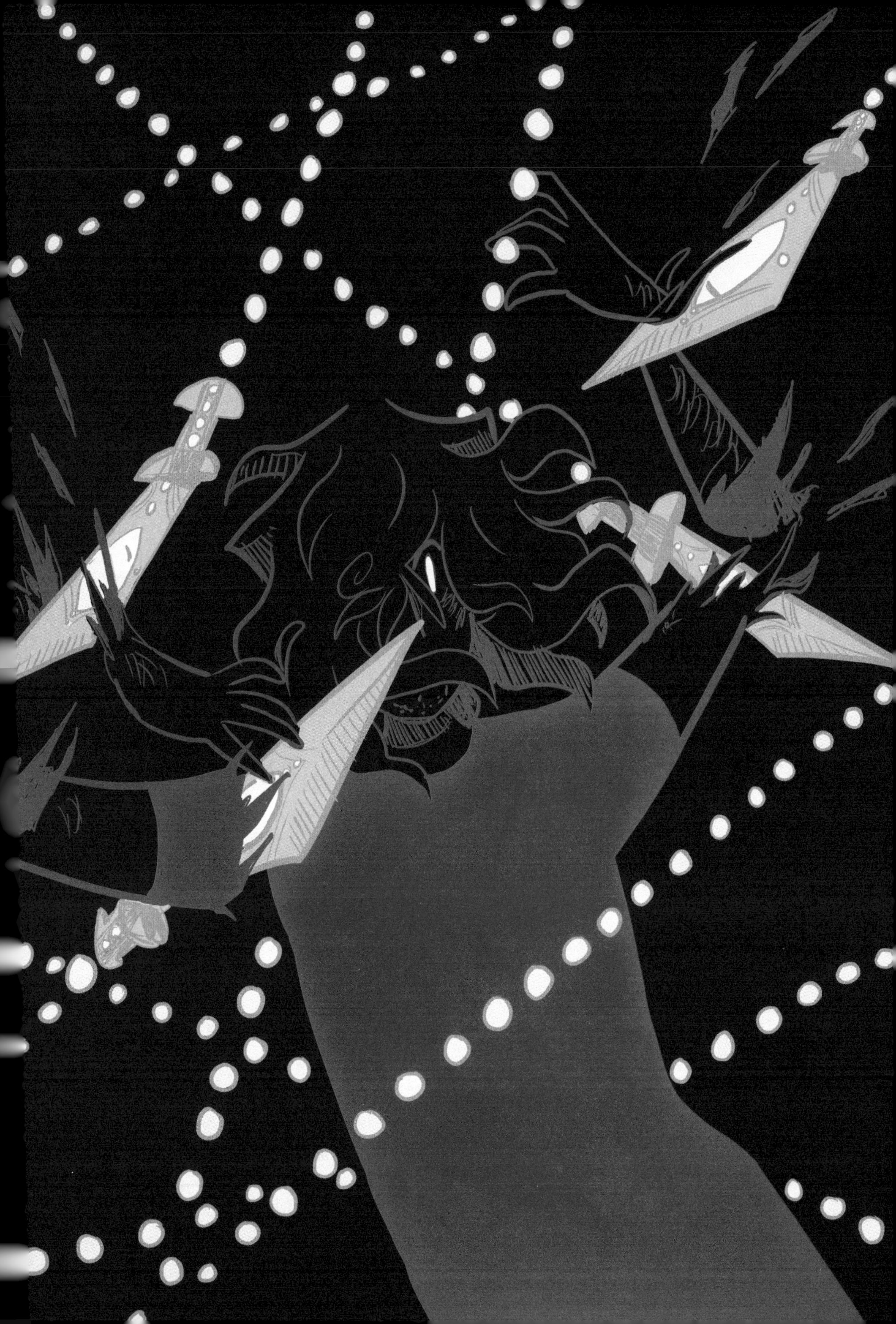

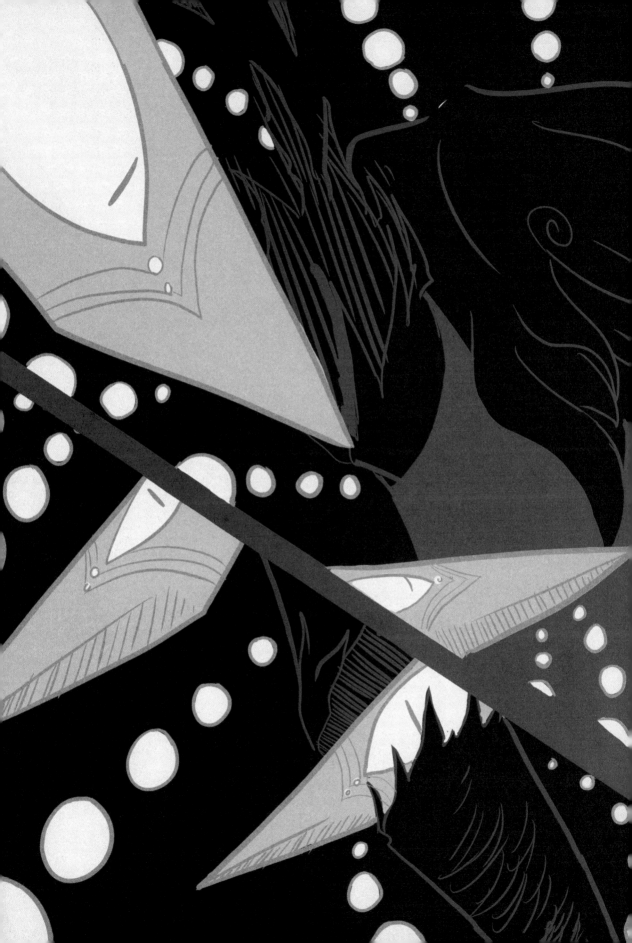

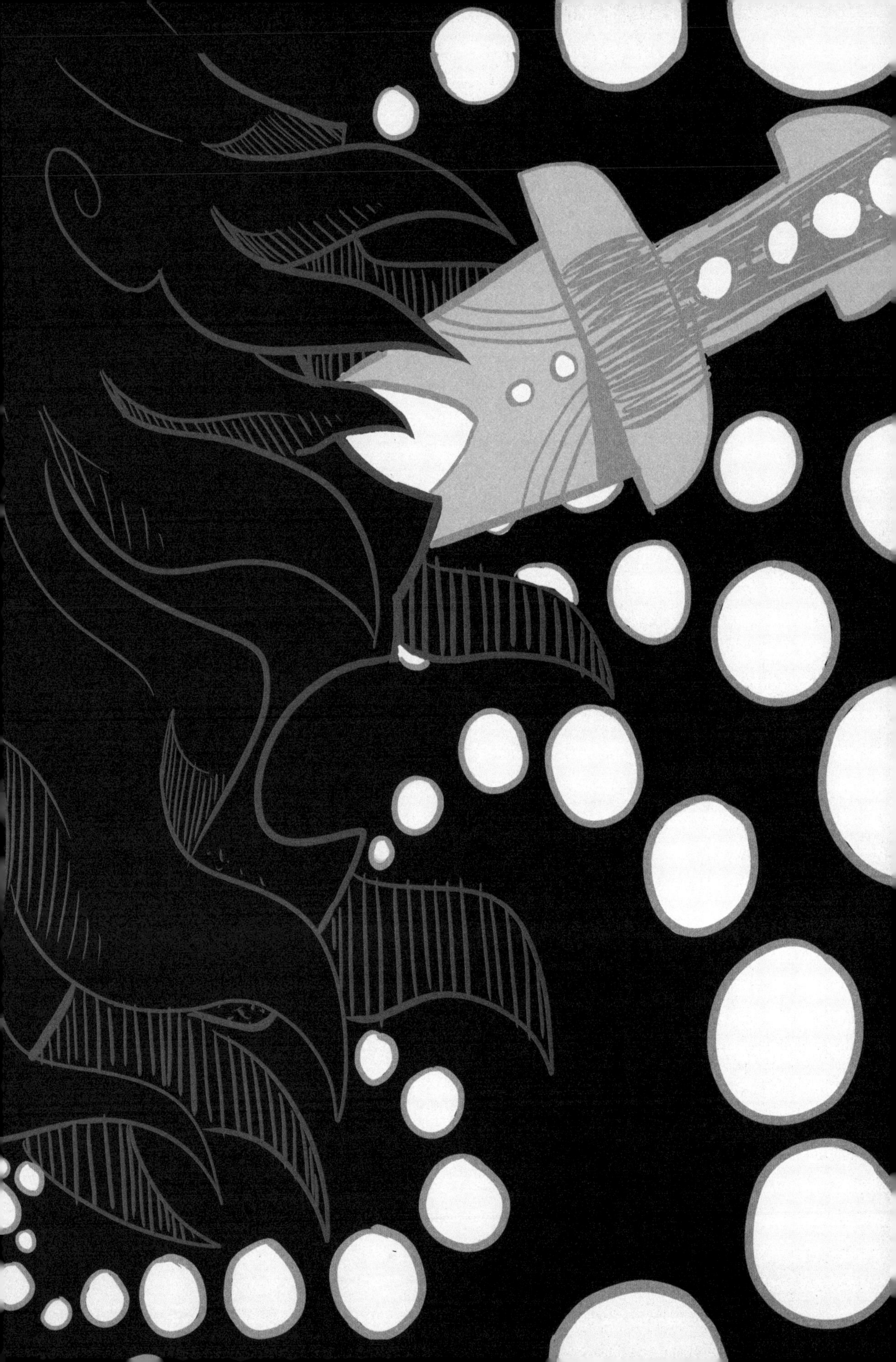

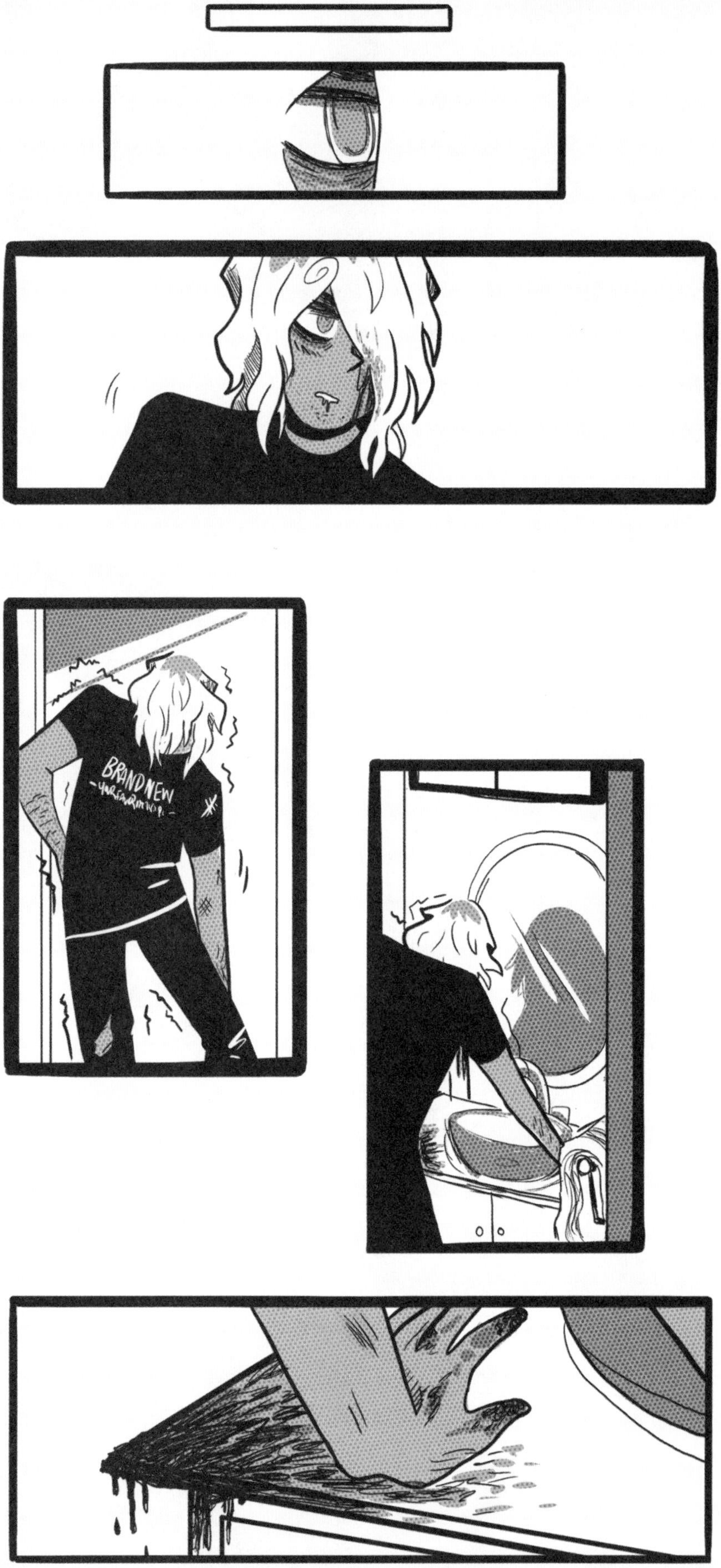
BRAND NEW

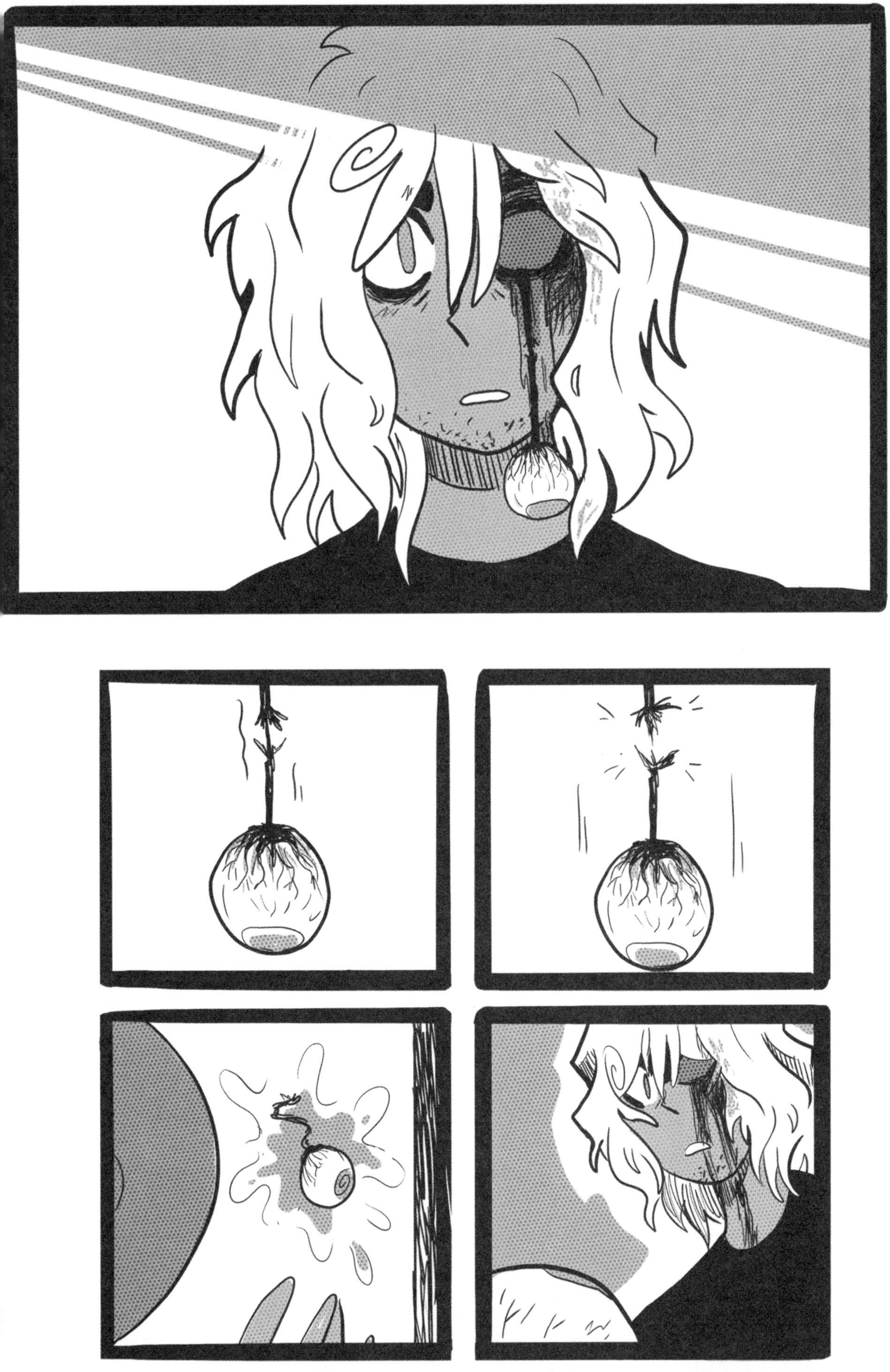

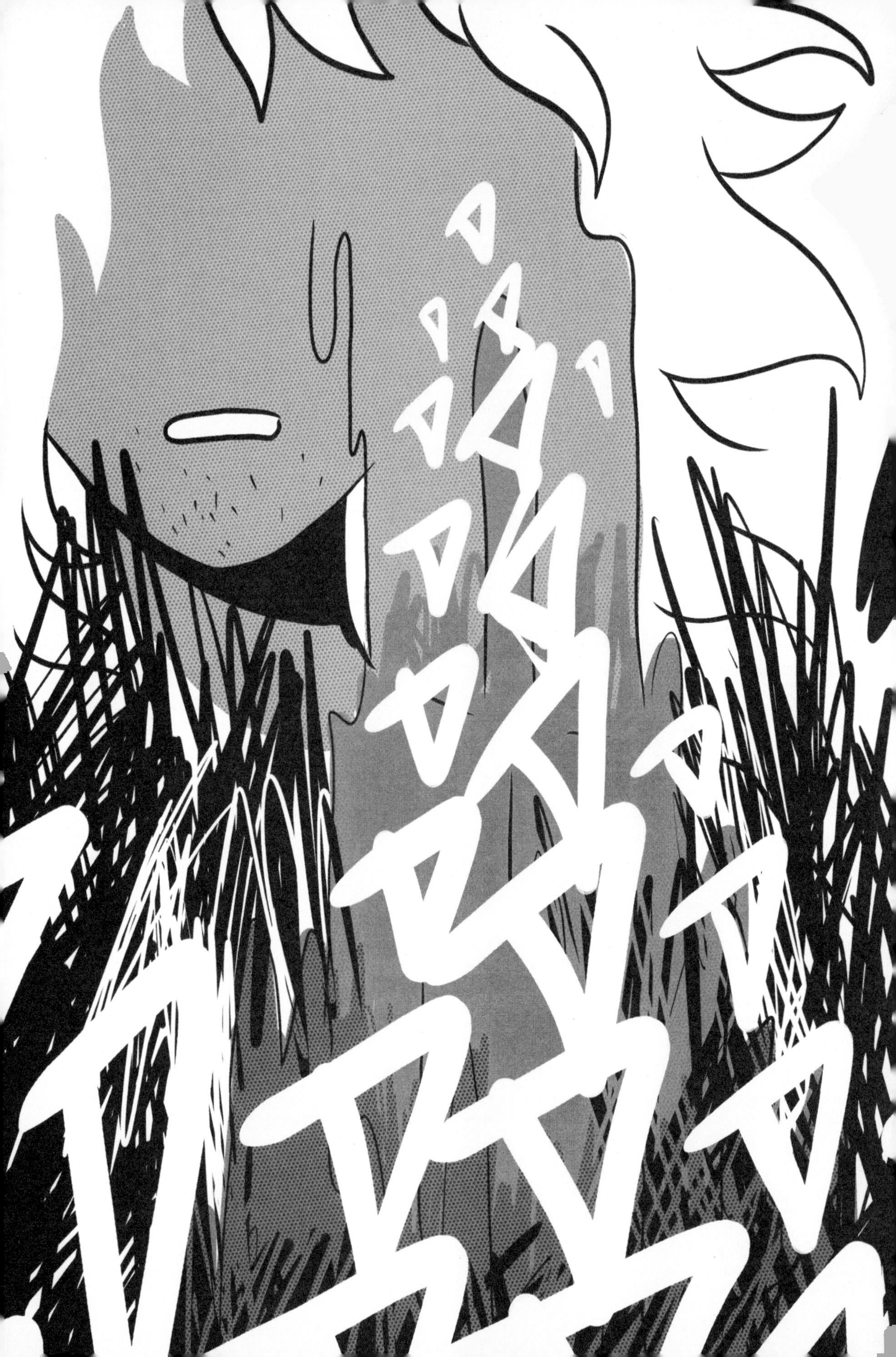

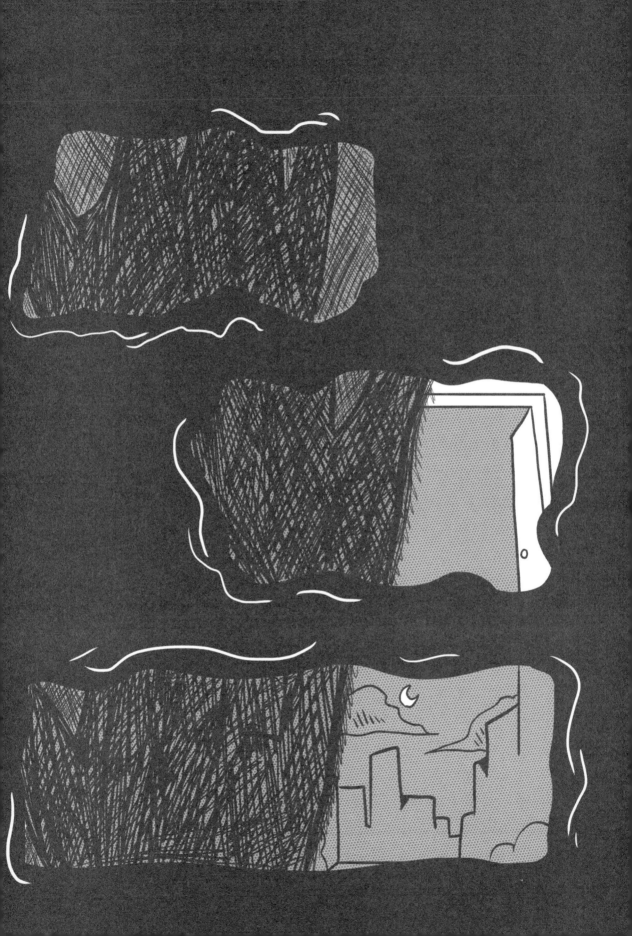

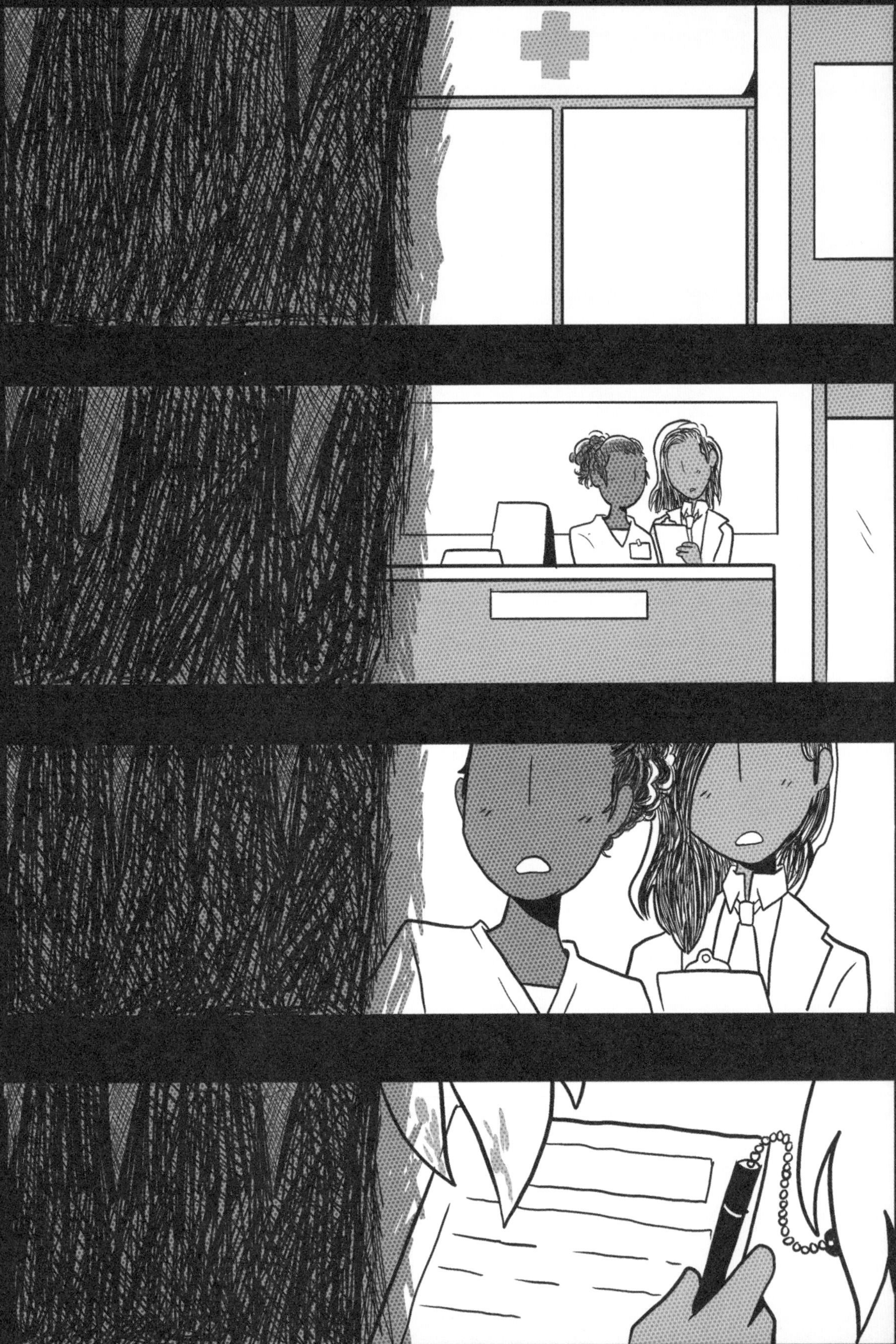

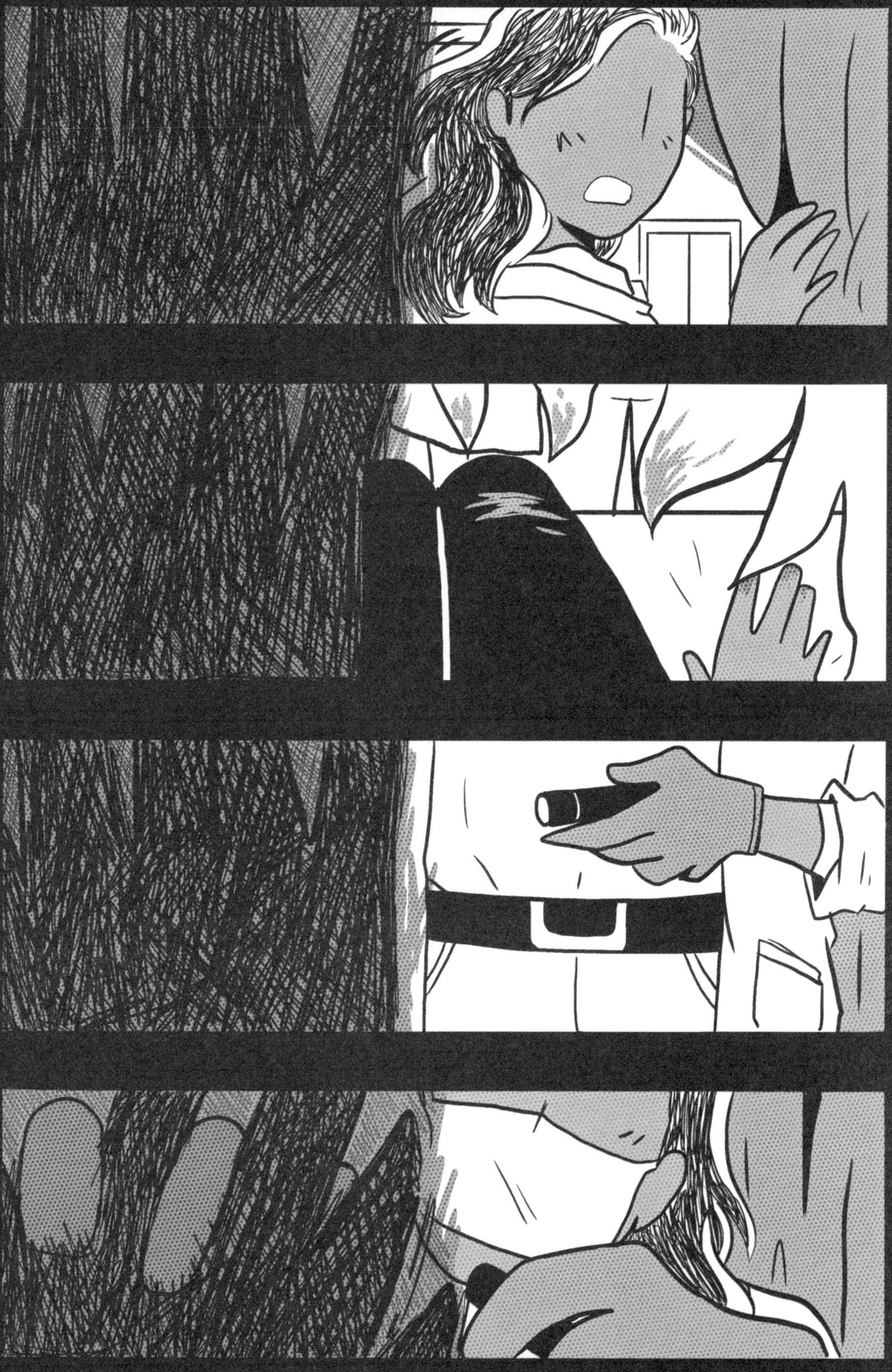

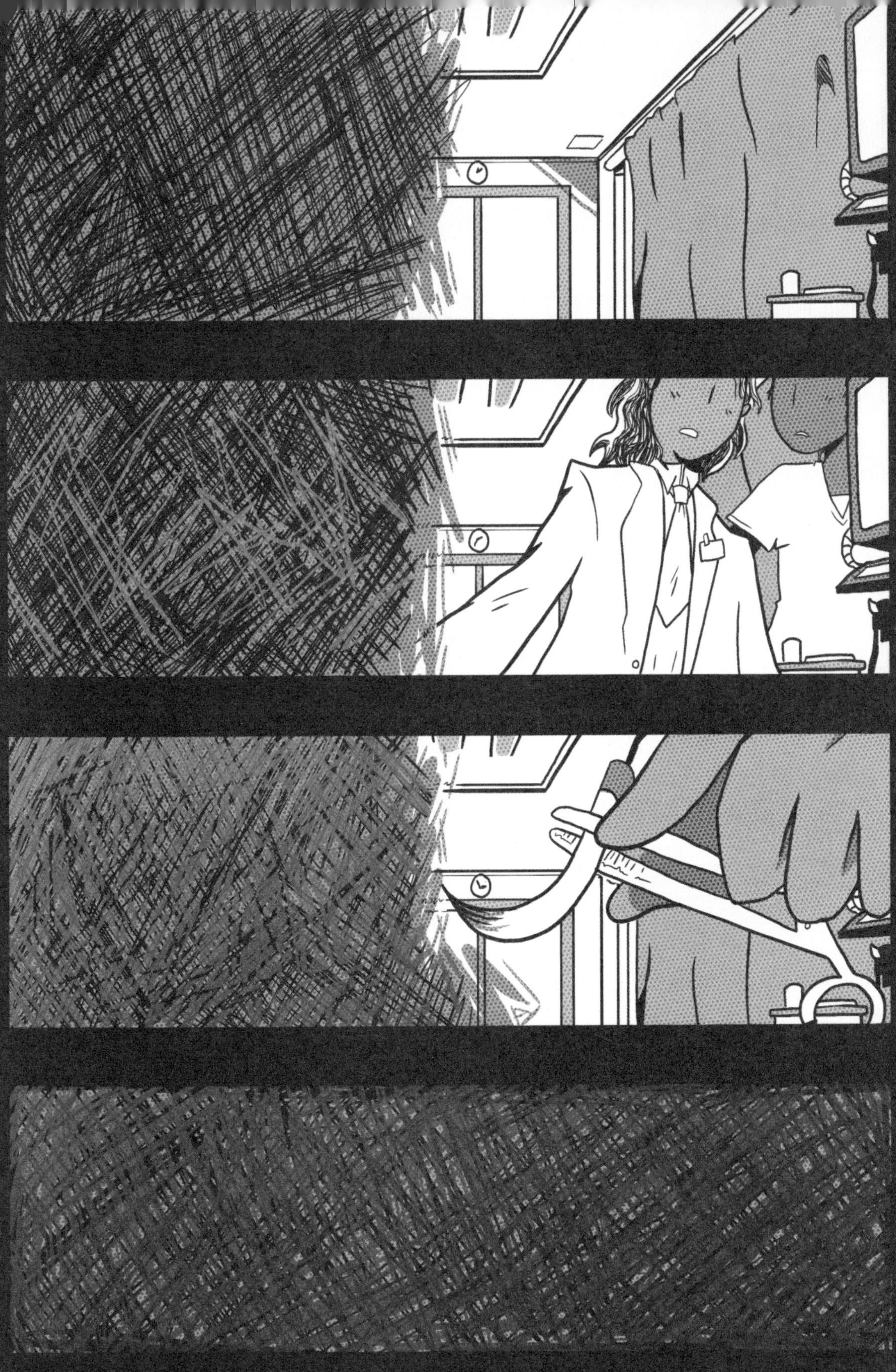

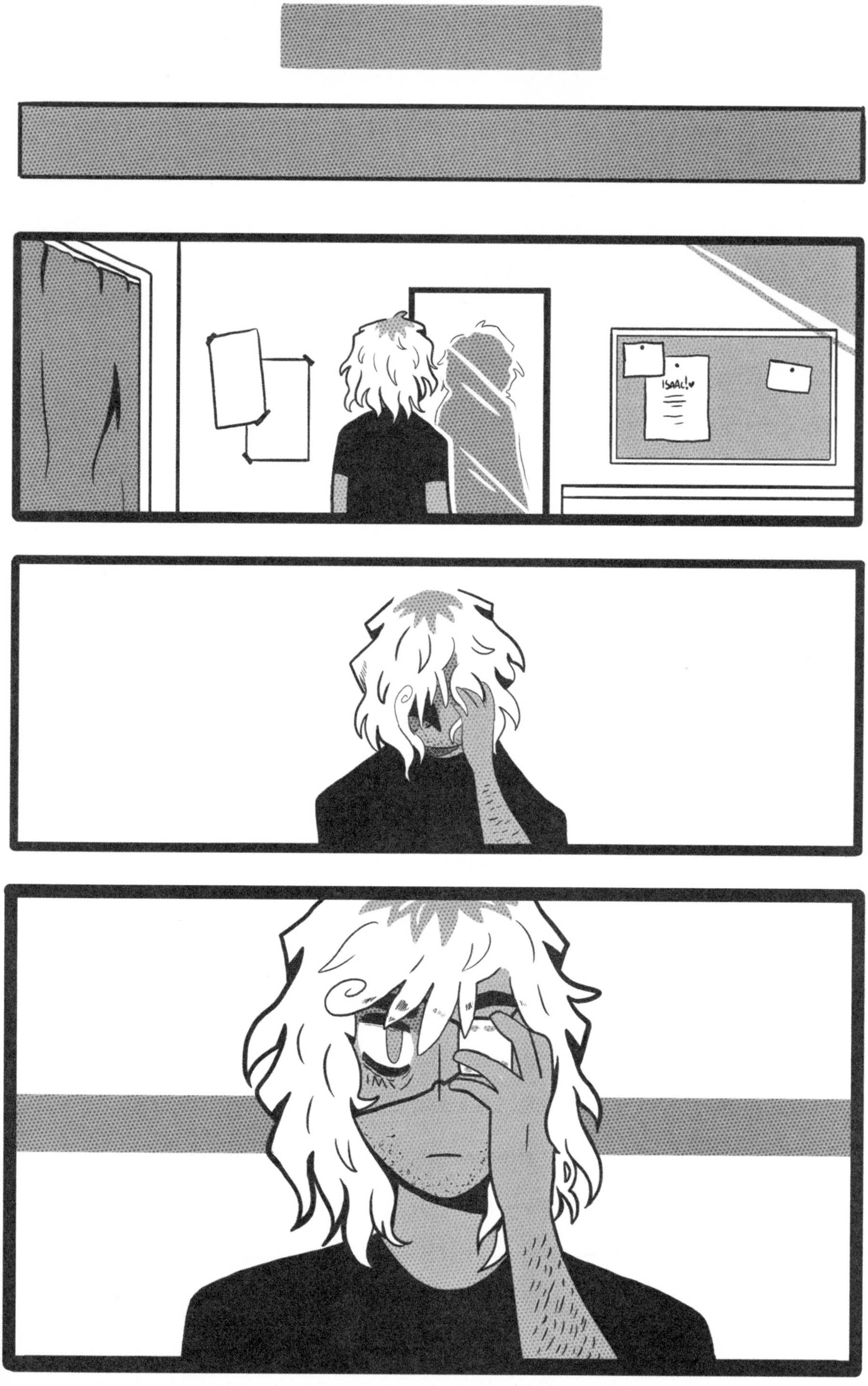
ISAAC!♥

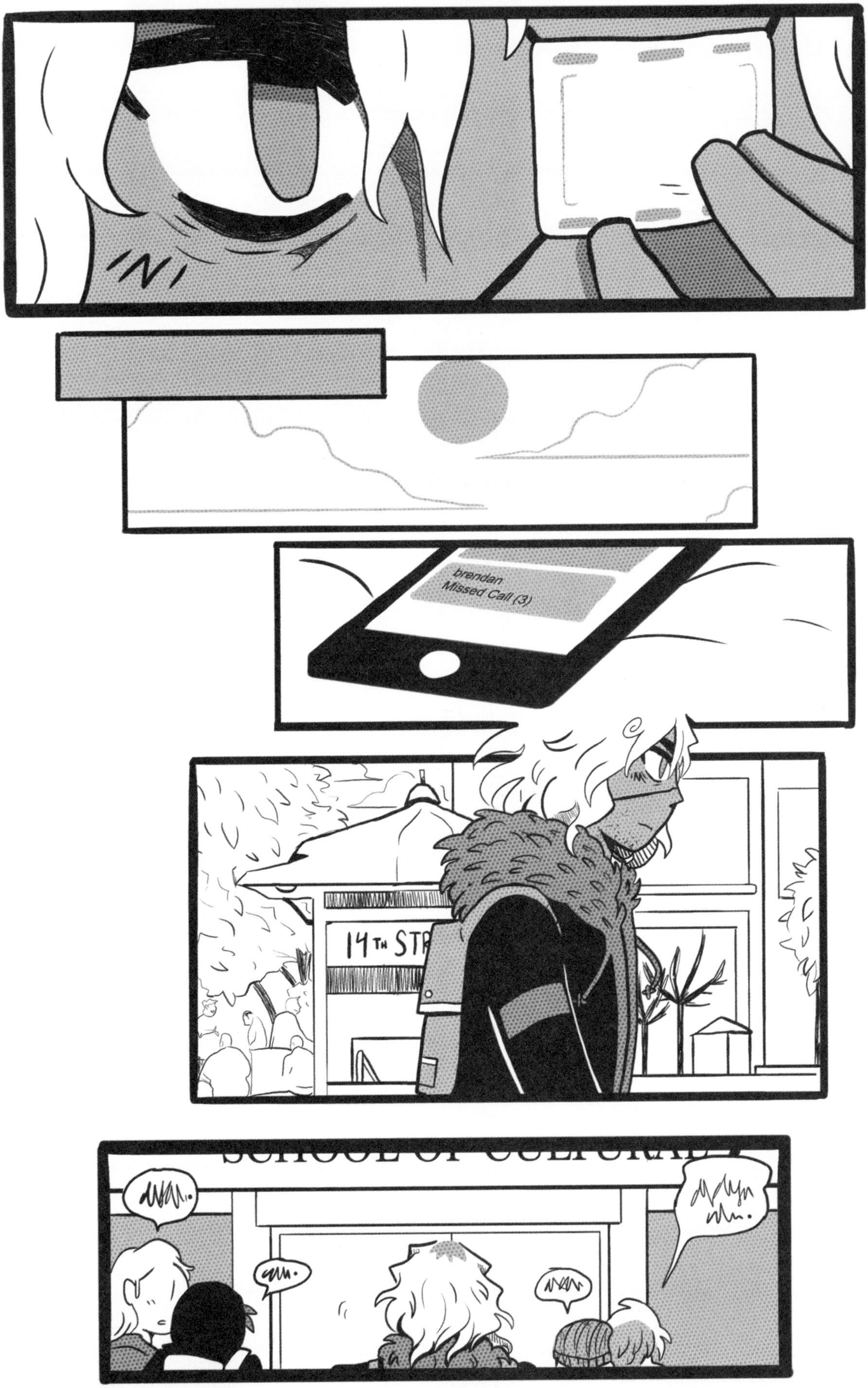
brendan
Missed Call (3)
14TH STR

CROWDED ELEVATOR...

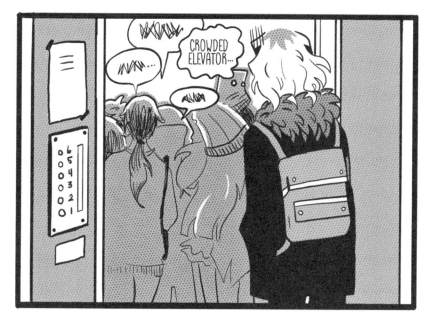

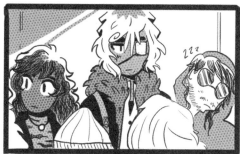

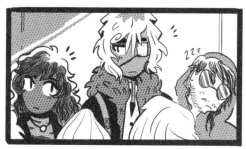

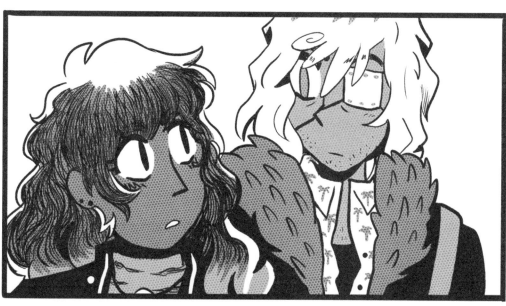

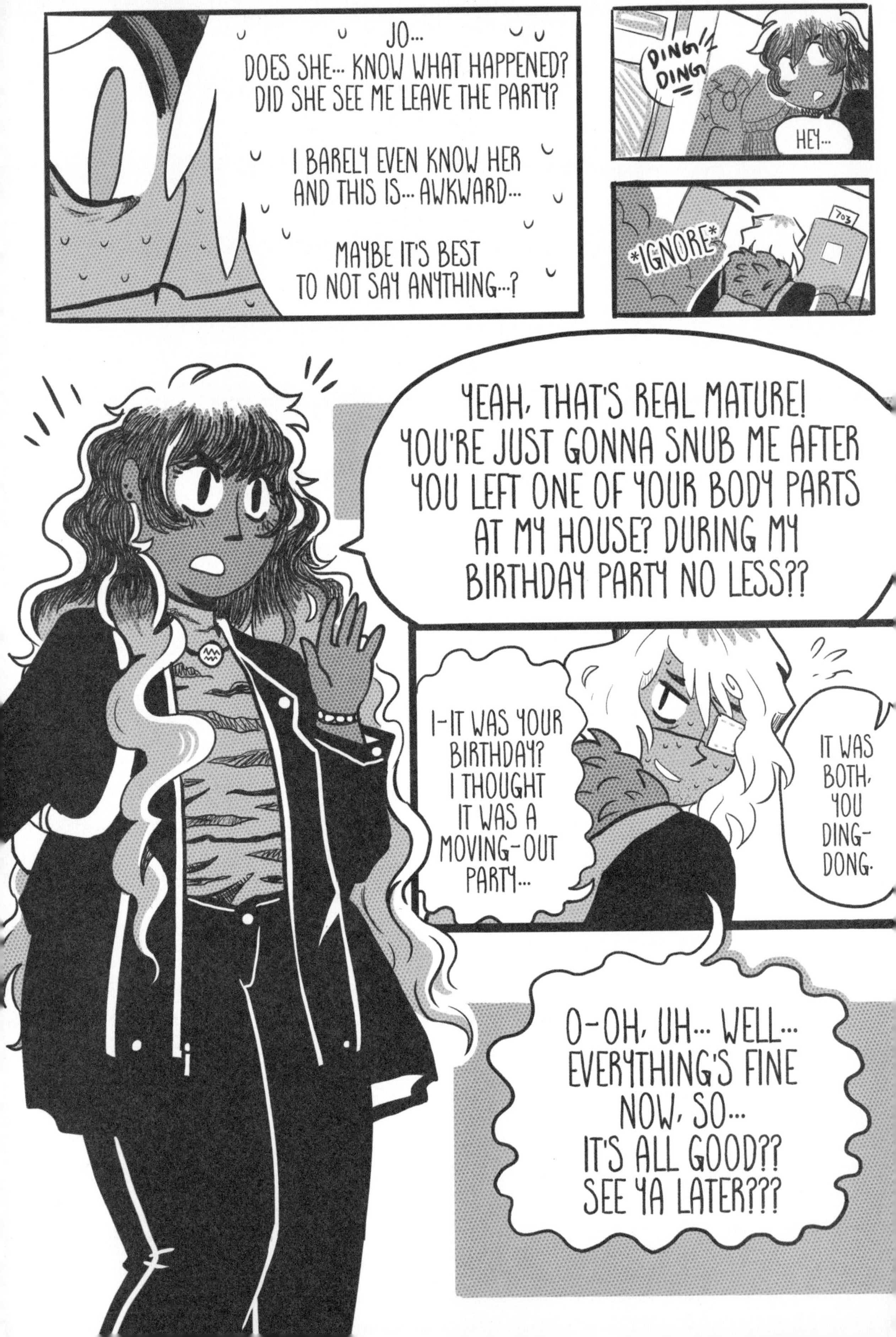
JO...
DOES SHE... KNOW WHAT HAPPENED? DID SHE SEE ME LEAVE THE PARTY?
I BARELY EVEN KNOW HER AND THIS IS... AWKWARD...
MAYBE IT'S BEST TO NOT SAY ANYTHING...?
DING DING
HEY...
IGNORE
703
YEAH, THAT'S REAL MATURE! YOU'RE JUST GONNA SNUB ME AFTER YOU LEFT ONE OF YOUR BODY PARTS AT MY HOUSE? DURING MY BIRTHDAY PARTY NO LESS??
I-IT WAS YOUR BIRTHDAY? I THOUGHT IT WAS A MOVING-OUT PARTY...
IT WAS BOTH, YOU DING-DONG.
O-OH, UH... WELL... EVERYTHING'S FINE NOW, SO... IT'S ALL GOOD?? SEE YA LATER???

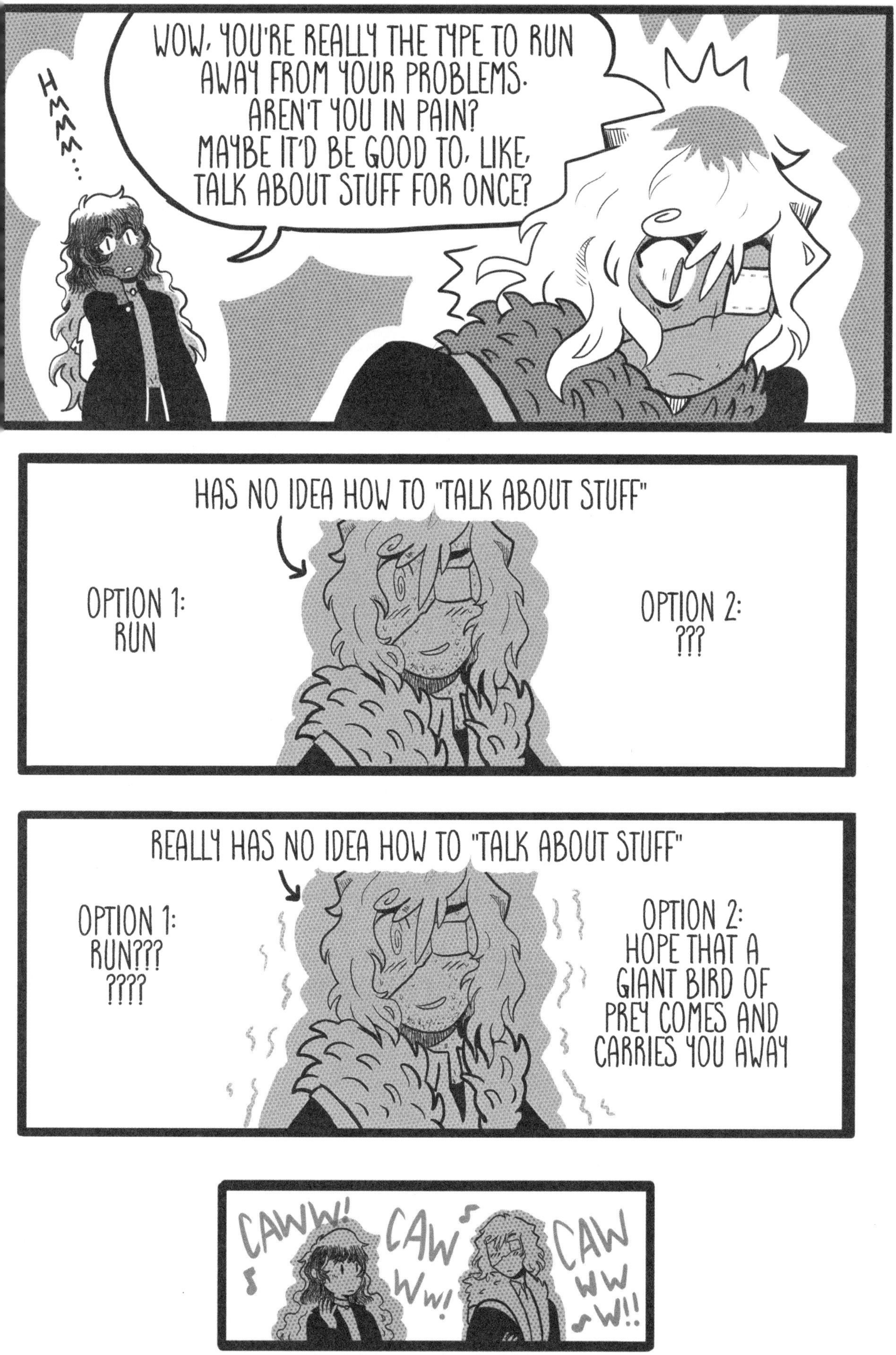
HMMM...
WOW, YOU'RE REALLY THE TYPE TO RUN AWAY FROM YOUR PROBLEMS. AREN'T YOU IN PAIN? MAYBE IT'D BE GOOD TO, LIKE, TALK ABOUT STUFF FOR ONCE?
HAS NO IDEA HOW TO "TALK ABOUT STUFF"
OPTION 1: RUN
OPTION 2: ???
REALLY HAS NO IDEA HOW TO "TALK ABOUT STUFF"
OPTION 1: RUN??? ????
OPTION 2: HOPE THAT A GIANT BIRD OF PREY COMES AND CARRIES YOU AWAY
CAWW!
CAW Ww!
CAW WW W!!

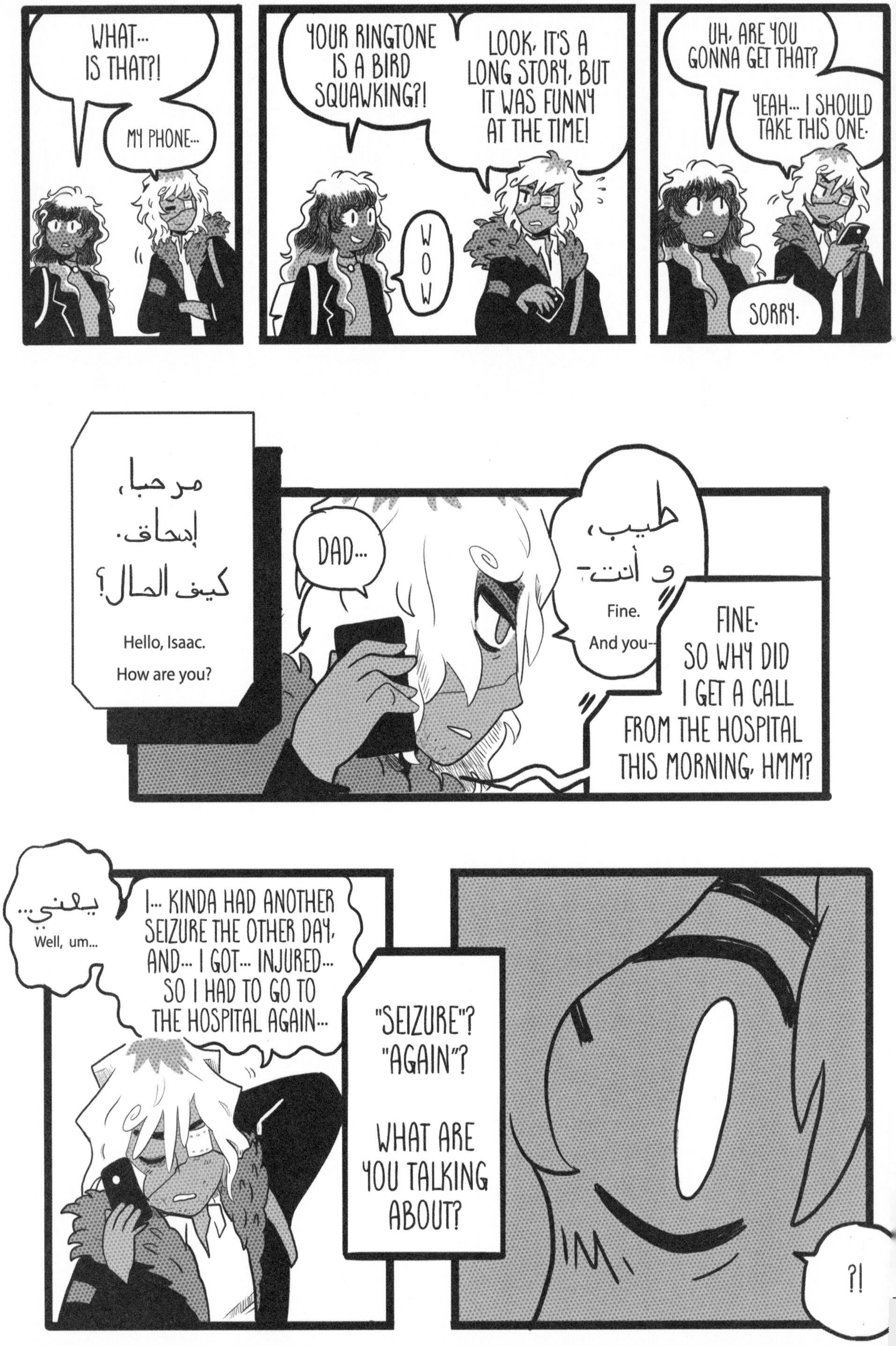
WHAT... IS THAT?!
MY PHONE...
YOUR RINGTONE IS A BIRD SQUAWKING?!
LOOK, IT'S A LONG STORY, BUT IT WAS FUNNY AT THE TIME!
WOW
UH, ARE YOU GONNA GET THAT?
YEAH... I SHOULD TAKE THIS ONE.
SORRY.
مرحبا، إسحاق. كيف الحال؟
Hello, Isaac. How are you?
DAD...
طيب، و أنت-
Fine. And you--
FINE. SO WHY DID I GET A CALL FROM THE HOSPITAL THIS MORNING, HMM?
يعني..
Well, um...
I... KINDA HAD ANOTHER SEIZURE THE OTHER DAY, AND... I GOT... INJURED... SO I HAD TO GO TO THE HOSPITAL AGAIN...
"SEIZURE"? "AGAIN"?
WHAT ARE YOU TALKING ABOUT?
?!

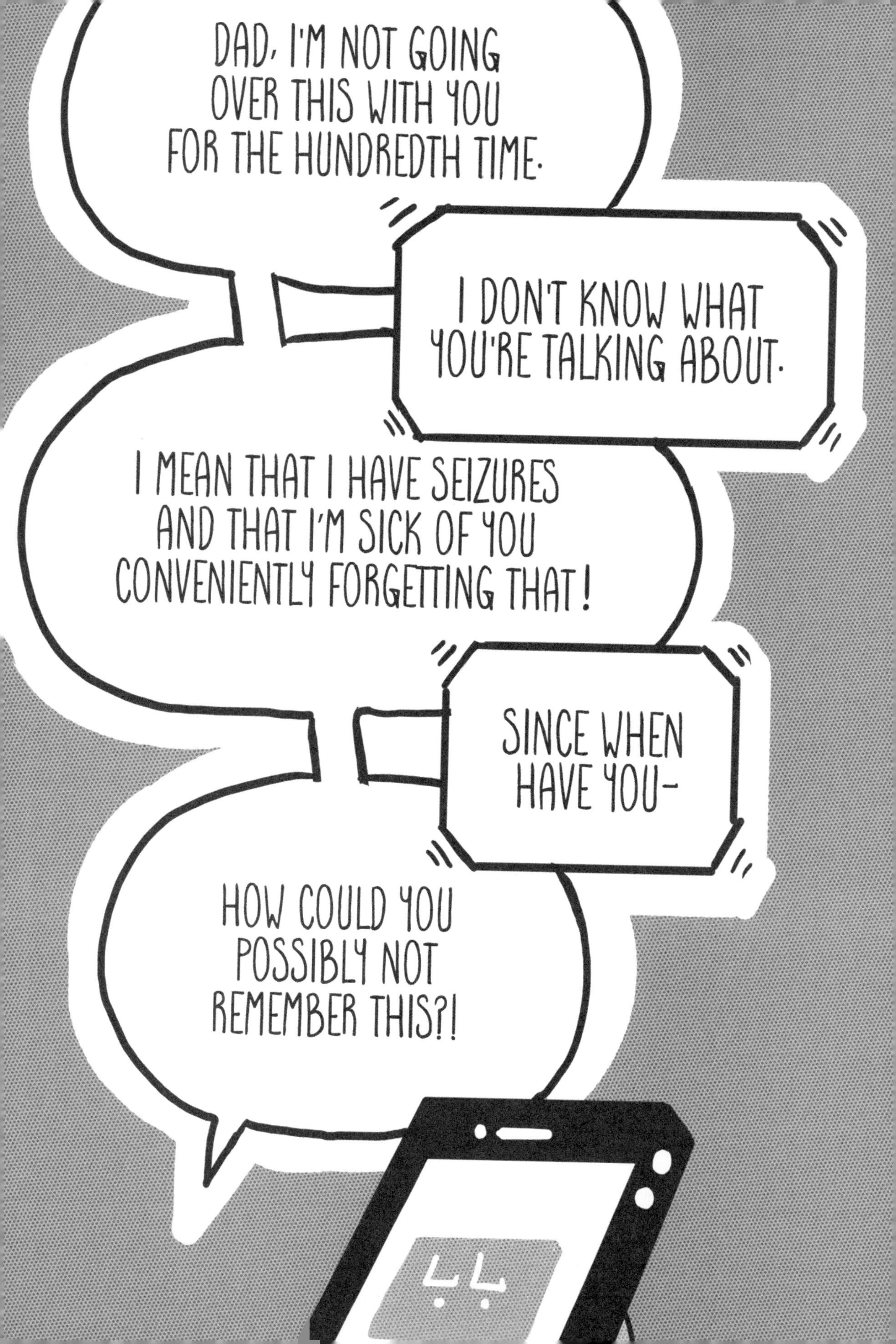
DAD, I'M NOT GOING OVER THIS WITH YOU FOR THE HUNDREDTH TIME.
I DON'T KNOW WHAT YOU'RE TALKING ABOUT.
I MEAN THAT I HAVE SEIZURES AND THAT I'M SICK OF YOU CONVENIENTLY FORGETTING THAT!
SINCE WHEN HAVE YOU-
HOW COULD YOU POSSIBLY NOT REMEMBER THIS?!

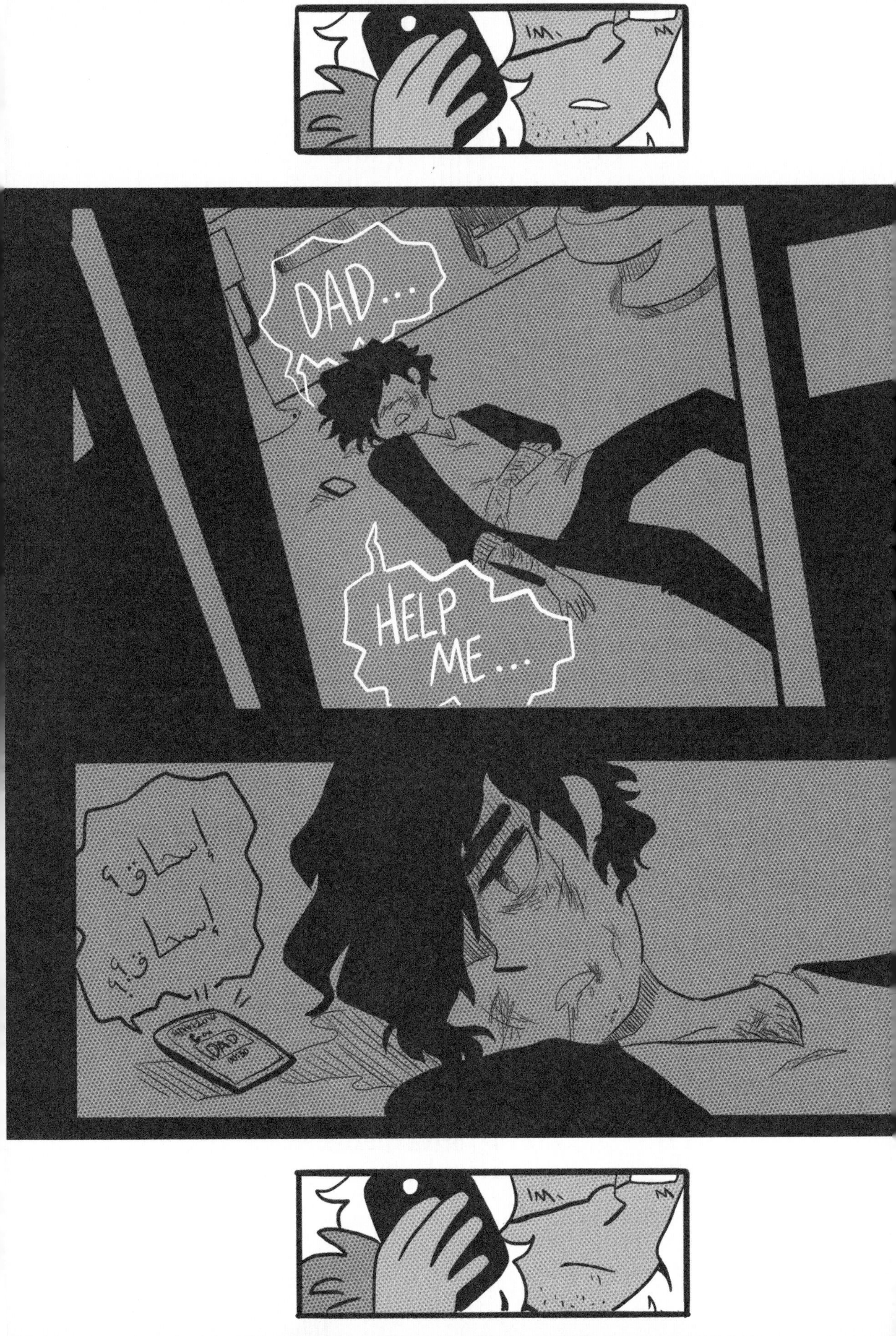
DAD...
HELP ME...
إسحاق؟
إسحاق؟؟
DAD

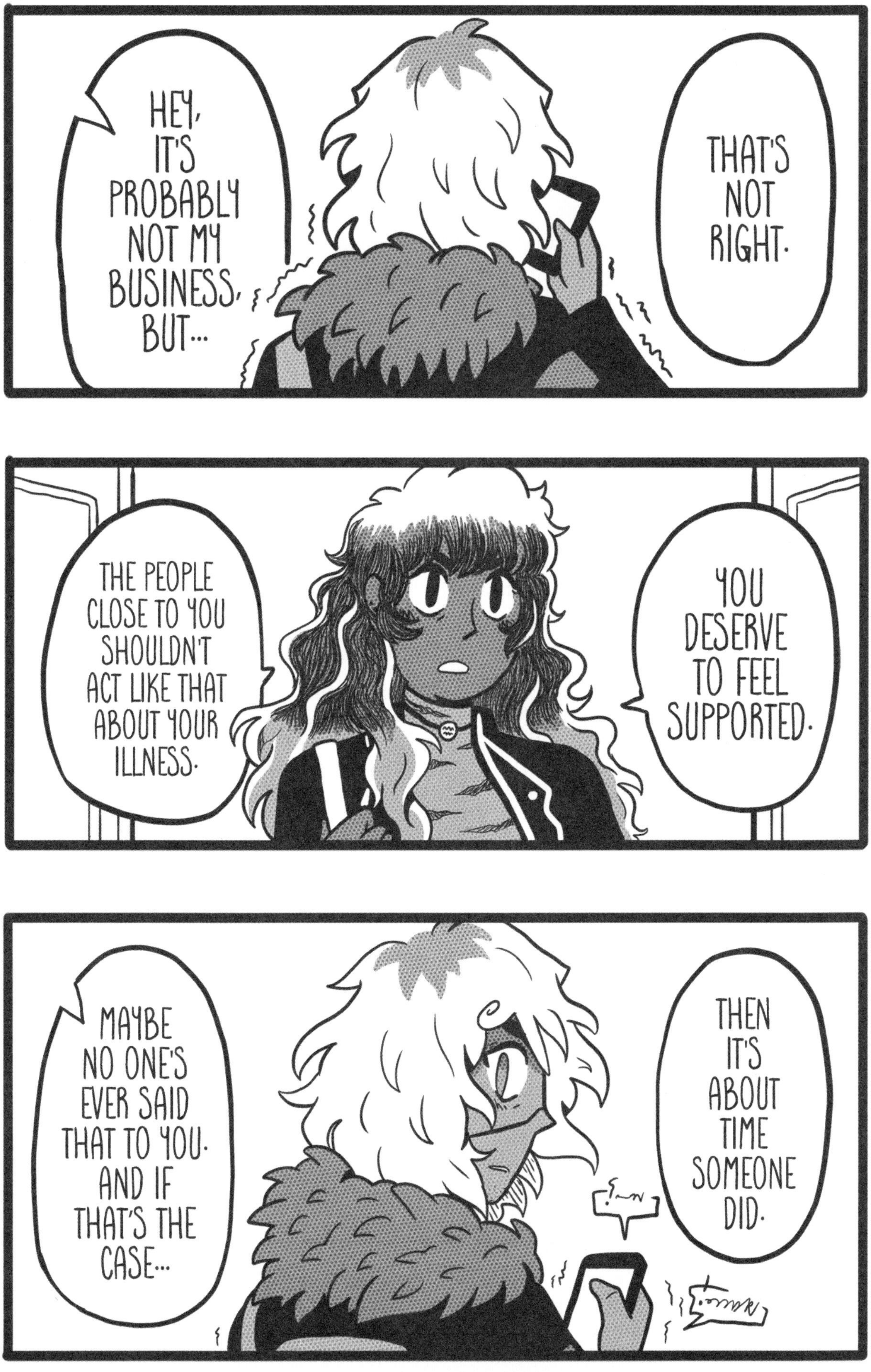

HEY, IT'S PROBABLY NOT MY BUSINESS, BUT...
THAT'S NOT RIGHT.
THE PEOPLE CLOSE TO YOU SHOULDN'T ACT LIKE THAT ABOUT YOUR ILLNESS.
YOU DESERVE TO FEEL SUPPORTED.
MAYBE NO ONE'S EVER SAID THAT TO YOU. AND IF THAT'S THE CASE...
THEN IT'S ABOUT TIME SOMEONE DID.

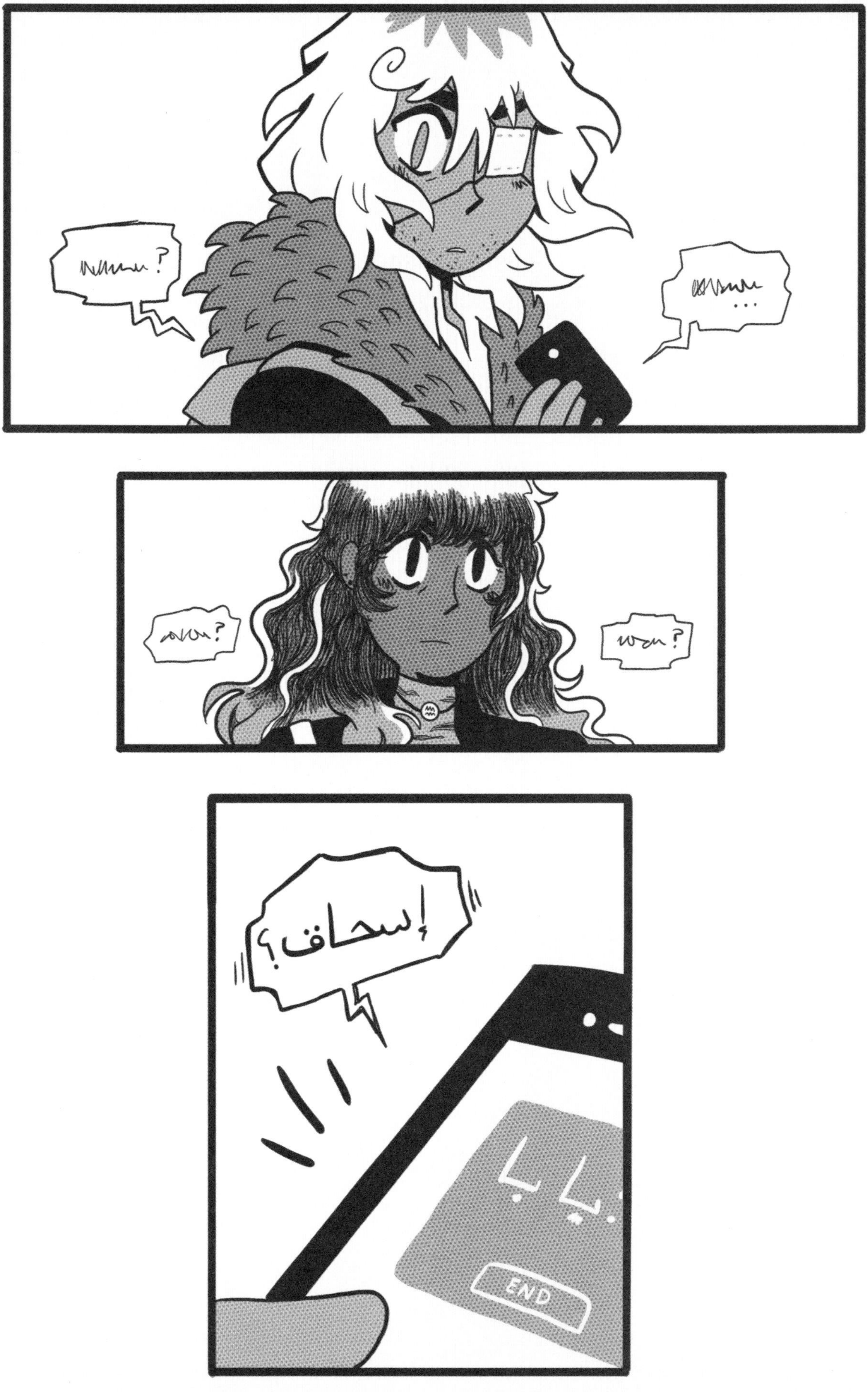
إسحاق؟
بابا
END

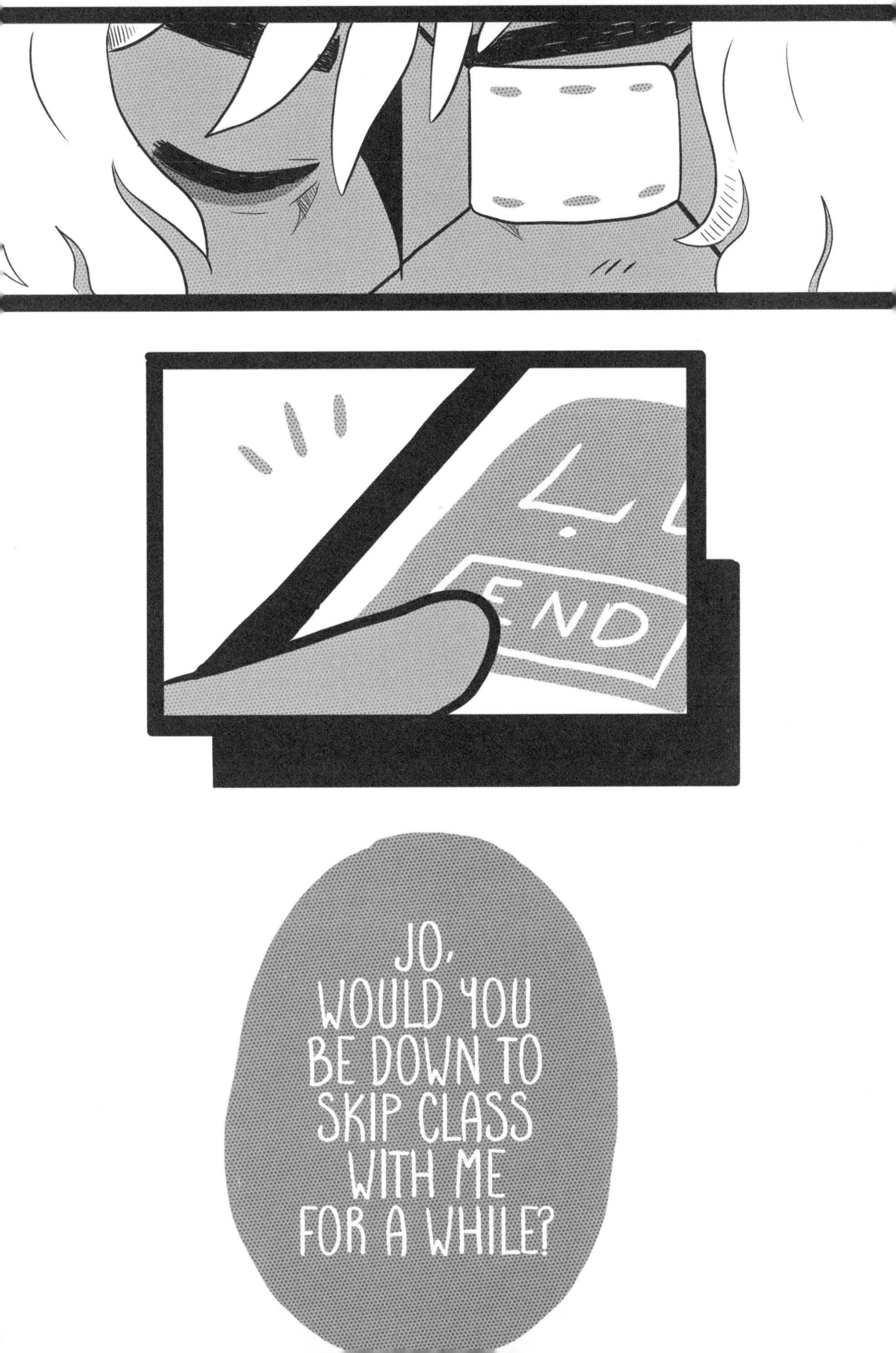
END
JO,
WOULD YOU
BE DOWN TO
SKIP CLASS
WITH ME
FOR A WHILE?

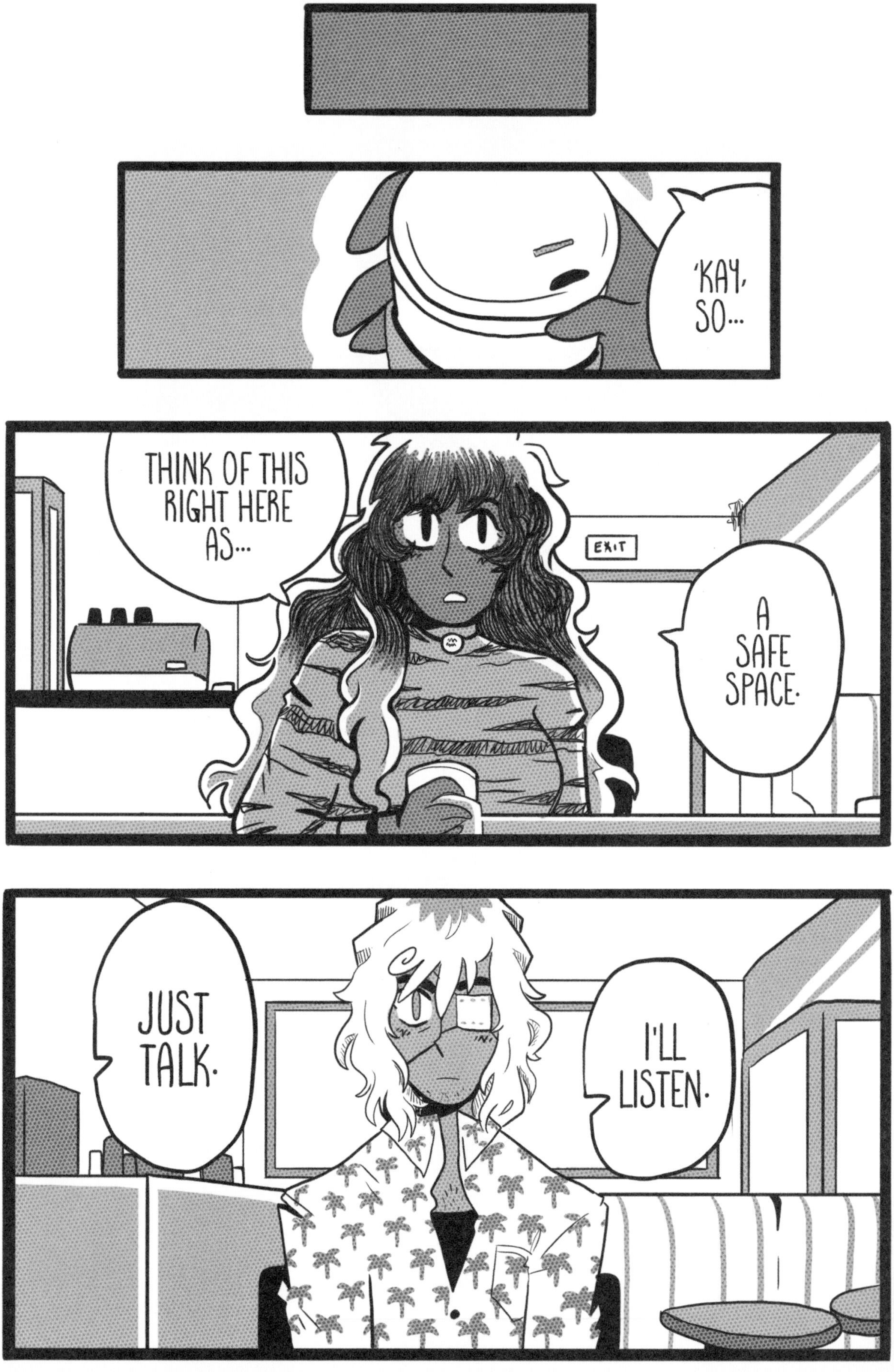
'KAY, SO...
THINK OF THIS RIGHT HERE AS...
A SAFE SPACE.
EXIT
JUST TALK.
I'LL LISTEN.

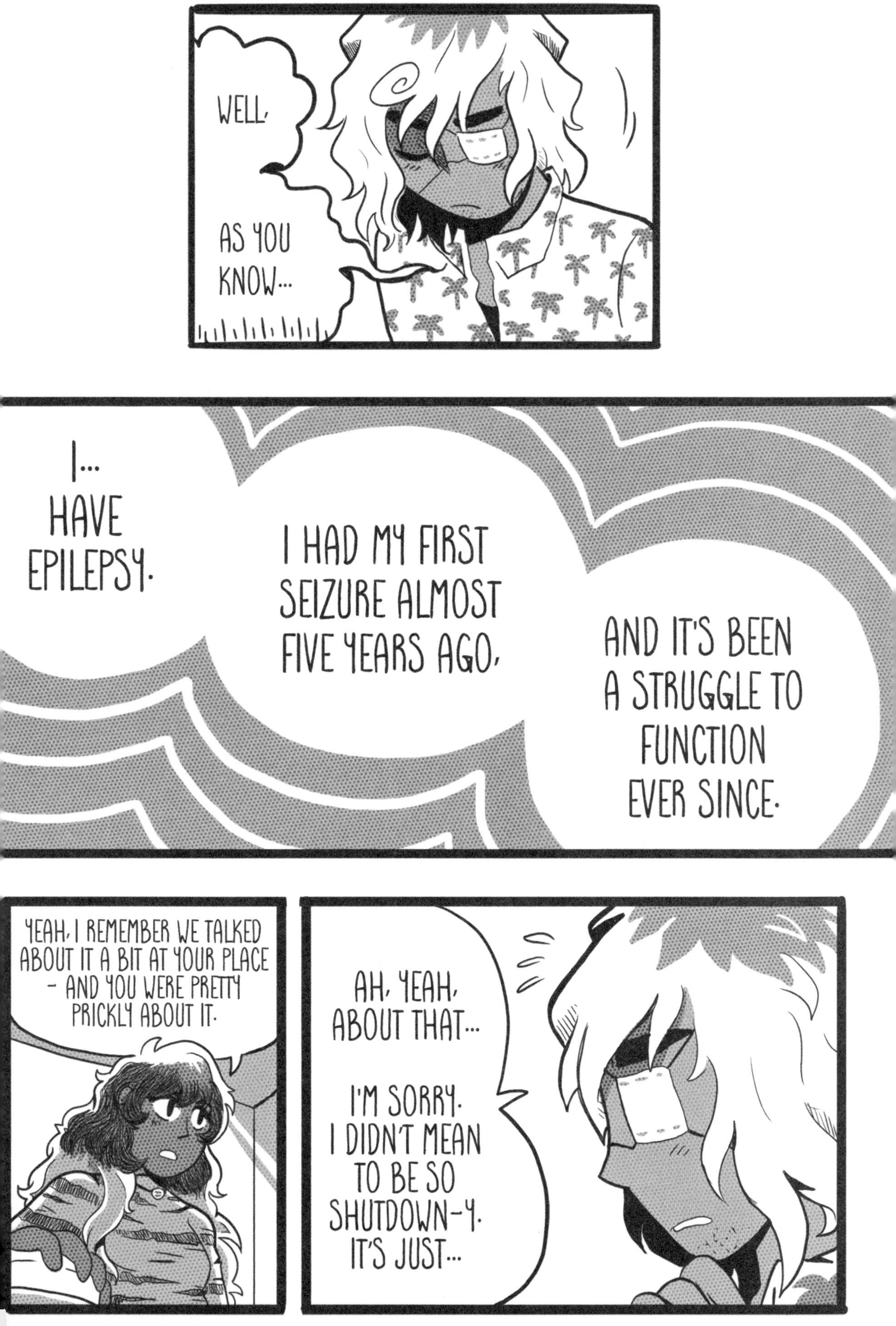
WELL,
AS YOU KNOW...
I... HAVE EPILEPSY.
I HAD MY FIRST SEIZURE ALMOST FIVE YEARS AGO,
AND IT'S BEEN A STRUGGLE TO FUNCTION EVER SINCE.
YEAH, I REMEMBER WE TALKED ABOUT IT A BIT AT YOUR PLACE - AND YOU WERE PRETTY PRICKLY ABOUT IT.
AH, YEAH, ABOUT THAT...
I'M SORRY. I DIDN'T MEAN TO BE SO SHUTDOWN-Y. IT'S JUST...

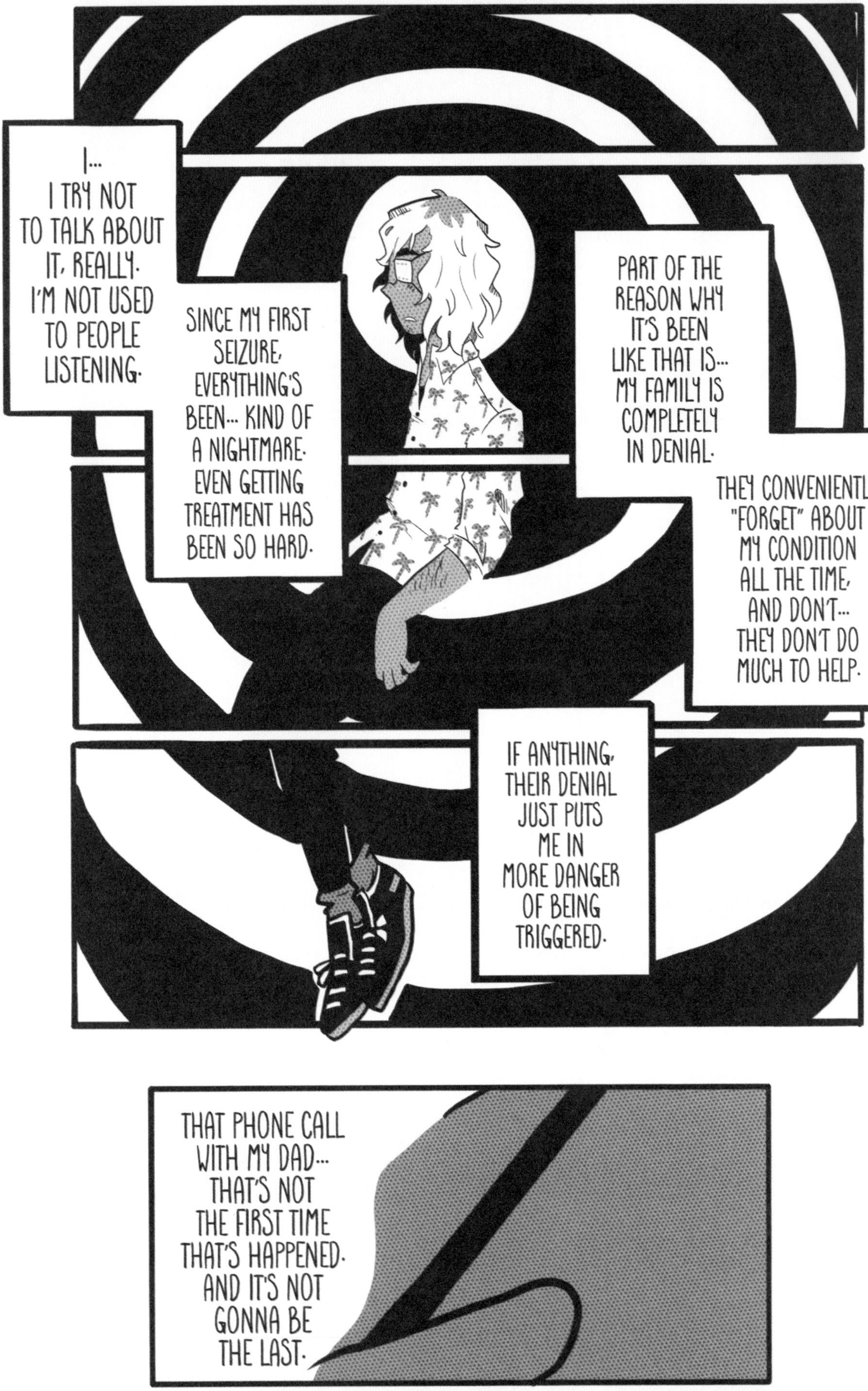

I...
I TRY NOT TO TALK ABOUT IT, REALLY. I'M NOT USED TO PEOPLE LISTENING.
SINCE MY FIRST SEIZURE, EVERYTHING'S BEEN... KIND OF A NIGHTMARE. EVEN GETTING TREATMENT HAS BEEN SO HARD.
PART OF THE REASON WHY IT'S BEEN LIKE THAT IS... MY FAMILY IS COMPLETELY IN DENIAL.
THEY CONVENIENTLY "FORGET" ABOUT MY CONDITION ALL THE TIME, AND DON'T... THEY DON'T DO MUCH TO HELP.
IF ANYTHING, THEIR DENIAL JUST PUTS ME IN MORE DANGER OF BEING TRIGGERED.
THAT PHONE CALL WITH MY DAD... THAT'S NOT THE FIRST TIME THAT'S HAPPENED. AND IT'S NOT GONNA BE THE LAST.

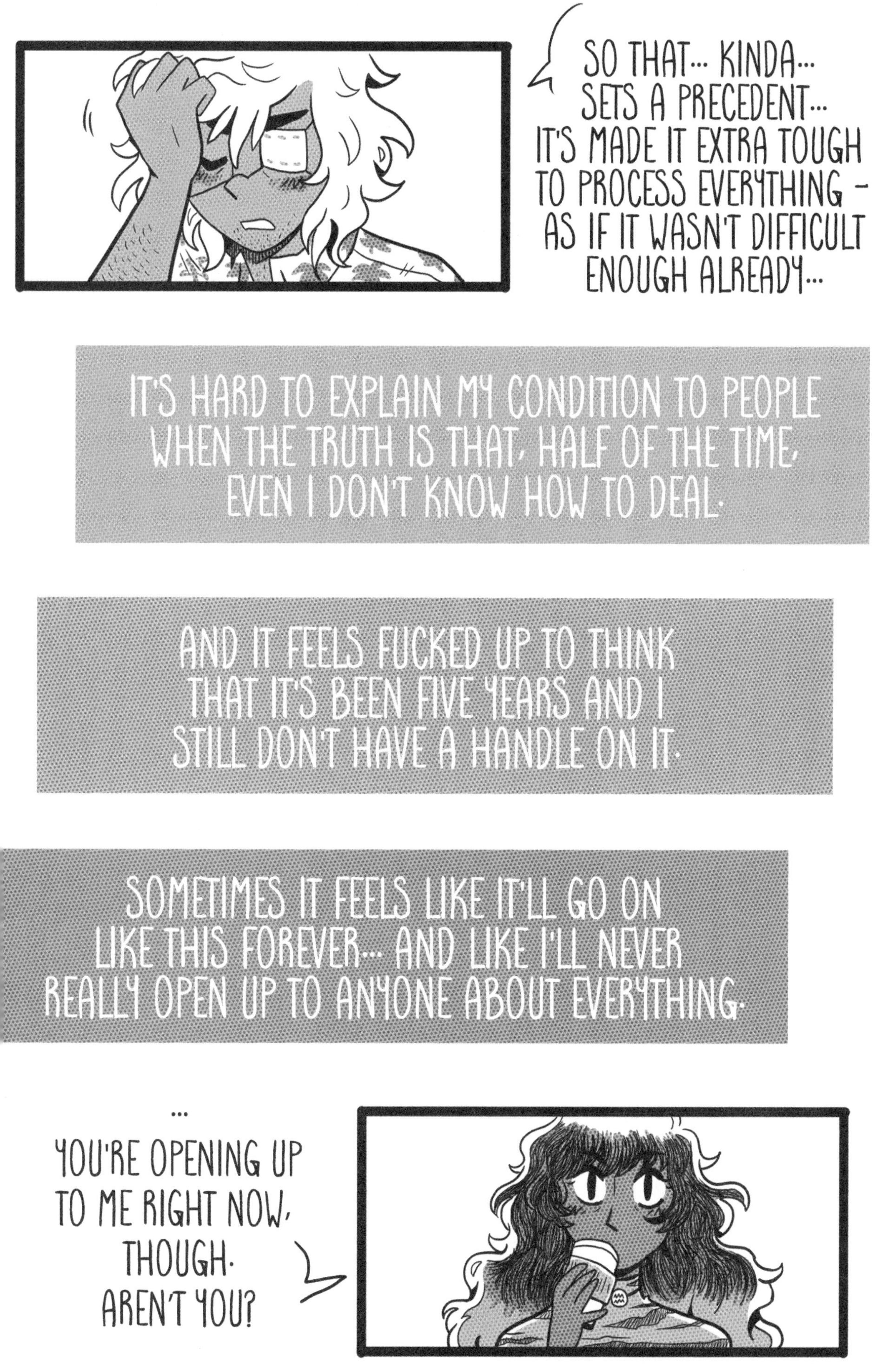
SO THAT... KINDA... SETS A PRECEDENT... IT'S MADE IT EXTRA TOUGH TO PROCESS EVERYTHING - AS IF IT WASN'T DIFFICULT ENOUGH ALREADY...
IT'S HARD TO EXPLAIN MY CONDITION TO PEOPLE WHEN THE TRUTH IS THAT, HALF OF THE TIME, EVEN I DON'T KNOW HOW TO DEAL.
AND IT FEELS FUCKED UP TO THINK THAT IT'S BEEN FIVE YEARS AND I STILL DON'T HAVE A HANDLE ON IT.
SOMETIMES IT FEELS LIKE IT'LL GO ON LIKE THIS FOREVER... AND LIKE I'LL NEVER REALLY OPEN UP TO ANYONE ABOUT EVERYTHING.
...
YOU'RE OPENING UP TO ME RIGHT NOW, THOUGH. AREN'T YOU?

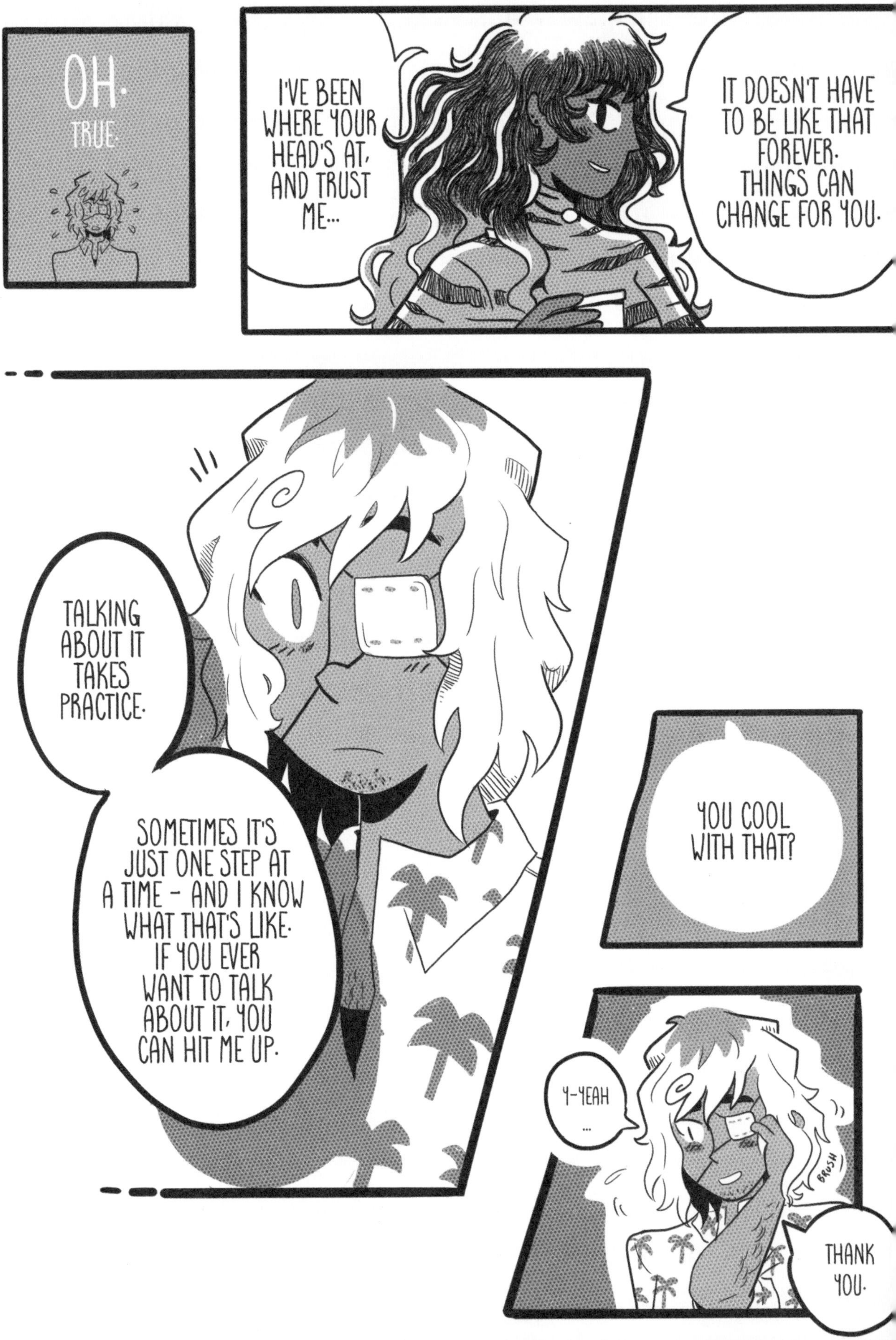
OH. TRUE.
I'VE BEEN WHERE YOUR HEAD'S AT, AND TRUST ME...
IT DOESN'T HAVE TO BE LIKE THAT FOREVER. THINGS CAN CHANGE FOR YOU.
TALKING ABOUT IT TAKES PRACTICE.
SOMETIMES IT'S JUST ONE STEP AT A TIME - AND I KNOW WHAT THAT'S LIKE. IF YOU EVER WANT TO TALK ABOUT IT, YOU CAN HIT ME UP.
YOU COOL WITH THAT?
Y-YEAH ...
BRUSH
THANK YOU.

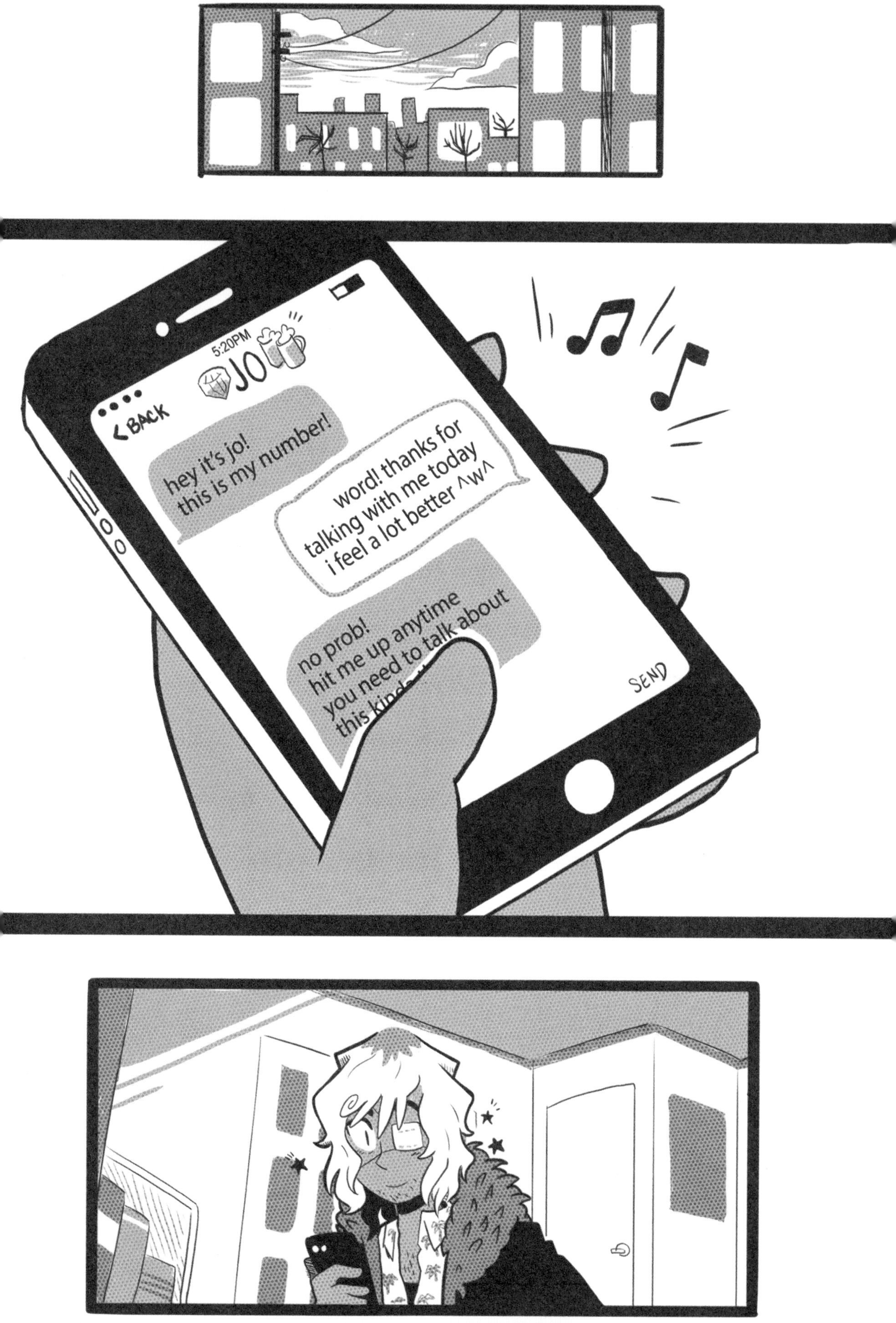
5:20PM
JO
< BACK
hey it's jo!
this is my number!
word! thanks for
talking with me today
i feel a lot better ^w^
no prob!
hit me up anytime
you need to talk about
SEND

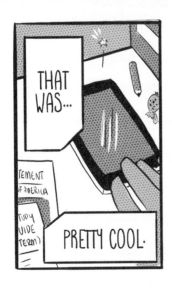

THAT WAS...

PRETTY COOL.

I'VE NEVER STARTED BEING FRIENDS WITH SOMEONE...

...WITH THEM ALREADY KNOWING.

USUALLY, THEY JUST KINDA FIND OUT – AND THEN ITS A FIFTY-FIFTY SHOT AS TO IF THEY'LL STICK AROUND.

IT SUCKS, BUT...

I DONT REALLY BLAME PEOPLE–

NOT EVERYONE WANTS TO DEAL WITH SOMETHING THAT HEAVY ABOUT SOMEONE THEY AREN'T VERY CLOSE WITH...

Hey buddy are we still on for tonight !??!?

Peter is coming over and he brought this ridiculous keg lol what time are you gonna come by?

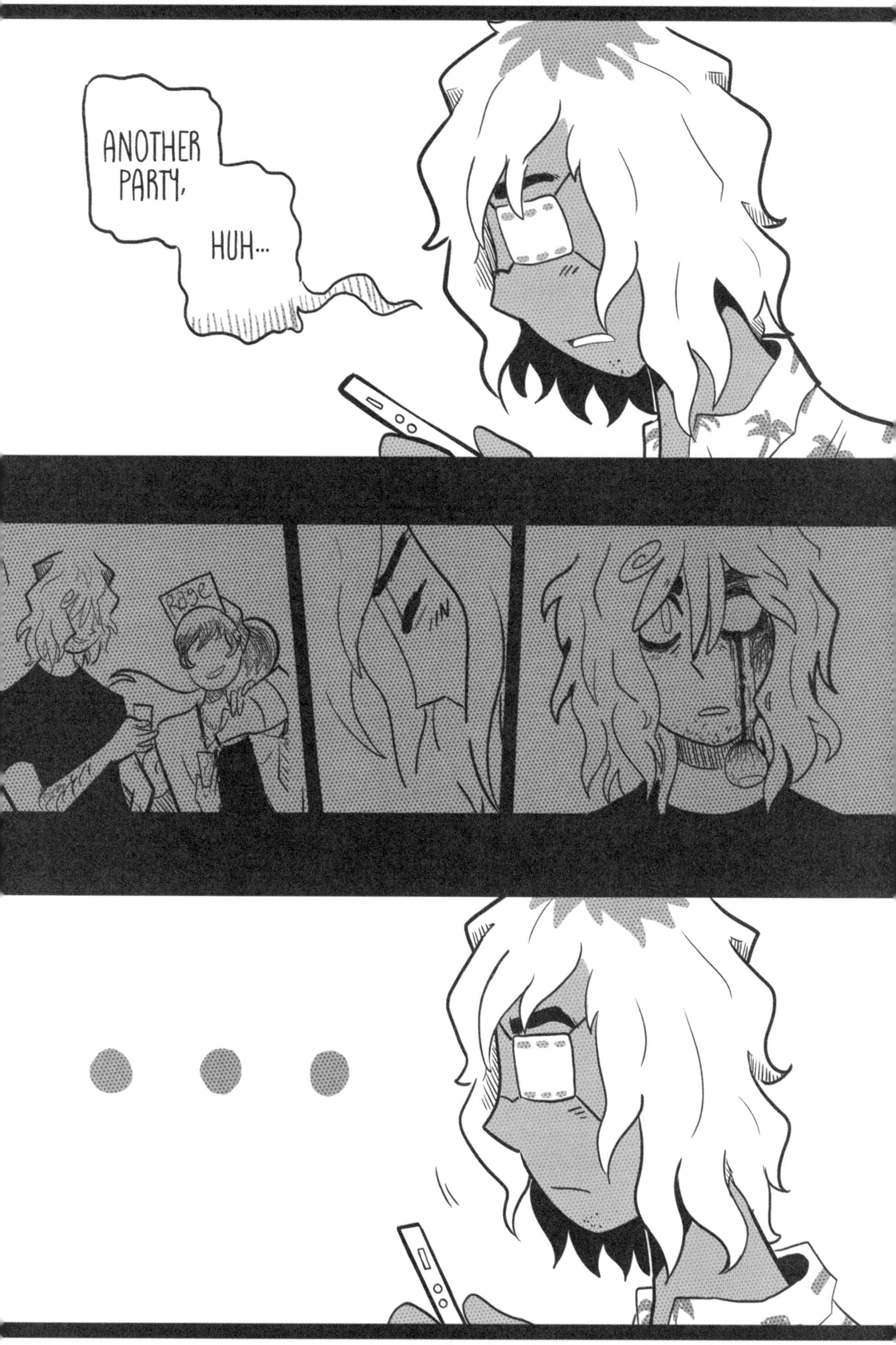
ANOTHER PARTY, HUH...

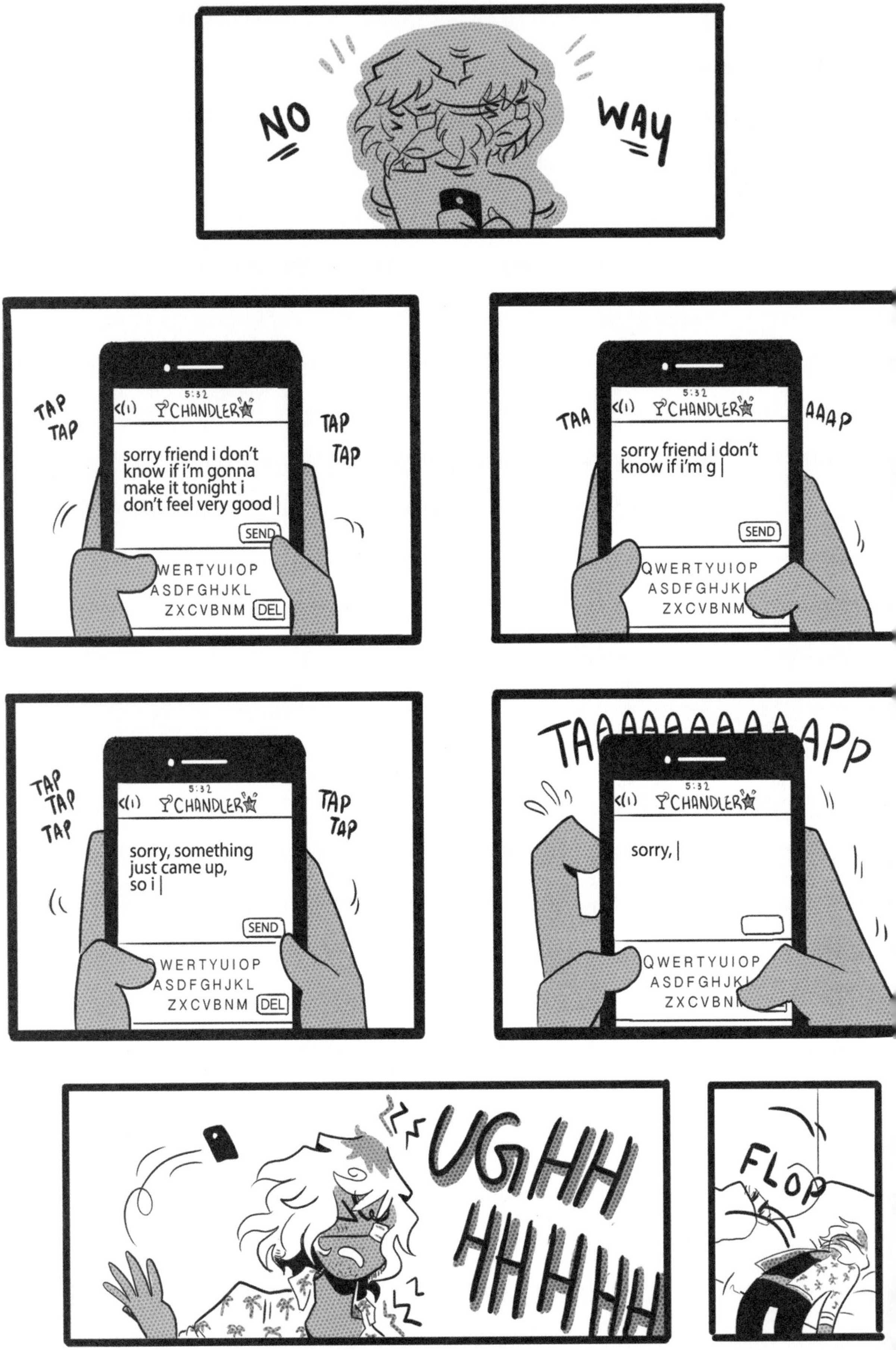
NO
WAY
TAP TAP
5:32
CHANDLER
sorry friend i don't know if i'm gonna make it tonight i don't feel very good
SEND
WERTYUIOP
ASDFGHJKL
ZXCVBNM DEL
TAP TAP
TAA
5:32
CHANDLER
sorry friend i don't know if i'm g
SEND
QWERTYUIOP
ASDFGHJKL
ZXCVBNM
AAAP
TAP TAP TAP
5:32
CHANDLER
sorry, something just came up, so i
SEND
WERTYUIOP
ASDFGHJKL
ZXCVBNM DEL
TAP TAP
TAAAAAAAAAAPP
5:32
CHANDLER
sorry,
QWERTYUIOP
ASDFGHJKL
ZXCVBNM
UGHHHHHHH
FLOP

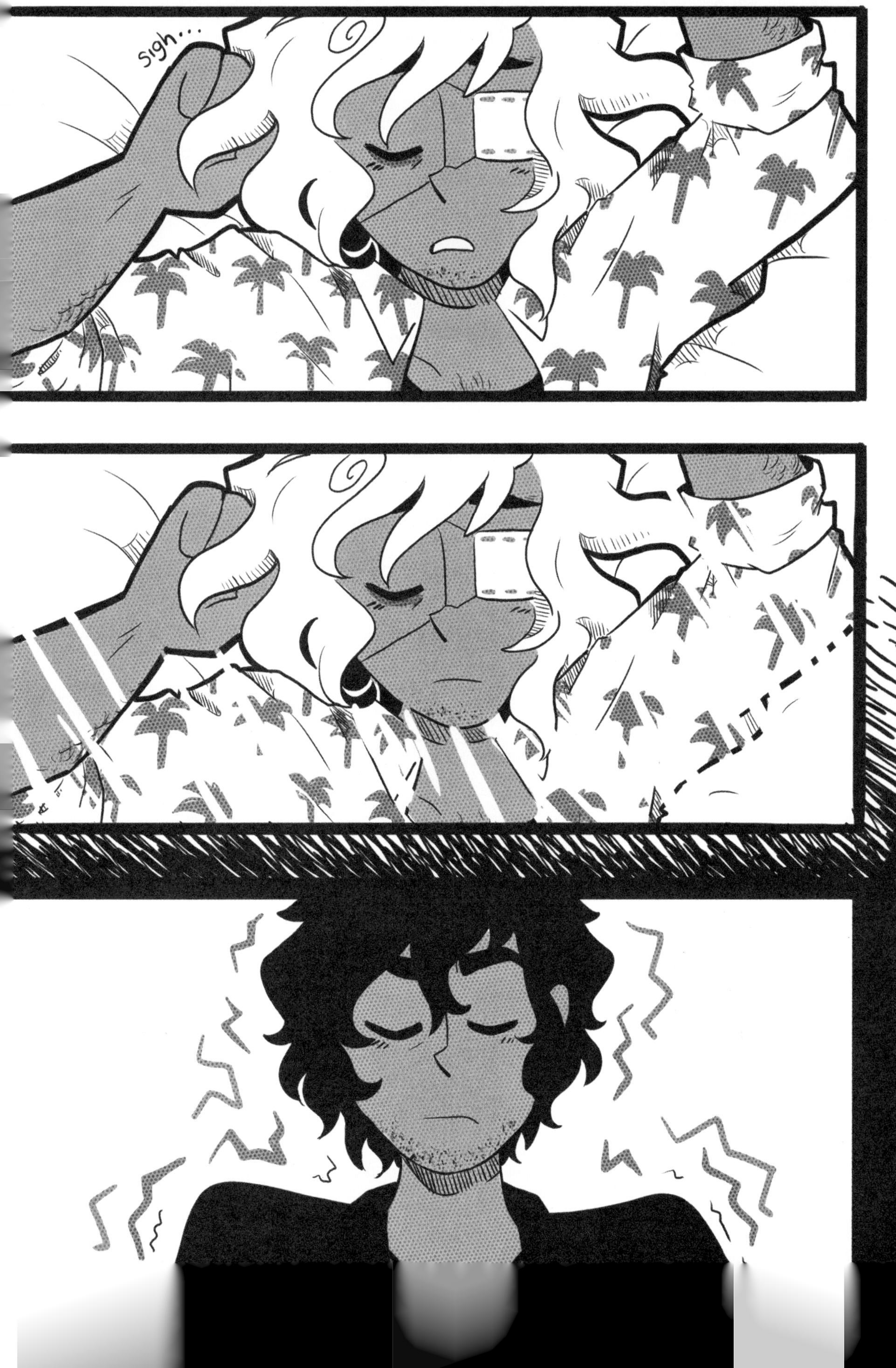
Sigh...

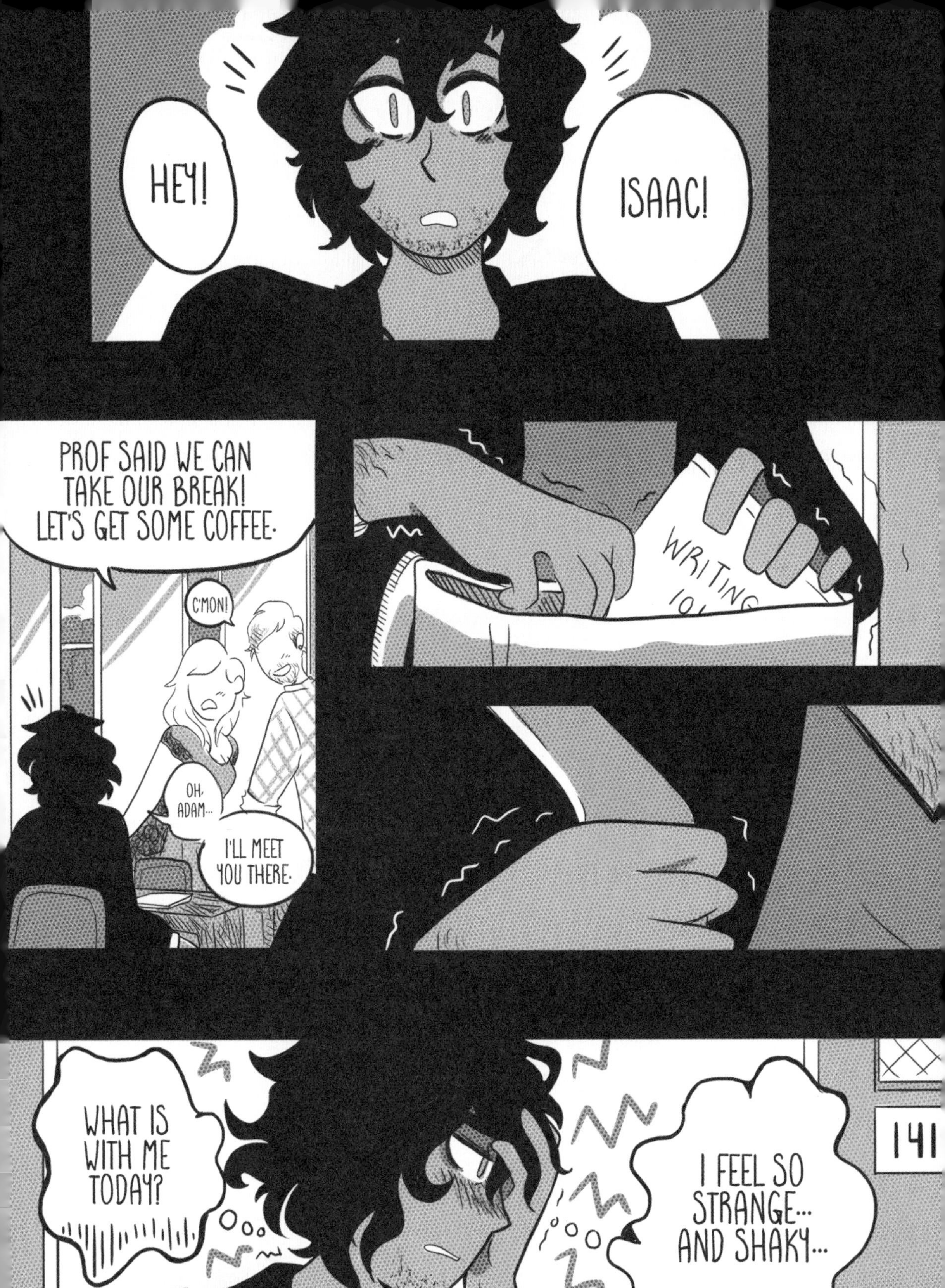
HEY!
ISAAC!
PROF SAID WE CAN TAKE OUR BREAK! LET'S GET SOME COFFEE.
C'MON!
OH, ADAM...
I'LL MEET YOU THERE.
WRITING 101
WHAT IS WITH ME TODAY?
I FEEL SO STRANGE... AND SHAKY...

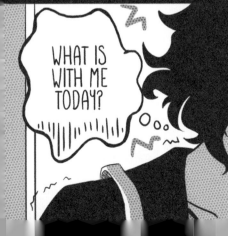

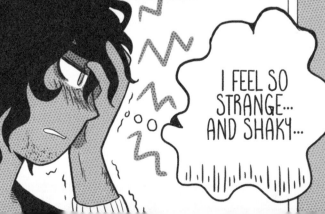

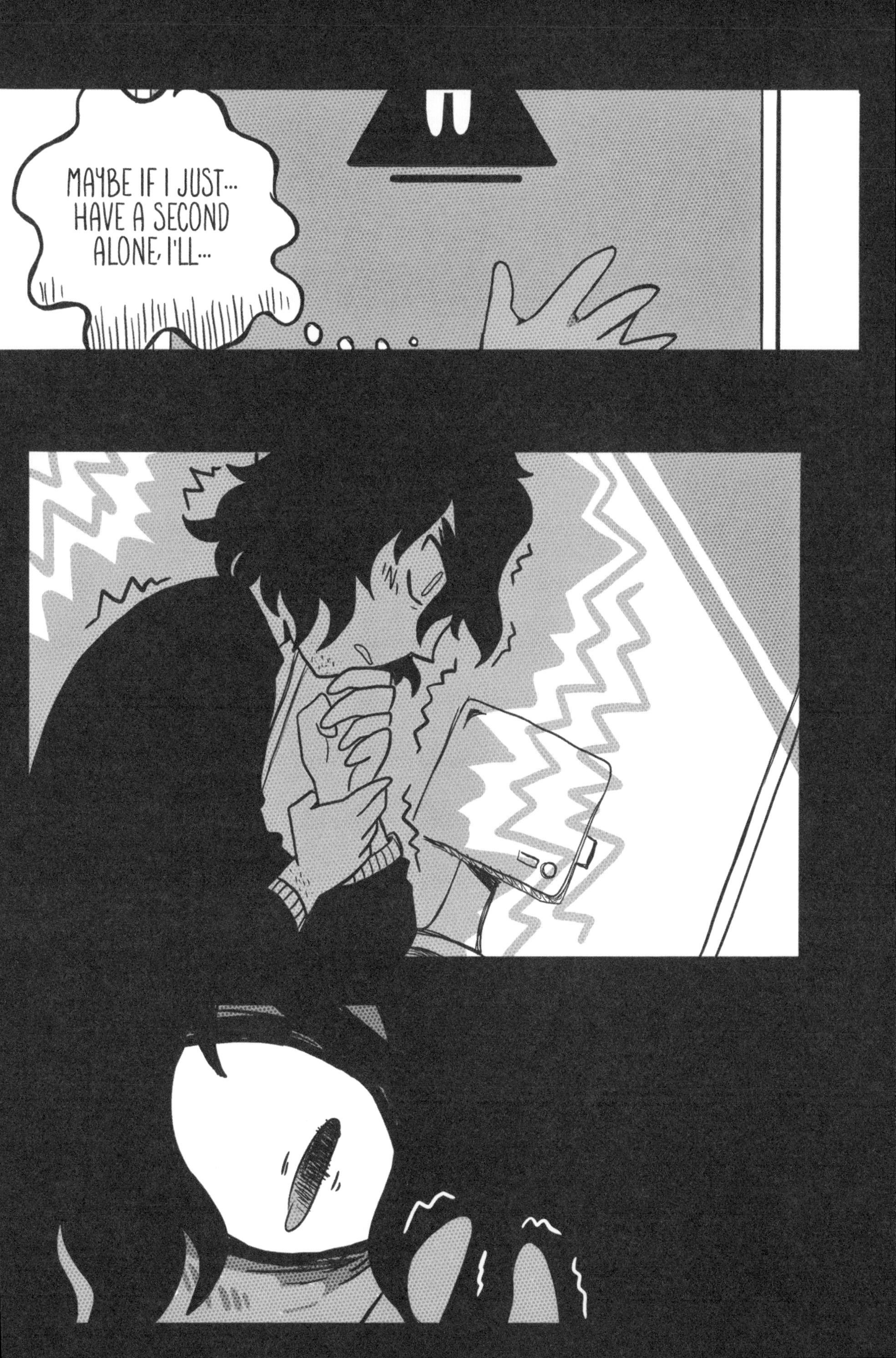
MAYBE IF I JUST... HAVE A SECOND ALONE, I'LL...

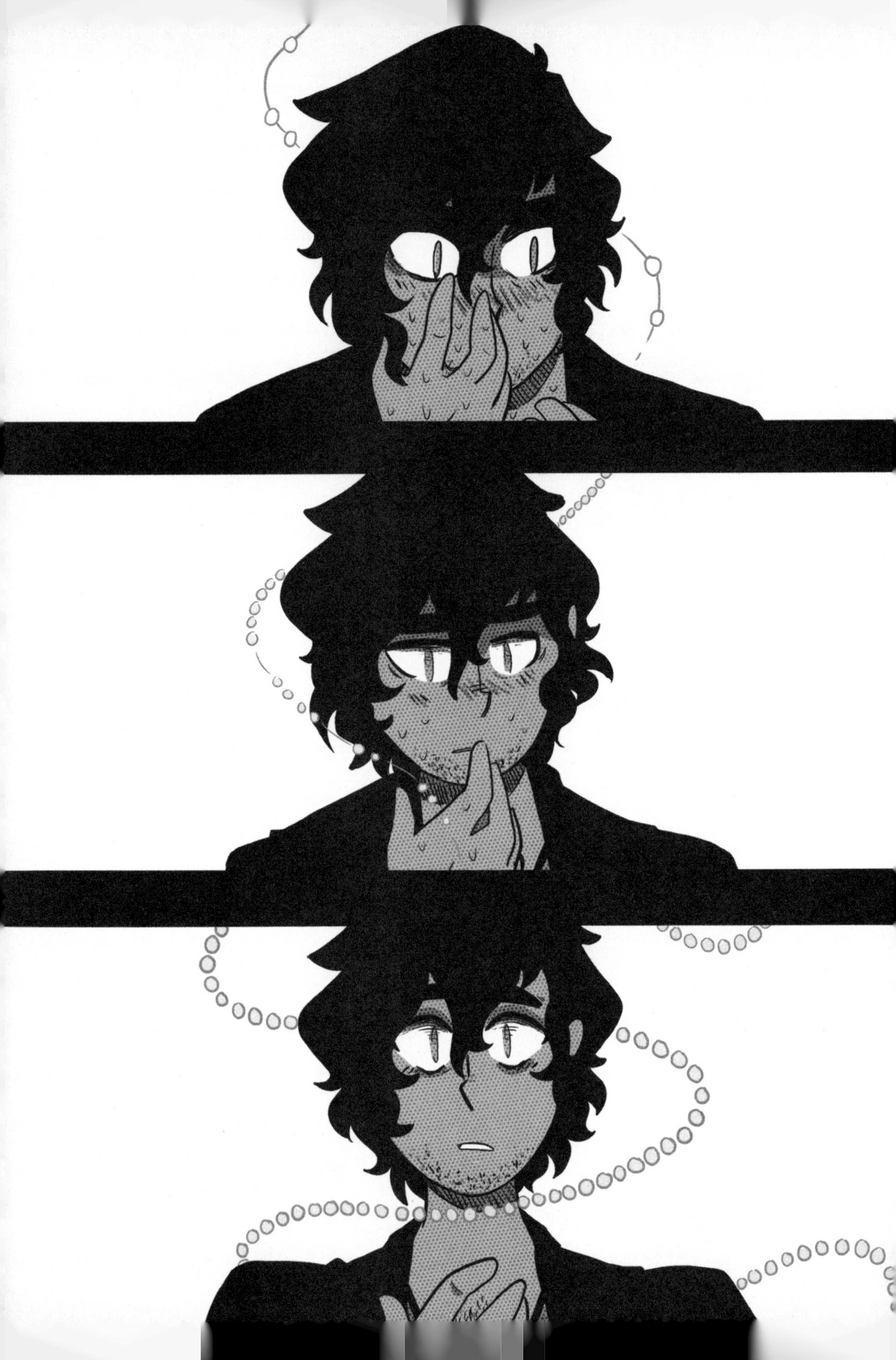

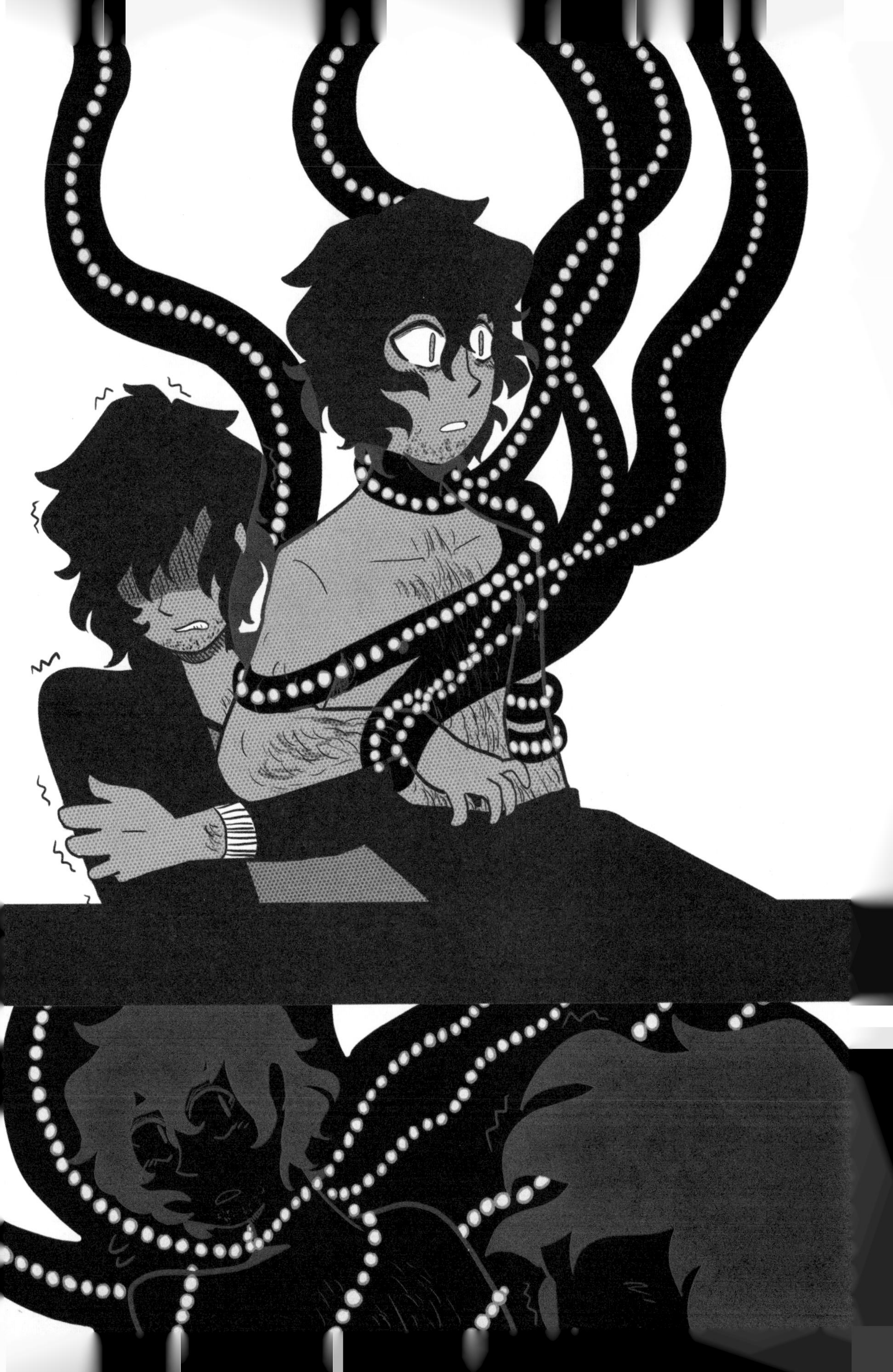

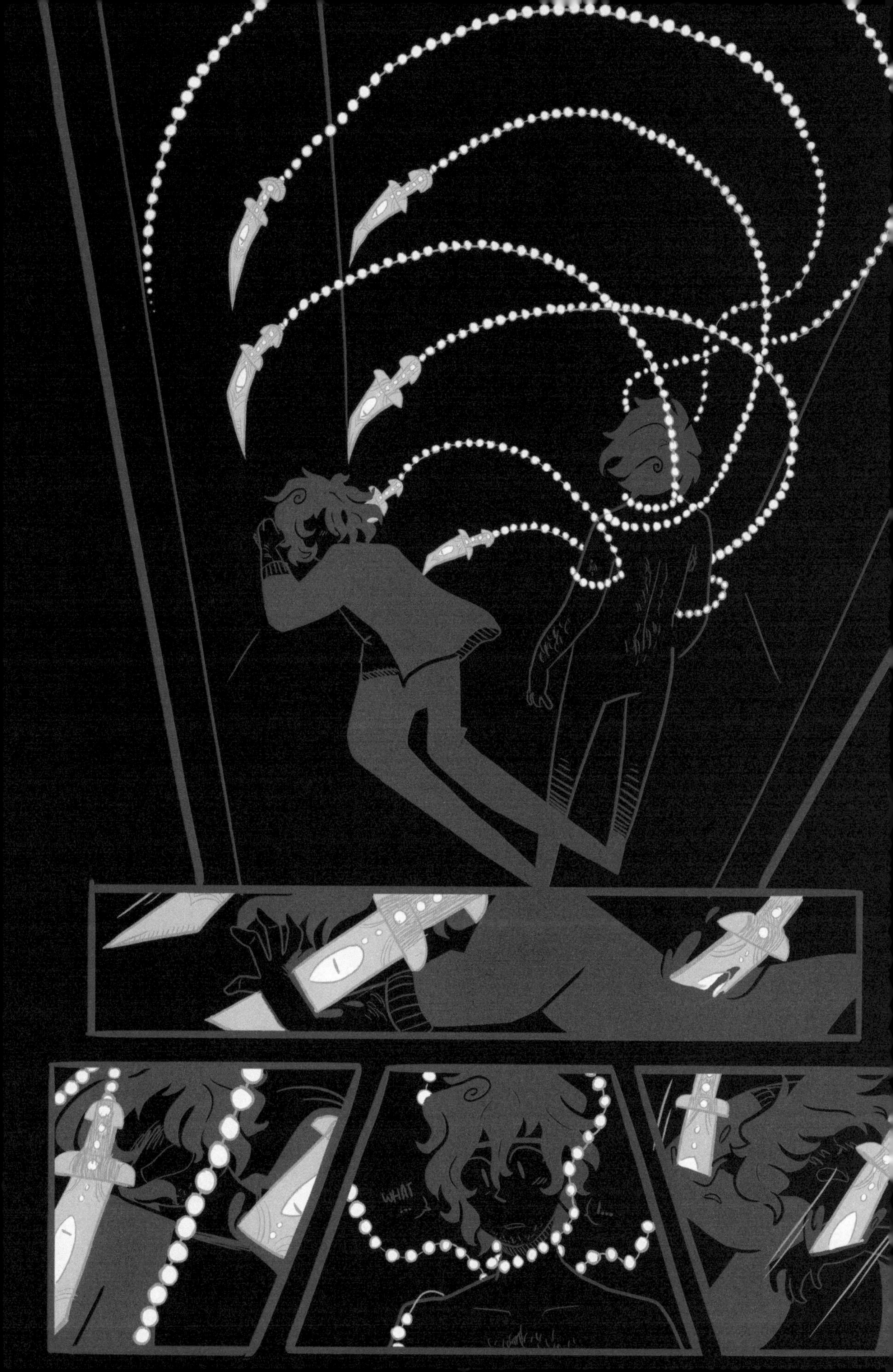
WHAT...
I...

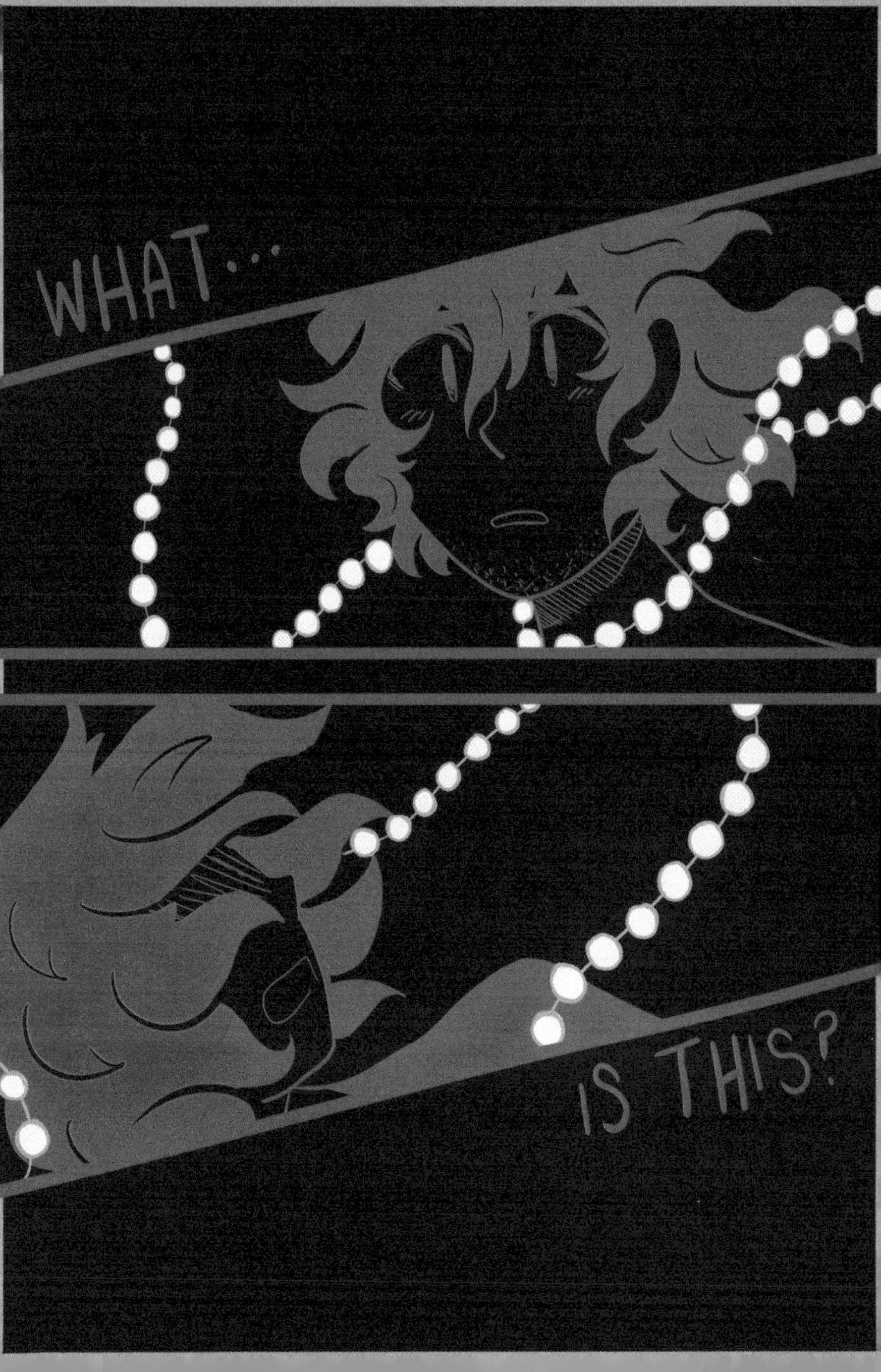
WHAT...
IS THIS?

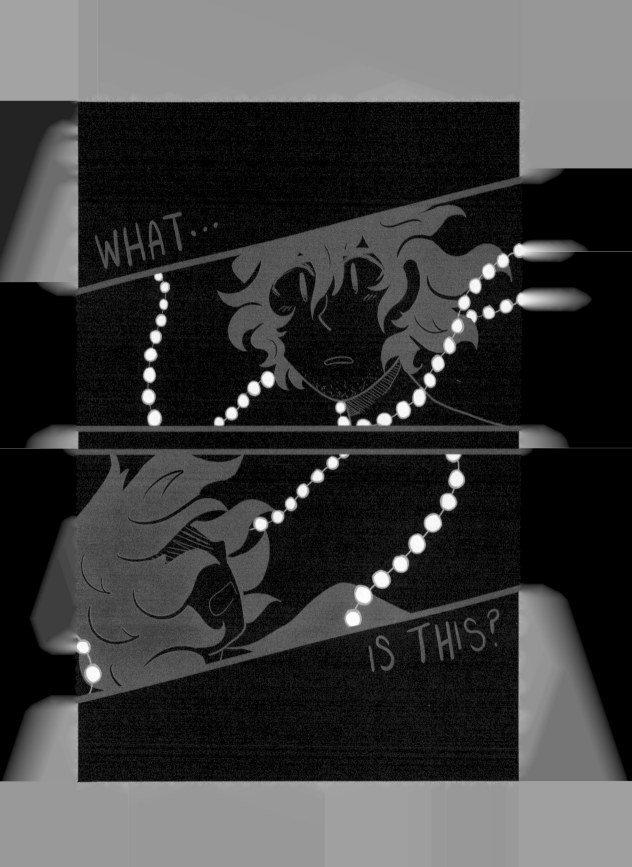

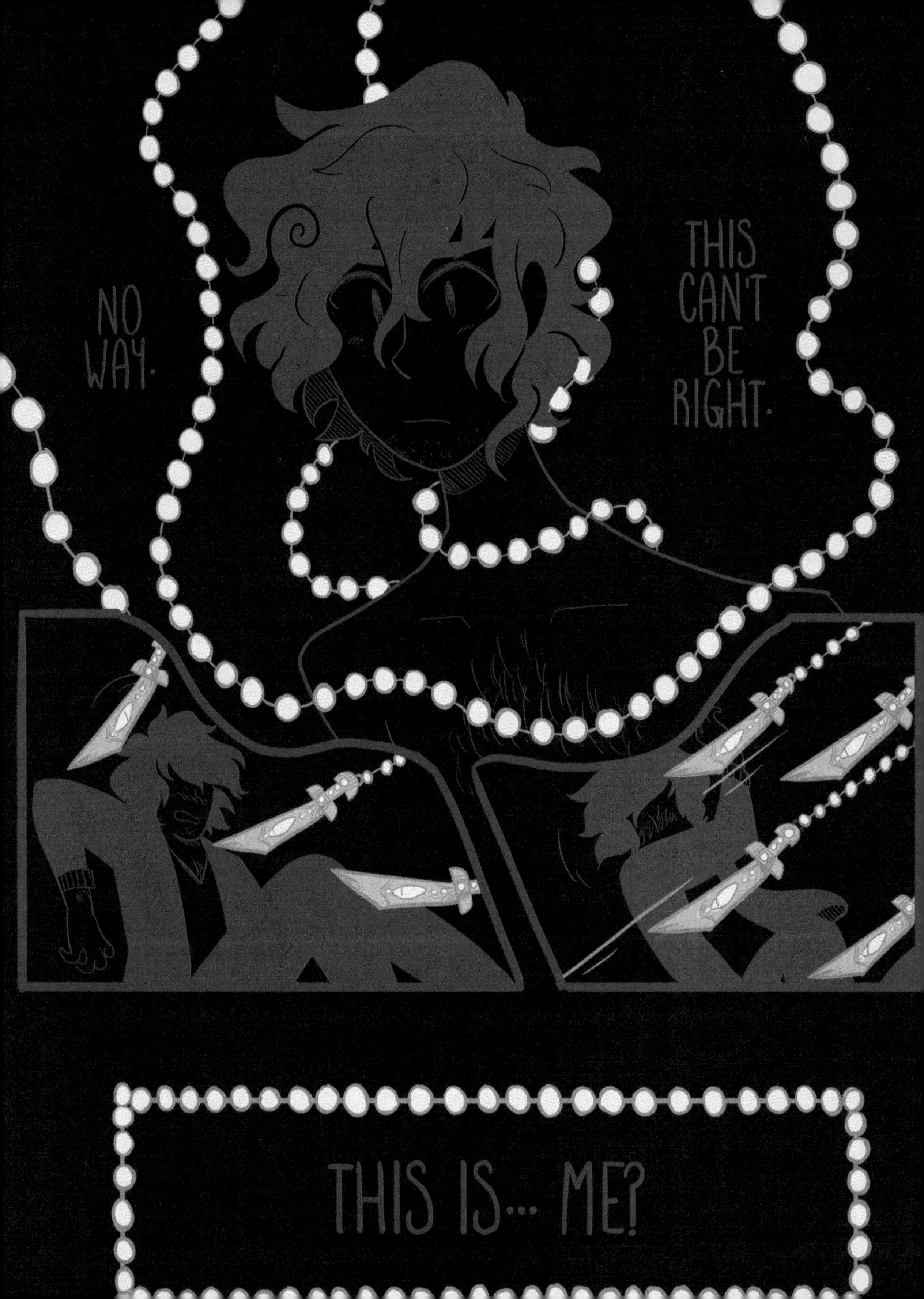
NO WAY.
THIS CAN'T BE RIGHT.
THIS IS... ME?

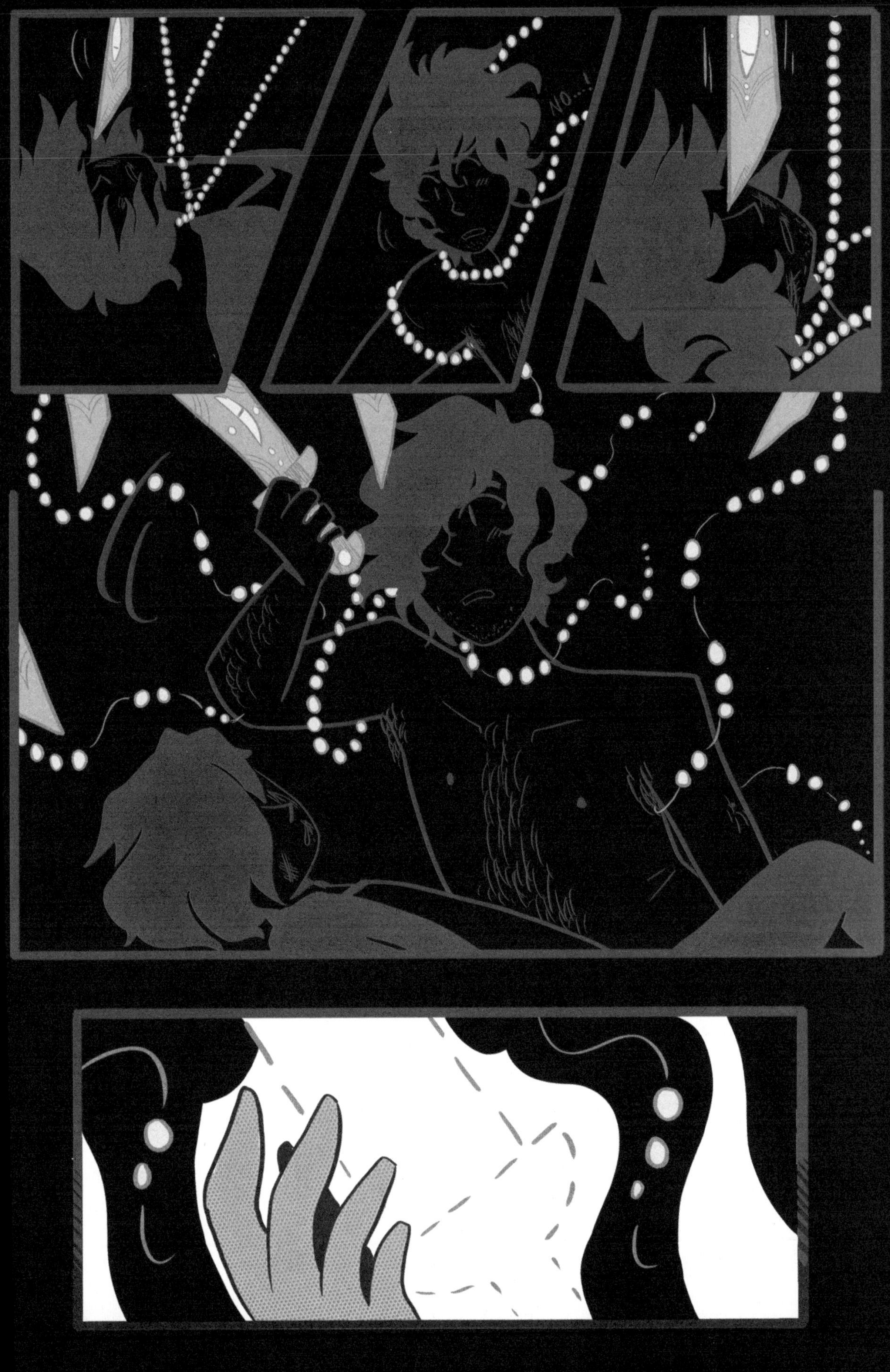
NO...!

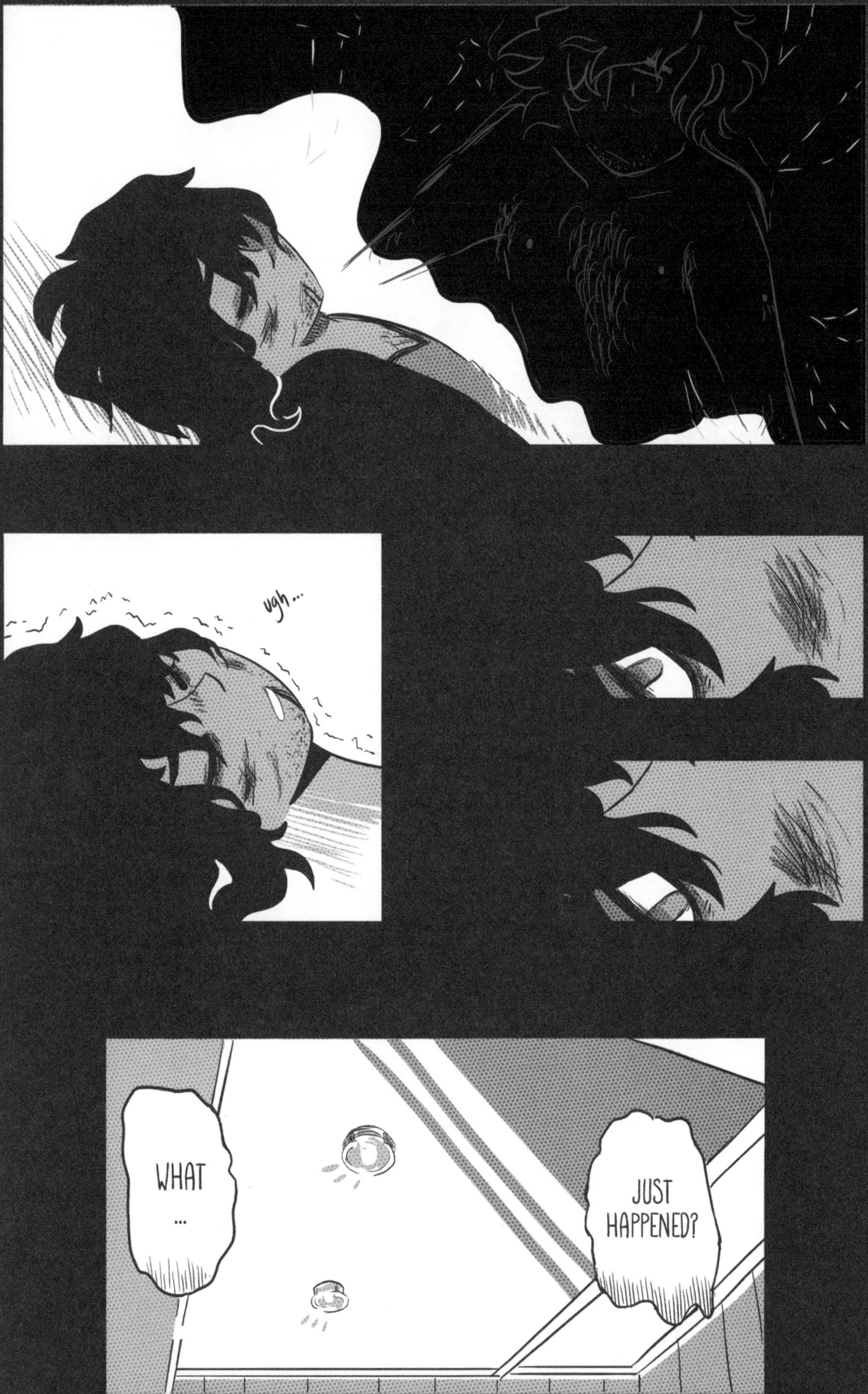
ugh...
WHAT
...
JUST HAPPENED?

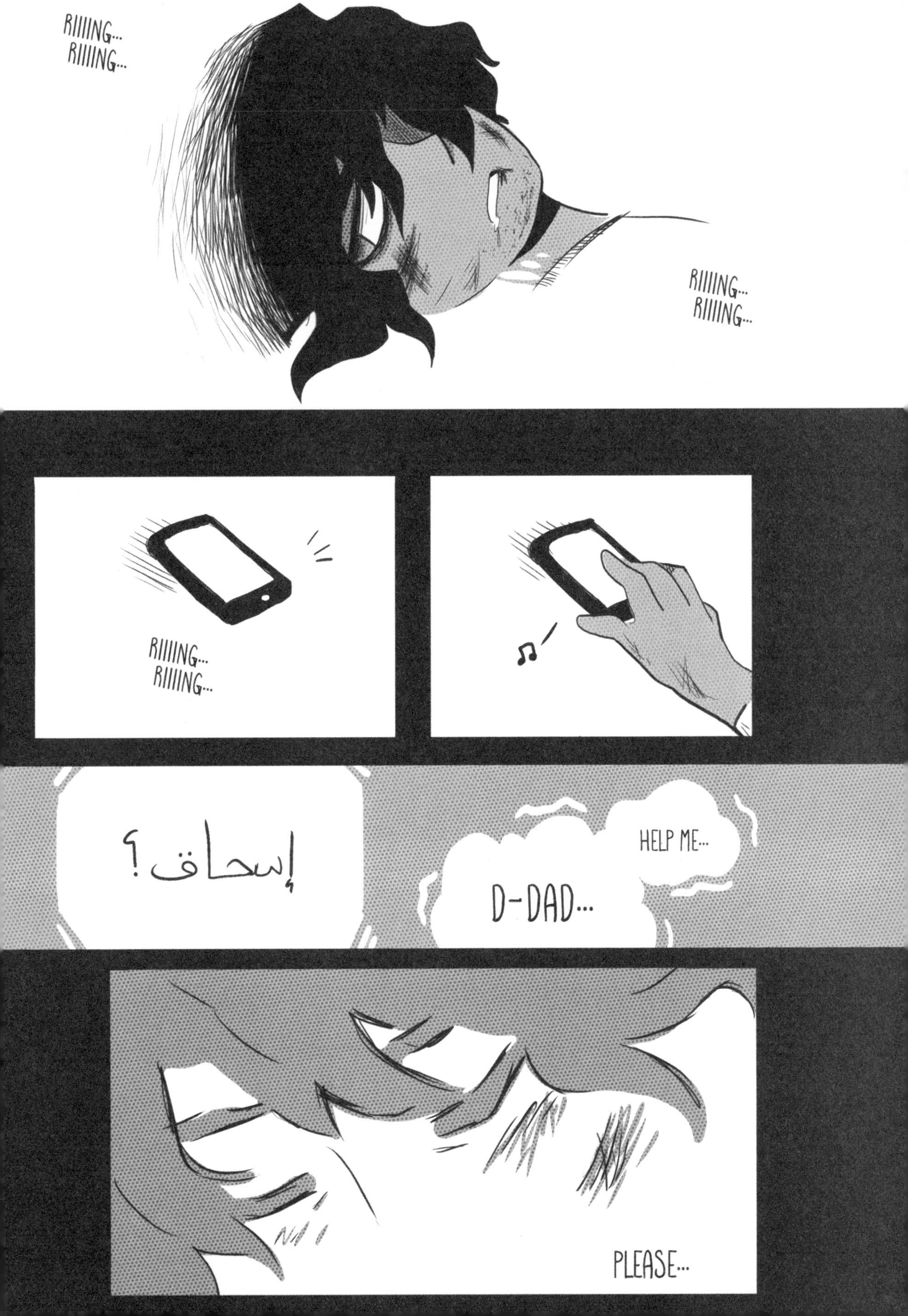
RIIIING...
RIIIING...
RIIIING...
RIIIING...
RIIIING...
RIIIING...
إسحاق؟
D-DAD...
HELP ME...
PLEASE...

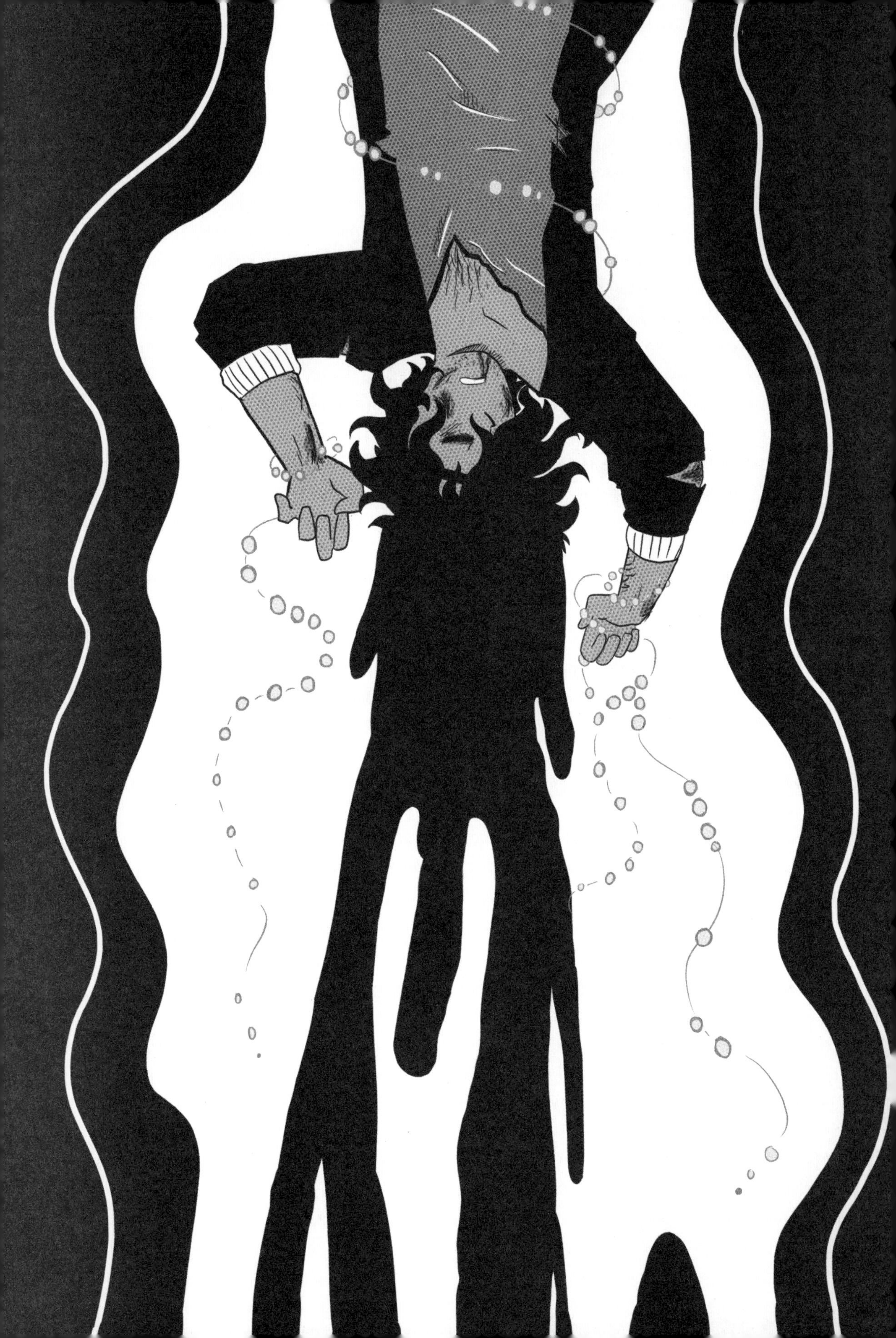

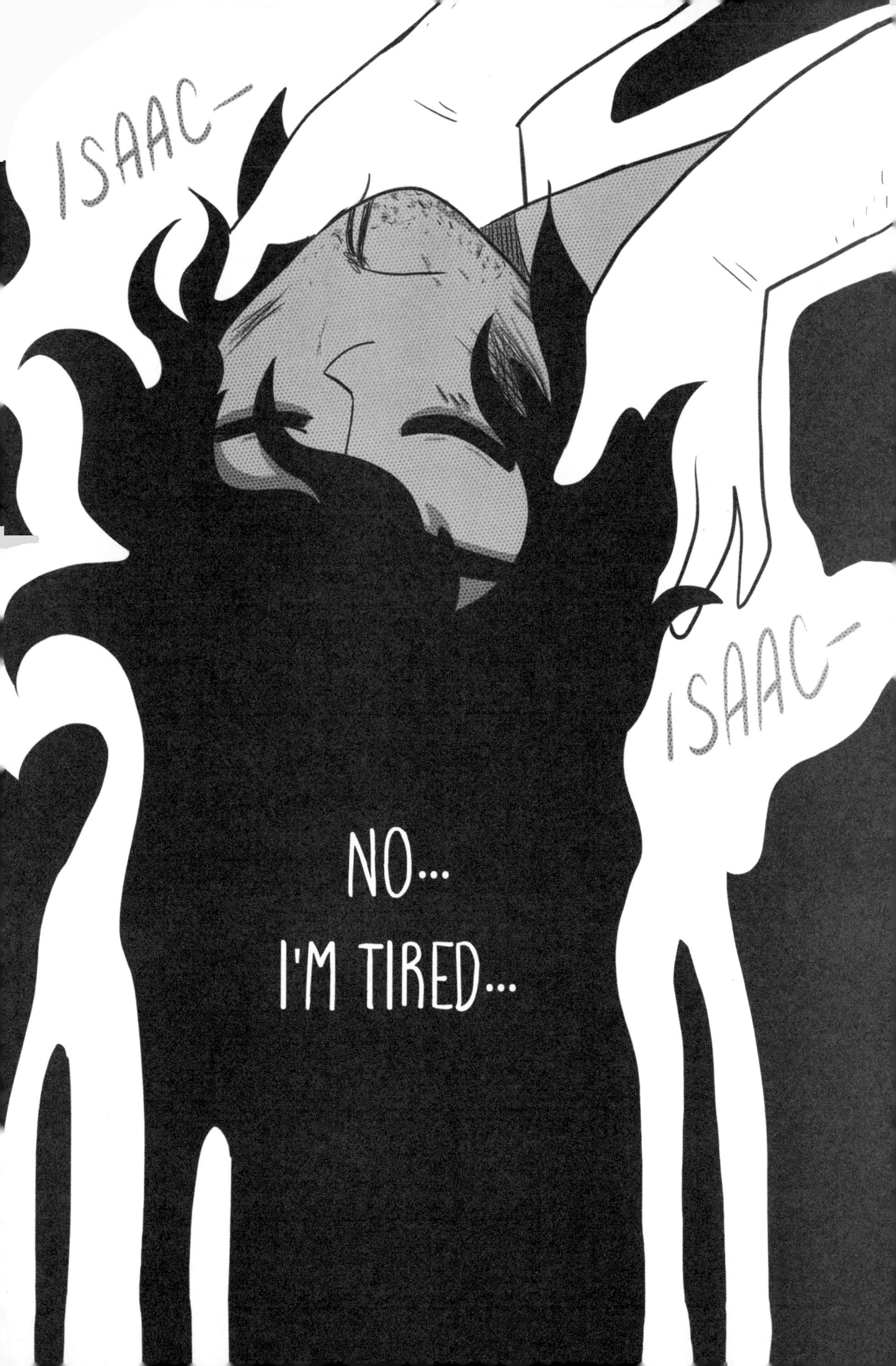
ISAAC–
ISAAC–
NO...
I'M TIRED...

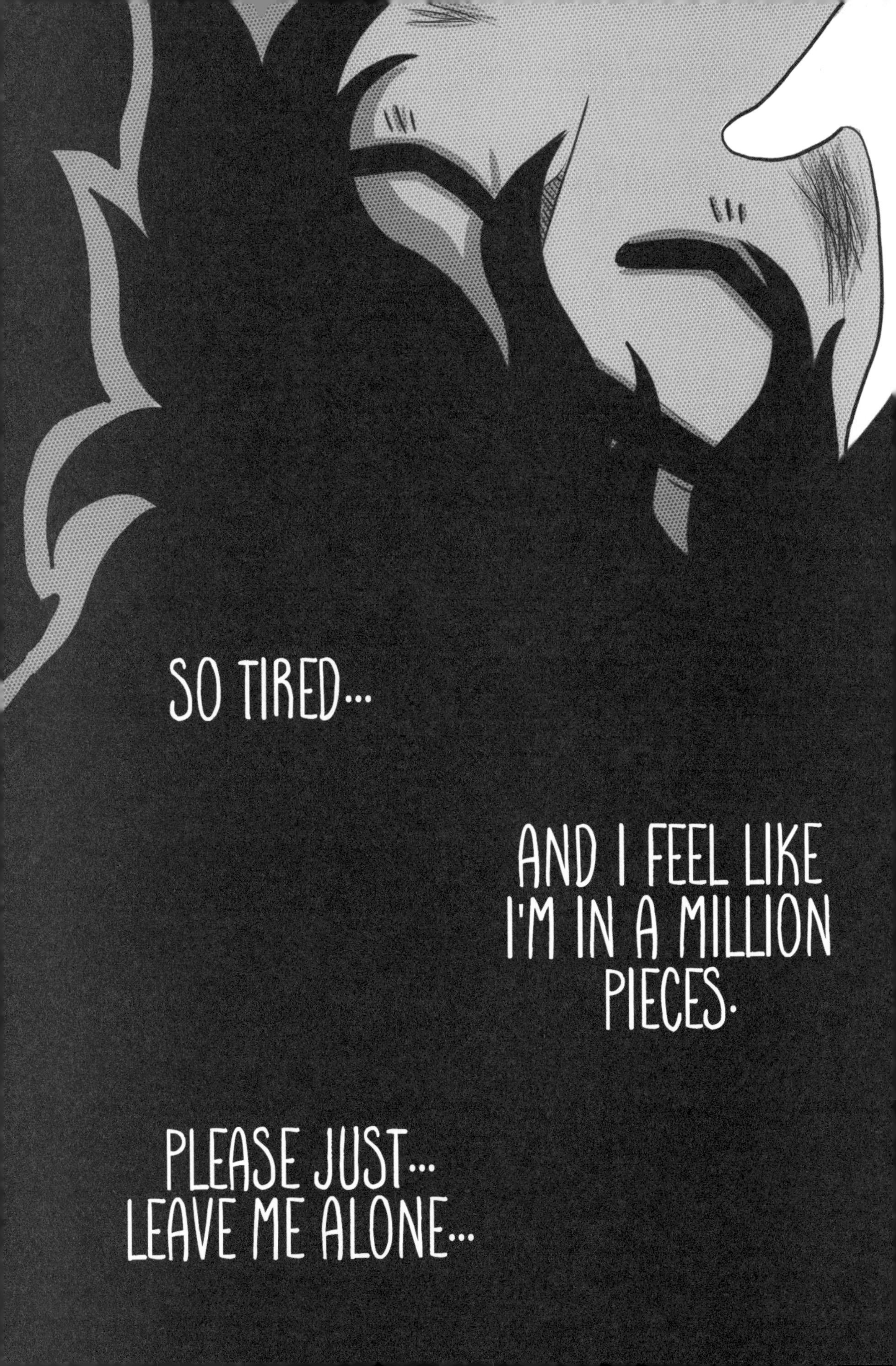
SO TIRED...
AND I FEEL LIKE I'M IN A MILLION PIECES.
PLEASE JUST... LEAVE ME ALONE...

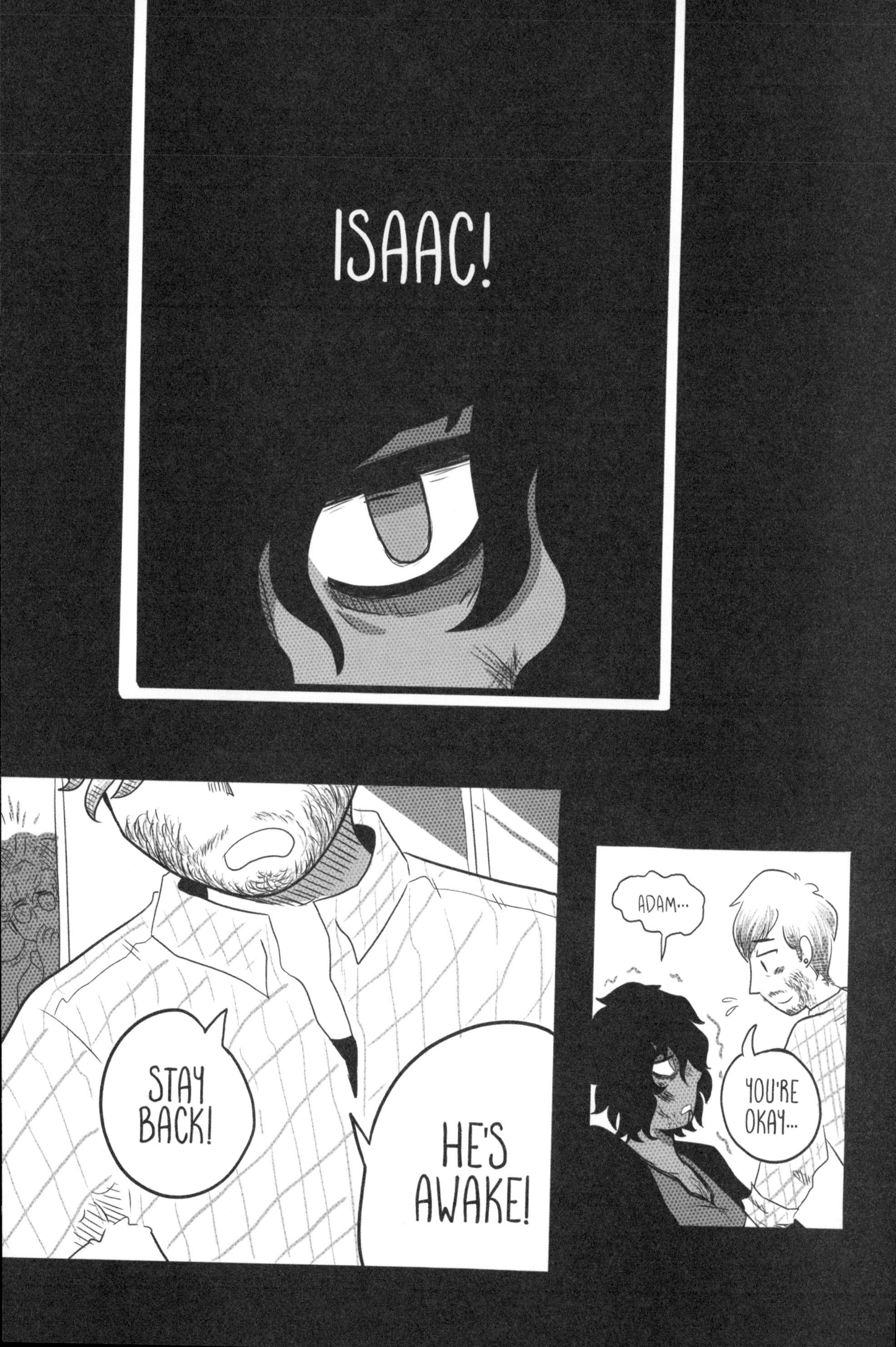
ISAAC!
STAY BACK!
HE'S AWAKE!
ADAM...
YOU'RE OKAY...

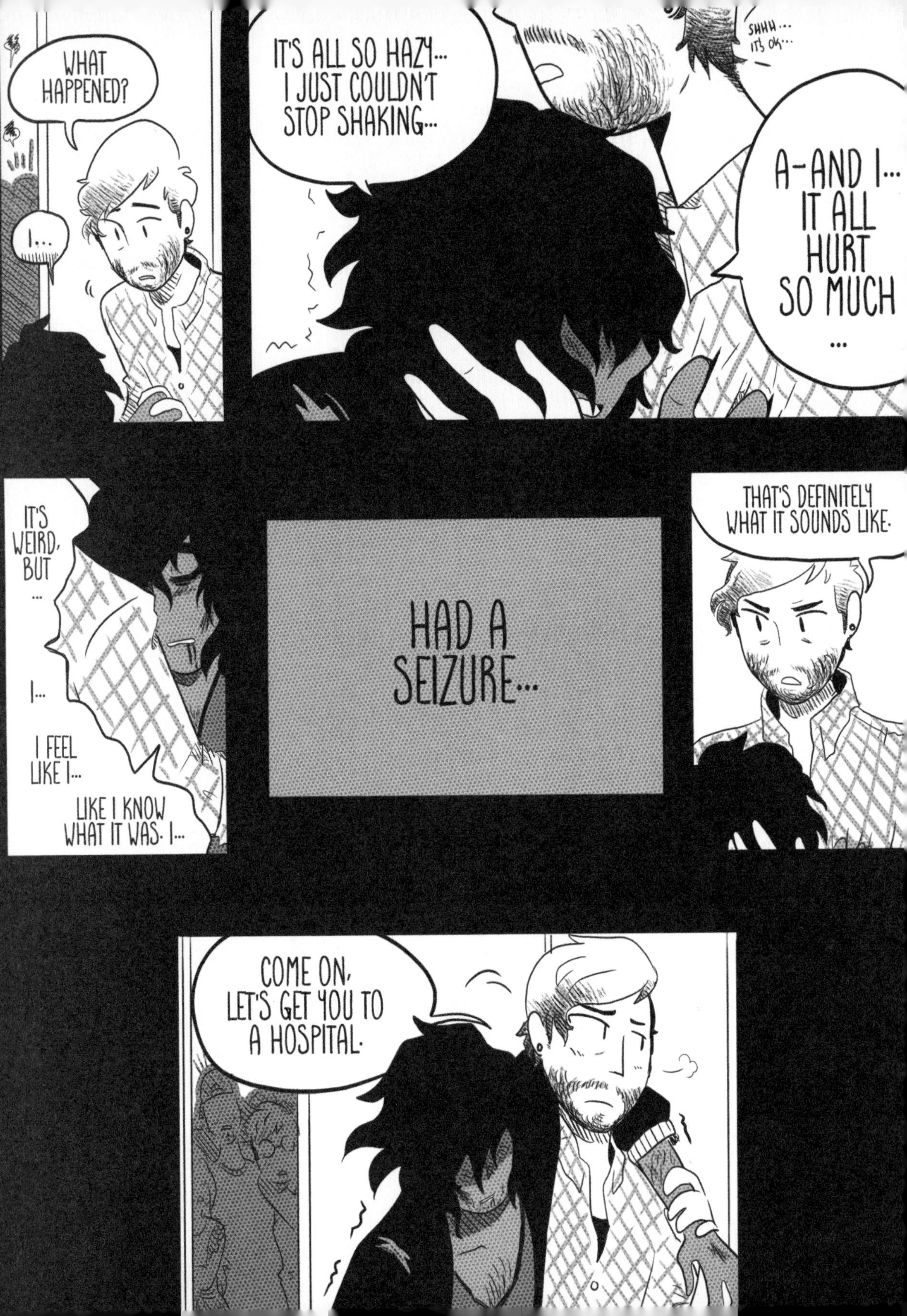
WHAT HAPPENED?
I...
IT'S ALL SO HAZY... I JUST COULDN'T STOP SHAKING...
SHHH... IT'S OK...
A-AND I... IT ALL HURT SO MUCH ...
IT'S WEIRD, BUT ...
I...
I FEEL LIKE I...
LIKE I KNOW WHAT IT WAS. I...
HAD A SEIZURE...
THAT'S DEFINITELY WHAT IT SOUNDS LIKE.
COME ON, LET'S GET YOU TO A HOSPITAL.

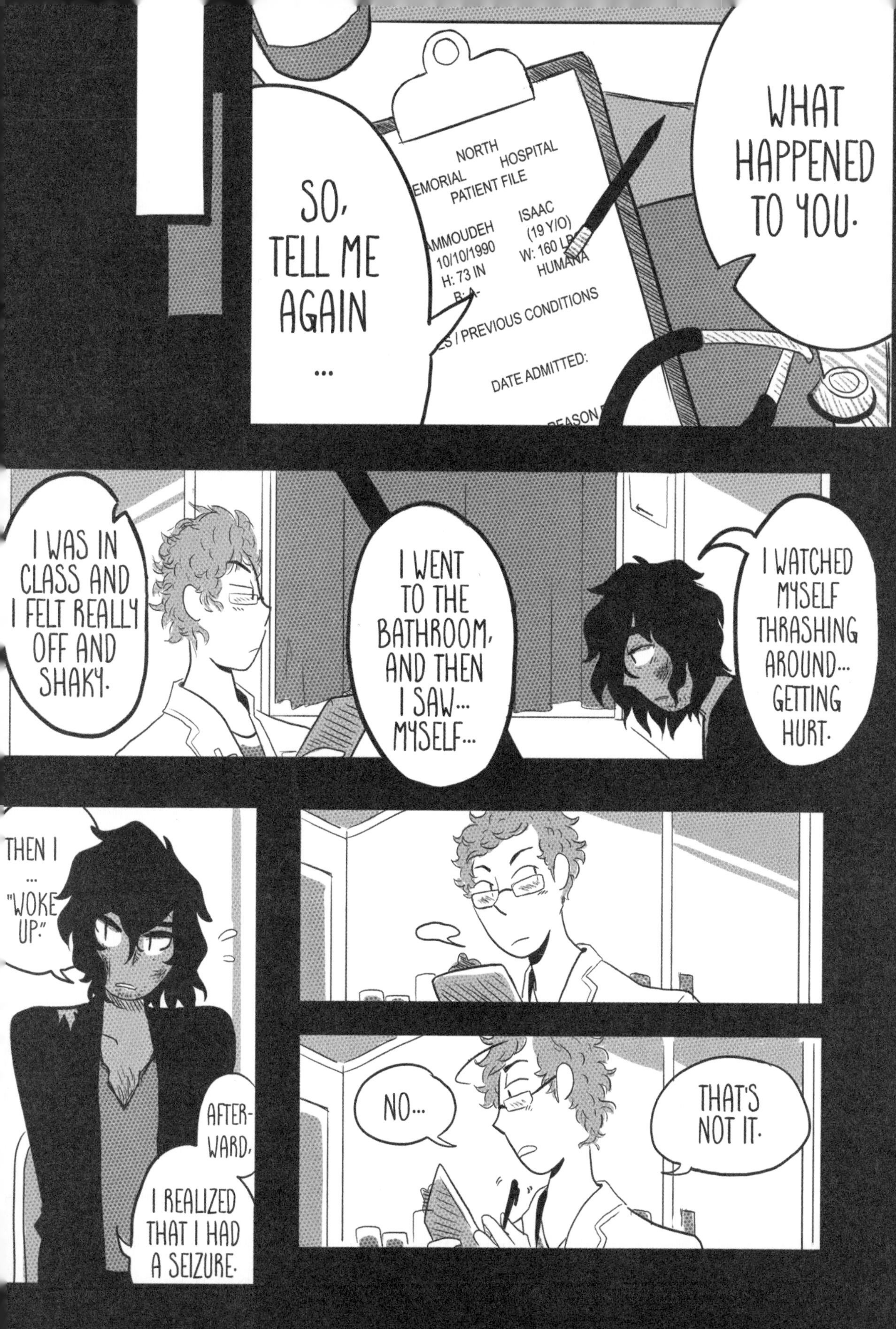
SO, TELL ME AGAIN ...
NORTH
EMORIAL HOSPITAL
PATIENT FILE
AMMOUDEH ISAAC
10/10/1990 (19 Y/O)
H: 73 IN W: 160 LB
HUMANA
ES / PREVIOUS CONDITIONS
DATE ADMITTED:
WHAT HAPPENED TO YOU.
I WAS IN CLASS AND I FELT REALLY OFF AND SHAKY.
I WENT TO THE BATHROOM, AND THEN I SAW... MYSELF...
I WATCHED MYSELF THRASHING AROUND... GETTING HURT.
THEN I ... "WOKE UP."
AFTER-WARD,
I REALIZED THAT I HAD A SEIZURE.
NO...
THAT'S NOT IT.

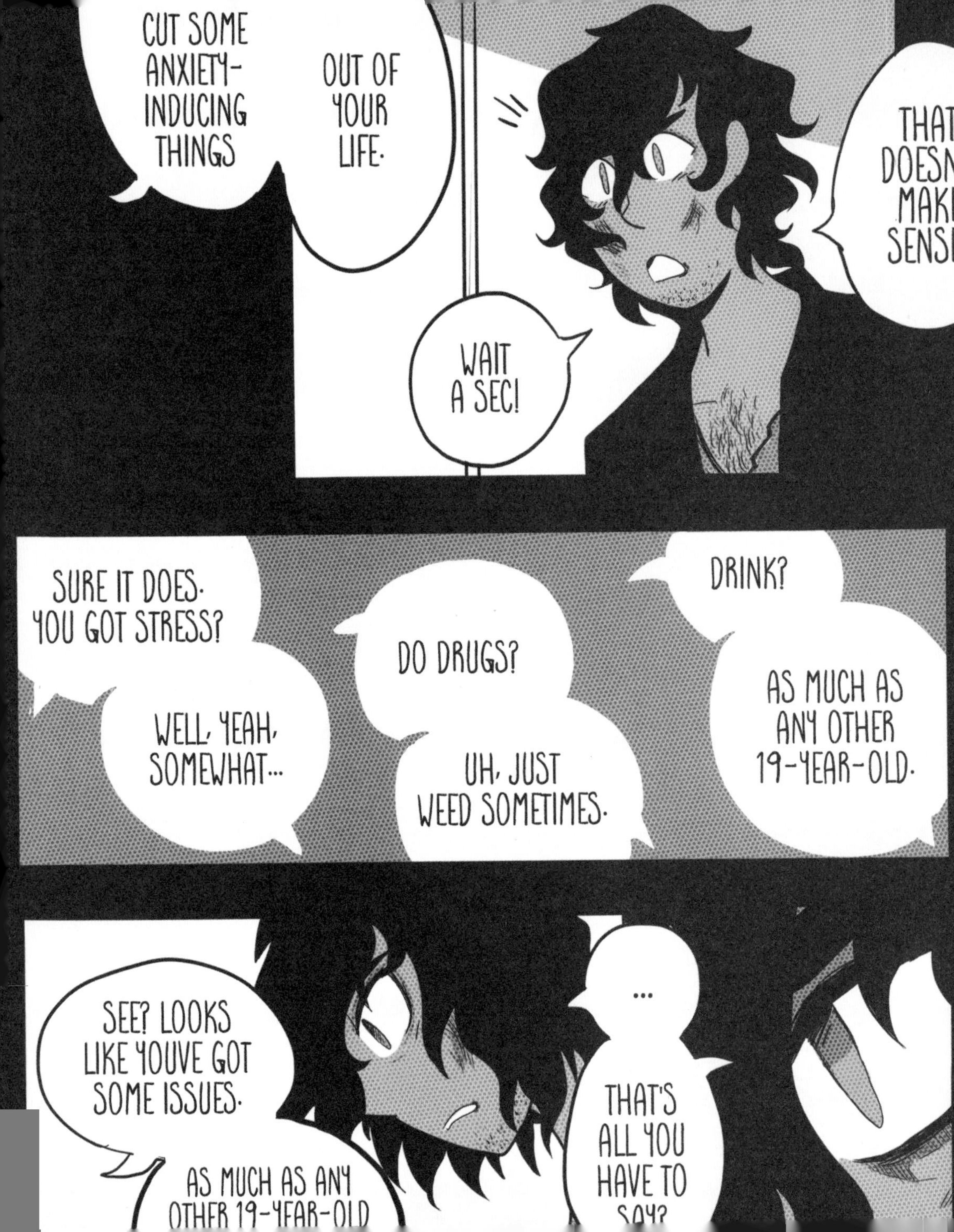
CUT SOME ANXIETY-INDUCING THINGS
OUT OF YOUR LIFE.
WAIT A SEC!
THAT DOESN'T MAKE SENSE!
SURE IT DOES. YOU GOT STRESS?
WELL, YEAH, SOMEWHAT...
DO DRUGS?
UH, JUST WEED SOMETIMES.
DRINK?
AS MUCH AS ANY OTHER 19-YEAR-OLD.
SEE? LOOKS LIKE YOUVE GOT SOME ISSUES.
AS MUCH AS ANY OTHER 19-YEAR-OLD
...
THAT'S ALL YOU HAVE TO SAY?

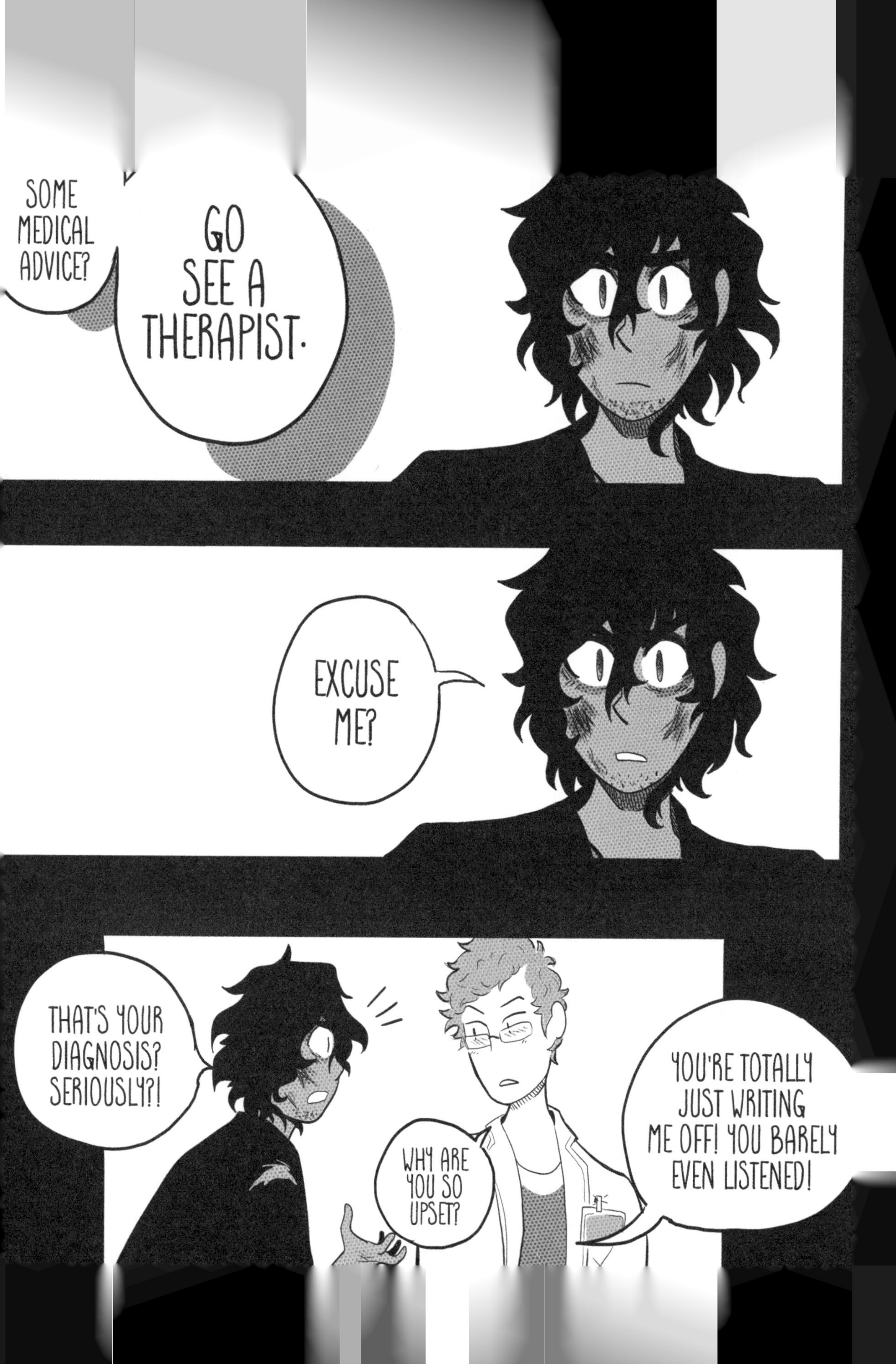
SOME MEDICAL ADVICE?
GO SEE A THERAPIST.
EXCUSE ME?
THAT'S YOUR DIAGNOSIS? SERIOUSLY?!
YOU'RE TOTALLY JUST WRITING ME OFF! YOU BARELY EVEN LISTENED!
WHY ARE YOU SO UPSET?

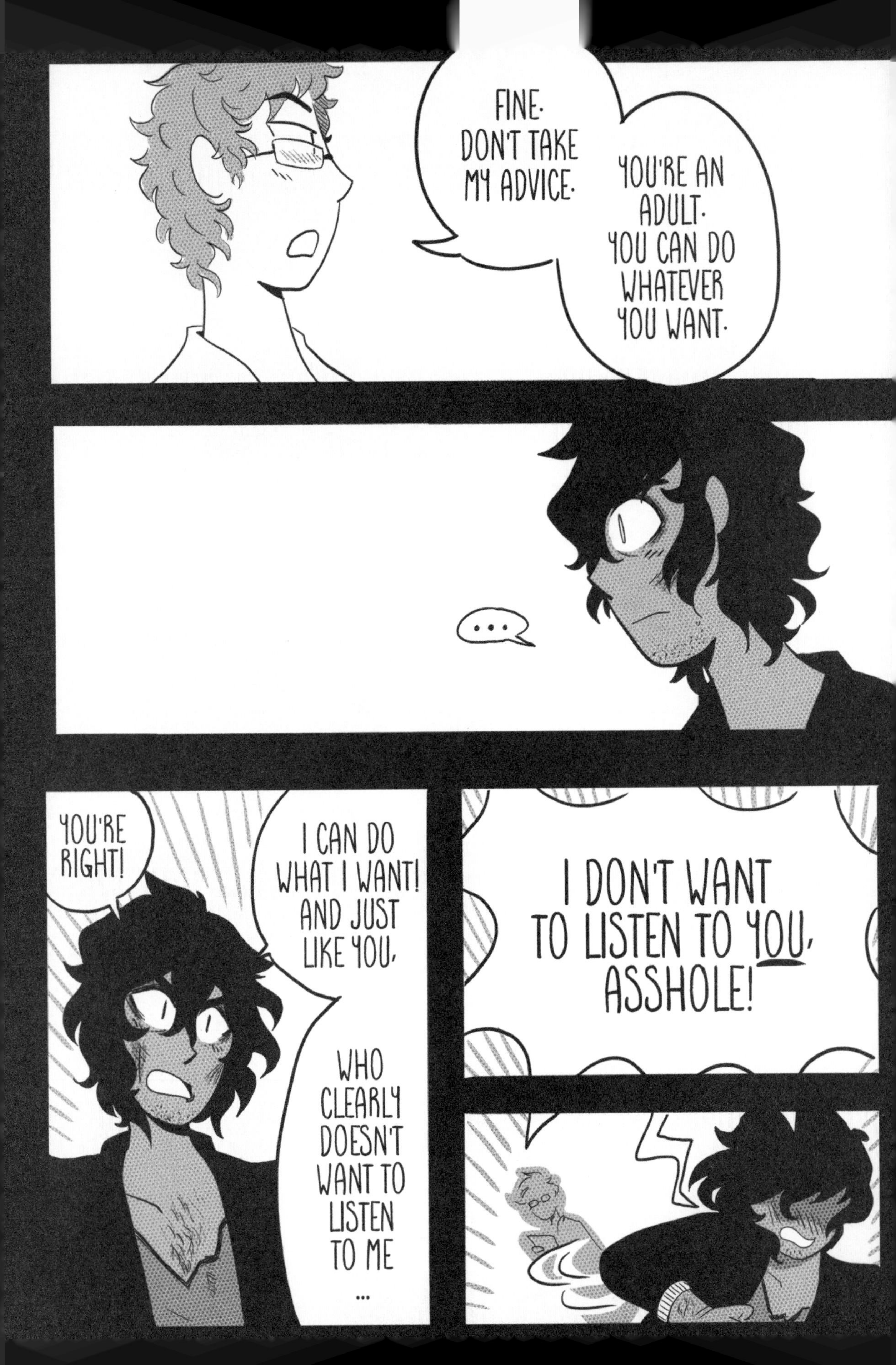
FINE. DON'T TAKE MY ADVICE.
YOU'RE AN ADULT. YOU CAN DO WHATEVER YOU WANT.
...
YOU'RE RIGHT!
I CAN DO WHAT I WANT! AND JUST LIKE YOU,
WHO CLEARLY DOESN'T WANT TO LISTEN TO ME ...
I DON'T WANT TO LISTEN TO YOU, ASSHOLE!

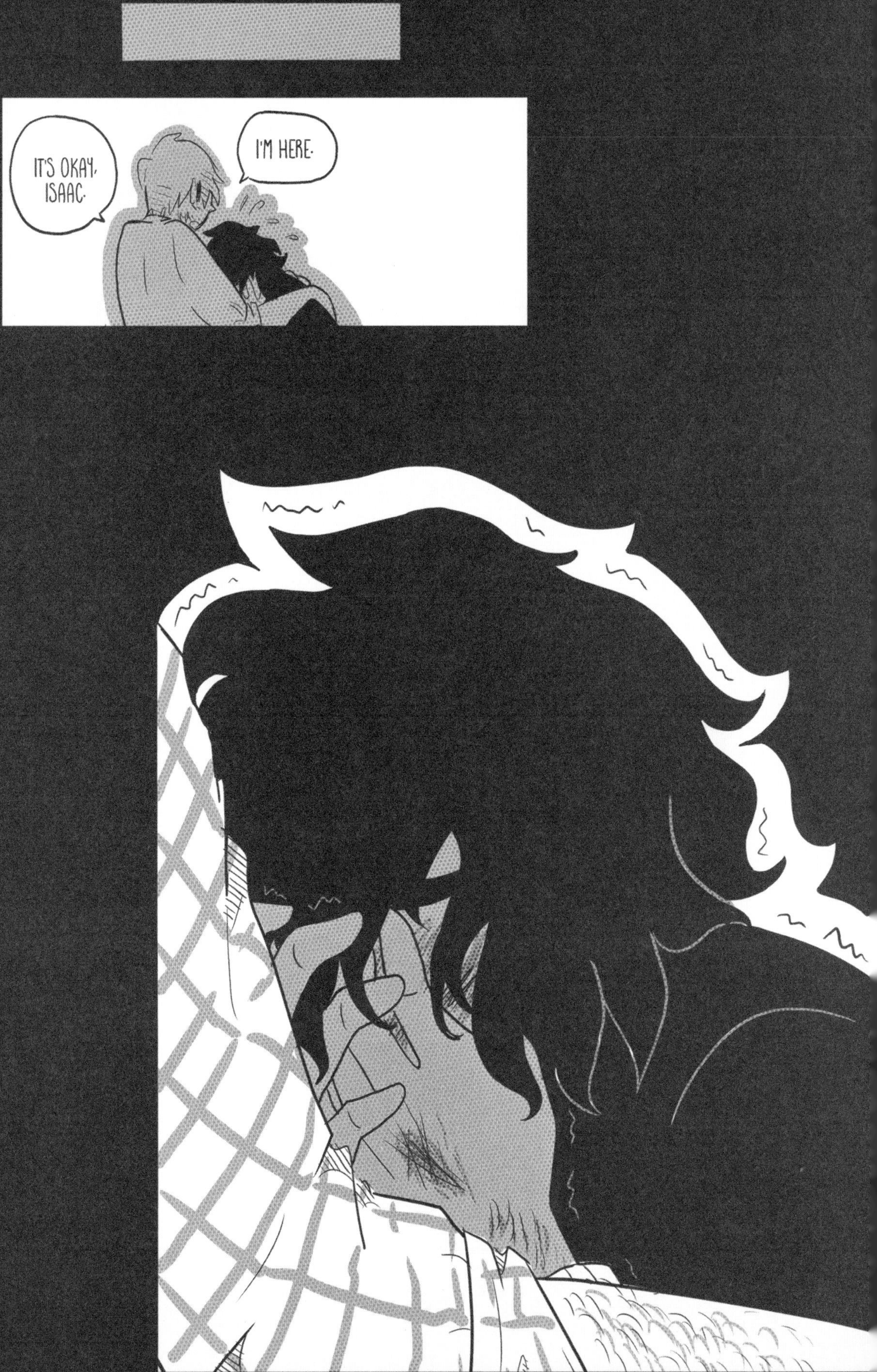
IT'S OKAY, ISAAC.
I'M HERE.

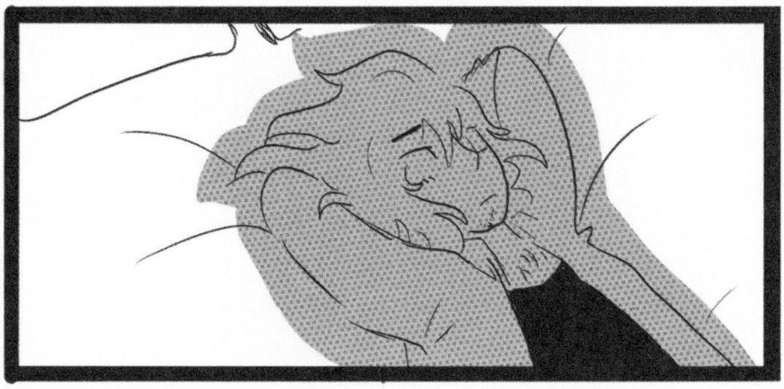

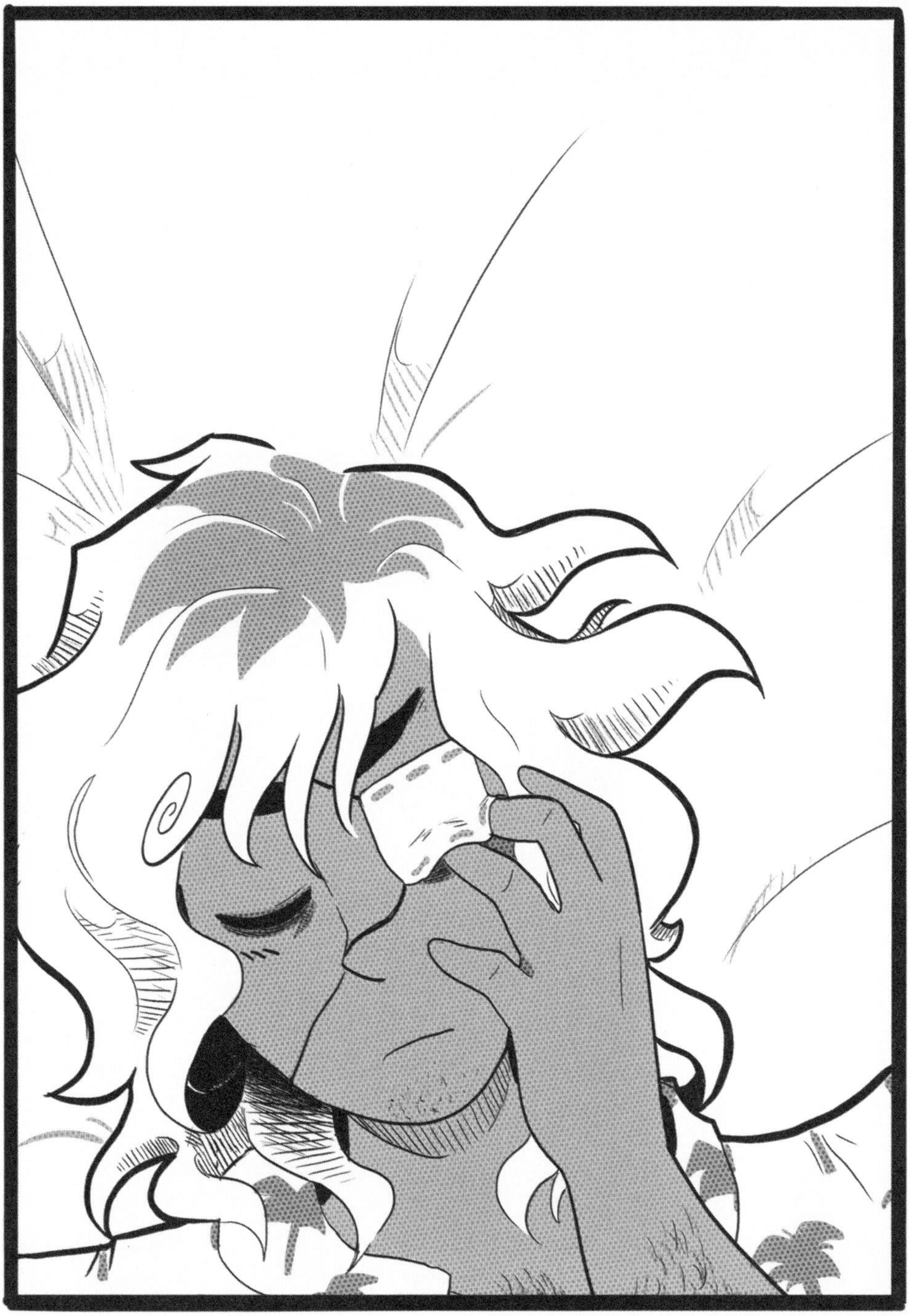

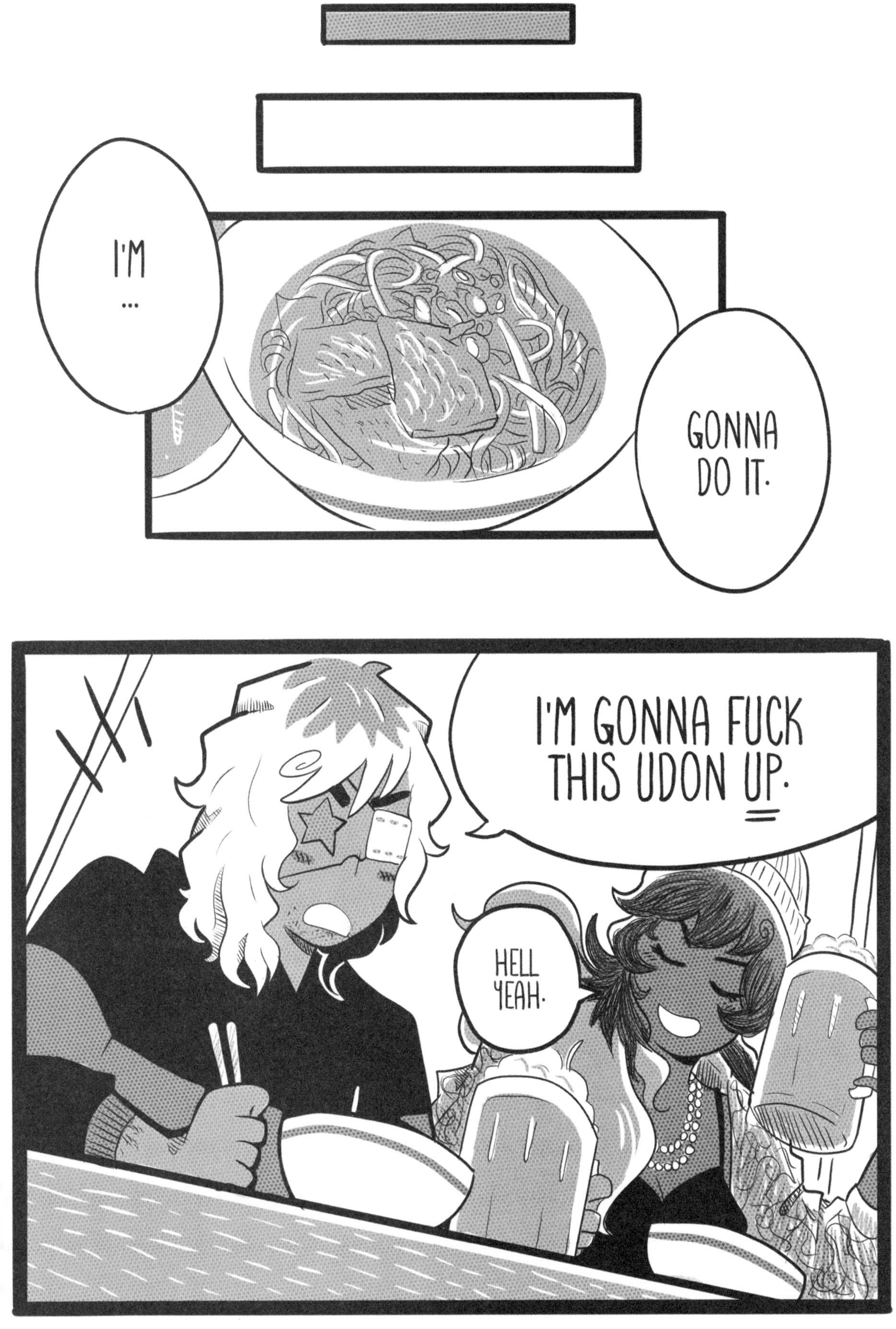
I'M
...
GONNA DO IT.
I'M GONNA FUCK THIS UDON UP.
HELL YEAH.

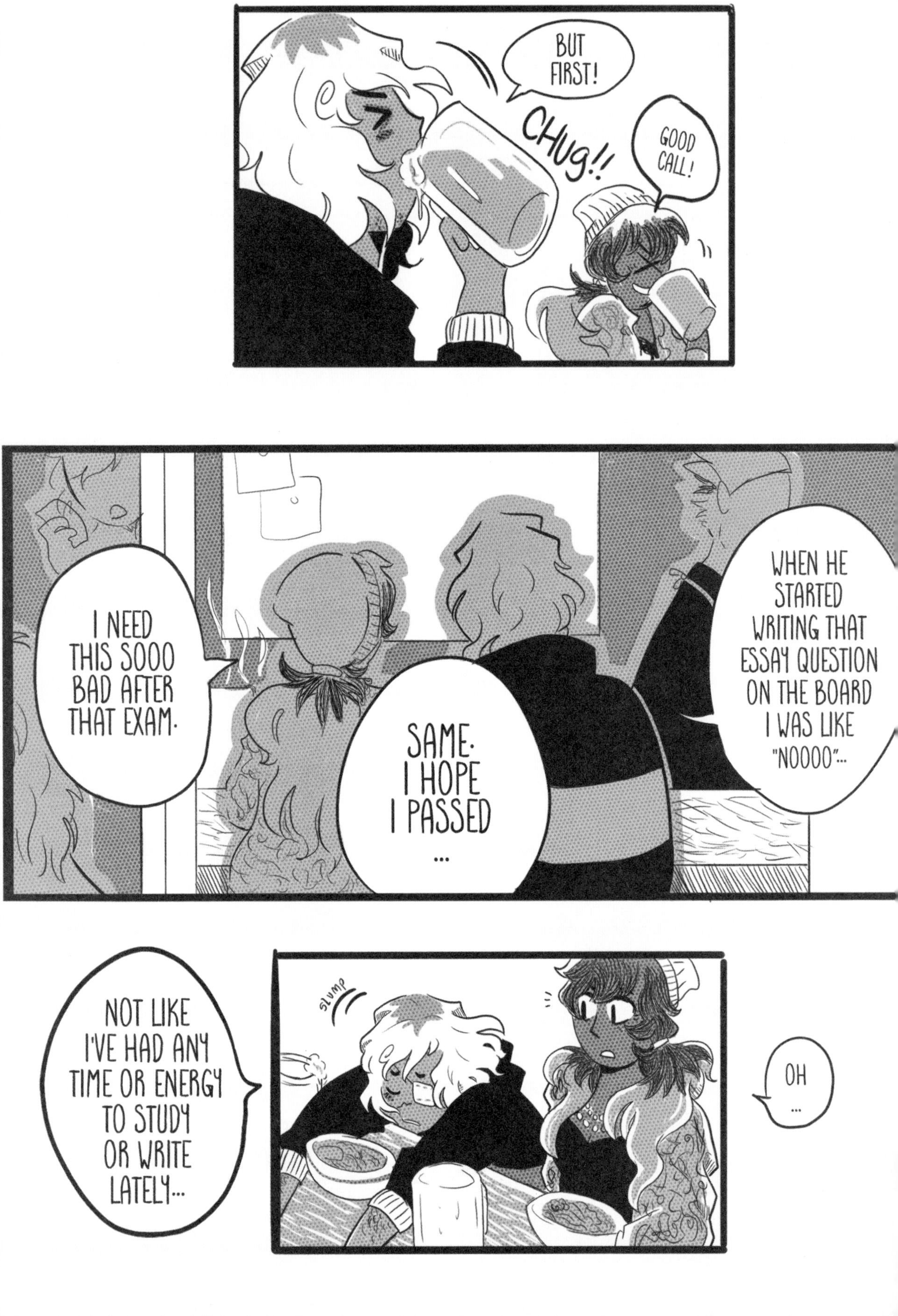
BUT FIRST!
CHUG!!
GOOD CALL!
I NEED THIS SOOO BAD AFTER THAT EXAM.
SAME. I HOPE I PASSED ...
WHEN HE STARTED WRITING THAT ESSAY QUESTION ON THE BOARD I WAS LIKE "NOOOO"...
SLUMP
NOT LIKE I'VE HAD ANY TIME OR ENERGY TO STUDY OR WRITE LATELY...
OH ...

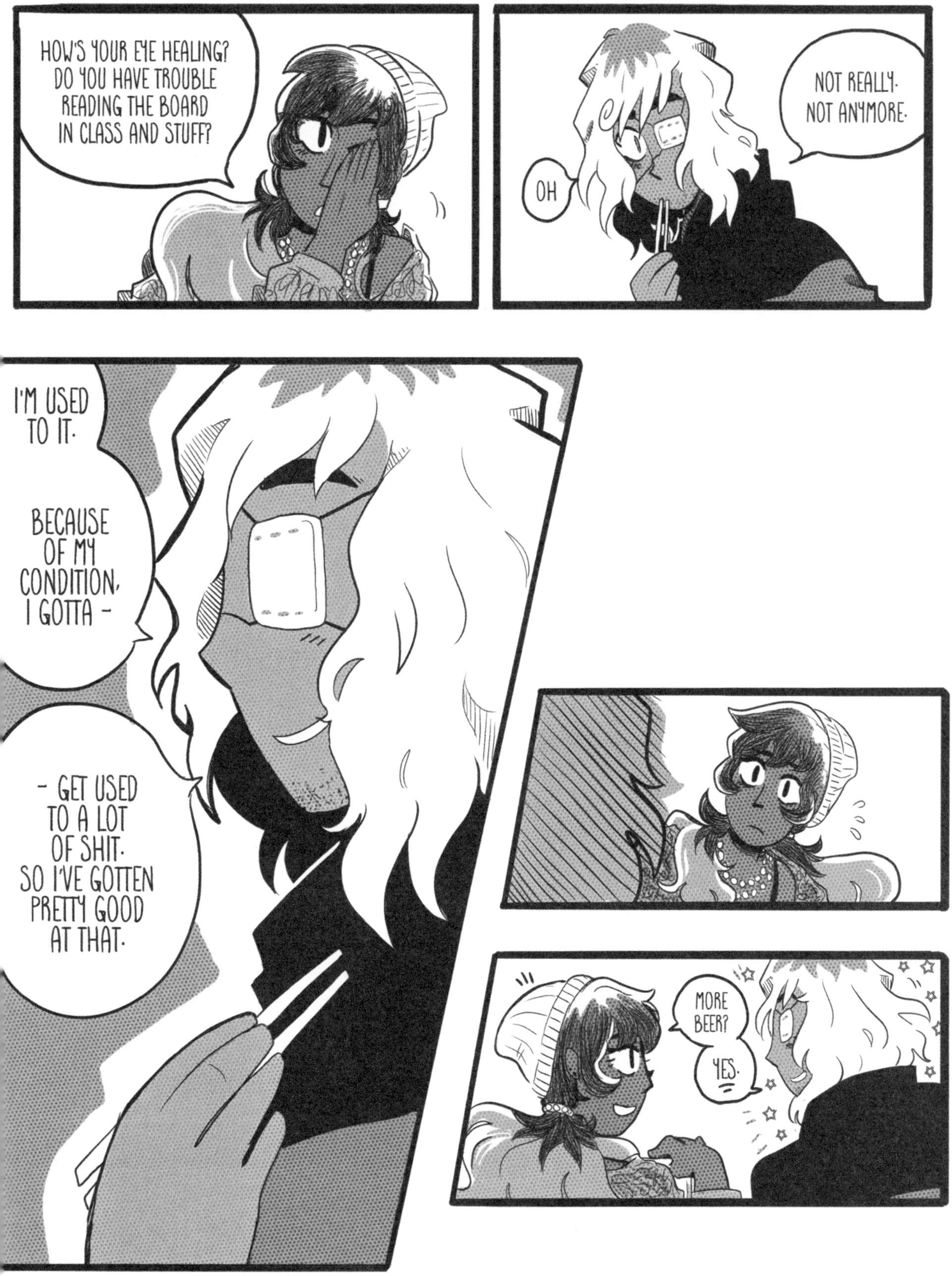

HOW'S YOUR EYE HEALING? DO YOU HAVE TROUBLE READING THE BOARD IN CLASS AND STUFF?
OH
NOT REALLY. NOT ANYMORE.
I'M USED TO IT.
BECAUSE OF MY CONDITION, I GOTTA -
- GET USED TO A LOT OF SHIT. SO I'VE GOTTEN PRETTY GOOD AT THAT.
MORE BEER?
YES.

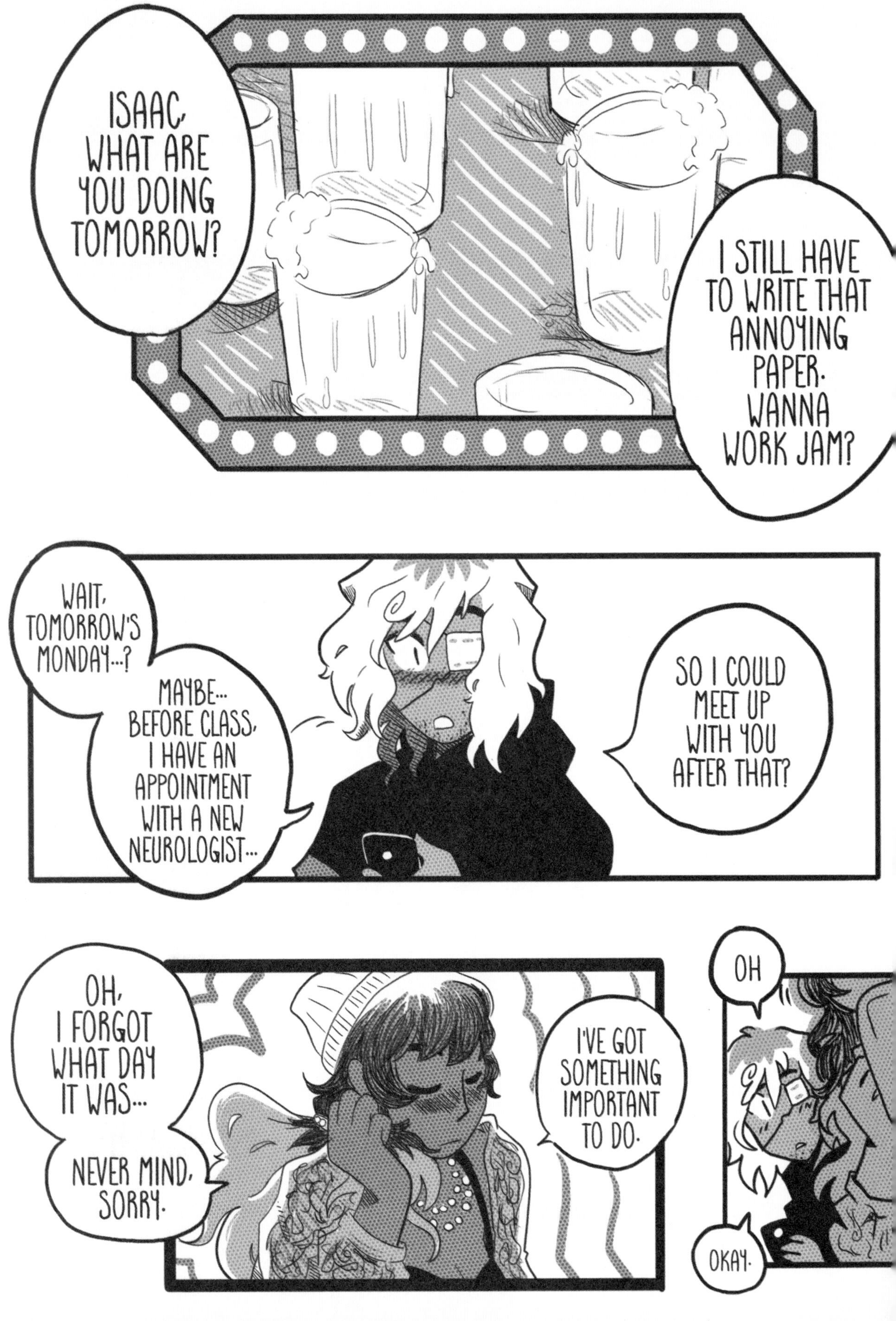
ISAAC, WHAT ARE YOU DOING TOMORROW?
I STILL HAVE TO WRITE THAT ANNOYING PAPER. WANNA WORK JAM?
WAIT, TOMORROW'S MONDAY...?
MAYBE... BEFORE CLASS, I HAVE AN APPOINTMENT WITH A NEW NEUROLOGIST...
SO I COULD MEET UP WITH YOU AFTER THAT?
OH, I FORGOT WHAT DAY IT WAS...
NEVER MIND, SORRY.
I'VE GOT SOMETHING IMPORTANT TO DO.
OH
OKAY.

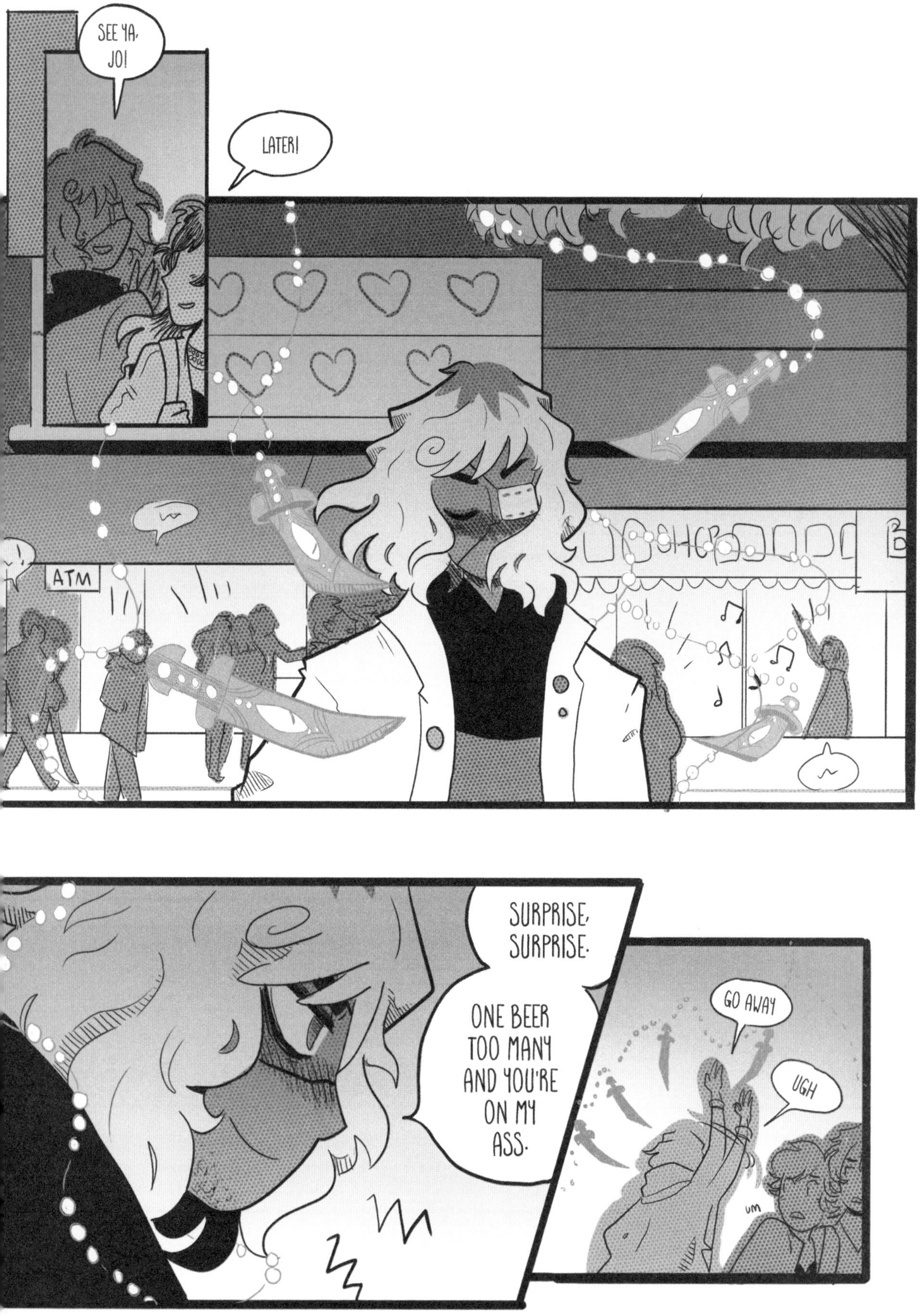
SEE YA, JO!
LATER!
ATM
SURPRISE, SURPRISE.
ONE BEER TOO MANY AND YOU'RE ON MY ASS.
GO AWAY
UGH
UM

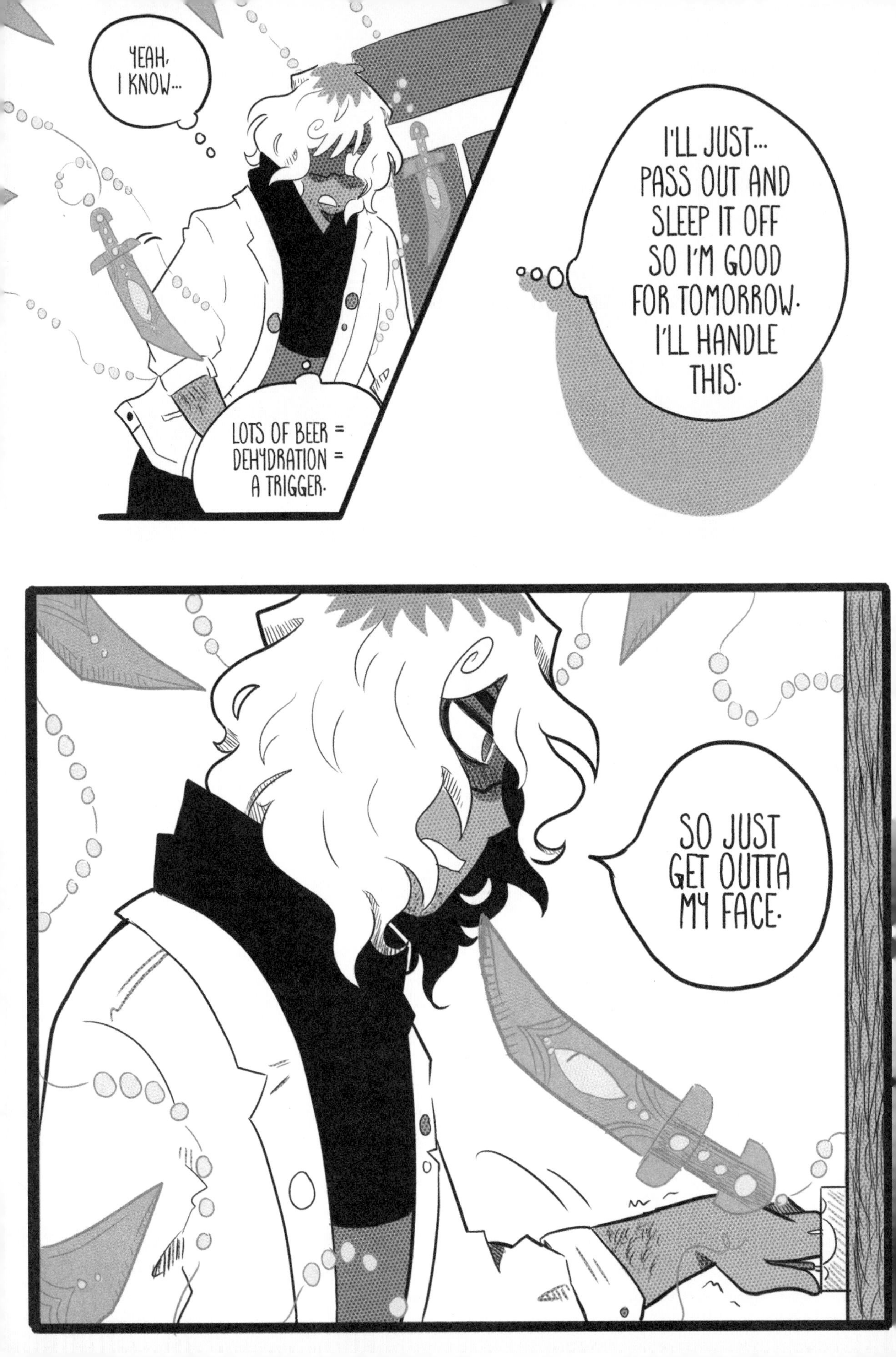
YEAH, I KNOW...
LOTS OF BEER = DEHYDRATION = A TRIGGER.
I'LL JUST... PASS OUT AND SLEEP IT OFF SO I'M GOOD FOR TOMORROW. I'LL HANDLE THIS.
SO JUST GET OUTTA MY FACE.

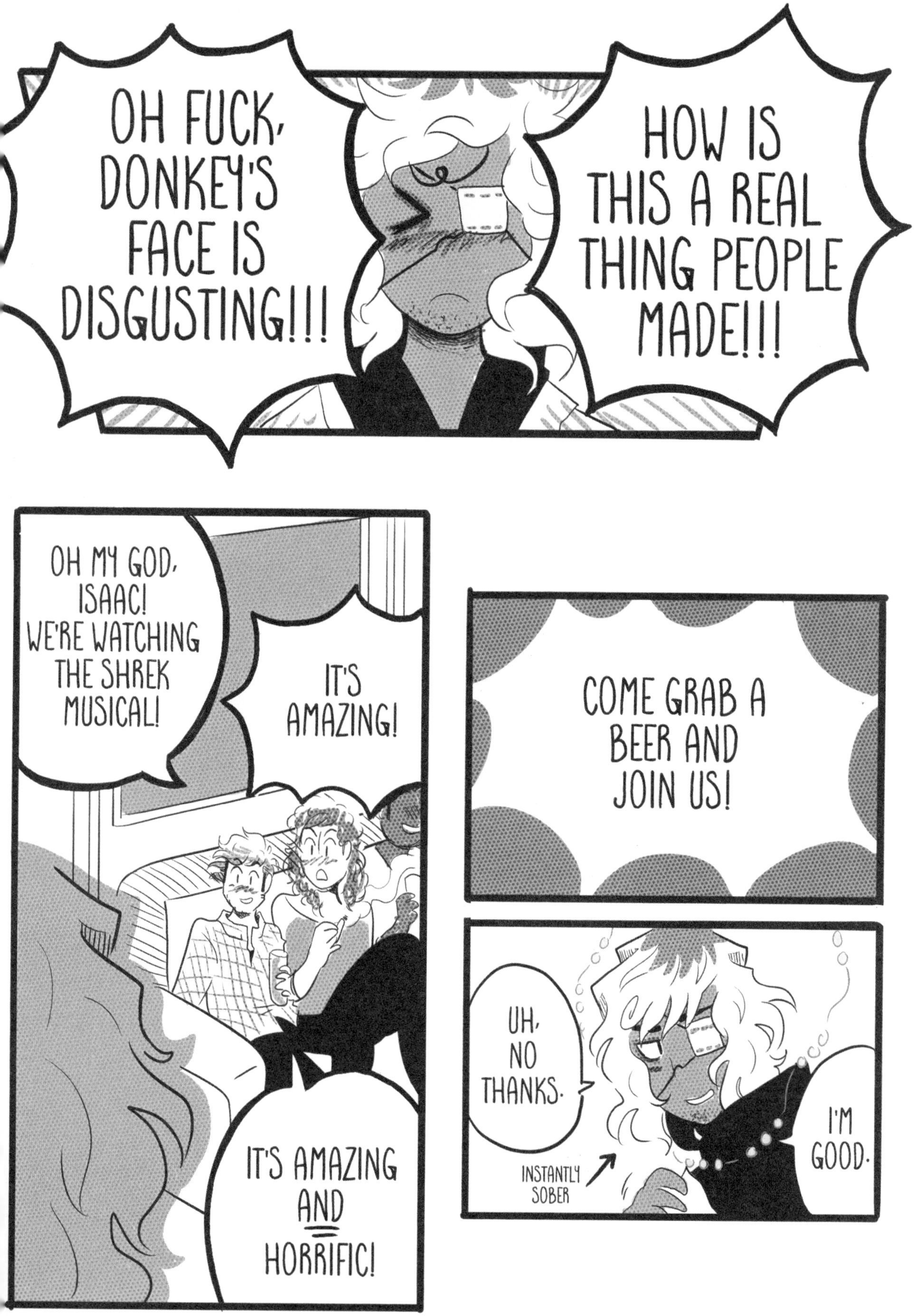
OH FUCK, DONKEY'S FACE IS DISGUSTING!!!
HOW IS THIS A REAL THING PEOPLE MADE!!!
OH MY GOD, ISAAC! WE'RE WATCHING THE SHREK MUSICAL!
IT'S AMAZING!
IT'S AMAZING AND HORRIFIC!
COME GRAB A BEER AND JOIN US!
UH, NO THANKS.
I'M GOOD.
INSTANTLY SOBER

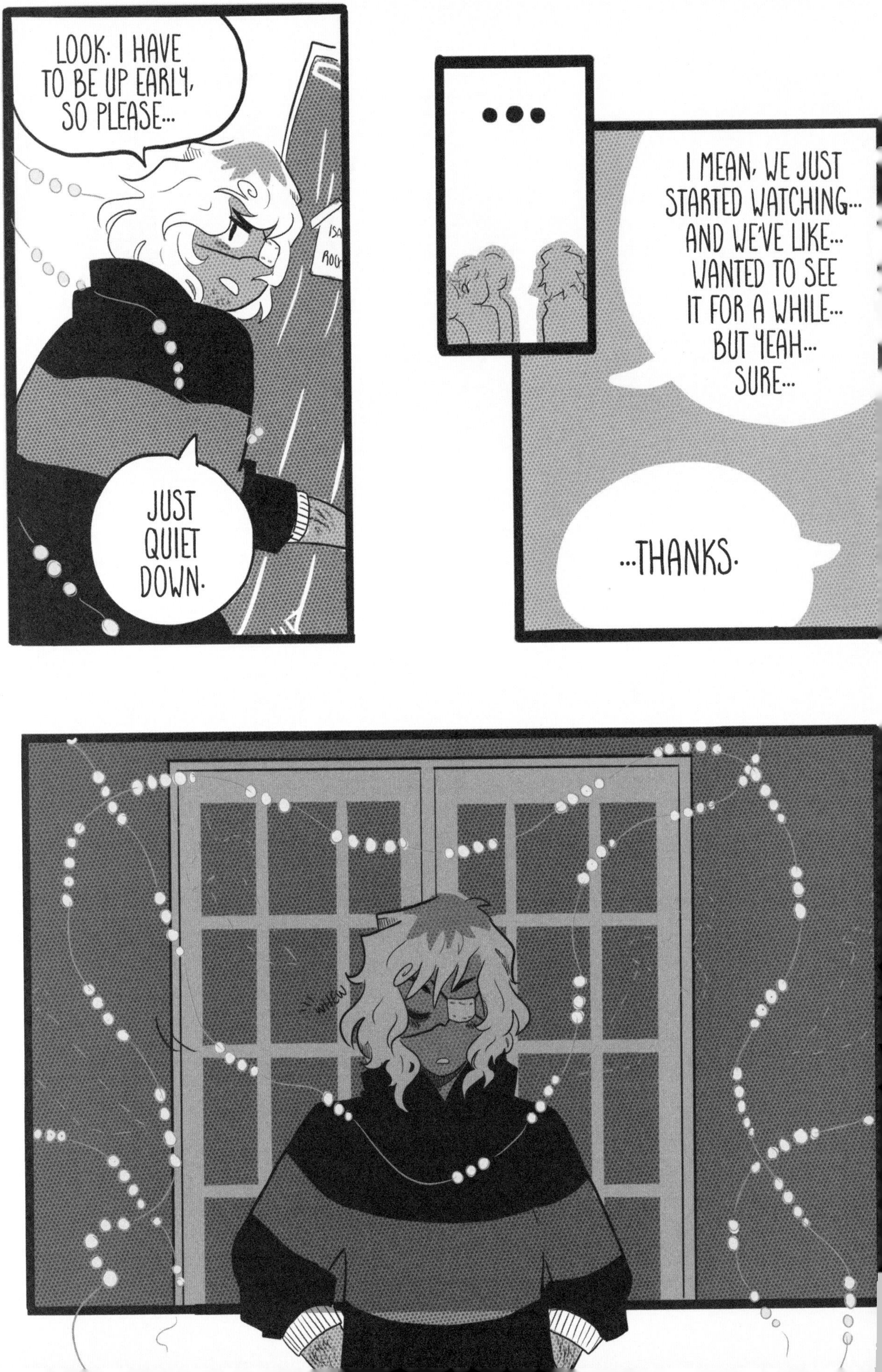
LOOK. I HAVE TO BE UP EARLY, SO PLEASE...
JUST QUIET DOWN.
...
I MEAN, WE JUST STARTED WATCHING... AND WE'VE LIKE... WANTED TO SEE IT FOR A WHILE... BUT YEAH... SURE...
...THANKS.
WHEW

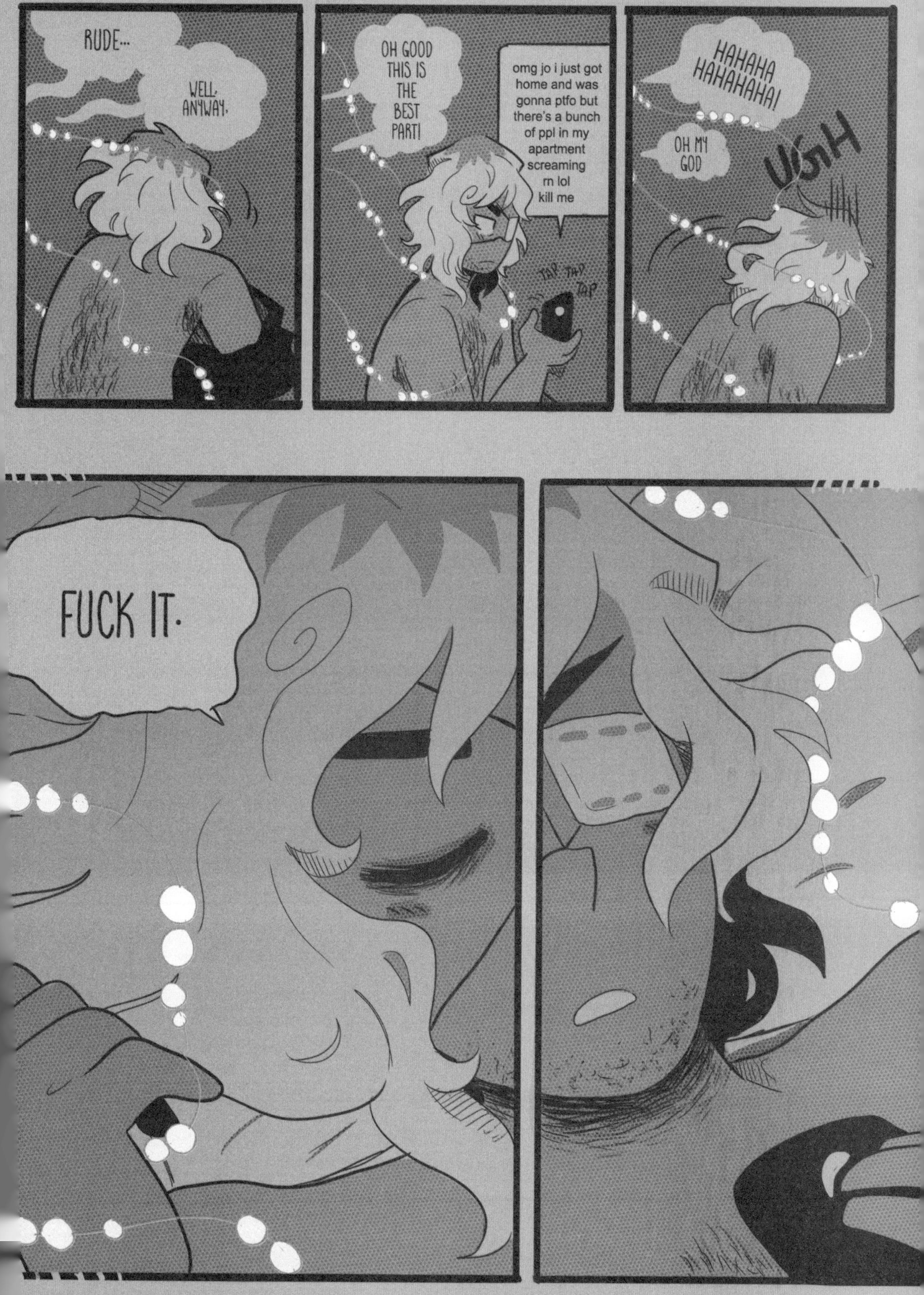
RUDE...
WELL, ANYWAY,
OH GOOD THIS IS THE BEST PART!
omg jo i just got home and was gonna ptfo but there's a bunch of ppl in my apartment screaming rn lol kill me
TAP TAP TAP
HAHAHA HAHAHAHA!
OH MY GOD
UGH
FUCK IT.

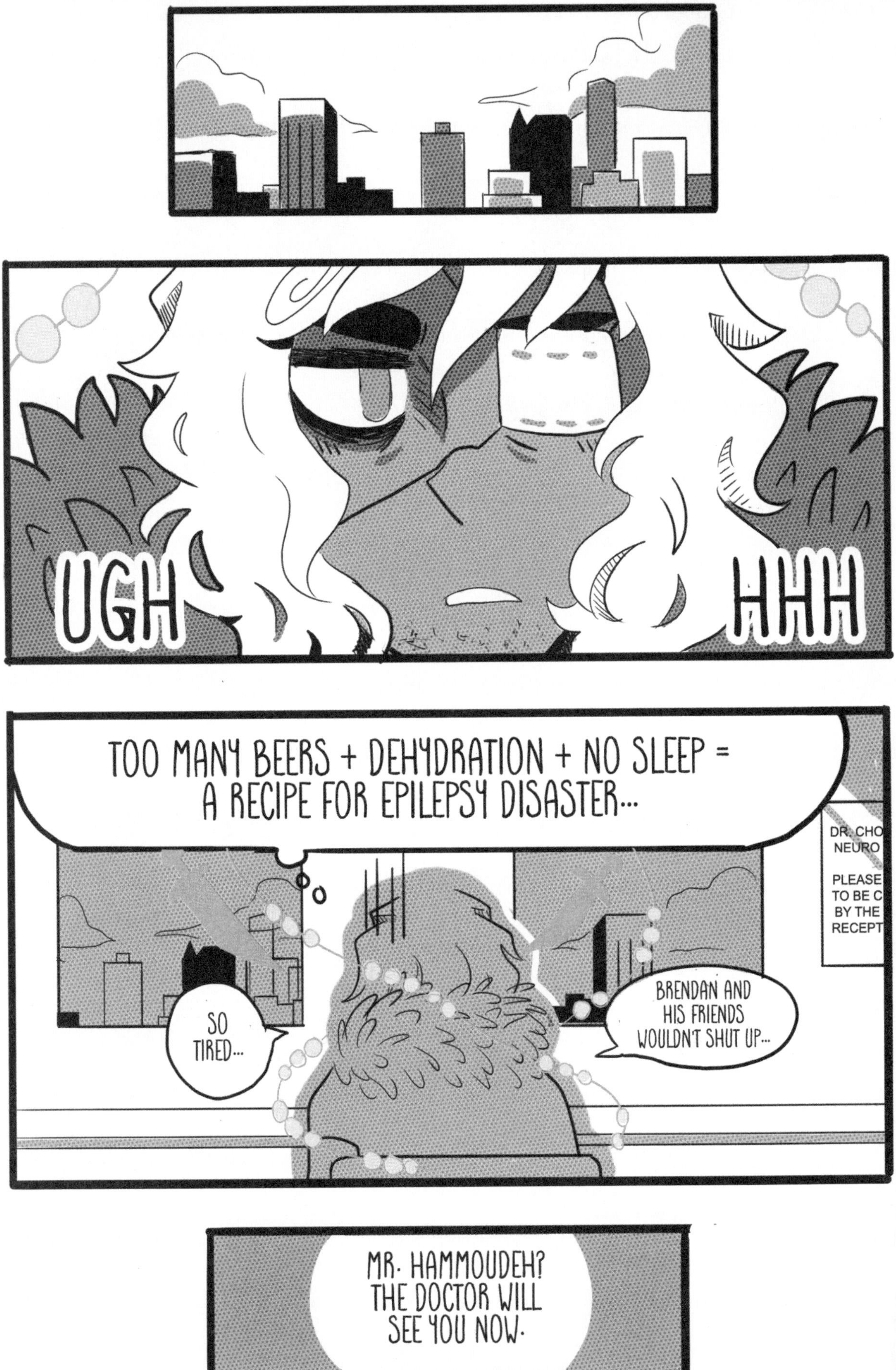
UGH
HHH
TOO MANY BEERS + DEHYDRATION + NO SLEEP = A RECIPE FOR EPILEPSY DISASTER...
DR. CHO
NEURO
PLEASE
TO BE C
BY THE
RECEPT
SO TIRED...
BRENDAN AND HIS FRIENDS WOULDN'T SHUT UP...
MR. HAMMOUDEH? THE DOCTOR WILL SEE YOU NOW.

WOW, IT LOOKS LIKE YOU'VE HAD A REALLY HARD TIME WITH ALL THIS.

THANK YOU FOR COMING TO ME.

SEEMS LIKE YOUR LAST NEURO—

—WAS A HUGE ASSHOLE.

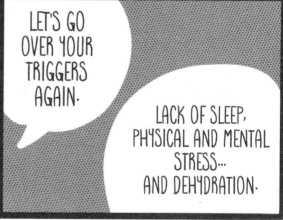

LET'S GO OVER YOUR TRIGGERS AGAIN.

LACK OF SLEEP, PHYSICAL AND MENTAL STRESS... AND DEHYDRATION.

WELL, I DON'T REALLY CONSIDER DEHYDRATION TO BE A REAL TRIGGER...

HEARD THAT ONE BEFORE...

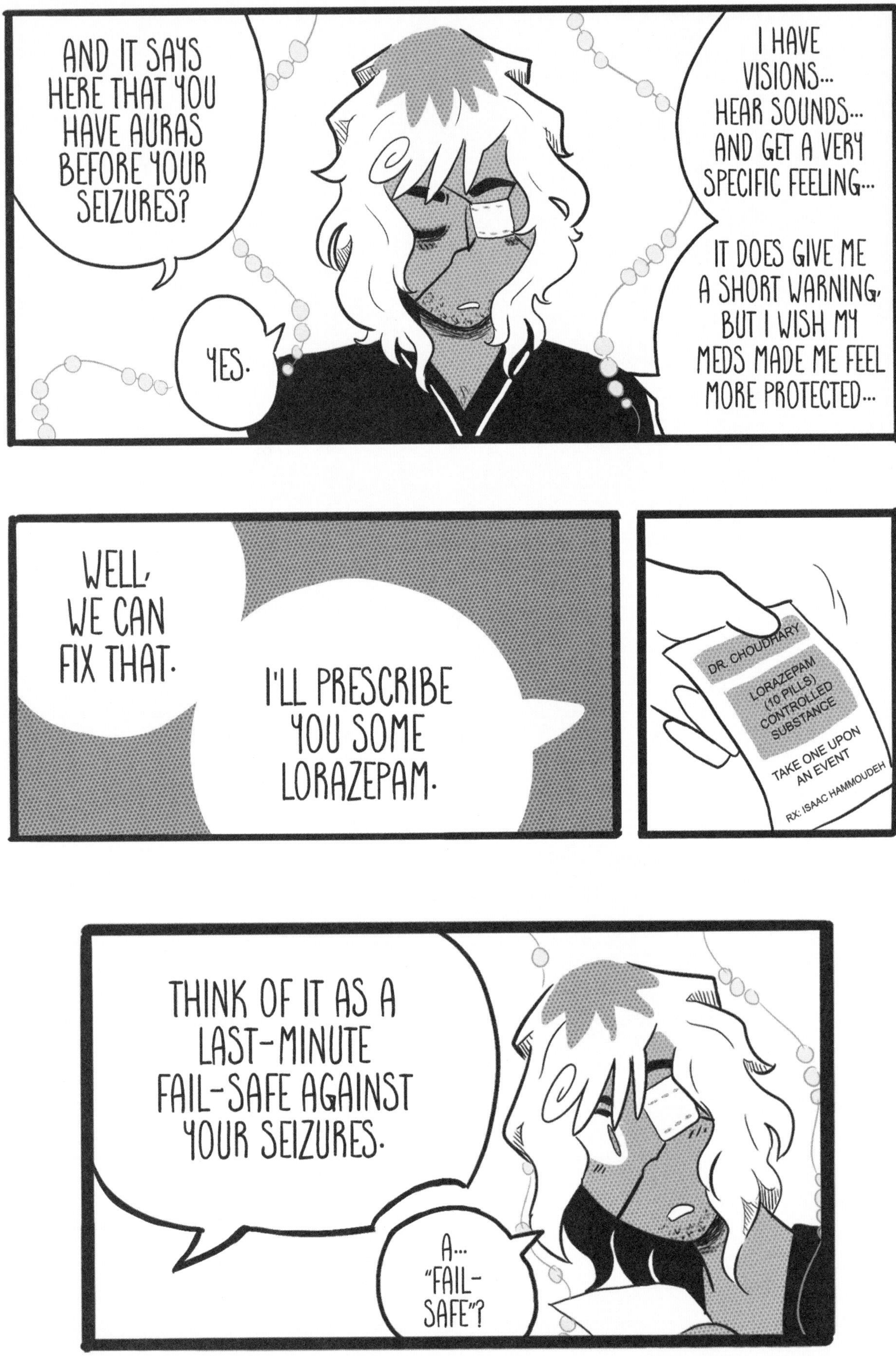
AND IT SAYS HERE THAT YOU HAVE AURAS BEFORE YOUR SEIZURES?
YES.
I HAVE VISIONS... HEAR SOUNDS... AND GET A VERY SPECIFIC FEELING...
IT DOES GIVE ME A SHORT WARNING, BUT I WISH MY MEDS MADE ME FEEL MORE PROTECTED...
WELL, WE CAN FIX THAT.
I'LL PRESCRIBE YOU SOME LORAZEPAM.
DR. CHOUDHARY
LORAZEPAM (10 PILLS) CONTROLLED SUBSTANCE
TAKE ONE UPON AN EVENT
RX: ISAAC HAMMOUDEH
THINK OF IT AS A LAST-MINUTE FAIL-SAFE AGAINST YOUR SEIZURES.
A... "FAIL-SAFE"?

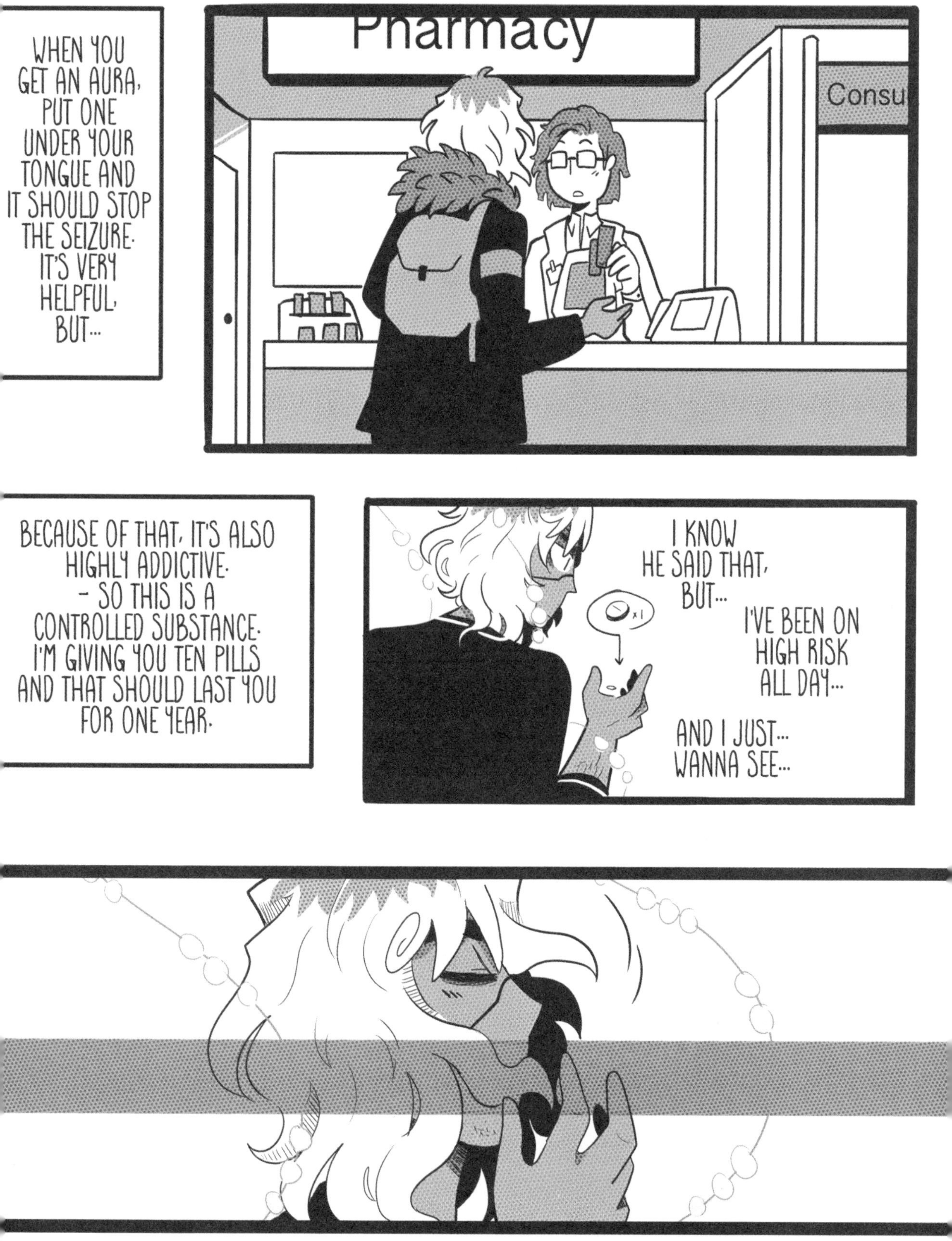
WHEN YOU GET AN AURA, PUT ONE UNDER YOUR TONGUE AND IT SHOULD STOP THE SEIZURE. IT'S VERY HELPFUL, BUT...
Pharmacy
Consu
BECAUSE OF THAT, IT'S ALSO HIGHLY ADDICTIVE. – SO THIS IS A CONTROLLED SUBSTANCE. I'M GIVING YOU TEN PILLS AND THAT SHOULD LAST YOU FOR ONE YEAR.
I KNOW HE SAID THAT, BUT...
I'VE BEEN ON HIGH RISK ALL DAY...
AND I JUST... WANNA SEE...

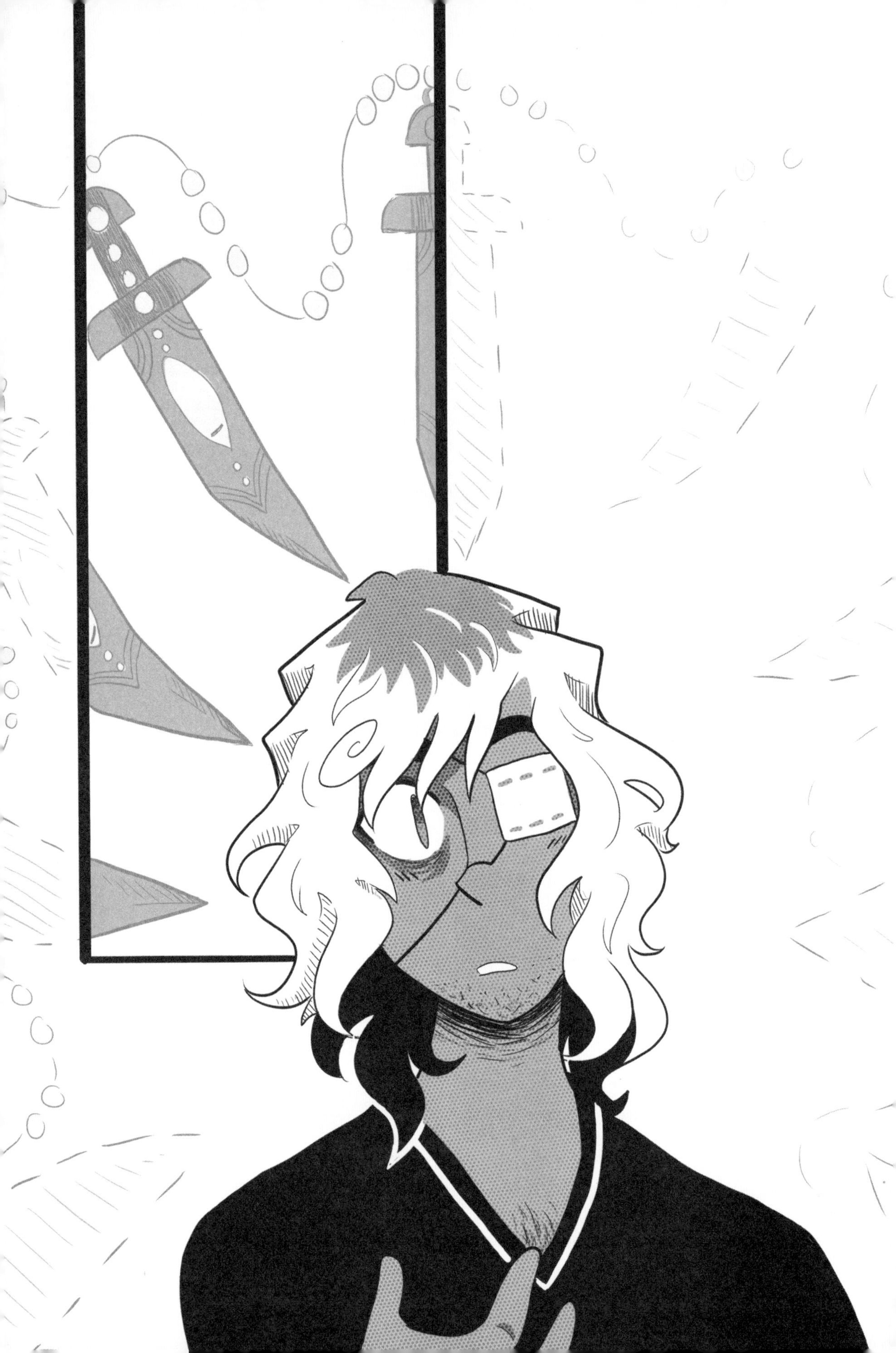

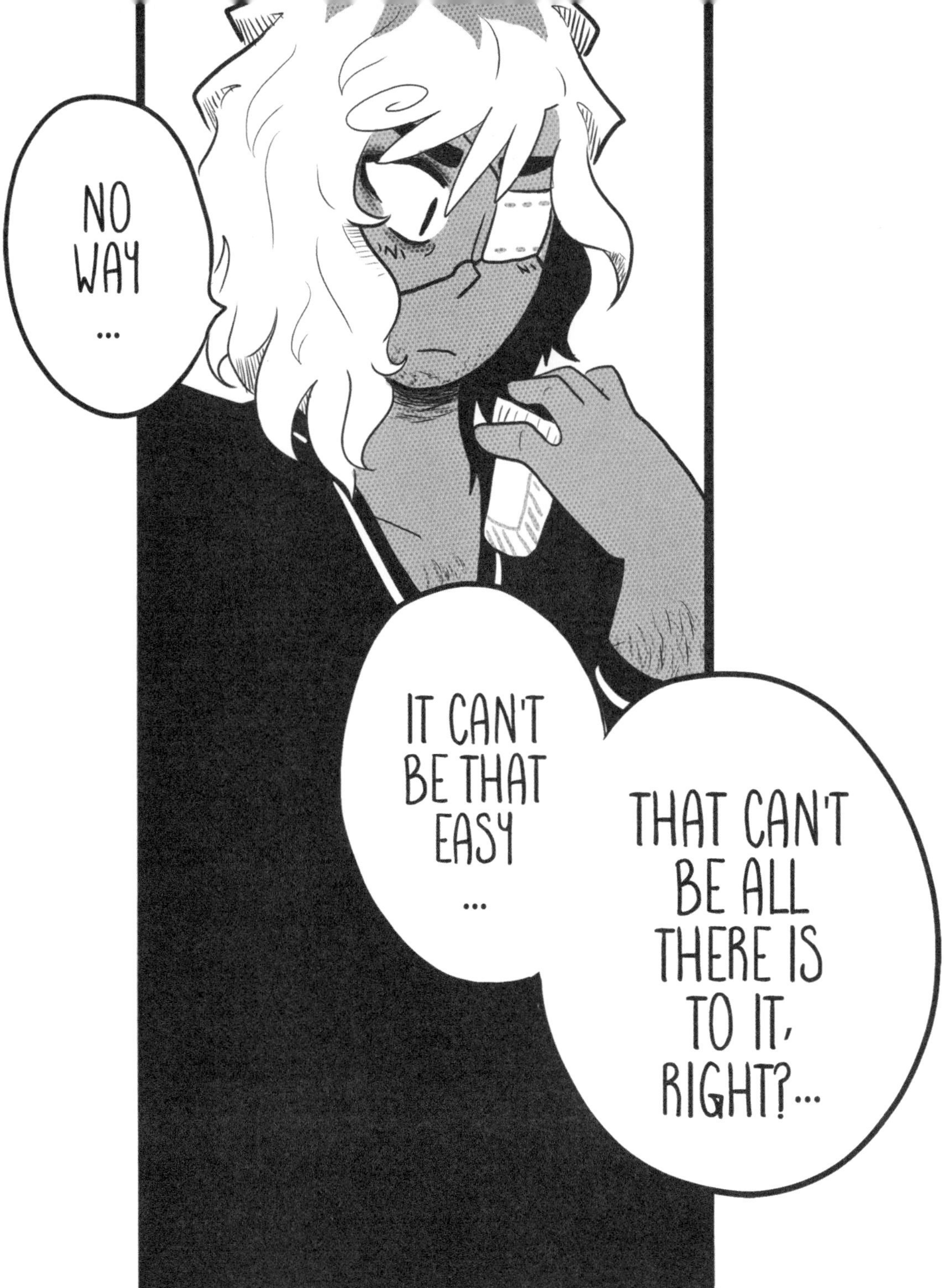
NO WAY ...
IT CAN'T BE THAT EASY ...
THAT CAN'T BE ALL THERE IS TO IT, RIGHT?...

[redacted]

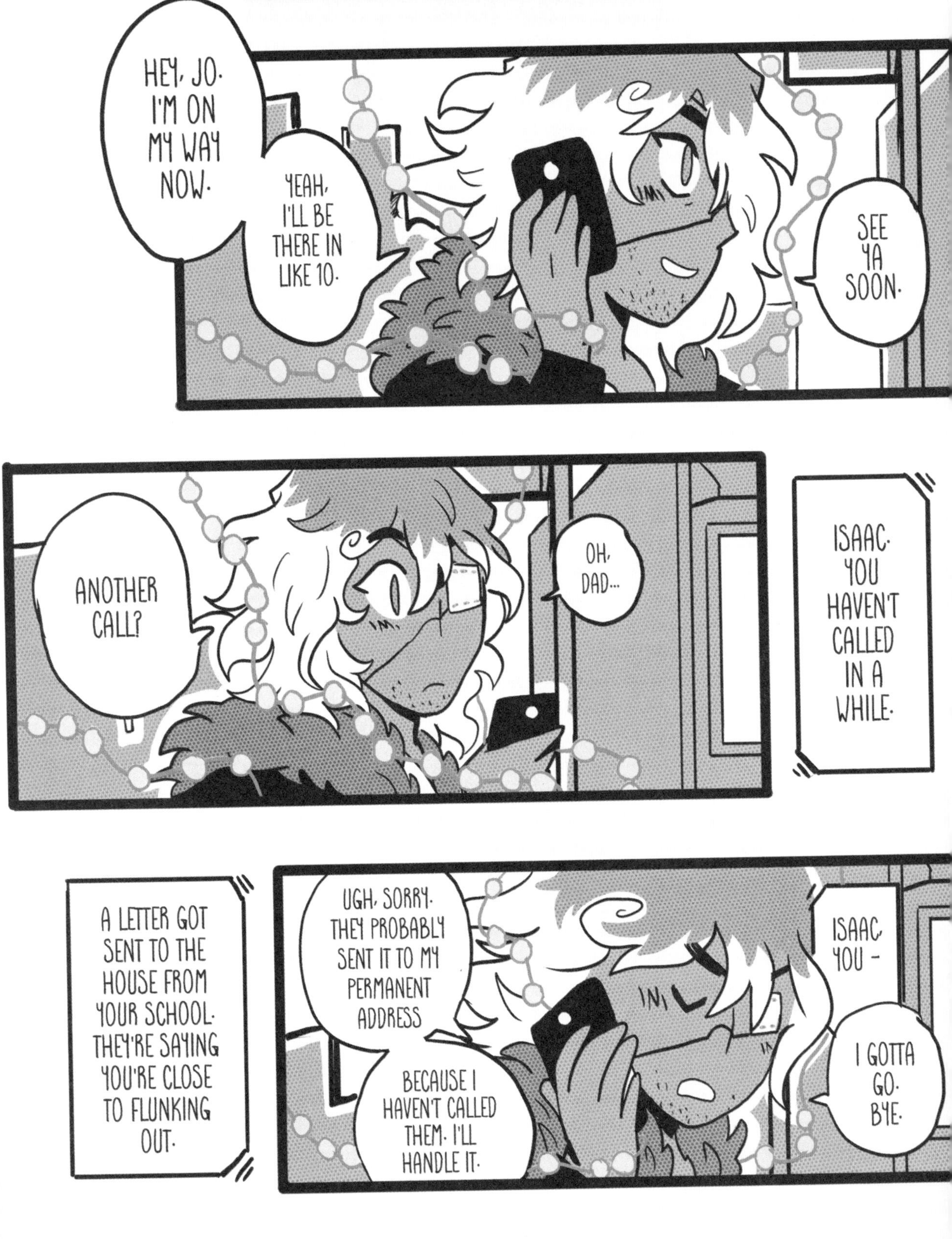

HEY, JO. I'M ON MY WAY NOW.
YEAH, I'LL BE THERE IN LIKE 10.
SEE YA SOON.
ANOTHER CALL?
OH, DAD...
ISAAC. YOU HAVEN'T CALLED IN A WHILE.
A LETTER GOT SENT TO THE HOUSE FROM YOUR SCHOOL. THEY'RE SAYING YOU'RE CLOSE TO FLUNKING OUT.
UGH, SORRY. THEY PROBABLY SENT IT TO MY PERMANENT ADDRESS
BECAUSE I HAVEN'T CALLED THEM. I'LL HANDLE IT.
ISAAC, YOU -
I GOTTA GO. BYE.

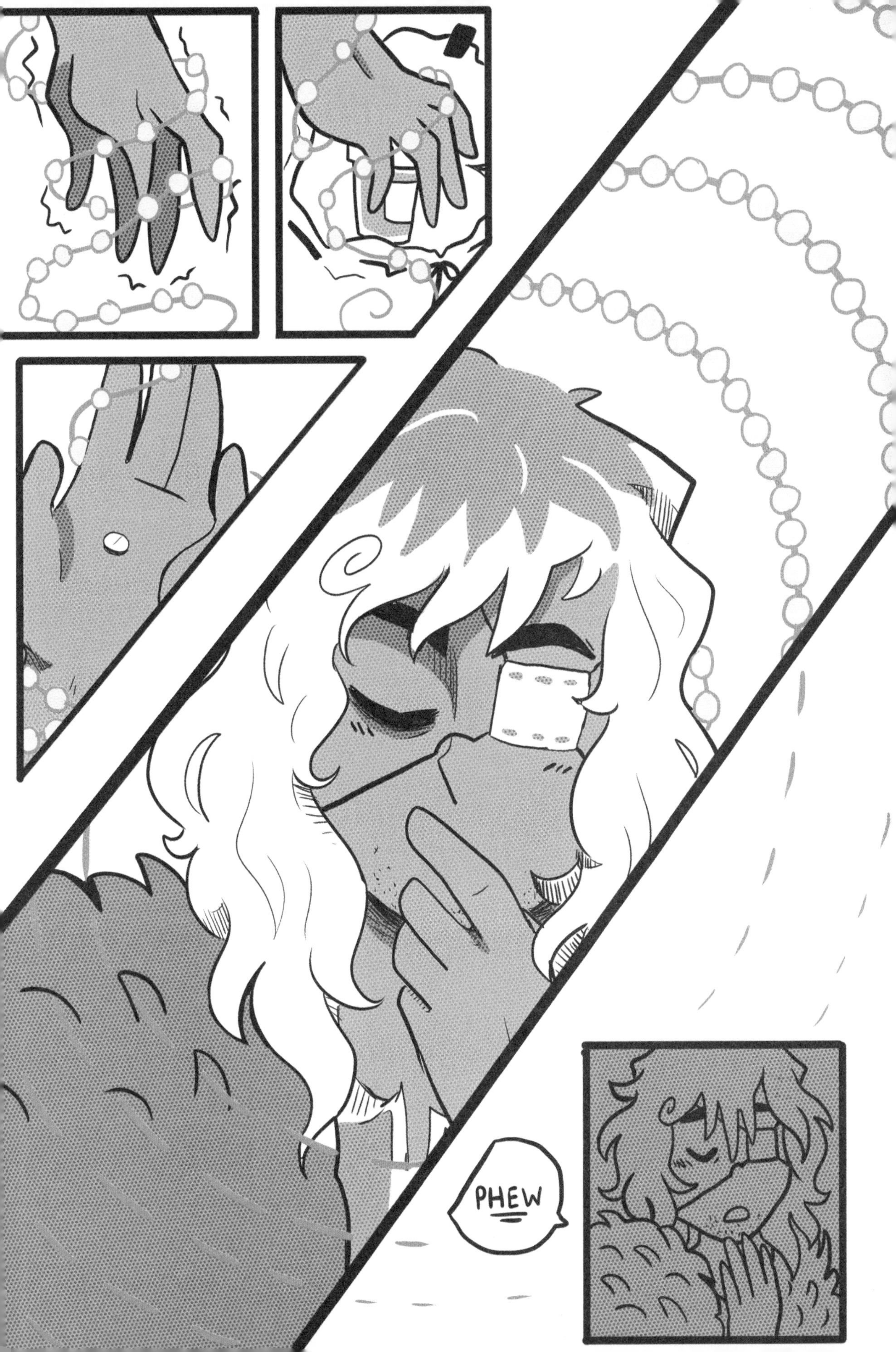
PHEW

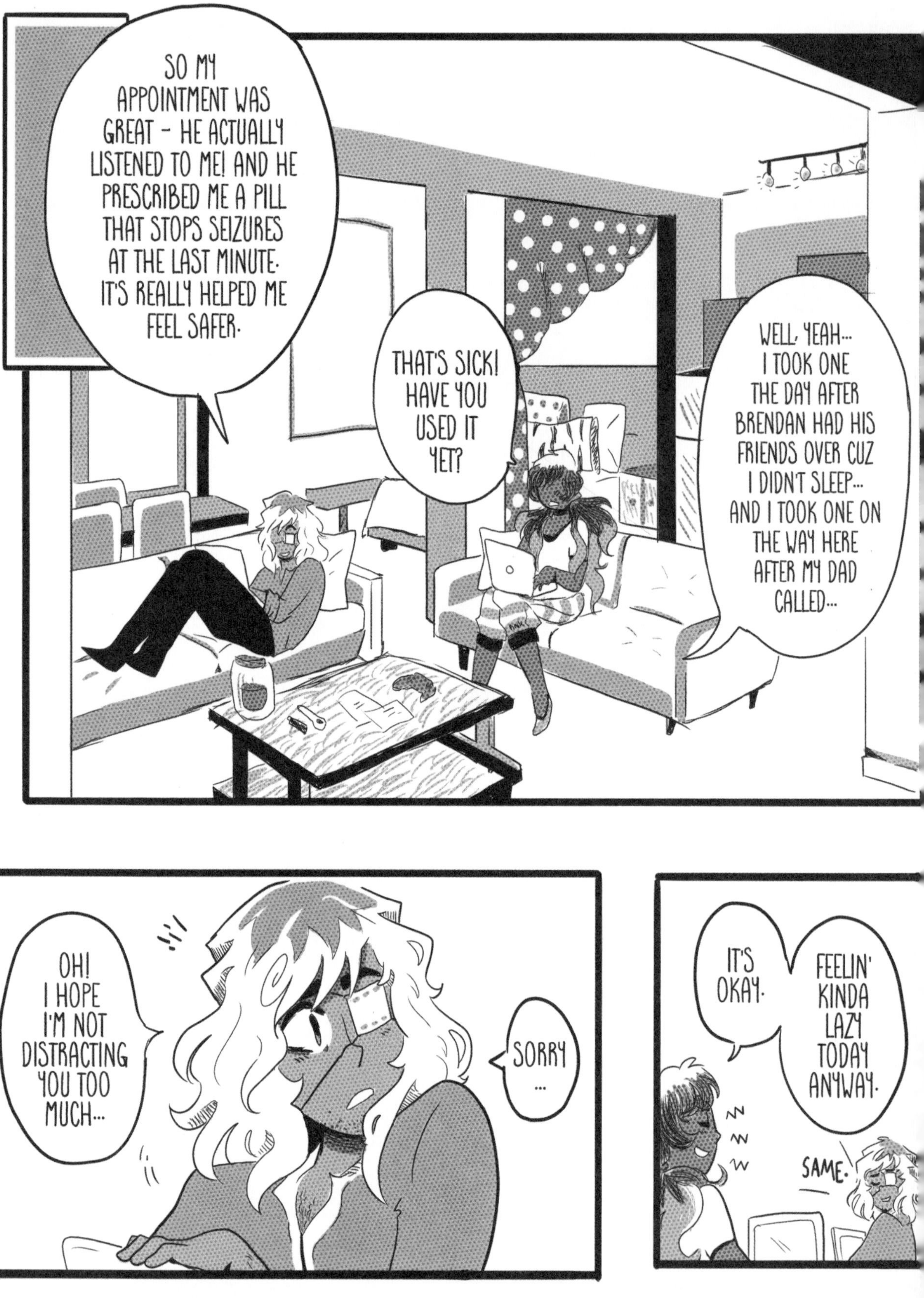
SO MY APPOINTMENT WAS GREAT - HE ACTUALLY LISTENED TO ME! AND HE PRESCRIBED ME A PILL THAT STOPS SEIZURES AT THE LAST MINUTE. IT'S REALLY HELPED ME FEEL SAFER.
THAT'S SICK! HAVE YOU USED IT YET?
WELL, YEAH... I TOOK ONE THE DAY AFTER BRENDAN HAD HIS FRIENDS OVER CUZ I DIDN'T SLEEP... AND I TOOK ONE ON THE WAY HERE AFTER MY DAD CALLED...
OH! I HOPE I'M NOT DISTRACTING YOU TOO MUCH...
SORRY...
IT'S OKAY.
FEELIN' KINDA LAZY TODAY ANYWAY.
SAME.

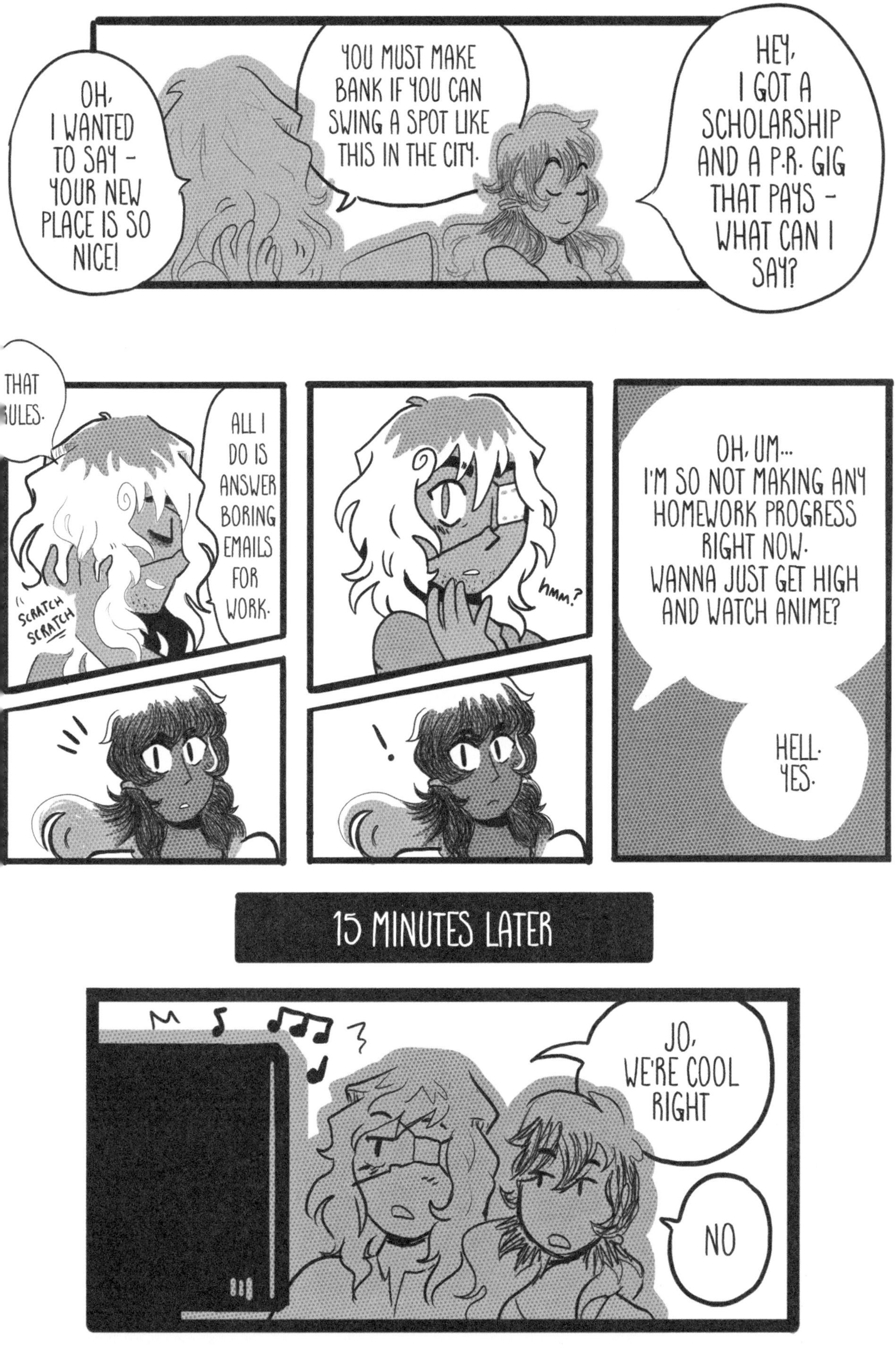
OH, I WANTED TO SAY - YOUR NEW PLACE IS SO NICE!
YOU MUST MAKE BANK IF YOU CAN SWING A SPOT LIKE THIS IN THE CITY.
HEY, I GOT A SCHOLARSHIP AND A P.R. GIG THAT PAYS - WHAT CAN I SAY?
THAT
ULES.
ALL I DO IS ANSWER BORING EMAILS FOR WORK.
SCRATCH SCRATCH
hmm?
!
OH, UM... I'M SO NOT MAKING ANY HOMEWORK PROGRESS RIGHT NOW. WANNA JUST GET HIGH AND WATCH ANIME?
HELL. YES.
15 MINUTES LATER
JO, WE'RE COOL RIGHT
NO

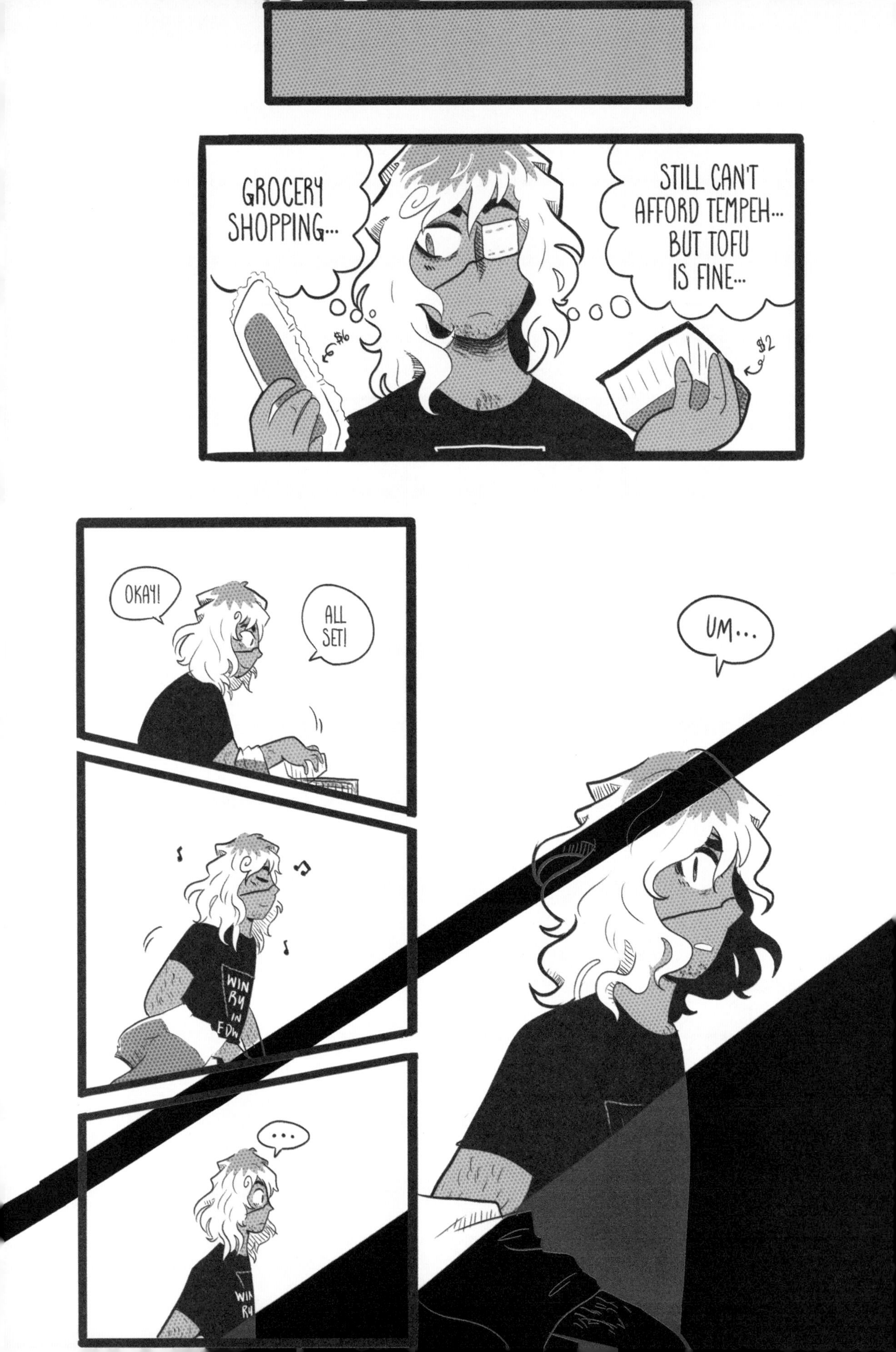
GROCERY SHOPPING...
$6
STILL CAN'T AFFORD TEMPEH... BUT TOFU IS FINE...
$2
OKAY!
ALL SET!
...
UM...

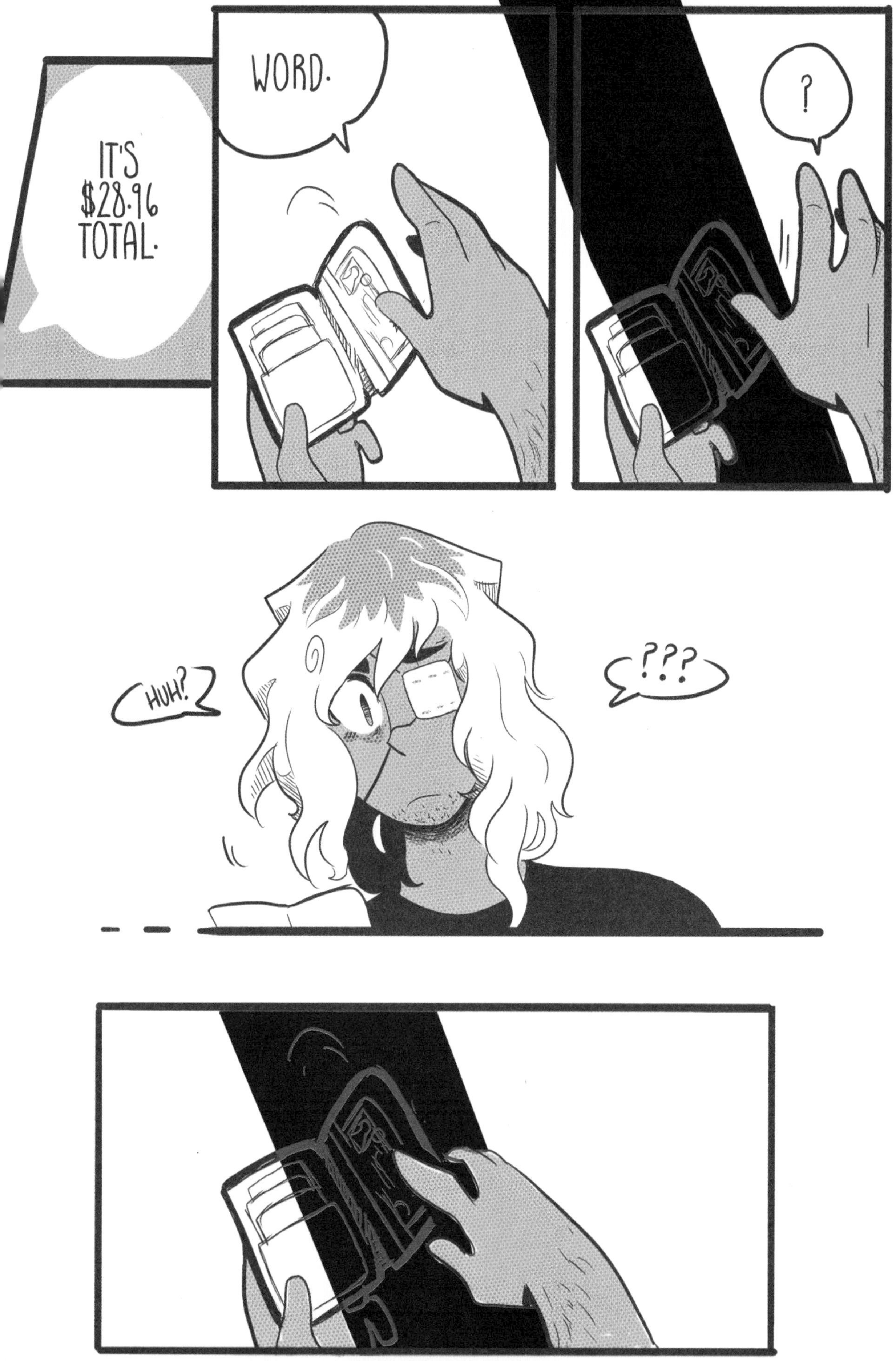
IT'S $28.96 TOTAL.
WORD.
?
HUH?
???

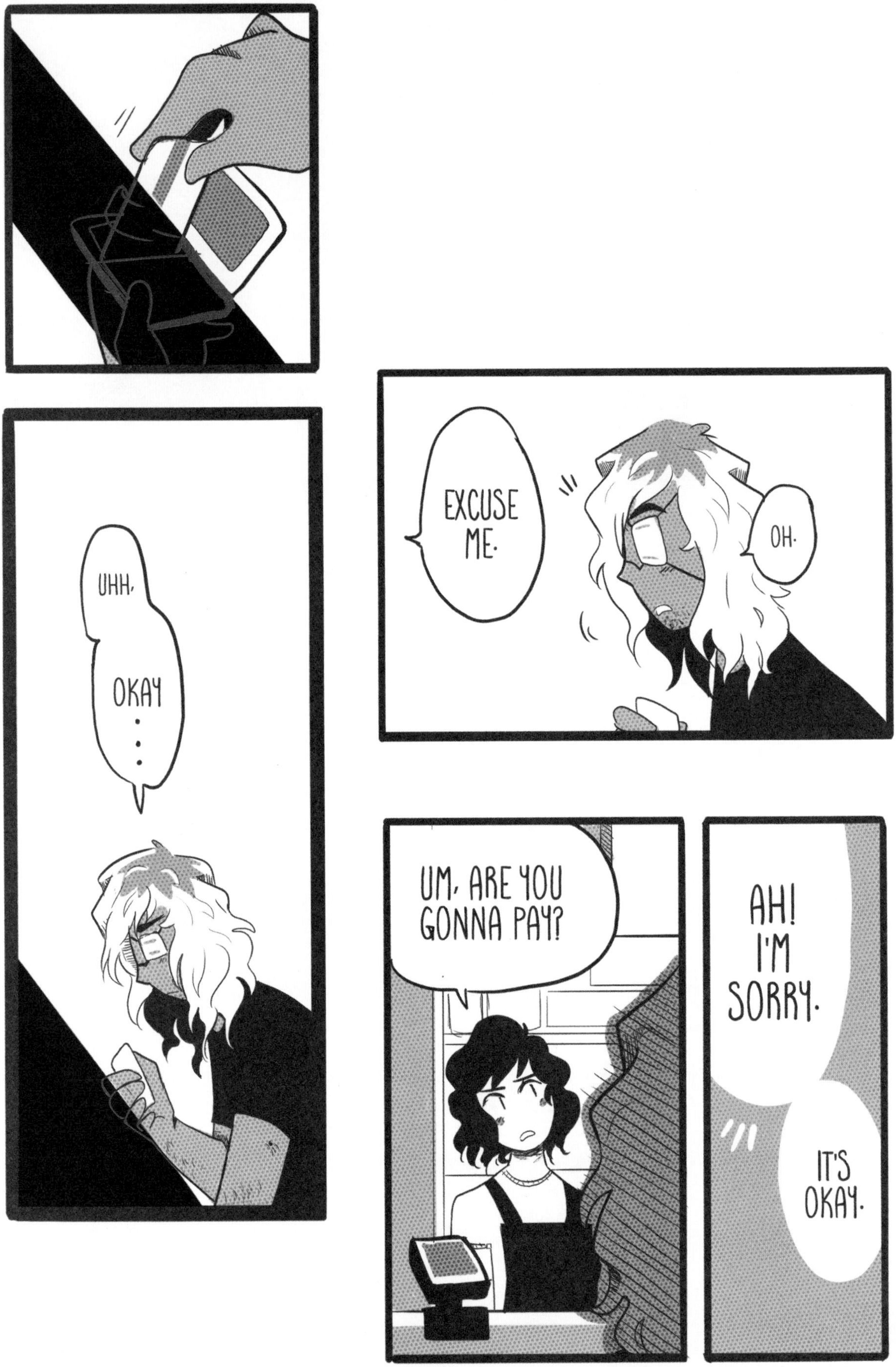
UHH,
OKAY....
EXCUSE ME.
OH.
UM, ARE YOU GONNA PAY?
AH! I'M SORRY.
IT'S OKAY.

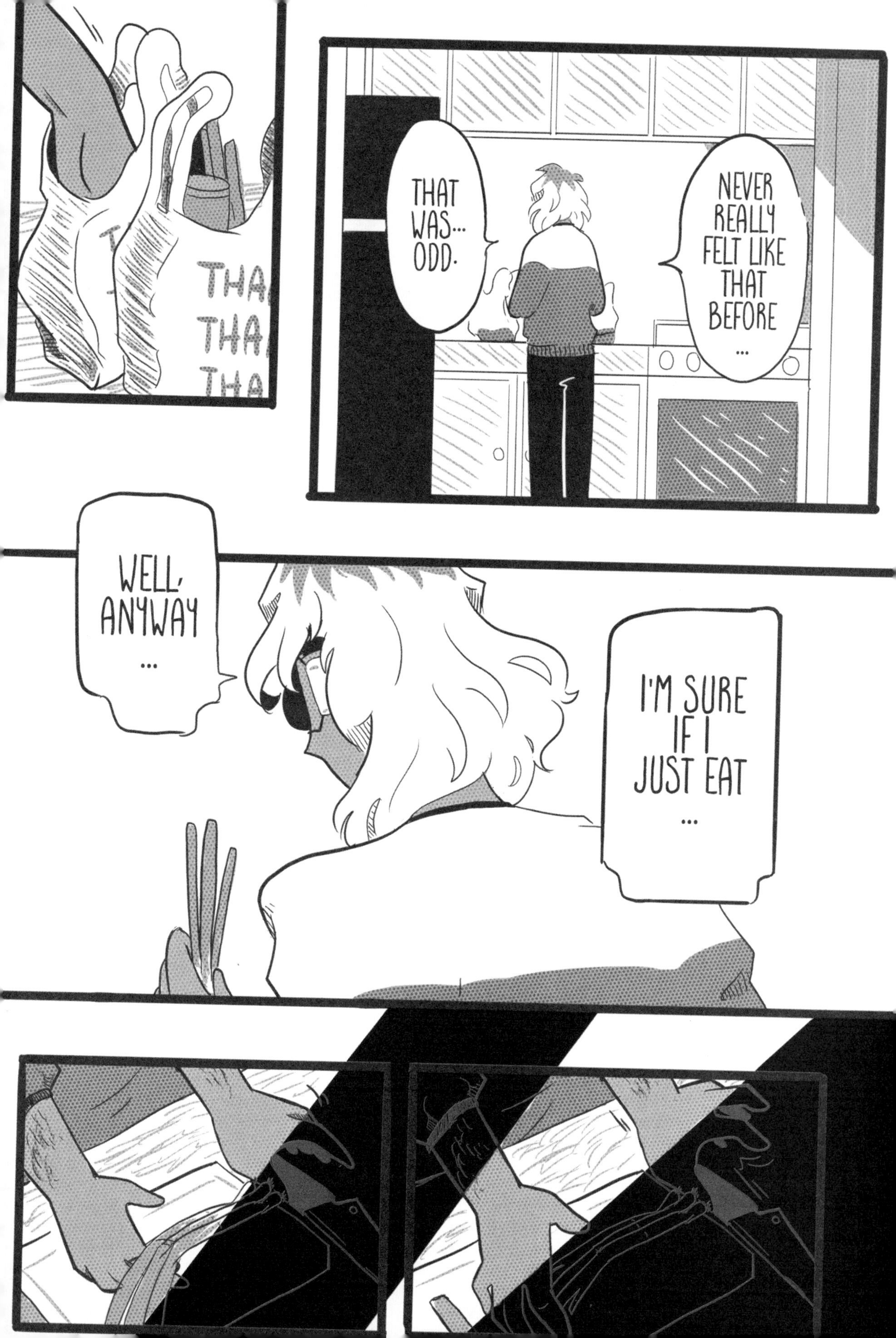
THAT WAS... ODD.
NEVER REALLY FELT LIKE THAT BEFORE ...
WELL, ANYWAY ...
I'M SURE IF I JUST EAT ...

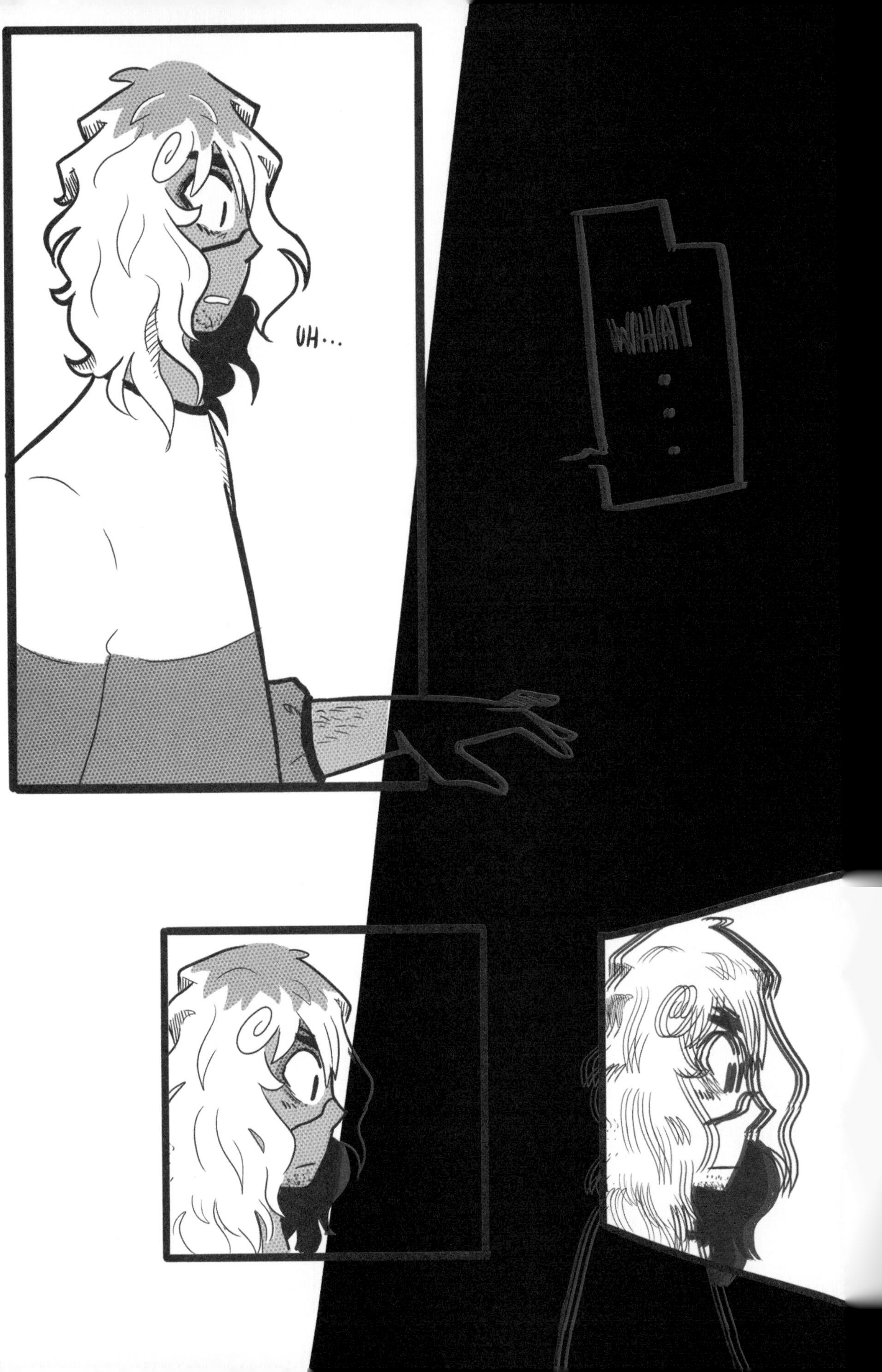
UH...
WHAT
...

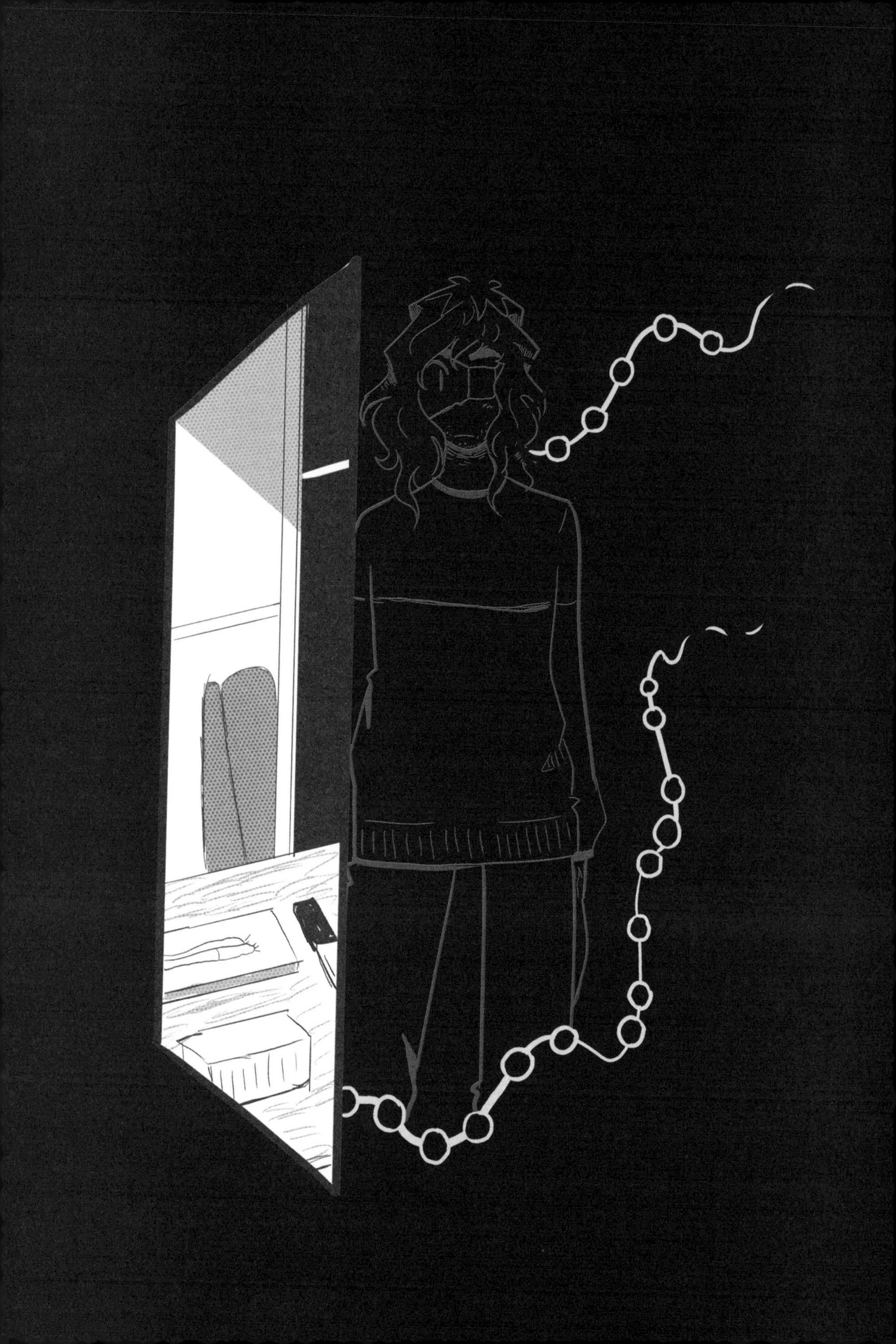

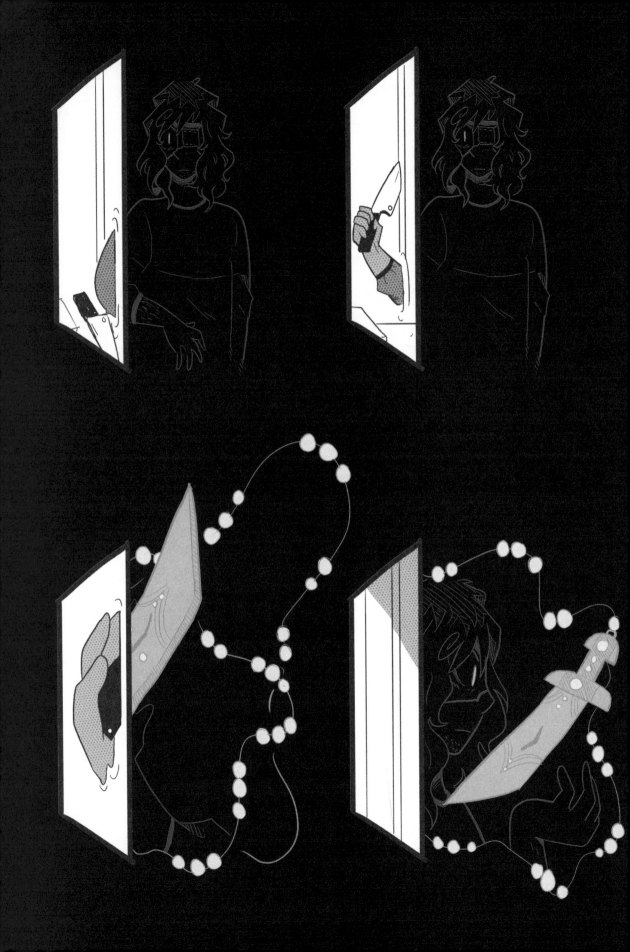

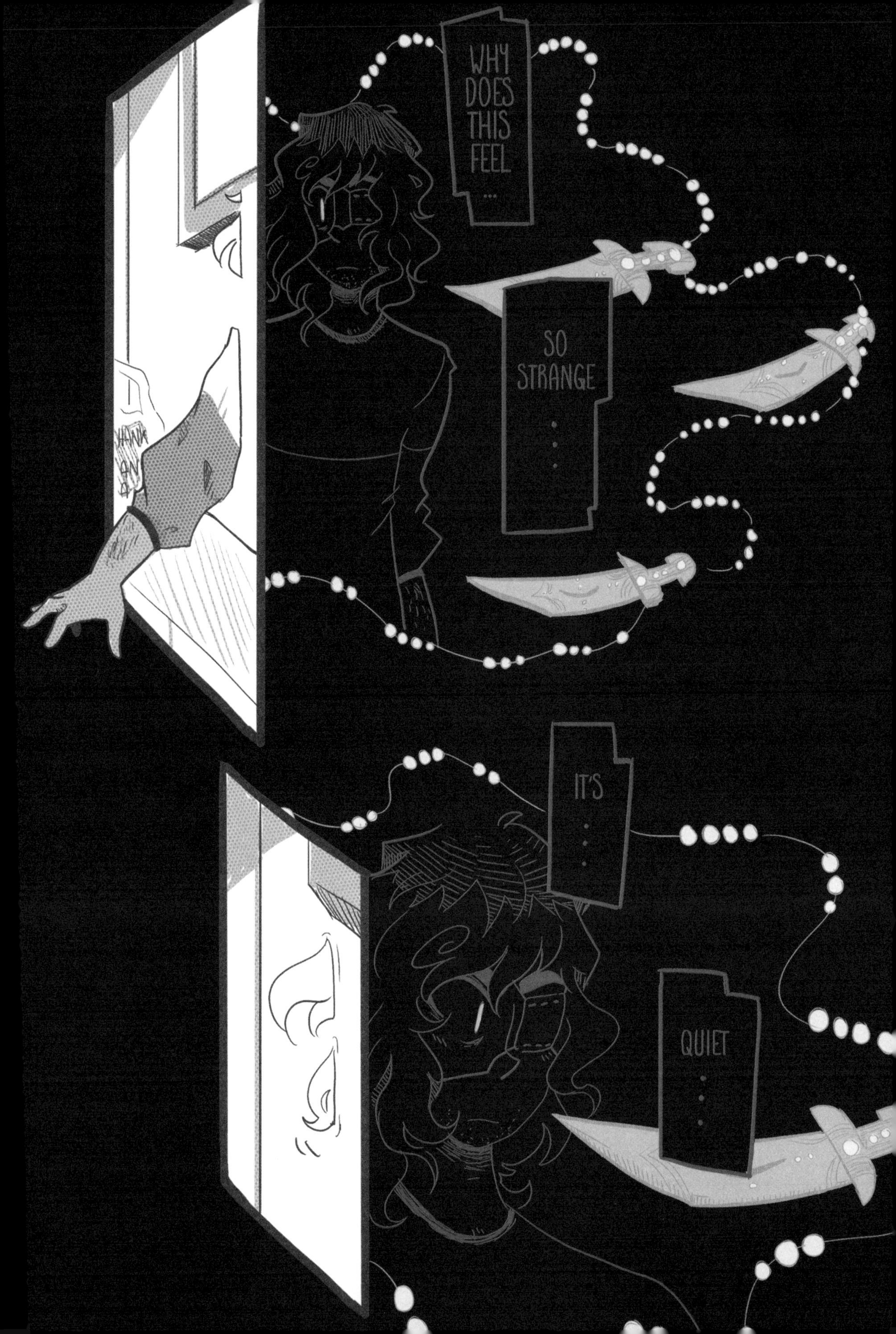
WHY DOES THIS FEEL ...
SO STRANGE ...
IT'S ...
QUIET ...

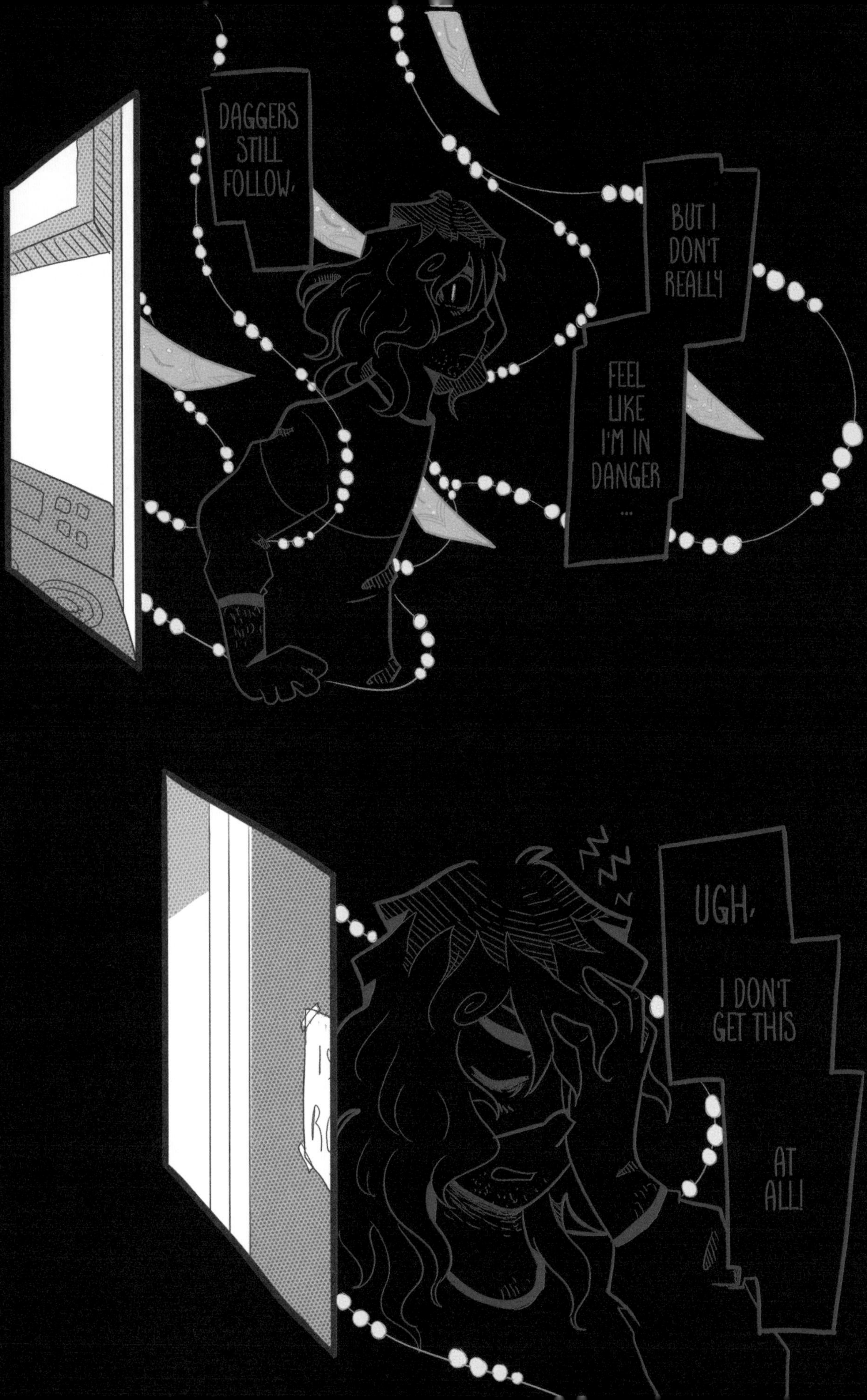
DAGGERS STILL FOLLOW,
BUT I DON'T REALLY
FEEL LIKE I'M IN DANGER ...
UGH,
I DON'T GET THIS
AT ALL!

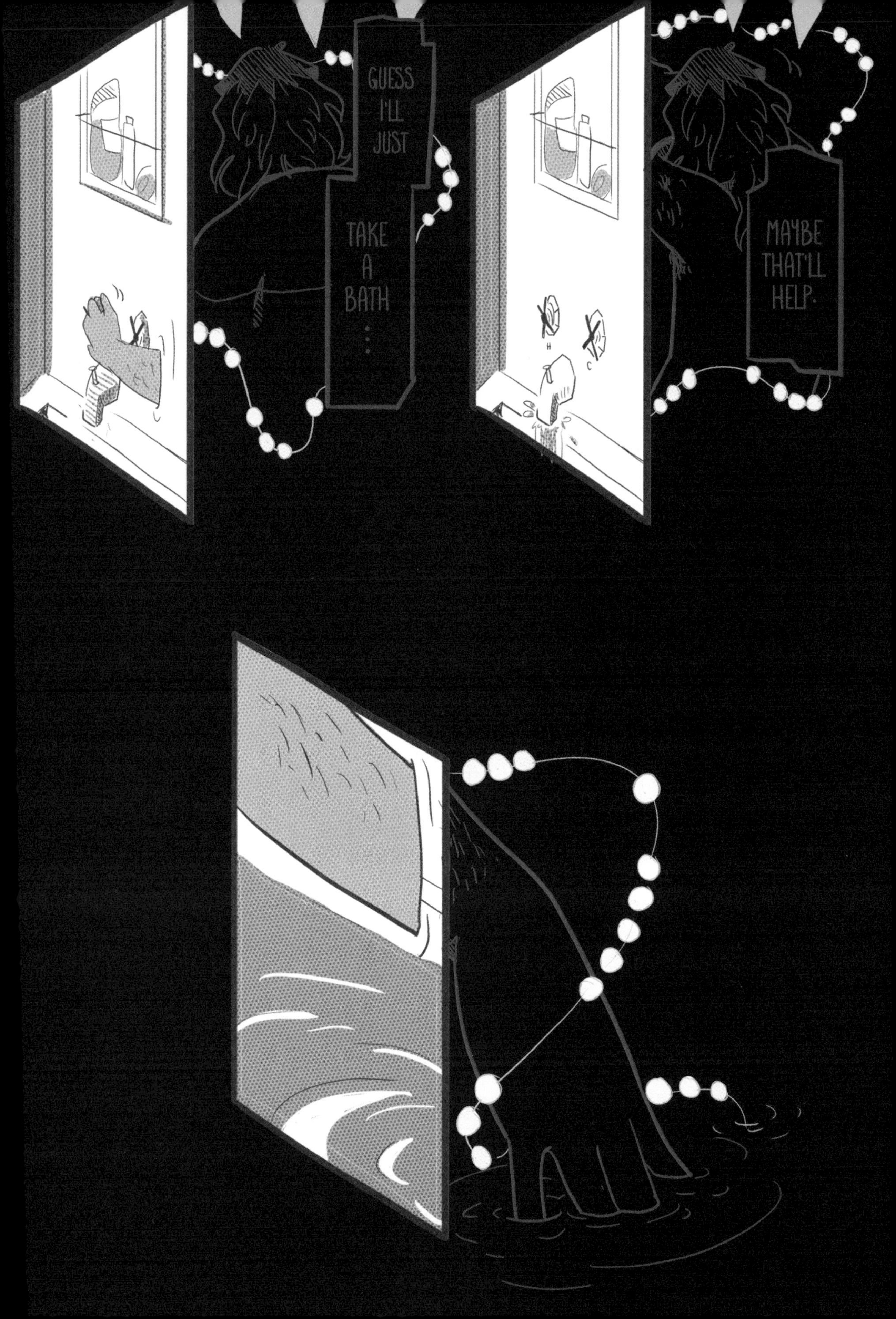
GUESS I'LL JUST
TAKE A BATH...
H
C
MAYBE THAT'LL HELP.

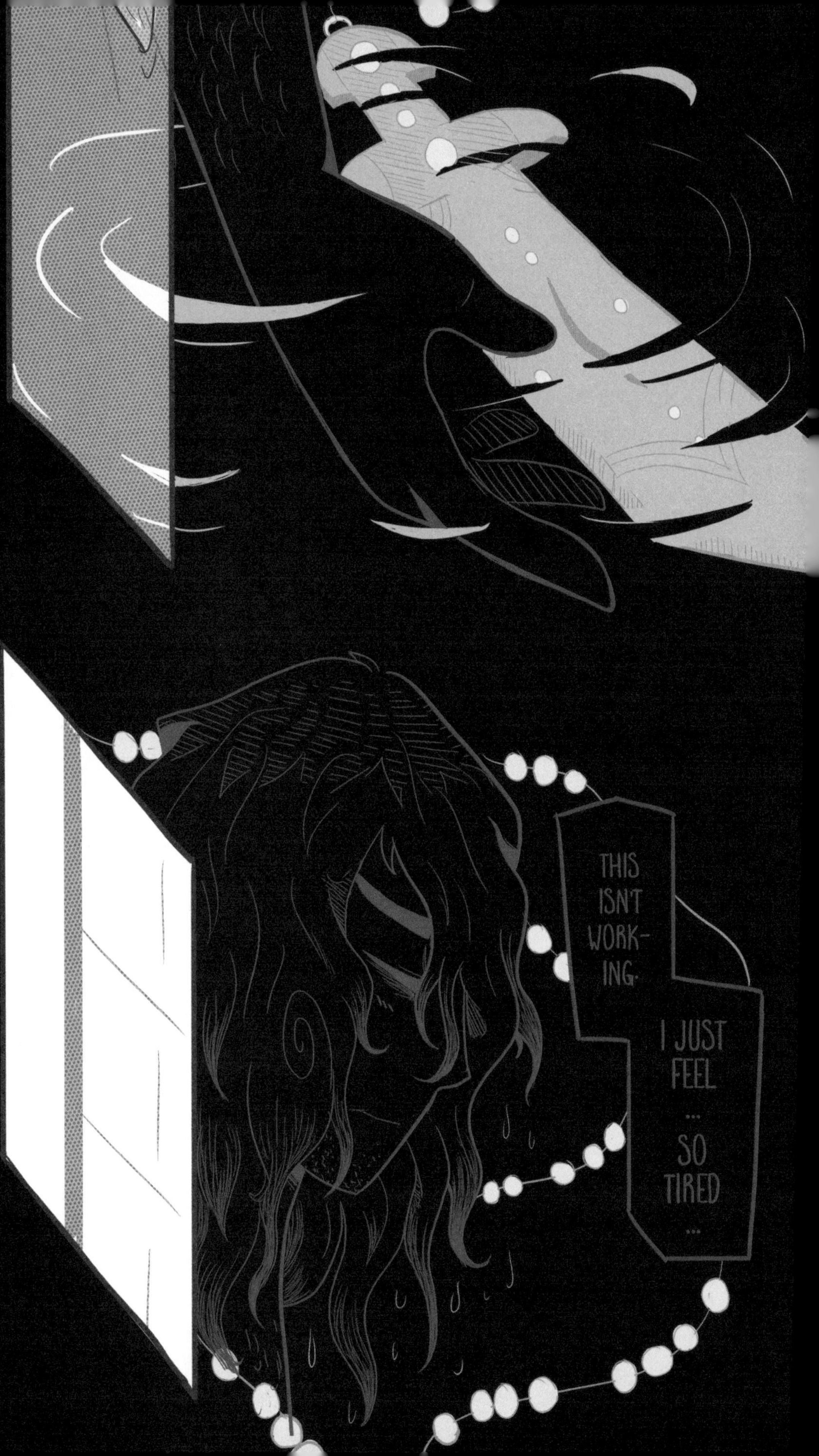
THIS ISN'T WORK-ING.
I JUST FEEL ... SO TIRED ...

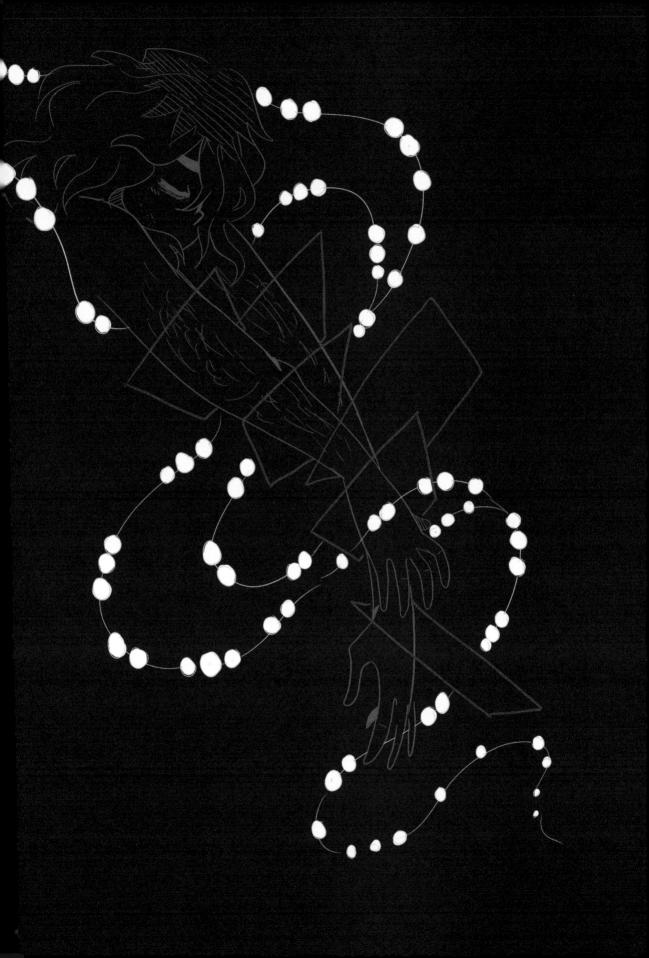

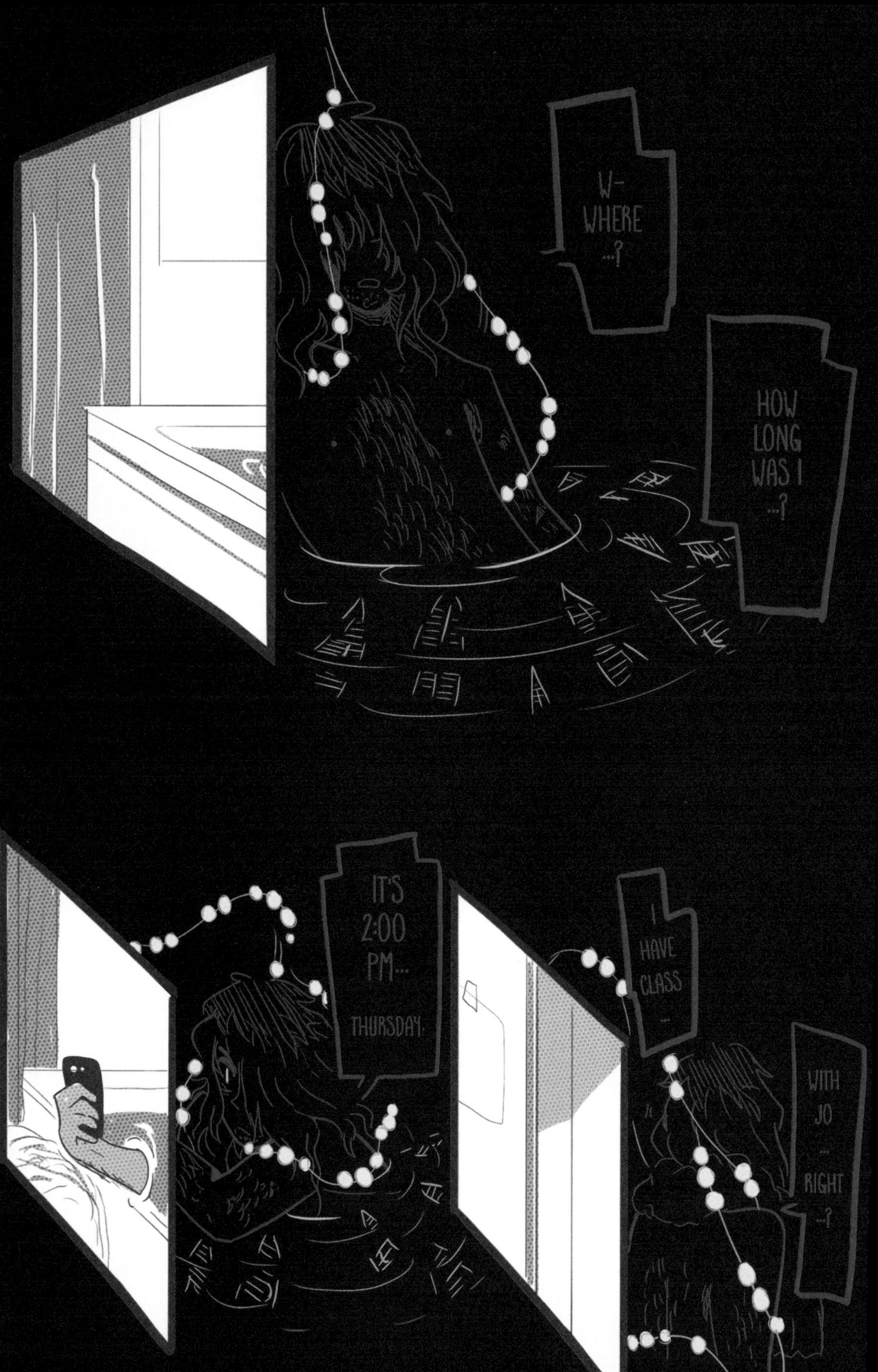
W- WHERE ...?
HOW LONG WAS I ...?
IT'S 2:00 PM... THURSDAY.
I HAVE CLASS ...
WITH JO ... RIGHT ...?

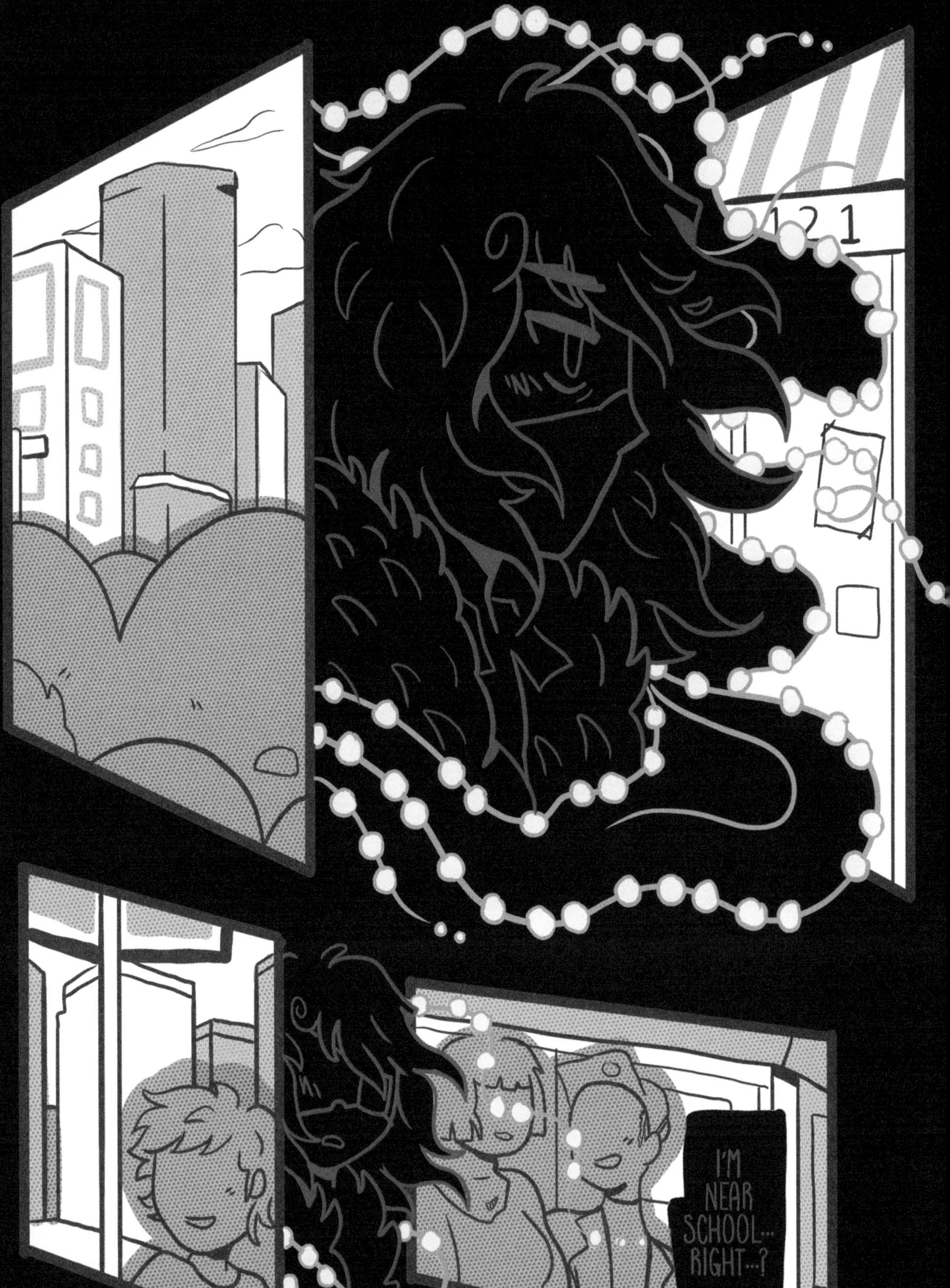
121
I'M NEAR SCHOOL... RIGHT...?

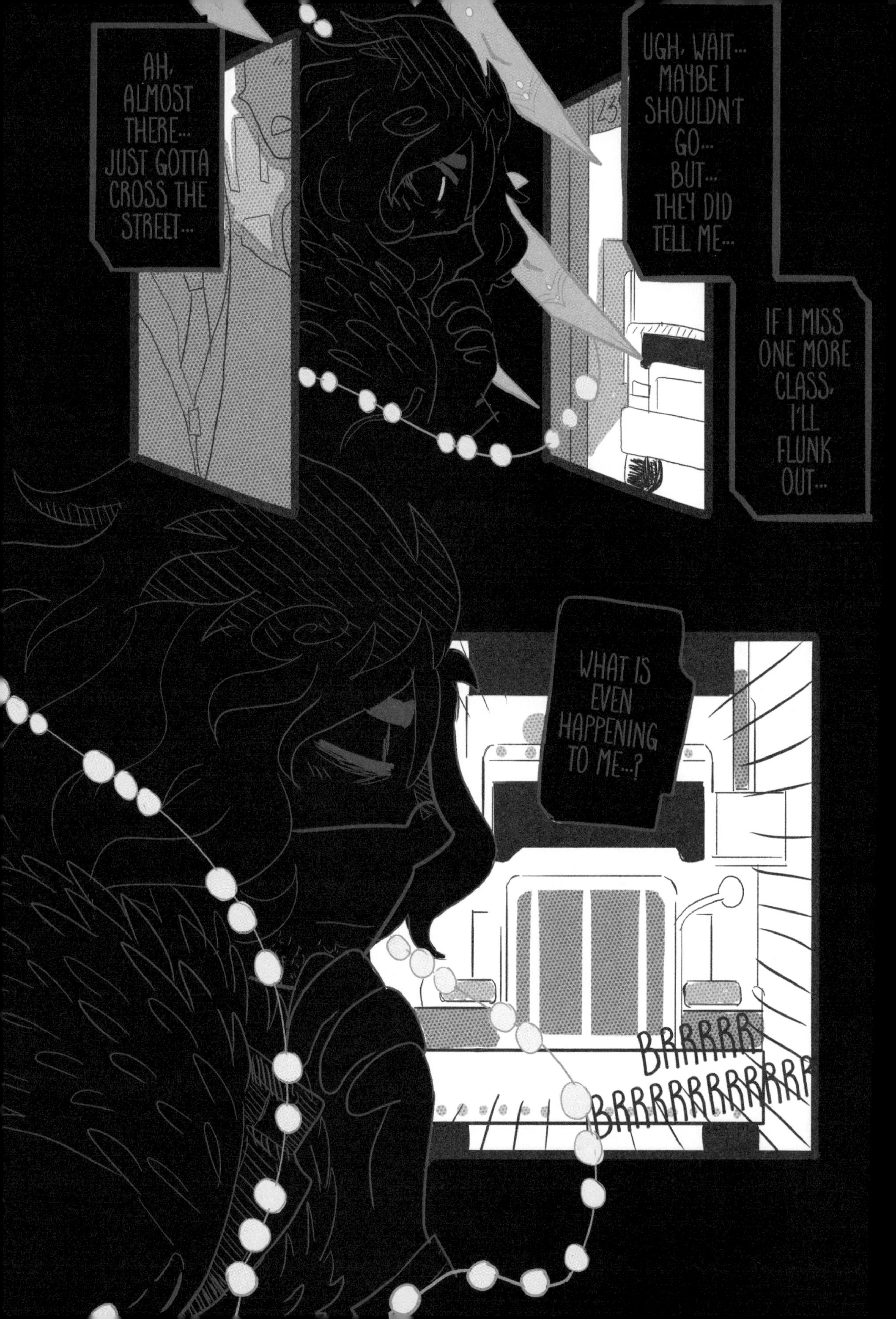
AH, ALMOST THERE... JUST GOTTA CROSS THE STREET...
UGH, WAIT... MAYBE I SHOULDN'T GO... BUT... THEY DID TELL ME...
IF I MISS ONE MORE CLASS, I'LL FLUNK OUT...
WHAT IS EVEN HAPPENING TO ME...?
BRRRRR
BRRRRRRRRRRRR

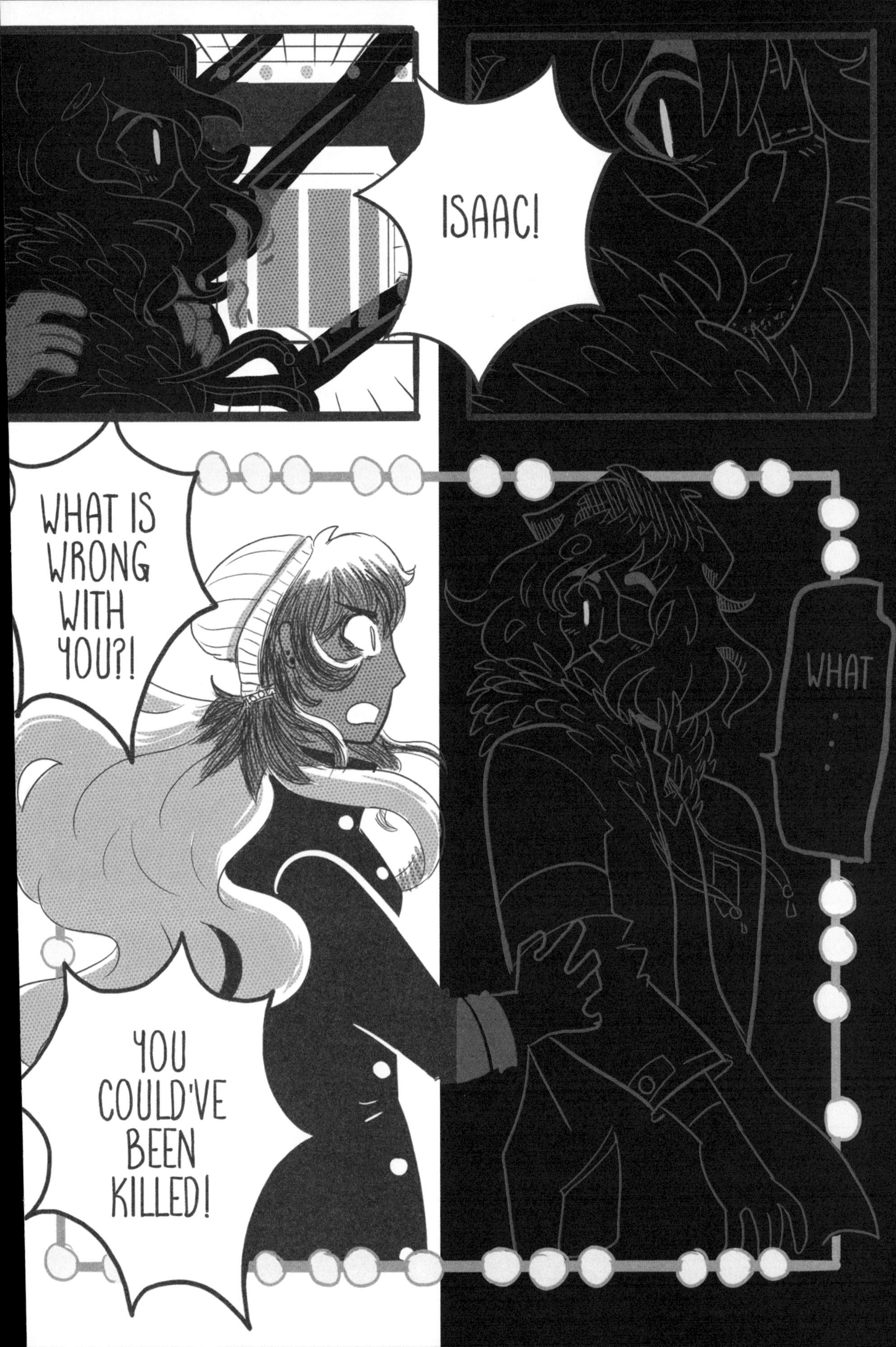
ISAAC!
WHAT IS WRONG WITH YOU?!
YOU COULD'VE BEEN KILLED!
WHAT...

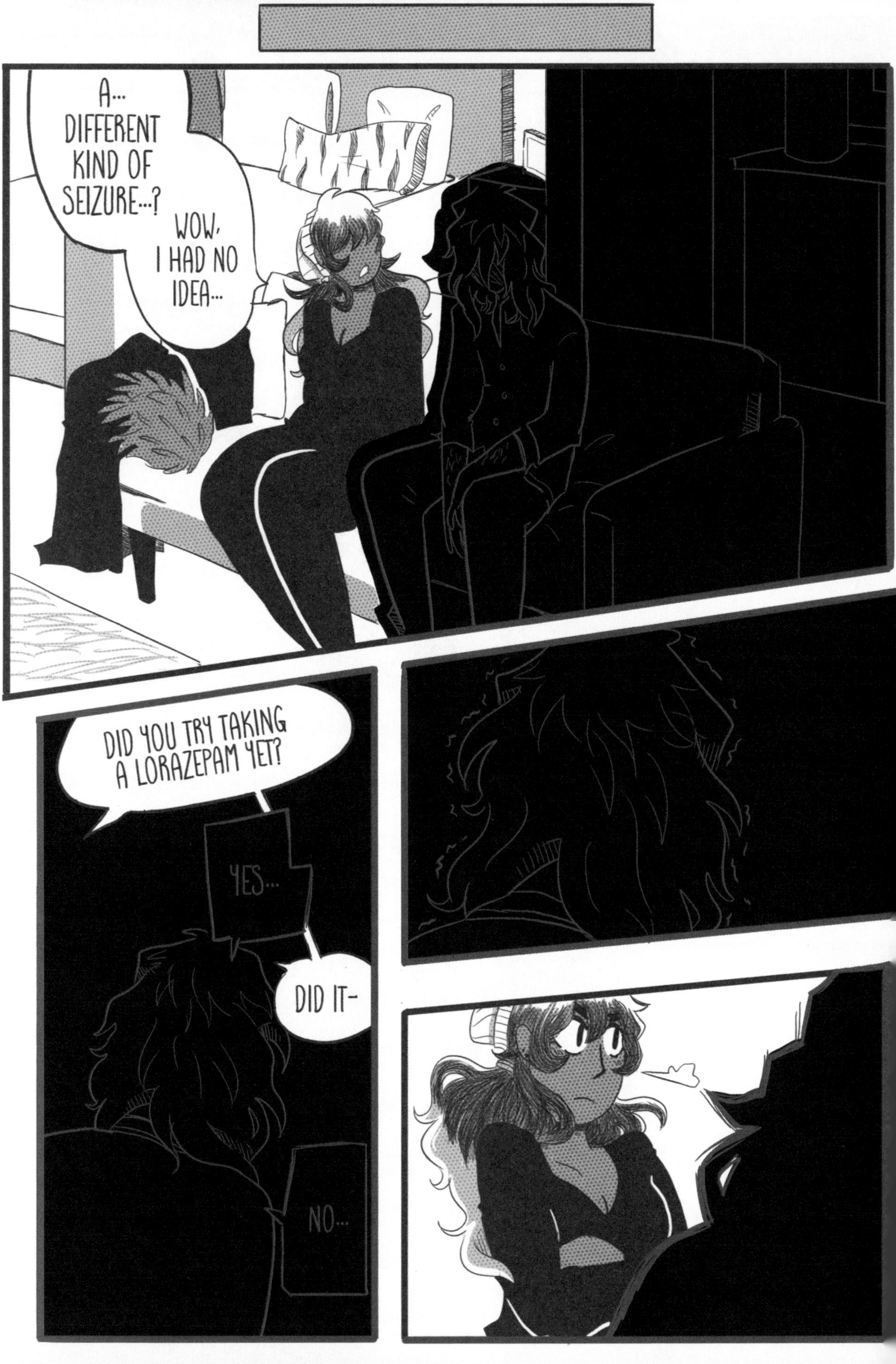
A... DIFFERENT KIND OF SEIZURE...?
WOW, I HAD NO IDEA...
DID YOU TRY TAKING A LORAZEPAM YET?
YES...
DID IT-
NO...

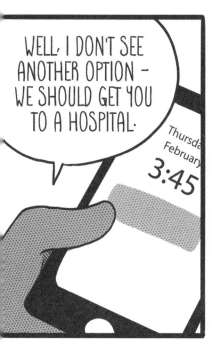

WELL, I DON'T SEE ANOTHER OPTION — WE SHOULD GET YOU TO A HOSPITAL.

Thursday February

3:45

BUT — WON'T YOU MISS CLASS, TOO?

ARE YOU SERIOUSLY WORRIED ABOUT THAT RIGHT NOW?

THIS IS JUST LIKE...

OKAY, GOTTA CALL A CAB...

THE FIRST TIME.

BACK THEN.

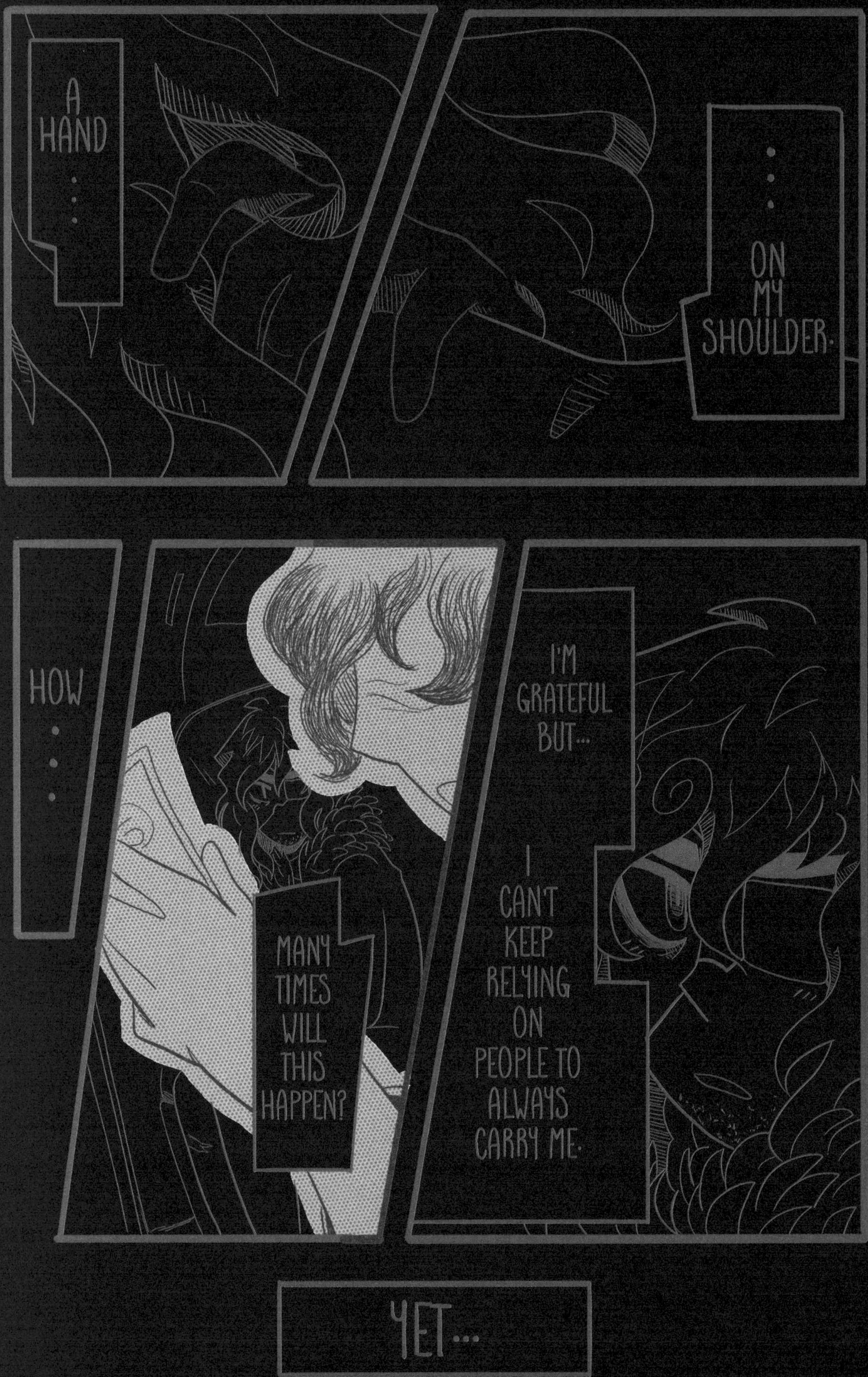
A HAND . . .
. . . ON MY SHOULDER.
HOW . . .
MANY TIMES WILL THIS HAPPEN?
I'M GRATEFUL BUT...
I CAN'T KEEP RELYING ON PEOPLE TO ALWAYS CARRY ME.
YET...

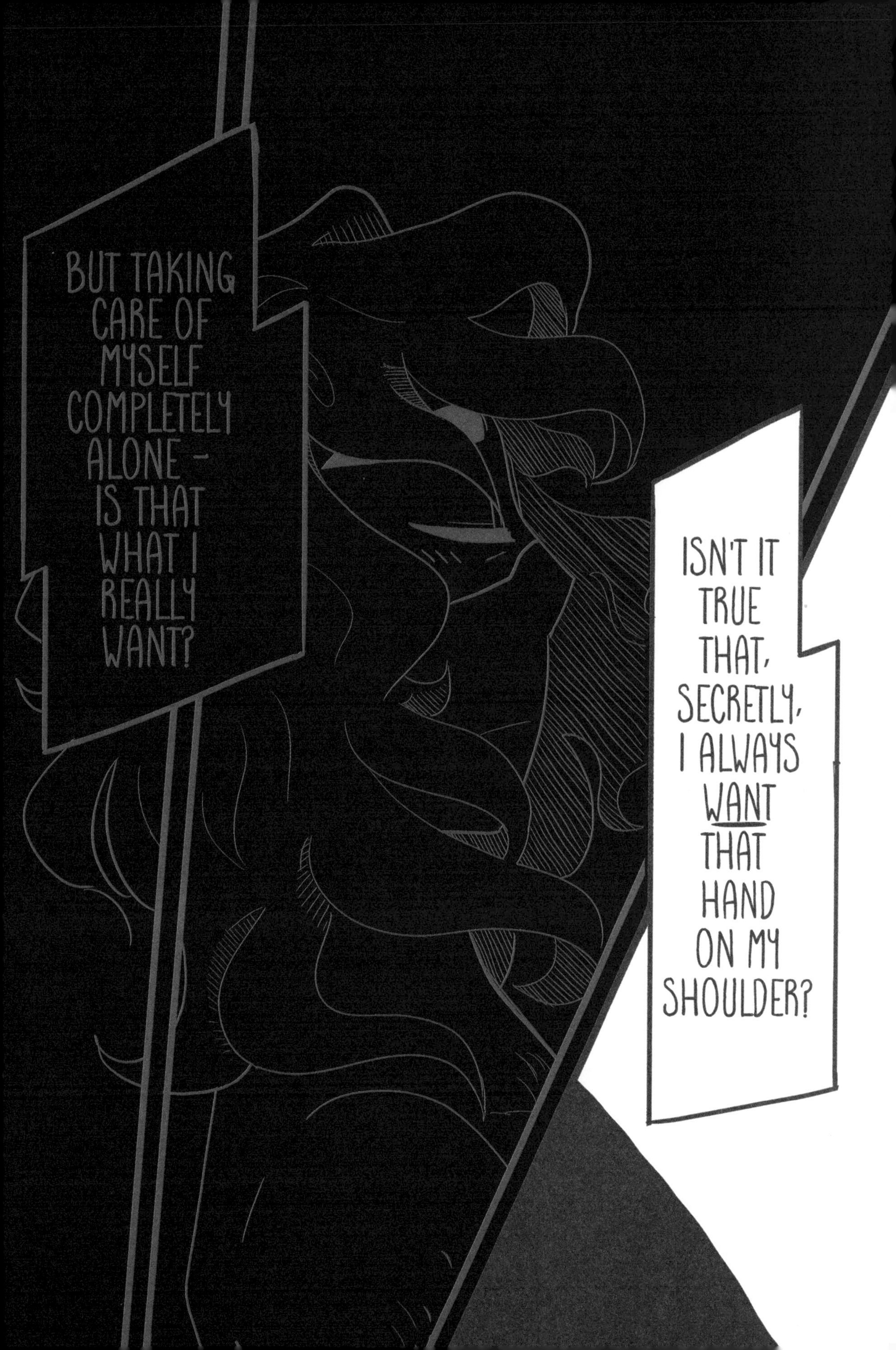
BUT TAKING CARE OF MYSELF COMPLETELY ALONE - IS THAT WHAT I REALLY WANT?
ISN'T IT TRUE THAT, SECRETLY, I ALWAYS WANT THAT HAND ON MY SHOULDER?

I DON'T...

KNOW...

ISAAC...

ISAAC!

WAKE UP ALREADY! THEY'RE CALLING FOR US!

WHA... WHAT TIME IS IT...

IT'S, LIKE, 7:00!

COME ON!

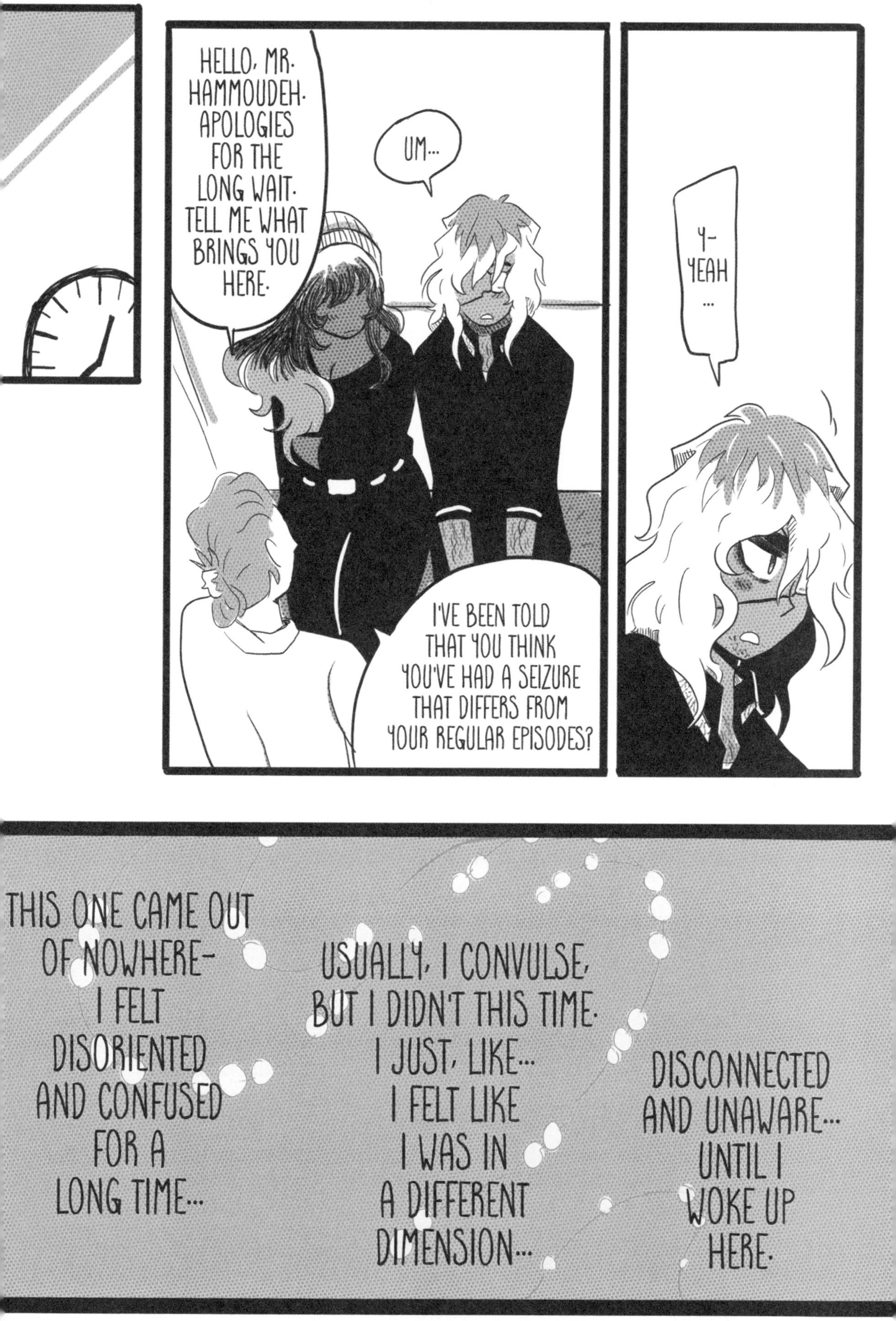
HELLO, MR. HAMMOUDEH. APOLOGIES FOR THE LONG WAIT. TELL ME WHAT BRINGS YOU HERE.
UM...
I'VE BEEN TOLD THAT YOU THINK YOU'VE HAD A SEIZURE THAT DIFFERS FROM YOUR REGULAR EPISODES?
Y-YEAH...
THIS ONE CAME OUT OF NOWHERE- I FELT DISORIENTED AND CONFUSED FOR A LONG TIME...
USUALLY, I CONVULSE, BUT I DIDN'T THIS TIME. I JUST, LIKE... I FELT LIKE I WAS IN A DIFFERENT DIMENSION...
DISCONNECTED AND UNAWARE... UNTIL I WOKE UP HERE.

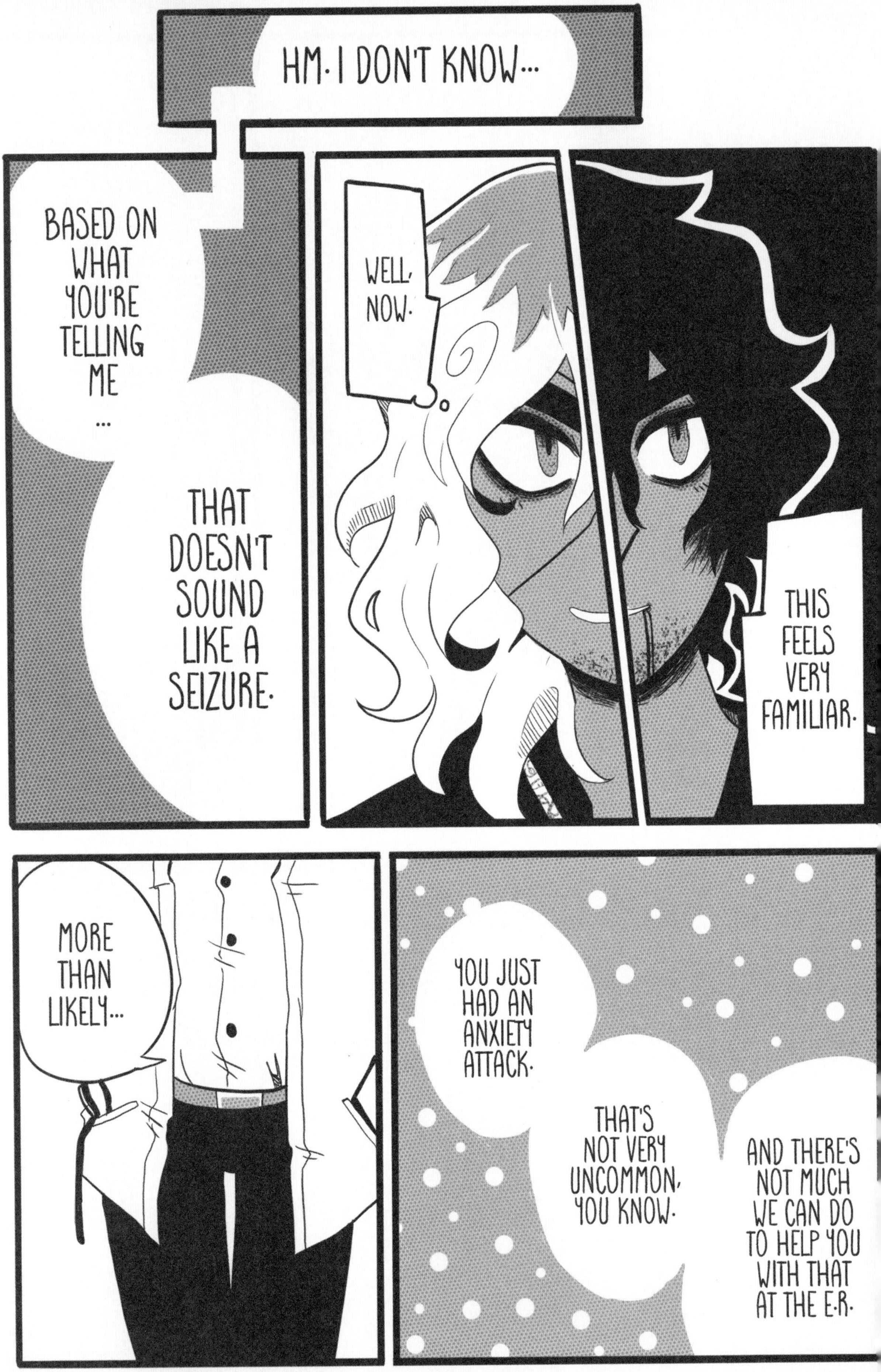

HM. I DON'T KNOW...
BASED ON WHAT YOU'RE TELLING ME ...
THAT DOESN'T SOUND LIKE A SEIZURE.
WELL, NOW.
THIS FEELS VERY FAMILIAR.
MORE THAN LIKELY...
YOU JUST HAD AN ANXIETY ATTACK.
THAT'S NOT VERY UNCOMMON, YOU KNOW.
AND THERE'S NOT MUCH WE CAN DO TO HELP YOU WITH THAT AT THE E.R.

THAT'S RIGHT. THEY'VE SAID THIS SO MANY TIMES BEFORE.

I EXPECTED THIS. SO WHY AM I...

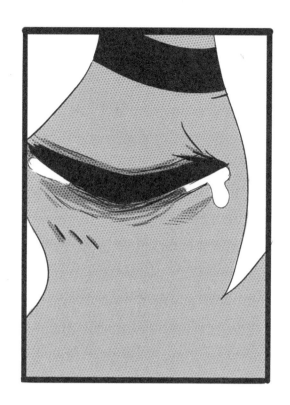

WAIT A MINUTE! THAT'S ALL YOU'VE GOT?!

AND YOU CALL YOURSELF A DOCTOR?!

UH...

WE WANT A SECOND OPINION! RIGHT NOW!

UM, I'LL... I'LL GO ASK ANOTHER DOCTOR, MA'AM...

YEAH, YOU'D BETTER.

...

YOU OKAY?

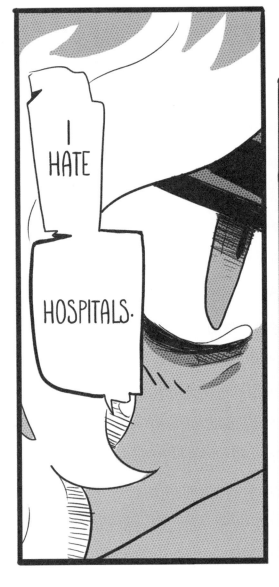

I HATE HOSPITALS.

YEAH.

ME, TOO.

THEY'RE THE WORST.

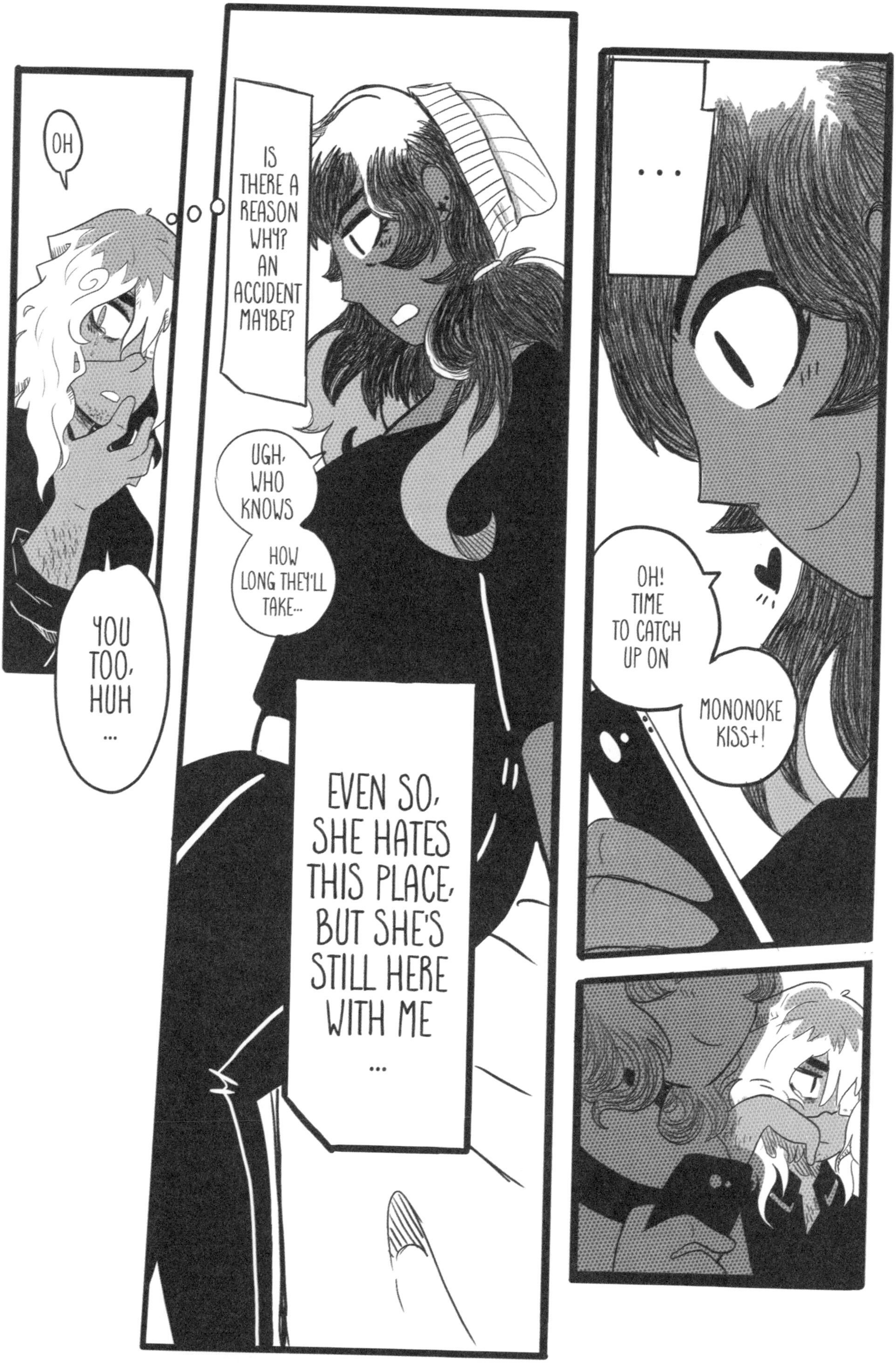
OH
YOU TOO, HUH ...
IS THERE A REASON WHY? AN ACCIDENT MAYBE?
UGH, WHO KNOWS
HOW LONG THEY'LL TAKE...
EVEN SO, SHE HATES THIS PLACE, BUT SHE'S STILL HERE WITH ME ...
. . .
OH! TIME TO CATCH UP ON
MONONOKE KISS+!

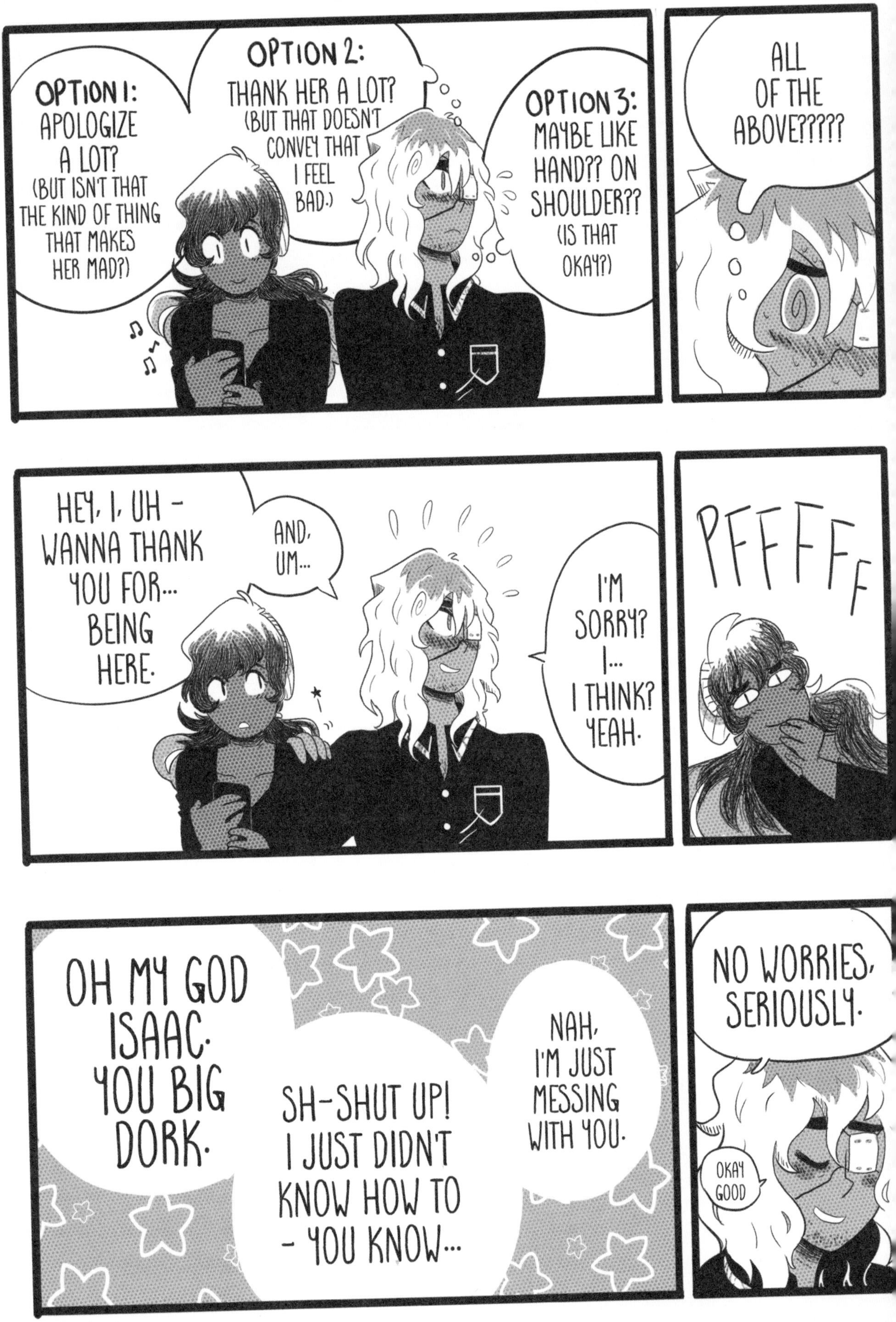
OPTION 1: APOLOGIZE A LOT? (BUT ISN'T THAT THE KIND OF THING THAT MAKES HER MAD?)
OPTION 2: THANK HER A LOT? (BUT THAT DOESN'T CONVEY THAT I FEEL BAD.)
OPTION 3: MAYBE LIKE HAND?? ON SHOULDER?? (IS THAT OKAY?)
ALL OF THE ABOVE?????
HEY, I, UH - WANNA THANK YOU FOR... BEING HERE.
AND, UM...
I'M SORRY? I... I THINK? YEAH.
PFFFFFF
OH MY GOD ISAAC. YOU BIG DORK.
SH-SHUT UP! I JUST DIDN'T KNOW HOW TO - YOU KNOW...
NAH, I'M JUST MESSING WITH YOU.
NO WORRIES, SERIOUSLY.
OKAY GOOD

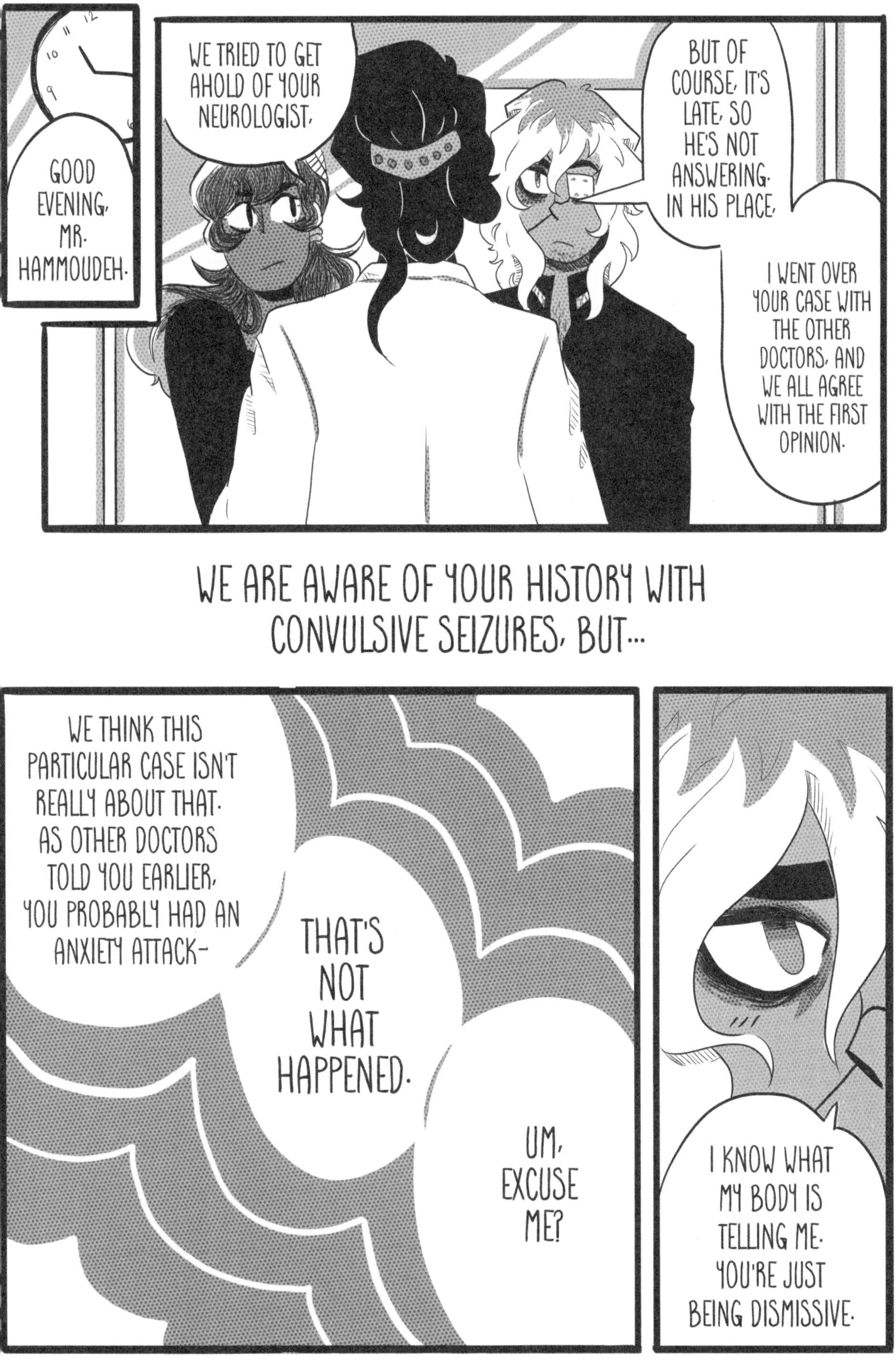
GOOD EVENING, MR. HAMMOUDEH.
WE TRIED TO GET AHOLD OF YOUR NEUROLOGIST,
BUT OF COURSE, IT'S LATE, SO HE'S NOT ANSWERING. IN HIS PLACE,
I WENT OVER YOUR CASE WITH THE OTHER DOCTORS, AND WE ALL AGREE WITH THE FIRST OPINION.
WE ARE AWARE OF YOUR HISTORY WITH CONVULSIVE SEIZURES, BUT...
WE THINK THIS PARTICULAR CASE ISN'T REALLY ABOUT THAT. AS OTHER DOCTORS TOLD YOU EARLIER, YOU PROBABLY HAD AN ANXIETY ATTACK-
THAT'S NOT WHAT HAPPENED.
UM, EXCUSE ME?
I KNOW WHAT MY BODY IS TELLING ME. YOU'RE JUST BEING DISMISSIVE.

...

I DON'T UNDERSTAND.

WHY ARE YOU SO UPSET?

YOU'RE JUST TOTALLY WRITING ME OFF!

YOU BARELY EVEN LISTENED TO ME!

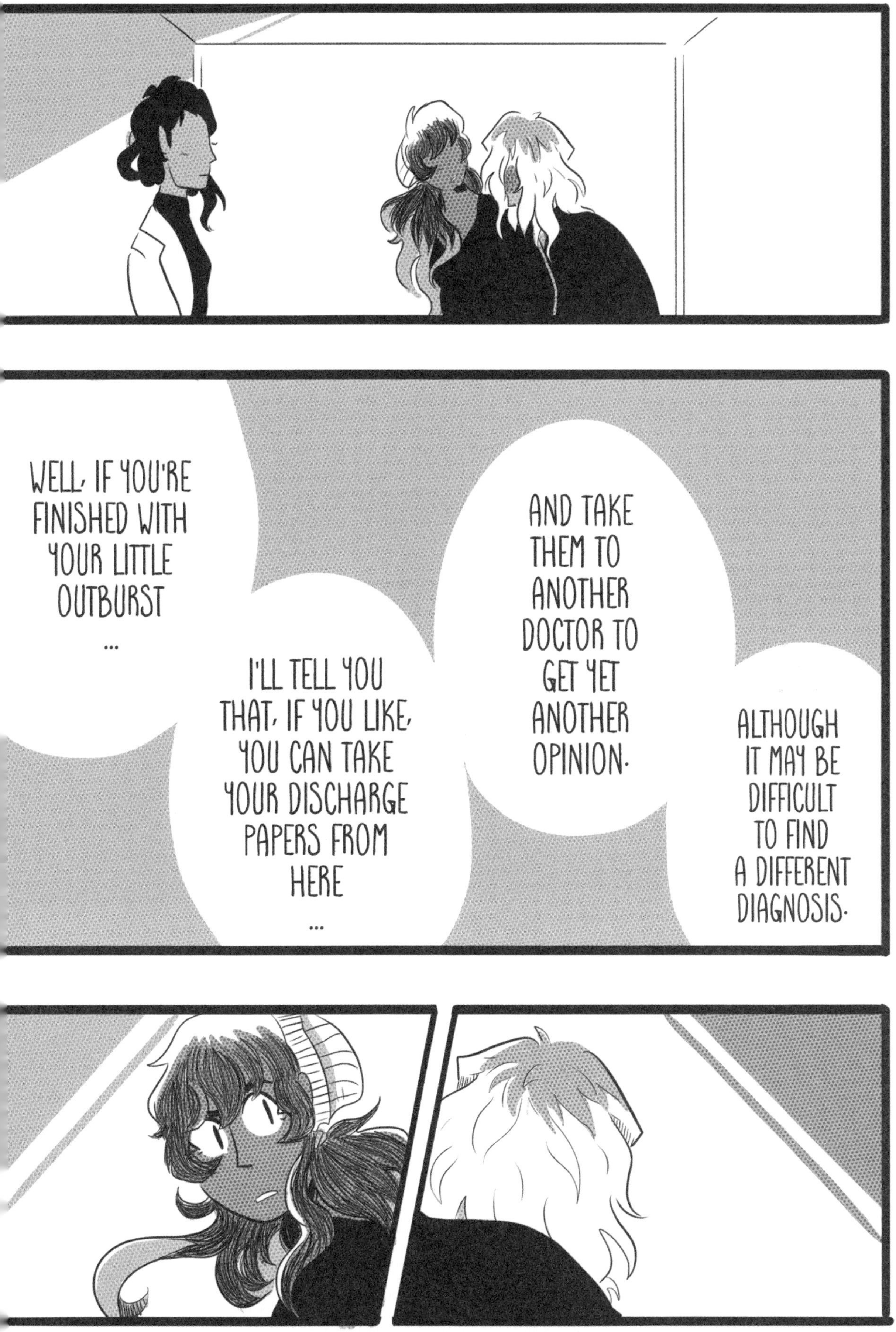
WELL, IF YOU'RE FINISHED WITH YOUR LITTLE OUTBURST ...
I'LL TELL YOU THAT, IF YOU LIKE, YOU CAN TAKE YOUR DISCHARGE PAPERS FROM HERE ...
AND TAKE THEM TO ANOTHER DOCTOR TO GET YET ANOTHER OPINION.
ALTHOUGH IT MAY BE DIFFICULT TO FIND A DIFFERENT DIAGNOSIS.

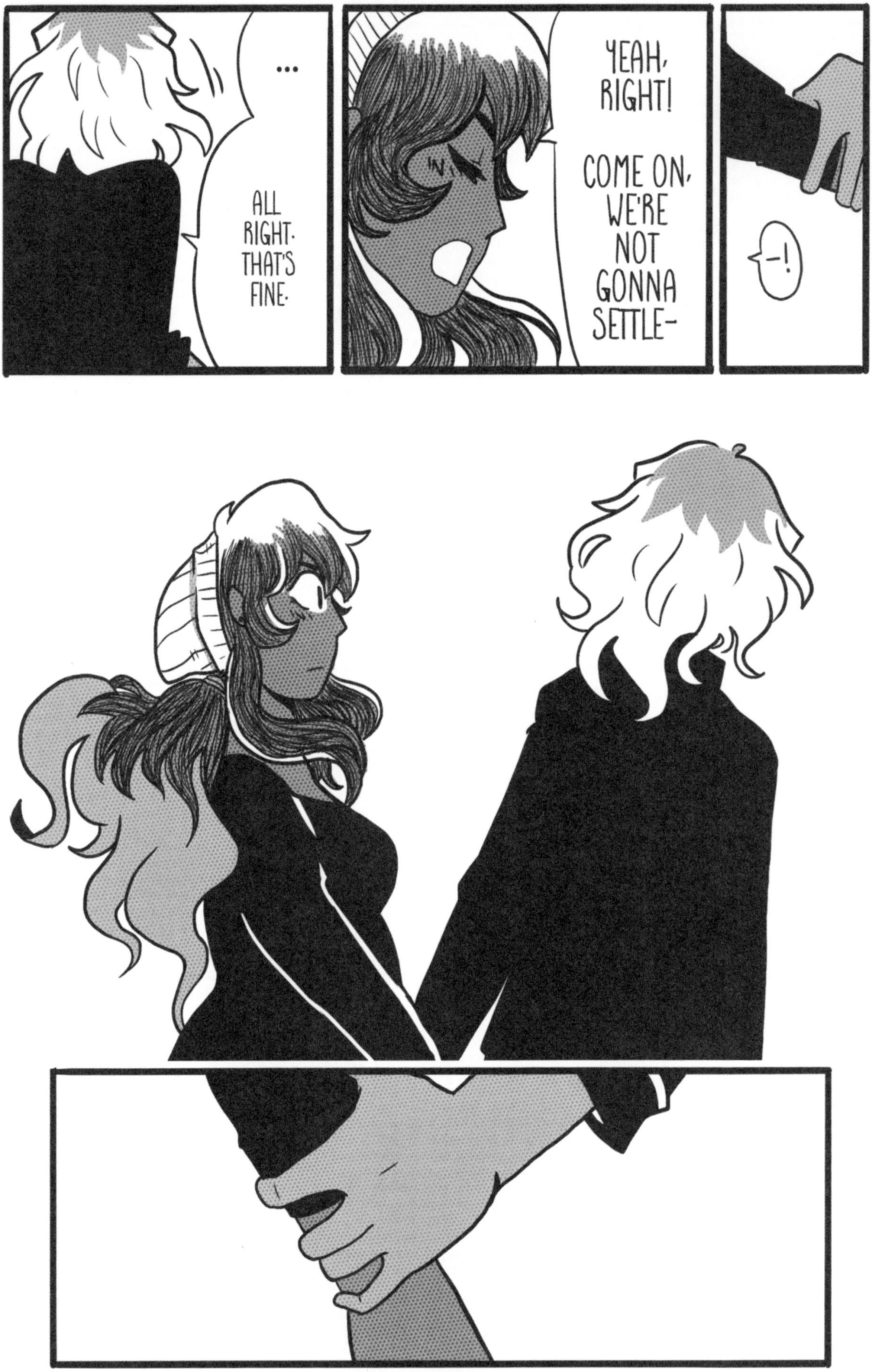
...
ALL RIGHT. THAT'S FINE.
YEAH, RIGHT!
COME ON, WE'RE NOT GONNA SETTLE-
--!

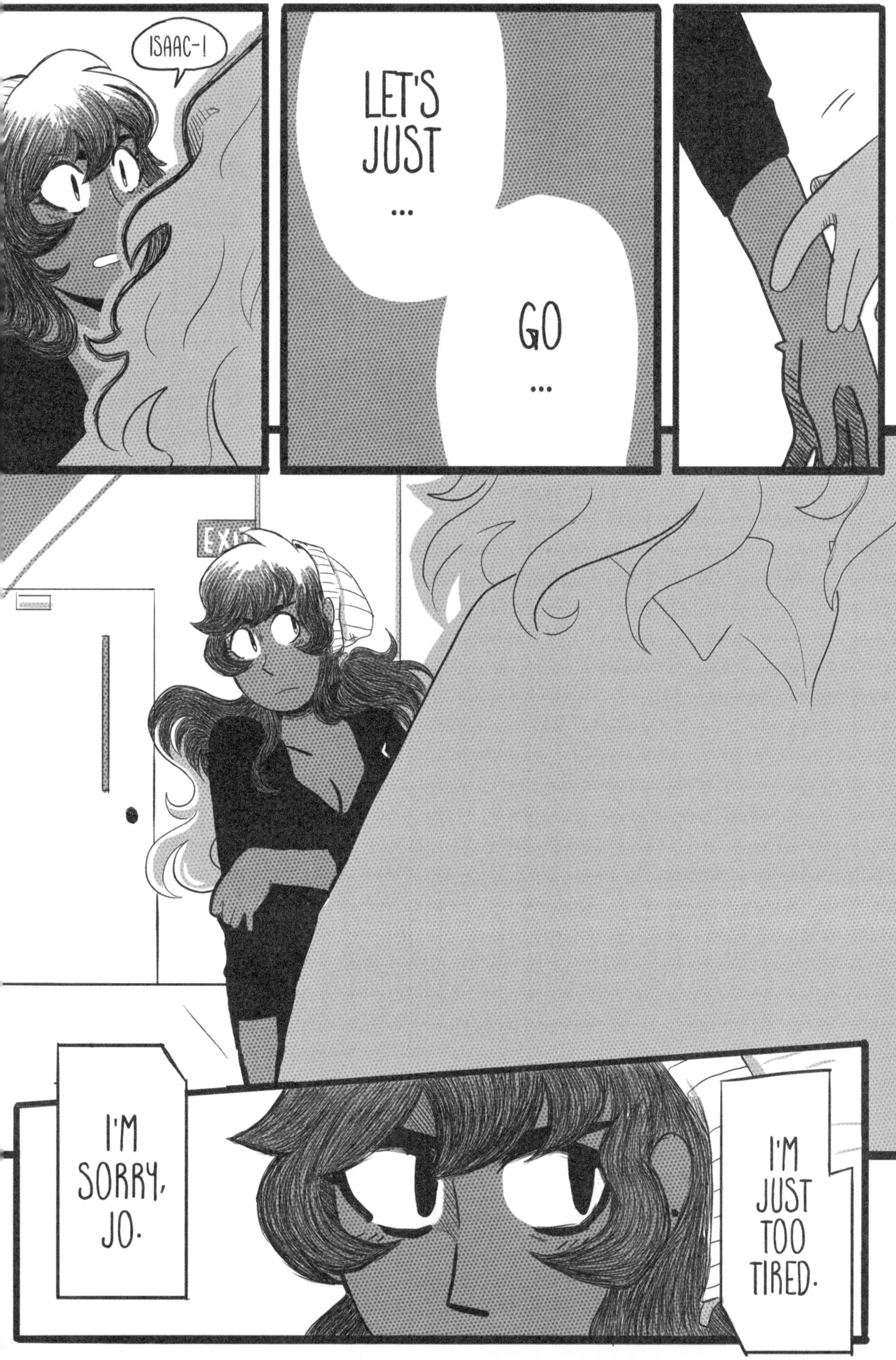
ISAAC-!
LET'S JUST ...
GO ...
I'M SORRY, JO.
I'M JUST TOO TIRED.

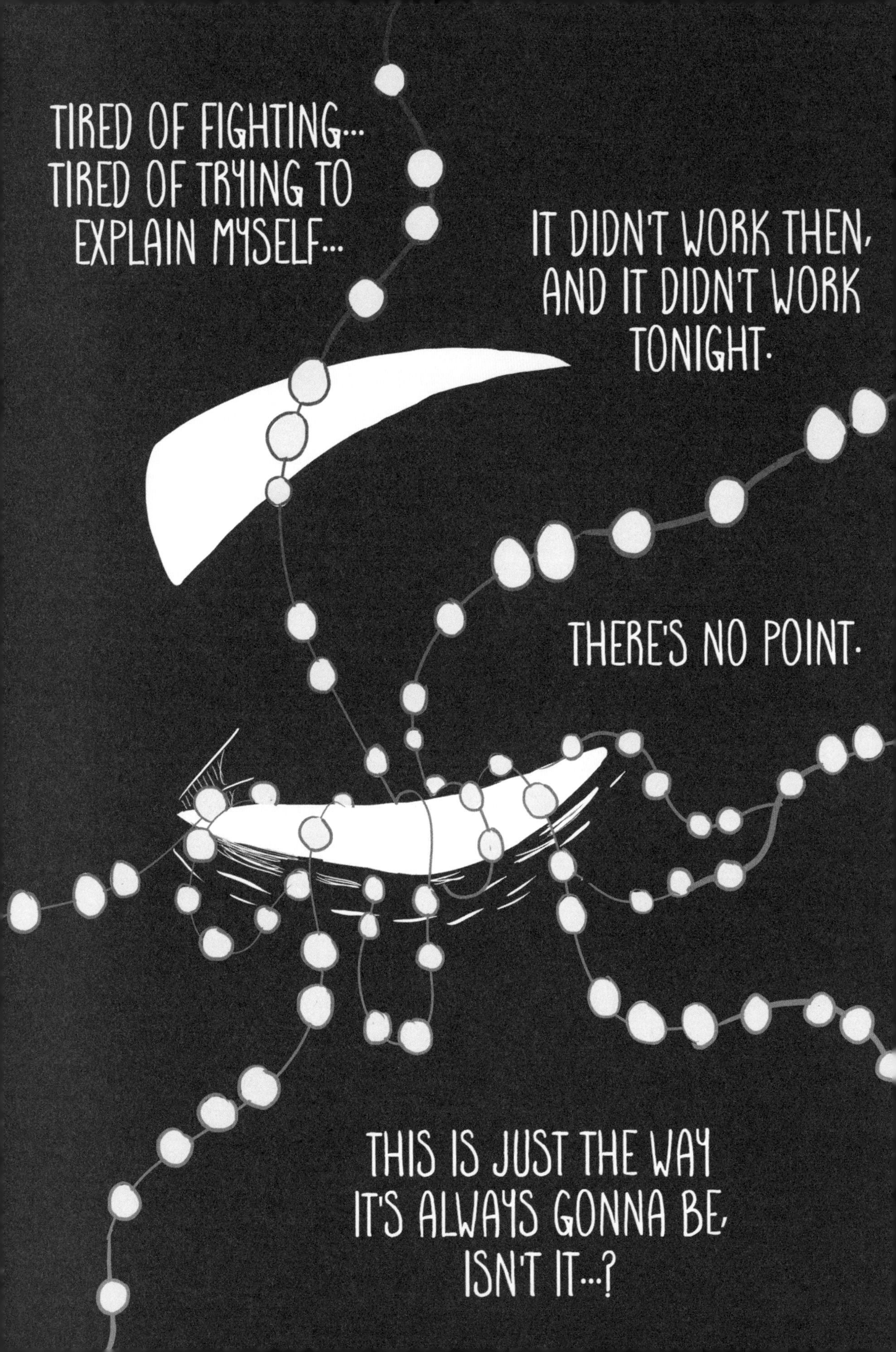
TIRED OF FIGHTING... TIRED OF TRYING TO EXPLAIN MYSELF...
IT DIDN'T WORK THEN, AND IT DIDN'T WORK TONIGHT.
THERE'S NO POINT.
THIS IS JUST THE WAY IT'S ALWAYS GONNA BE, ISN'T IT...?

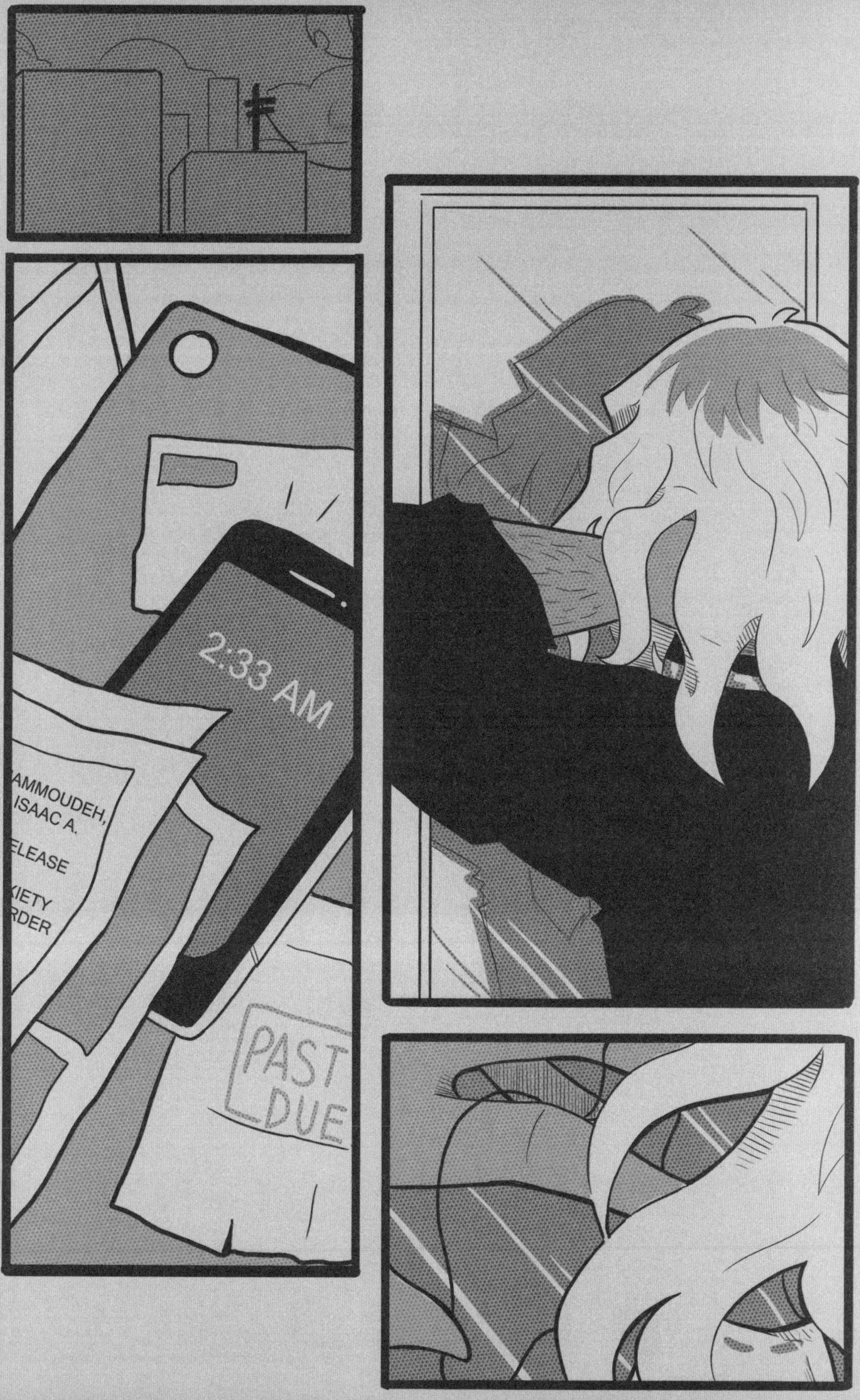

2:33 AM
AMMOUDEH,
ISAAC A.
ELEASE
XIETY
RDER
PAST DUE

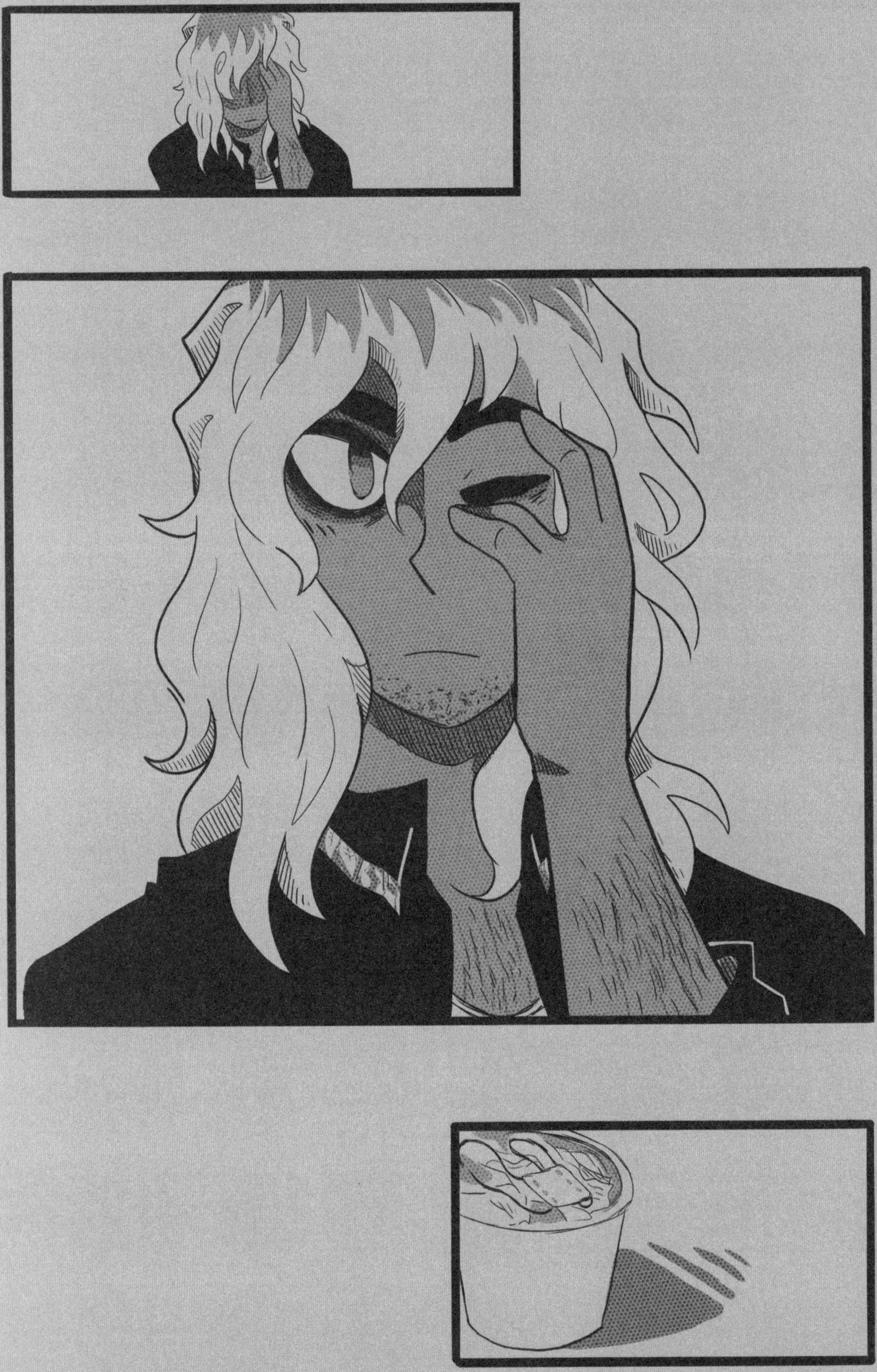

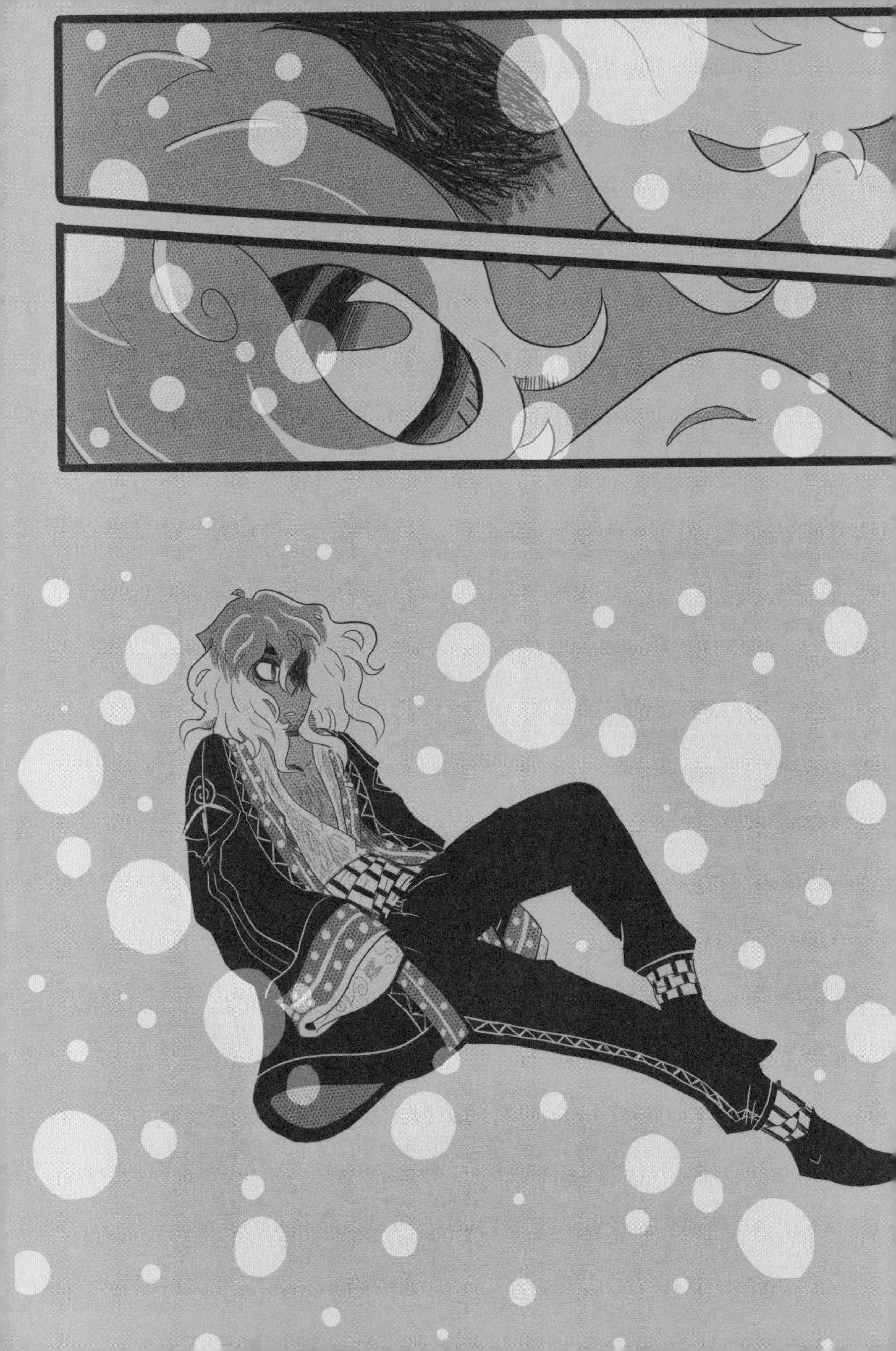

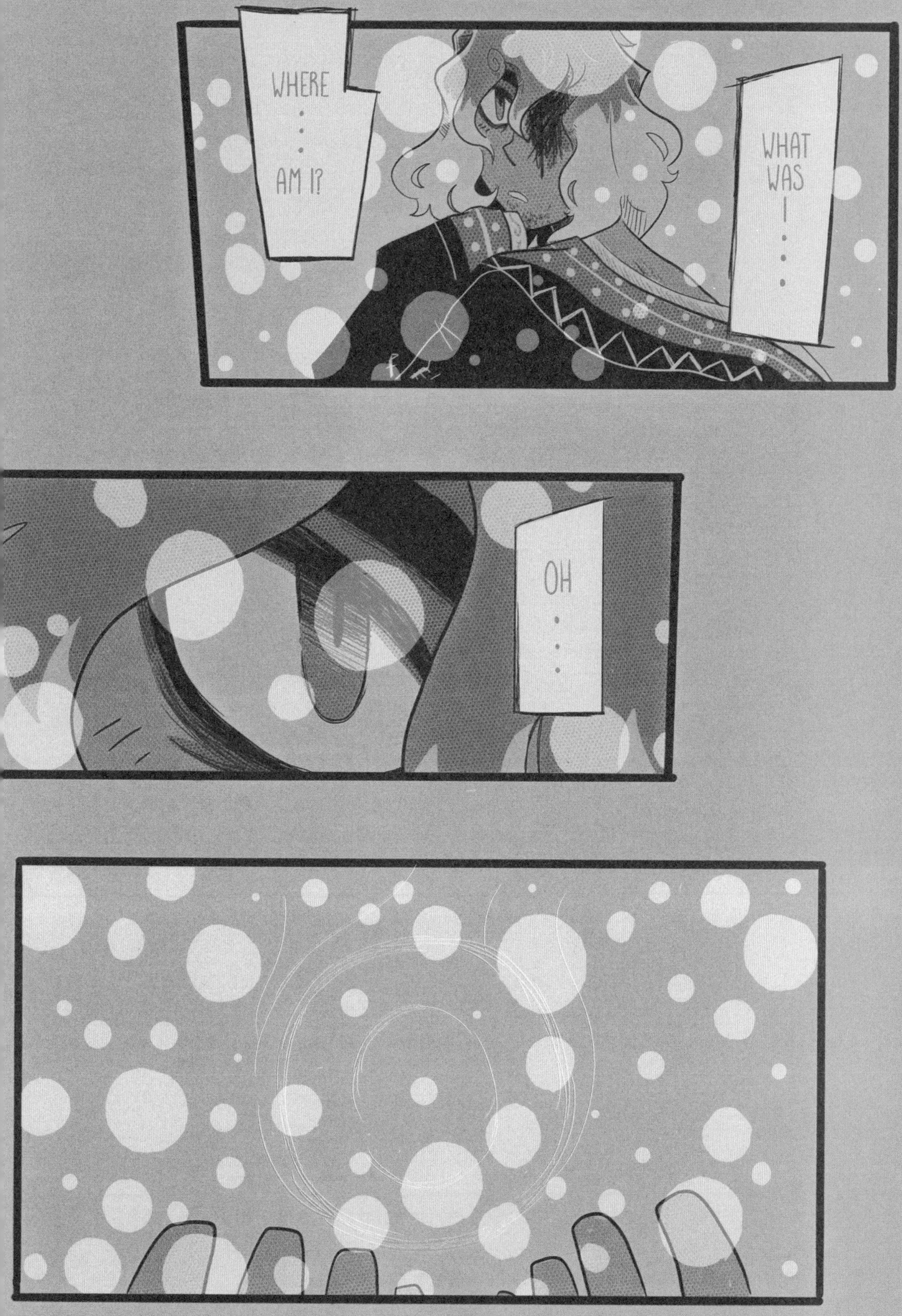
WHERE . . . AM I?
WHAT WAS I . . .
OH . . .

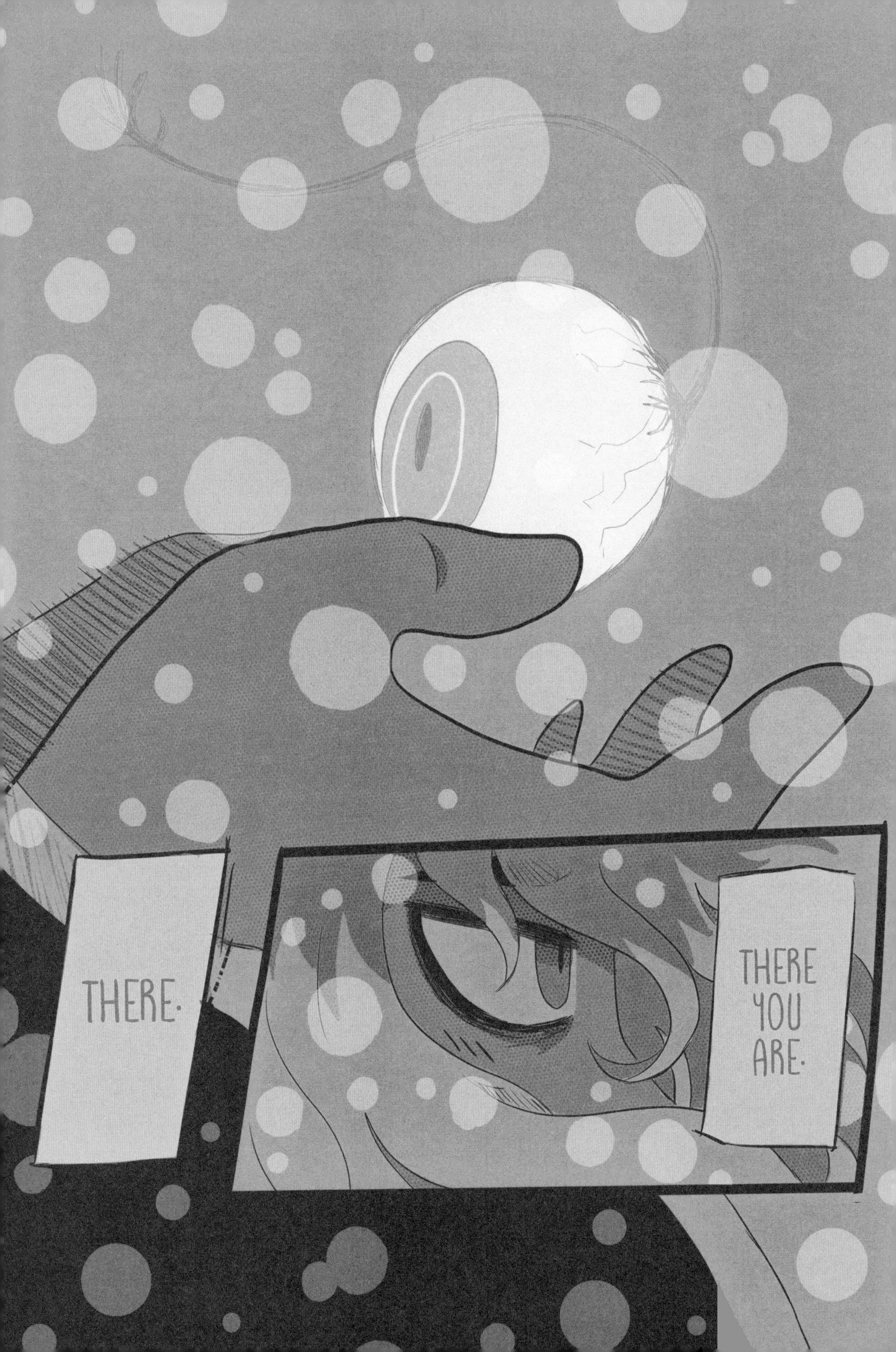
THERE.
THERE YOU ARE.

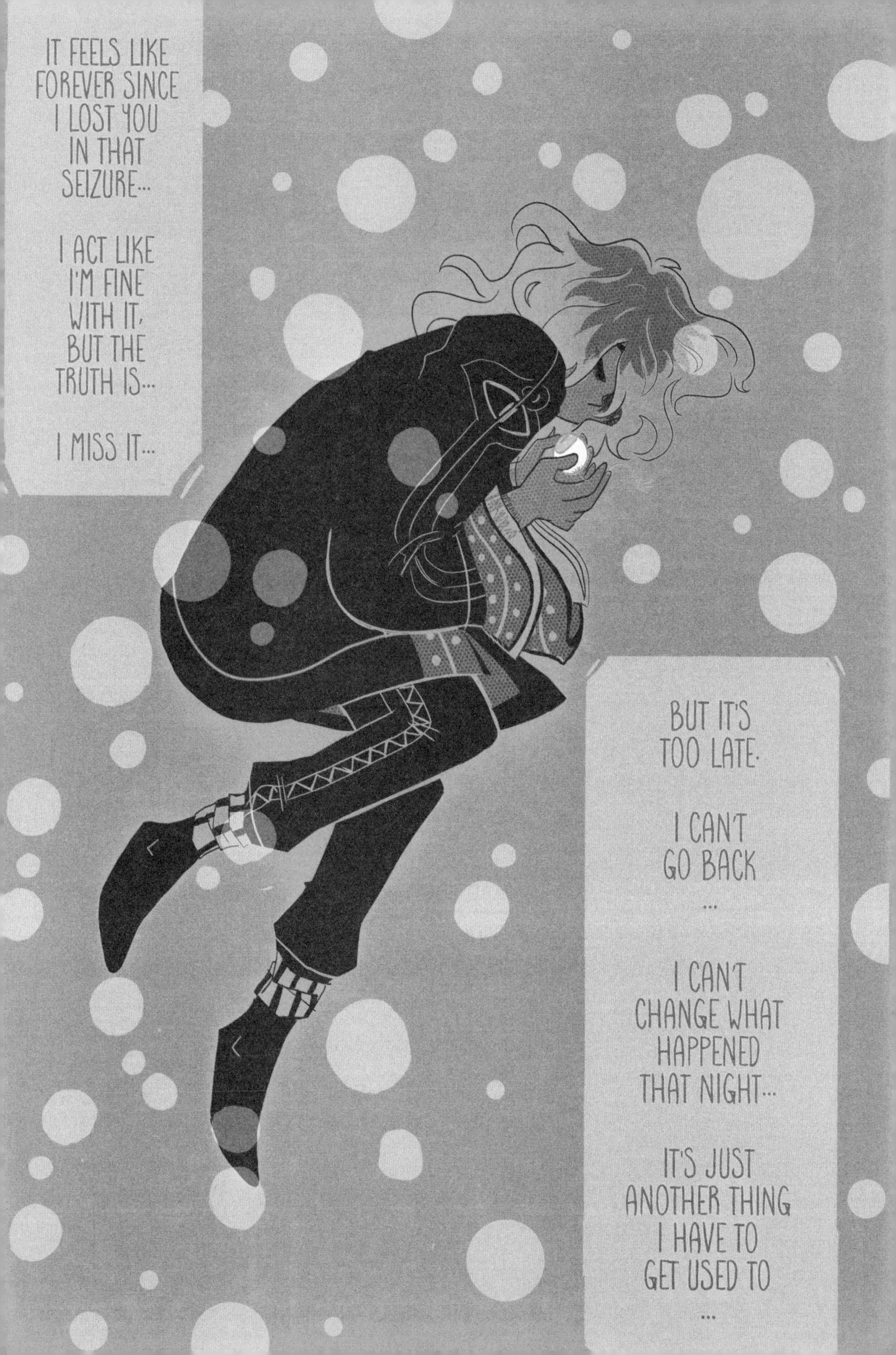
IT FEELS LIKE FOREVER SINCE I LOST YOU IN THAT SEIZURE...
I ACT LIKE I'M FINE WITH IT, BUT THE TRUTH IS...
I MISS IT...
BUT IT'S TOO LATE.
I CAN'T GO BACK
...
I CAN'T CHANGE WHAT HAPPENED THAT NIGHT...
IT'S JUST ANOTHER THING I HAVE TO GET USED TO
...

BUT YOU'RE USED TO GETTING USED TO THINGS.
ISN'T THAT RIGHT?
WH...
WHAT?

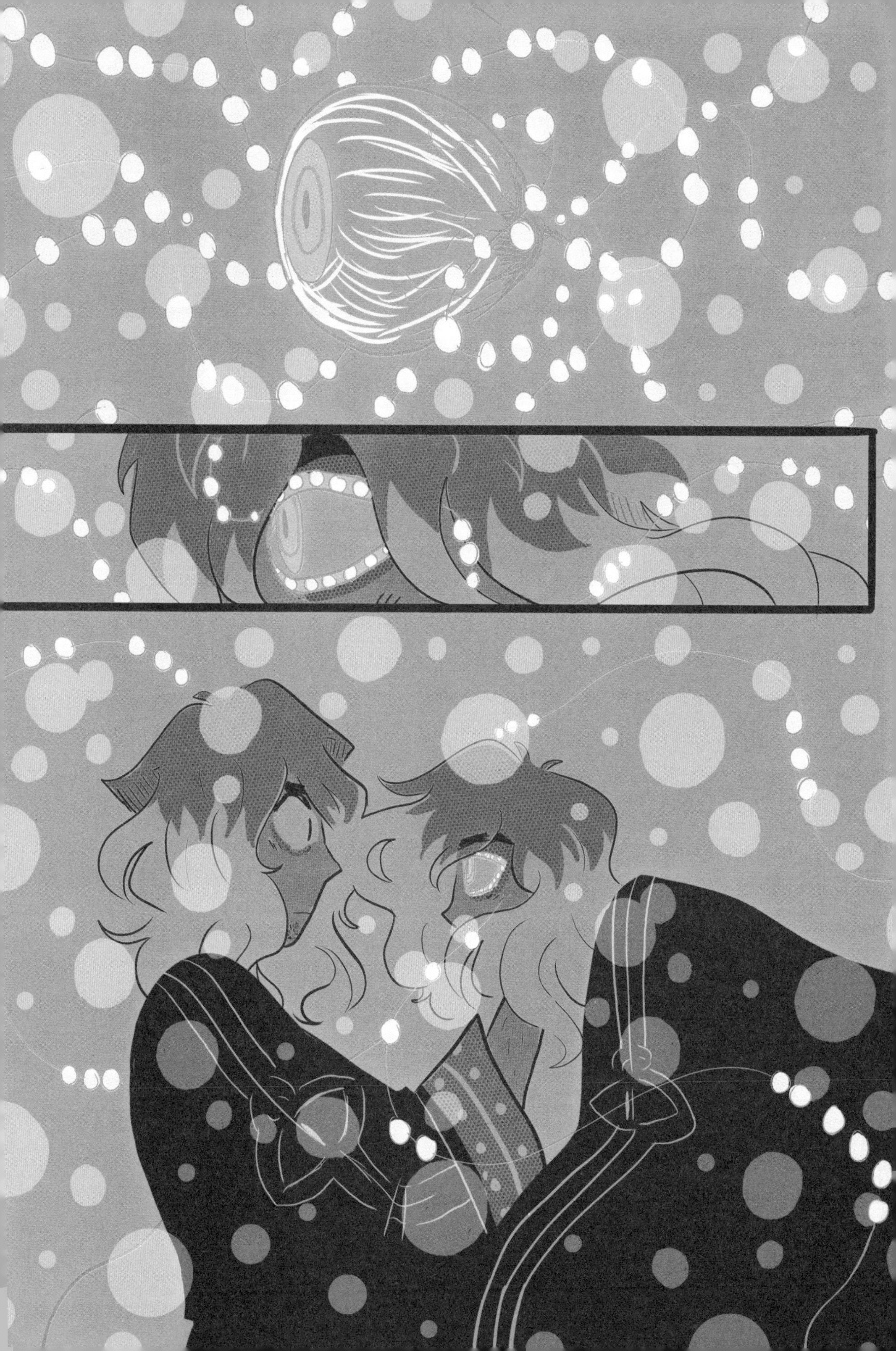

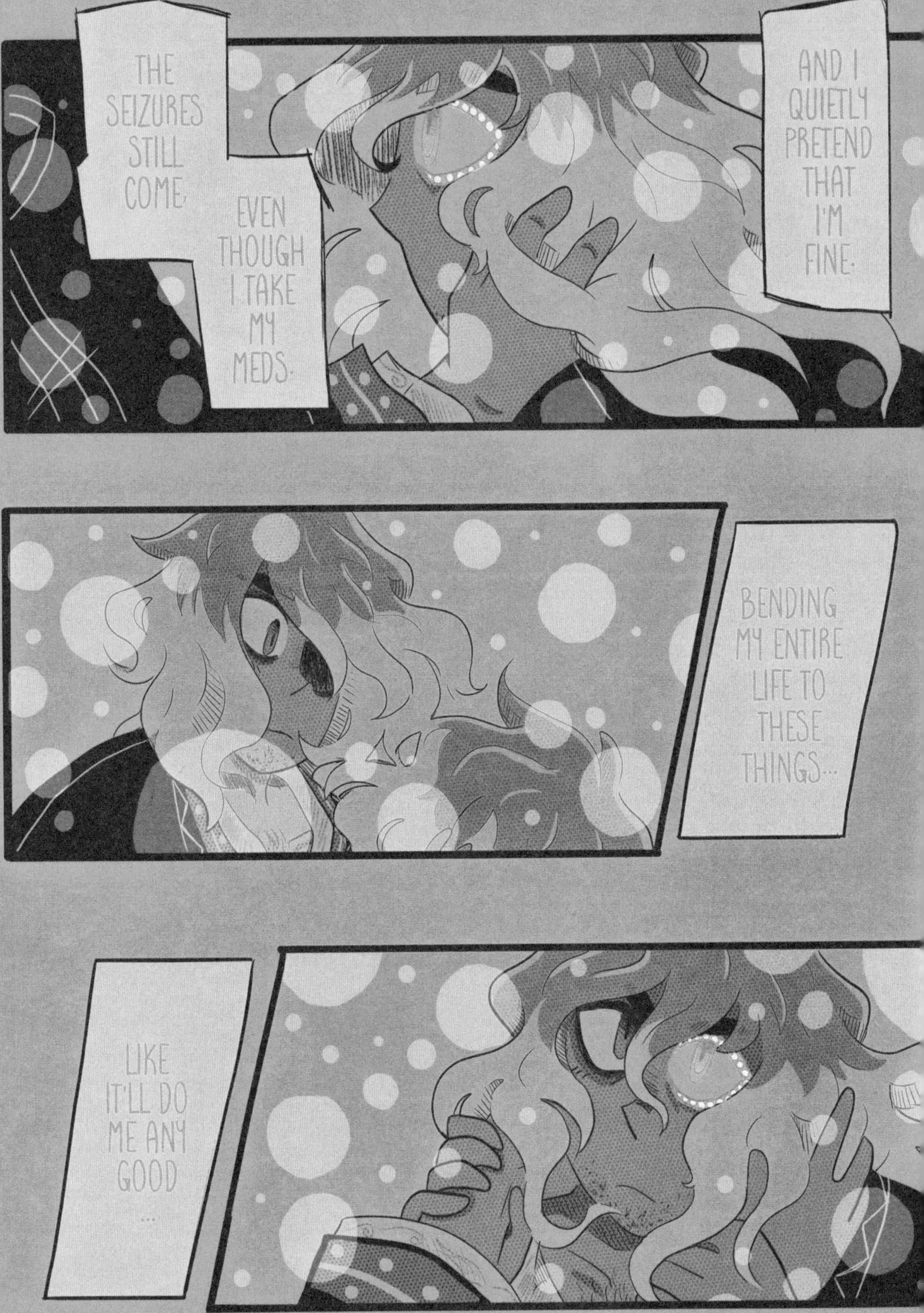
THE SEIZURES STILL COME,
EVEN THOUGH I TAKE MY MEDS.
AND I QUIETLY PRETEND THAT I'M FINE.
BENDING MY ENTIRE LIFE TO THESE THINGS...
LIKE IT'LL DO ME ANY GOOD
...

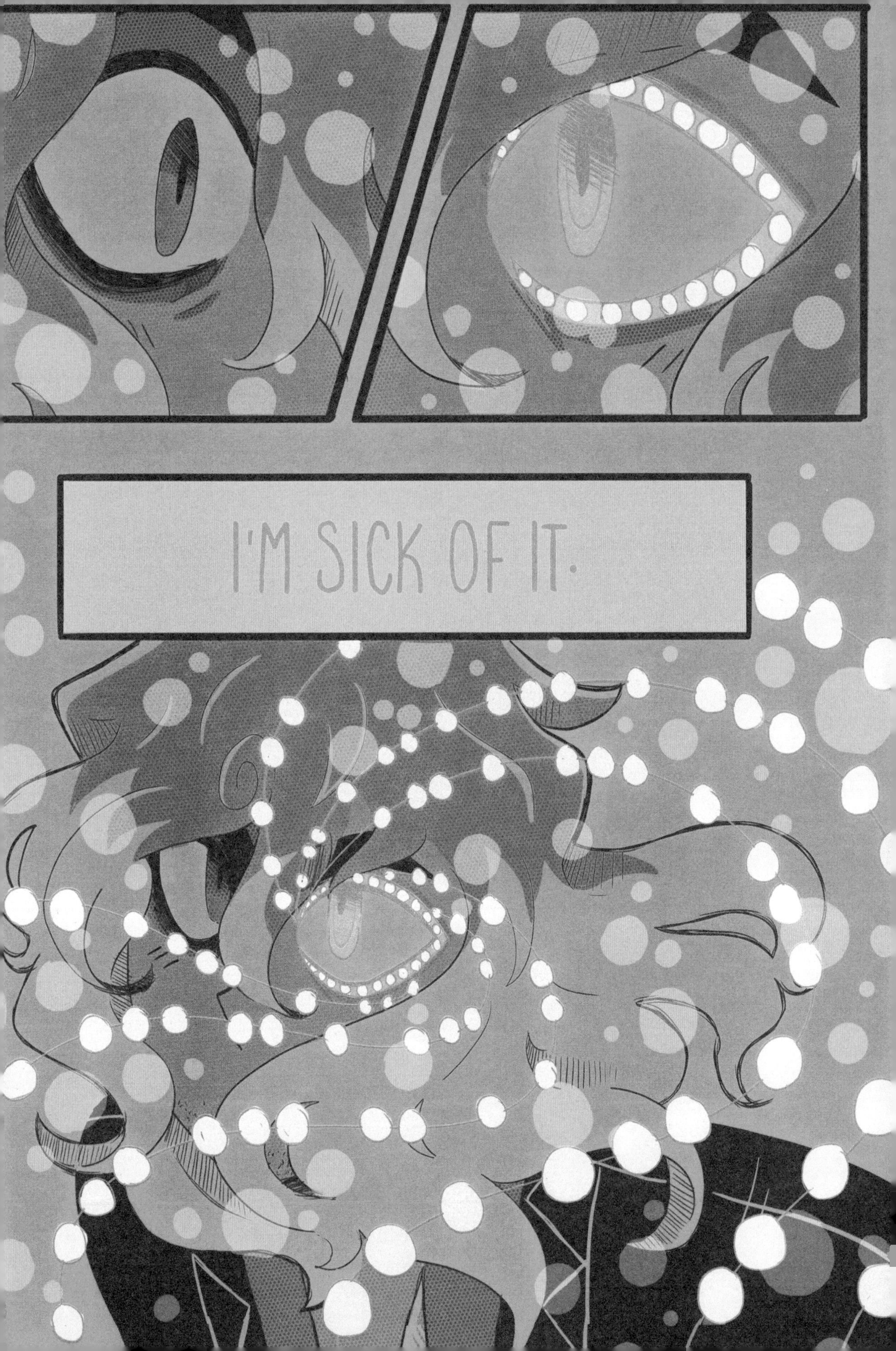
I'M SICK OF IT.

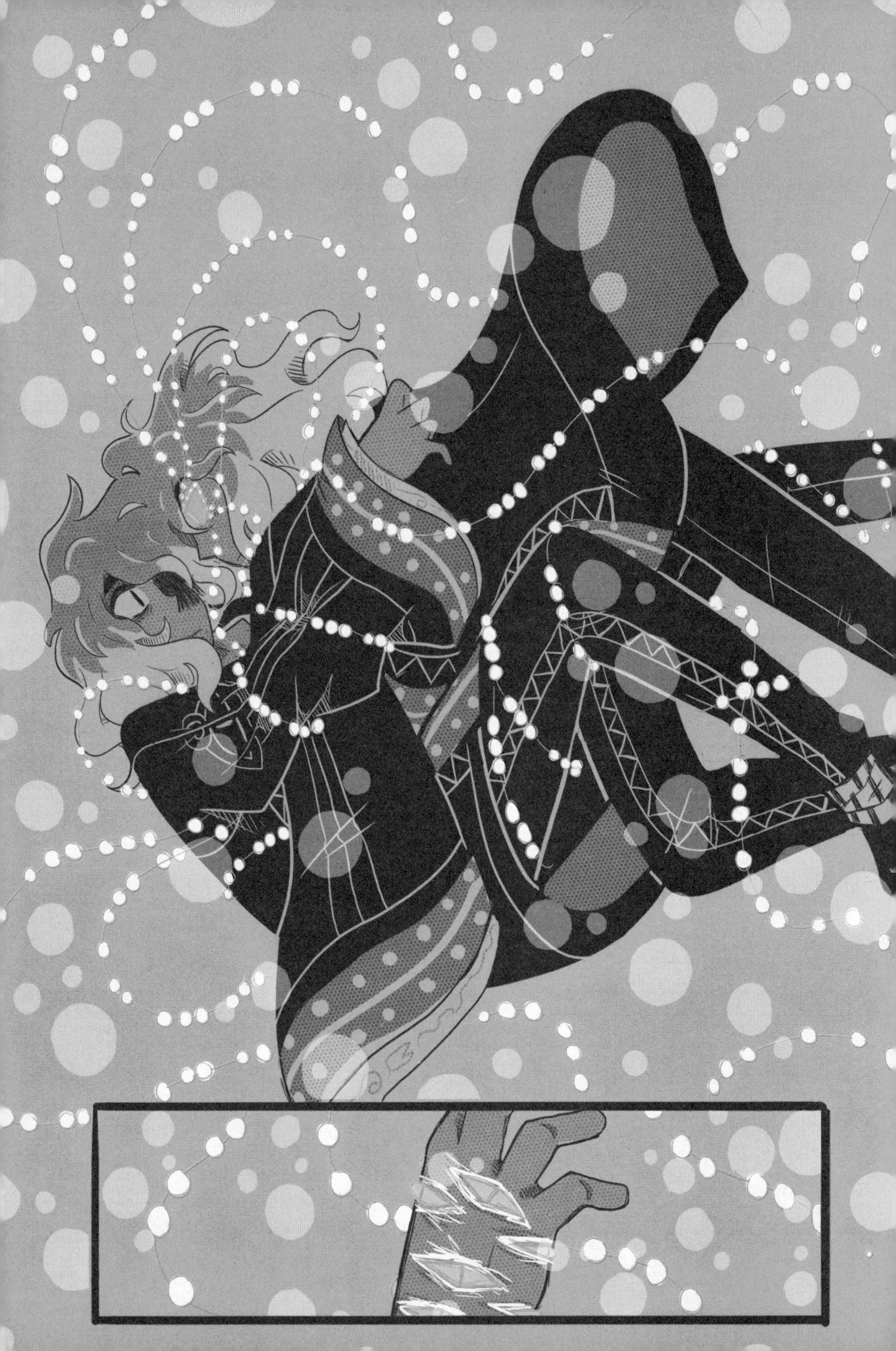

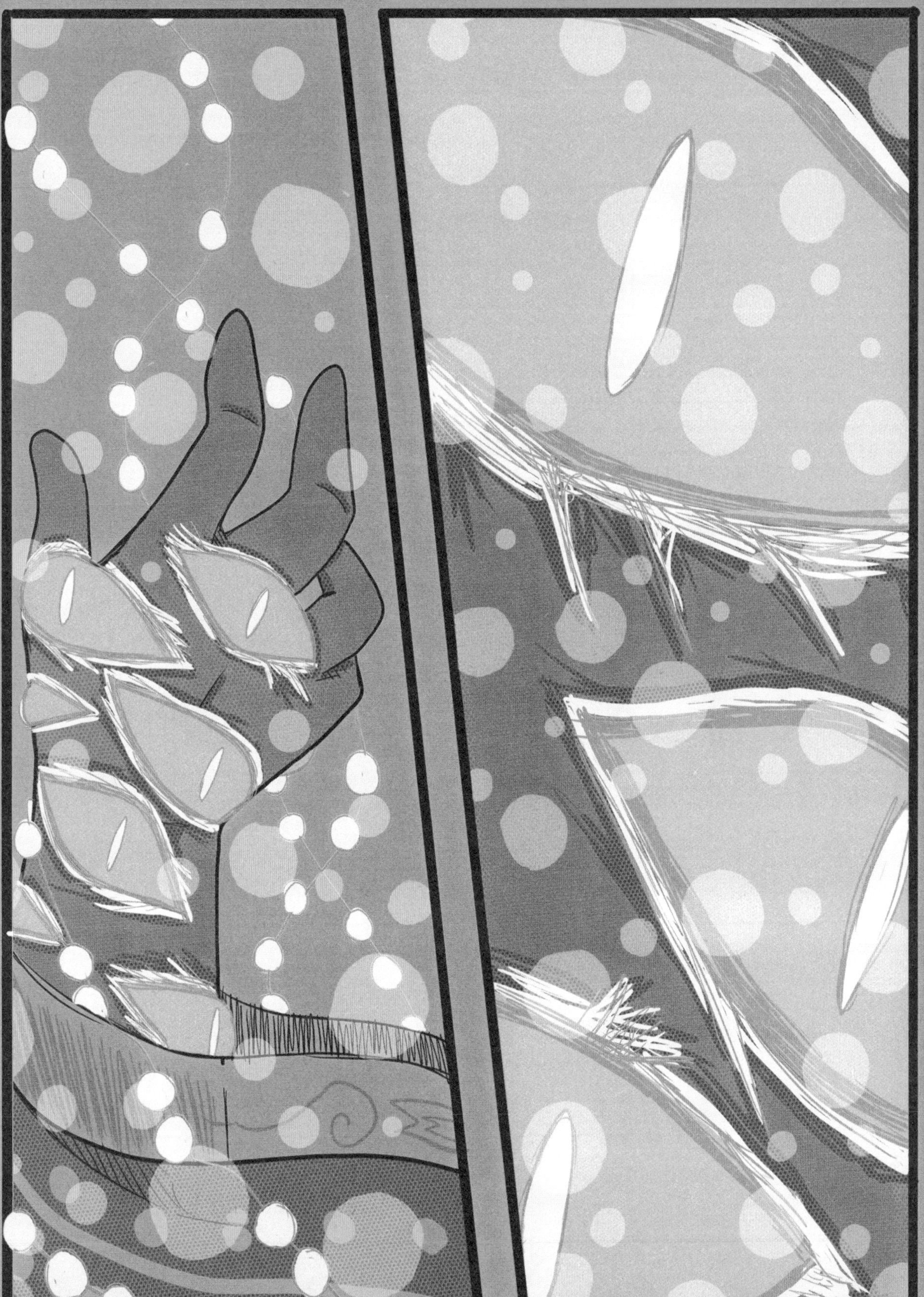

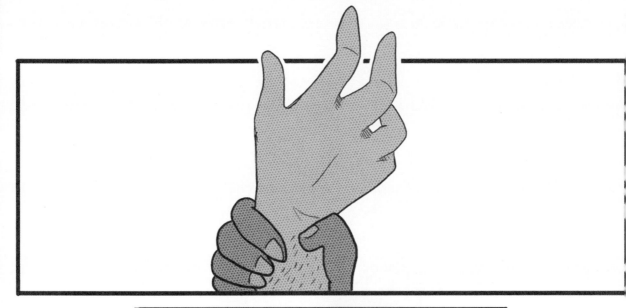

JO...?

UH, YEAH... WE HAD PLANS TODAY... REMEMBER?

OH... RIGHT...

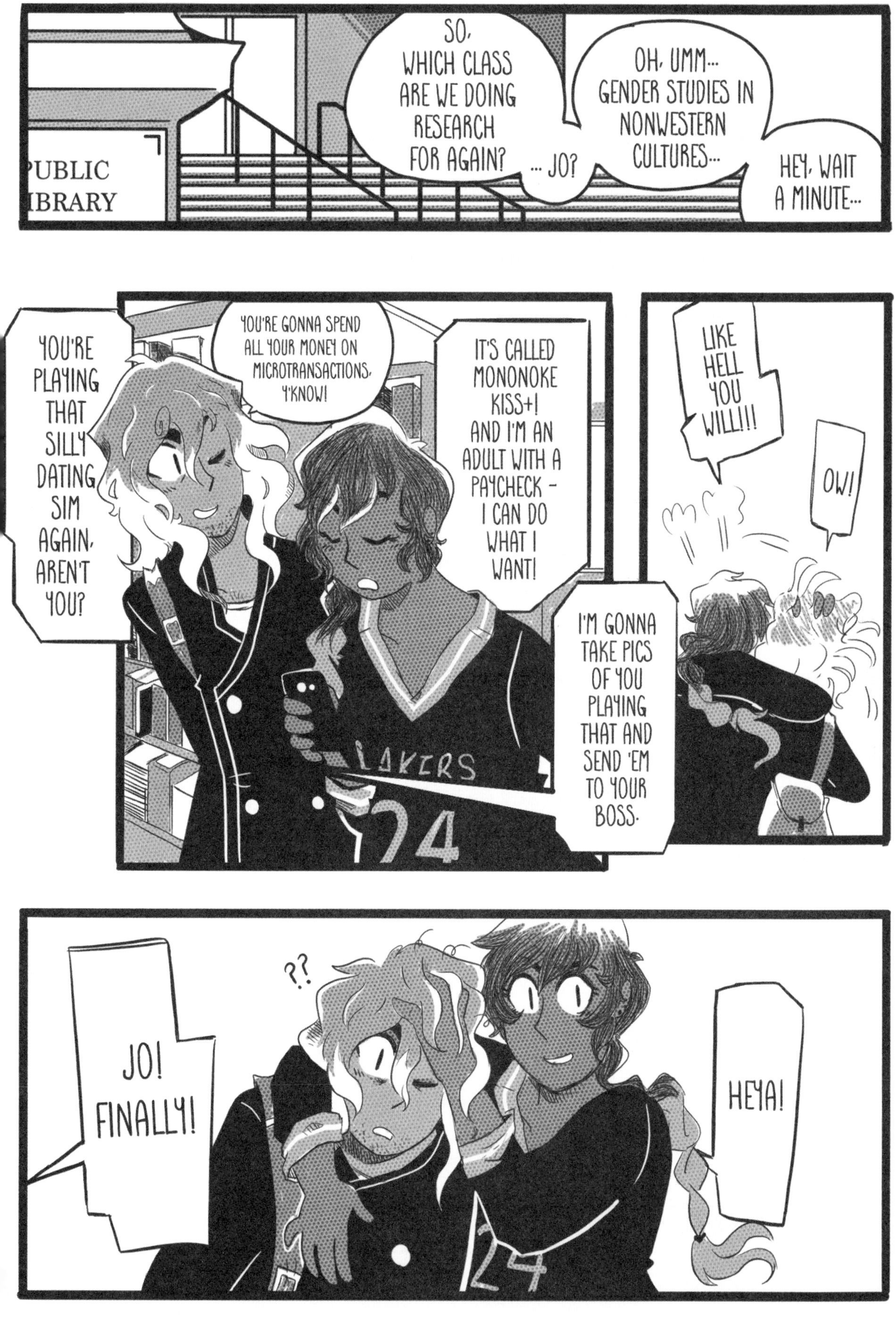
PUBLIC
LIBRARY
SO, WHICH CLASS ARE WE DOING RESEARCH FOR AGAIN?
... JO?
OH, UMM... GENDER STUDIES IN NONWESTERN CULTURES...
HEY, WAIT A MINUTE...
YOU'RE PLAYING THAT SILLY DATING SIM AGAIN, AREN'T YOU?
YOU'RE GONNA SPEND ALL YOUR MONEY ON MICROTRANSACTIONS, Y'KNOW!
IT'S CALLED MONONOKE KISS+! AND I'M AN ADULT WITH A PAYCHECK - I CAN DO WHAT I WANT!
I'M GONNA TAKE PICS OF YOU PLAYING THAT AND SEND 'EM TO YOUR BOSS.
LAKERS
24
LIKE HELL YOU WILL!!!
OW!
??
JO! FINALLY!
HEYA!

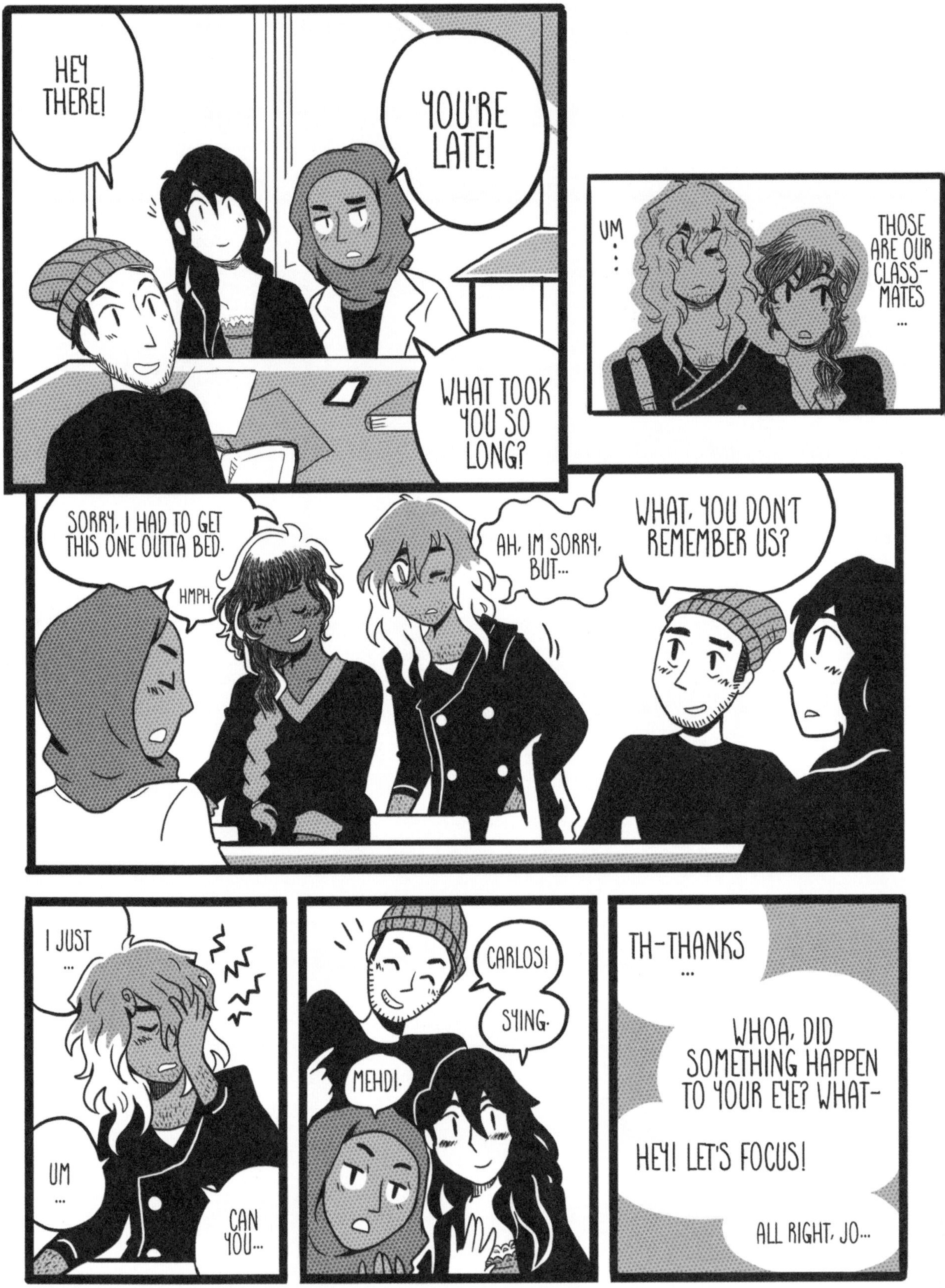
HEY THERE!
YOU'RE LATE!
WHAT TOOK YOU SO LONG?
UM...
THOSE ARE OUR CLASS-MATES...
SORRY, I HAD TO GET THIS ONE OUTTA BED.
HMPH.
AH, IM SORRY, BUT...
WHAT, YOU DON'T REMEMBER US?
I JUST...
UM...
CAN YOU...
CARLOS!
SYING.
MEHDI.
TH-THANKS...
WHOA, DID SOMETHING HAPPEN TO YOUR EYE? WHAT-
HEY! LET'S FOCUS!
ALL RIGHT, JO...

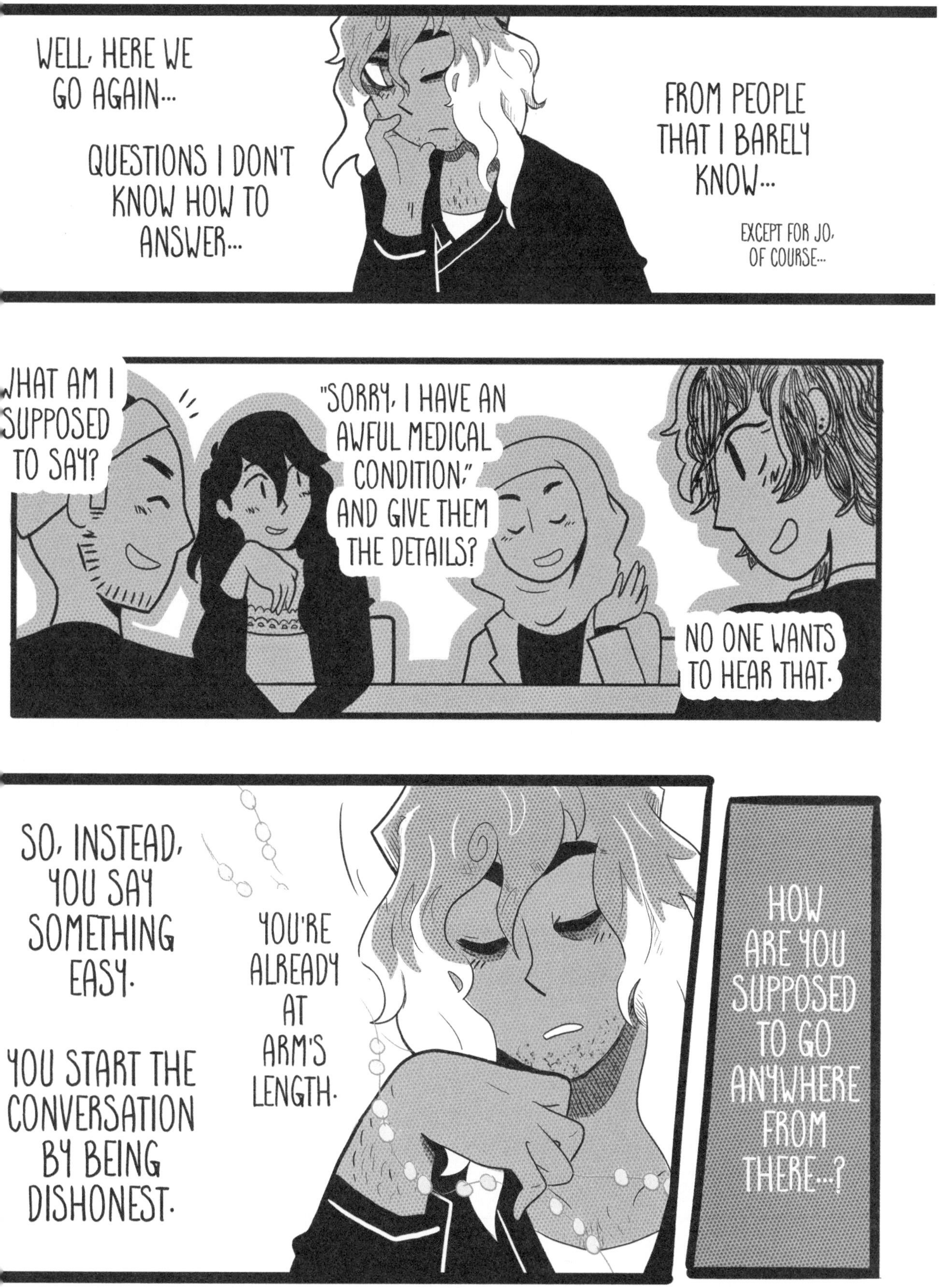
WELL, HERE WE GO AGAIN...
QUESTIONS I DON'T KNOW HOW TO ANSWER...
FROM PEOPLE THAT I BARELY KNOW...
EXCEPT FOR JO, OF COURSE...
WHAT AM I SUPPOSED TO SAY?
"SORRY, I HAVE AN AWFUL MEDICAL CONDITION," AND GIVE THEM THE DETAILS?
NO ONE WANTS TO HEAR THAT.
SO, INSTEAD, YOU SAY SOMETHING EASY.
YOU START THE CONVERSATION BY BEING DISHONEST.
YOU'RE ALREADY AT ARM'S LENGTH.
HOW ARE YOU SUPPOSED TO GO ANYWHERE FROM THERE...?

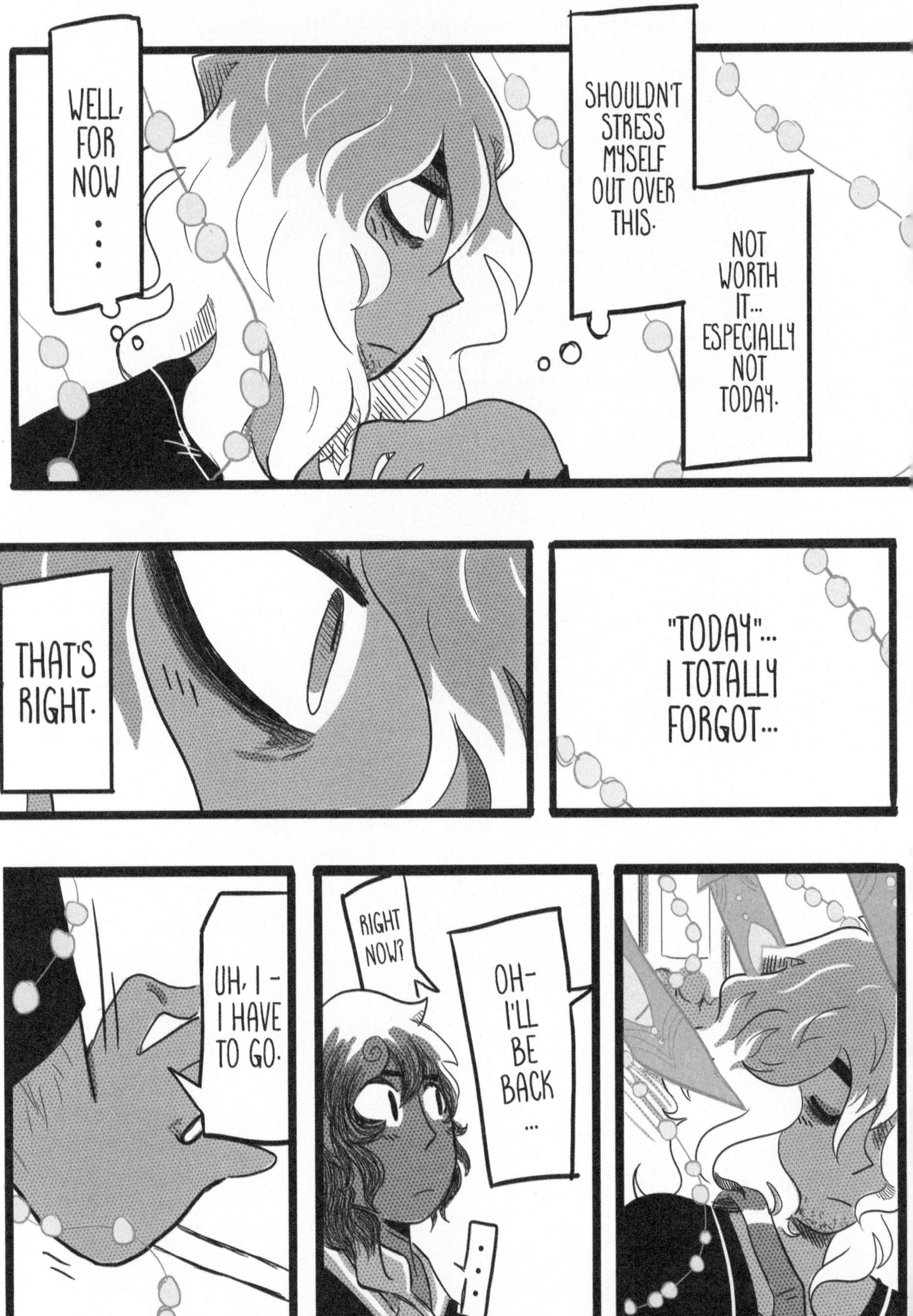
WELL, FOR NOW ...
SHOULDN'T STRESS MYSELF OUT OVER THIS.
NOT WORTH IT... ESPECIALLY NOT TODAY.
THAT'S RIGHT.
"TODAY"... I TOTALLY FORGOT...
UH, I - I HAVE TO GO.
RIGHT NOW?
OH- I'LL BE BACK ...
...

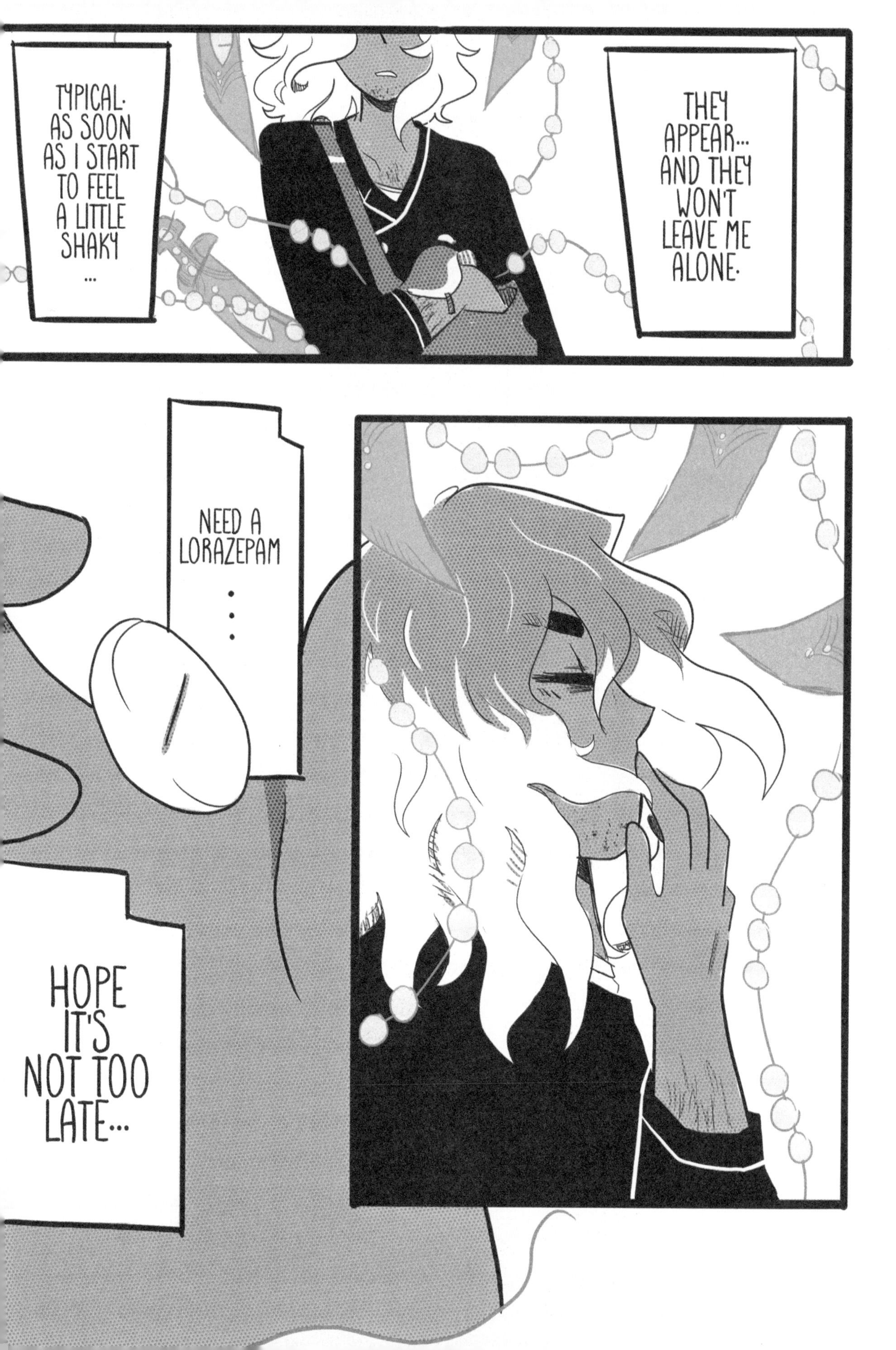
TYPICAL. AS SOON AS I START TO FEEL A LITTLE SHAKY ...
THEY APPEAR... AND THEY WON'T LEAVE ME ALONE.
NEED A LORAZEPAM ...
HOPE IT'S NOT TOO LATE...

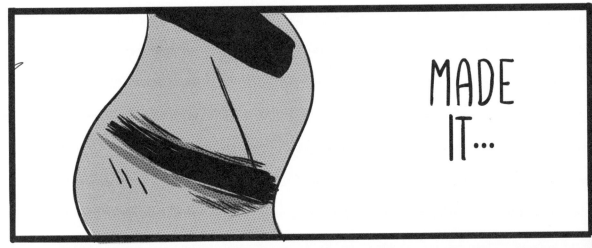

MADE IT...

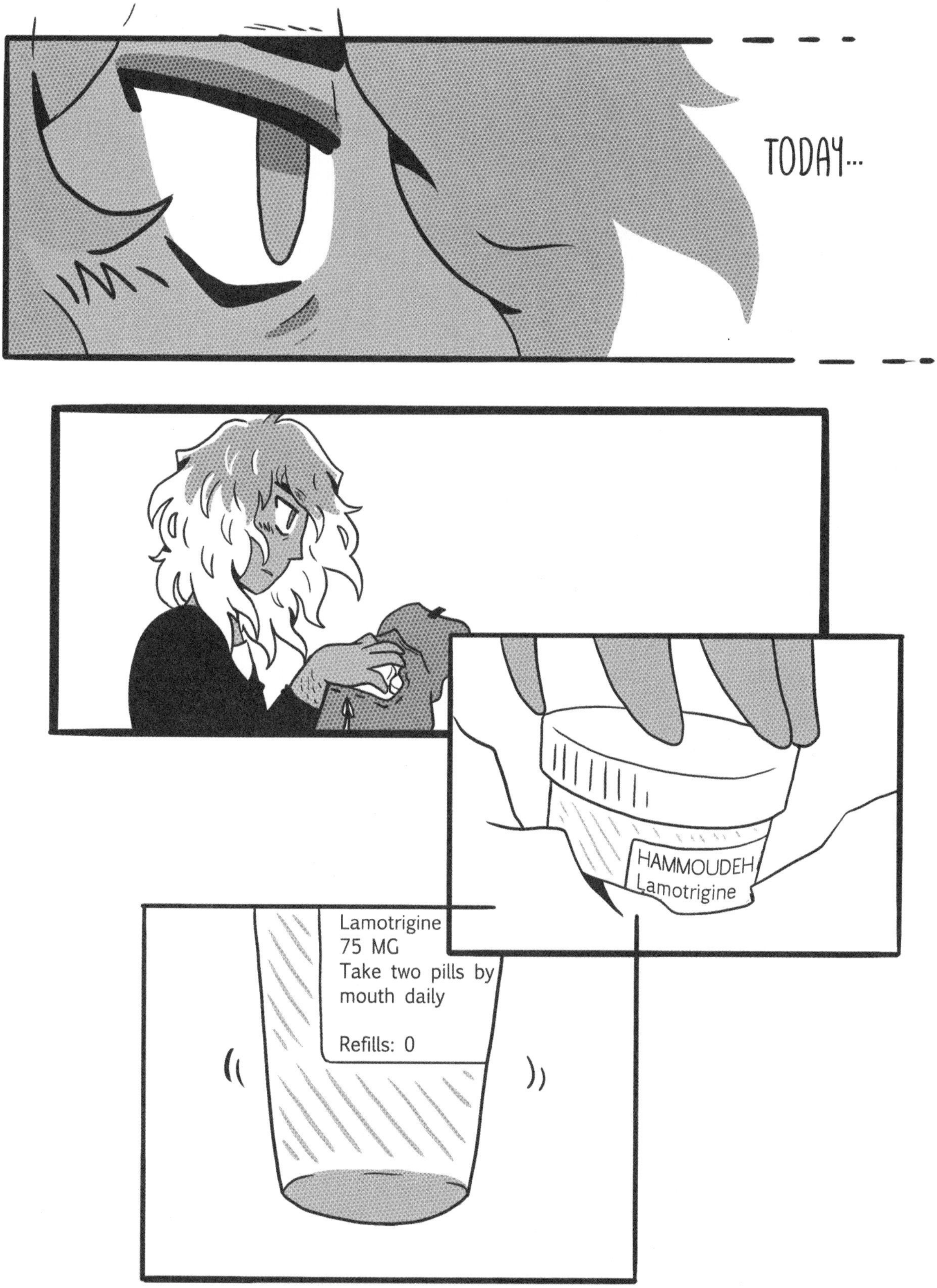
TODAY...
HAMMOUDEH
Lamotrigine
Lamotrigine
75 MG
Take two pills by
mouth daily
Refills: 0

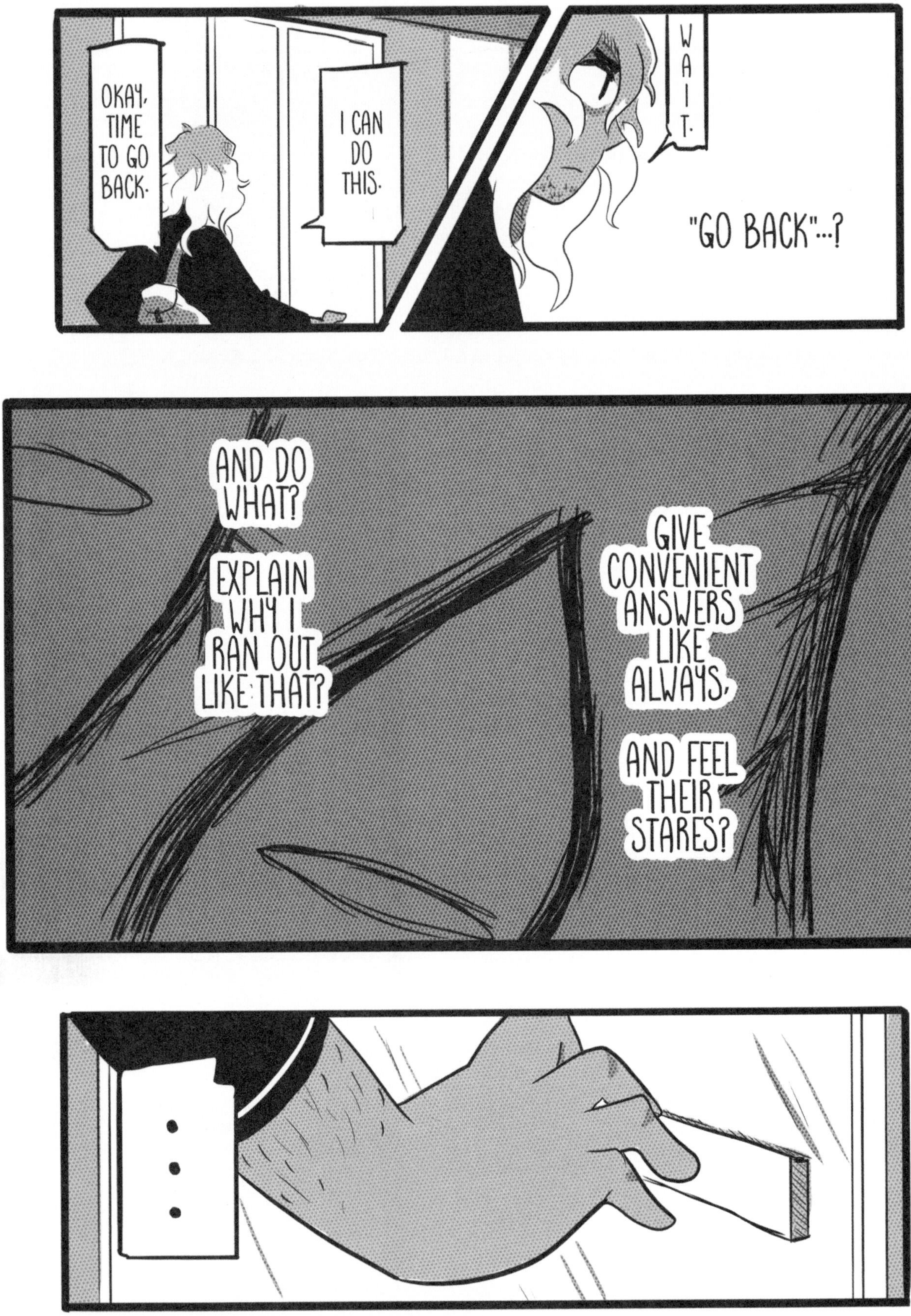
OKAY, TIME TO GO BACK.
I CAN DO THIS.
WAIT.
"GO BACK"...?
AND DO WHAT?
EXPLAIN WHY I RAN OUT LIKE THAT?
GIVE CONVENIENT ANSWERS LIKE ALWAYS,
AND FEEL THEIR STARES?
...

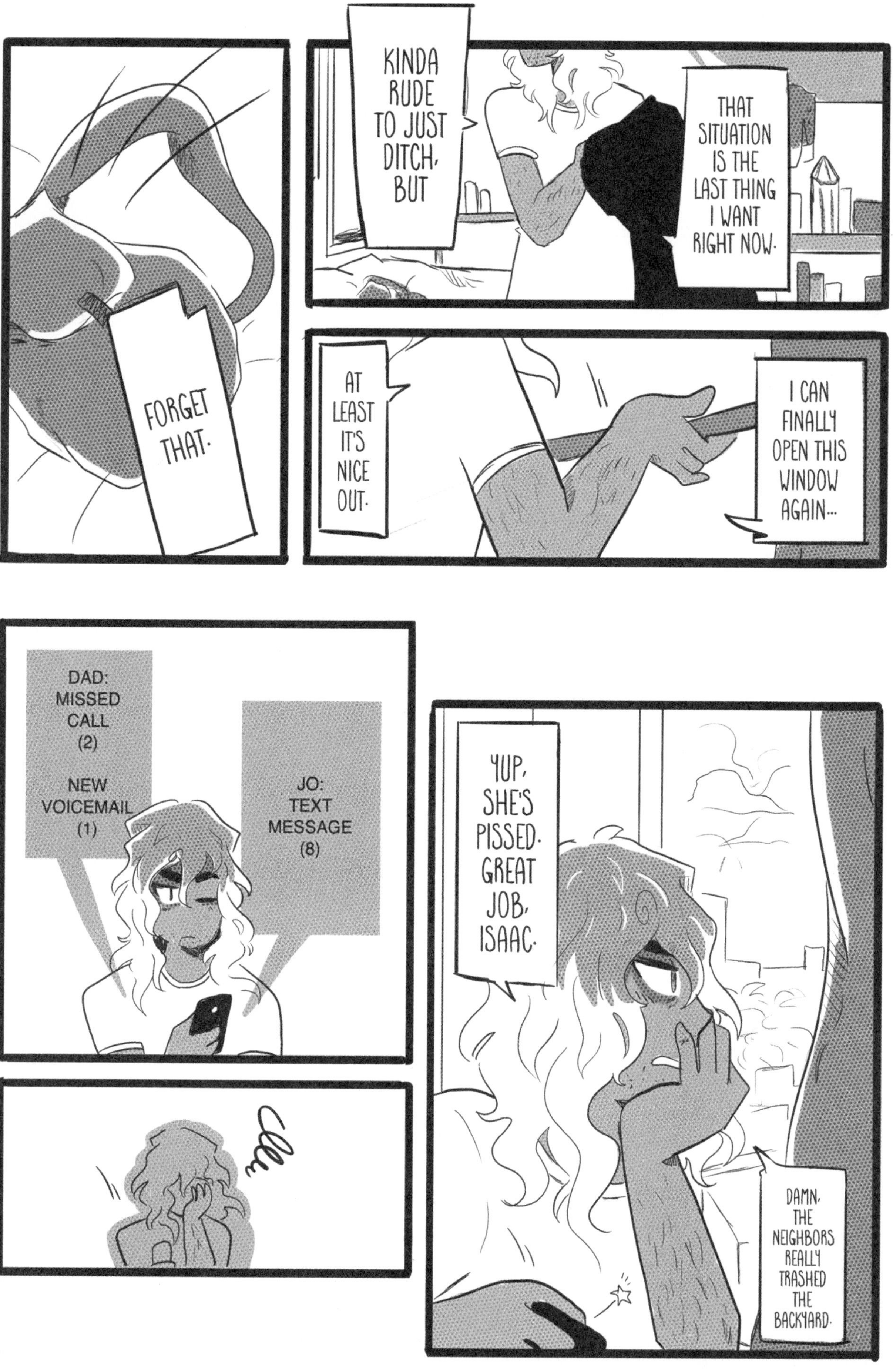
FORGET THAT.
KINDA RUDE TO JUST DITCH, BUT
THAT SITUATION IS THE LAST THING I WANT RIGHT NOW.
AT LEAST IT'S NICE OUT.
I CAN FINALLY OPEN THIS WINDOW AGAIN...
DAD: MISSED CALL (2) NEW VOICEMAIL (1)
JO: TEXT MESSAGE (8)
YUP, SHE'S PISSED. GREAT JOB, ISAAC.
DAMN. THE NEIGHBORS REALLY TRASHED THE BACKYARD.

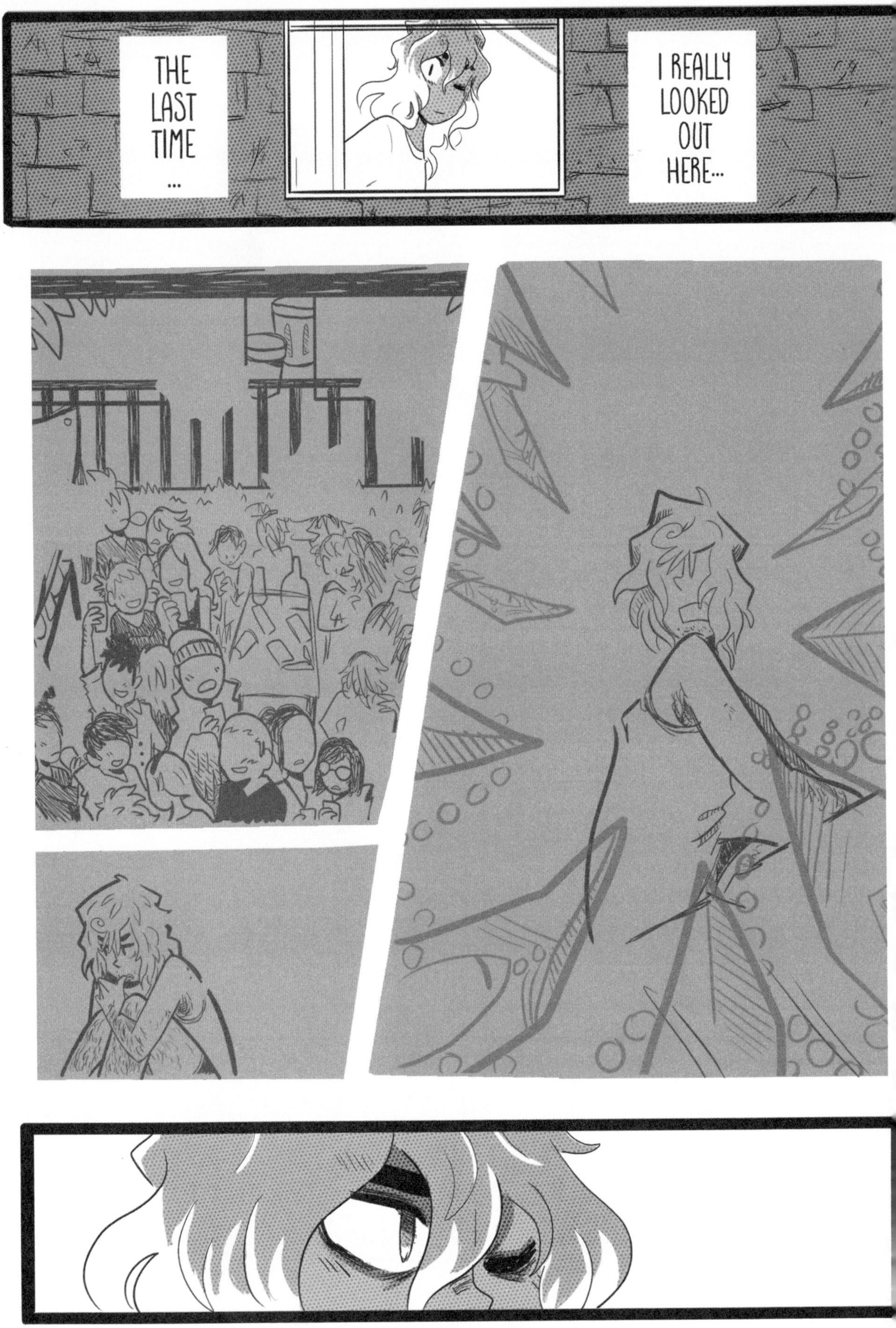
THE LAST TIME ...
I REALLY LOOKED OUT HERE...

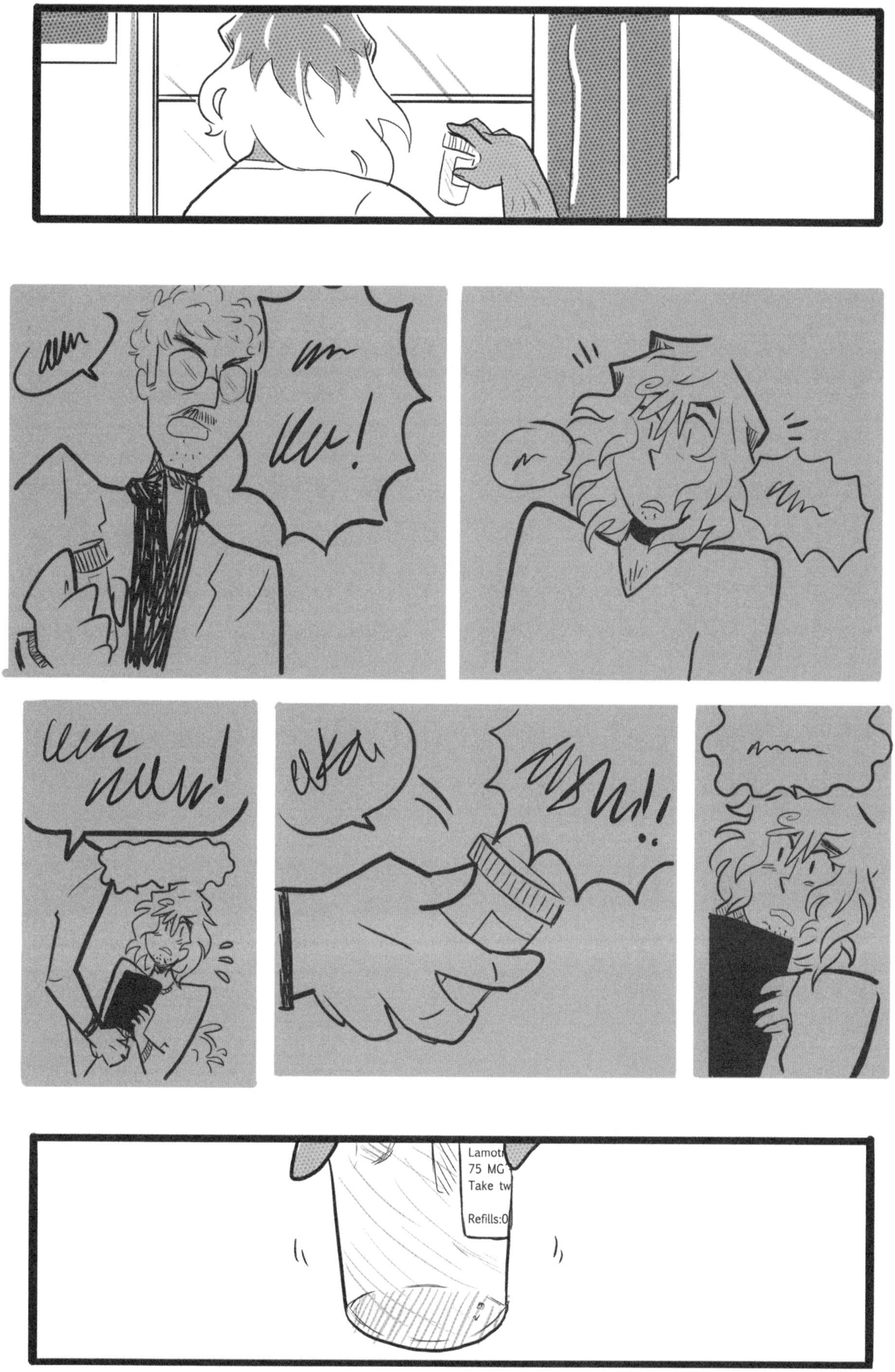
Lamotr
75 MG
Take tw
Refills:0

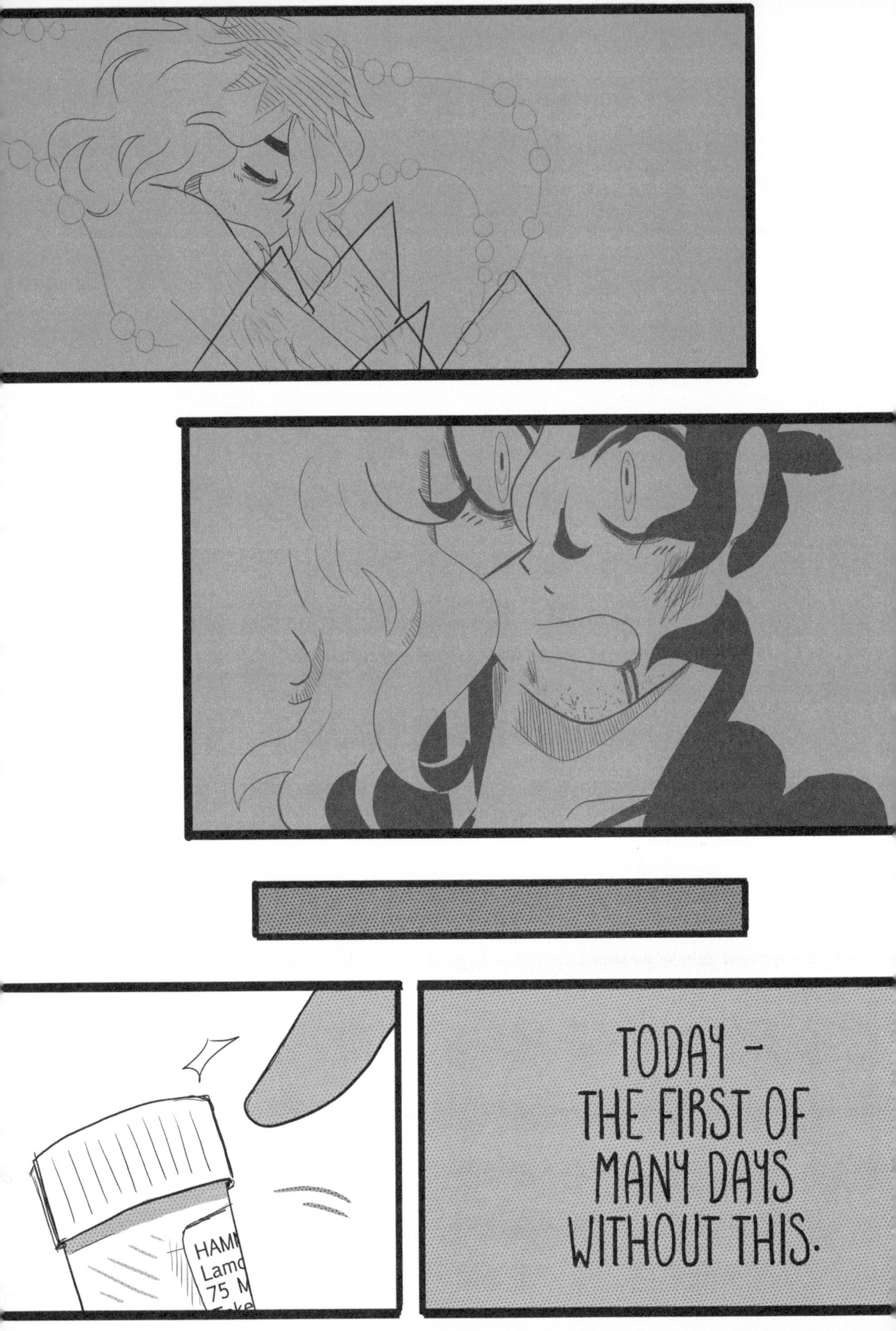
TODAY -
THE FIRST OF
MANY DAYS
WITHOUT THIS.

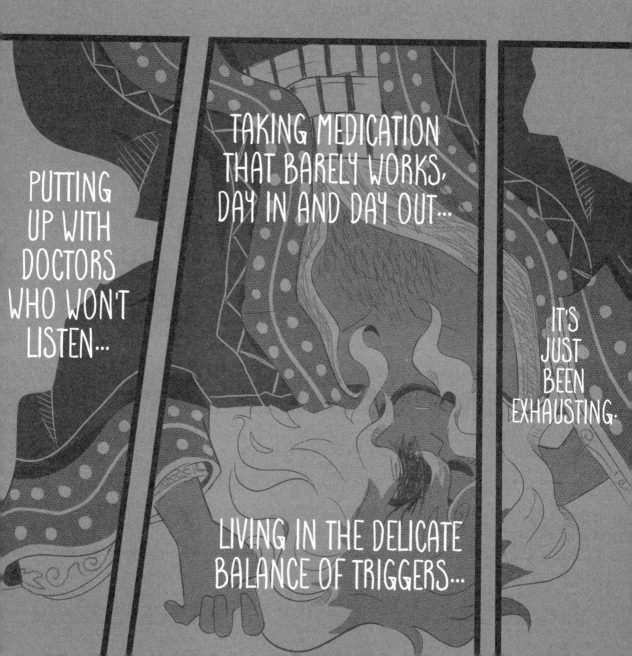

ALL I HAVE LEFT IS A
HANDFUL OF THE FAIL-SAFE DRUG.

THAT'S FINE.
I'LL BE ALL RIGHT.

AFTER ALL...

PUTTING
UP WITH
DOCTORS
WHO WON'T
LISTEN...

TAKING MEDICATION
THAT BARELY WORKS,
DAY IN AND DAY OUT...

IT'S
JUST
BEEN
EXHAUSTING.

LIVING IN THE DELICATE
BALANCE OF TRIGGERS...

HAMMOUDEH, ISAAC
LORAZEPAM
TAKE ONE AT
ONSET OF EPISODE
REFILLS: 0

ISAAC, LOOK!
ISN'T THIS LIKE
THAT ONE KIND
OF SEIZURE
YOU HAD?

IT SOUNDS
FAMILIAR!

HUH?
LET
ME
SEE.

Complex-partial status epileptica (also known as CPSE) is a unique form of non-convulsive epilepsy that occurs periodically, and is often described as a long-lasting dreamlike state. Patients who experience CPSE report symptoms suc as unresponsiveness, blank staring, di altered senses, and difficulty speaki

CPSE is notoriously difficult diagnose and treat because o symptoms and thus is a highly dangerous and misunderstood condit in the medical fie

ISN'T
THAT IT?

DURING THE 8 HOURS
WE SPENT AT THE
HOSPITAL, NONE OF
THE DOCTORS
THOUGHT OF THIS?

AND HOW MUCH DID
YOU HAVE TO PAY
FOR THAT VISIT?

THOSE WERE
ALL MY
SYMPTOMS.
THAT'S
TOTALLY IT.

LOOKS
LIKE IT.

DON'T
ASK...

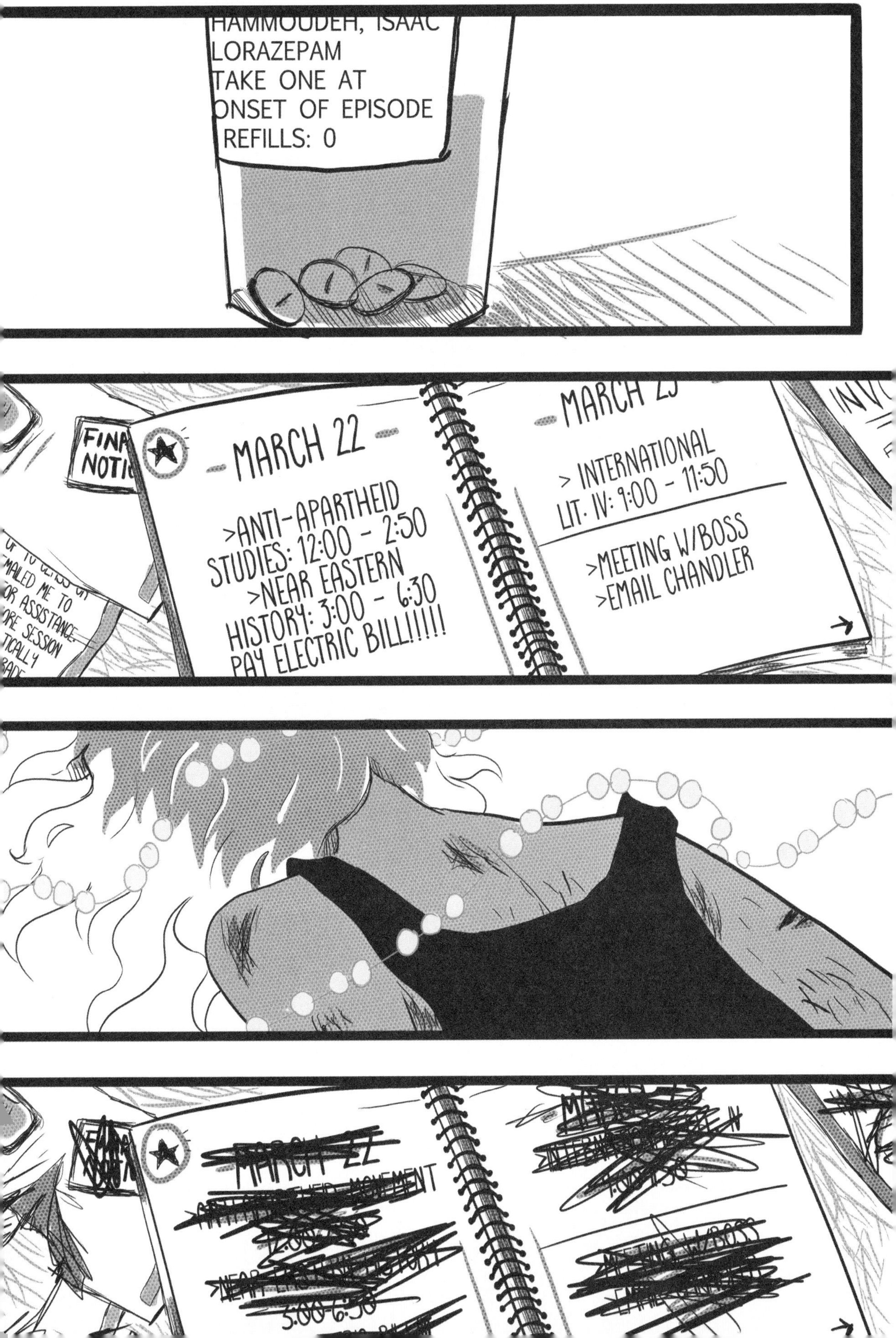
HAMMOUDEH, ISAAC
LORAZEPAM
TAKE ONE AT
ONSET OF EPISODE
REFILLS: 0
MARCH 22
>ANTI-APARTHEID
STUDIES: 12:00 - 2:50
>NEAR EASTERN
HISTORY: 3:00 - 6:30
PAY ELECTRIC BILL!!!!!
> INTERNATIONAL
LIT. IV: 9:00 - 11:50
>MEETING W/BOSS
>EMAIL CHANDLER

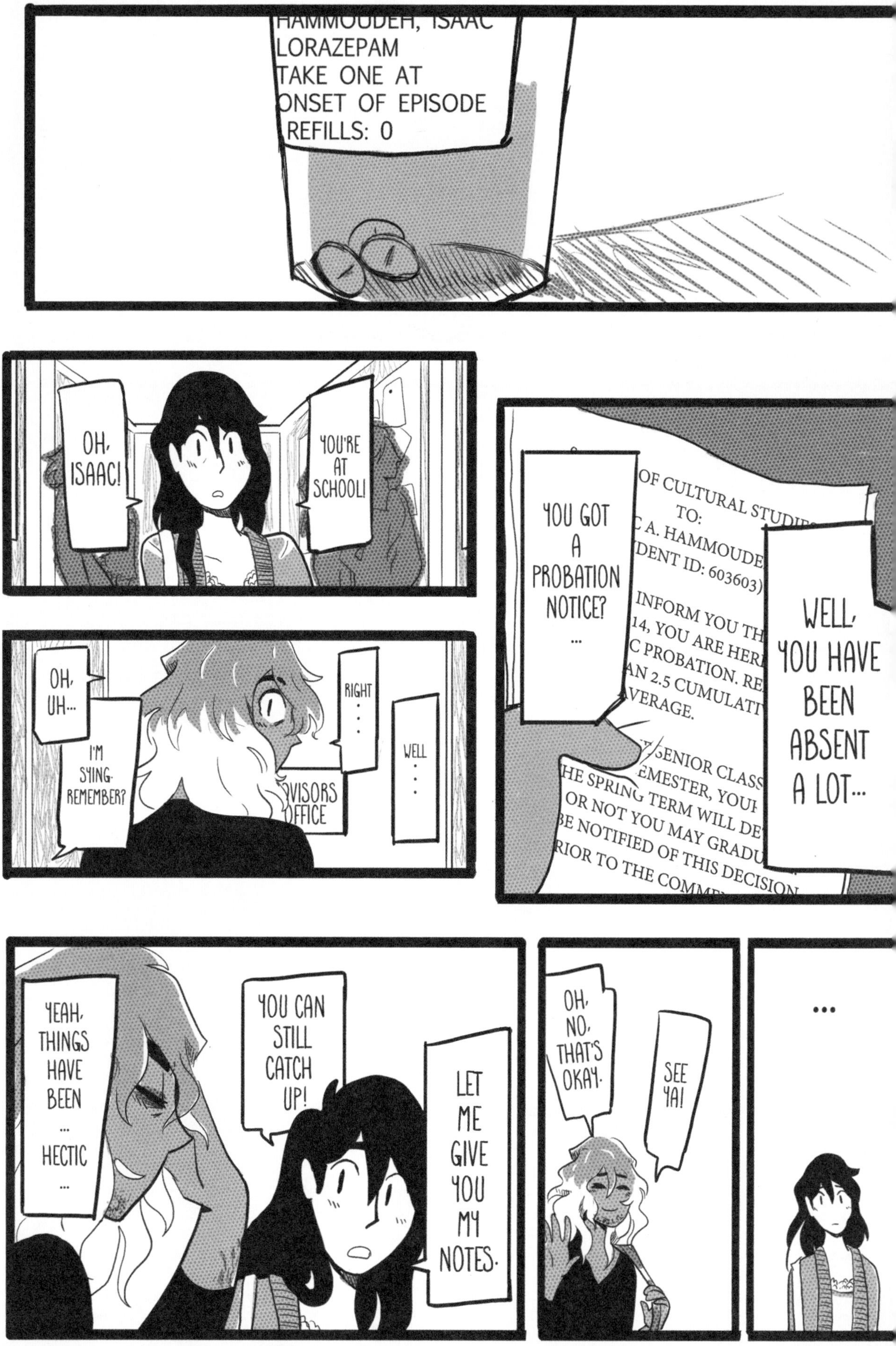
HAMMOUDEH, ISAAC
LORAZEPAM
TAKE ONE AT
ONSET OF EPISODE
REFILLS: 0
OH, ISAAC!
YOU'RE AT SCHOOL!
OH, UH...
I'M SYING. REMEMBER?
RIGHT . . .
VISORS
OFFICE
WELL . . .
YOU GOT A PROBATION NOTICE? ...
OF CULTURAL STUDI
TO:
C A. HAMMOUDE
DENT ID: 603603)
INFORM YOU TH
14, YOU ARE HER
C PROBATION. RE
AN 2.5 CUMULATI
VERAGE.
SENIOR CLASS
EMESTER, YOU
HE SPRING TERM WILL DE
OR NOT YOU MAY GRADU
BE NOTIFIED OF THIS DECISION
RIOR TO THE COMM
WELL, YOU HAVE BEEN ABSENT A LOT...
YEAH, THINGS HAVE BEEN ... HECTIC ...
YOU CAN STILL CATCH UP!
LET ME GIVE YOU MY NOTES.
OH, NO, THAT'S OKAY.
SEE YA!
...

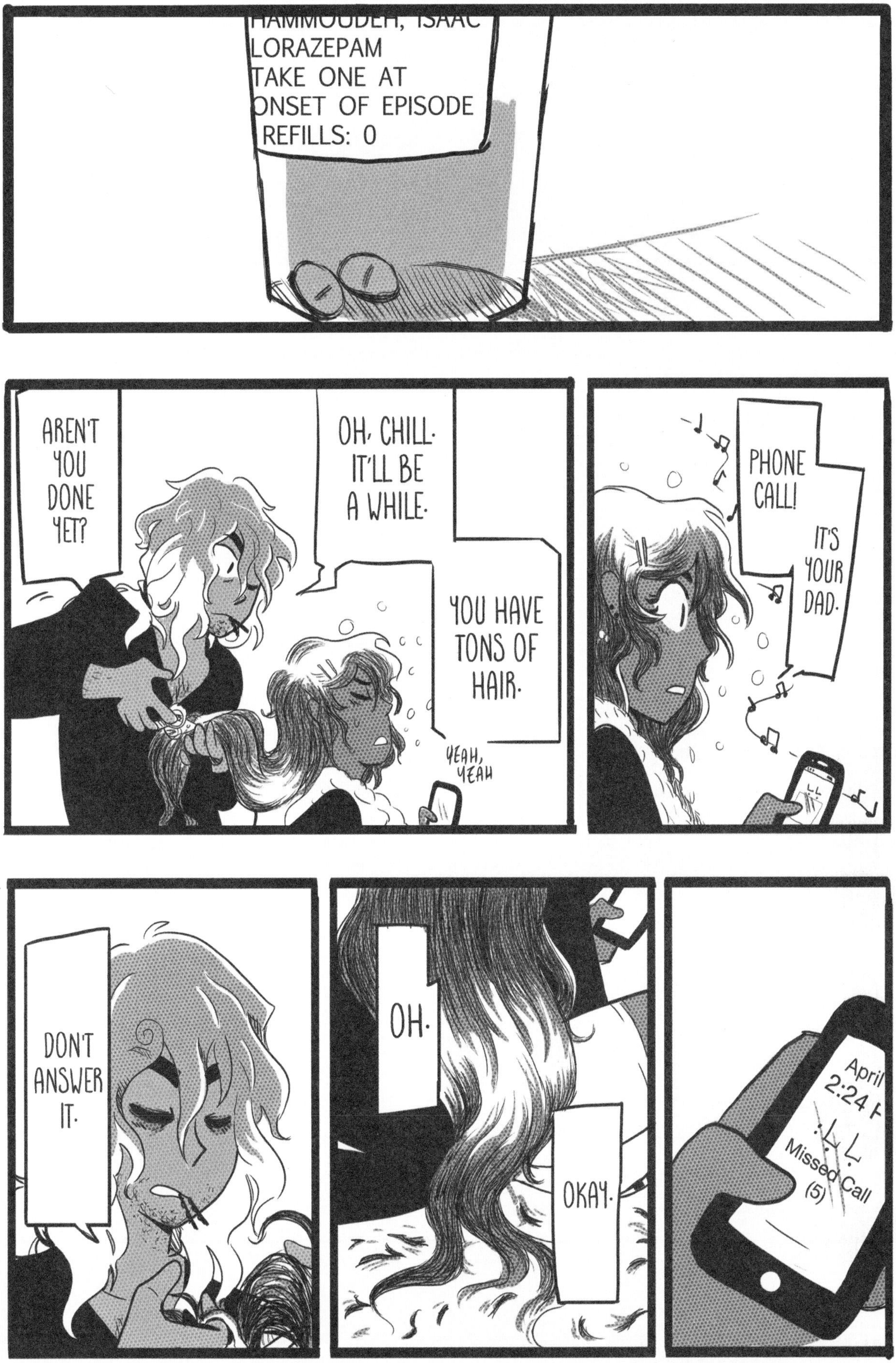
HAMMOUDEH, ISAAC
LORAZEPAM
TAKE ONE AT
ONSET OF EPISODE
REFILLS: 0
AREN'T YOU DONE YET?
OH, CHILL. IT'LL BE A WHILE.
YOU HAVE TONS OF HAIR.
YEAH, YEAH
PHONE CALL!
IT'S YOUR DAD.
DON'T ANSWER IT.
OH.
OKAY.
April
2:24
Missed Call
(5)

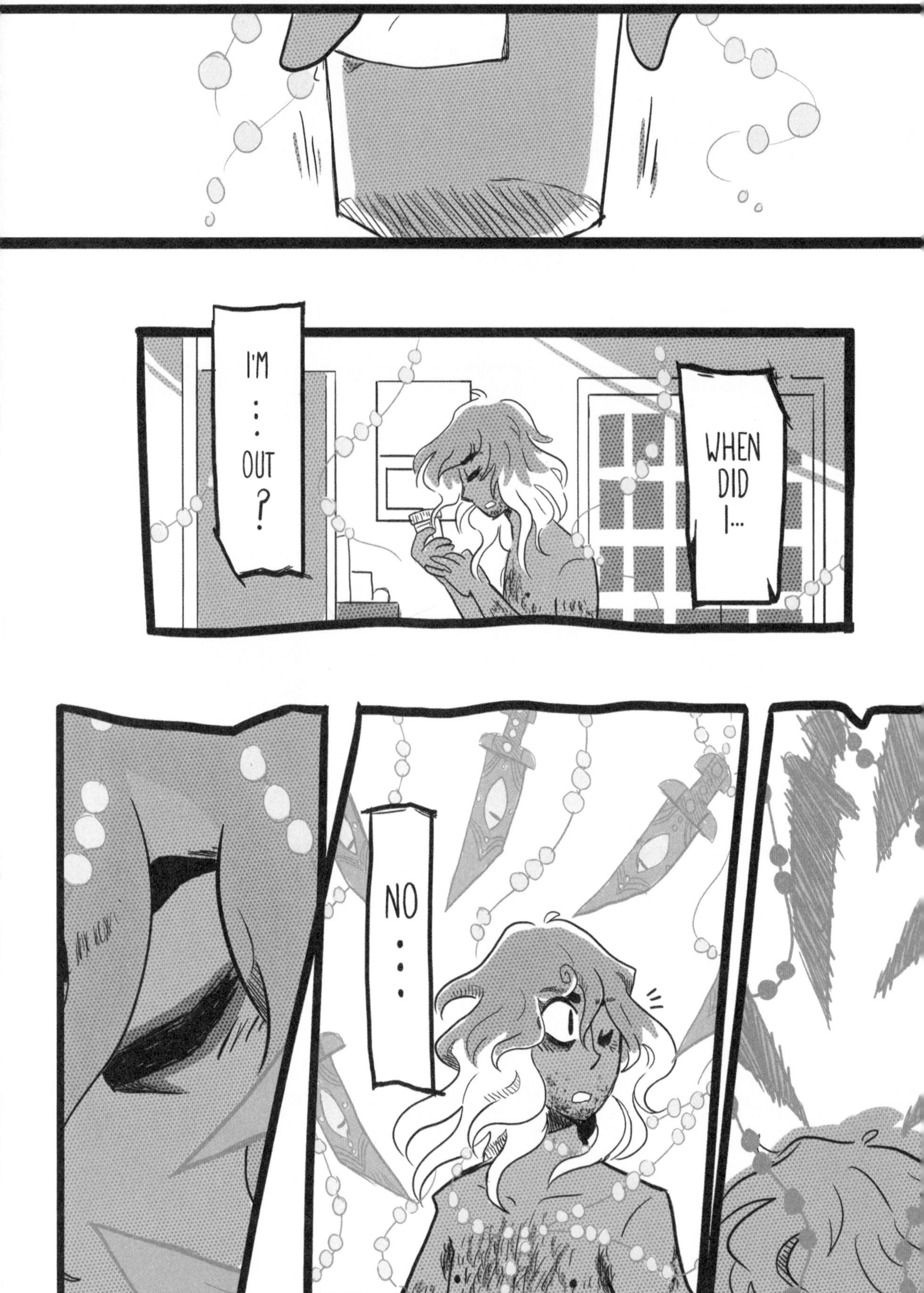
I'M ... OUT?
WHEN DID I...
NO...

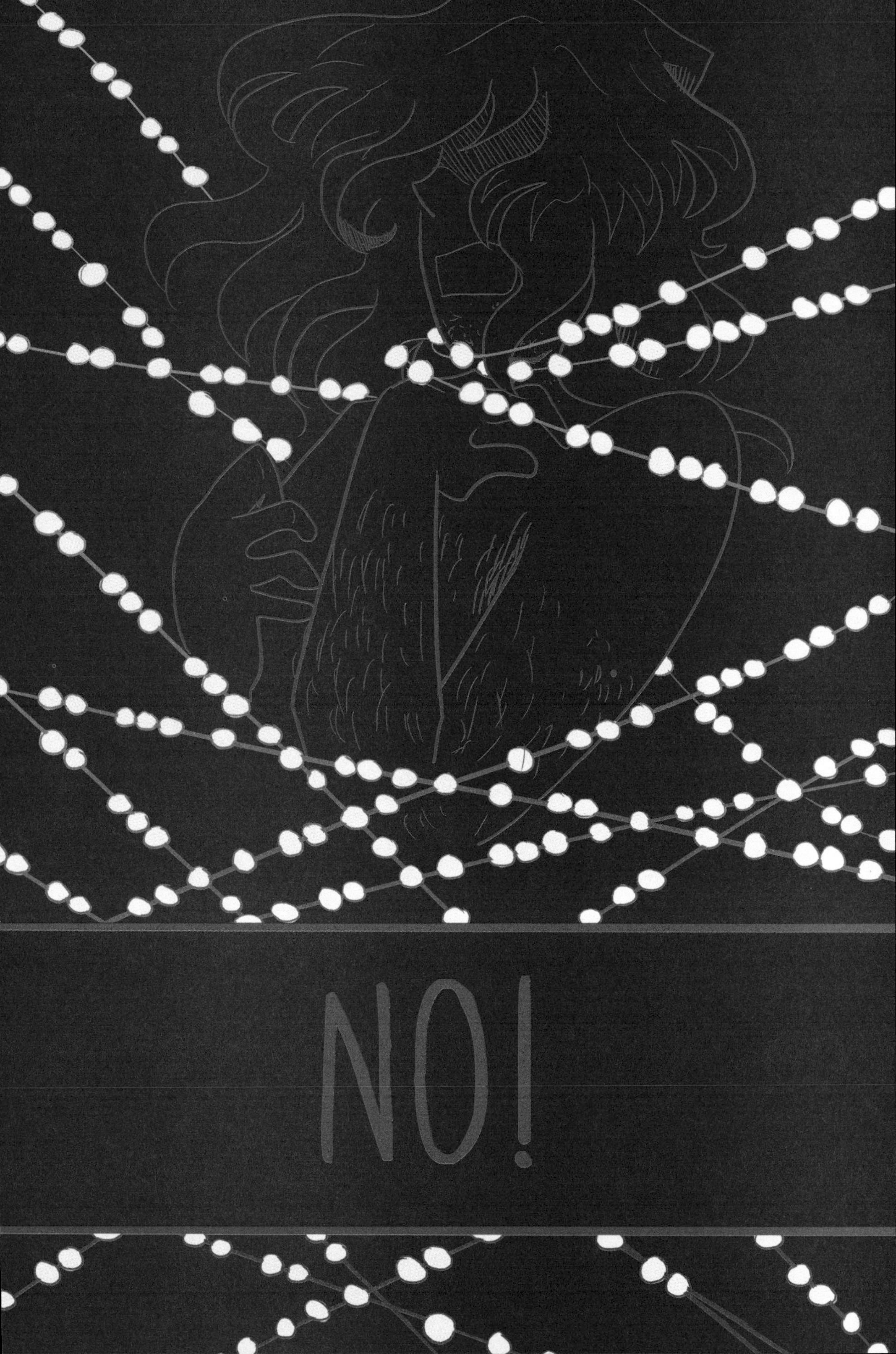
NO!

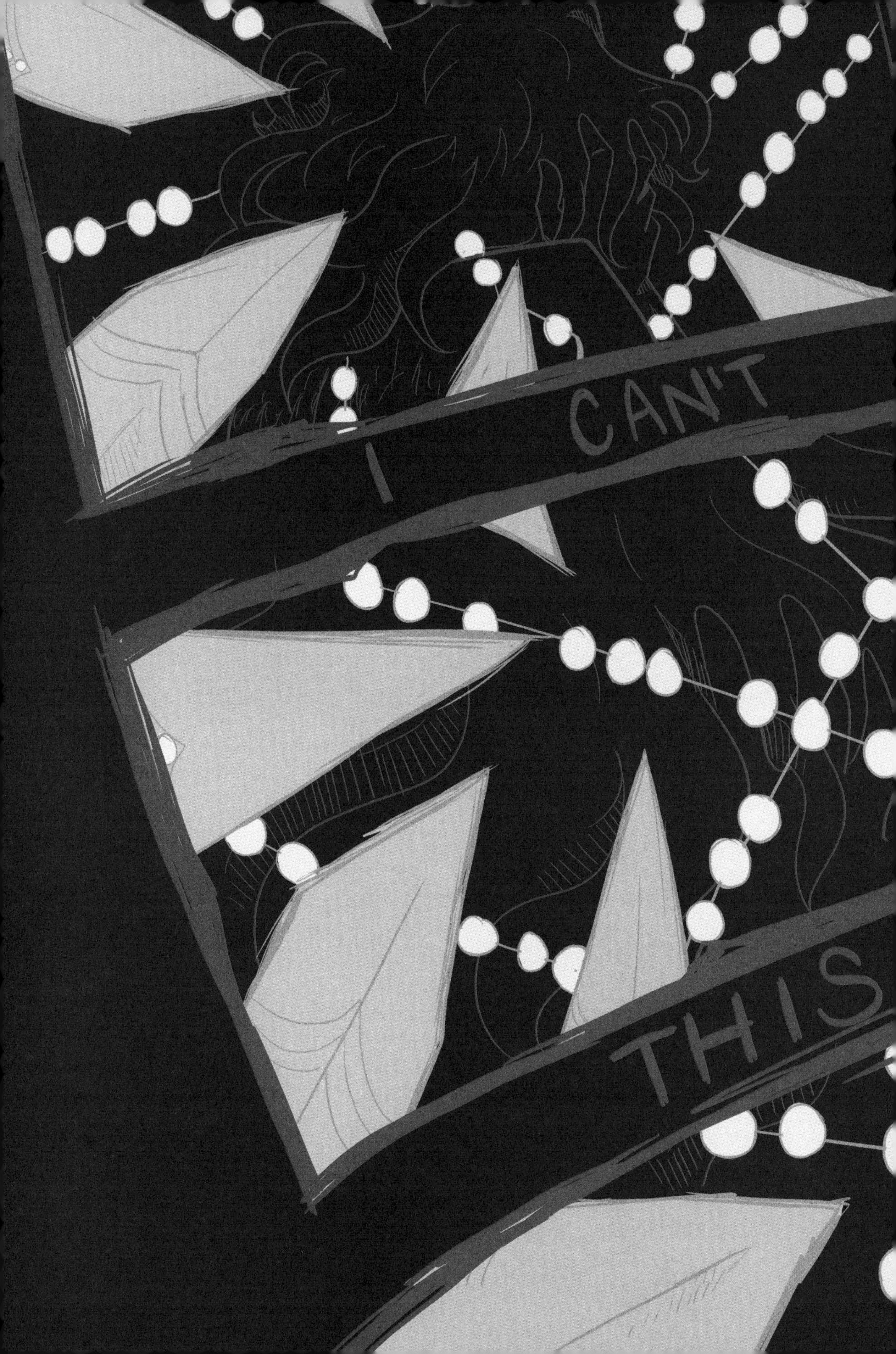
I CAN'T
THIS

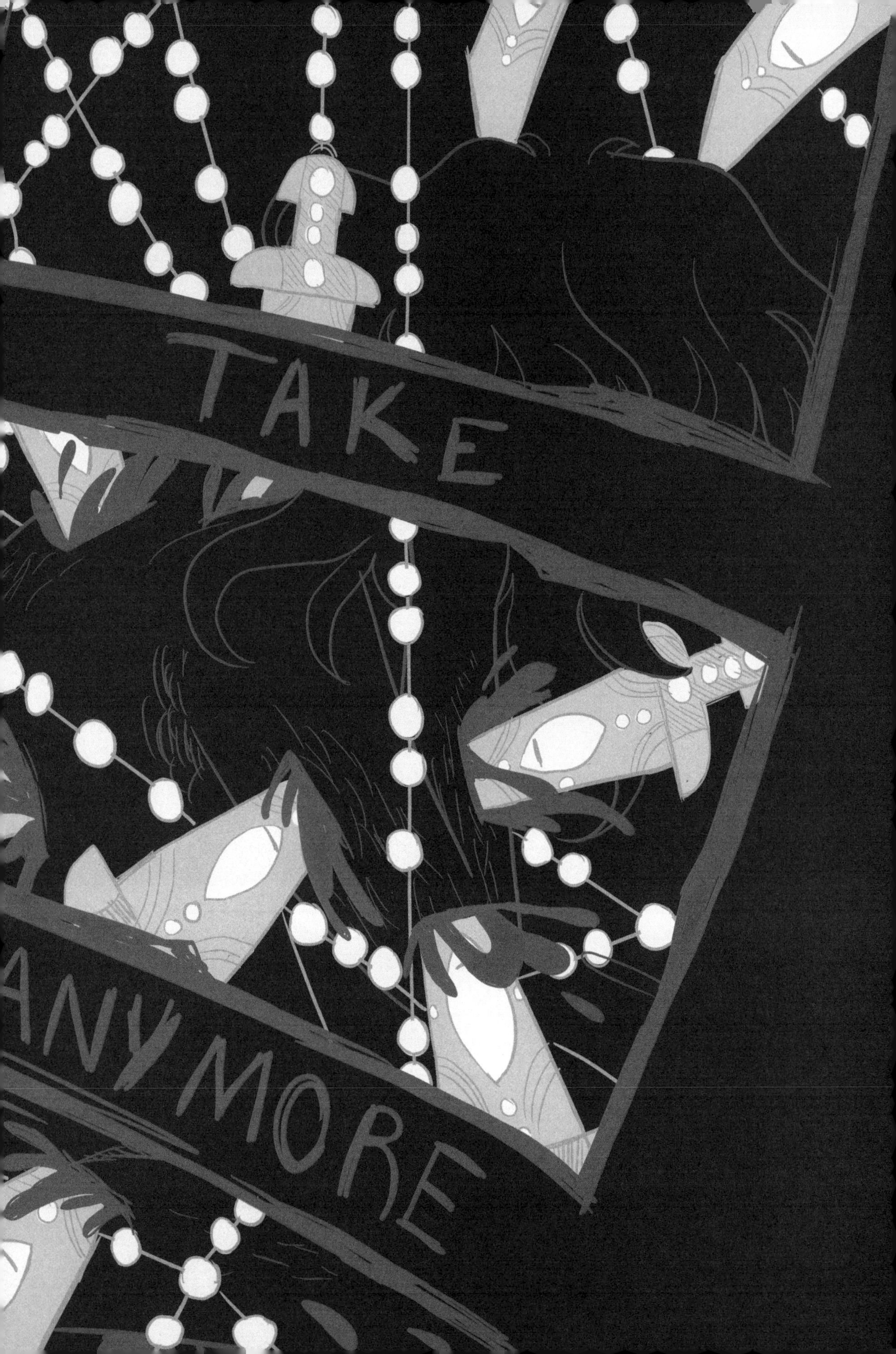
TAKE
ANYMORE

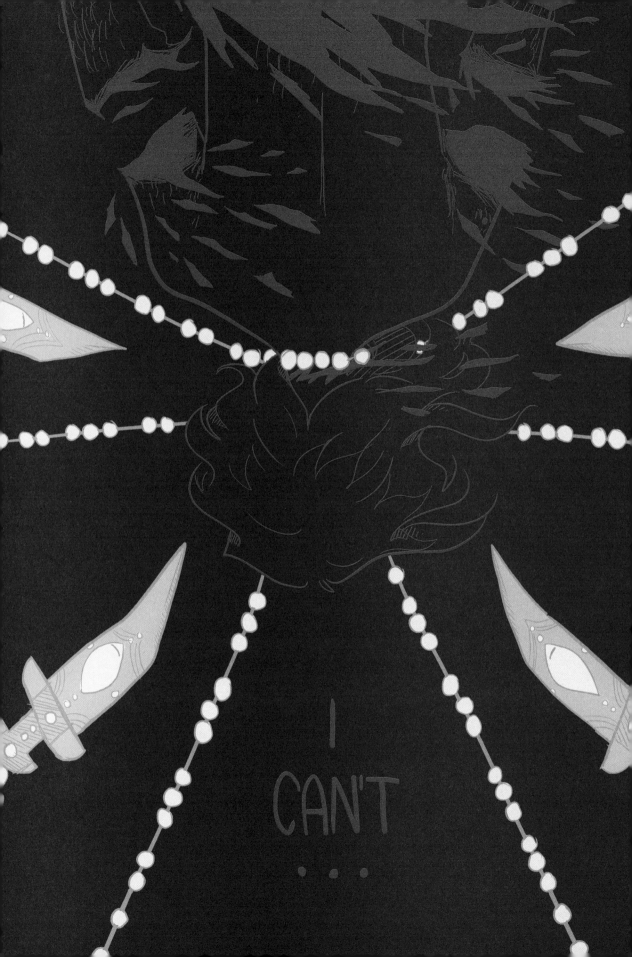

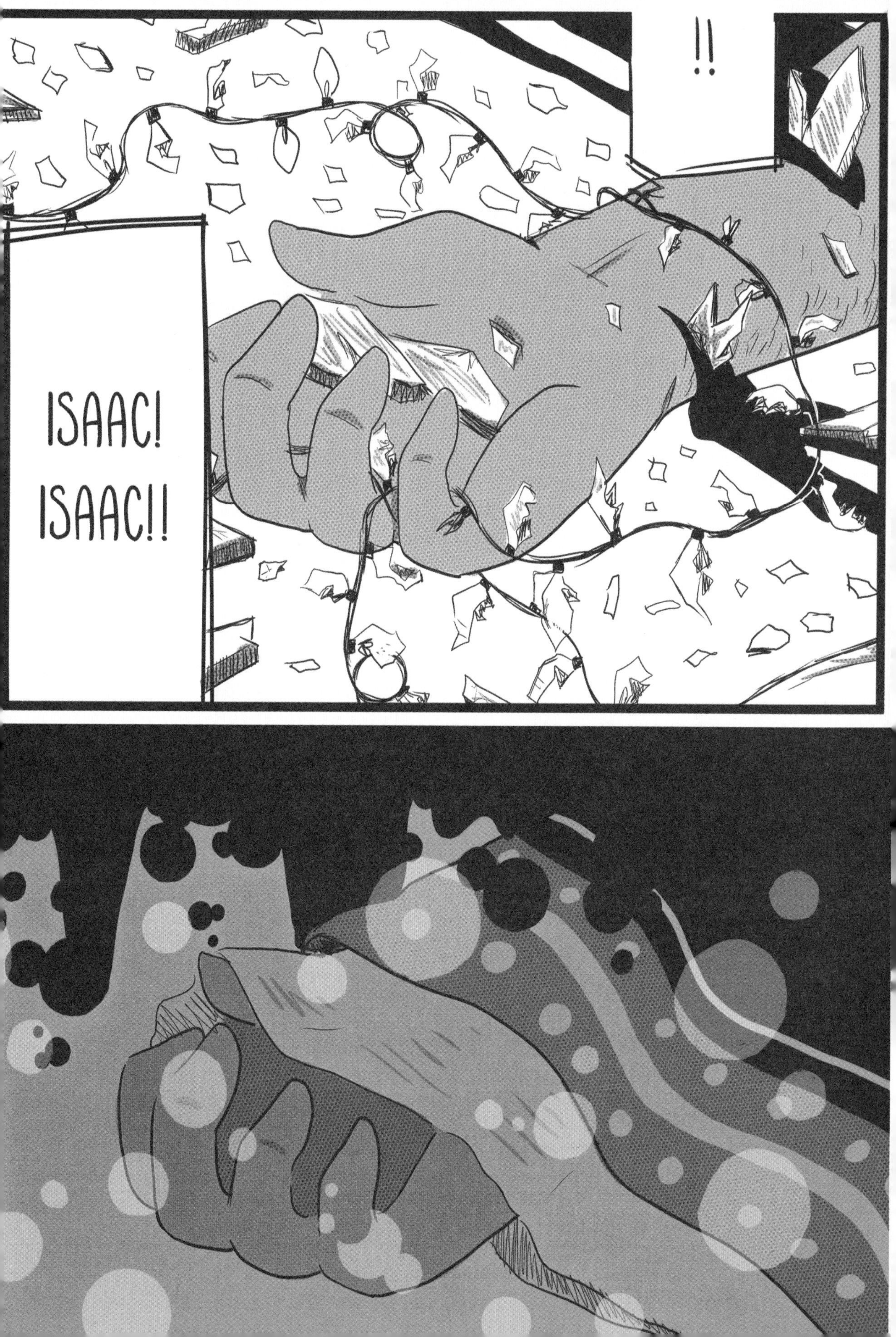
!!
ISAAC! ISAAC!!

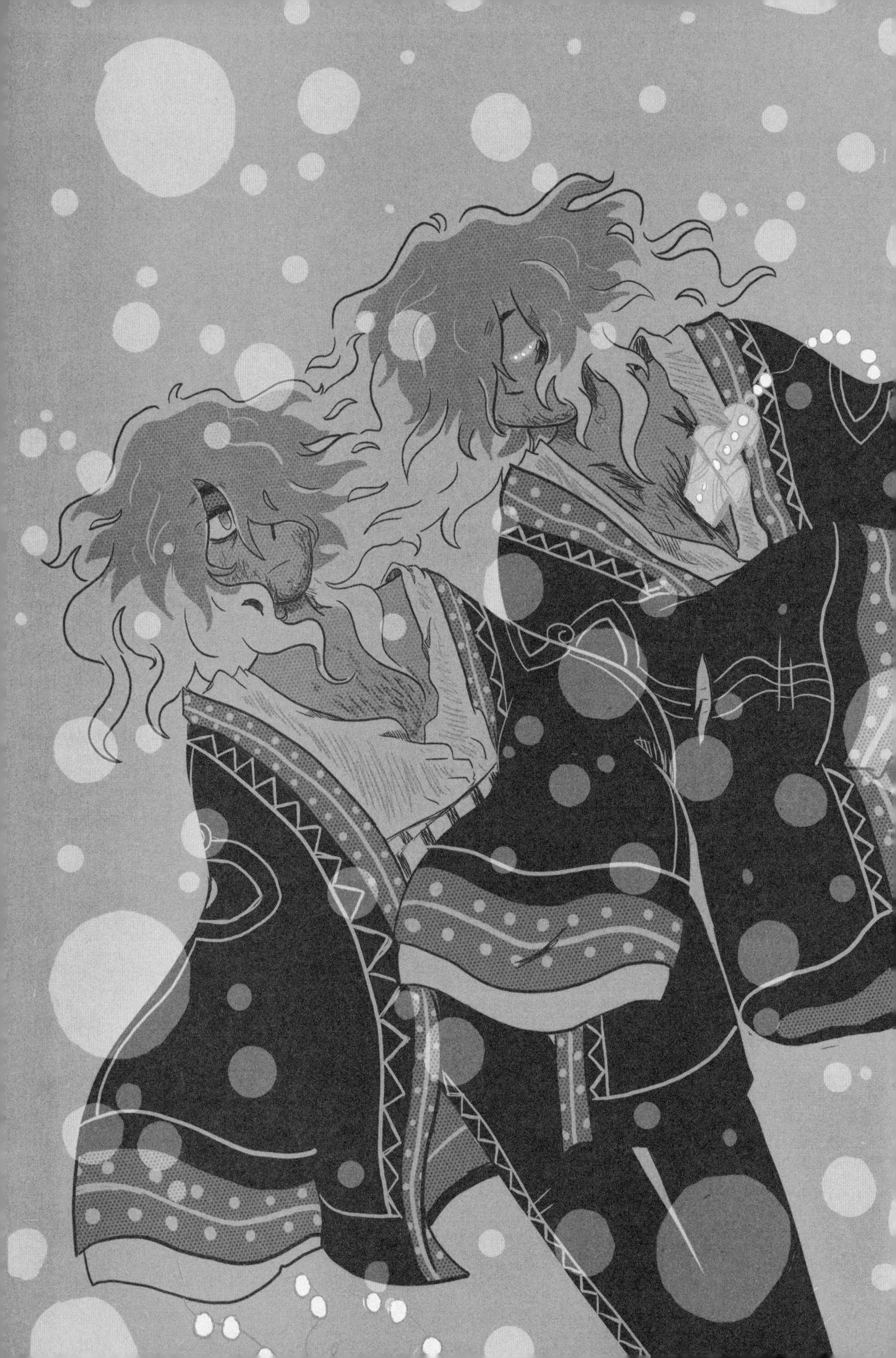

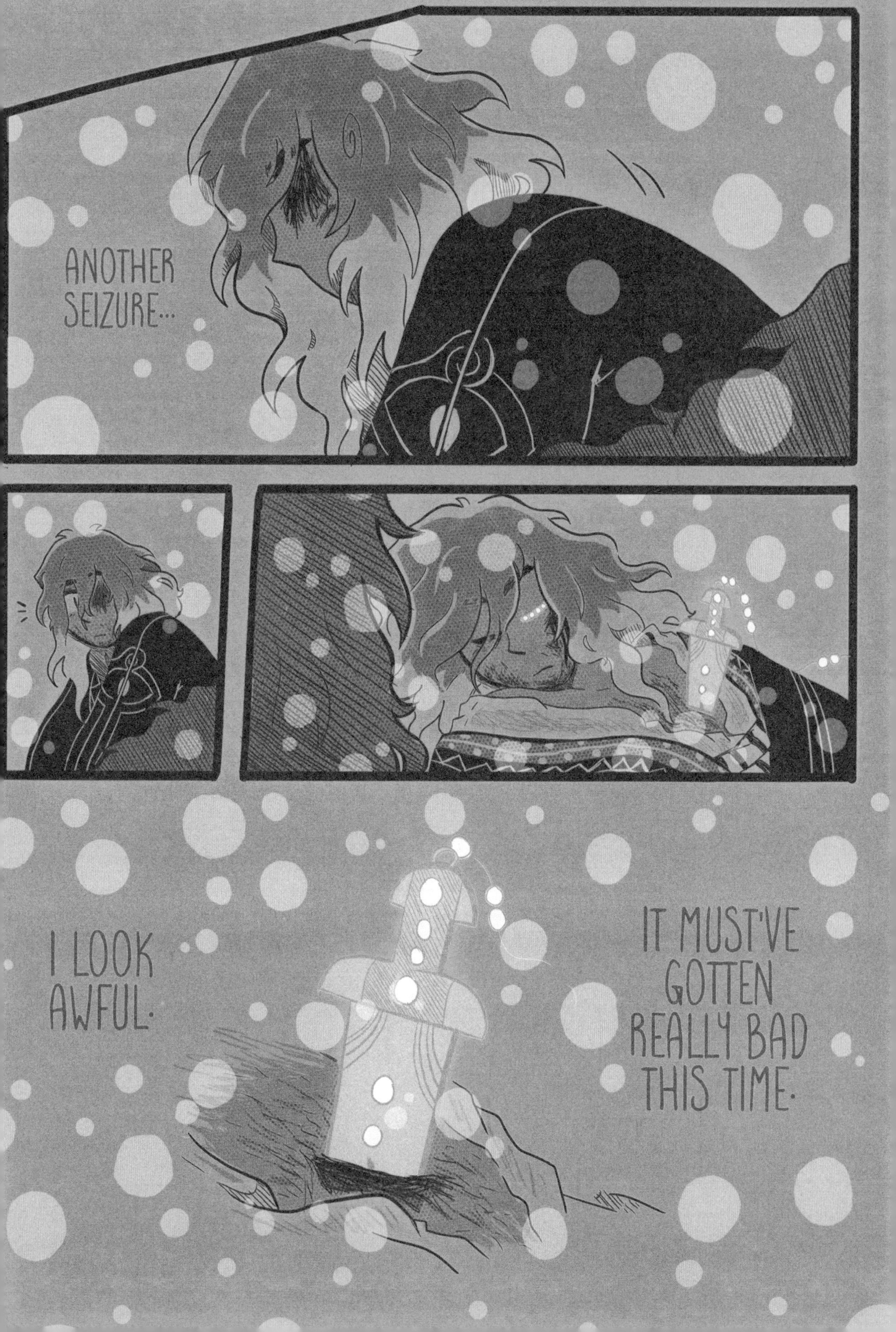
ANOTHER SEIZURE...
I LOOK AWFUL.
IT MUST'VE GOTTEN REALLY BAD THIS TIME.

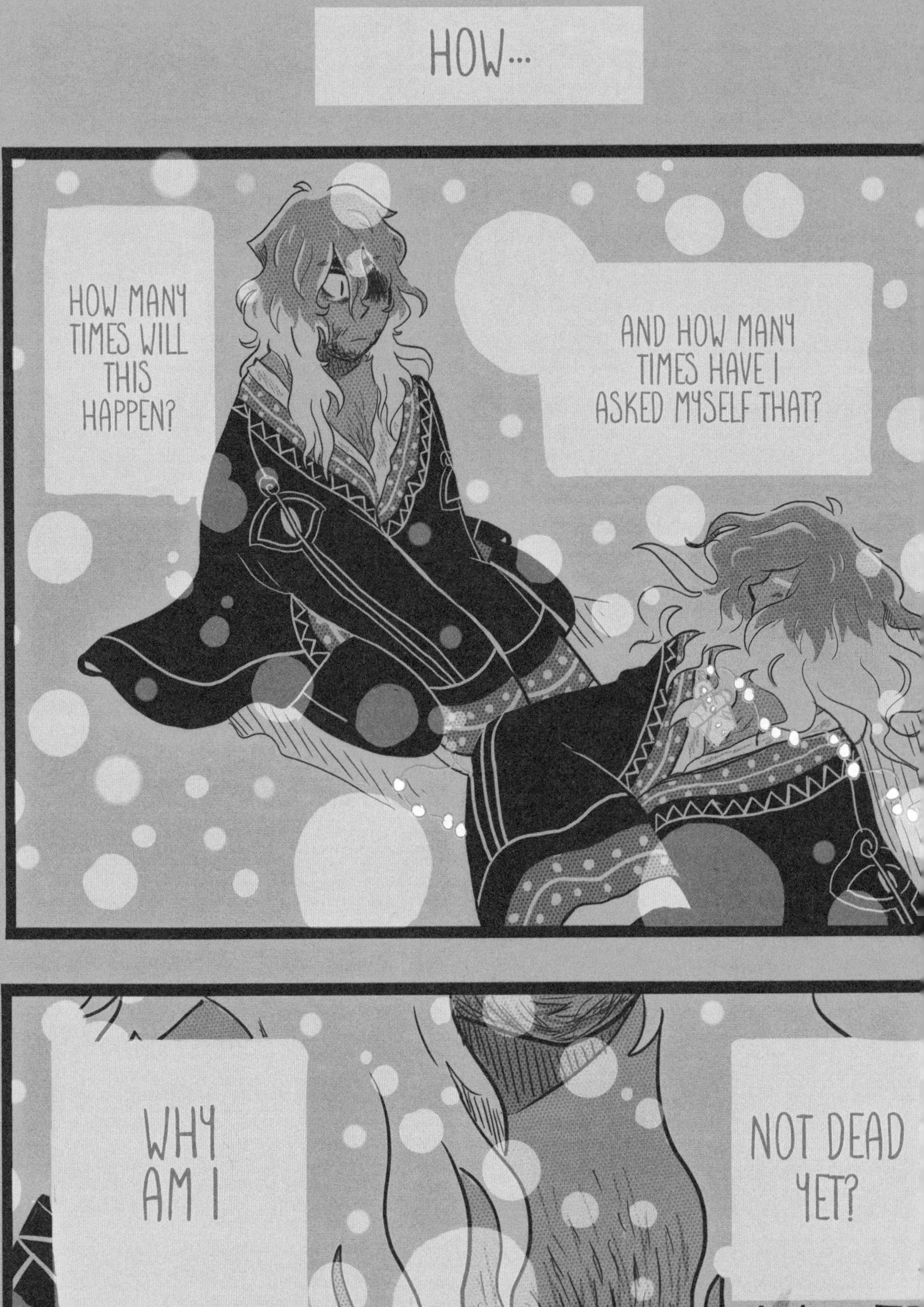
HOW...
HOW MANY TIMES WILL THIS HAPPEN?
AND HOW MANY TIMES HAVE I ASKED MYSELF THAT?
WHY AM I
NOT DEAD YET?

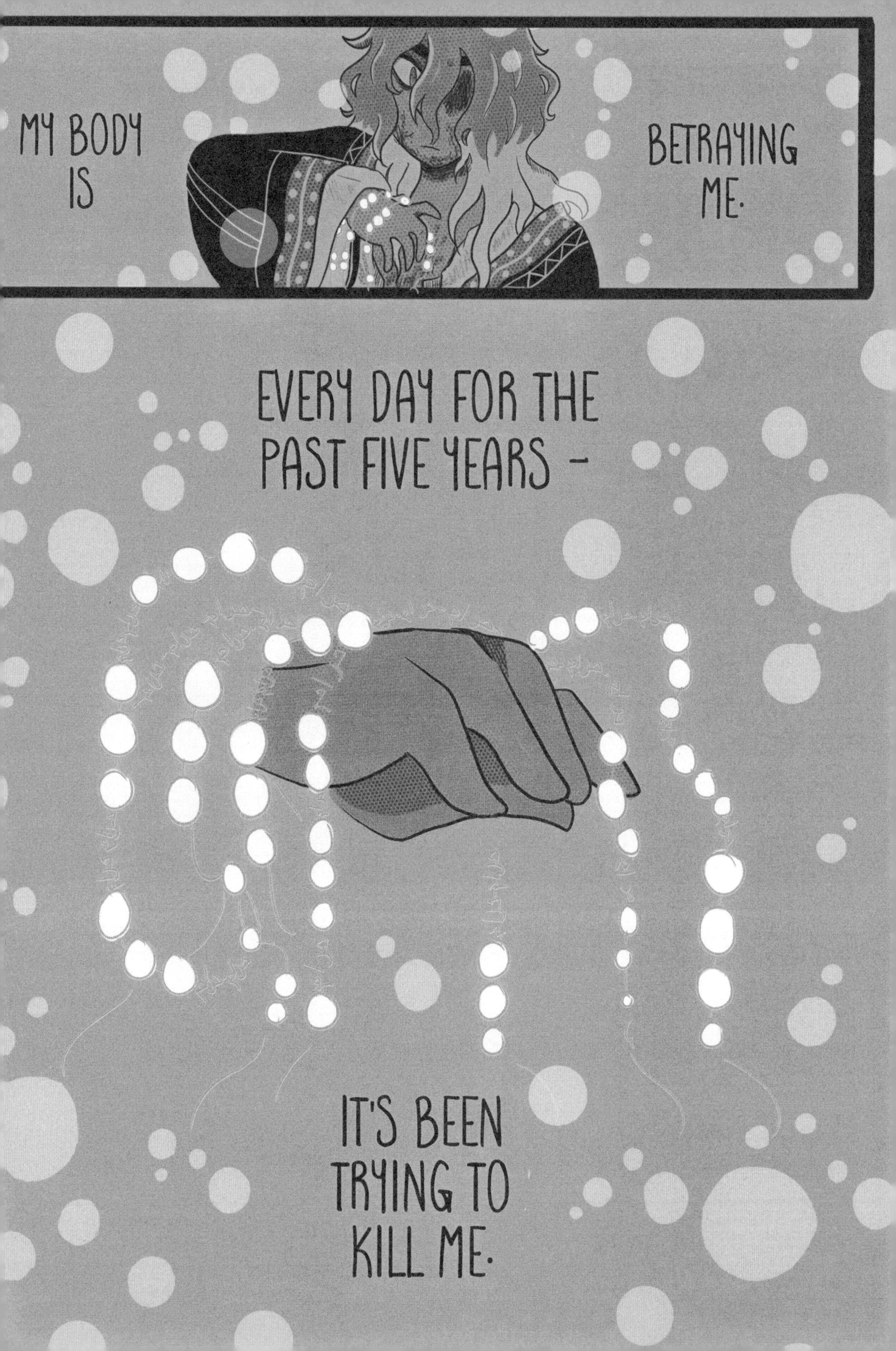
MY BODY IS
BETRAYING ME.
EVERY DAY FOR THE PAST FIVE YEARS –
IT'S BEEN TRYING TO KILL ME.

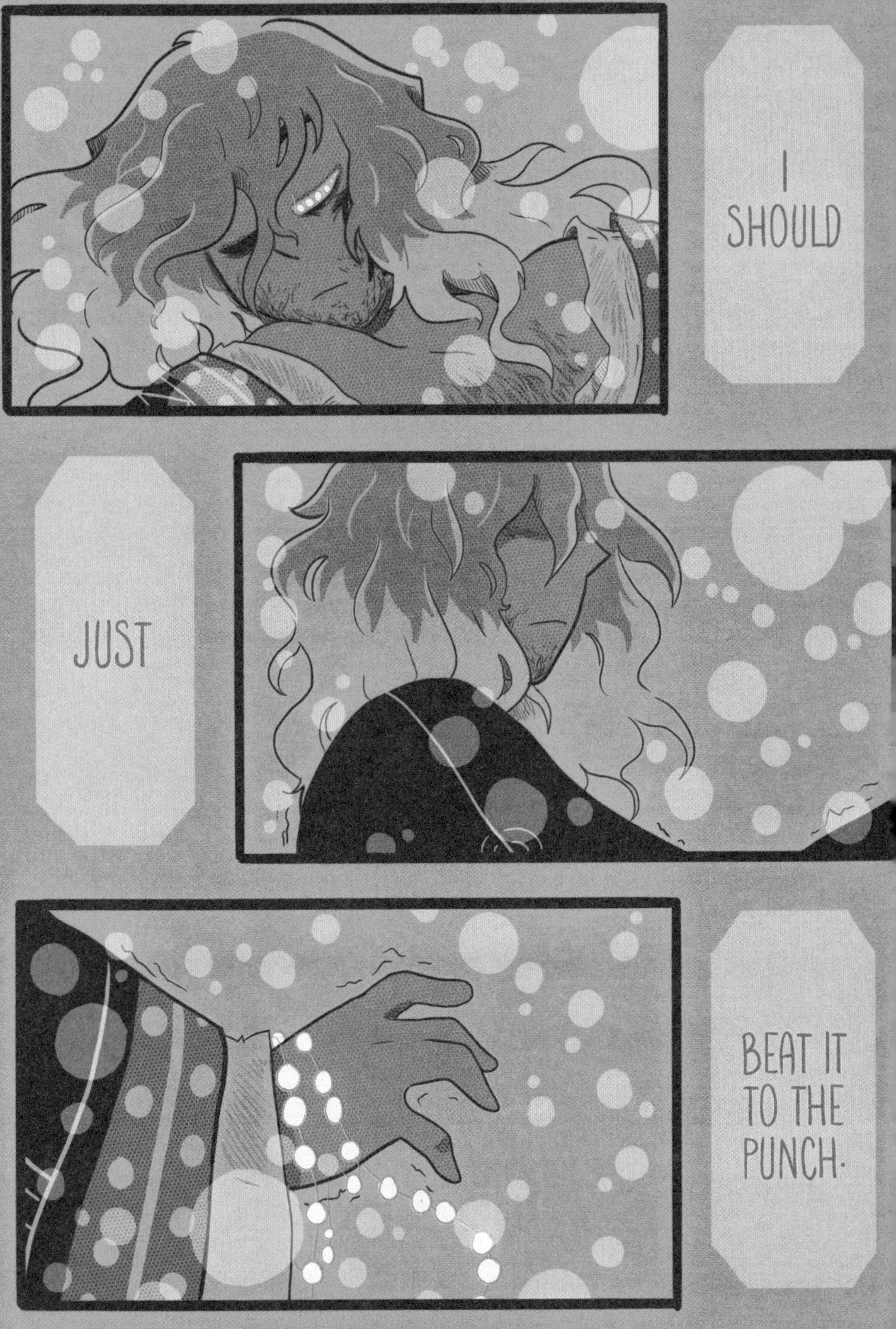
I SHOULD
JUST
BEAT IT TO THE PUNCH.

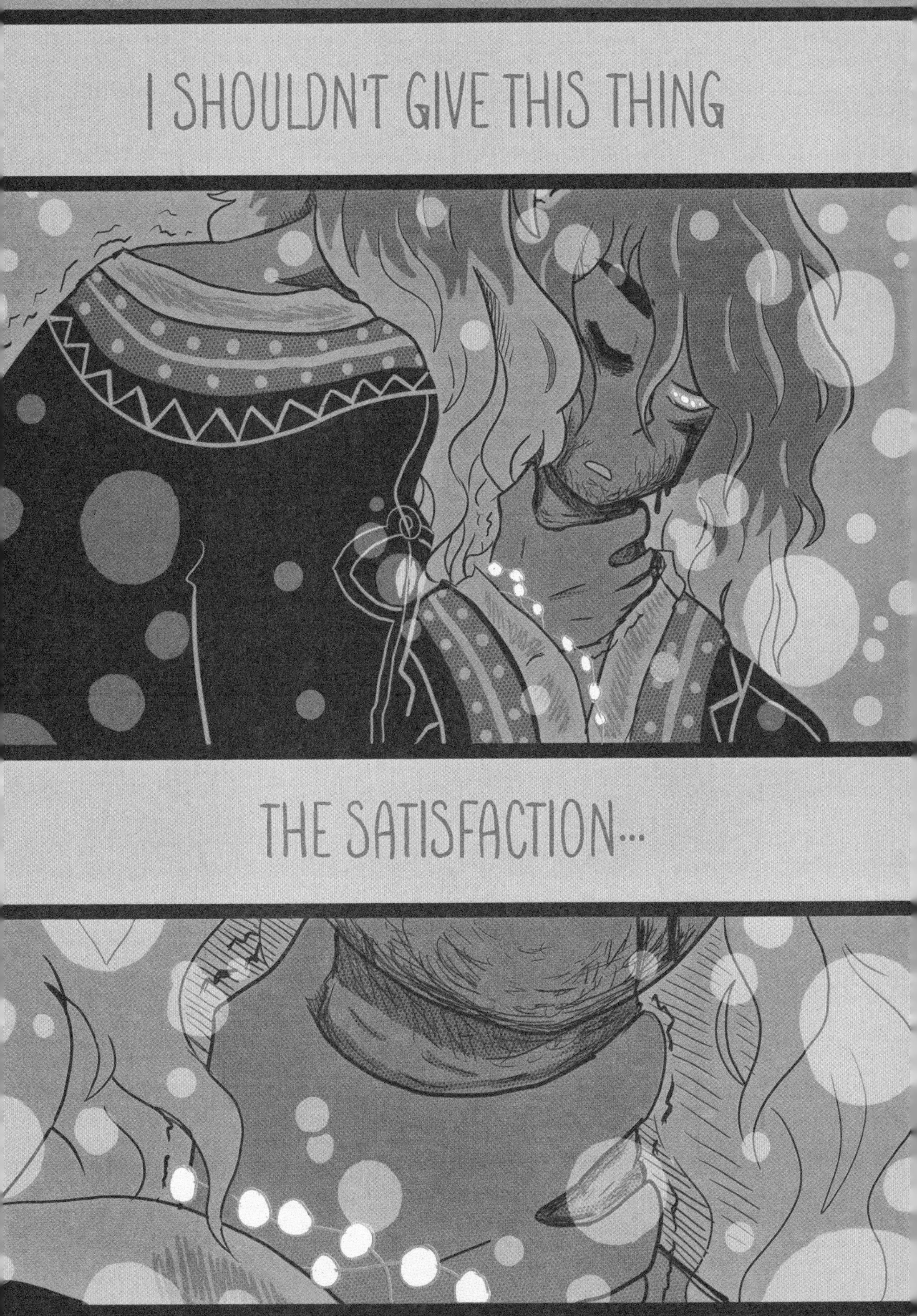
I SHOULDN'T GIVE THIS THING
THE SATISFACTION...

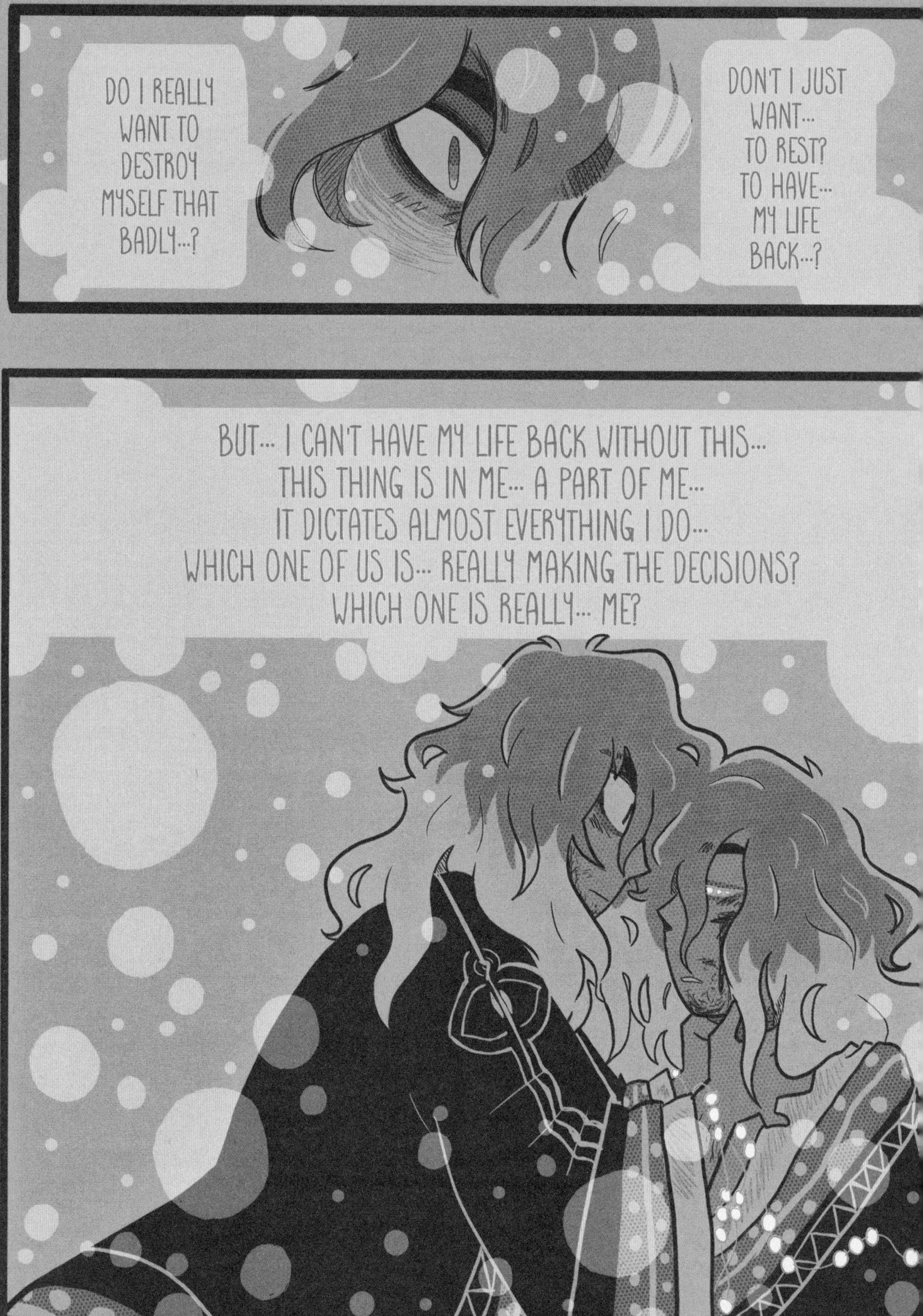
DO I REALLY WANT TO DESTROY MYSELF THAT BADLY...?
DON'T I JUST WANT... TO REST? TO HAVE... MY LIFE BACK...?
BUT... I CAN'T HAVE MY LIFE BACK WITHOUT THIS...
THIS THING IS IN ME... A PART OF ME...
IT DICTATES ALMOST EVERYTHING I DO...
WHICH ONE OF US IS... REALLY MAKING THE DECISIONS?
WHICH ONE IS REALLY... ME?

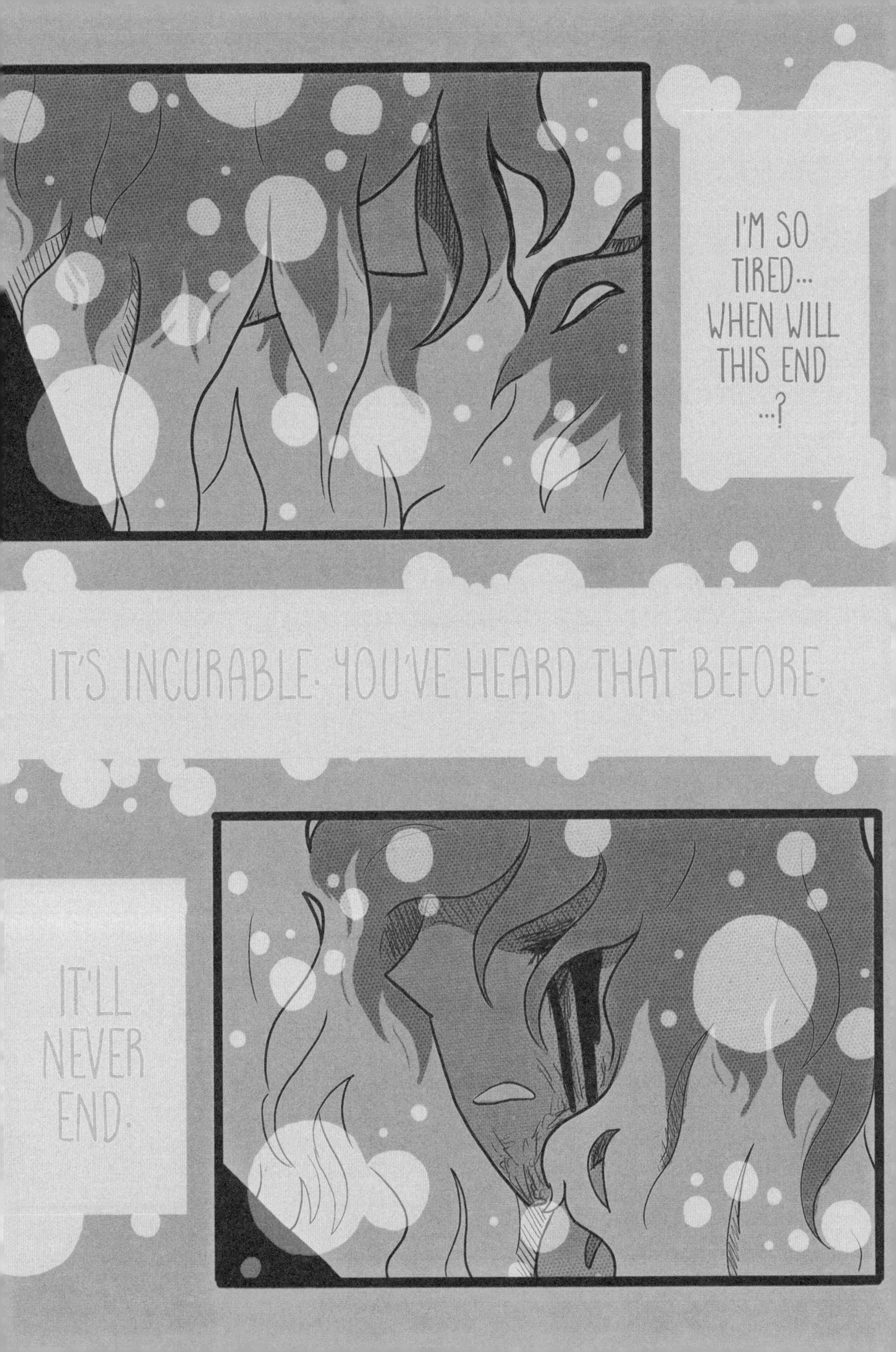
I'M SO TIRED... WHEN WILL THIS END ...?
IT'S INCURABLE. YOU'VE HEARD THAT BEFORE.
IT'LL NEVER END.

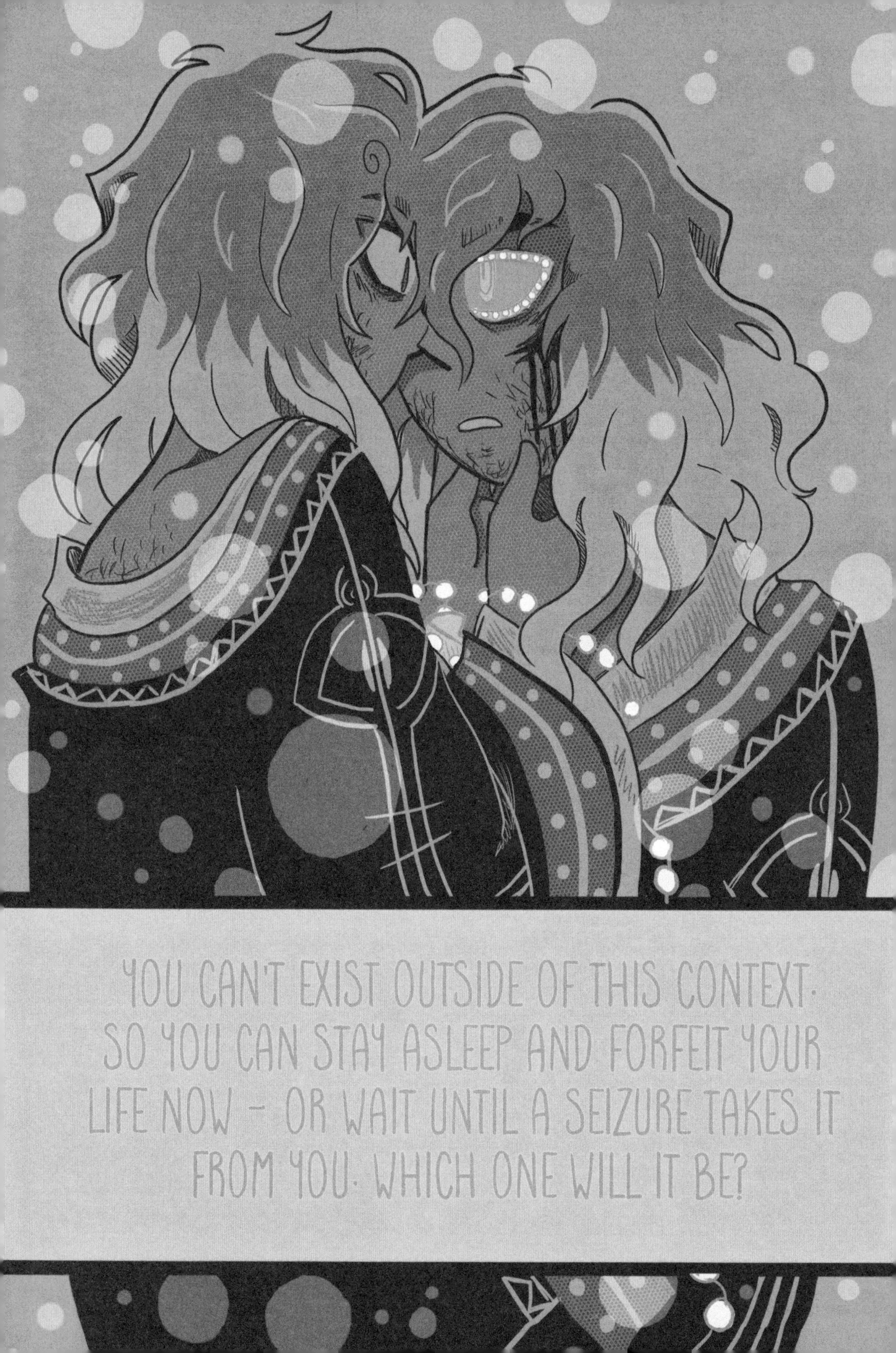
YOU CAN'T EXIST OUTSIDE OF THIS CONTEXT. SO YOU CAN STAY ASLEEP AND FORFEIT YOUR LIFE NOW – OR WAIT UNTIL A SEIZURE TAKES IT FROM YOU. WHICH ONE WILL IT BE?

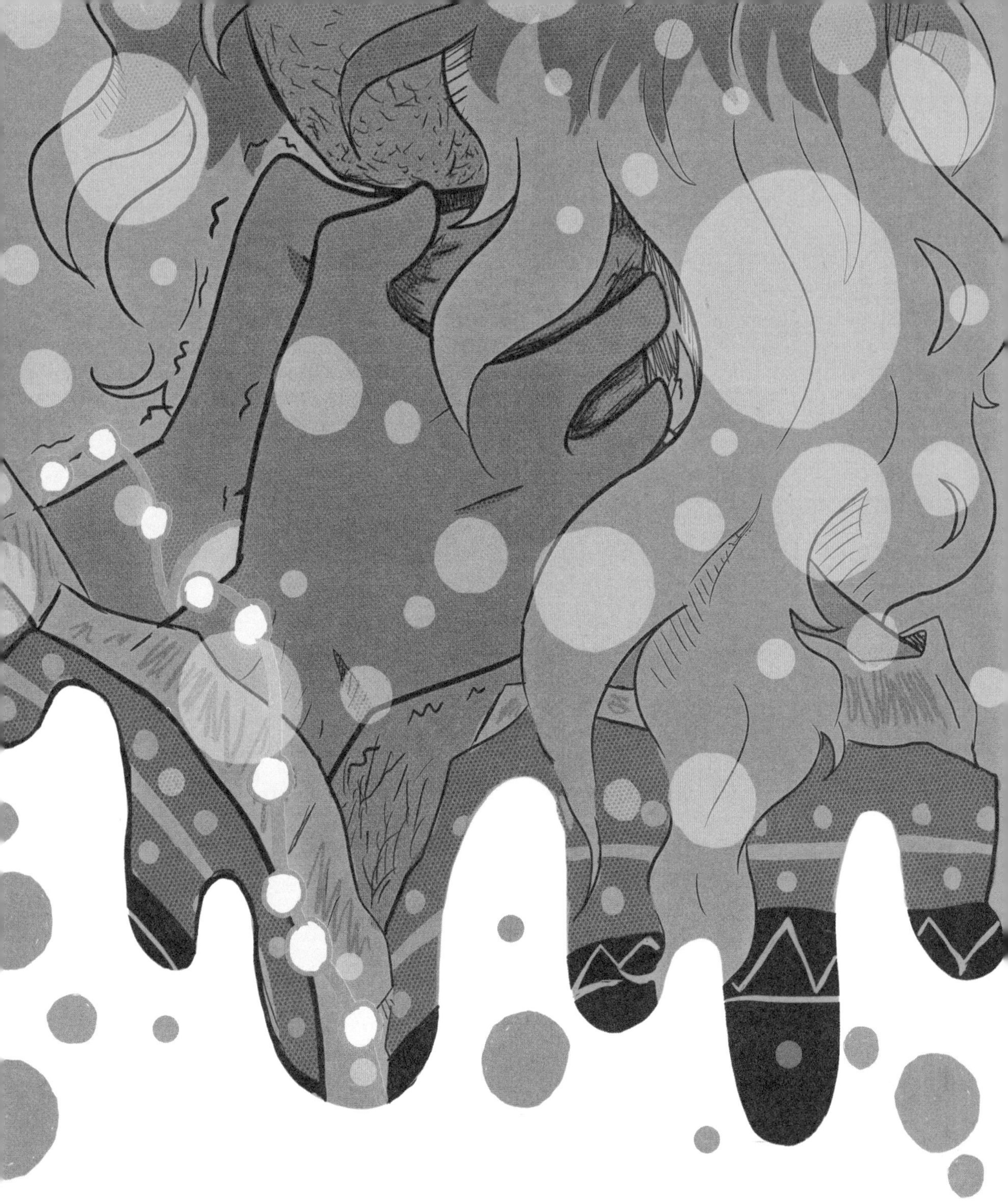

YOU'D BETTER WAKE UP SOON;
OTHERWISE, YOU WON'T
GET TO CHOOSE.

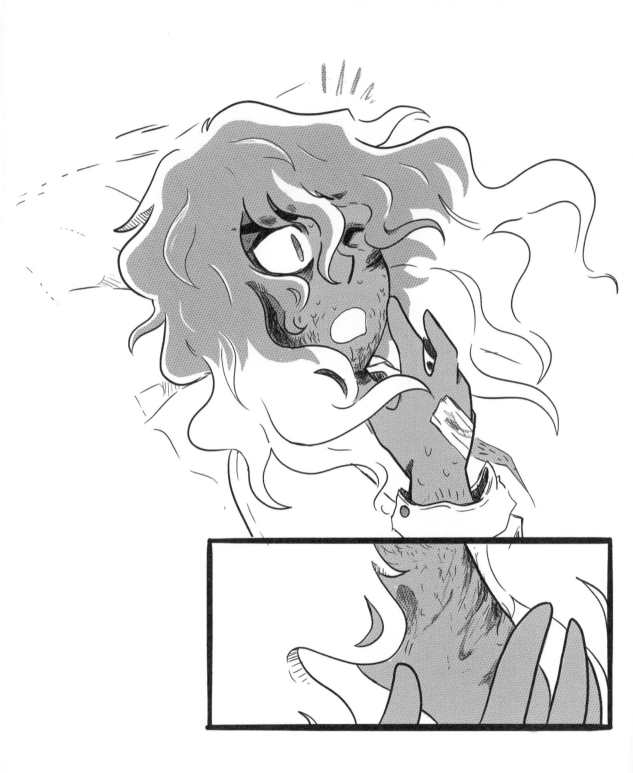

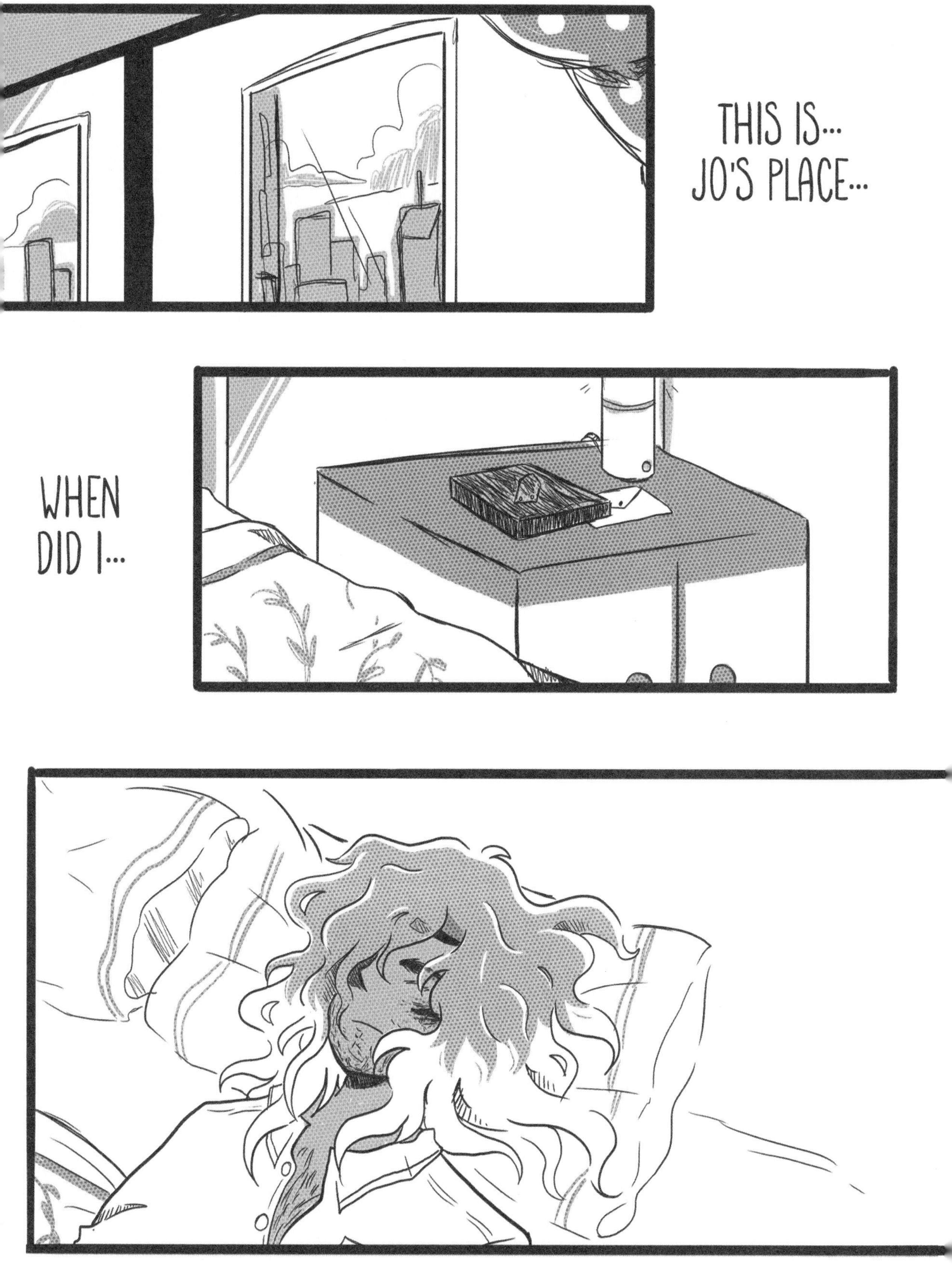
THIS IS... JO'S PLACE...
WHEN DID I...

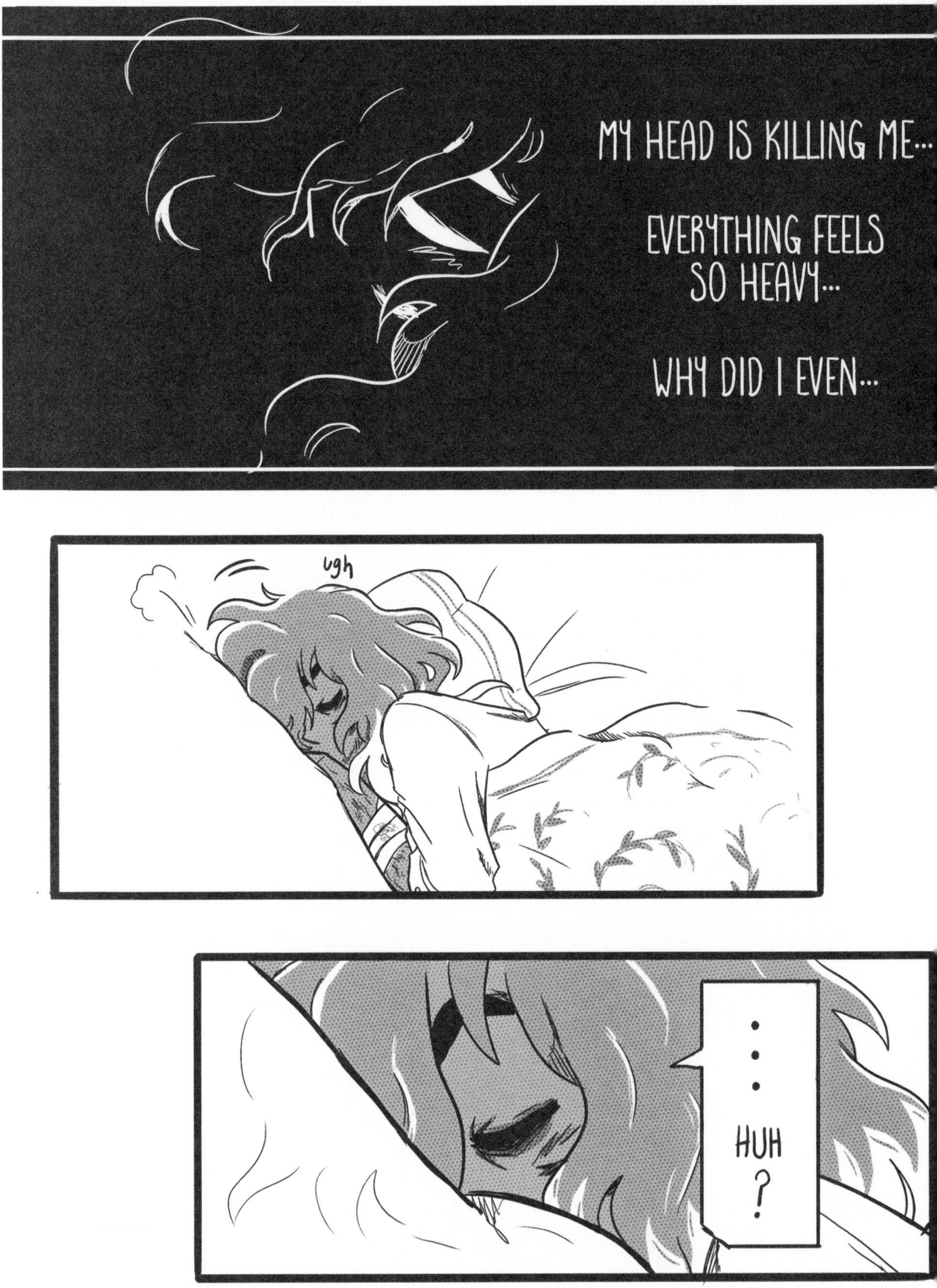

MY HEAD IS KILLING ME...
EVERYTHING FEELS SO HEAVY...
WHY DID I EVEN...
ugh
...
HUH?

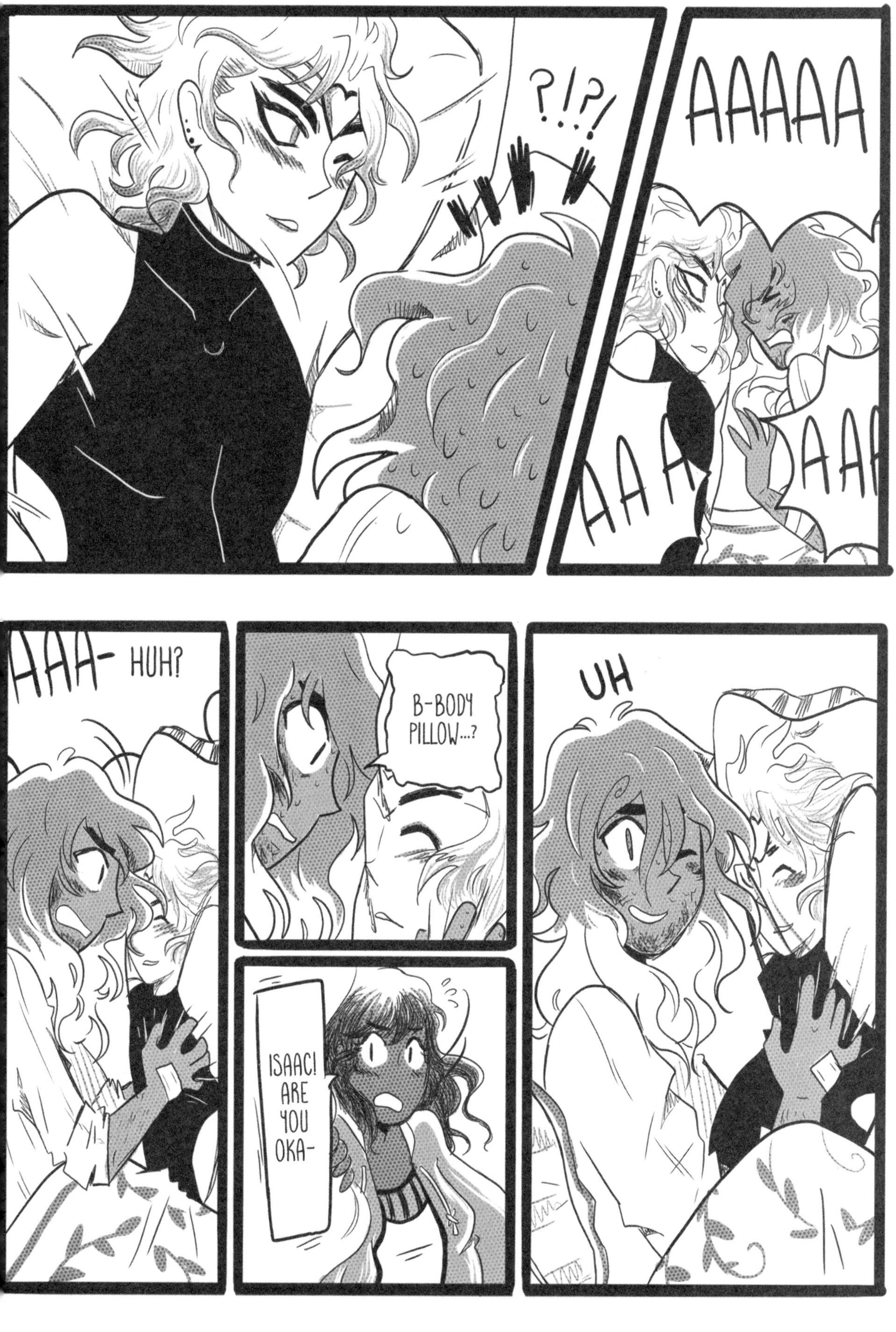
?!?!
AAAAA
AAA
AAA
AAA-
HUH?
B-BODY PILLOW...?
ISAAC! ARE YOU OKA-
UH

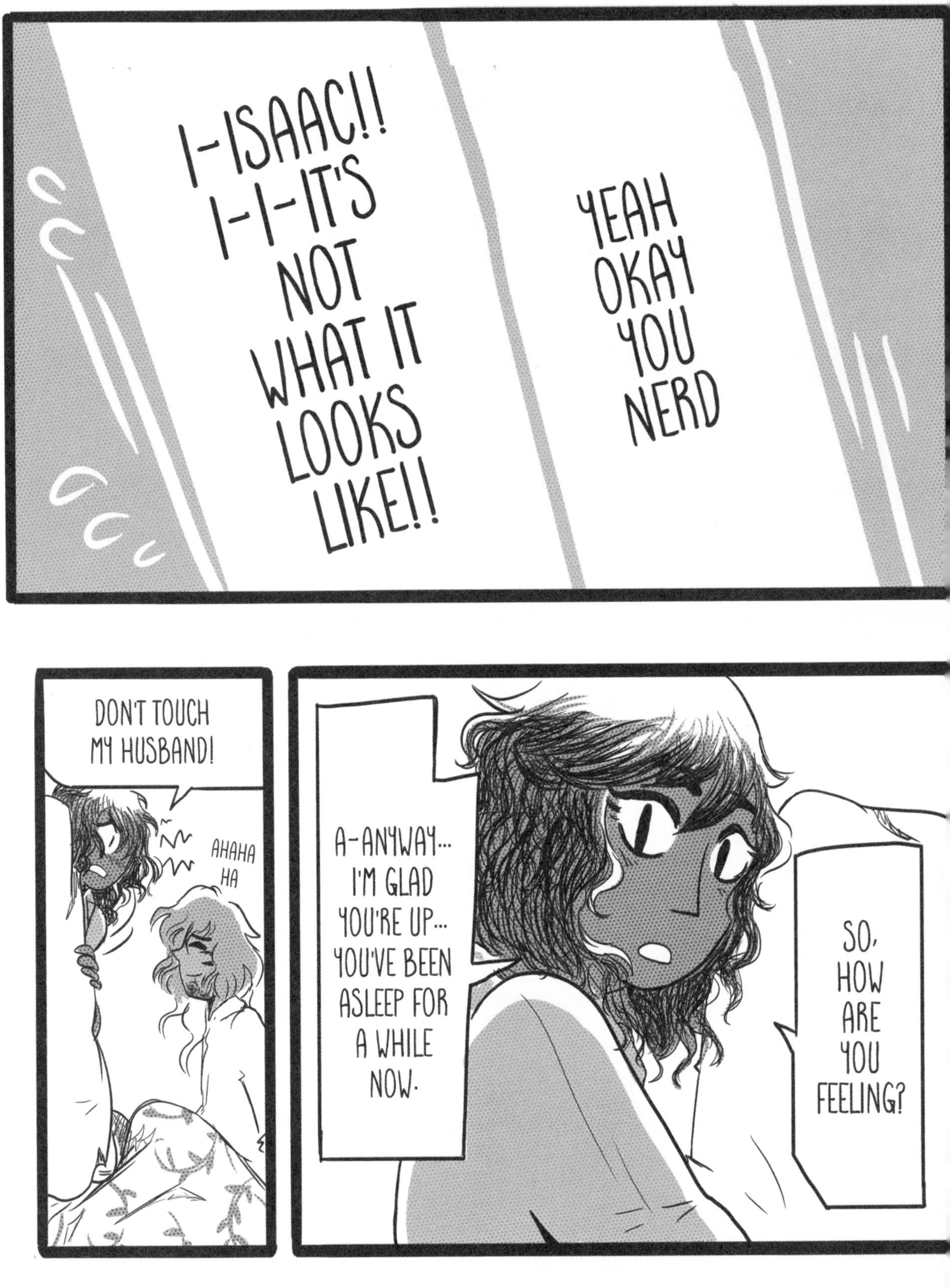

I-ISAAC!! I-I-IT'S NOT WHAT IT LOOKS LIKE!!
YEAH OKAY YOU NERD
DON'T TOUCH MY HUSBAND!
AHAHA HA
A-ANYWAY... I'M GLAD YOU'RE UP... YOU'VE BEEN ASLEEP FOR A WHILE NOW.
SO, HOW ARE YOU FEELING?

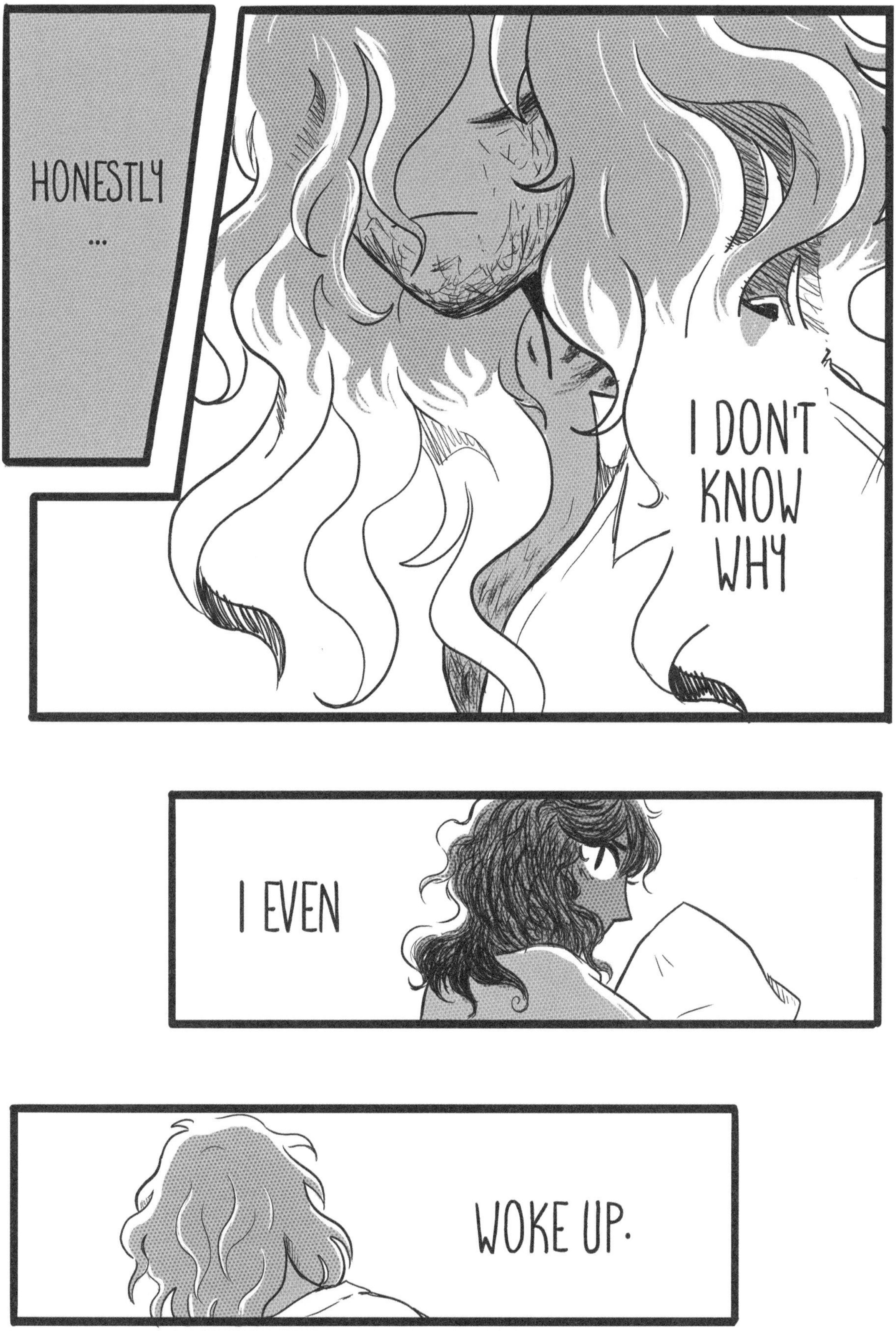
HONESTLY
...
I DON'T KNOW WHY
I EVEN
WOKE UP.

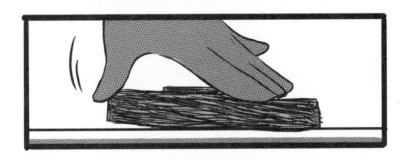

...
YOU'RE GONNA SAY SHIT LIKE THAT SO EASILY?

THAT'S PATHETIC.

YOU WERE LUCKY. YOU HAD THREE SEIZURES IN A ROW AND YOU CAME OUT SOMEWHAT FINE.

YOU NEED TO BE STRONGER THAN THIS.

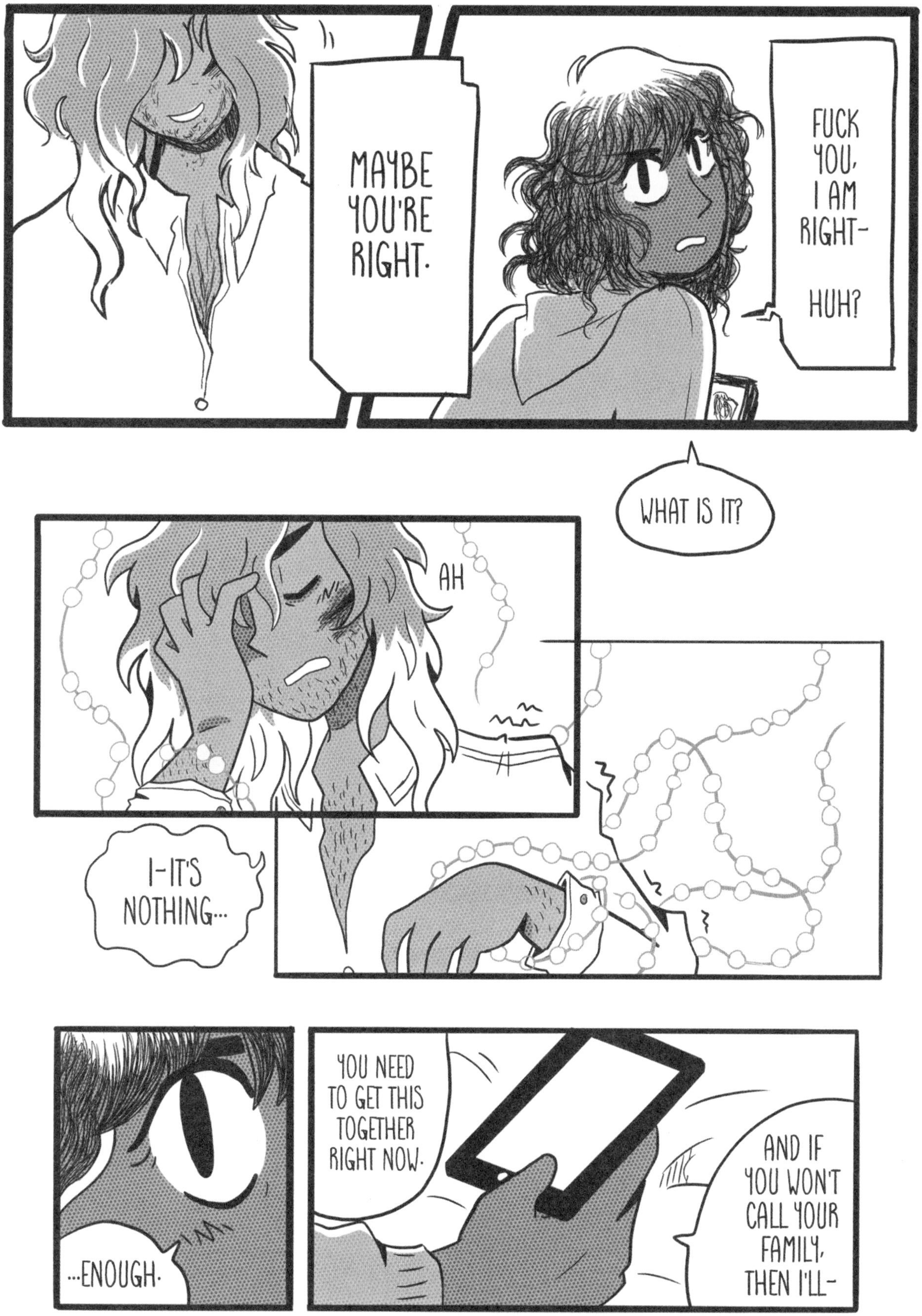
MAYBE YOU'RE RIGHT.
FUCK YOU, I AM RIGHT-
HUH?
WHAT IS IT?
AH
I-IT'S NOTHING...
...ENOUGH.
YOU NEED TO GET THIS TOGETHER RIGHT NOW.
AND IF YOU WON'T CALL YOUR FAMILY, THEN I'LL-

WAIT.
PLEASE
...
DON'T
...

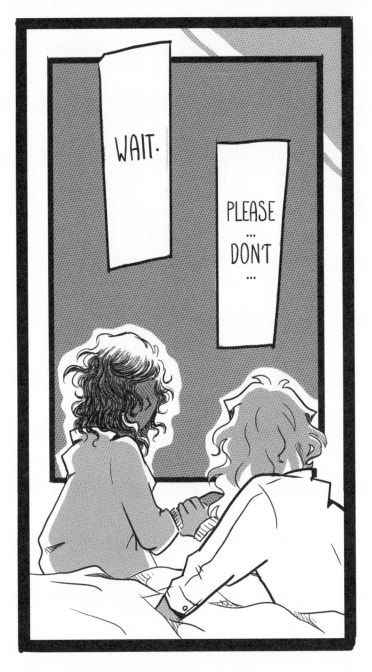

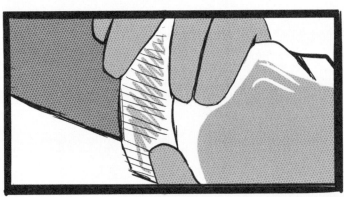

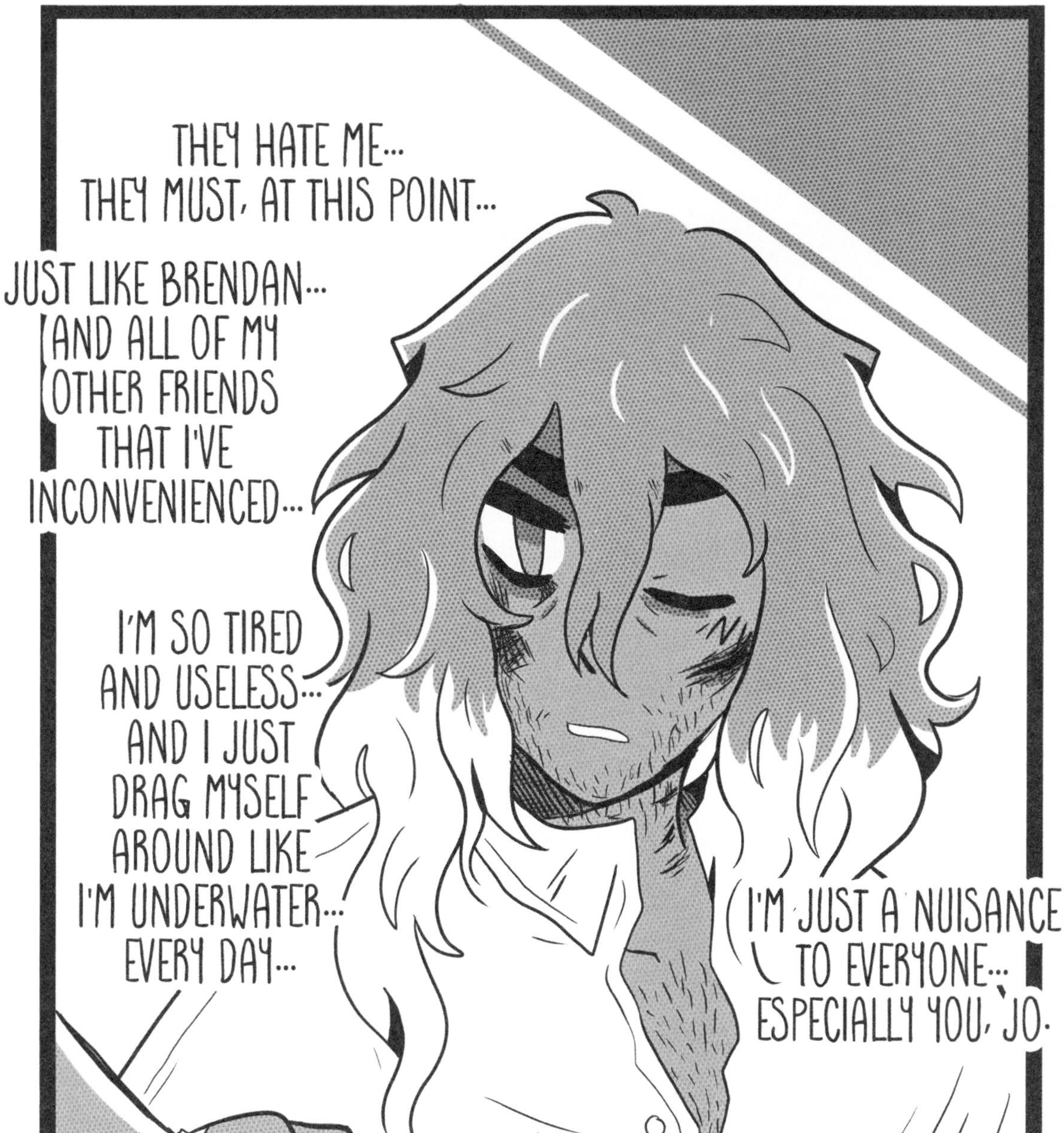
THEY HATE ME... THEY MUST, AT THIS POINT...
JUST LIKE BRENDAN... AND ALL OF MY OTHER FRIENDS THAT I'VE INCONVENIENCED...
I'M SO TIRED AND USELESS... AND I JUST DRAG MYSELF AROUND LIKE I'M UNDERWATER... EVERY DAY...
I'M JUST A NUISANCE TO EVERYONE... ESPECIALLY YOU, JO.

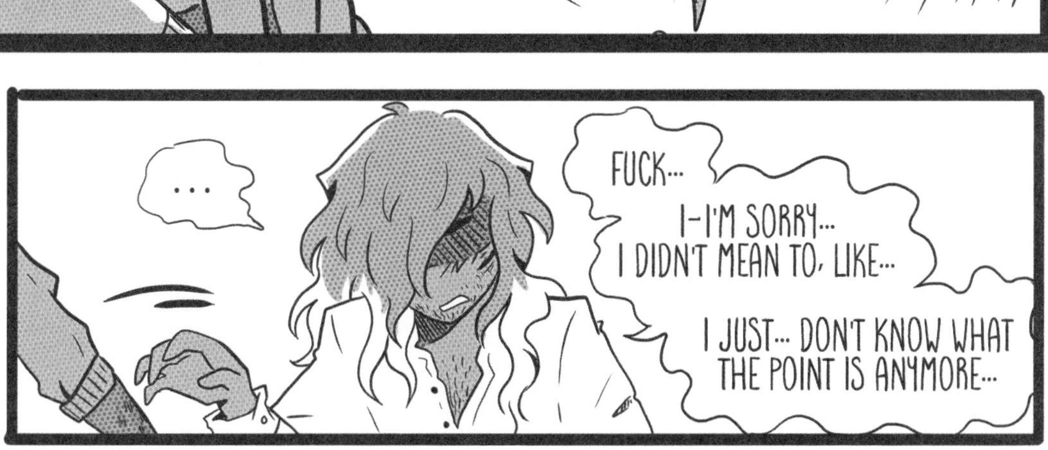
...
FUCK...
I-I'M SORRY... I DIDN'T MEAN TO, LIKE...
I JUST... DON'T KNOW WHAT THE POINT IS ANYMORE...

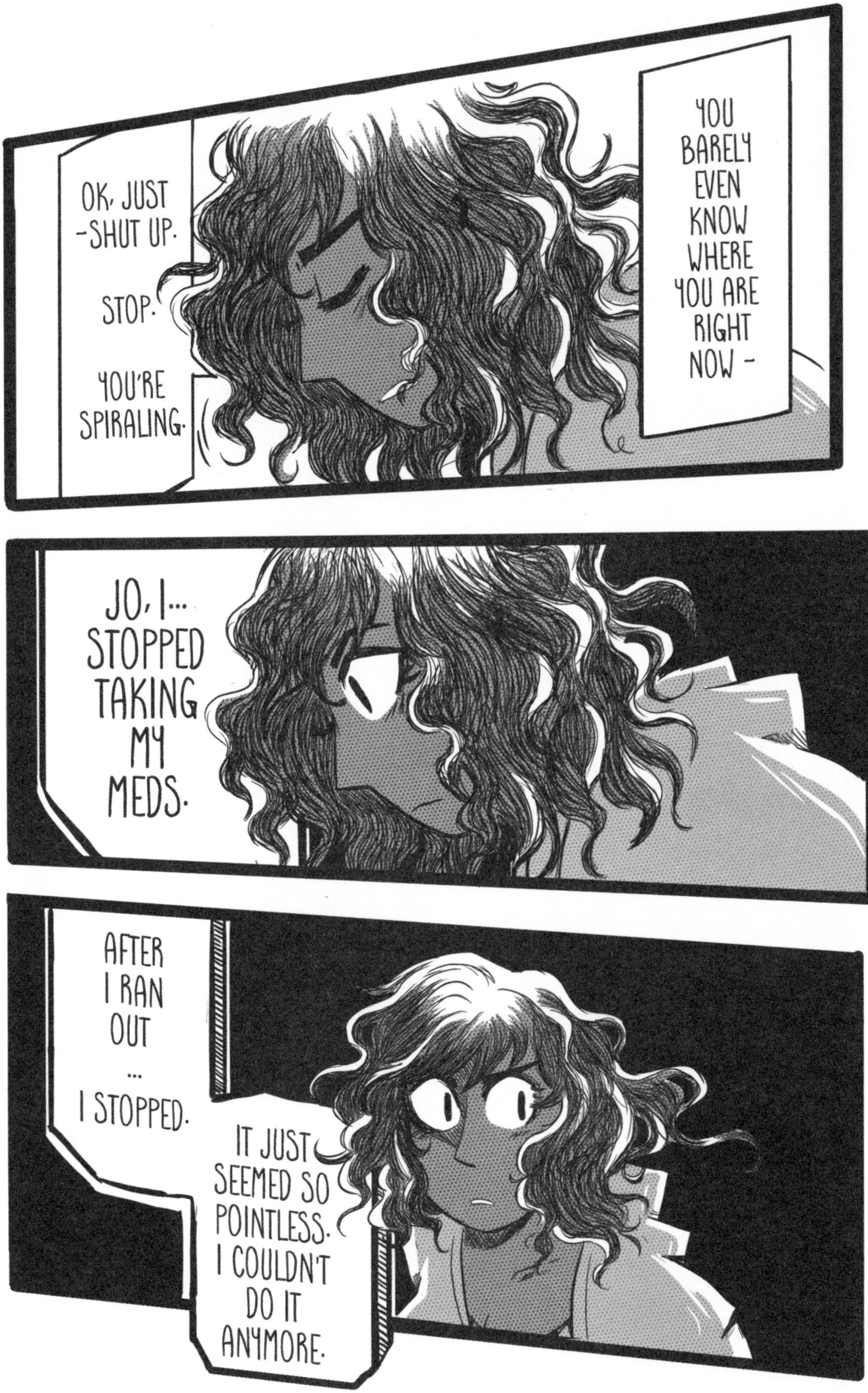
OK, JUST -SHUT UP.
STOP.
YOU'RE SPIRALING.
YOU BARELY EVEN KNOW WHERE YOU ARE RIGHT NOW -
JO, I... STOPPED TAKING MY MEDS.
AFTER I RAN OUT ... I STOPPED.
IT JUST SEEMED SO POINTLESS. I COULDN'T DO IT ANYMORE.

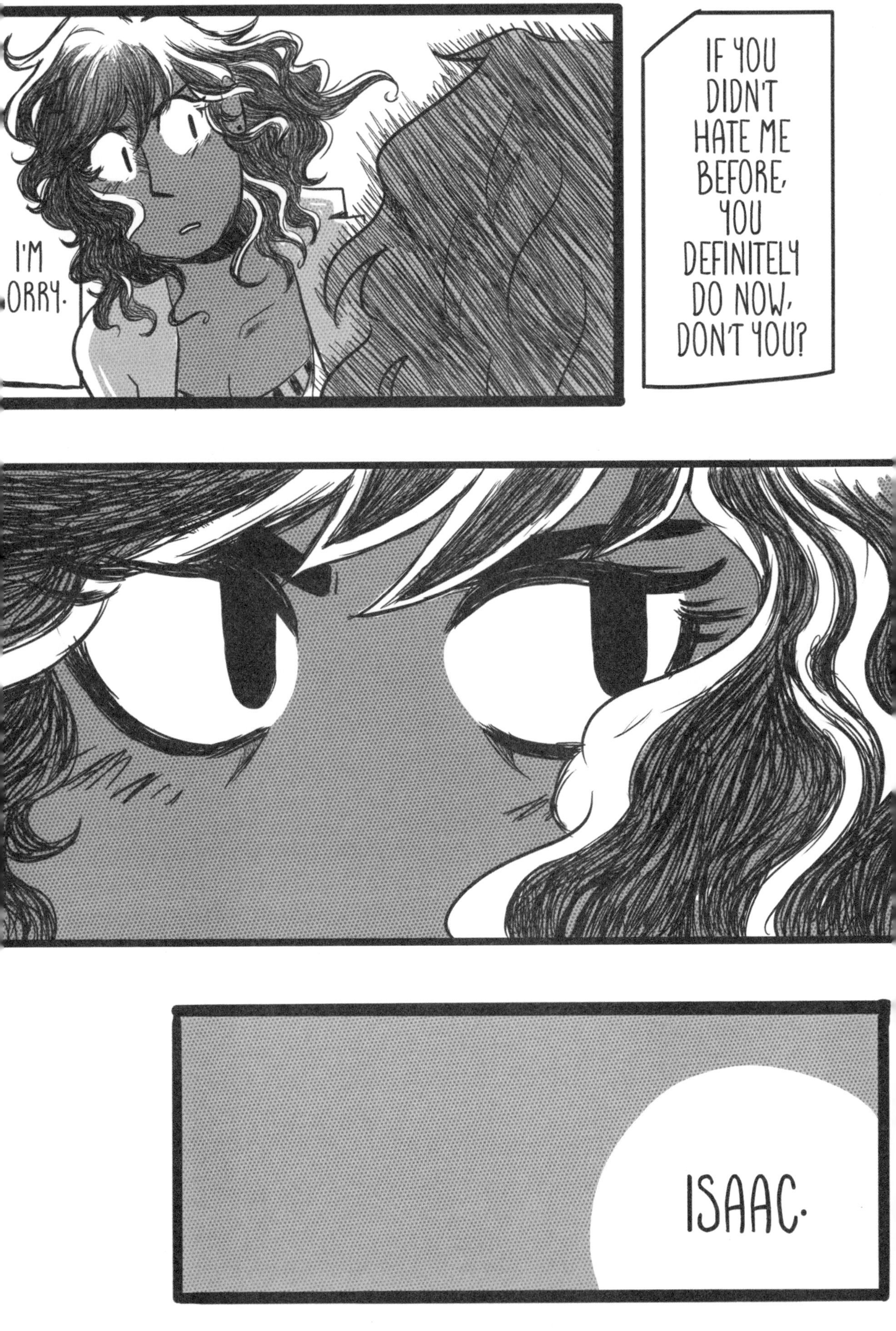
I'M
SORRY.
IF YOU DIDN'T HATE ME BEFORE, YOU DEFINITELY DO NOW, DON'T YOU?
ISAAC.

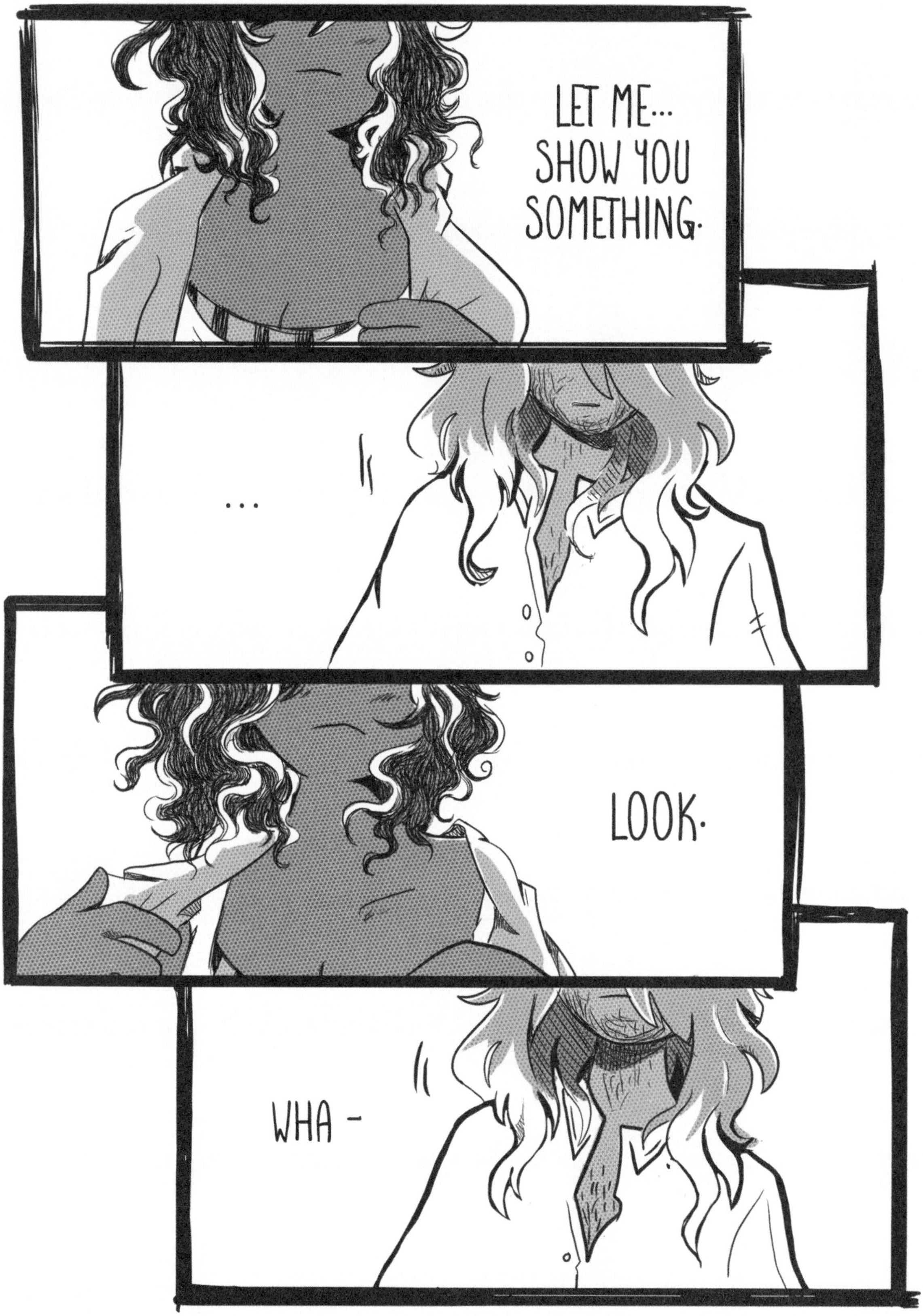
LET ME... SHOW YOU SOMETHING.
...
LOOK.
WHA -

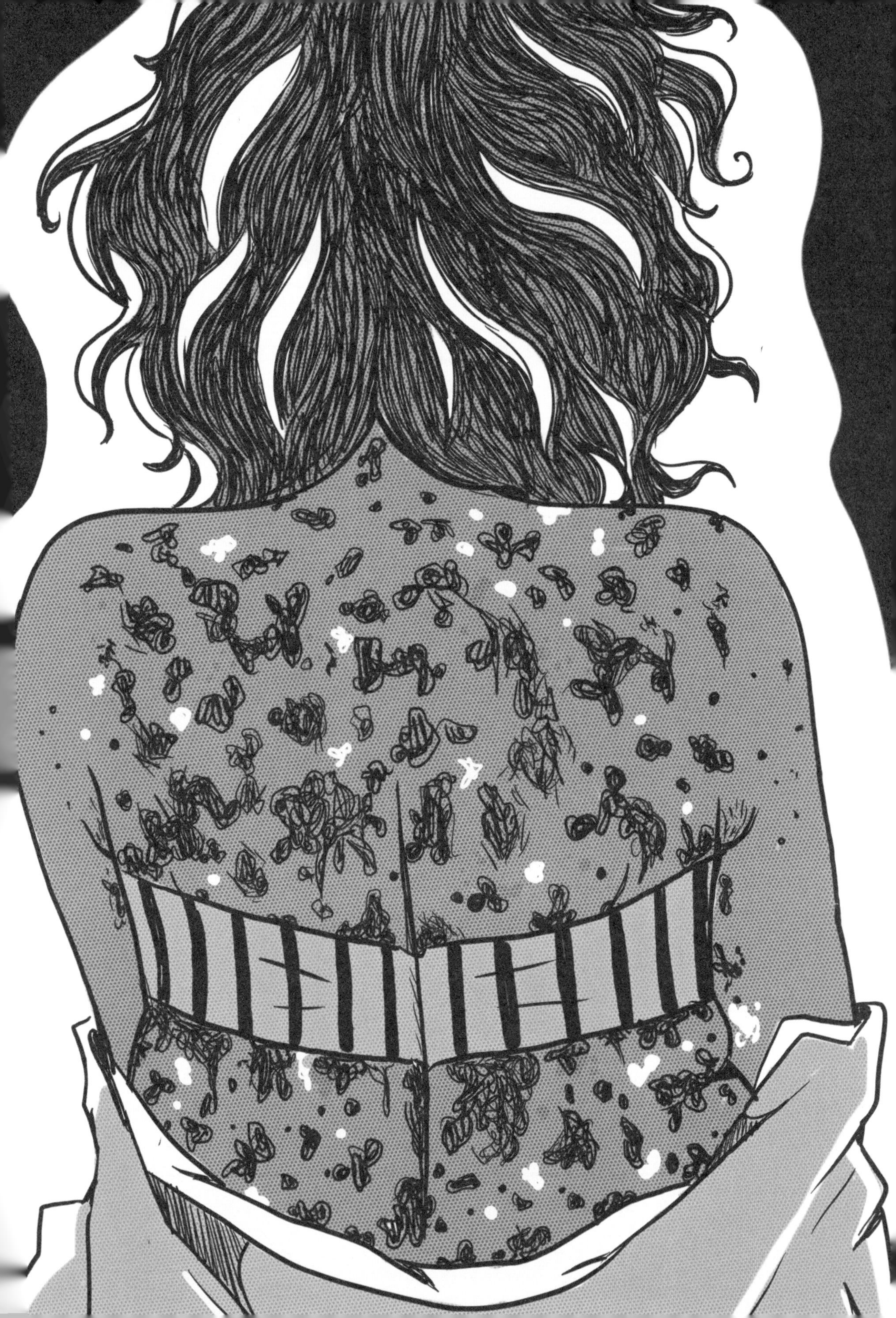

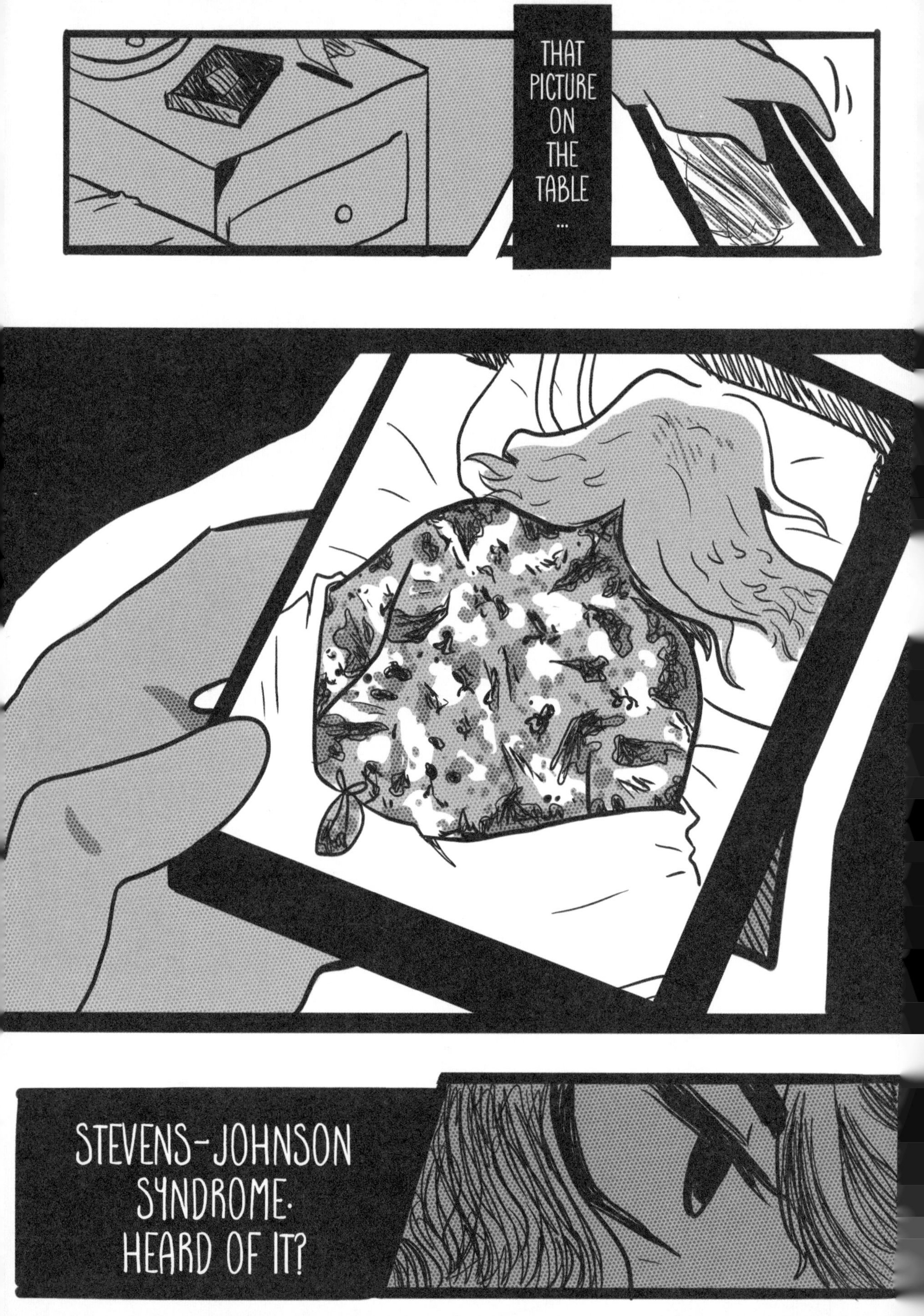
THAT PICTURE ON THE TABLE ...
STEVENS-JOHNSON SYNDROME. HEARD OF IT?

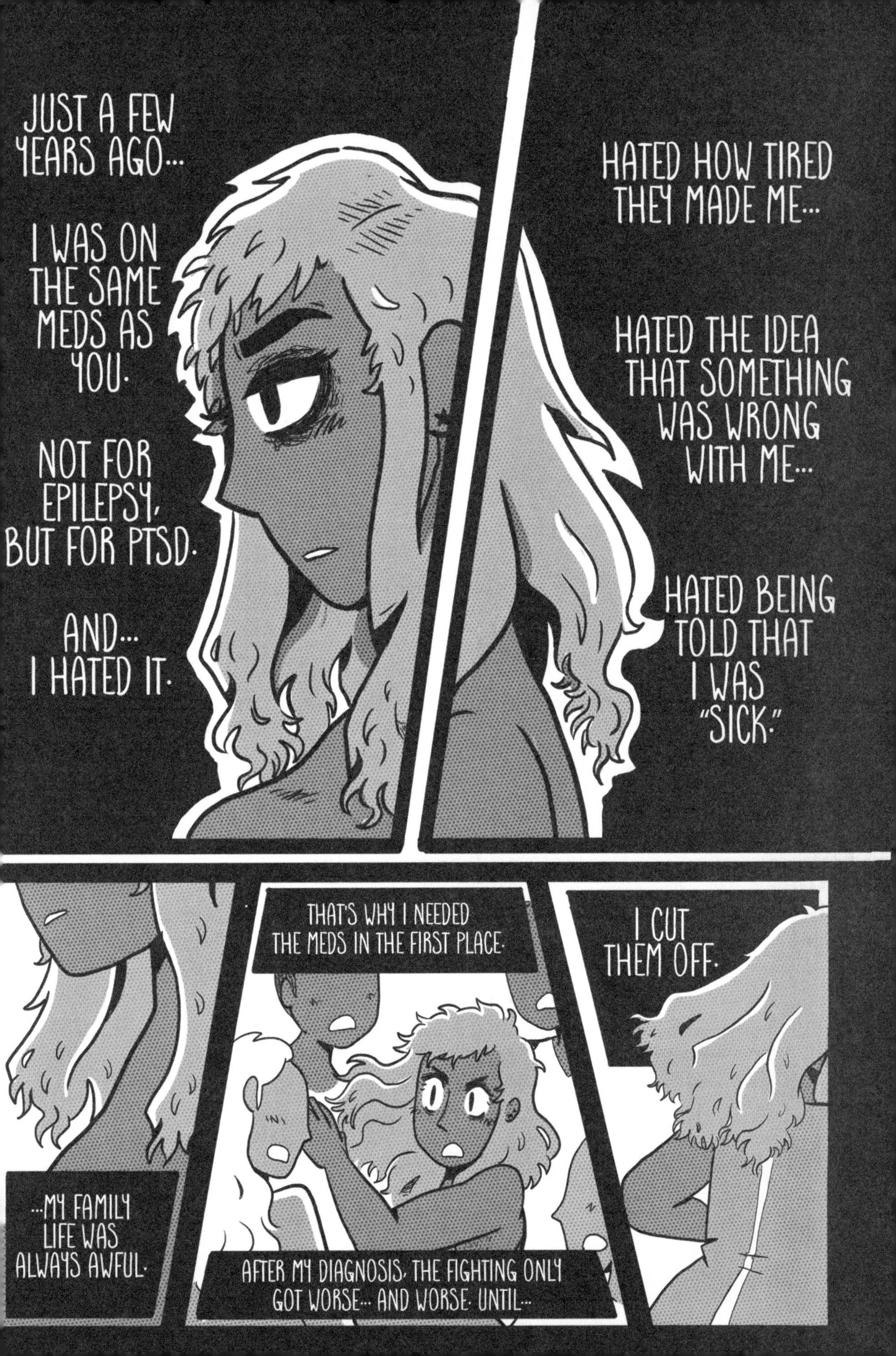
JUST A FEW YEARS AGO...
I WAS ON THE SAME MEDS AS YOU.
NOT FOR EPILEPSY, BUT FOR PTSD.
AND... I HATED IT.
HATED HOW TIRED THEY MADE ME...
HATED THE IDEA THAT SOMETHING WAS WRONG WITH ME...
HATED BEING TOLD THAT I WAS "SICK."
...MY FAMILY LIFE WAS ALWAYS AWFUL.
THAT'S WHY I NEEDED THE MEDS IN THE FIRST PLACE.
AFTER MY DIAGNOSIS, THE FIGHTING ONLY GOT WORSE... AND WORSE. UNTIL...
I CUT THEM OFF.

I STARTED TO TAKE MY MEDS ON AND OFF.

MEDS ALARM: SNOOZE

IT WAS A DIFFICULT TIME... AND IT MADE ME RECKLESS. LIKE YOU.

NOT LONG AFTER THAT...
IT... STARTED OFF AS JUST A RASH...
BUT IT GREW, AND I FELT ILL...

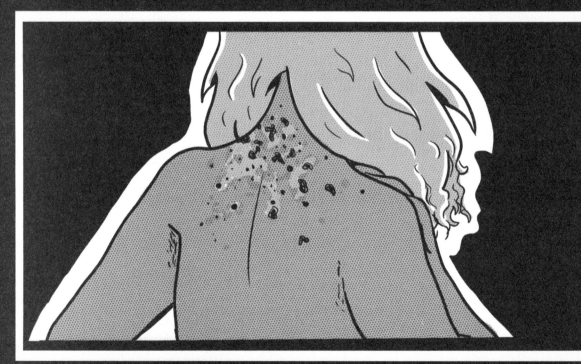

MY FAMILY, WELL...
THEY'RE THE WHOLE REASON I WAS IN THIS MESS,
SO I WASN'T ABOUT TO CALL THEM.
I TOOK MYSELF TO THE HOSPITAL.

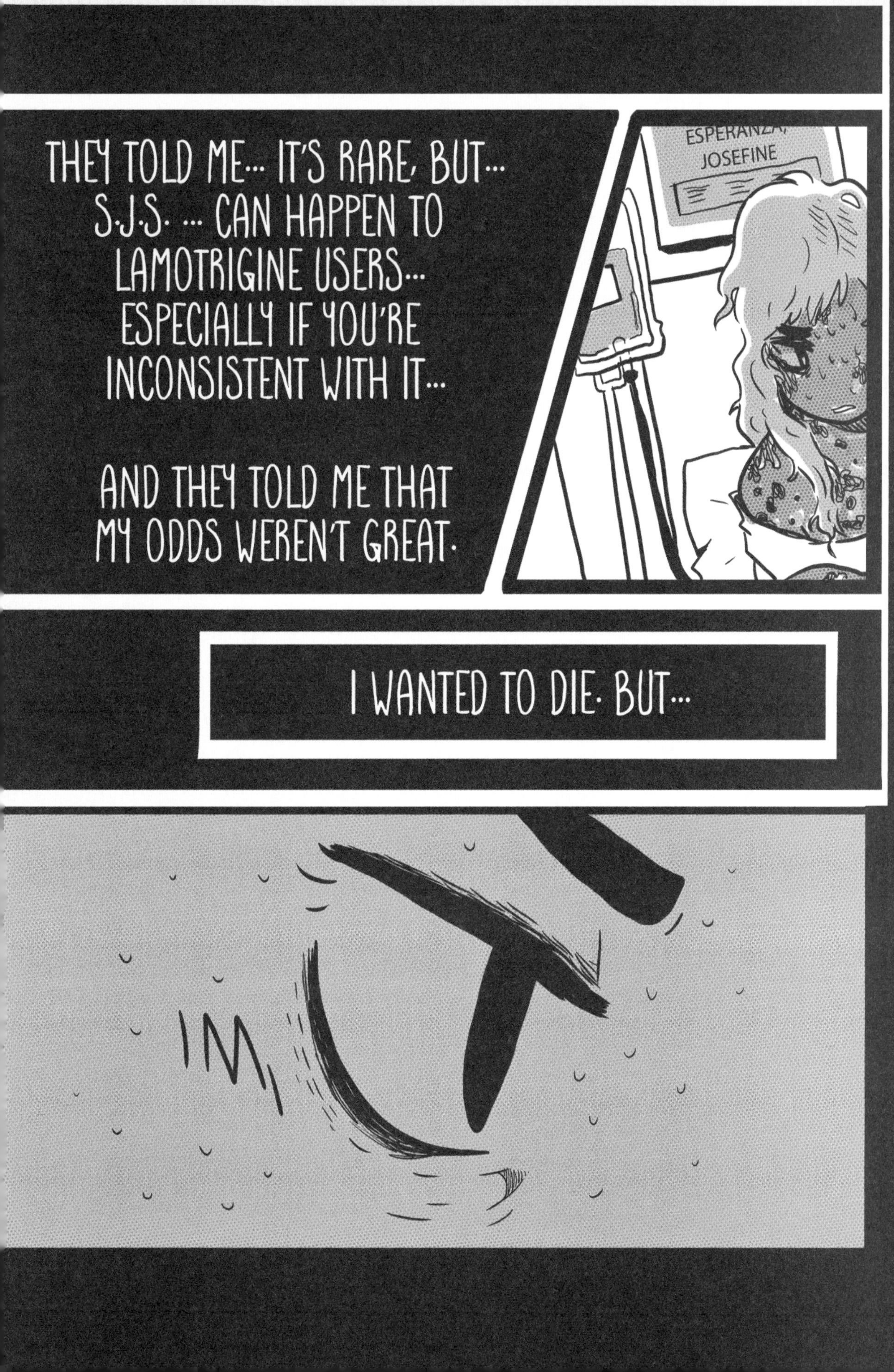
THEY TOLD ME... IT'S RARE, BUT... S.J.S. ... CAN HAPPEN TO LAMOTRIGINE USERS... ESPECIALLY IF YOU'RE INCONSISTENT WITH IT...
AND THEY TOLD ME THAT MY ODDS WEREN'T GREAT.
ESPERANZA, JOSEFINE
I WANTED TO DIE. BUT...

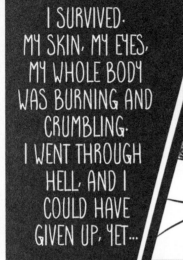

I SURVIVED. MY SKIN, MY EYES, MY WHOLE BODY WAS BURNING AND CRUMBLING. I WENT THROUGH HELL. AND I COULD HAVE GIVEN UP, YET...

I SWORE TO NOT LET THIS... THING... DO WHAT IT WANTED TO ME...

I WAS GOING TO DO WHATEVER IT TOOK

TO BECOME THE PERSON I AM NOW.

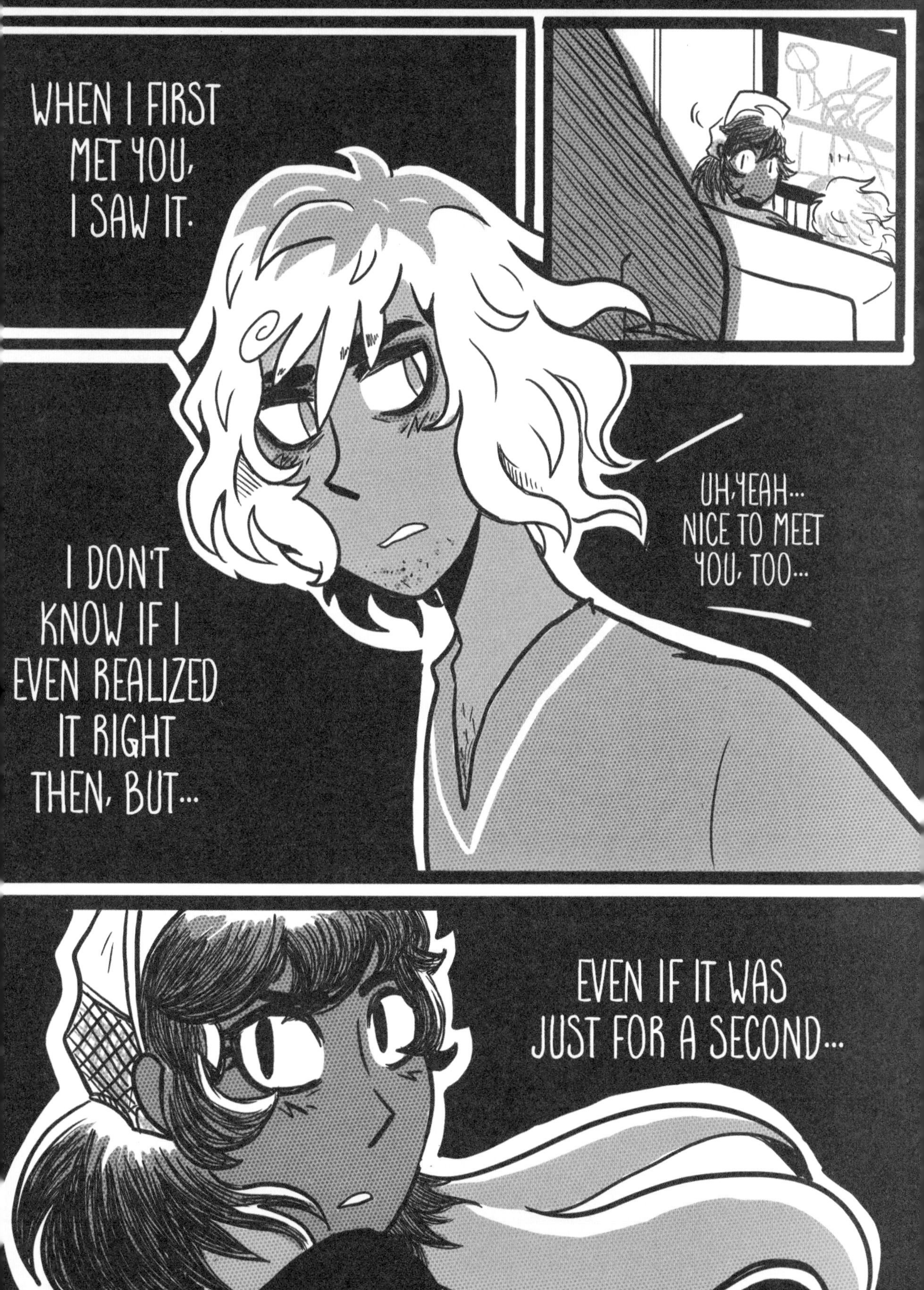
WHEN I FIRST MET YOU, I SAW IT.
UH, YEAH... NICE TO MEET YOU, TOO...
I DON'T KNOW IF I EVEN REALIZED IT RIGHT THEN, BUT...
EVEN IF IT WAS JUST FOR A SECOND...

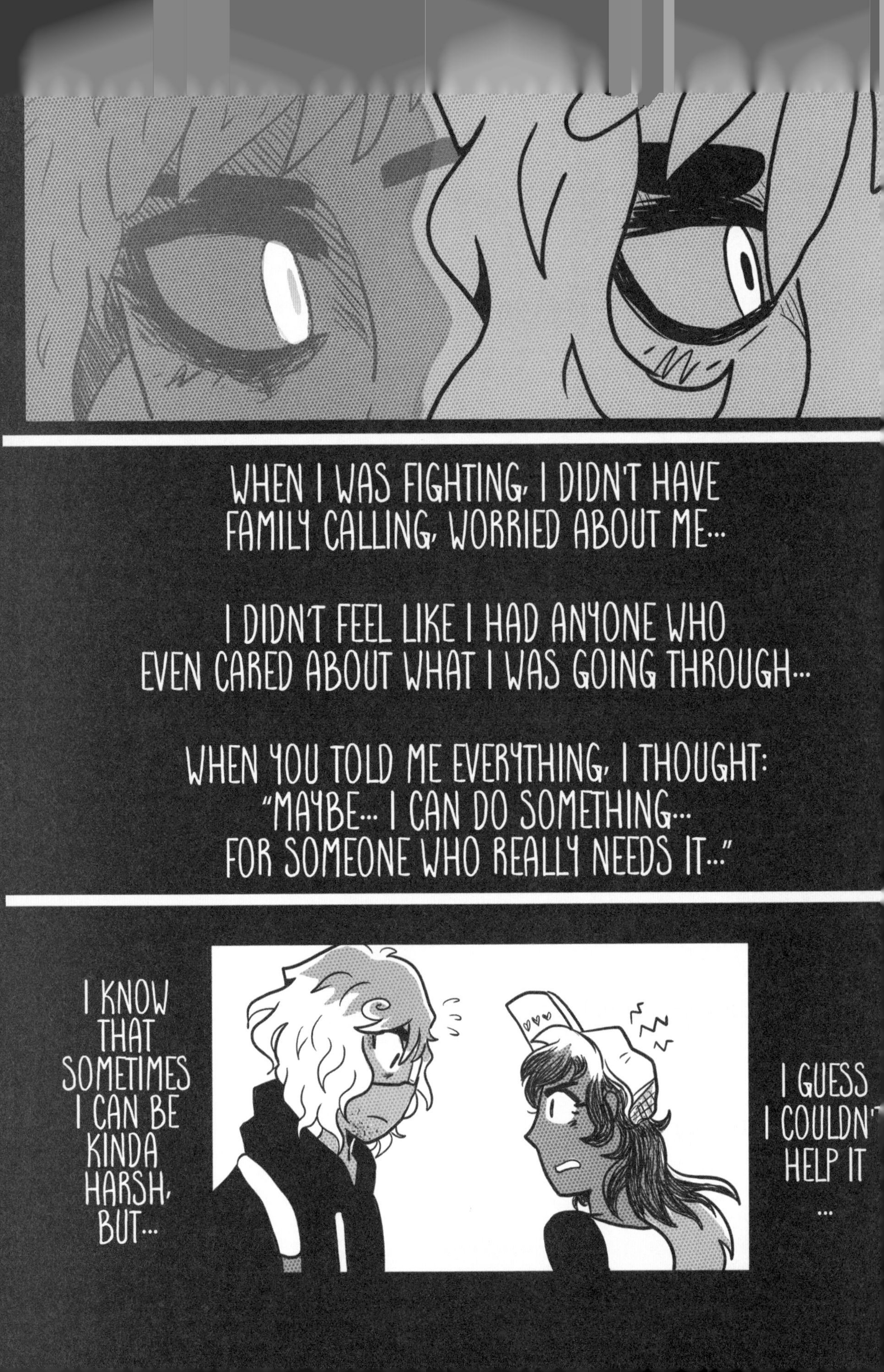
WHEN I WAS FIGHTING, I DIDN'T HAVE FAMILY CALLING, WORRIED ABOUT ME...
I DIDN'T FEEL LIKE I HAD ANYONE WHO EVEN CARED ABOUT WHAT I WAS GOING THROUGH...
WHEN YOU TOLD ME EVERYTHING, I THOUGHT: "MAYBE... I CAN DO SOMETHING... FOR SOMEONE WHO REALLY NEEDS IT..."
I KNOW THAT SOMETIMES I CAN BE KINDA HARSH, BUT...
I GUESS I COULDN'T HELP IT ...

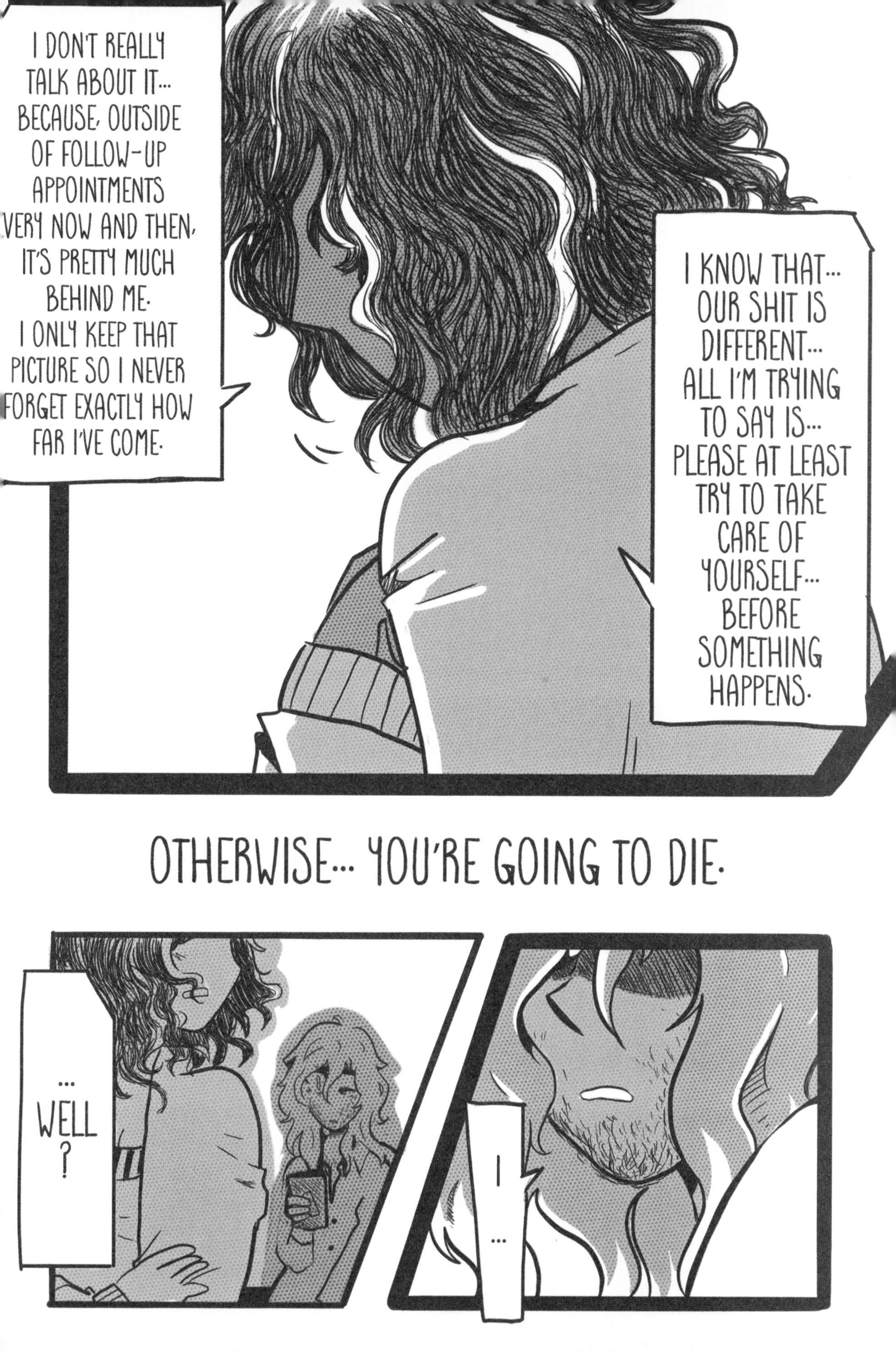
I DON'T REALLY TALK ABOUT IT... BECAUSE, OUTSIDE OF FOLLOW-UP APPOINTMENTS VERY NOW AND THEN, IT'S PRETTY MUCH BEHIND ME. I ONLY KEEP THAT PICTURE SO I NEVER FORGET EXACTLY HOW FAR I'VE COME.
I KNOW THAT... OUR SHIT IS DIFFERENT... ALL I'M TRYING TO SAY IS... PLEASE AT LEAST TRY TO TAKE CARE OF YOURSELF... BEFORE SOMETHING HAPPENS.
OTHERWISE... YOU'RE GOING TO DIE.
... WELL ?
I ...

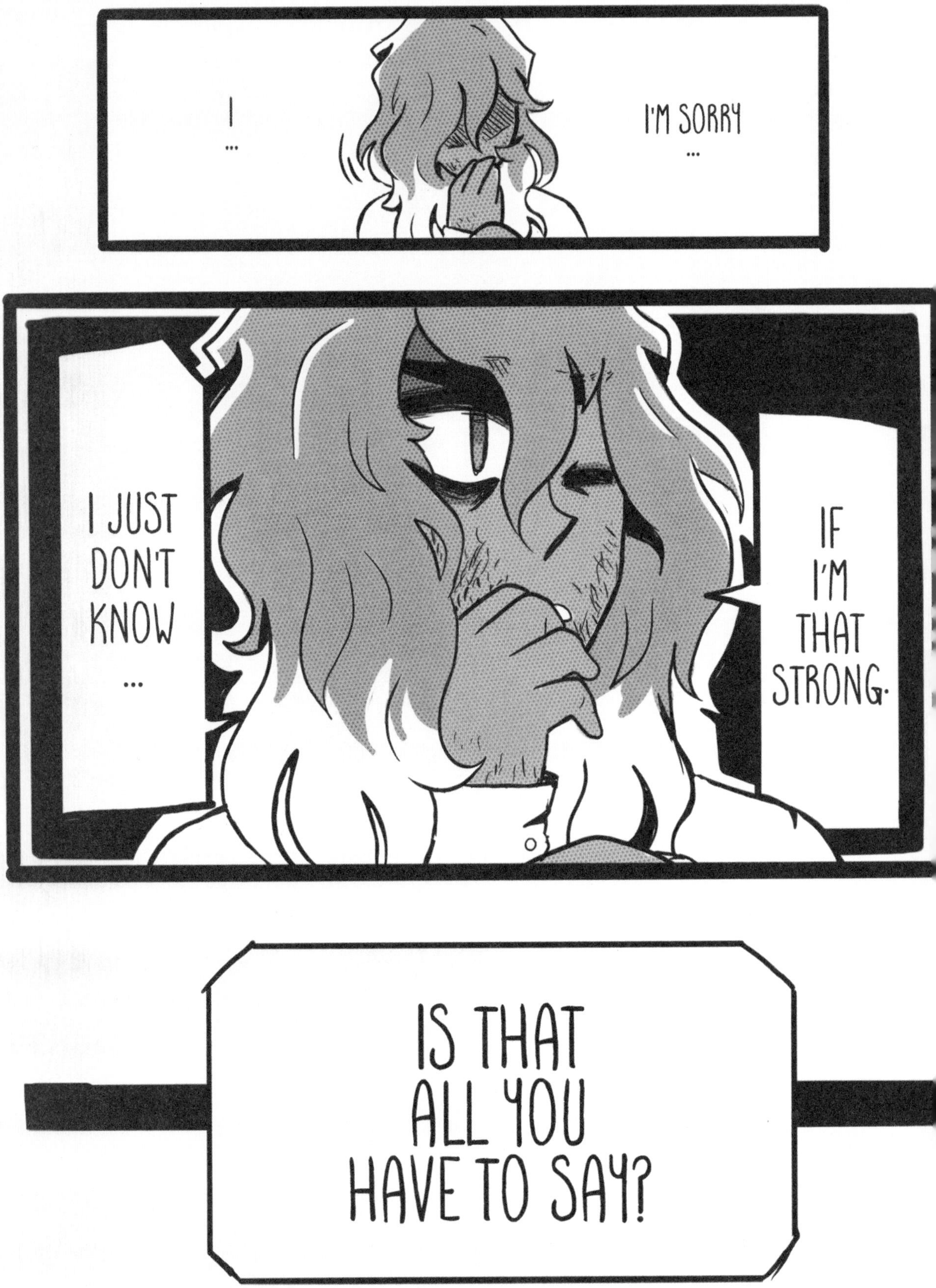

I
...
I'M SORRY
...
I JUST DON'T KNOW
...
IF I'M THAT STRONG.
IS THAT ALL YOU HAVE TO SAY?

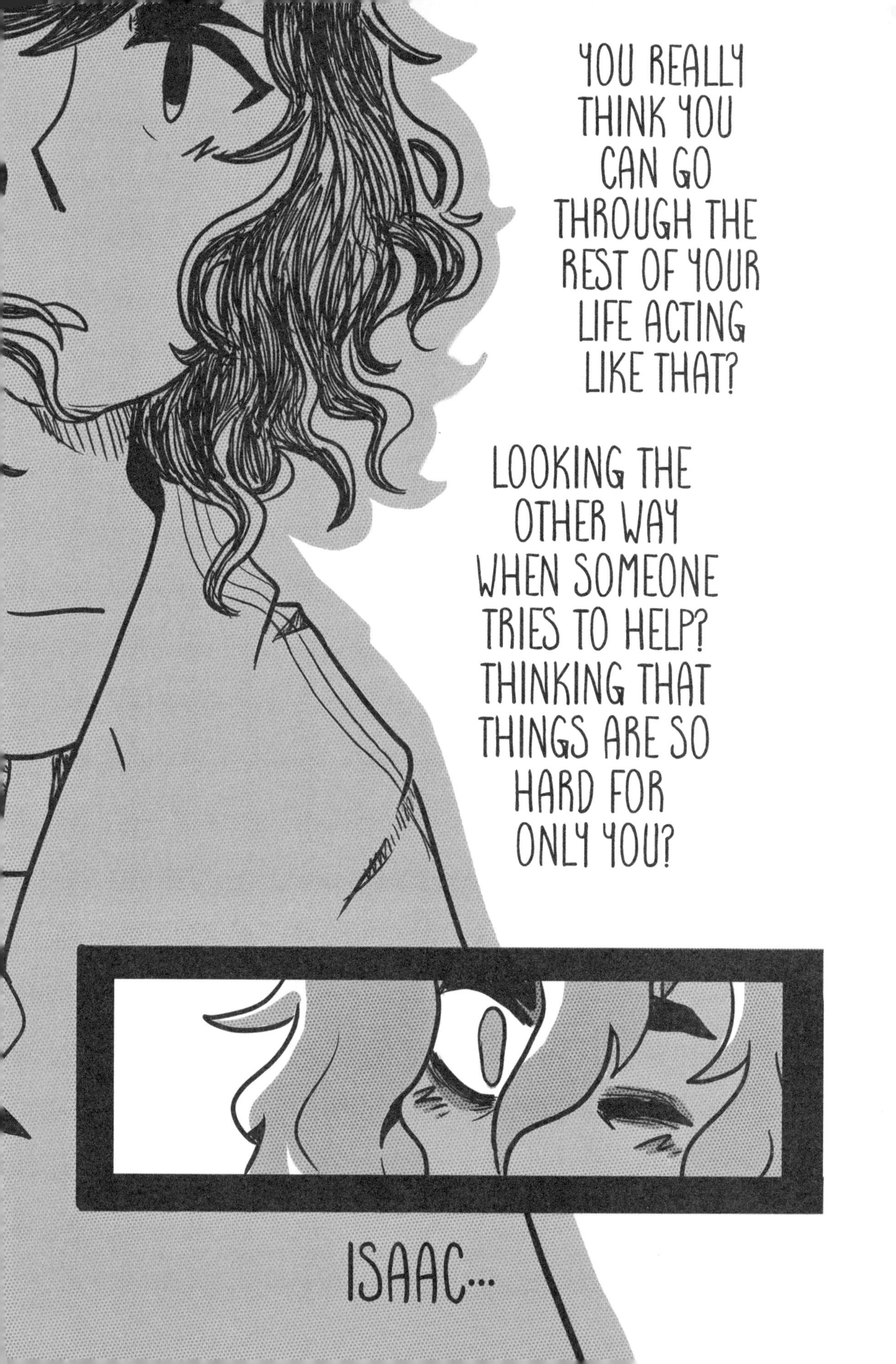
YOU REALLY THINK YOU CAN GO THROUGH THE REST OF YOUR LIFE ACTING LIKE THAT?
LOOKING THE OTHER WAY WHEN SOMEONE TRIES TO HELP? THINKING THAT THINGS ARE SO HARD FOR ONLY YOU?
ISAAC...

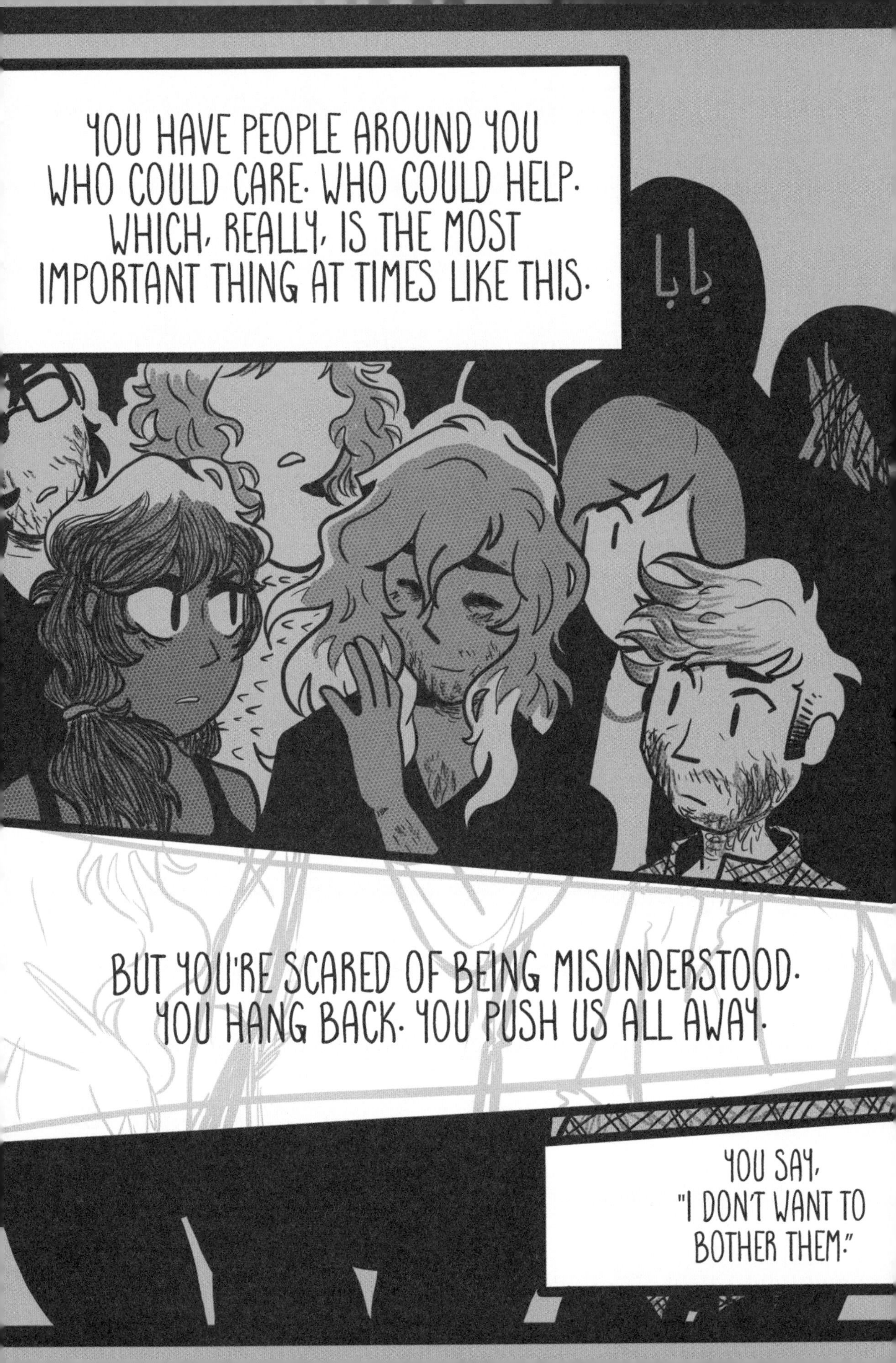
YOU HAVE PEOPLE AROUND YOU WHO COULD CARE. WHO COULD HELP. WHICH, REALLY, IS THE MOST IMPORTANT THING AT TIMES LIKE THIS.
بابا
BUT YOU'RE SCARED OF BEING MISUNDERSTOOD. YOU HANG BACK. YOU PUSH US ALL AWAY.
YOU SAY, "I DON'T WANT TO BOTHER THEM."

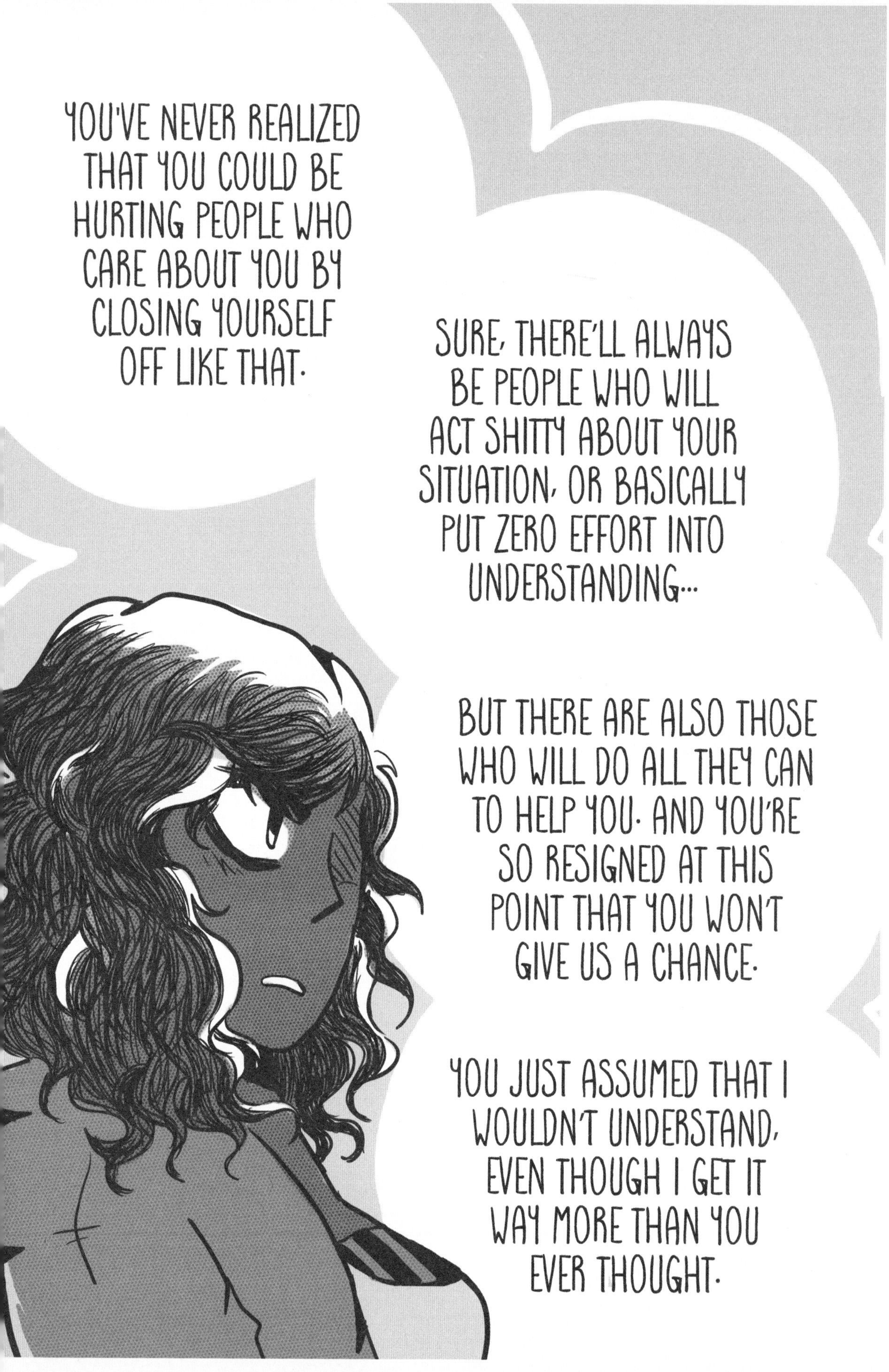
YOU'VE NEVER REALIZED THAT YOU COULD BE HURTING PEOPLE WHO CARE ABOUT YOU BY CLOSING YOURSELF OFF LIKE THAT.
SURE, THERE'LL ALWAYS BE PEOPLE WHO WILL ACT SHITTY ABOUT YOUR SITUATION, OR BASICALLY PUT ZERO EFFORT INTO UNDERSTANDING...
BUT THERE ARE ALSO THOSE WHO WILL DO ALL THEY CAN TO HELP YOU. AND YOU'RE SO RESIGNED AT THIS POINT THAT YOU WON'T GIVE US A CHANCE.
YOU JUST ASSUMED THAT I WOULDN'T UNDERSTAND, EVEN THOUGH I GET IT WAY MORE THAN YOU EVER THOUGHT.

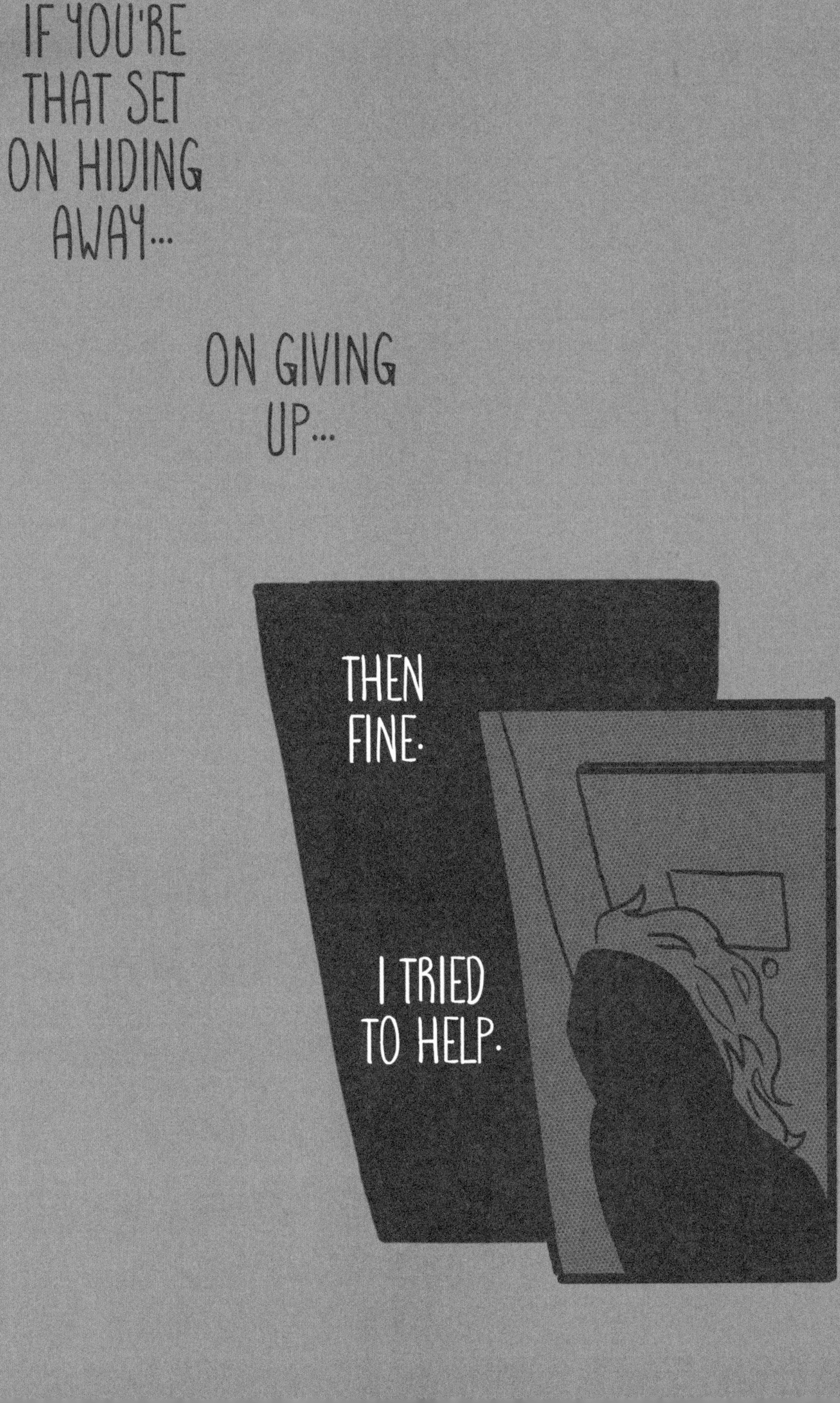
IF YOU'RE THAT SET ON HIDING AWAY...
ON GIVING UP...
THEN FINE.
I TRIED TO HELP.

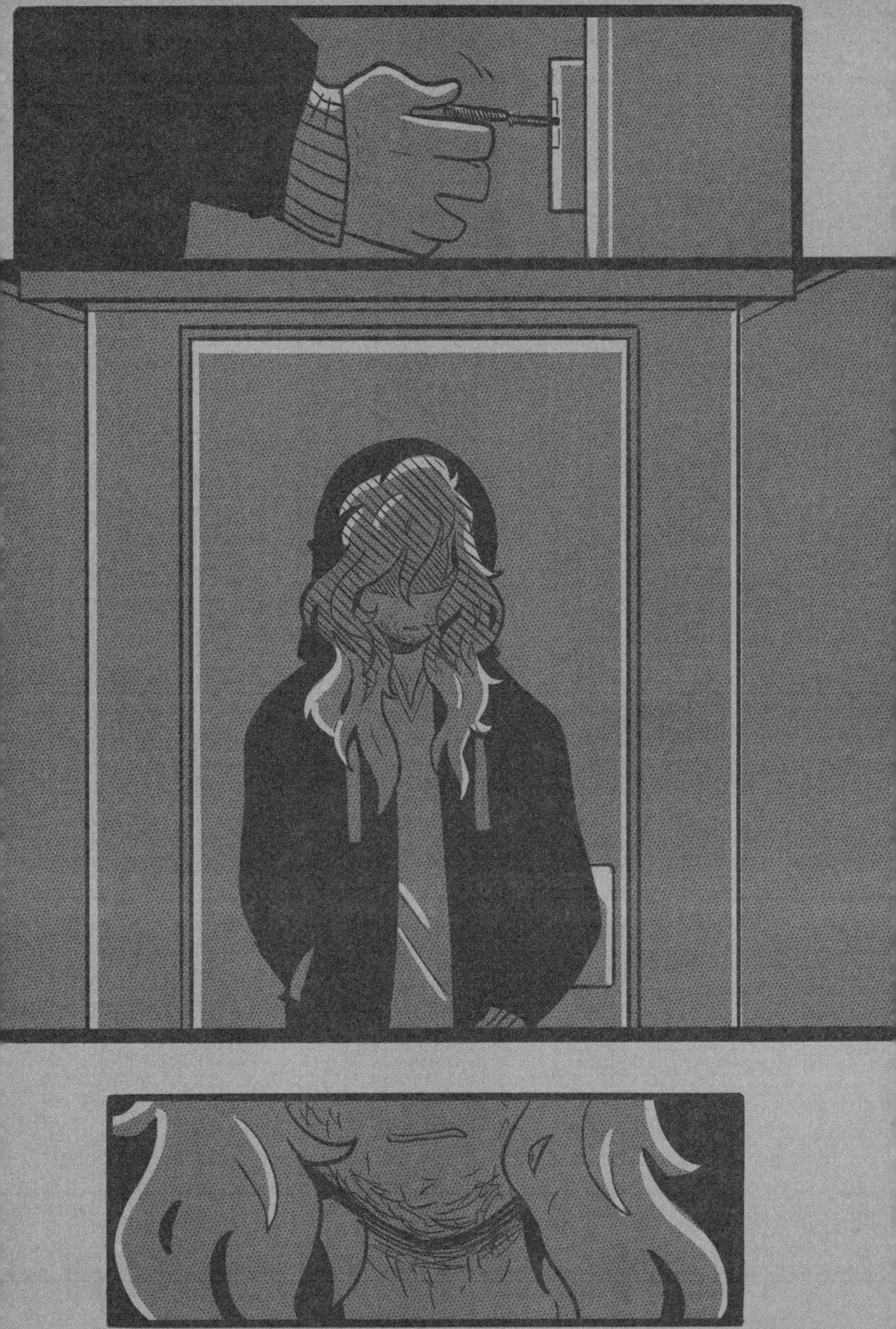

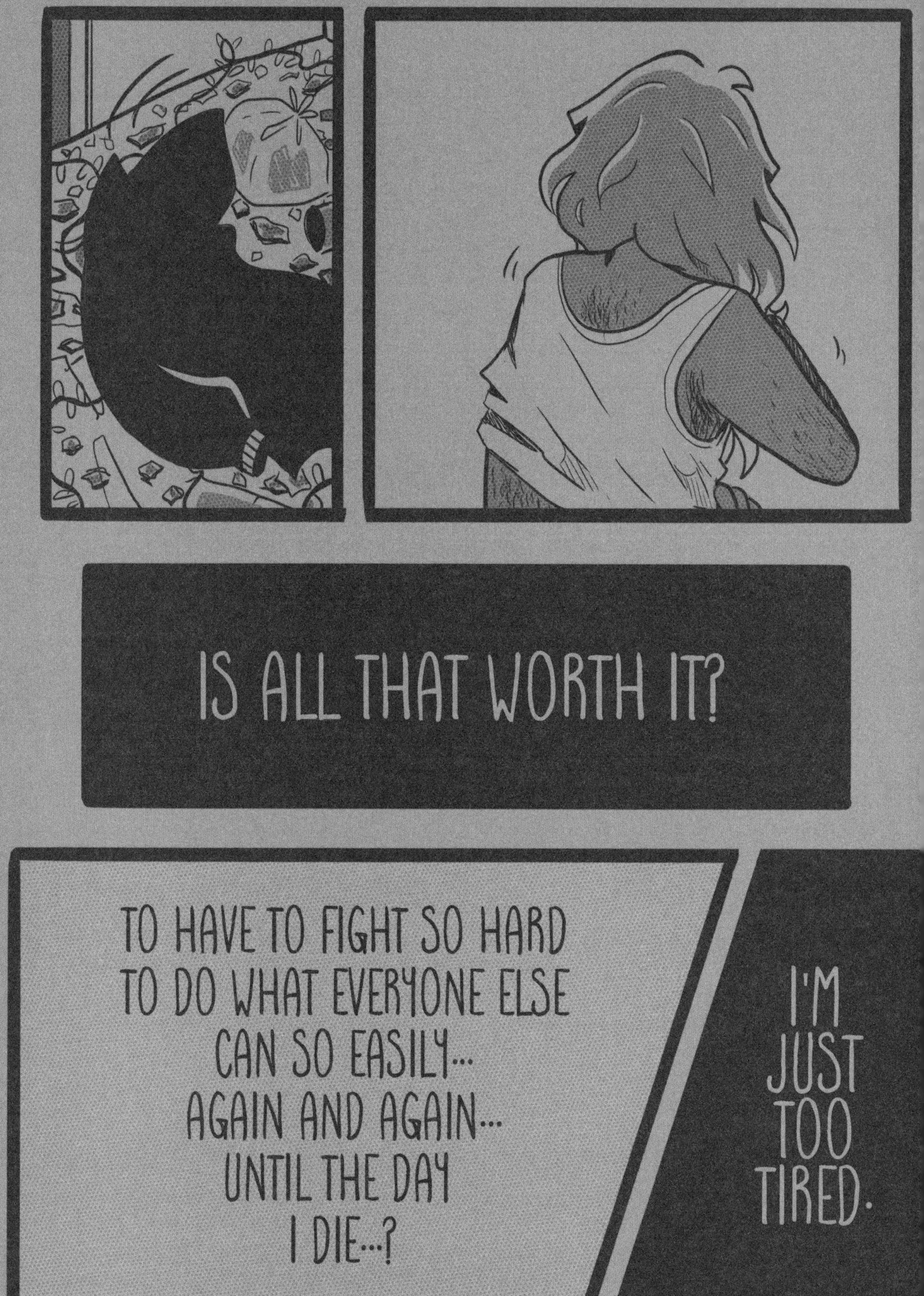
IS ALL THAT WORTH IT?
TO HAVE TO FIGHT SO HARD TO DO WHAT EVERYONE ELSE CAN SO EASILY... AGAIN AND AGAIN... UNTIL THE DAY I DIE...?
I'M JUST TOO TIRED.

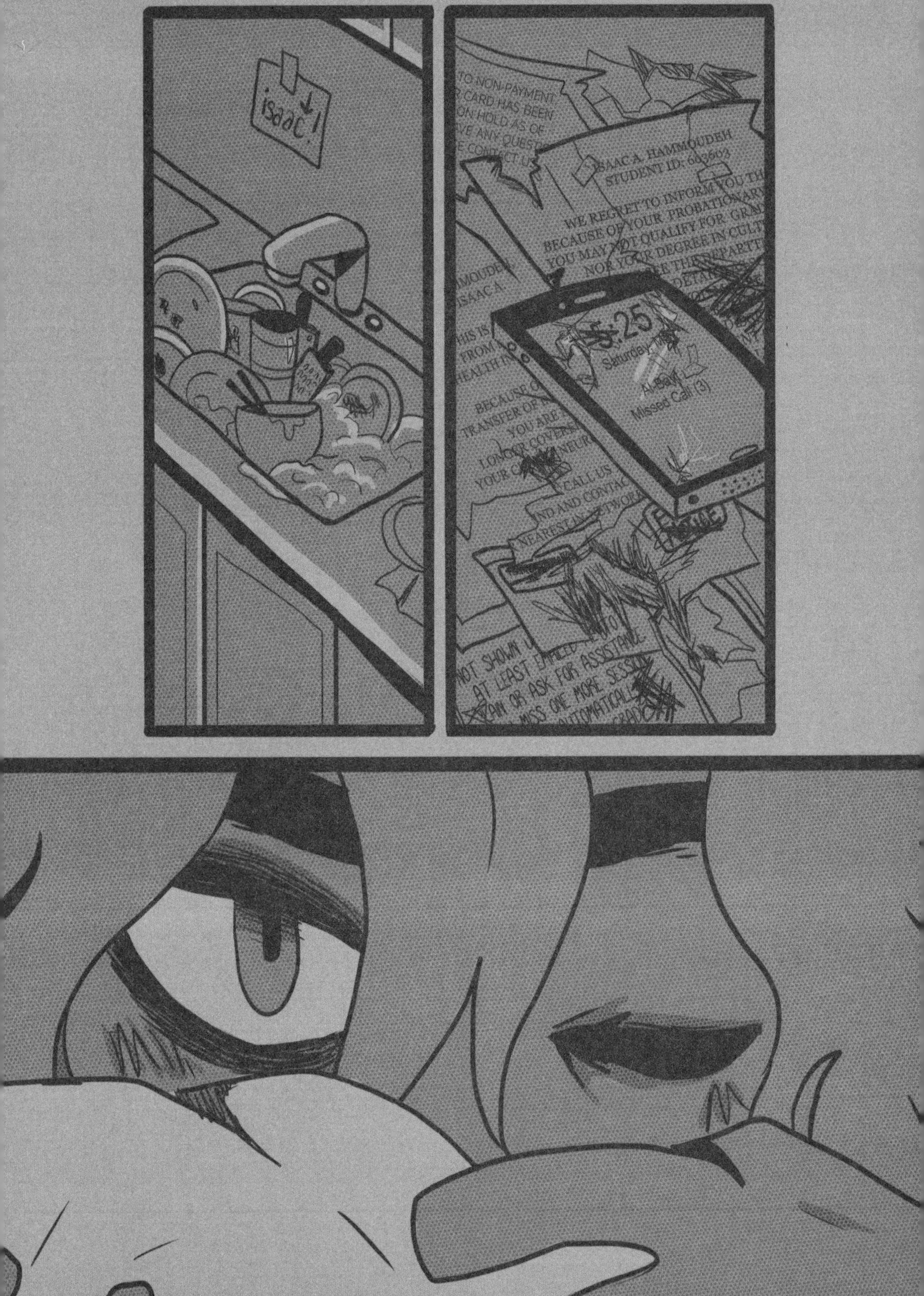
isaac!
ISAAC A. HAMMOUDEH
STUDENT ID:
WE REGRET TO INFORM YOU
BECAUSE OF YOUR PROBATIONARY
Saturday
Missed Call (3)
OR ASK FOR ASSISTANCE

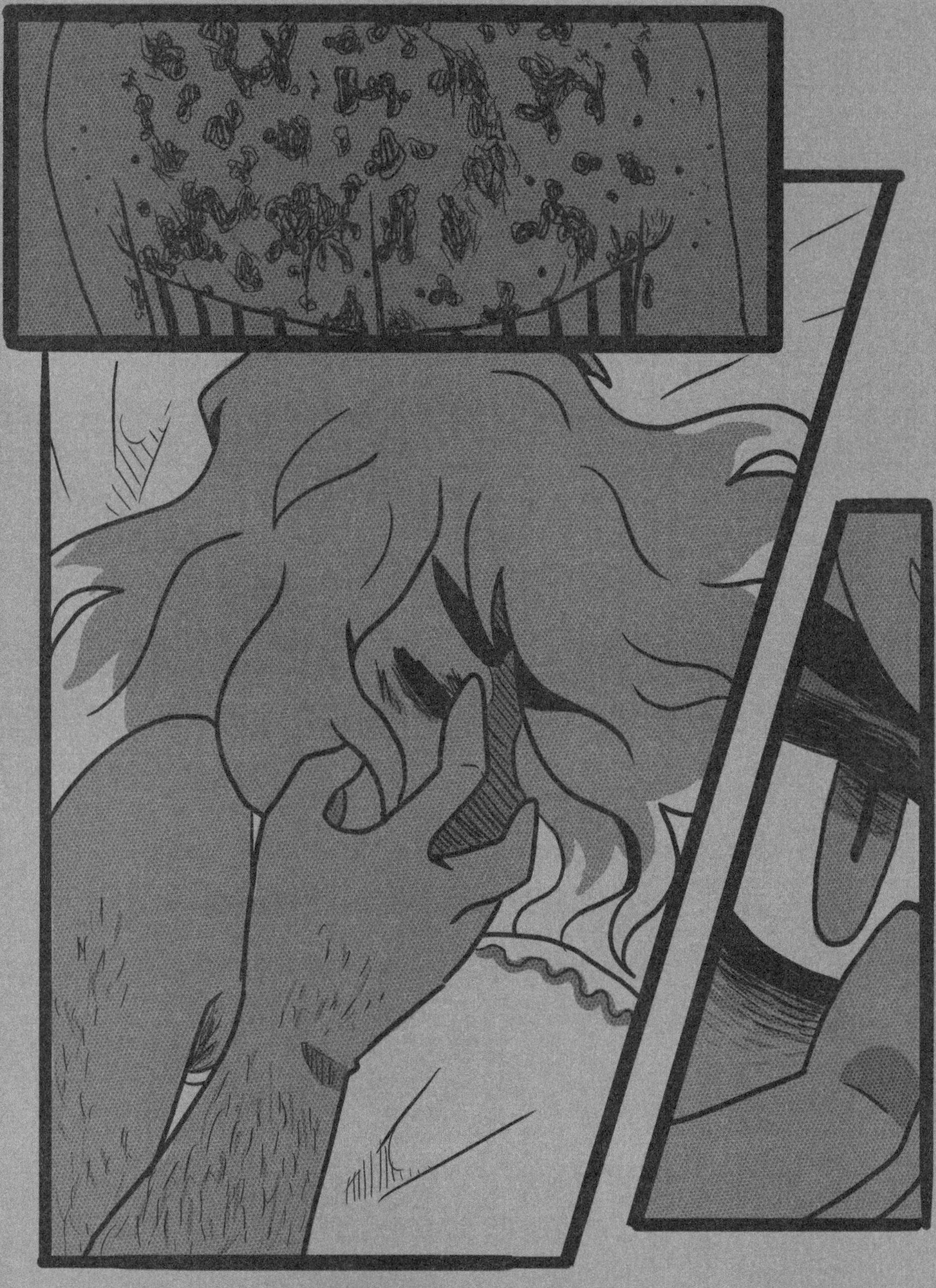

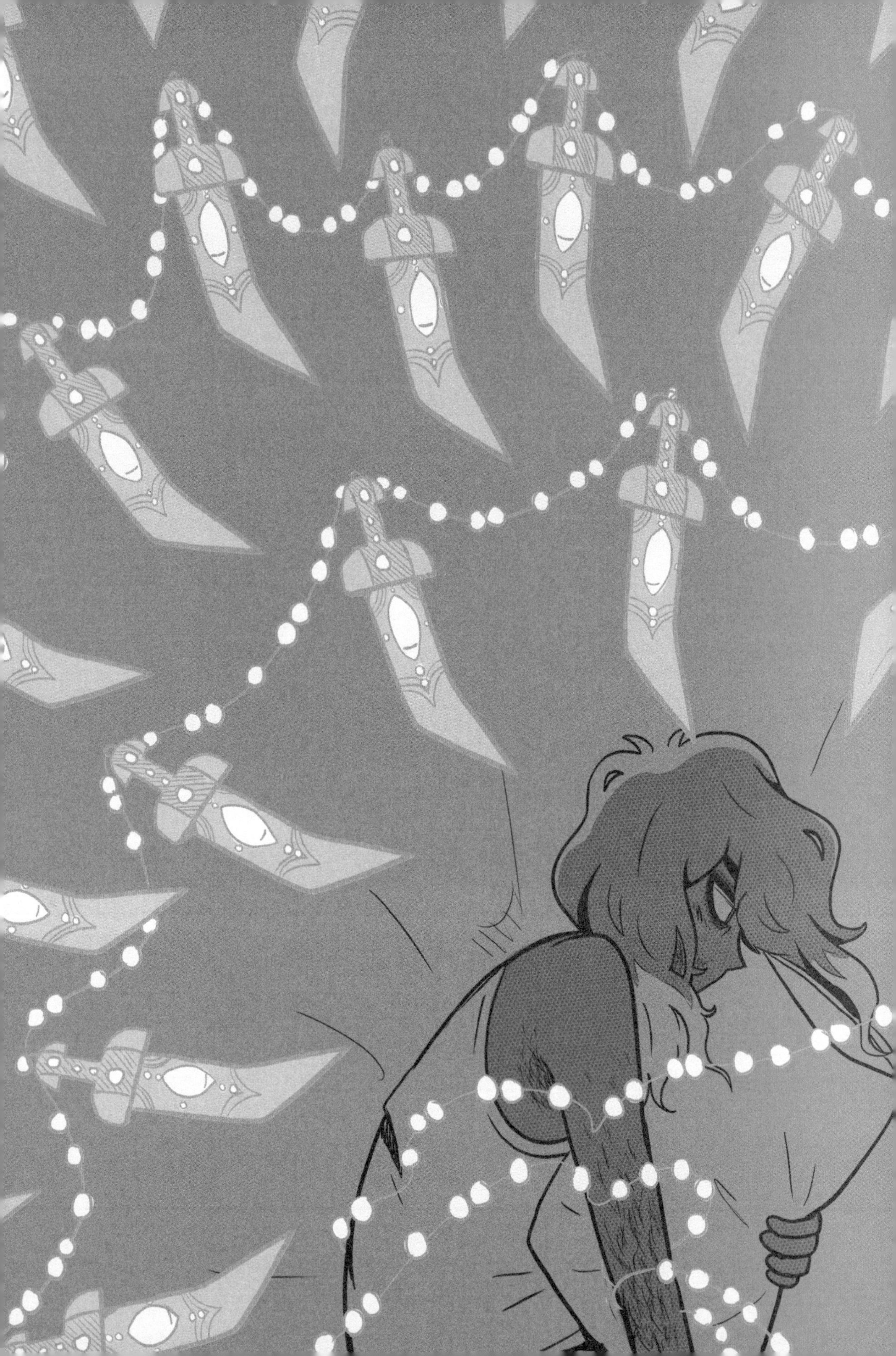

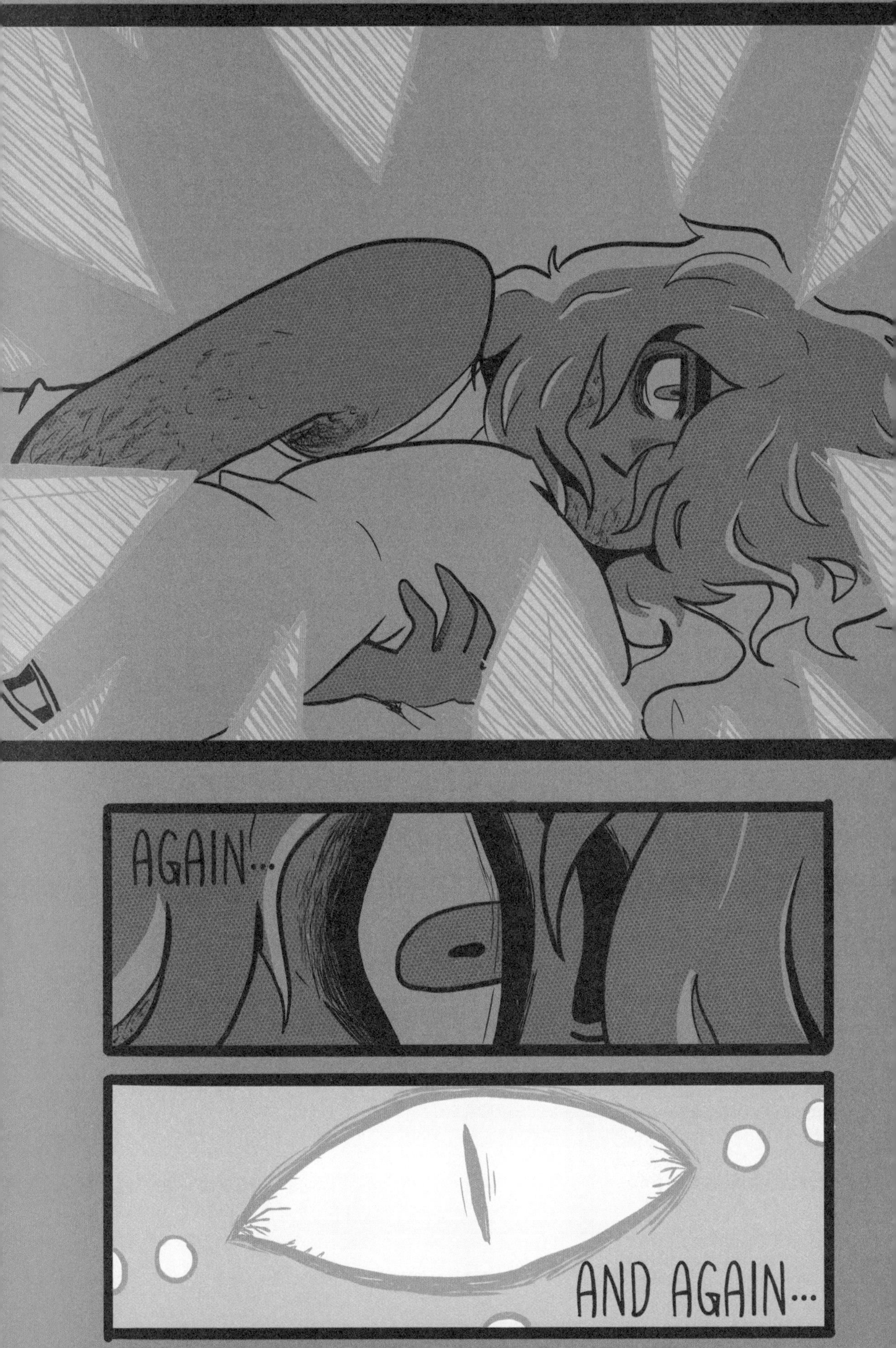
AGAIN...
AND AGAIN...

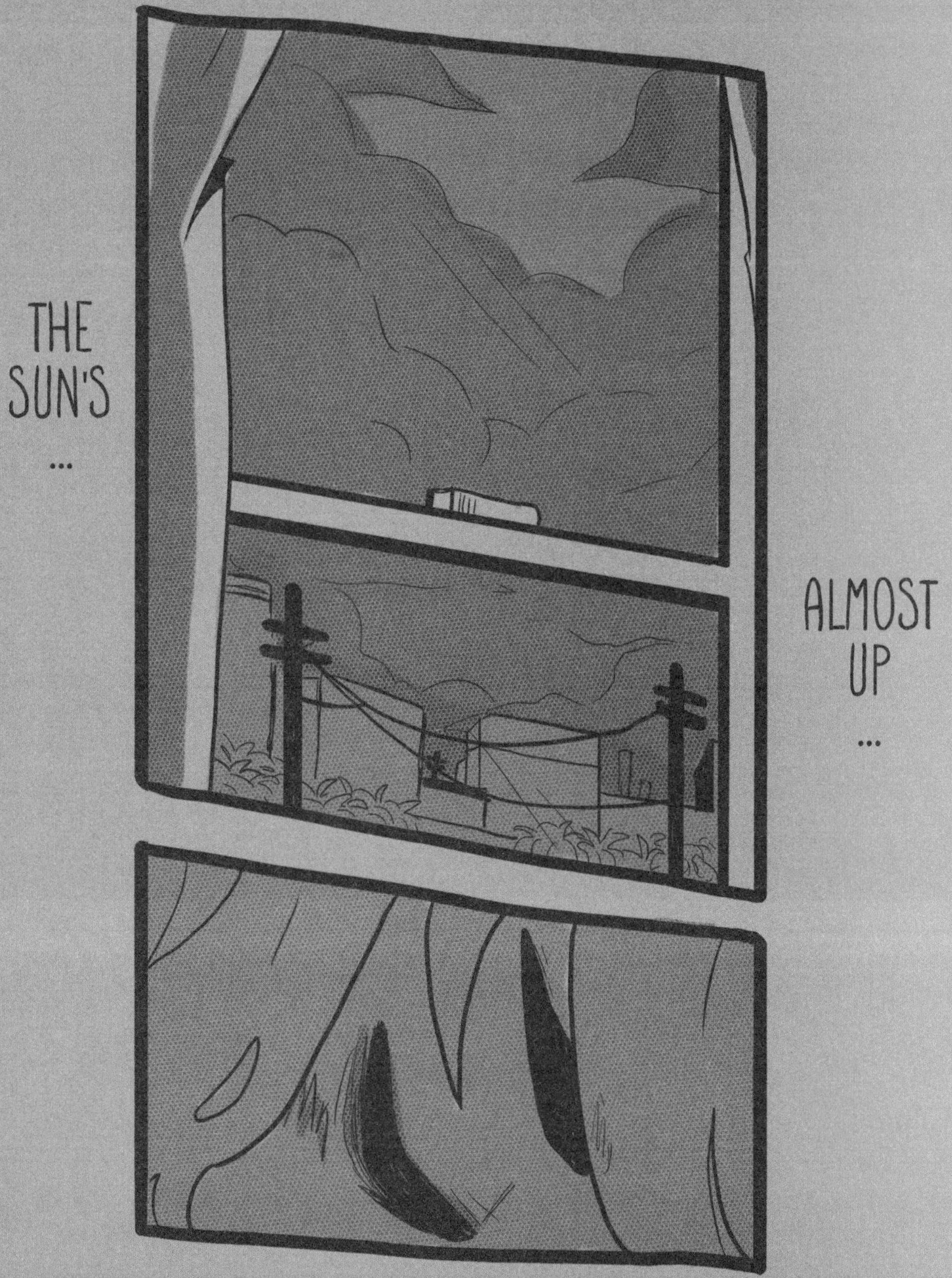
THE SUN'S
...
ALMOST UP
...

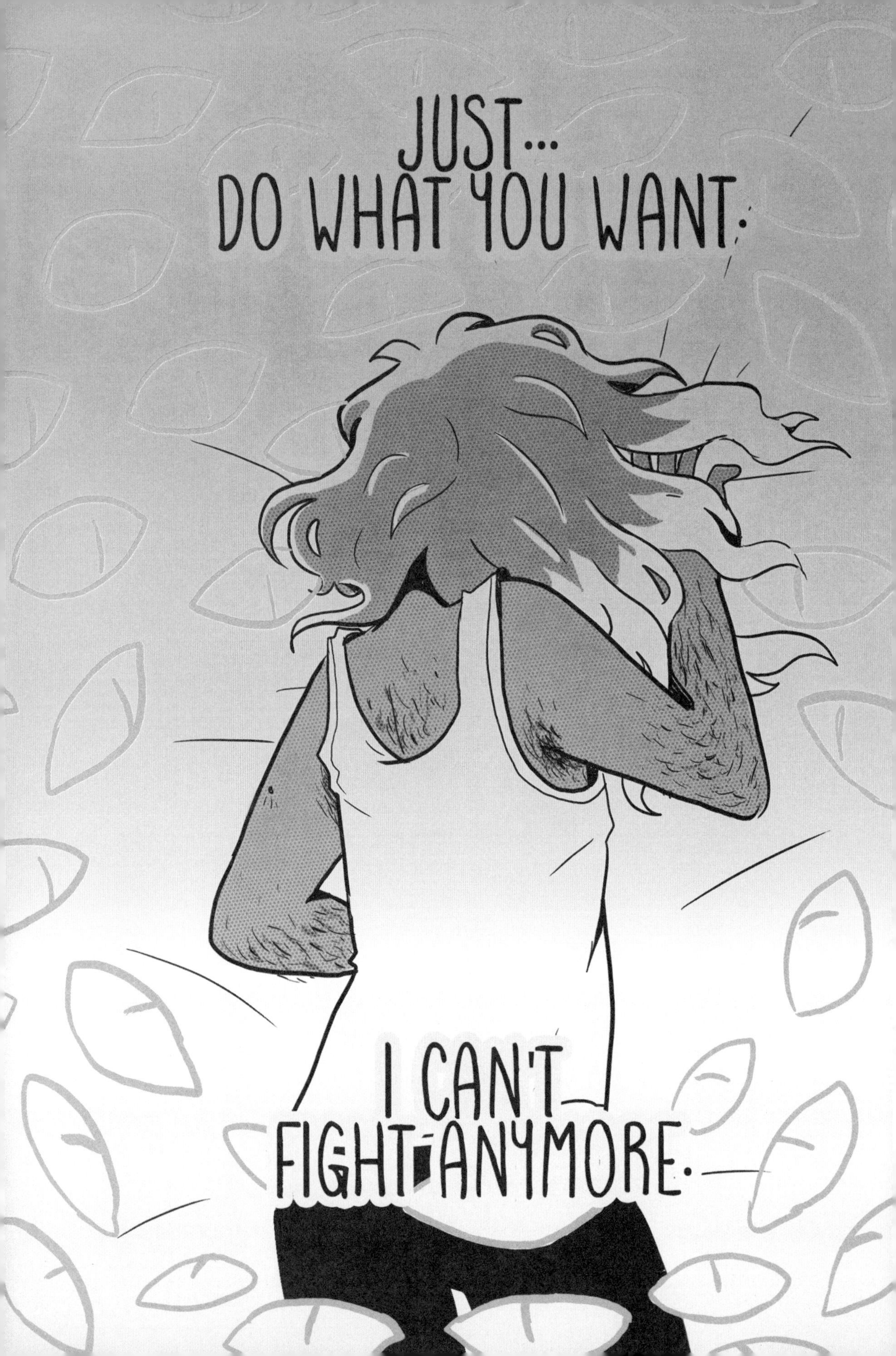
JUST...
DO WHAT YOU WANT.
I CAN'T
FIGHT ANYMORE.

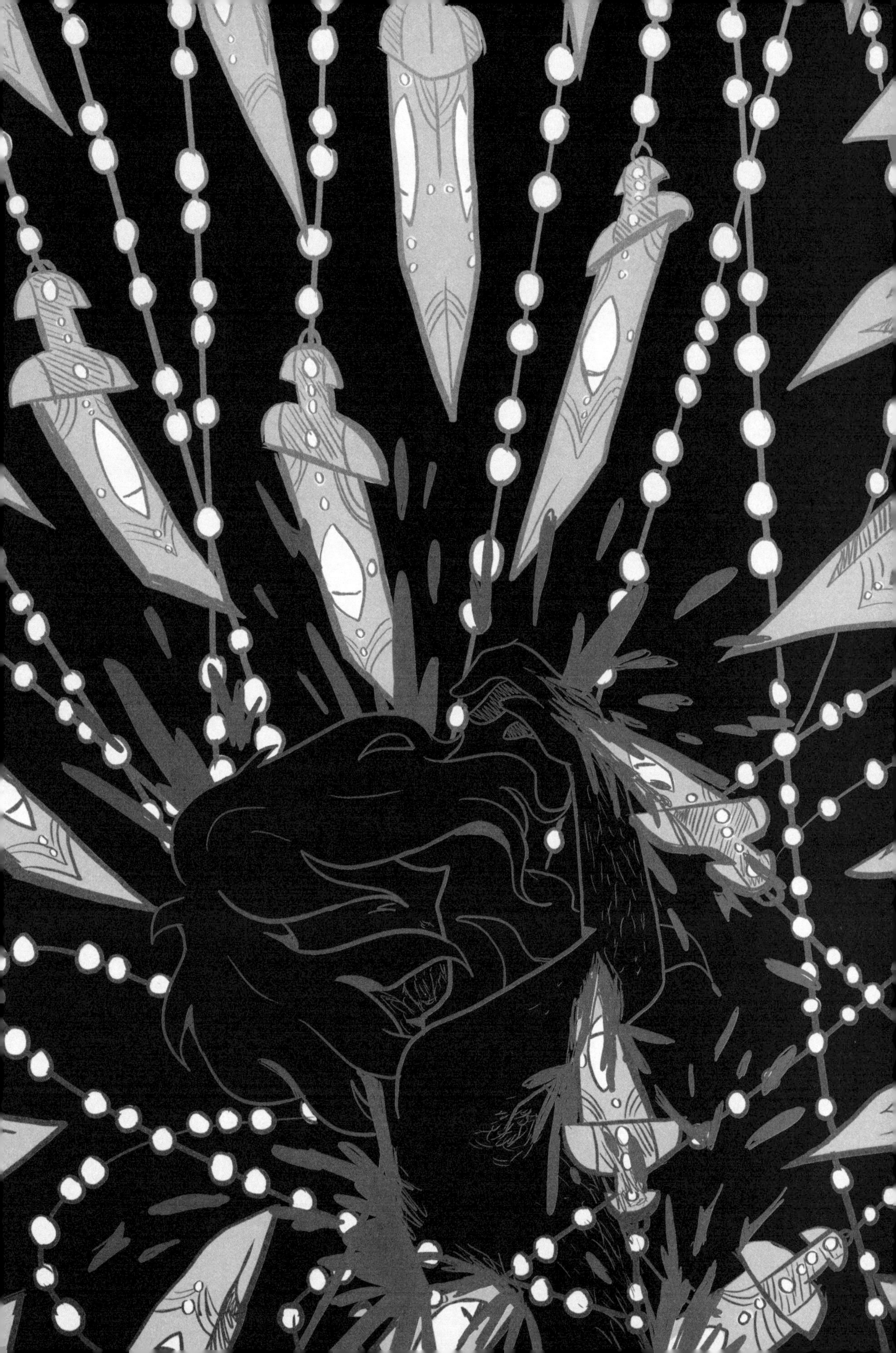

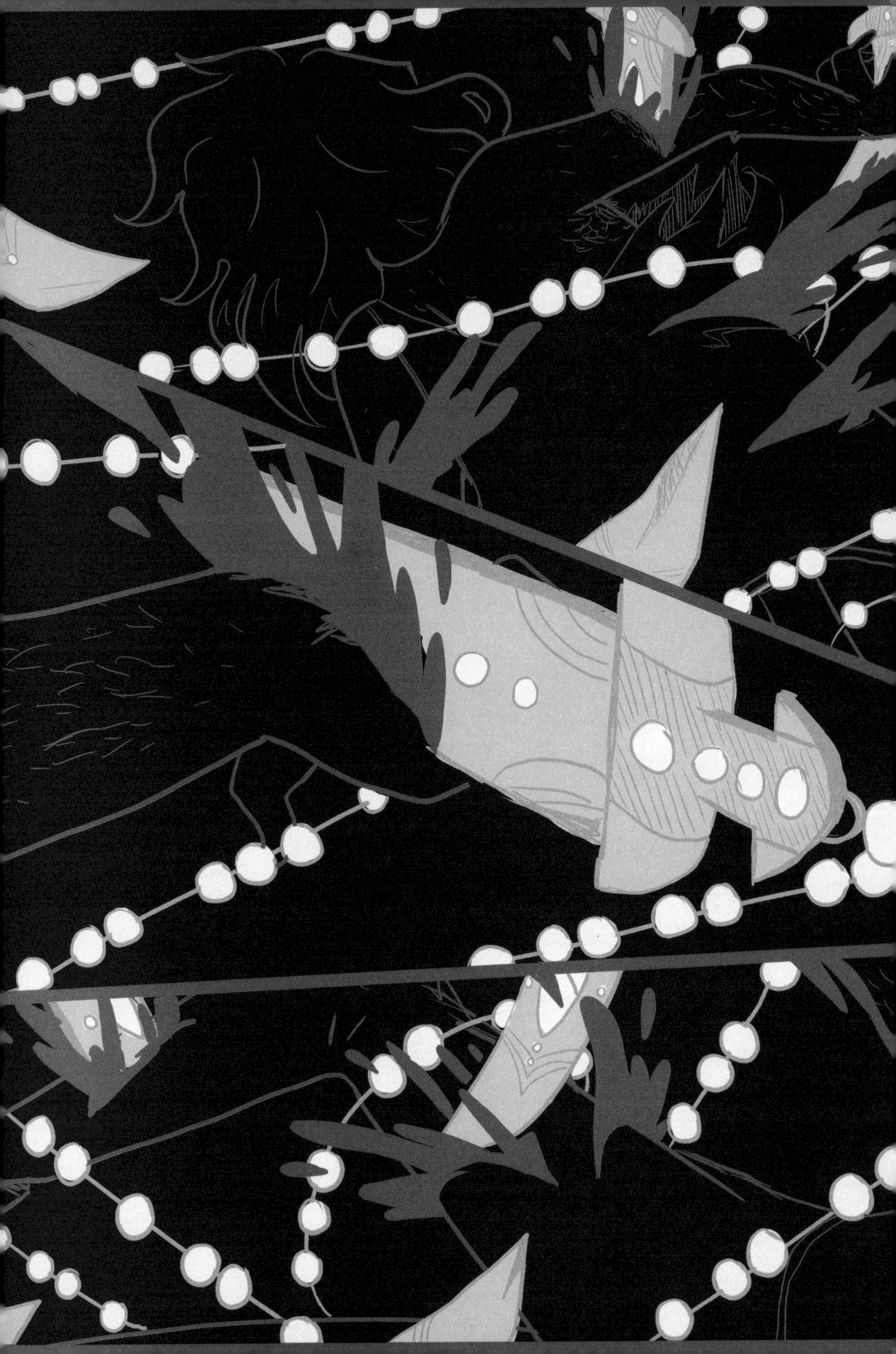

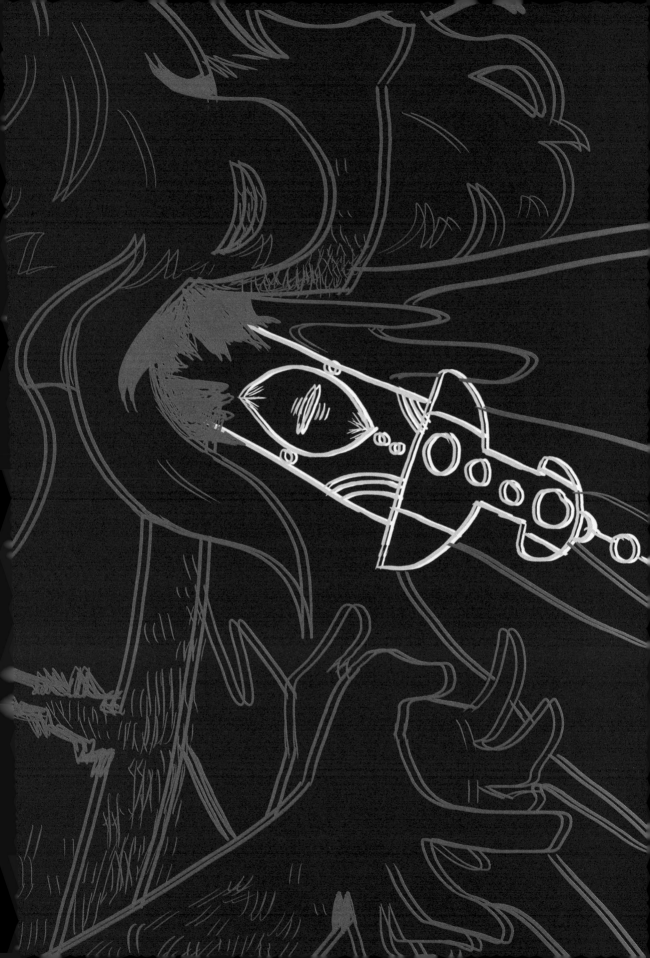

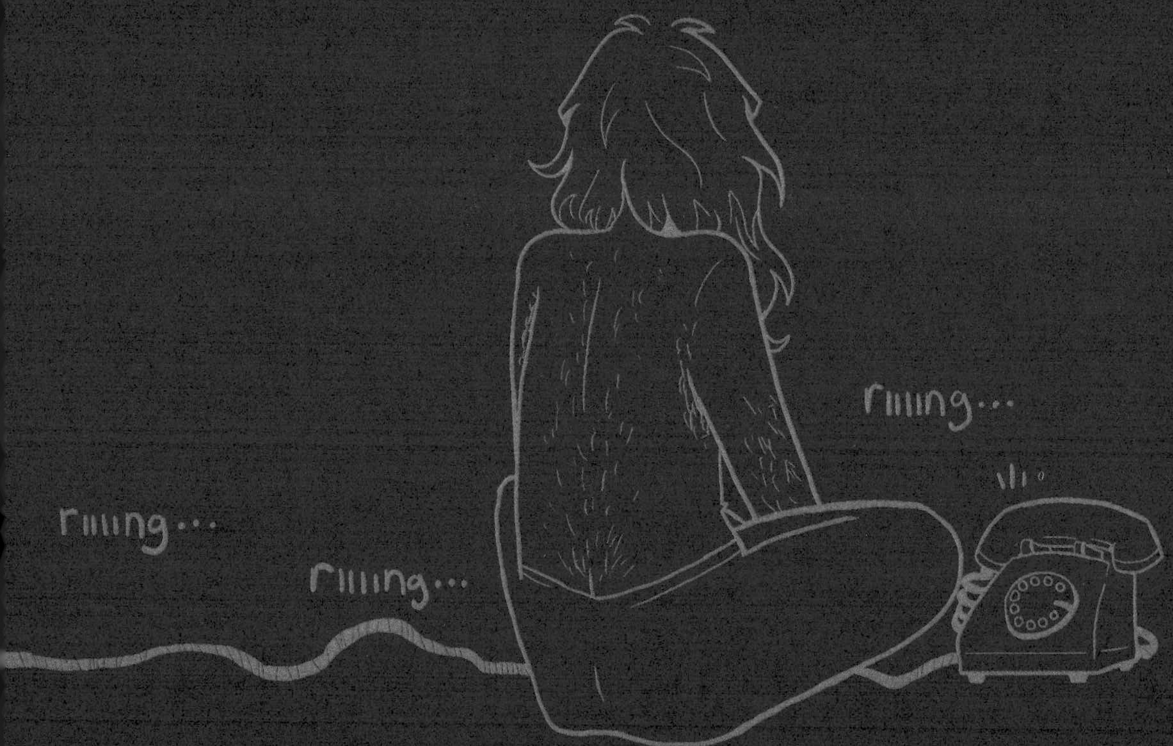
rilling...
rilling...
rilling...

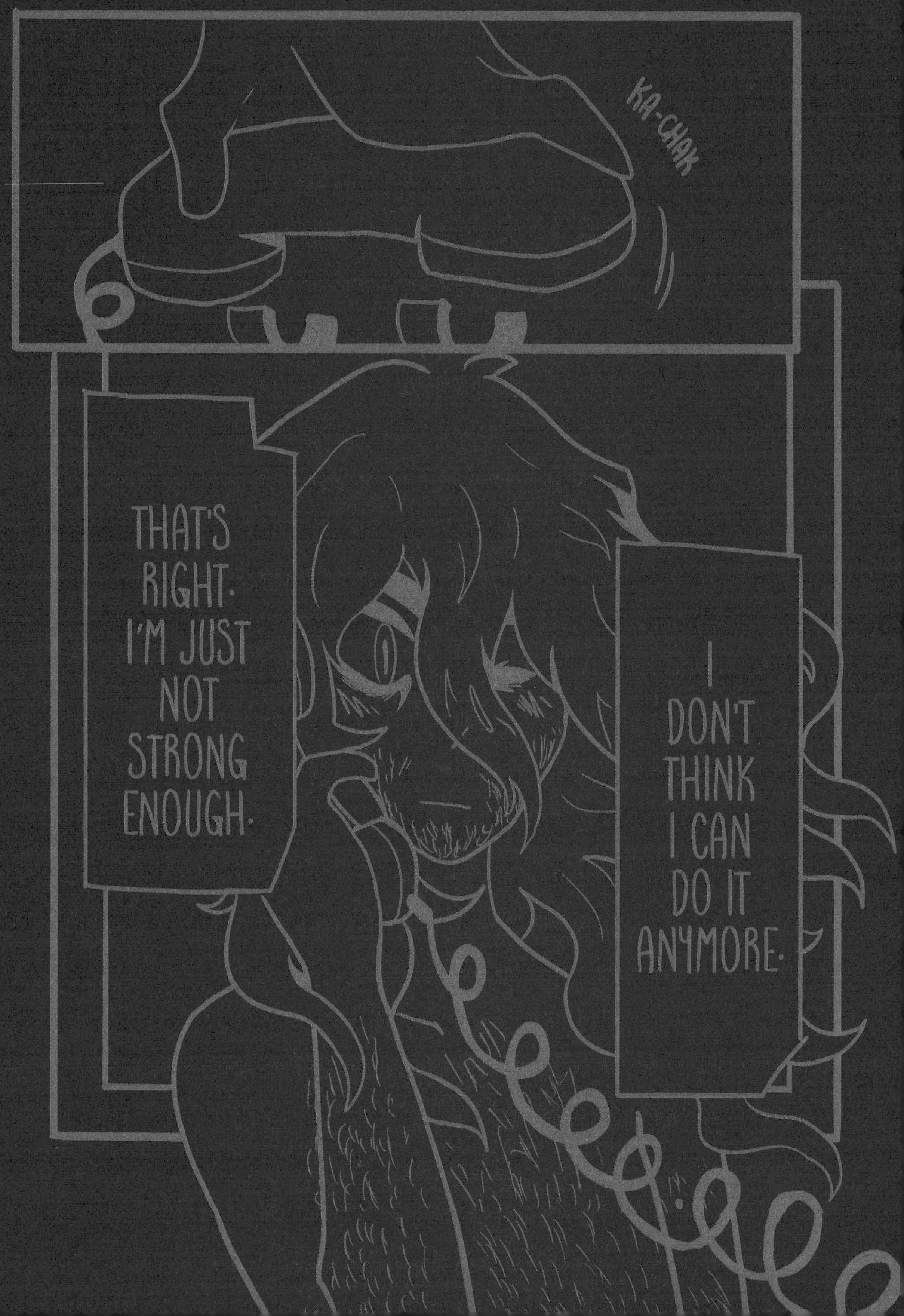
KA-CHAK
THAT'S RIGHT. I'M JUST NOT STRONG ENOUGH.
I DON'T THINK I CAN DO IT ANYMORE.

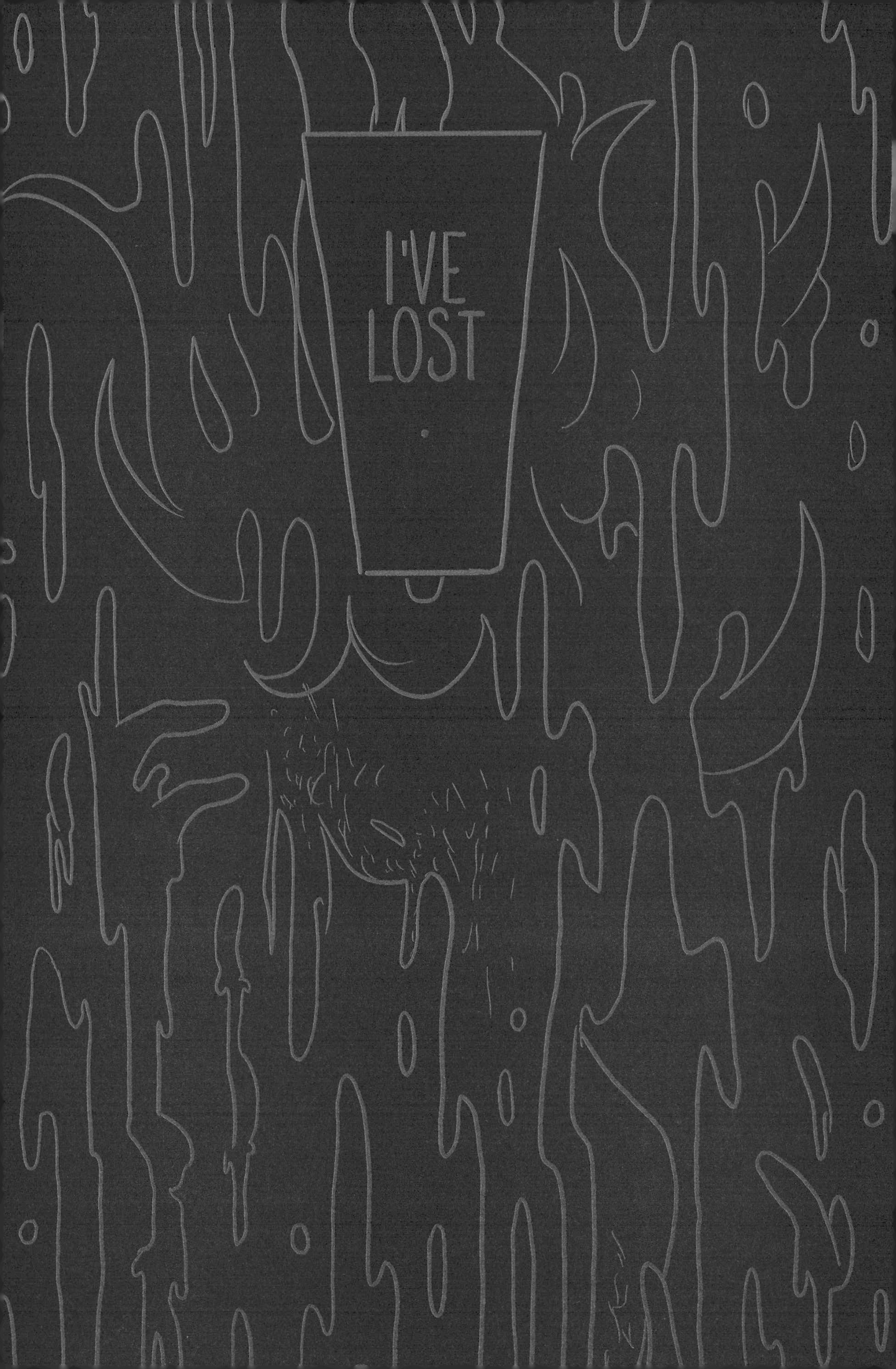
I'VE LOST

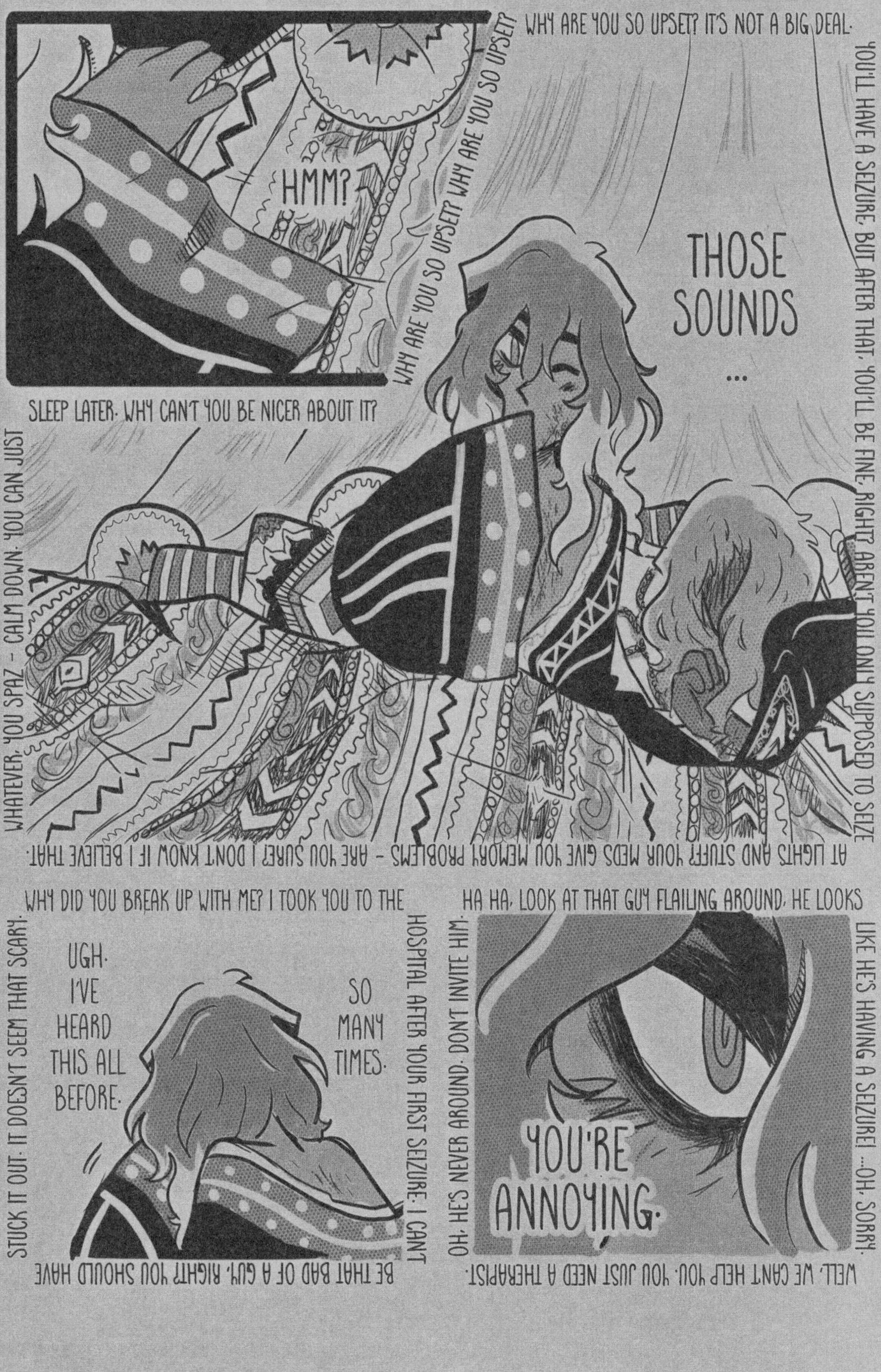
HMM?
WHY ARE YOU SO UPSET? WHY ARE YOU SO UPSET? WHY ARE YOU SO UPSET?
WHY ARE YOU SO UPSET? IT'S NOT A BIG DEAL. YOU'LL HAVE A SEIZURE, BUT AFTER THAT, YOU'LL BE FINE, RIGHT? ARENT YOU ONLY SUPPOSED TO SEIZE AT LIGHTS AND STUFF? YOUR MEDS GIVE YOU MEMORY PROBLEMS - ARE YOU SURE? I DONT KNOW IF I BELIEVE THAT. WHATEVER. YOU SPAZ - CALM DOWN. YOU CAN JUST SLEEP LATER. WHY CAN'T YOU BE NICER ABOUT IT?
THOSE SOUNDS ...
WHY DID YOU BREAK UP WITH ME? I TOOK YOU TO THE HOSPITAL AFTER YOUR FIRST SEIZURE. I CANT BE THAT BAD OF A GUY, RIGHT? YOU SHOULD HAVE STUCK IT OUT. IT DOESNT SEEM THAT SCARY.
UGH. I'VE HEARD THIS ALL BEFORE.
SO MANY TIMES.
HA HA, LOOK AT THAT GUY FLAILING AROUND, HE LOOKS LIKE HE'S HAVING A SEIZURE! ...OH, SORRY. WELL, WE CANT HELP YOU. YOU JUST NEED A THERAPIST. OH, HE'S NEVER AROUND. DONT INVITE HIM.
YOU'RE ANNOYING.

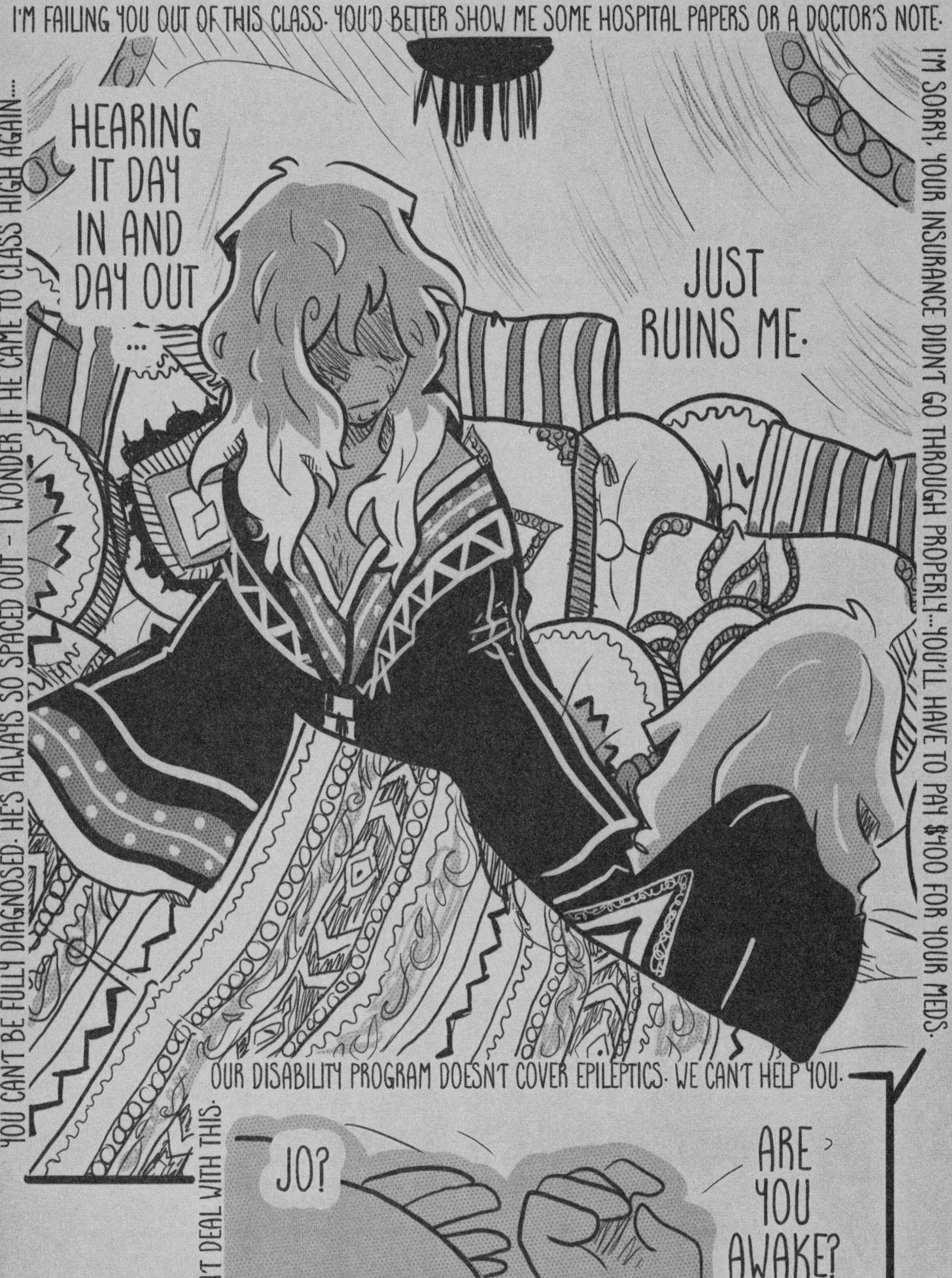
I'M FAILING YOU OUT OF THIS CLASS. YOU'D BETTER SHOW ME SOME HOSPITAL PAPERS OR A DOCTOR'S NOTE.
I'M SORRY. YOUR INSURANCE DIDN'T GO THROUGH PROPERLY...YOU'LL HAVE TO PAY $400 FOR YOUR MEDS.
YOU CAN'T BE FULLY DIAGNOSED. HE'S ALWAYS SO SPACED OUT - I WONDER IF HE CAME TO CLASS HIGH AGAIN....
HEARING IT DAY IN AND DAY OUT
...
JUST RUINS ME.
OUR DISABILITY PROGRAM DOESN'T COVER EPILEPTICS. WE CAN'T HELP YOU.
I CAN'T DEAL WITH THIS.
JO?
ARE YOU AWAKE?

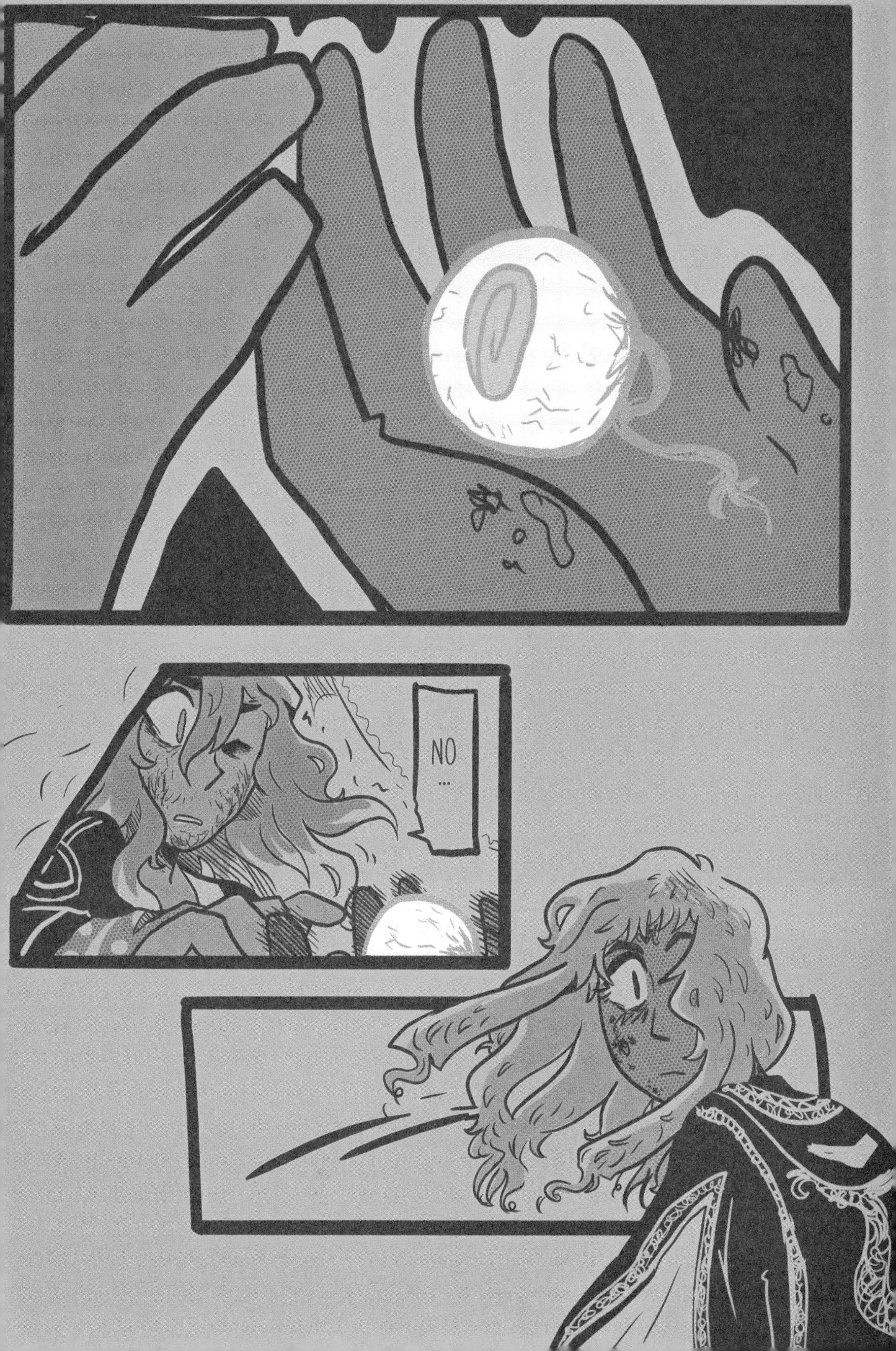
NO
...

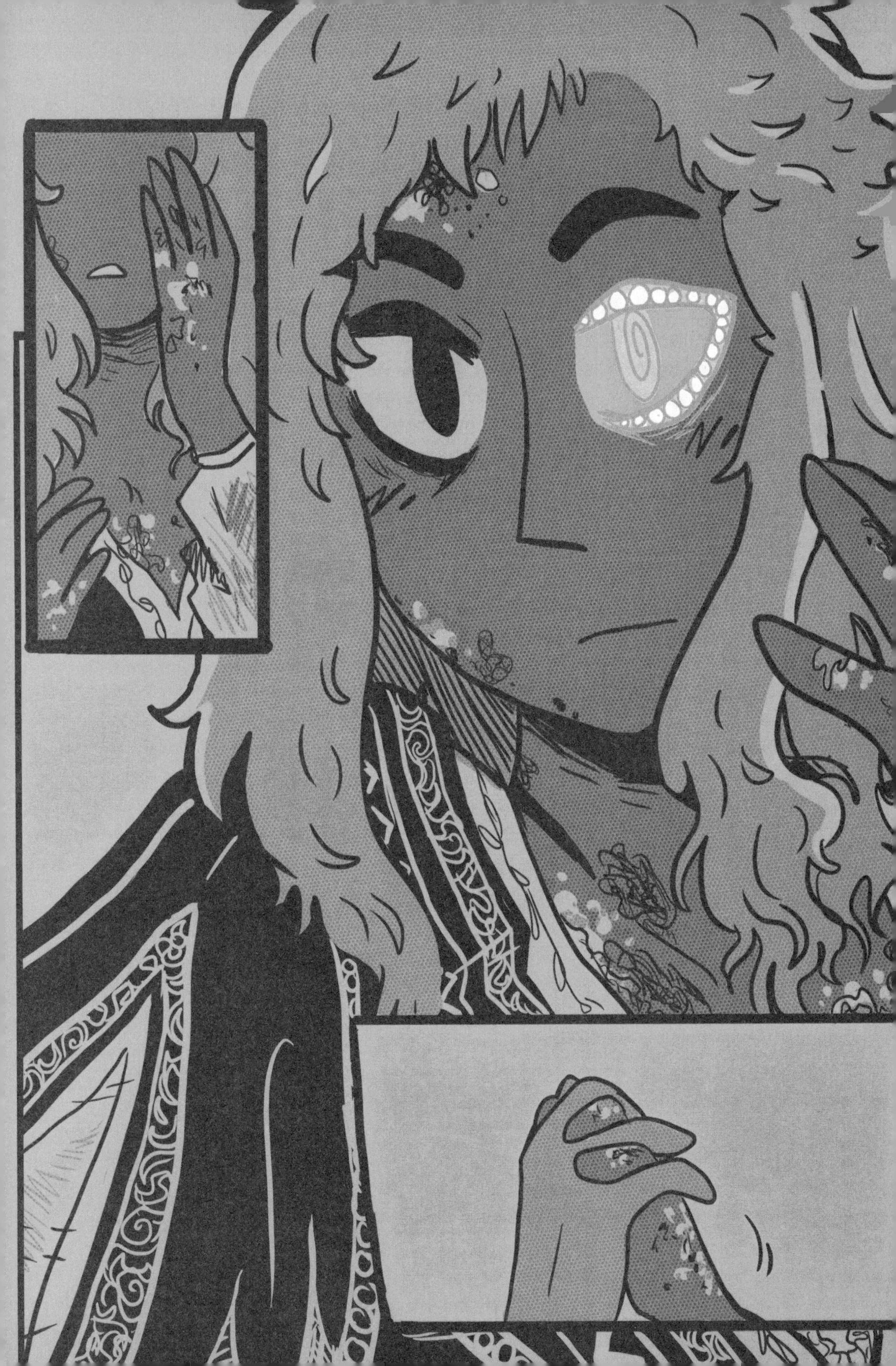

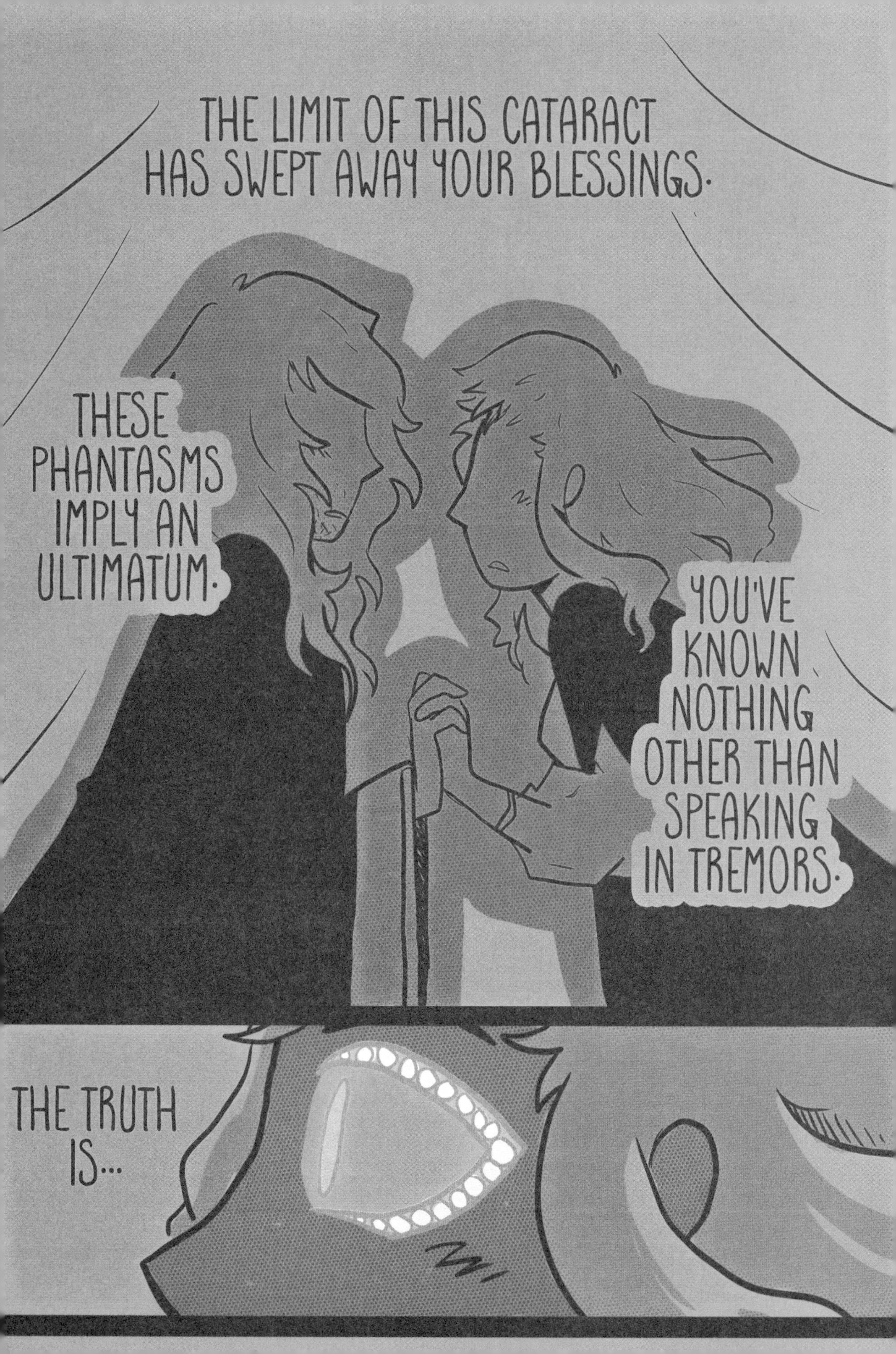
THE LIMIT OF THIS CATARACT HAS SWEPT AWAY YOUR BLESSINGS.
THESE PHANTASMS IMPLY AN ULTIMATUM.
YOU'VE KNOWN NOTHING OTHER THAN SPEAKING IN TREMORS.
THE TRUTH IS...

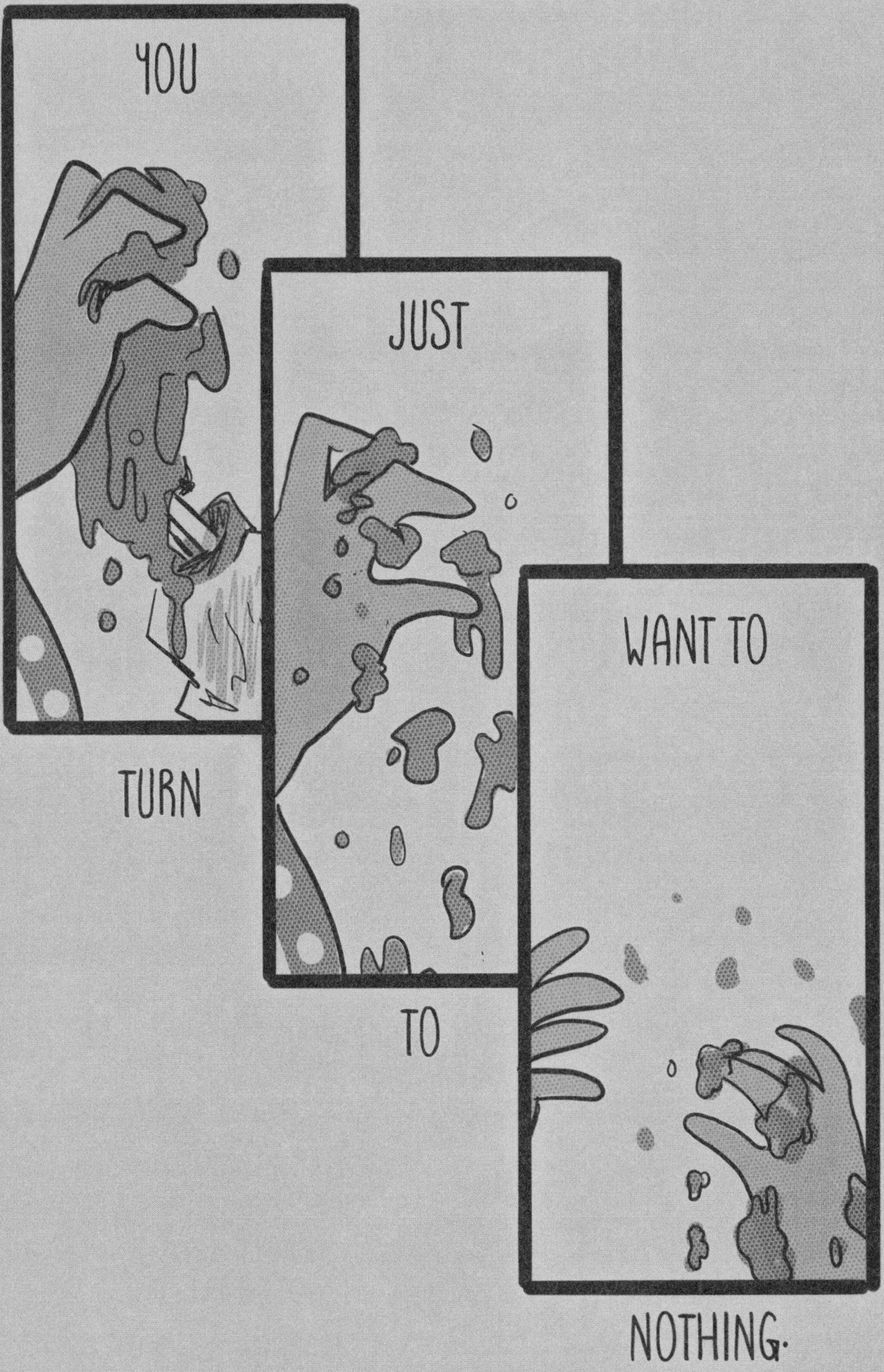
YOU
JUST
WANT TO
TURN
TO
NOTHING.

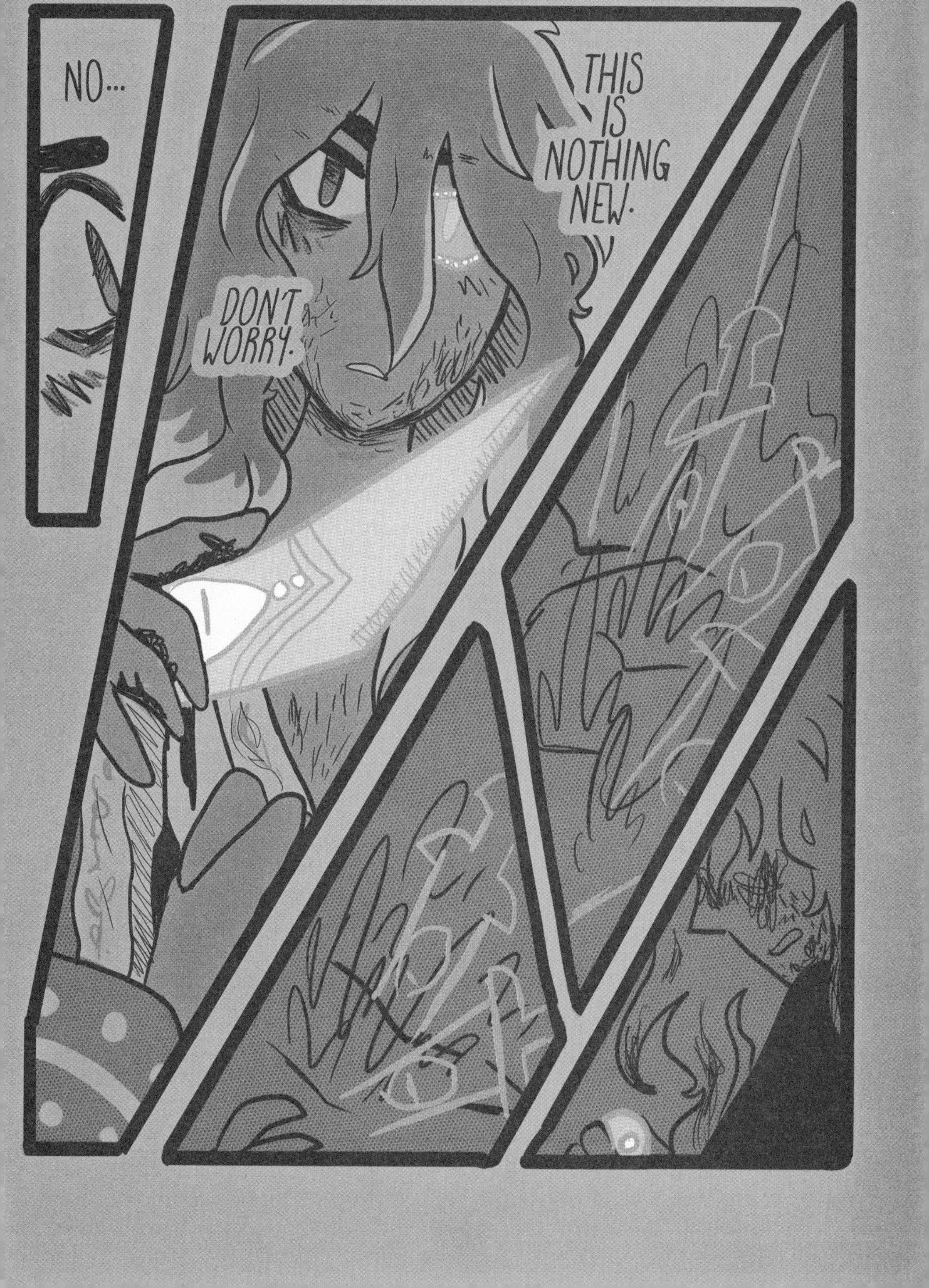
NO...
THIS IS NOTHING NEW.
DON'T WORRY.

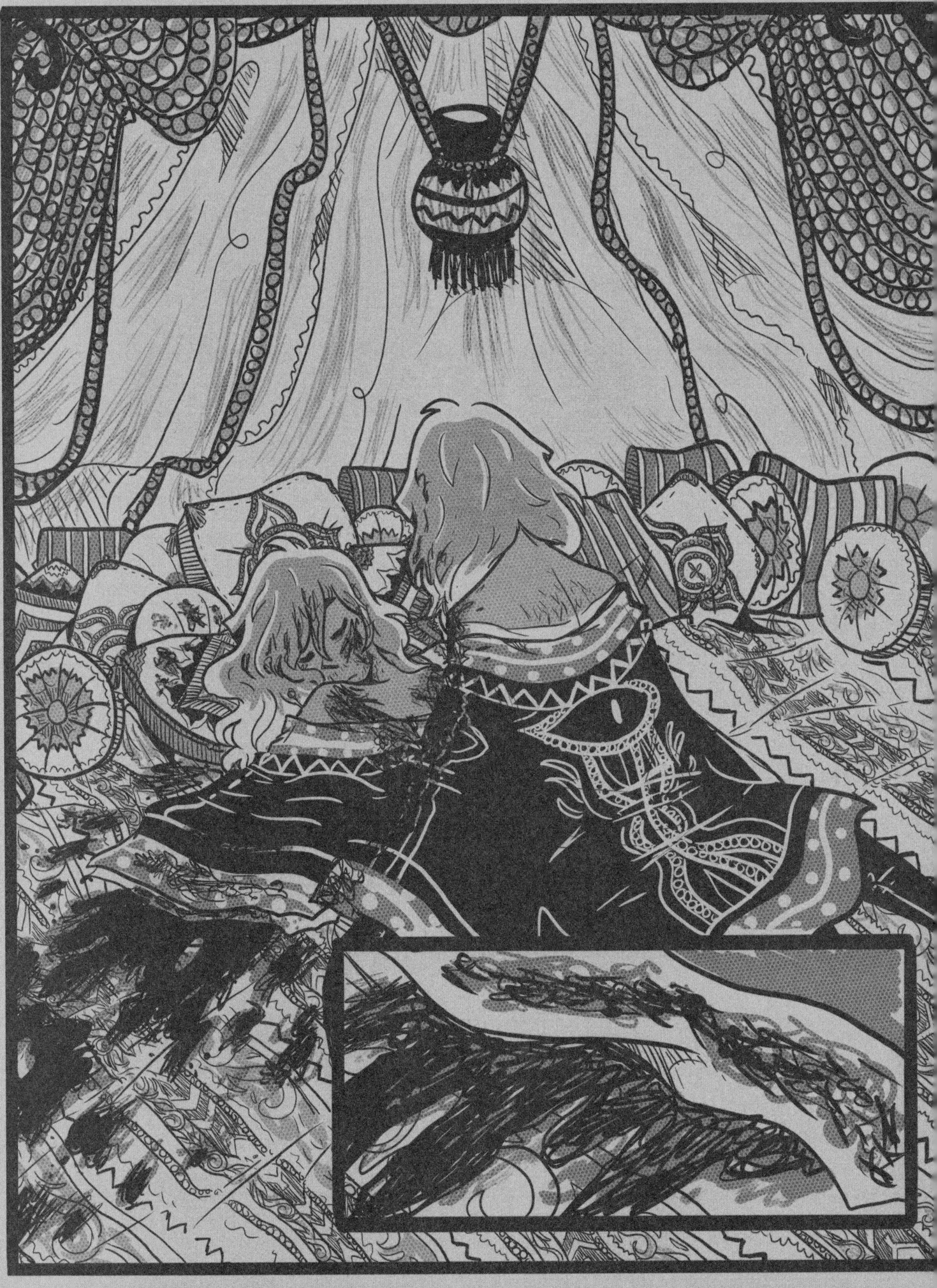

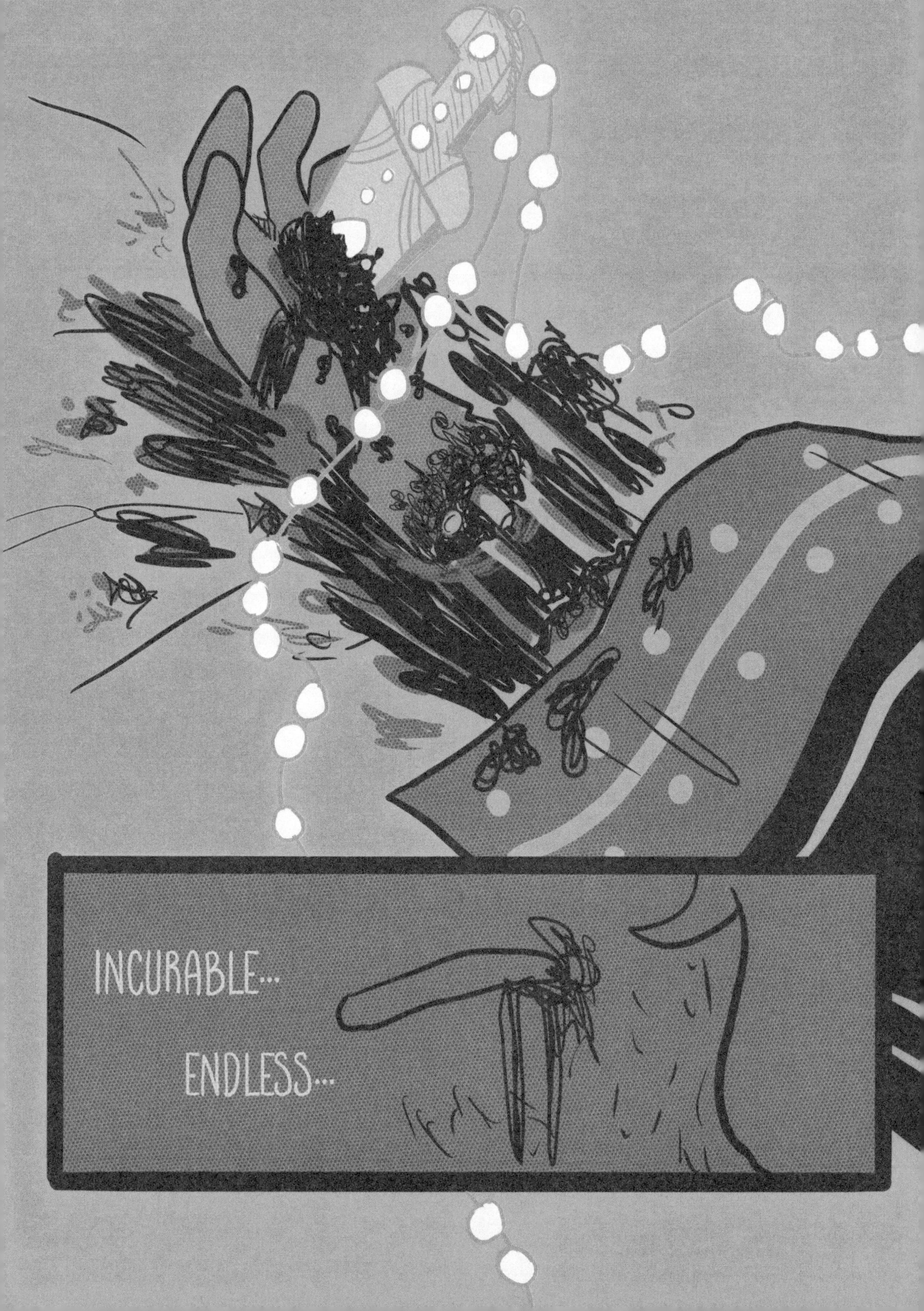
INCURABLE...
ENDLESS...

ALL I
EVER
WANTED

WAS FOR
SOMEONE
TO TELL
ME I WAS
DOING A
GOOD JOB.

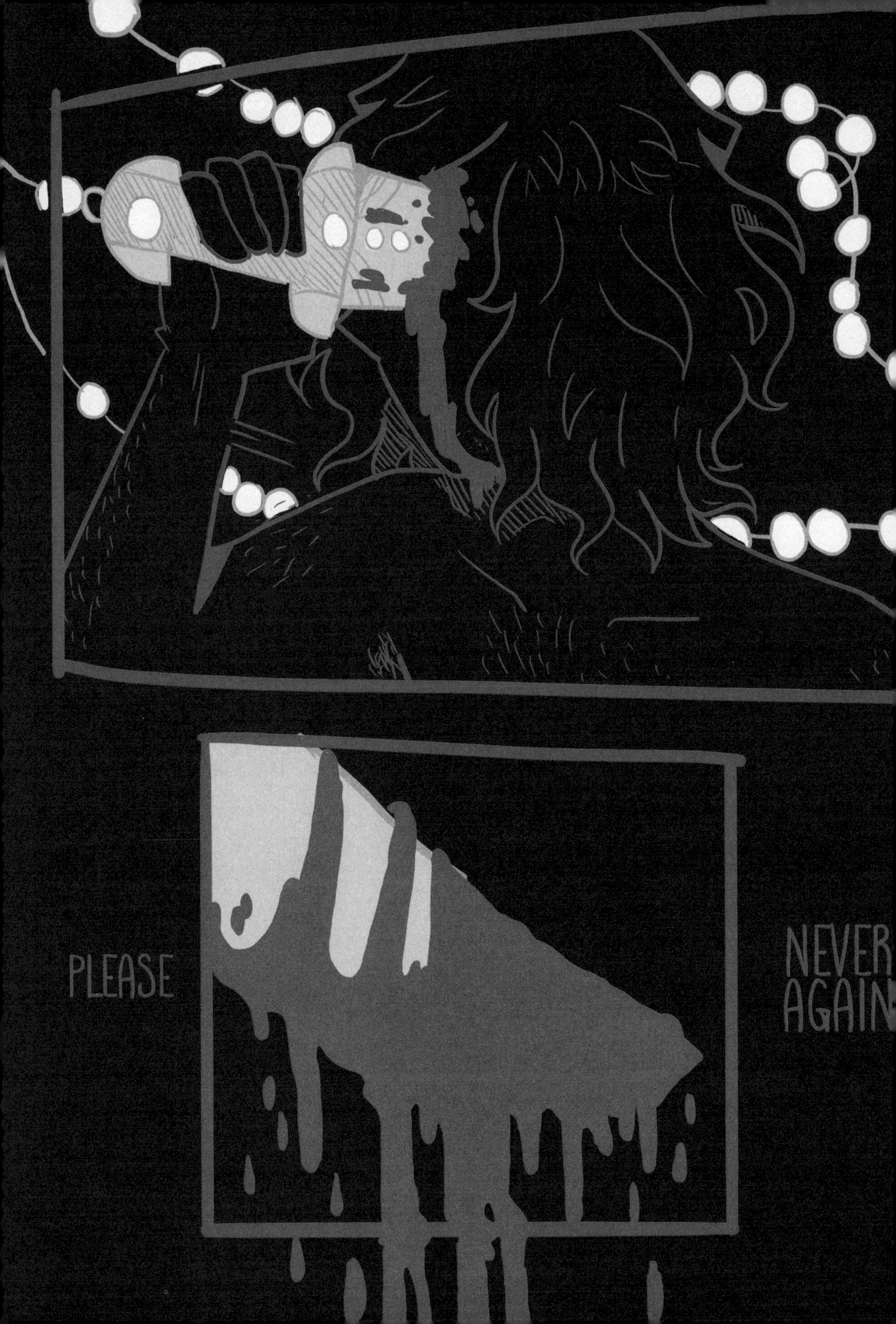
PLEASE
NEVER
AGAIN

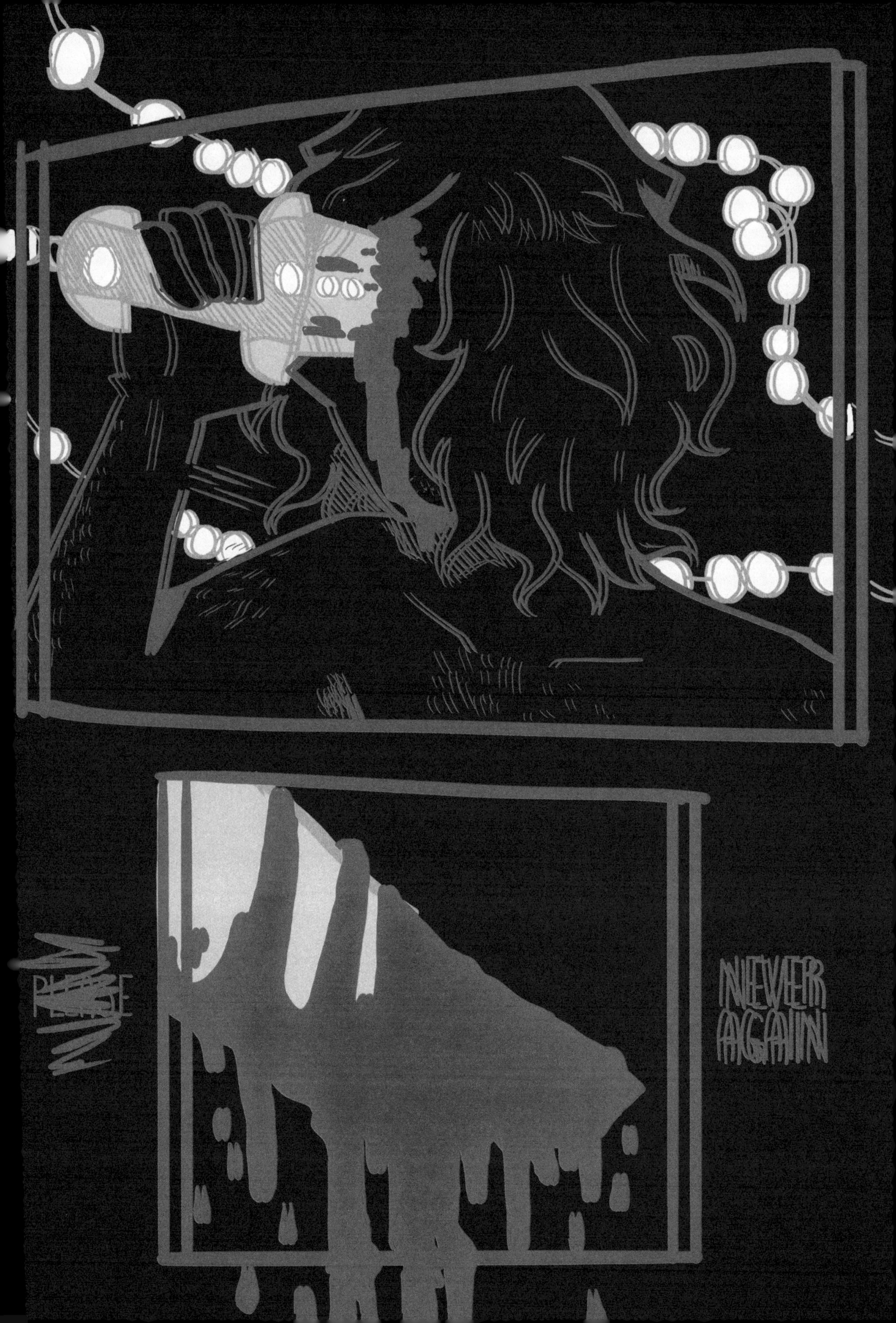
NEVER
AGAIN

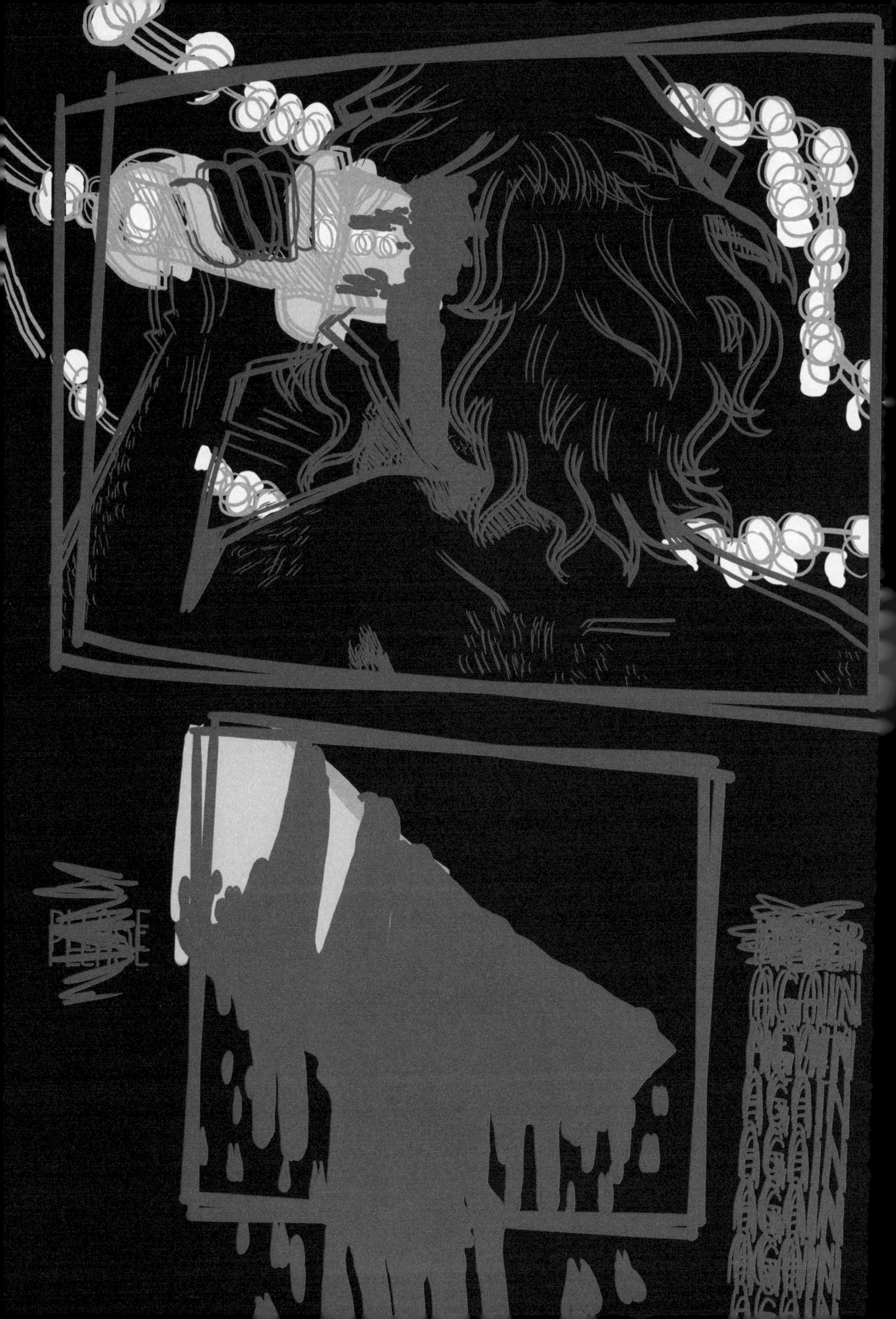
PLEASE
AGAIN
AGAIN
AGAIN
AGAIN
AGAIN
AGAIN

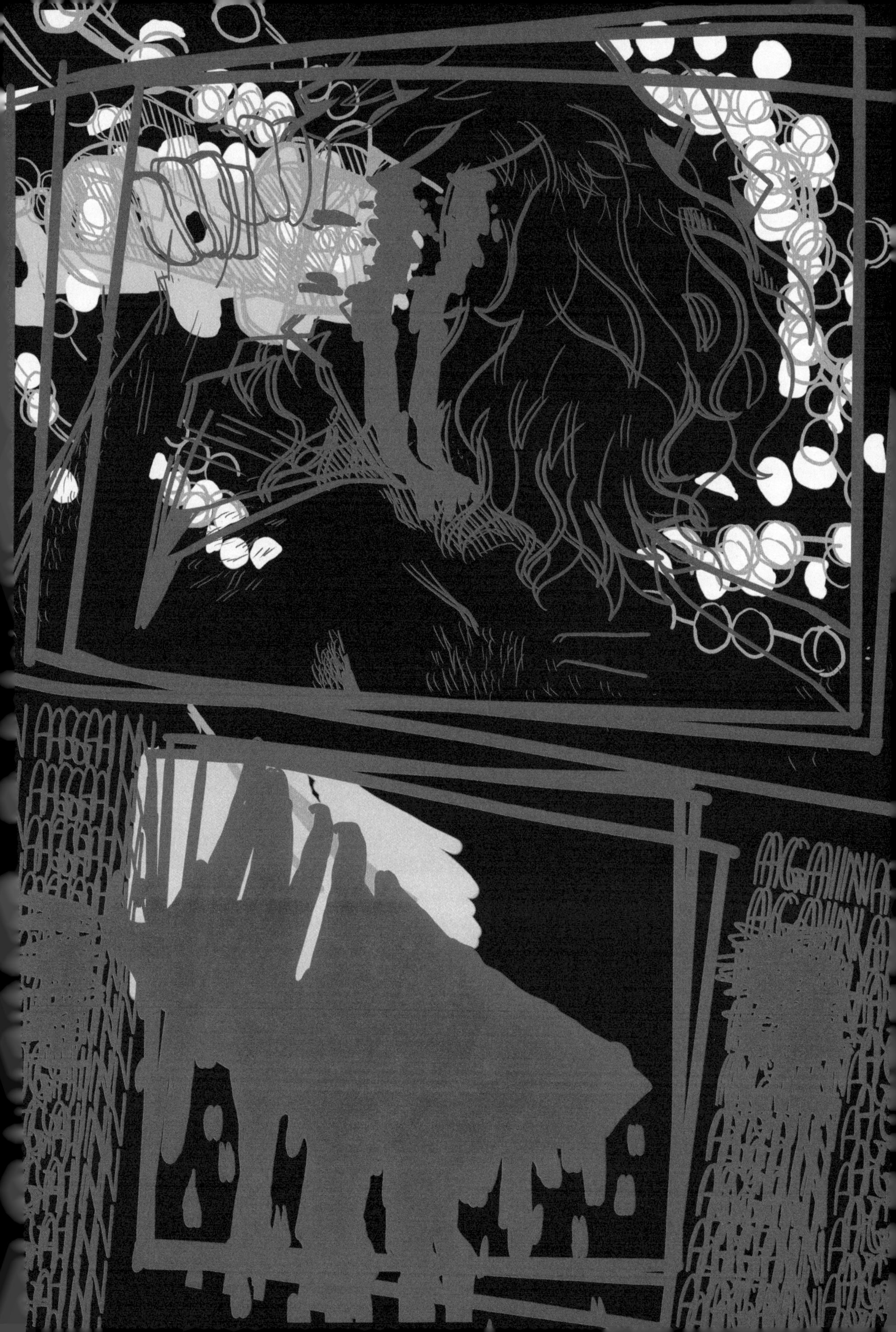

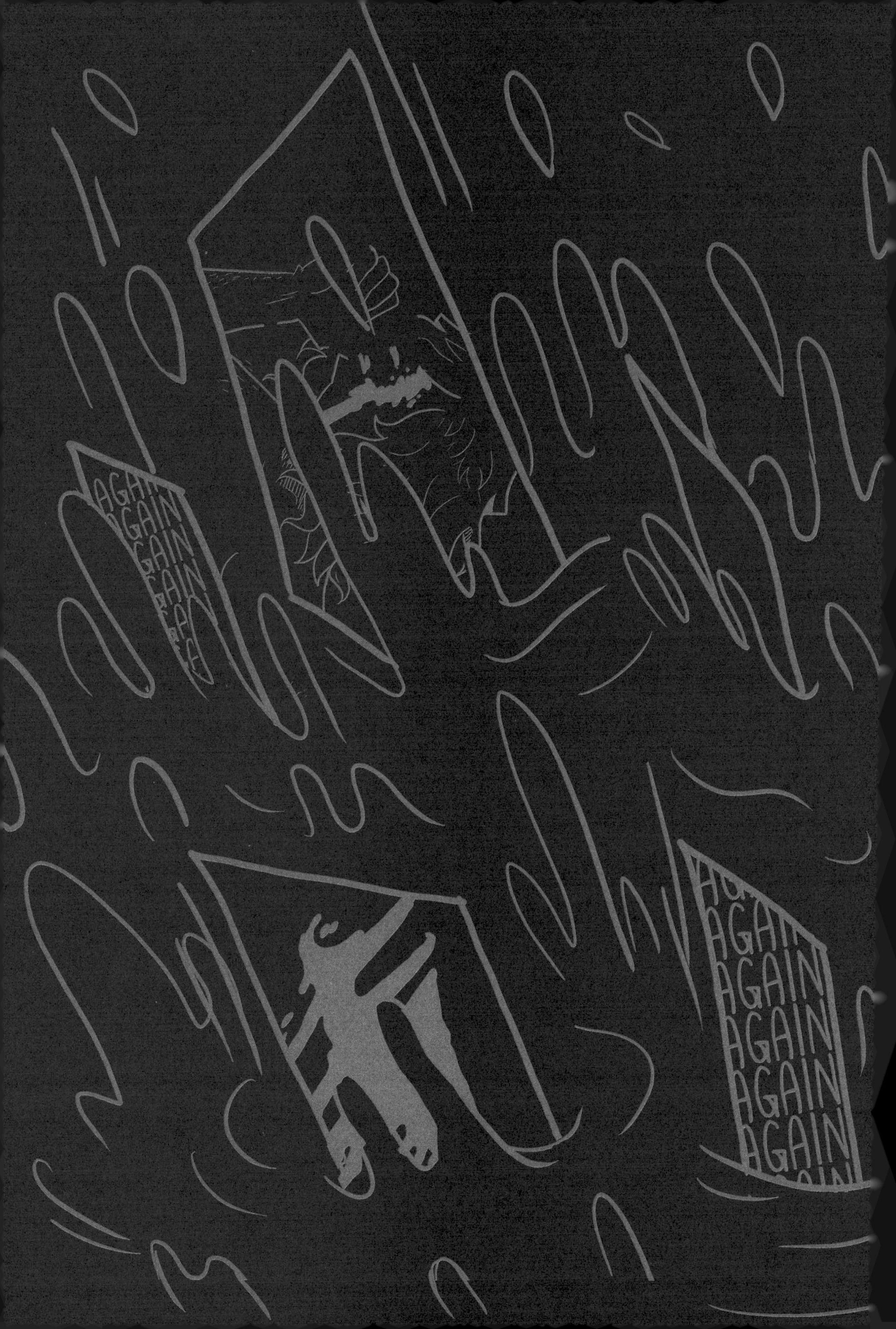
AGAIN
AGAIN
AGAIN
AGAIN
AGAIN
AGAIN
AGAIN
AGAIN
AGAIN

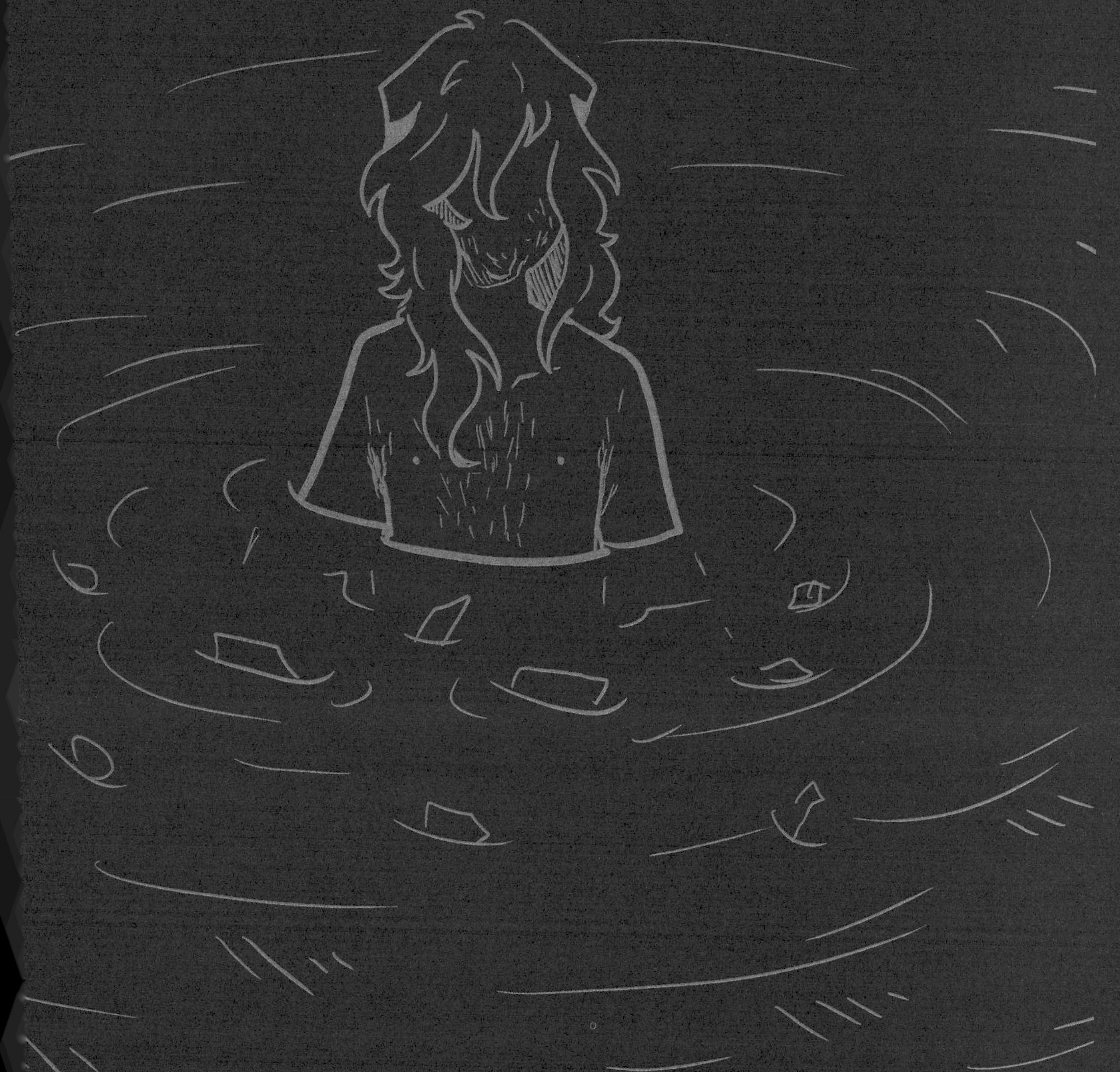

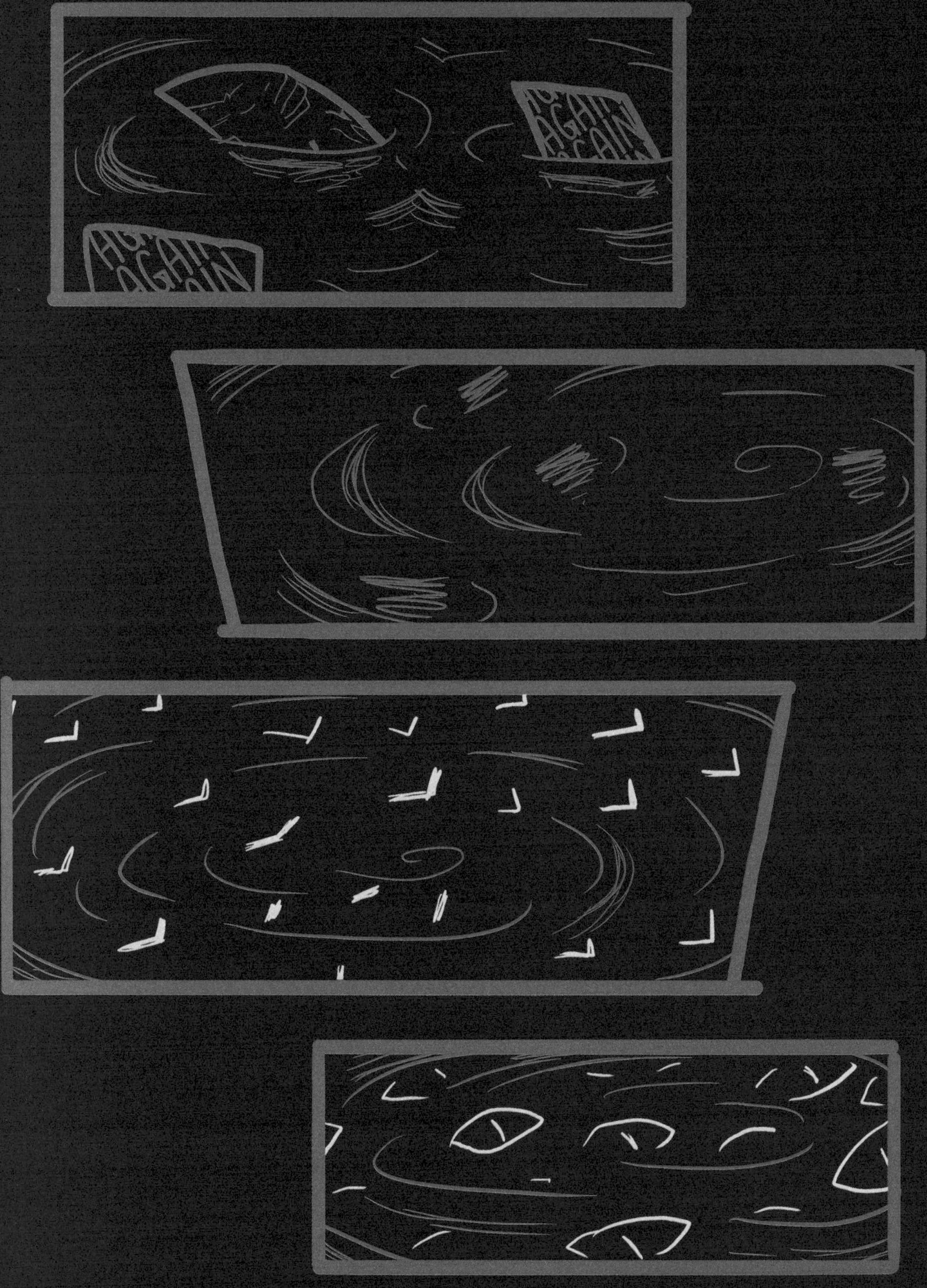
AGAIN
AGAIN

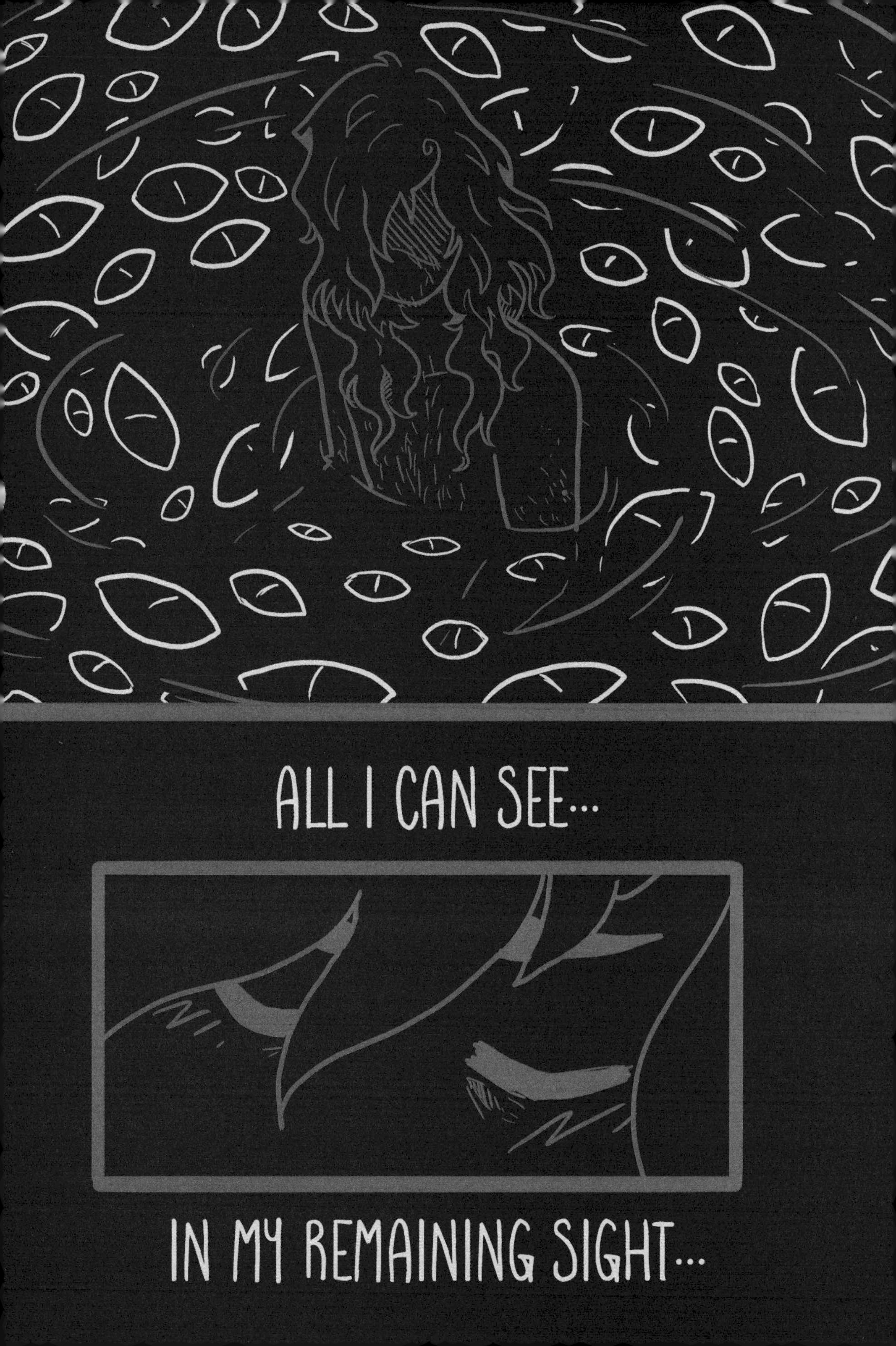
ALL I CAN SEE...
IN MY REMAINING SIGHT...

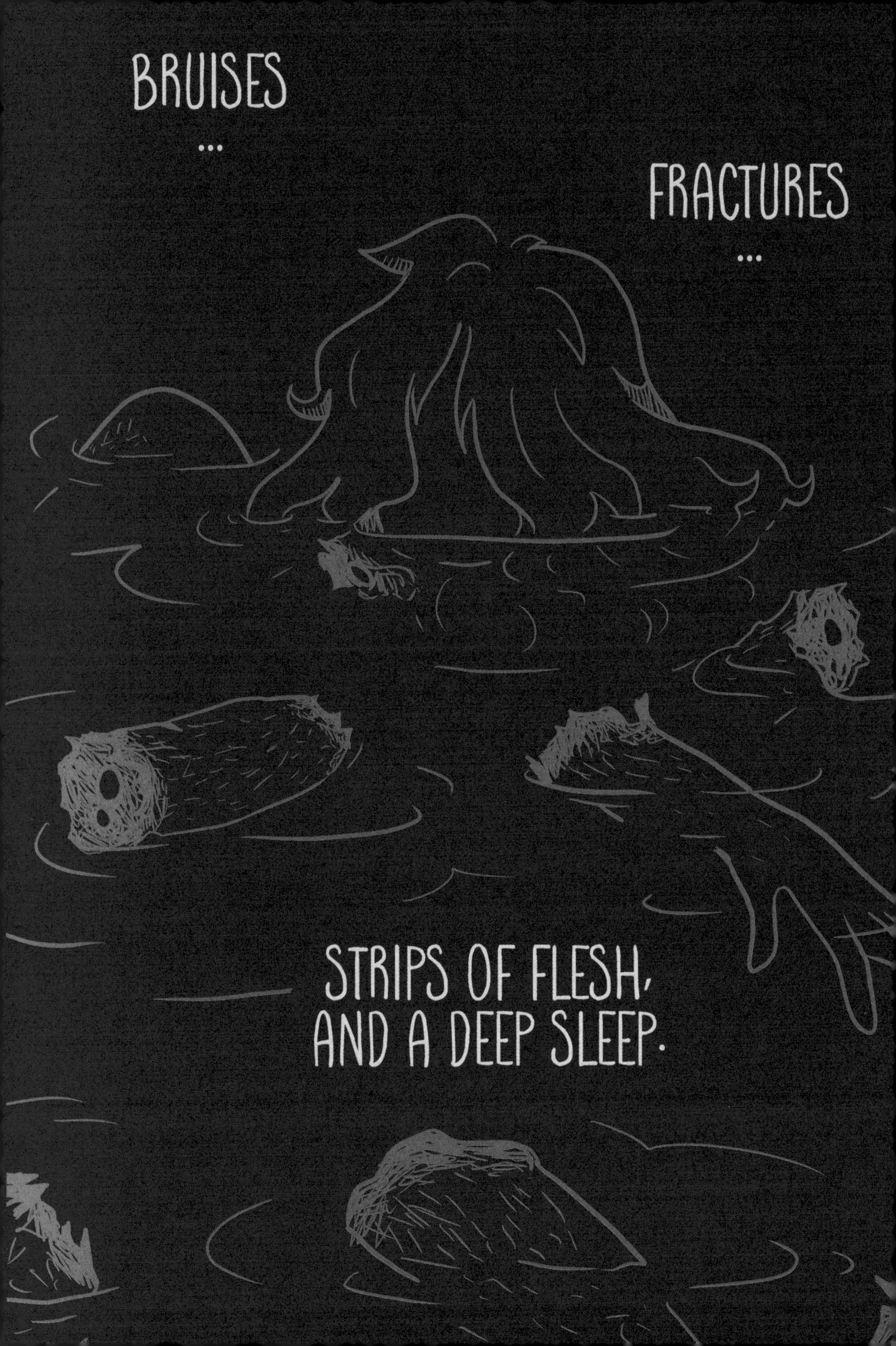
BRUISES
...
FRACTURES
...
STRIPS OF FLESH,
AND A DEEP SLEEP.

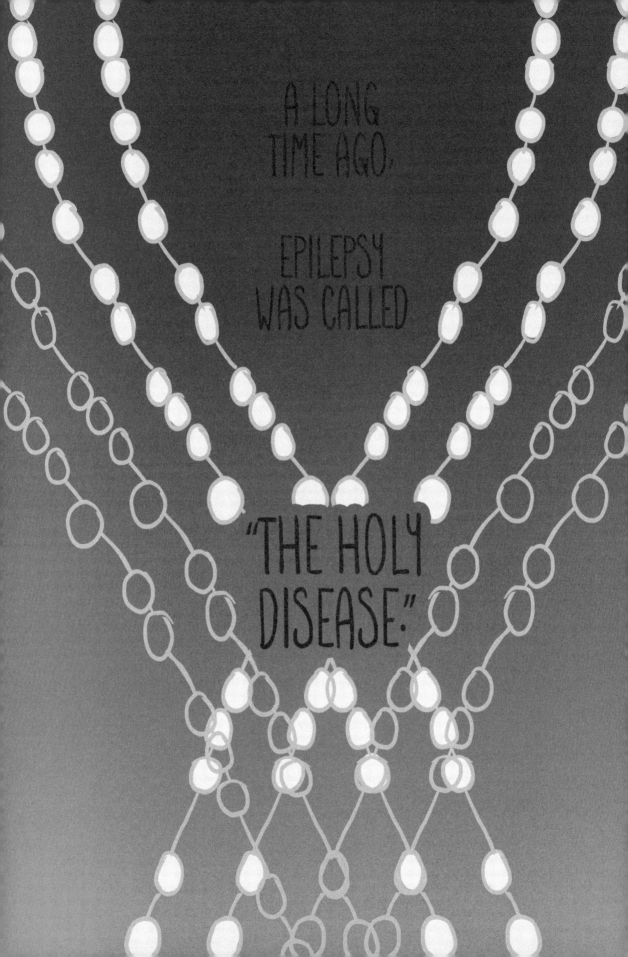

A LONG
TIME AGO,

EPILEPSY
WAS CALLED

"THE HOLY
DISEASE."

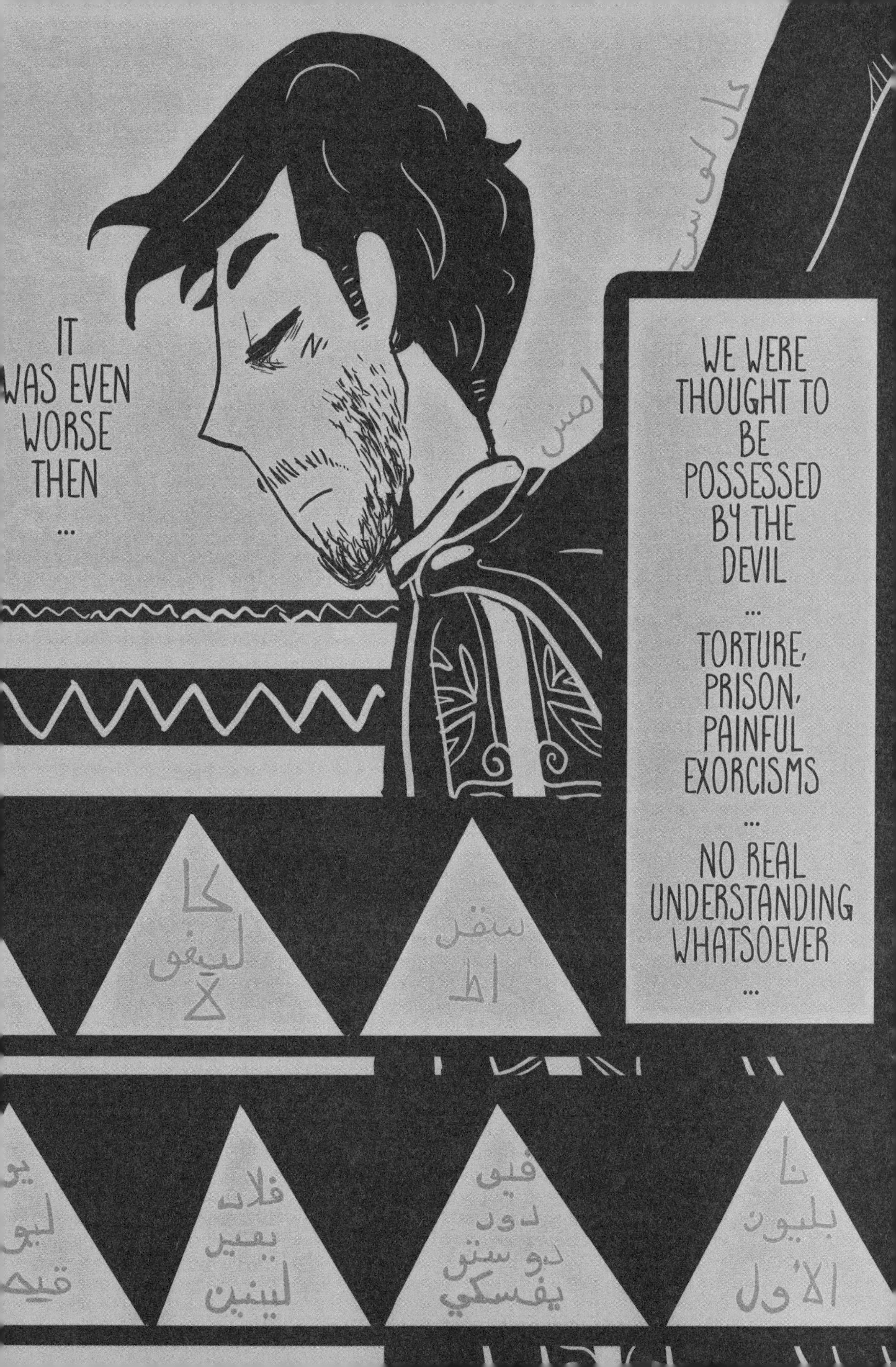
IT WAS EVEN WORSE THEN ...
WE WERE THOUGHT TO BE POSSESSED BY THE DEVIL ... TORTURE, PRISON, PAINFUL EXORCISMS ... NO REAL UNDERSTANDING WHATSOEVER ...

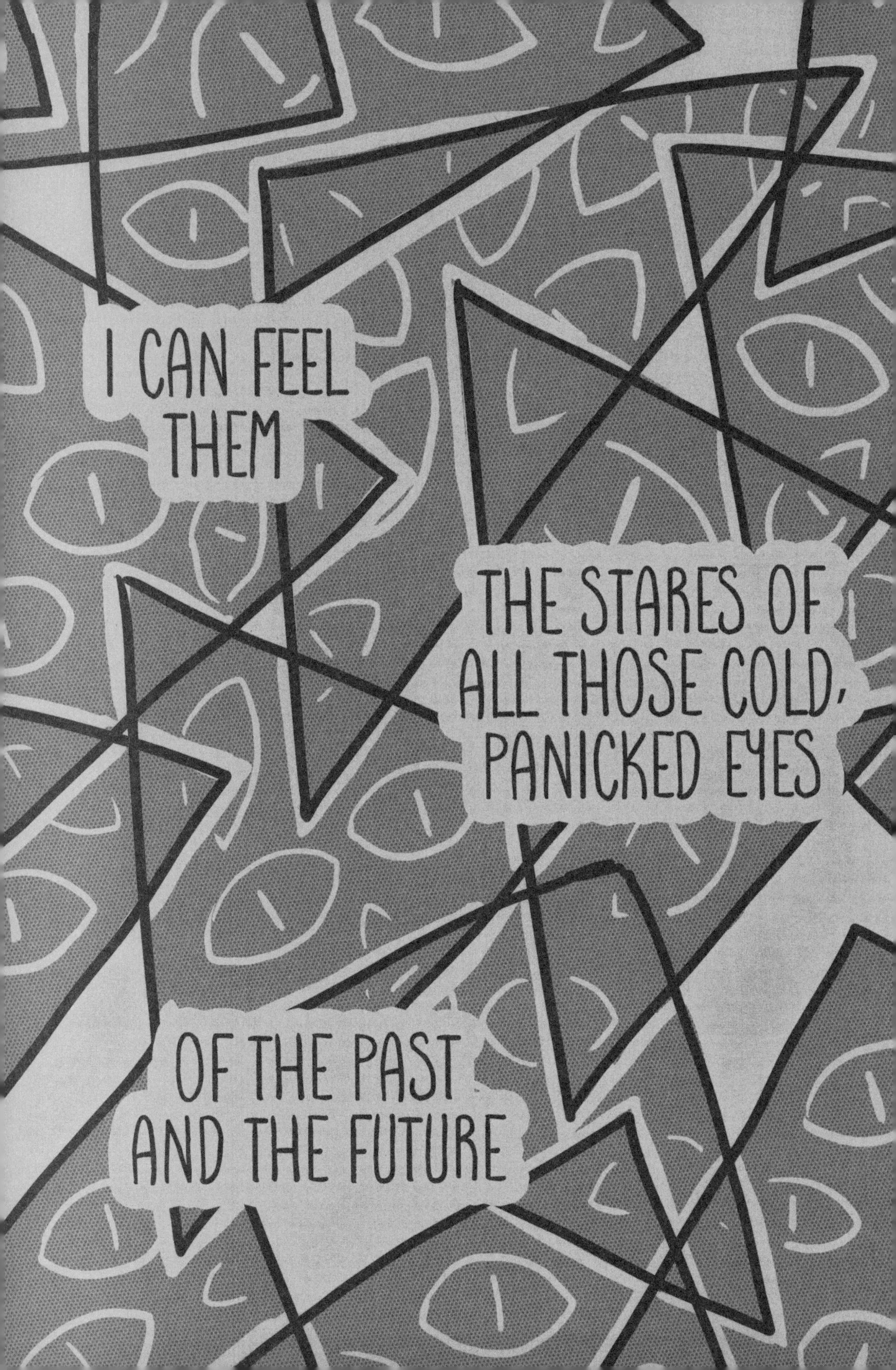
I CAN FEEL THEM
THE STARES OF ALL THOSE COLD, PANICKED EYES
OF THE PAST AND THE FUTURE

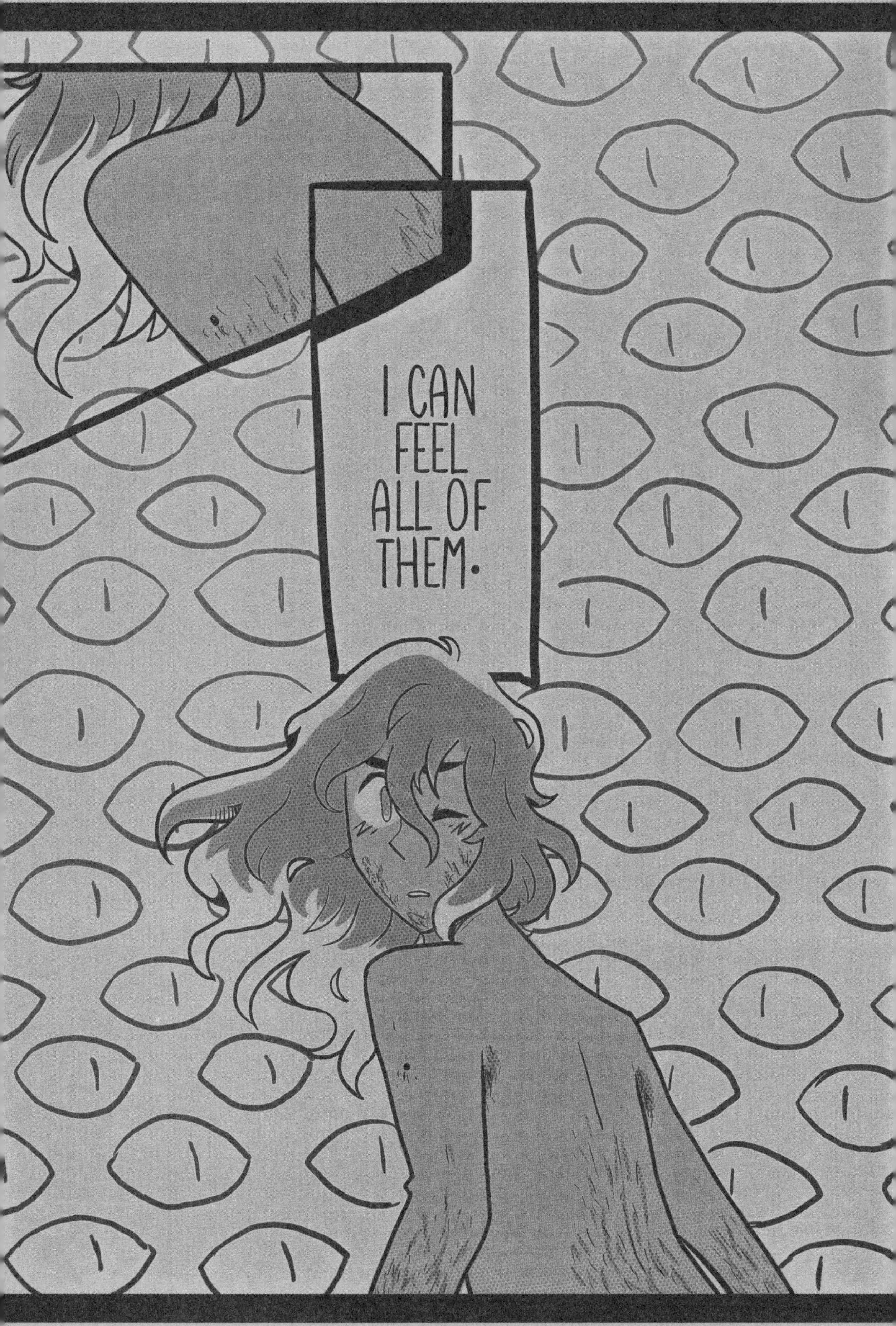
I CAN FEEL ALL OF THEM.

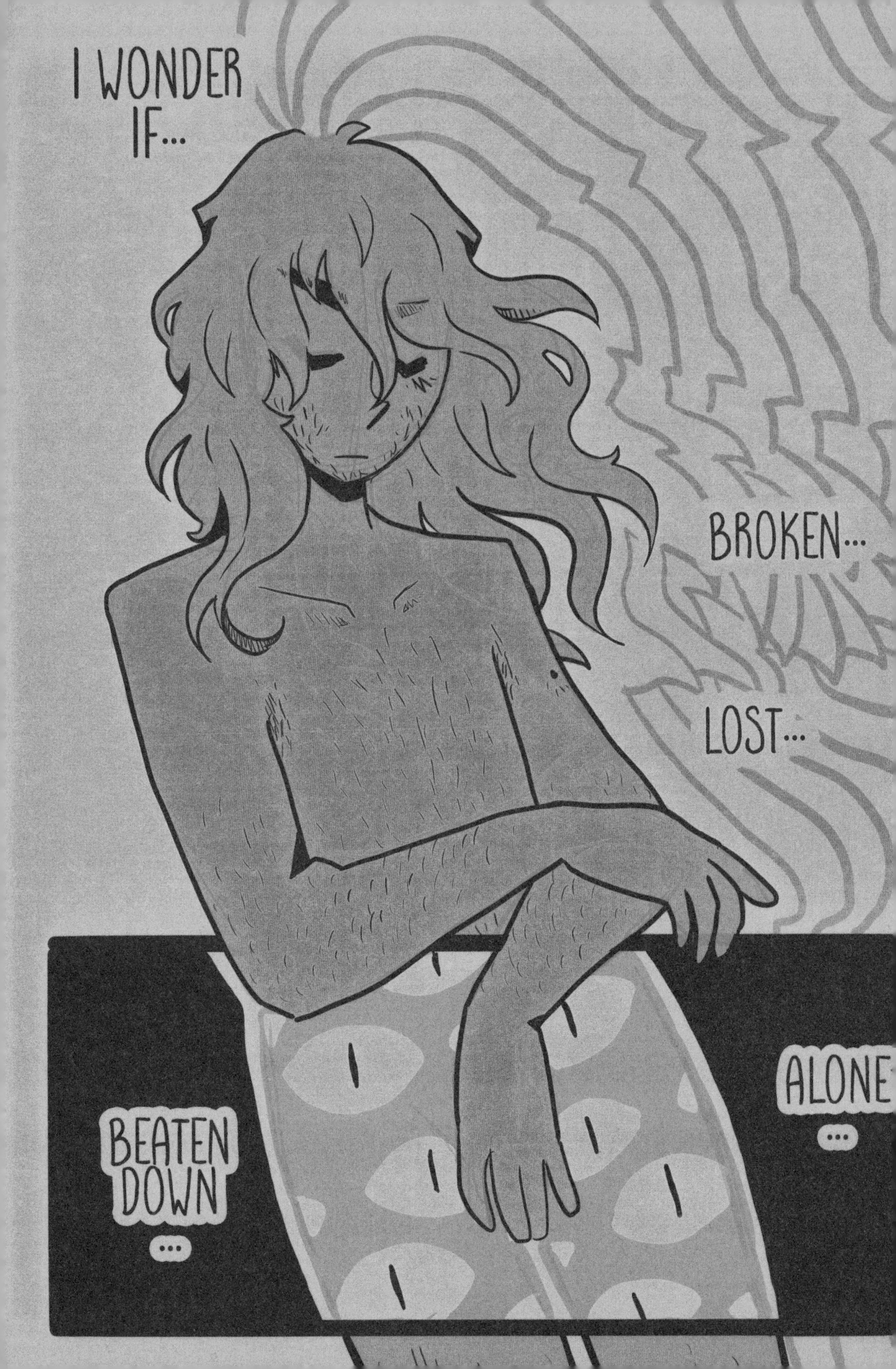
I WONDER IF...
BROKEN...
LOST...
BEATEN DOWN
...
ALONE
...

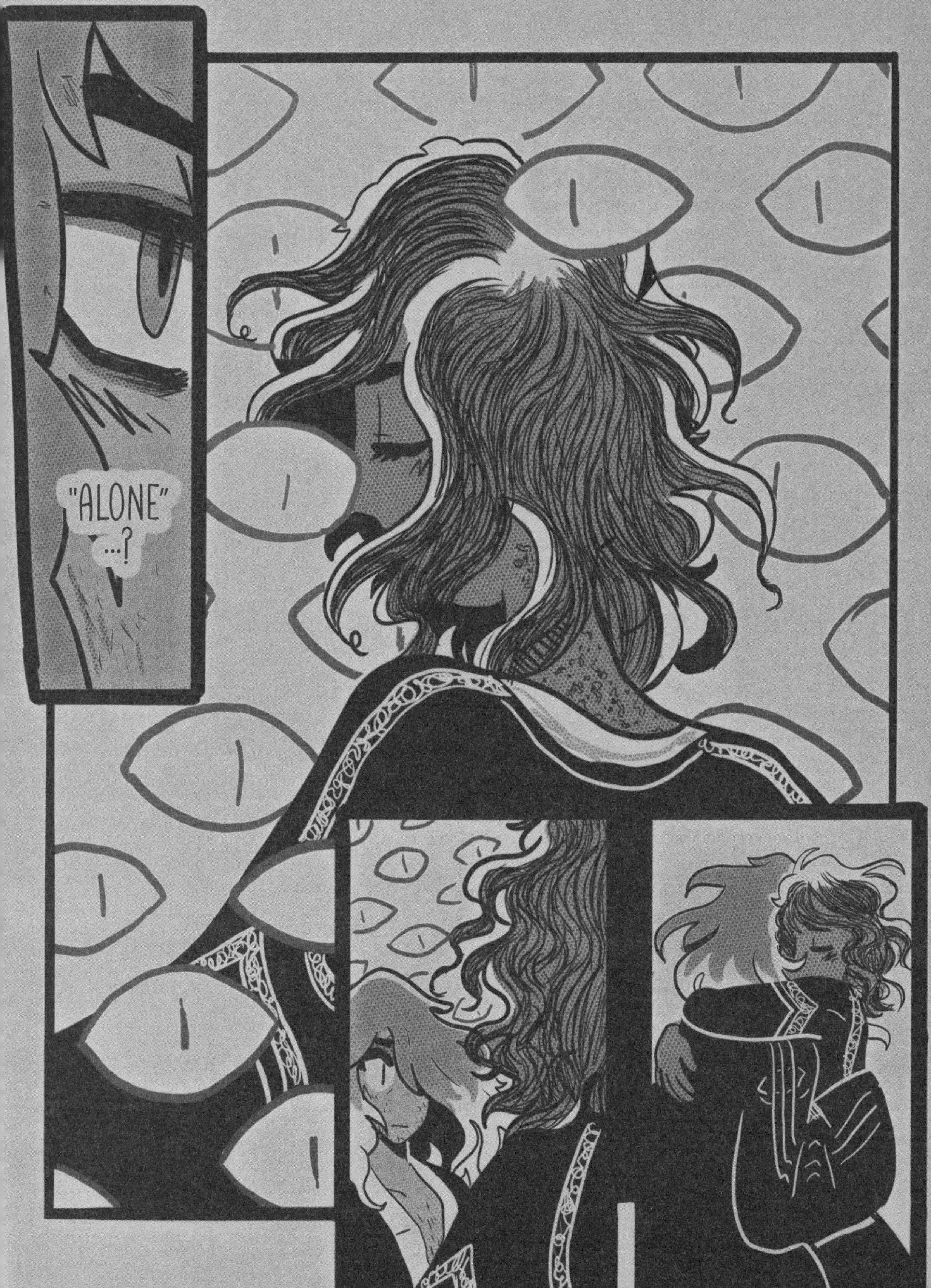
"ALONE"
...?

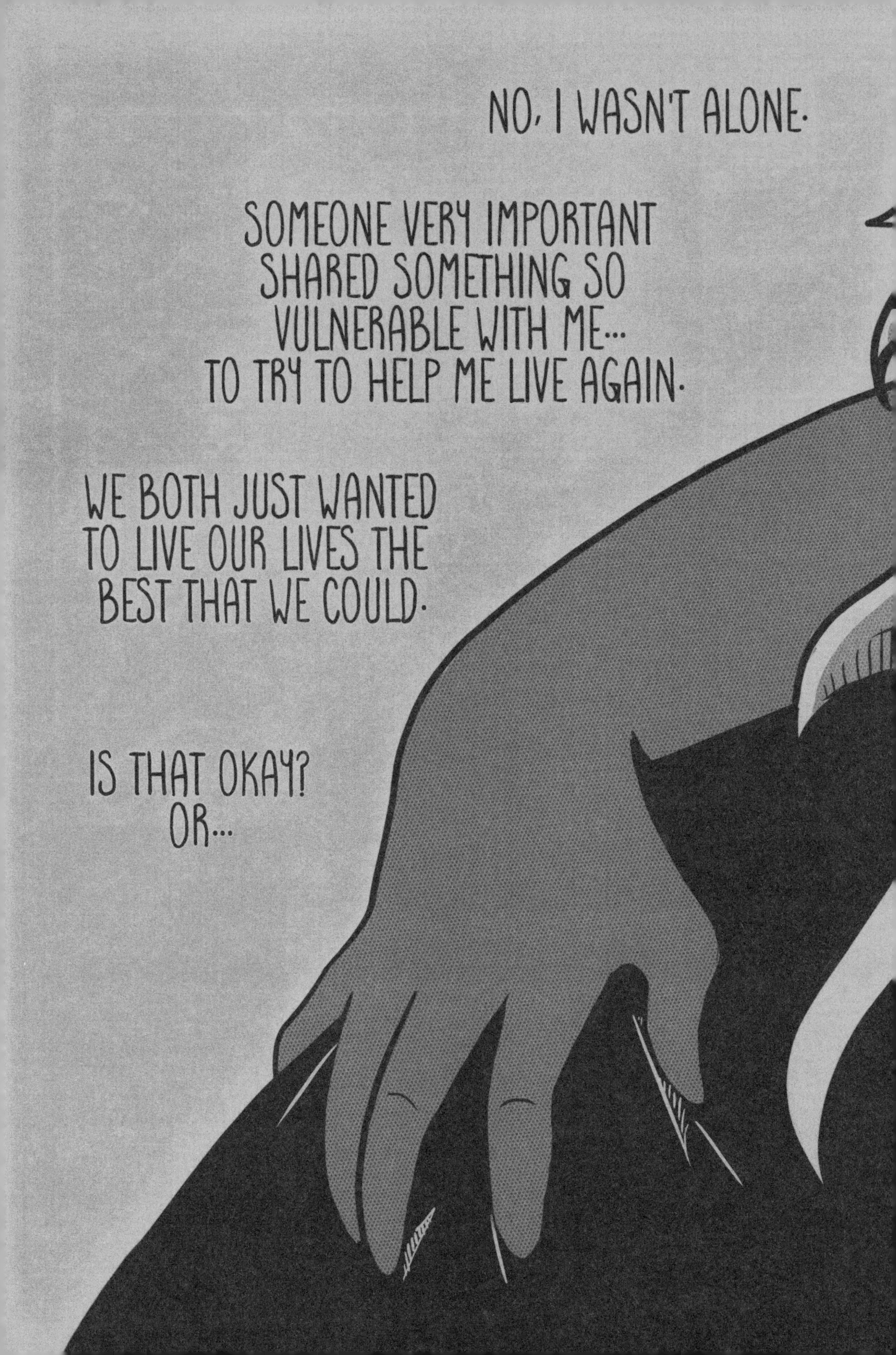
NO, I WASN'T ALONE.
SOMEONE VERY IMPORTANT SHARED SOMETHING SO VULNERABLE WITH ME... TO TRY TO HELP ME LIVE AGAIN.
WE BOTH JUST WANTED TO LIVE OUR LIVES THE BEST THAT WE COULD.
IS THAT OKAY? OR...

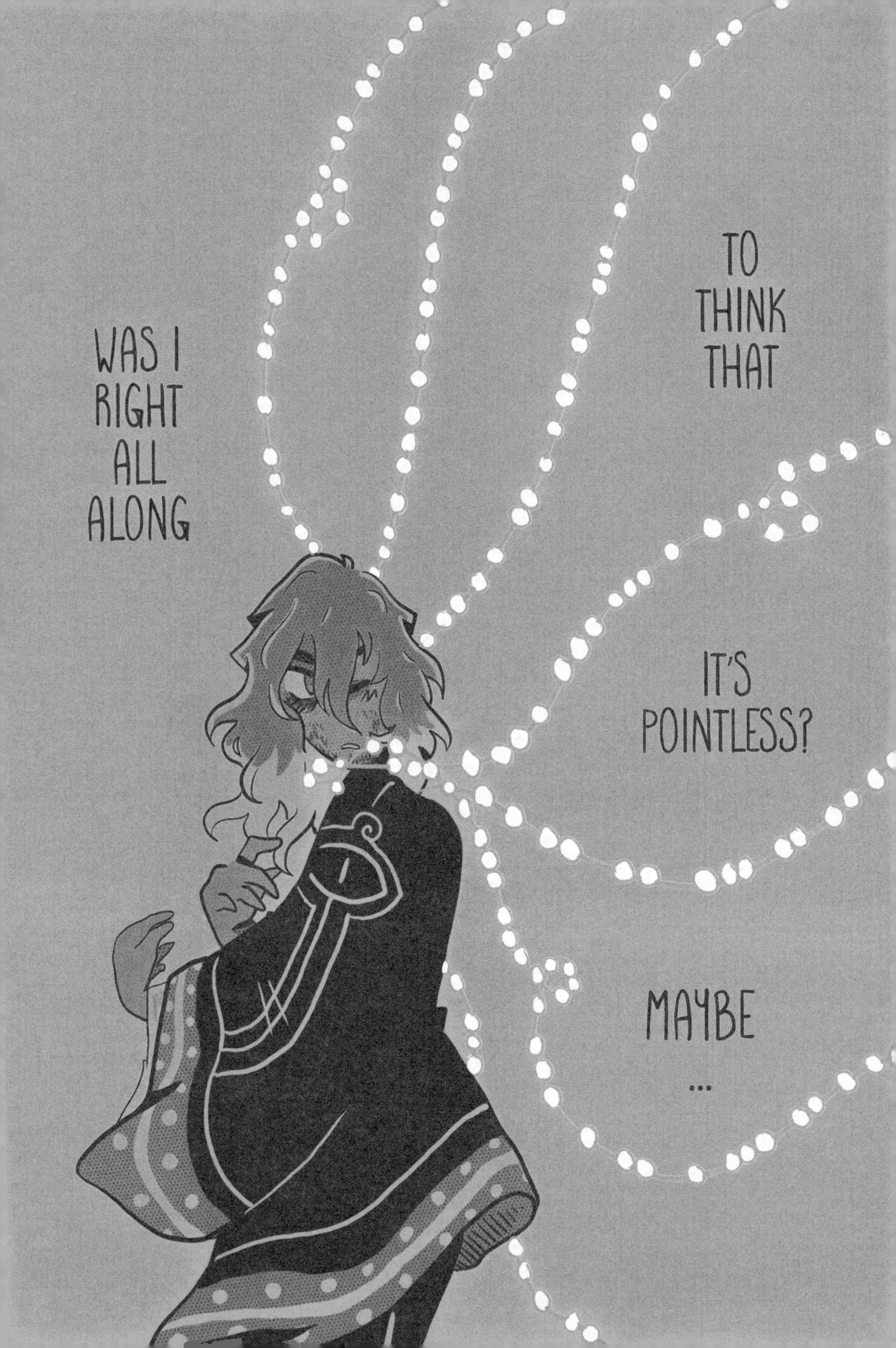
WAS I RIGHT ALL ALONG
TO THINK THAT
IT'S POINTLESS?
MAYBE
...

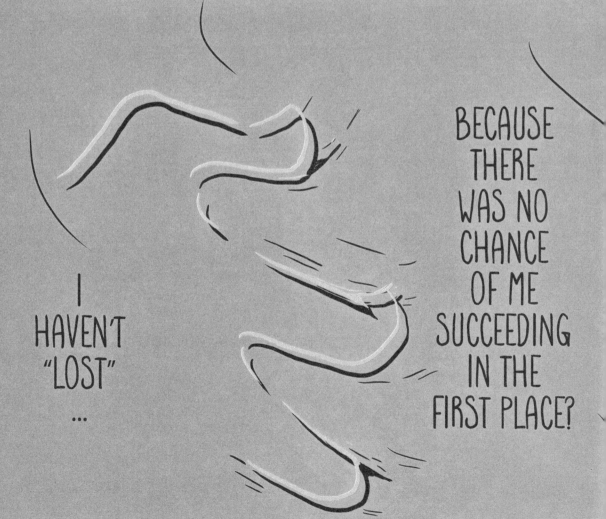

I HAVEN'T "LOST" ...

BECAUSE THERE WAS NO CHANCE OF ME SUCCEEDING IN THE FIRST PLACE?

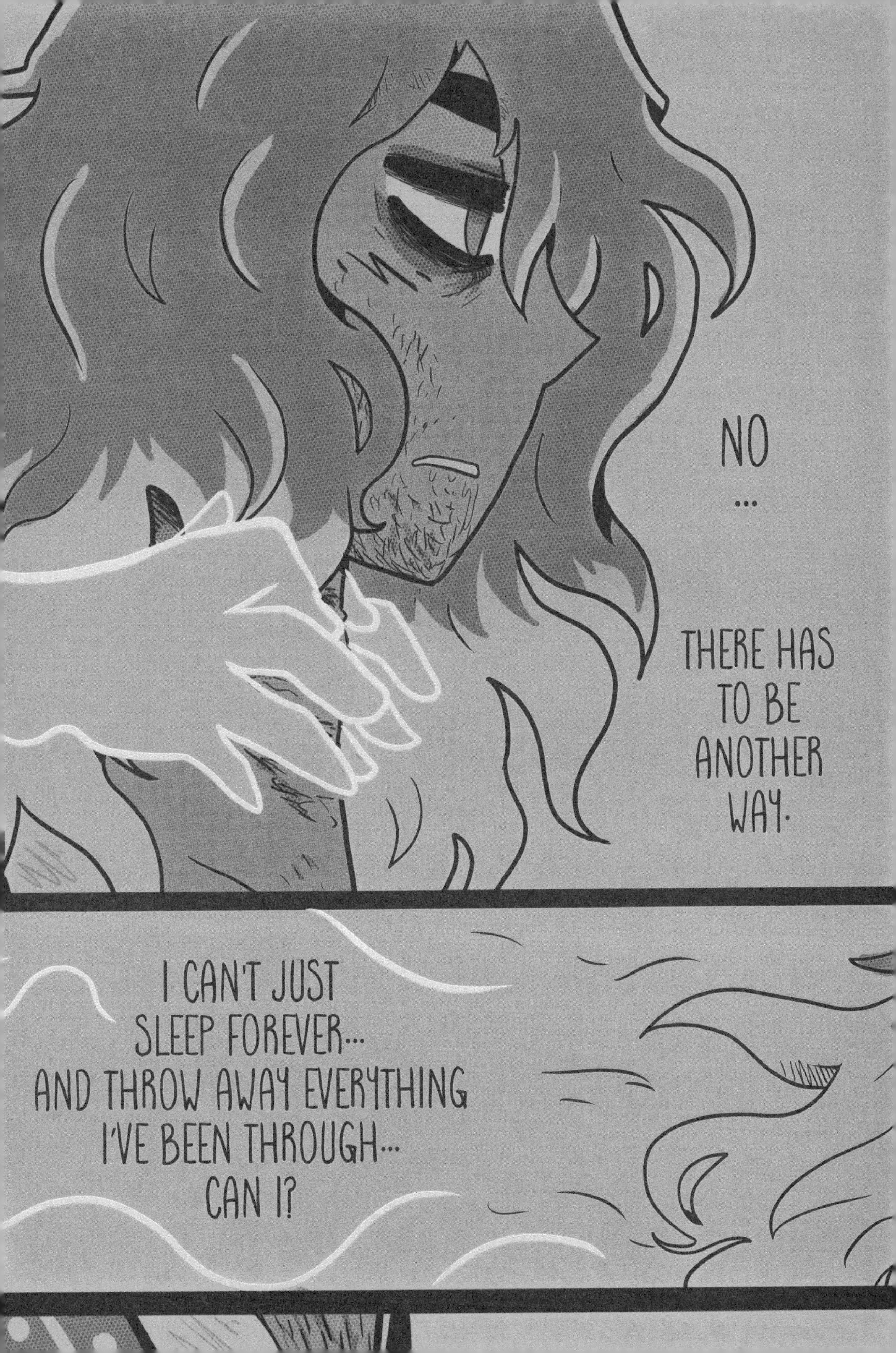
NO
...
THERE HAS TO BE ANOTHER WAY.
I CAN'T JUST SLEEP FOREVER...
AND THROW AWAY EVERYTHING I'VE BEEN THROUGH...
CAN I?

I DON'T WANT
TO JUST DRAG
MYSELF AROUND
ANYMORE...

I WANT
TO DO...
SOMETHING...

I WANT
...

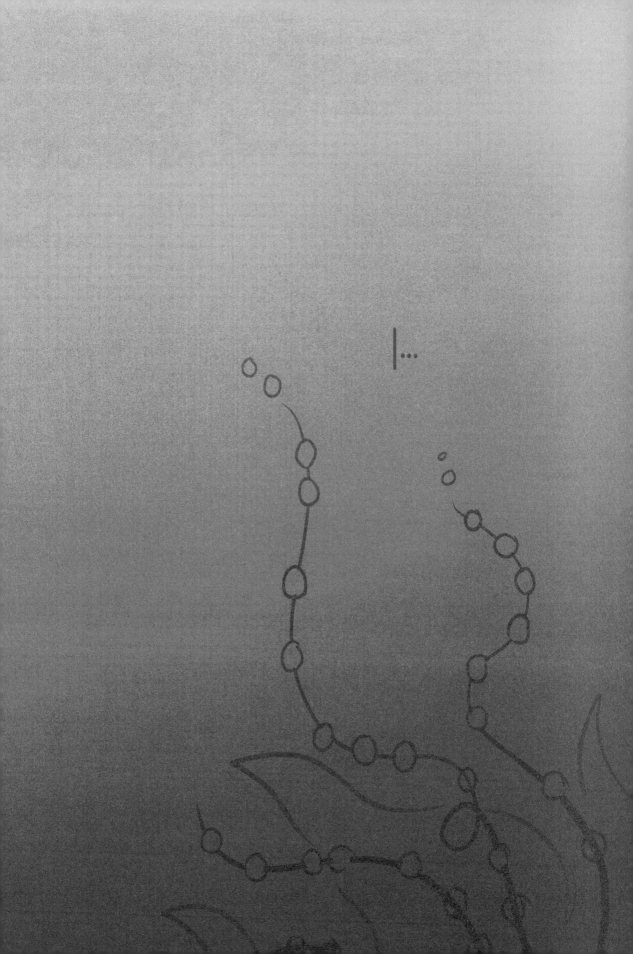

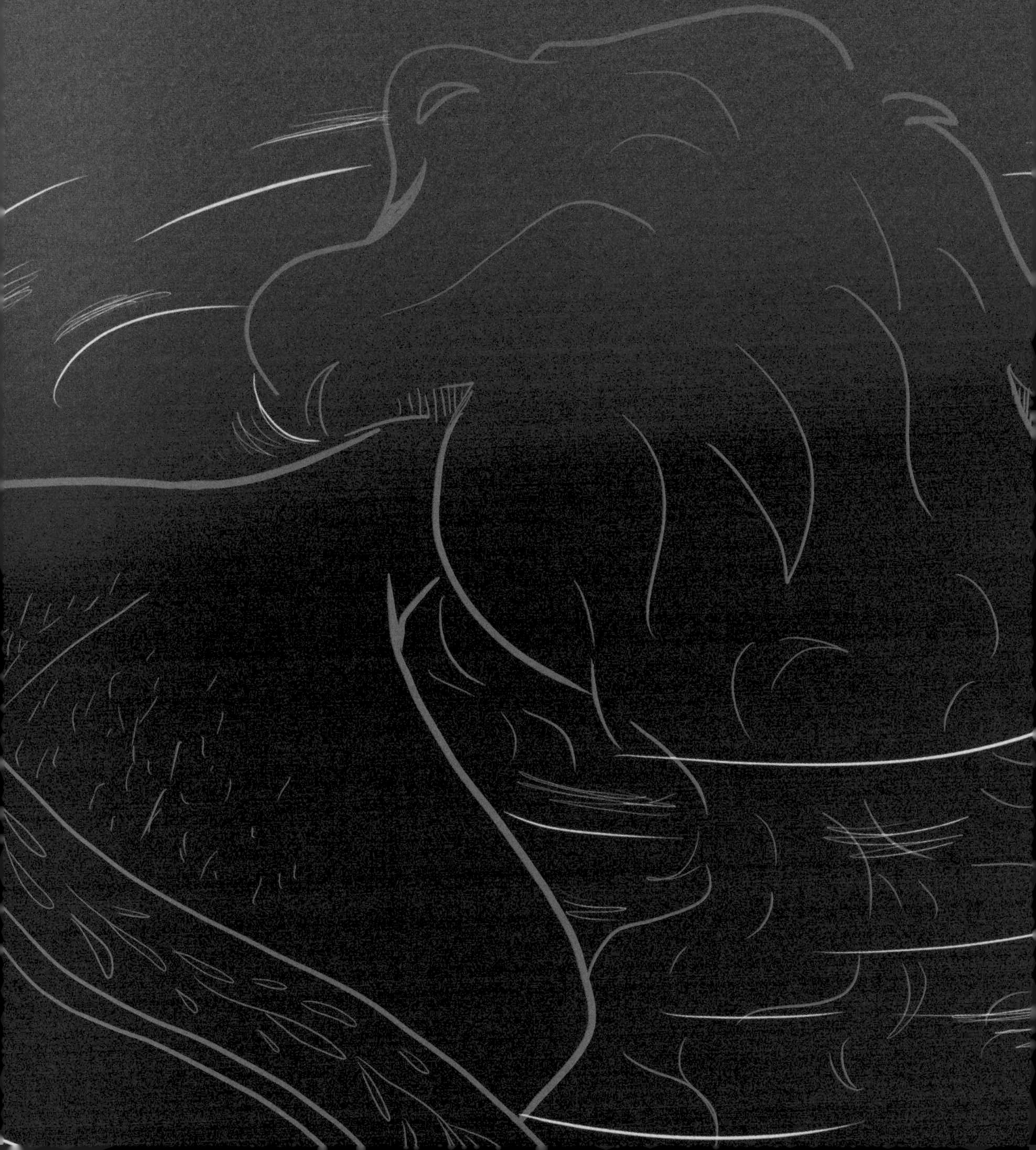

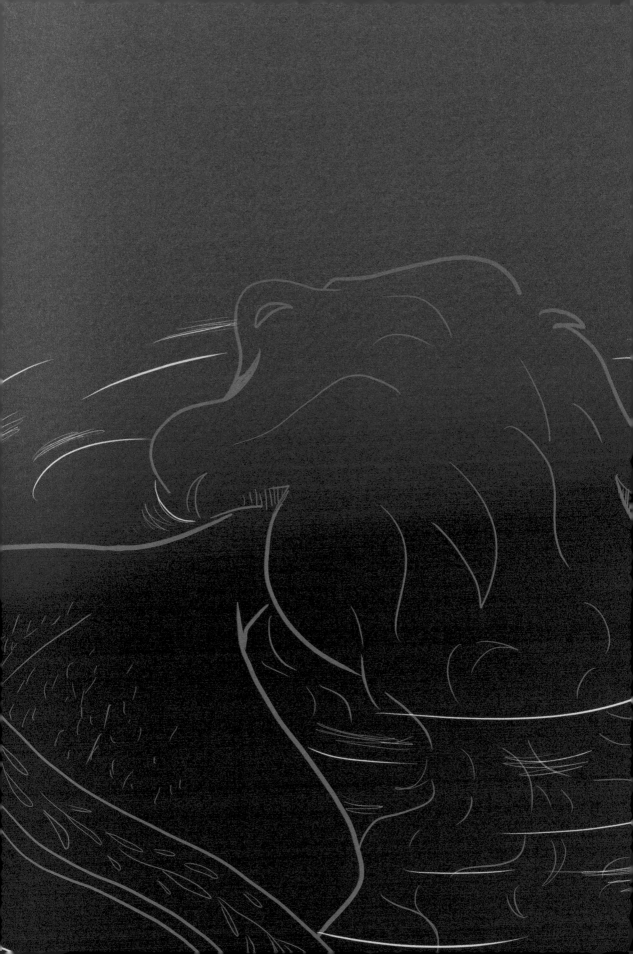

MAYBE I DON'T KNOW EXACTLY
WHAT I WANT YET
ugh

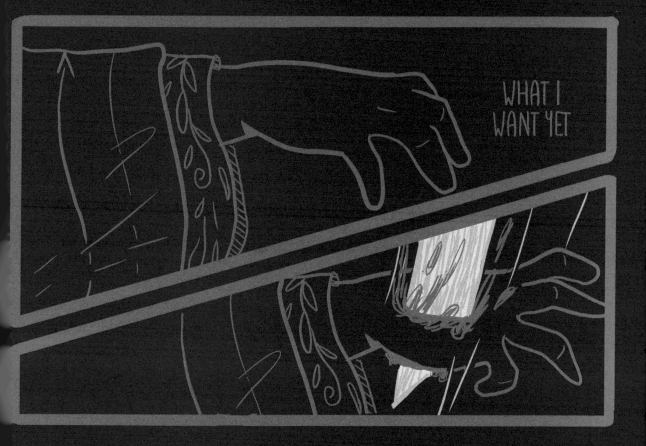

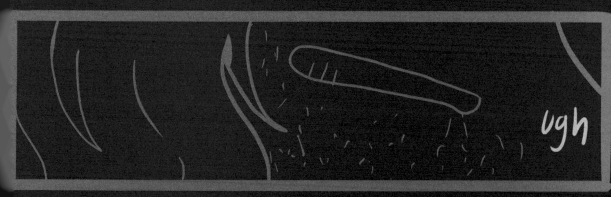

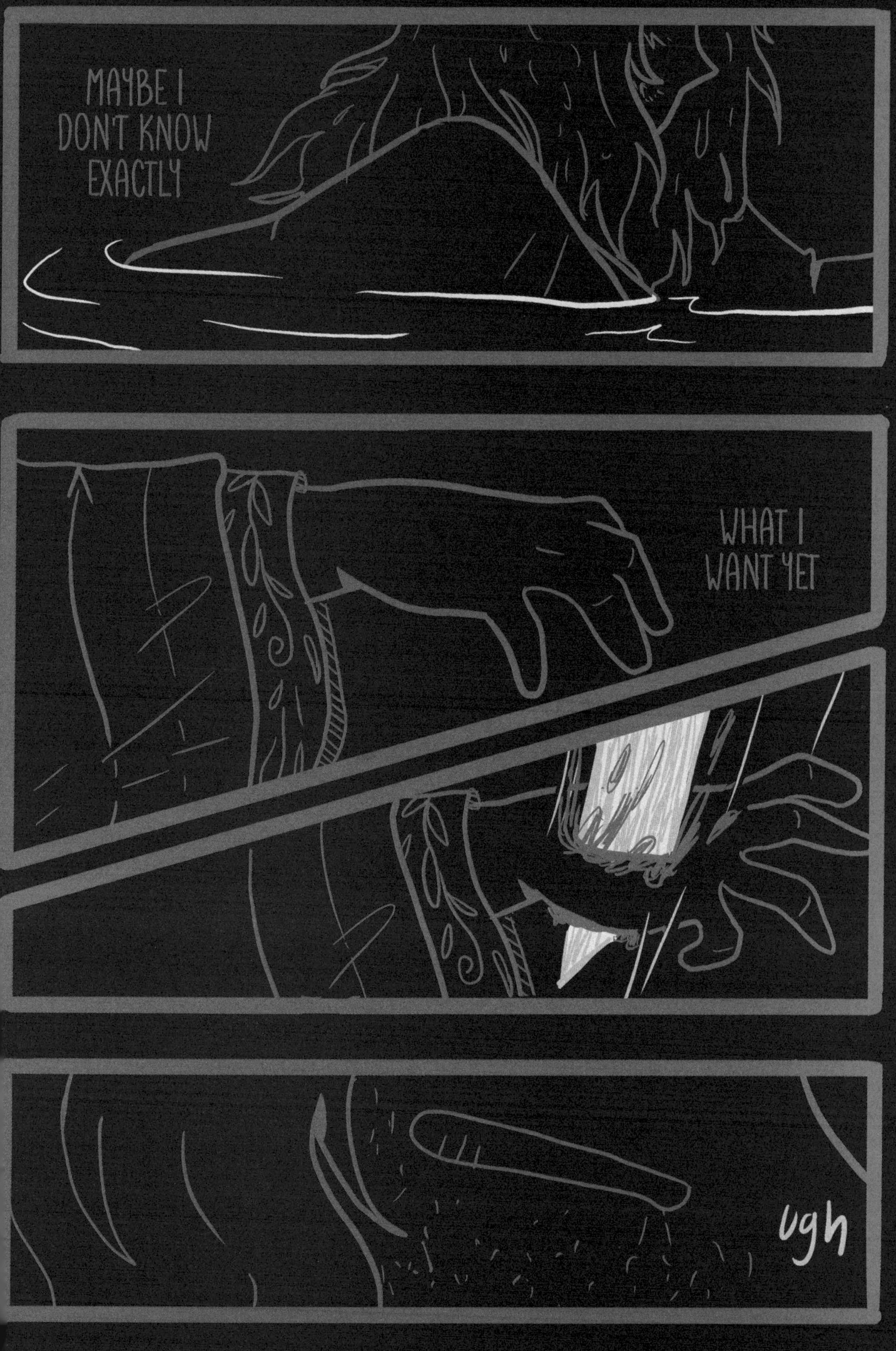

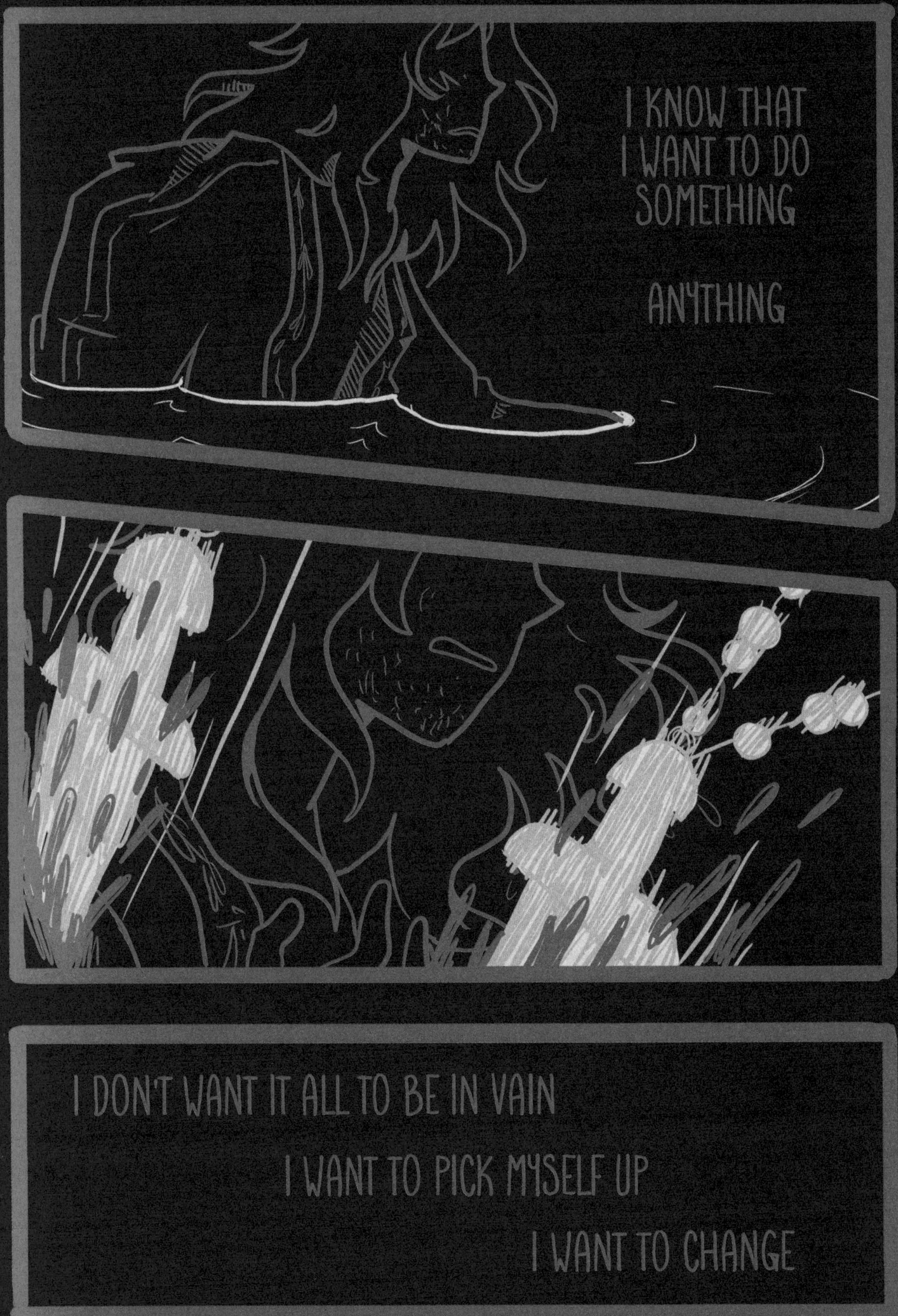
I KNOW THAT I WANT TO DO SOMETHING
ANYTHING
I DON'T WANT IT ALL TO BE IN VAIN
I WANT TO PICK MYSELF UP
I WANT TO CHANGE

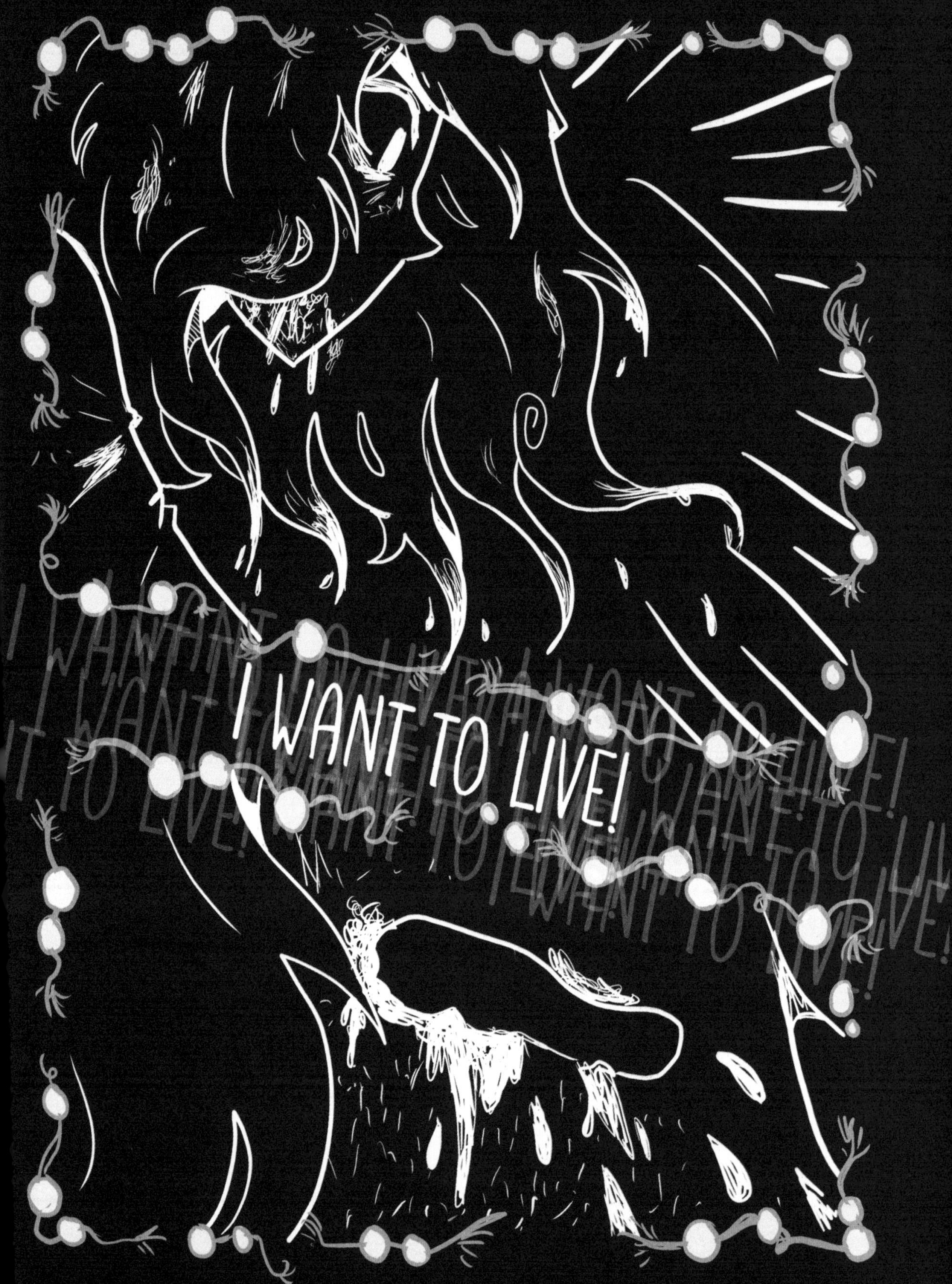
I WANT TO LIVE!

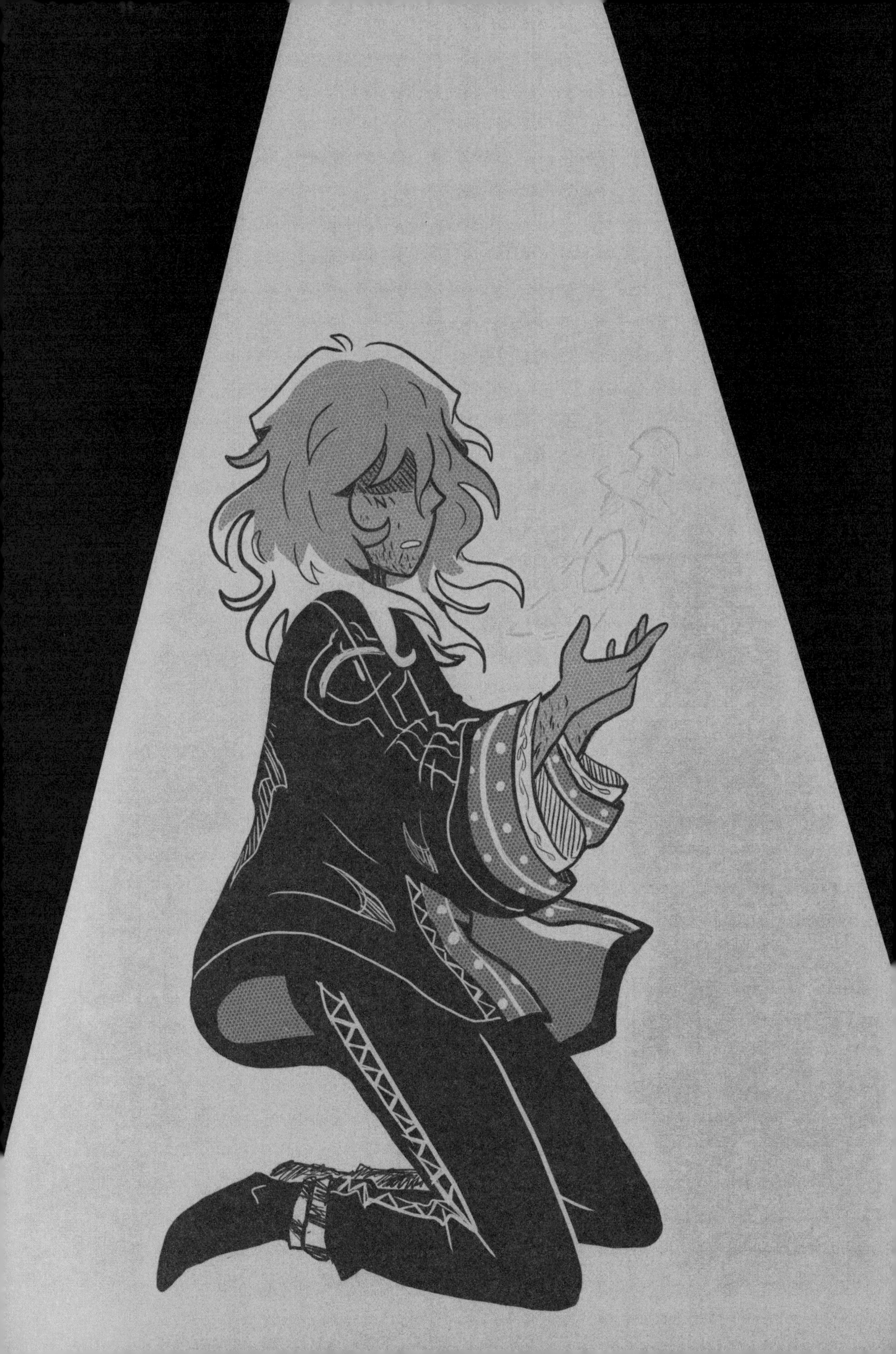

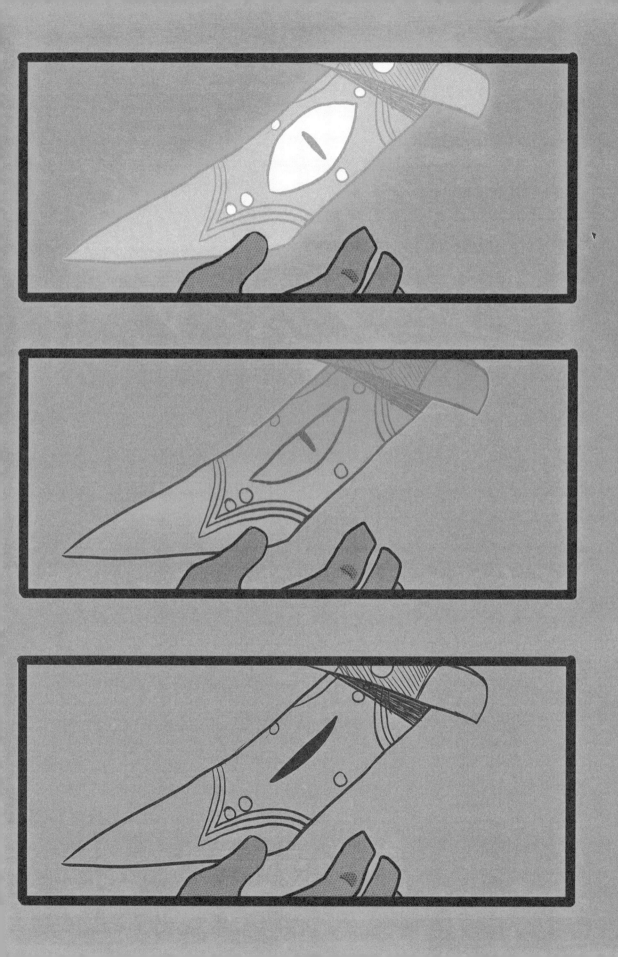

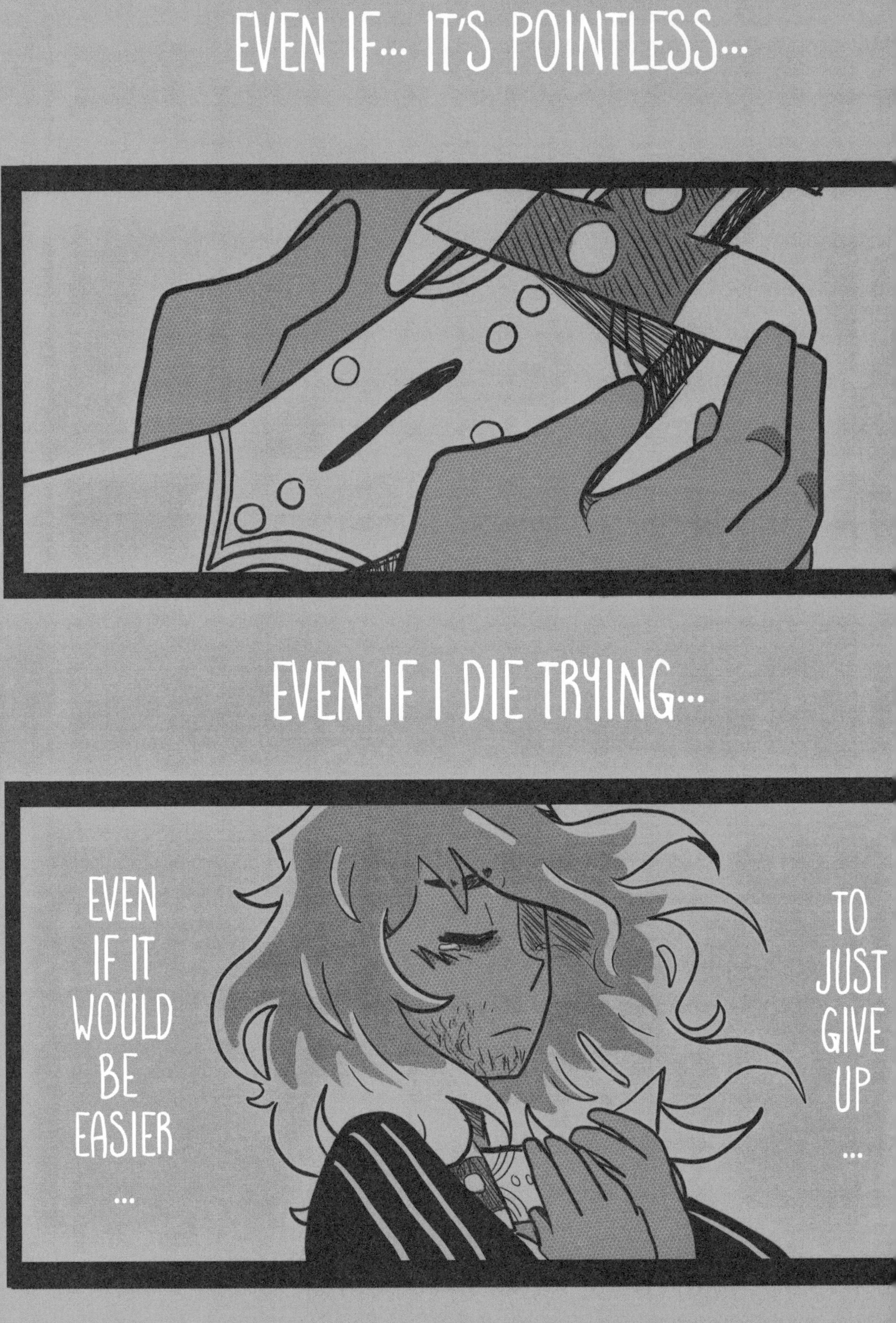
EVEN IF... IT'S POINTLESS...
EVEN IF I DIE TRYING...
EVEN IF IT WOULD BE EASIER ...
TO JUST GIVE UP ...

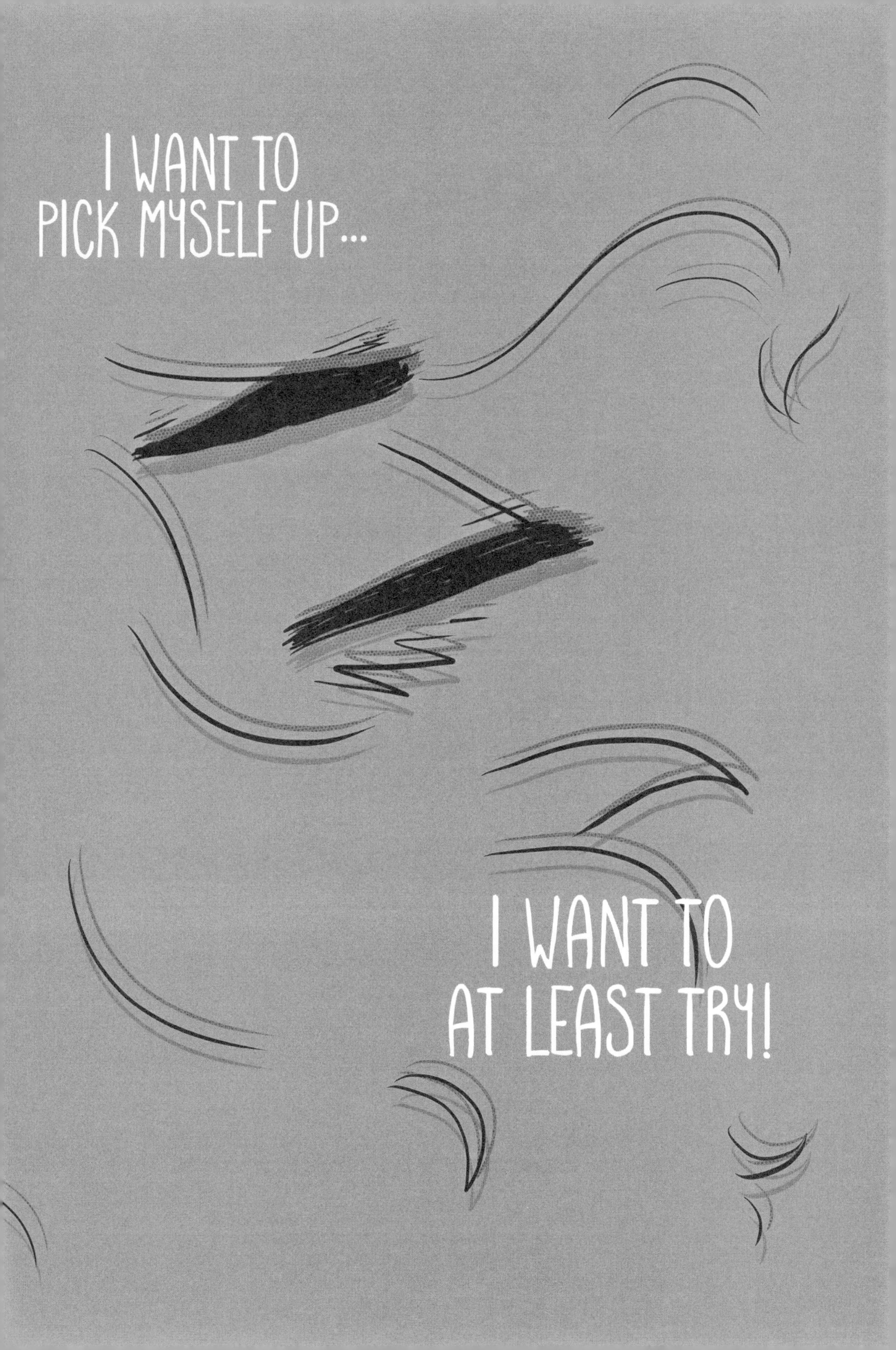
I WANT TO
PICK MYSELF UP...
I WANT TO
AT LEAST TRY!

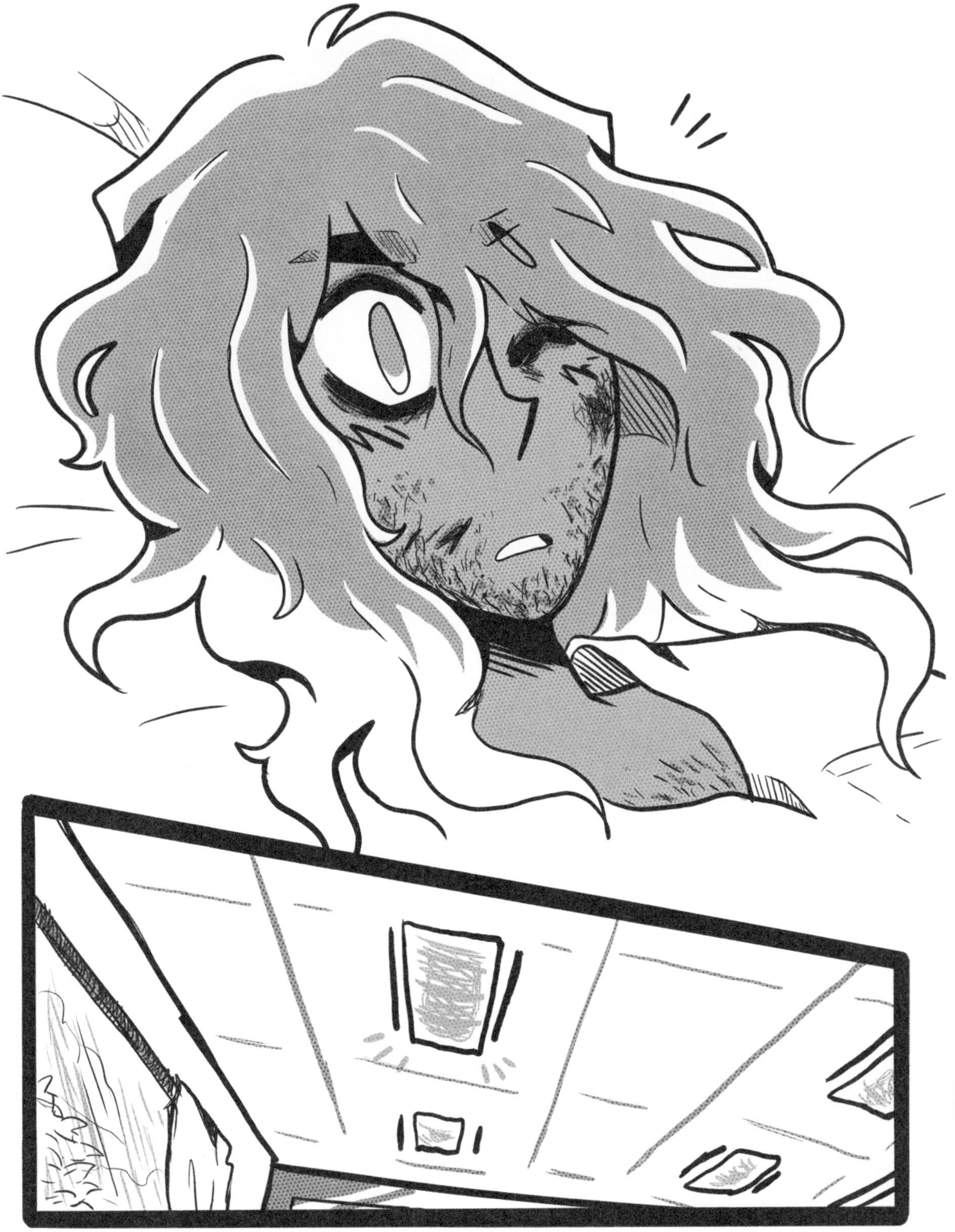

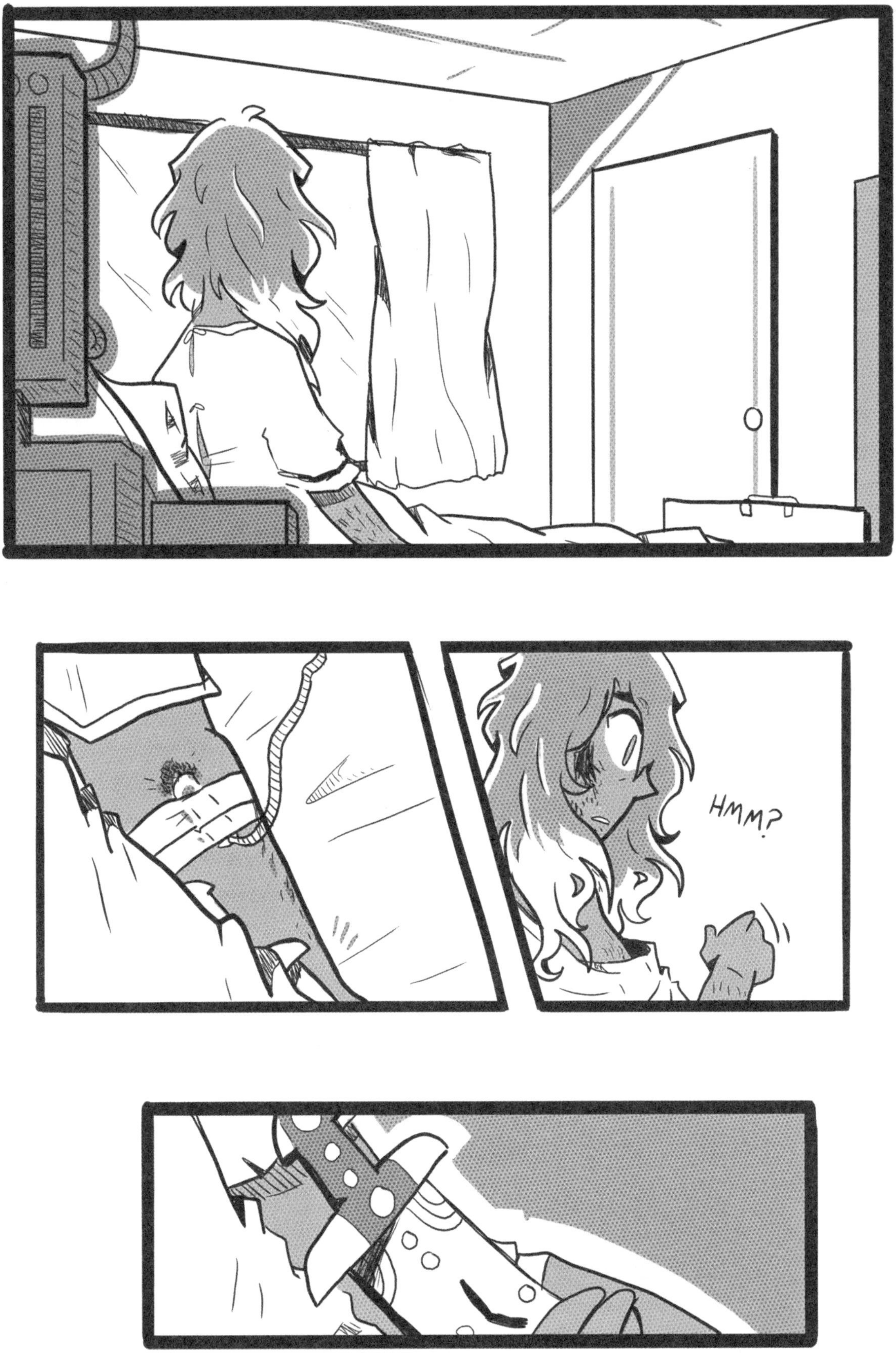
HMM?

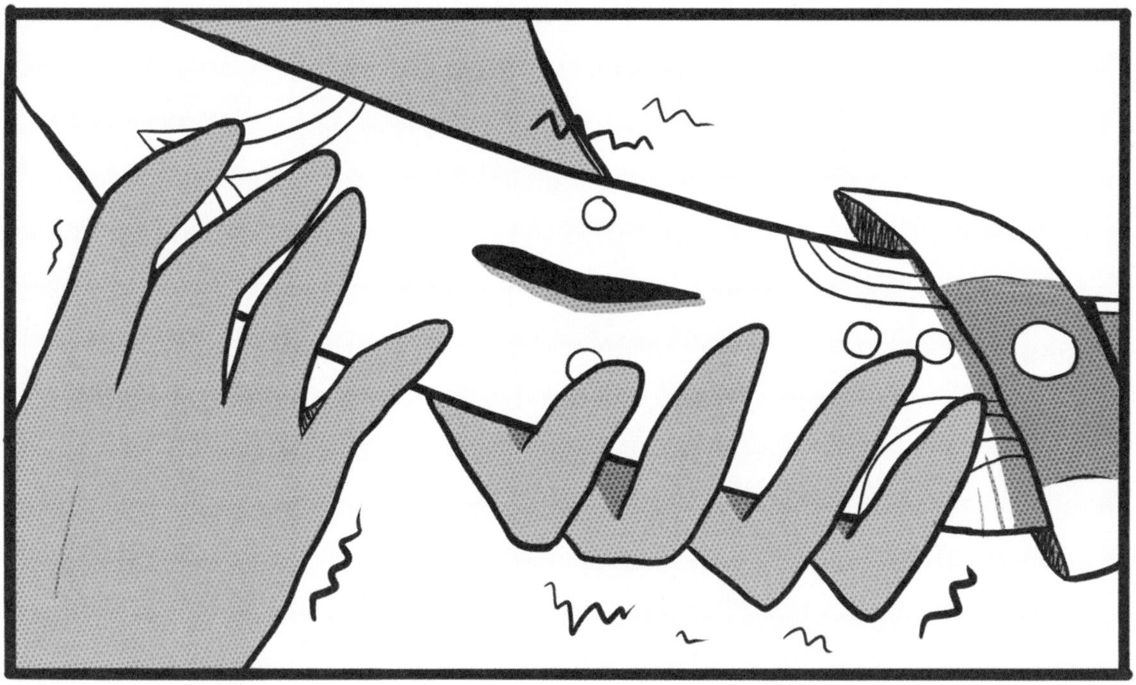

THAT'S RIGHT. THINGS CAN CHANGE. IT'S JUST... GONNA TAKE SOME TIME, I GUESS.

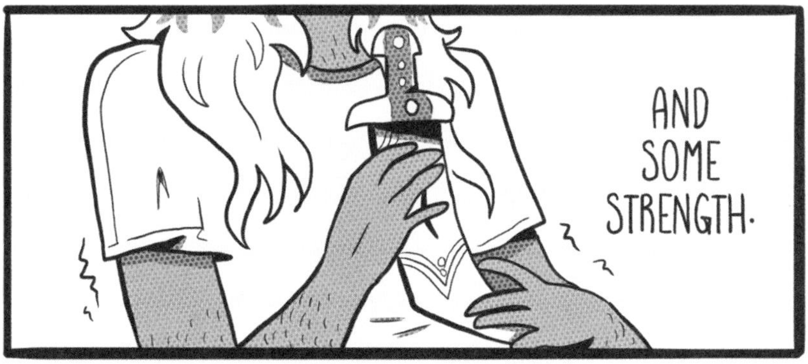
AND SOME STRENGTH.

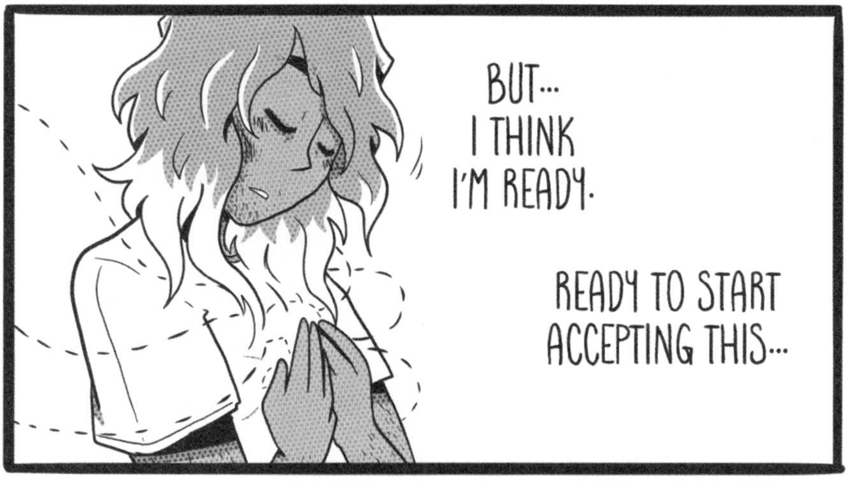
BUT... I THINK I'M READY.
READY TO START ACCEPTING THIS...

READY TO TAKE A STEP FORWARD.

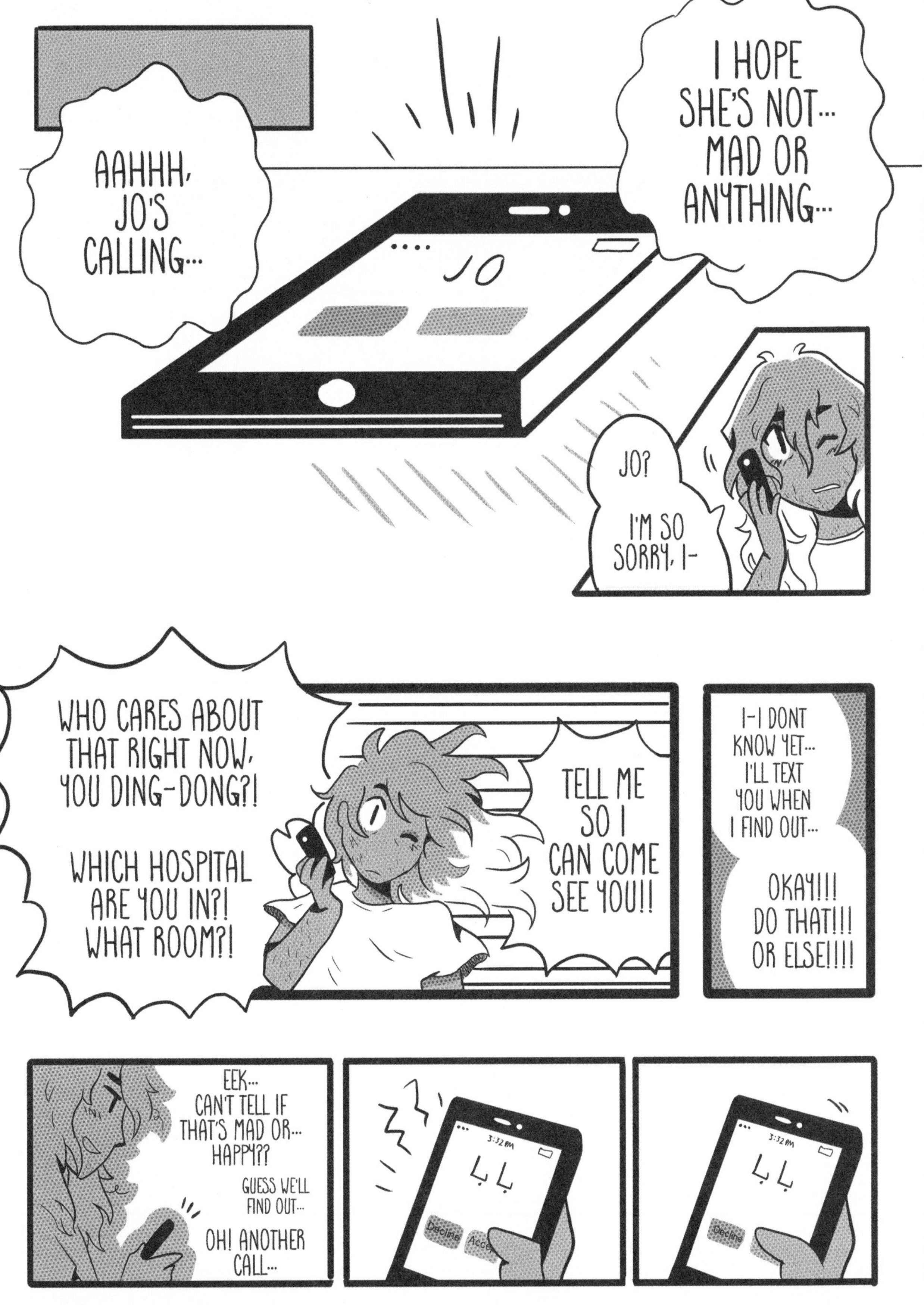

AAHHH, JO'S CALLING...
JO
I HOPE SHE'S NOT... MAD OR ANYTHING...
JO?
I'M SO SORRY, I-
WHO CARES ABOUT THAT RIGHT NOW, YOU DING-DONG?!
WHICH HOSPITAL ARE YOU IN?! WHAT ROOM?!
TELL ME SO I CAN COME SEE YOU!!
I-I DONT KNOW YET... I'LL TEXT YOU WHEN I FIND OUT...
OKAY!!! DO THAT!!! OR ELSE!!!!
EEK... CAN'T TELL IF THAT'S MAD OR... HAPPY??
GUESS WE'LL FIND OUT...
OH! ANOTHER CALL...
3:32 PM
بابا
Decline
3:32 PM
بابا
Decline

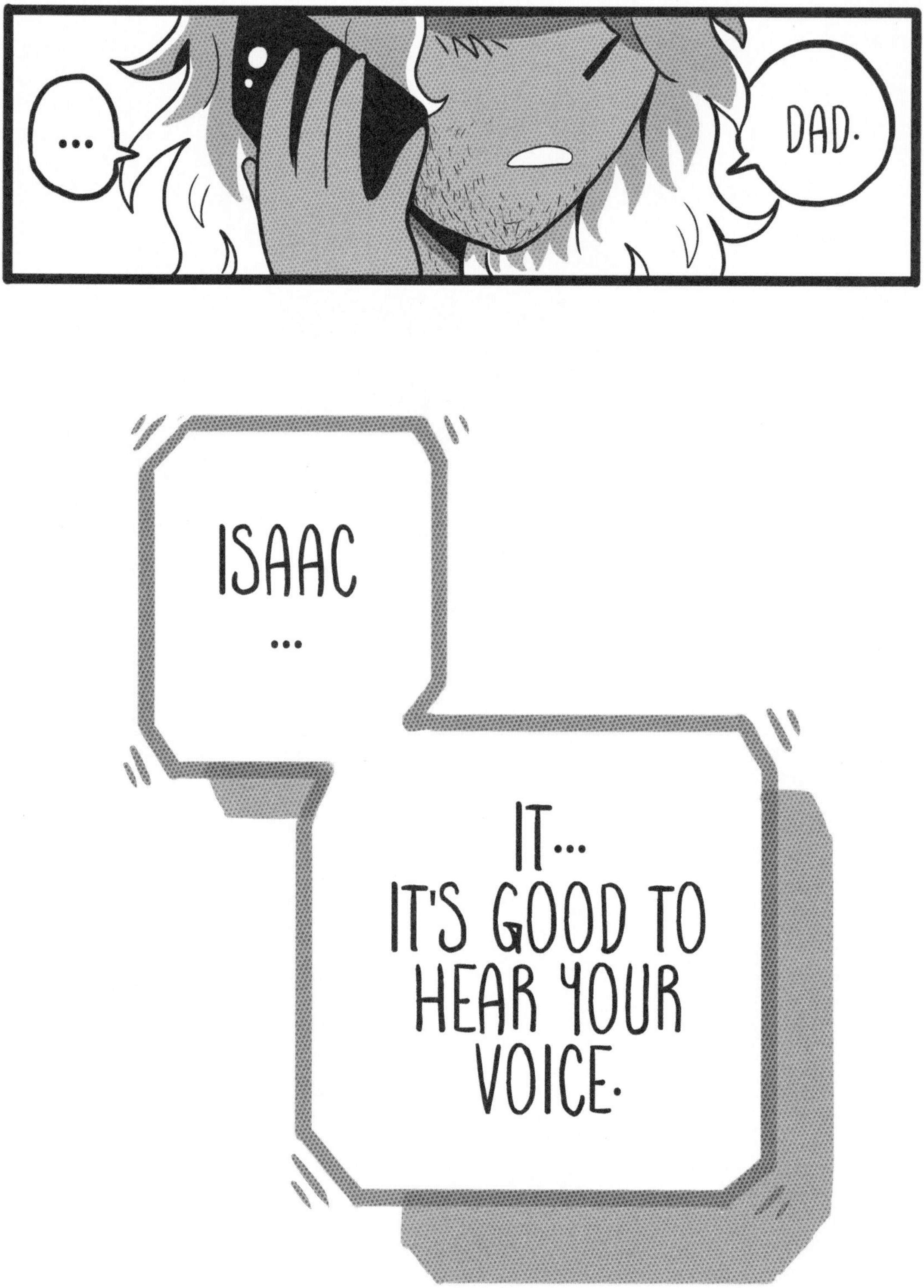
...
DAD.
ISAAC ...
IT... IT'S GOOD TO HEAR YOUR VOICE.

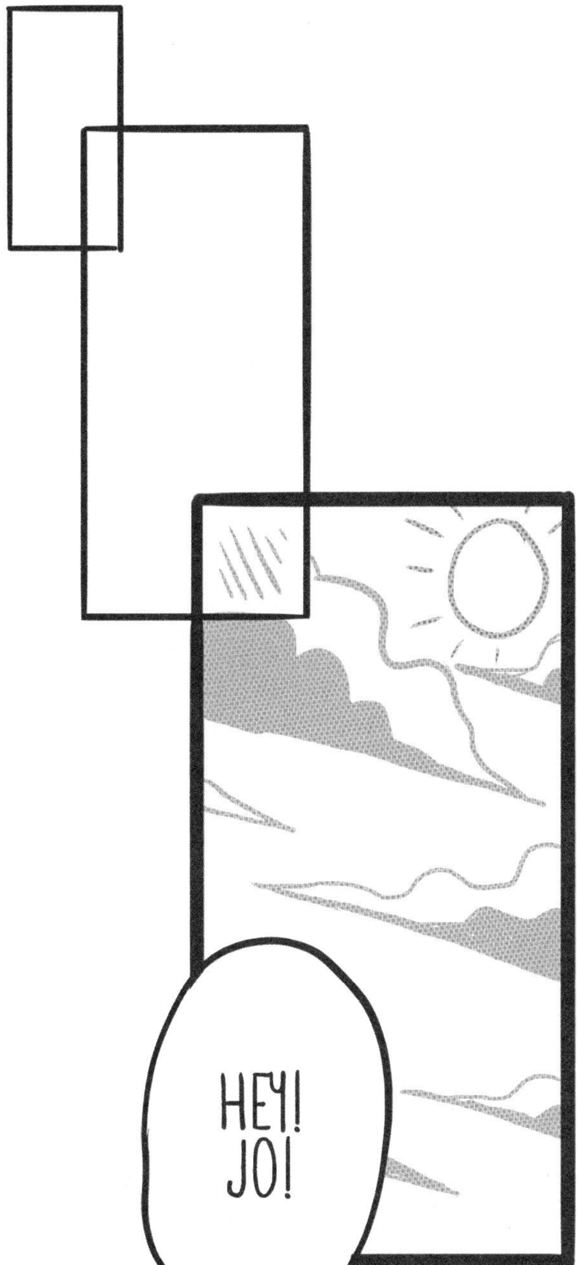
HEY! JO!

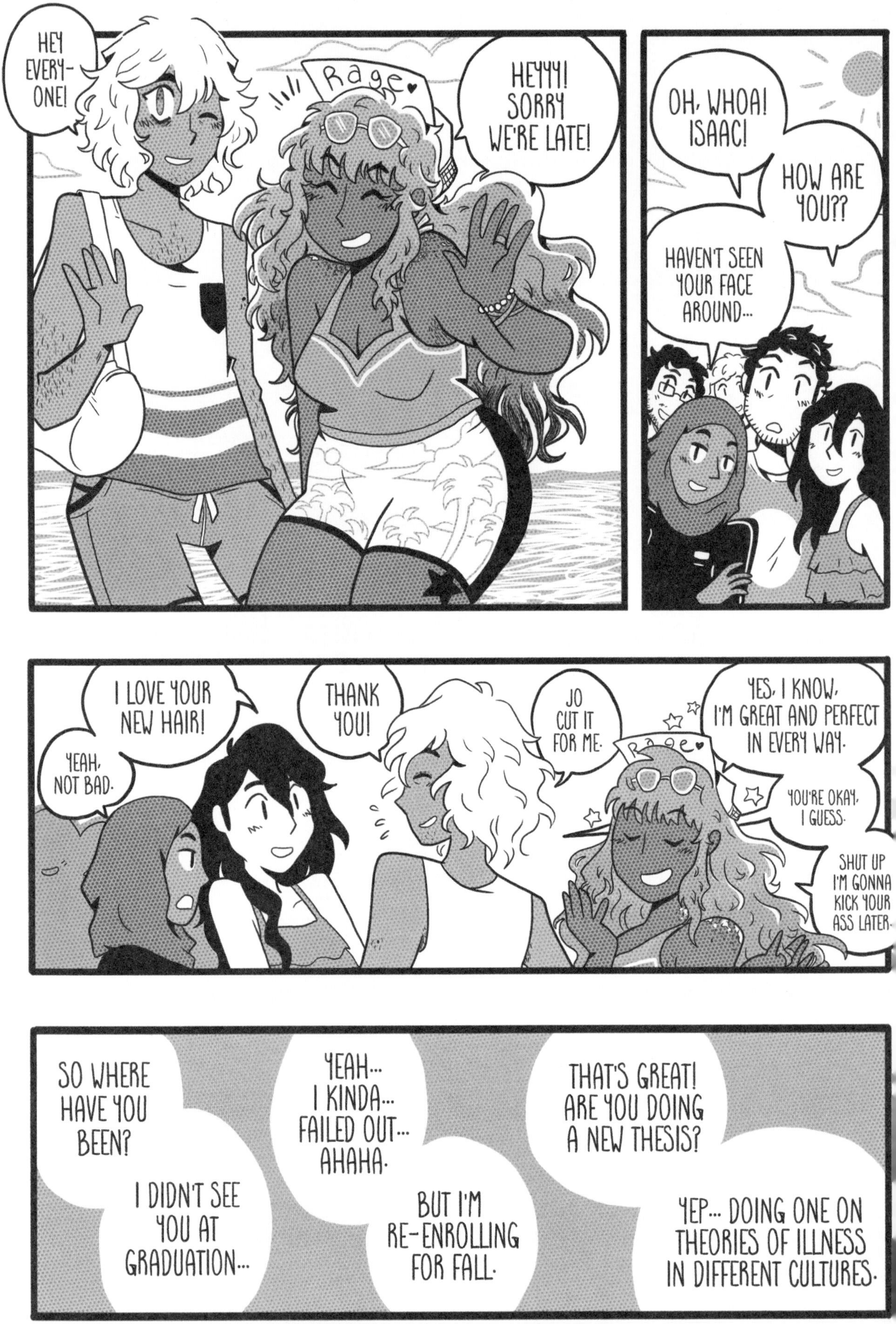
HEY EVERY-ONE!
HEYYY! SORRY WE'RE LATE!
Rage
OH, WHOA! ISAAC!
HOW ARE YOU??
HAVEN'T SEEN YOUR FACE AROUND...
I LOVE YOUR NEW HAIR!
YEAH, NOT BAD.
THANK YOU!
JO CUT IT FOR ME.
YES, I KNOW, I'M GREAT AND PERFECT IN EVERY WAY.
Rage
YOU'RE OKAY, I GUESS.
SHUT UP I'M GONNA KICK YOUR ASS LATER.
SO WHERE HAVE YOU BEEN?
I DIDN'T SEE YOU AT GRADUATION...
YEAH... I KINDA... FAILED OUT... AHAHA.
BUT I'M RE-ENROLLING FOR FALL.
THAT'S GREAT! ARE YOU DOING A NEW THESIS?
YEP... DOING ONE ON THEORIES OF ILLNESS IN DIFFERENT CULTURES.

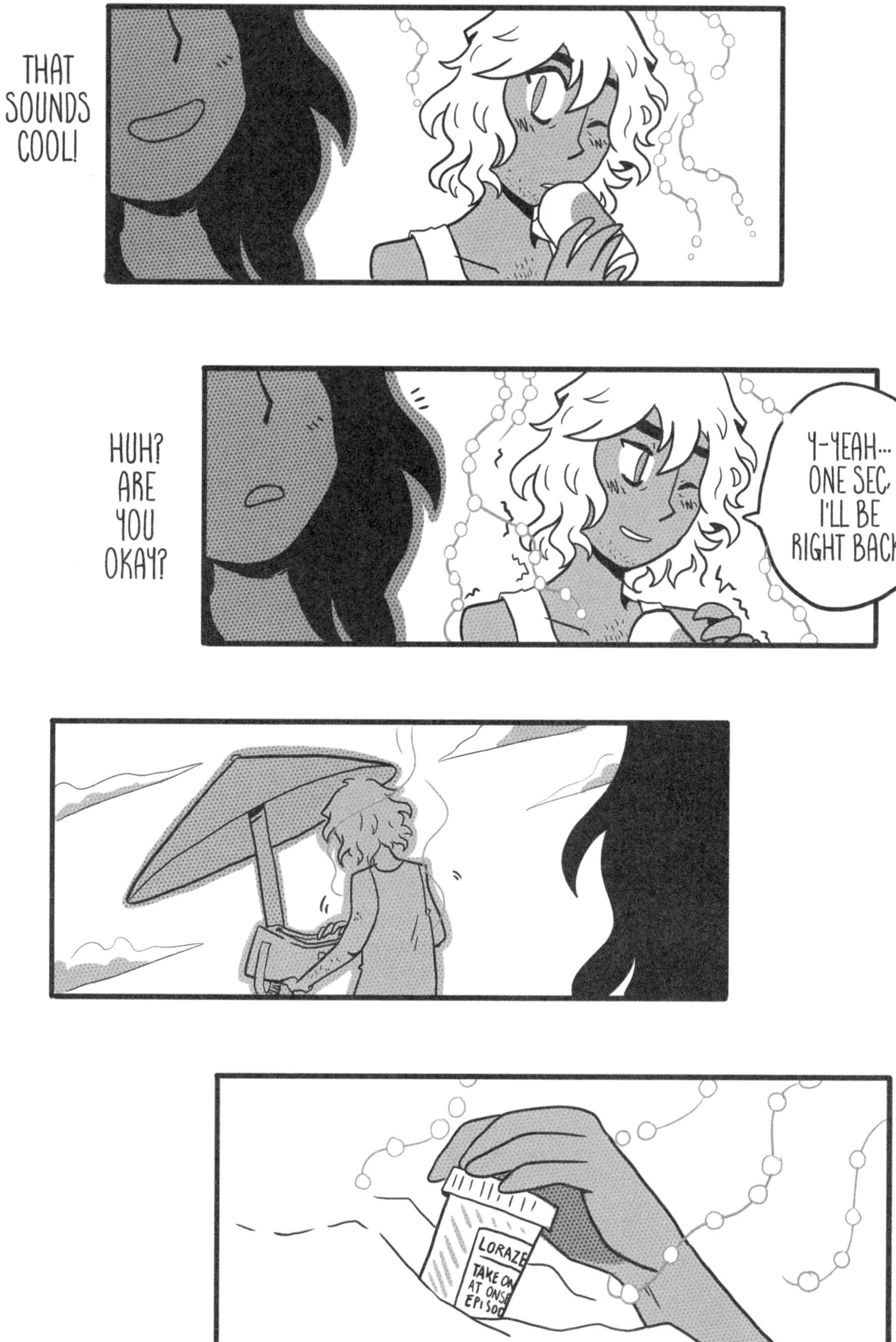
THAT SOUNDS COOL!
HUH? ARE YOU OKAY?
Y-YEAH... ONE SEC, I'LL BE RIGHT BACK.
LORAZE
TAKE ON
AT ONSE
EPISOD

... I AM OKAY.

RIGHT NOW, AT LEAST.

MAYBE I WON'T FEEL OKAY TOMORROW.

OR THE NEXT DAY.

BUT...

THAT'S ALL RIGHT, I THINK.

IT'S ALL RIGHT TO TAKE IT DAY BY DAY.

IT'S ALL RIGHT THAT THINGS WON'T GET BETTER OVERNIGHT.

IT TOOK SOME TIME TO REALIZE, BUT...

I KNOW NOW THAT I HAVE SOME STRENGTH IN ME.

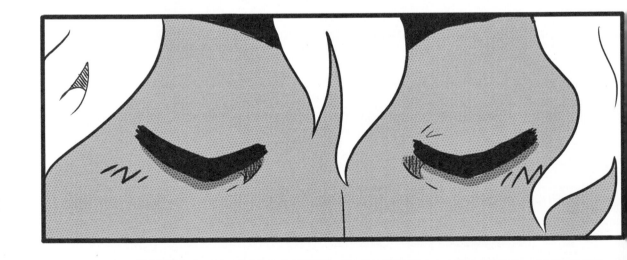

I CAN HOLD ON TO EVERYTHING
I'VE BEEN THROUGH...

AND I CAN STAY STRONG.

This book is dedicated to my dad, who, since the comic's original run,
has come to better understand and consider my epilepsy.
Thank you for your eternal love and support.

And big thank-yous/ILUs to: Joey, Chelsea, Pablo, Kat, Alex,
Gray, Vreni, Jesse, Karina, Bryan, Leslie, Lacey, Sam, Ananth, Yuko,
Rook & Cricket, Kris, Sloane, Em, Sophia, David & Kate & Ben, Maré,
Leia, Caldy, Conrad, Jo, Cassie, Isaac, Mercedes, Meeks, Christina, Geneva,
Emely, Sommer & David & Novalie & Ender & Rin, Rob & Michelle,
and all the others who have stood by me through my illness.

If you're struggling with epilepsy,
there are resources explicitly designed to help you.
Visit www.epilepsy.com/helpline
or call the Epilepsy Foundation 24/7 Helpline
at 1-800-332-1000 for support, advice, and treatment information.

Additional resources:
National Suicide Prevention Lifeline: 1-800-273-8255
Crisis Text Line: Text "Home" to 741741
LGBT National Help Center: www.glbthotline.org or 1-888-843-4564
Naseeha Muslim Youth Helpline: 1-866-627-3342